CORDELIA'S HONOR

LOIS McMASTER BUJOLD

CORDELIA'S HONOR

This is a work of fiction. All the characters and events portrayed in this book are fictional, and any resemblance to real people or incidents is purely coincidental.

A Baen Book

Baen Publishing Enterprises
P.O. Box 1403
Riverdale, NY 10471

ISBN: 0-671-57828-6

Cover art by Gary Ruddell

First mass market printing, September 1999

Distributed by Simon & Schuster
1230 Avenue of the Americas
New York, NY 10020

Typeset by Windhaven Press, Auburn, NH
Printed in the United States of America

SHARDS OF HONOR
"Superb . . . science fiction . . . adventure and war . . . *hugely enjoyable.*"
—*Booklist*

"This author is bound to becme a favorite on everyone's list."
—*Romantic Times*

BARRAYAR
" . . . a **tour de force** of topnotch characterization and **thrilling** adventure."
—*Rave Reviews*

"In the course of an often **spine-tingling** adventure, Bujold and her heroine deal with these crucial subjects: militarism, feminism, eugenics, and the dead hand of tradition, with a **marvelous** mixture of grace and cunning. . . . This is sf fully equipped with brains, humor, and heart."
—*Locus*

"**All the virtues,** including prose that sings."
—*Chicago Sun-Times*

"**Bujold has a genius** for blending technological speculation . . . classic military science fiction, and cultural anthropology . . . in wonderfully plotted stories. Cordelia is the most competent female protagonist I can remember in one of the most enjoyable books."
—*VOYA*

". . . **A phenomenal success.** . . . Bujold's Barrayar series has it all . . . carefully plotted and full of action.
—*Cleveland Plain Dealer*

". . . **Her best book yet.** This is not faint praise; her last novel, *The Vor Game,* won the 1991 Hugo, and *Falling Free* won a Nebula in 1989 . . . it's the swashbuckling that makes this story fun."
—*Philadelphia Inquirer*

Baen Books by Lois McMaster Bujold

CONTENTS

SHARDS OF HONOR

To Pat Wrede
for being a voice
in the wilderness

CHAPTER ONE

A sea of mist drifted through the cloud forest: soft, grey, luminescent. On the high ridges the fog showed brighter as the morning sun began to warm and lift the moisture, although in the ravine a cool, soundless dimness still counterfeited a pre-dawn twilight.

Commander Cordelia Naismith glanced at her team botanist and adjusted the straps of her biological collecting equipment a bit more comfortably before continuing her breathless climb. She pushed a long tendril of fog-dampened copper hair out of her eyes, clawing it impatiently toward the clasp at the nape of her neck. Their next survey area would definitely be at a lower altitude. The gravity of this planet was slightly lower than their home world of Beta Colony, but it did not quite make up for the physiological strain imposed by the thin mountain air.

Denser vegetation marked the upper boundary of the forest patch. Following the splashy path of the ravine's brook, they bent and scrambled through the living tunnel, then broke into the open air.

A morning breeze was ribboning away the last of the fog on the golden uplands. They stretched endlessly, rise after rise, culminating at last in the great grey shoulders

3

of a central peak crowned by glittering ice. This world's sun shone in the deep turquoise sky giving an overwhelming richness to the golden grasses, tiny flowers, tussocks of a silvery plant like powdered lace dotted everywhere. The two explorers gazed entranced at the mountain above, enveloped by the silence.

The botanist, Ensign Dubauer, grinned over his shoulder at Cordelia and fell to his knees beside one of the silvery tussocks. She strolled to the nearest rise for a look at the panorama behind them. The patchy forest grew denser down the gentle slopes. Five hundred meters below, banks of clouds stretched like a white sea to the horizon. Far to the west, their mountain's smaller sister just broke through the updraft-curdled tops.

Cordelia was just wishing herself on the plains below, to see the novelty of water falling from the sky, when she was jarred from her reverie. "Now what the devil can Rosemont be burning to make a stink like that?" she murmured.

An oily black column of smoke was rising beyond the next spur of the mountain slope, to be smudged, thinned, and dissipated by the upper breezes. It certainly appeared to be coming from the location of their base camp. She studied it intently.

A distant whining, rising to a howl, pierced the silence. Their planetary shuttle burst from behind the ridge and boomed across the sky above them, leaving a sparkling trail of ionized gases.

"What a takeoff!" cried Dubauer, his attention wrenched skyward.

Cordelia keyed her short-range wrist communicator and spoke into it. "Naismith to Base One. Come in, please."

A small, empty hiss was her sole reply. She called again, twice, with the same result. Ensign Dubauer hovered anxiously at her elbow.

"Try yours," she said. But his luck was no better. "Pack up your stuff, we're going back to camp," she ordered. "Double time."

They struggled toward the next ridge at a gasping jog, and plunged back into the forest. The spindly bearded seemed artistically wild on the way up; on the way down they made a menacing obstacle course. Cordelia's mind ratcheted over a dozen possible disasters, each more bizarre than the last. So the unknown breeds dragons in map margins, she reflected, and suppressed her panic.

They slid down through the last patch of woods for their first clear view of the large glade selected for their primary base camp. Cordelia gaped, shocked. Reality had surpassed imagination.

Smoke was rising from five slagged and lumpy black mounds, formerly a neat ring of tents. A smouldering scar was burned in the grasses where the shuttle had been parked, opposite the camp from the ravine. Smashed equipment was scattered everywhere. Their bacteriologically sealed sanitary facilities had been just downslope; yes, she saw, even the privy had been torched.

"My God," breathed Ensign Dubauer, and started forward like a sleepwalker. Cordelia collared him.

"Get down and cover me," she ordered, then walked cautiously toward the silent ruins.

The grass all around the camp was trampled and churned. Her stunned mind struggled to account for the carnage. Previously undetected aborigines? No, nothing short of a plasma arc could have melted the fabric of their tents. The long-looked-for but still undiscovered advanced aliens? Perhaps some unexpected disease outbreak, not forestalled by their monthlong robotic microbiological survey and immunizations—could it have been an attempt at sterilization? An attack by some other planetary government? Their attackers could scarcely have come through the same wormhole exit they had discovered, still, they had only mapped about ten percent of the volume of space within a light-month of this system. Aliens?

She was miserably conscious of her mind coming full circle, like one of her team zoologist's captive animals racing frantically in an exercise wheel. She poked grimly through the rubbish for some clue.

She found it in the high grass halfway to the ravine.

The long body in the baggy tan fatigues of the Betan Astronomical Survey was stretched out full length, arms and legs askew, as though hit while running for the shelter of the forest. Her breath drew inward in pain of recognition. She turned him over gently.

It was the conscientious Lieutenant Rosemont. His eyes were glazed and fixed and somehow worried, as though they still held a mirror to his spirit. She closed them for him.

She searched him for the cause of his death. No blood, no burns, no broken bones—her long white fingers probed his scalp. The skin beneath his blond hair was blistered, the telltale signature of a nerve disruptor. That let out aliens. She cradled his head in her lap a moment, stroking his familiar features helplessly, like a blind woman. No time now for mourning.

She returned to the blackened ring on her hands and knees, and began to search through the mess for comm equipment. The attackers had been quite thorough in that department, the twisted lumps of plastic and metal she found testified. Much valuable equipment seemed to be missing altogether.

There was a rustle in the grass. She snapped her stun gun to the aim and froze. The tense face of Ensign Dubauer pushed through the straw-colored vegetation.

"It's me, don't shoot," he called in a strangled tone meant to be a whisper.

"I almost did. Why didn't you stay put?" she hissed back. "Never mind, help me look for a comm unit that can reach the ship. And stay down, they could come back at any time."

"Who could? Who did this?"

"Multiple choice, take your pick—Nuovo Brasilians, Barrayarans, Cetagandans, could be any of that crowd. Reg Rosemont's dead. Nerve disruptor."

Cordelia crawled over to the mound of the specimen tent and carefully considered its lumps. "Hand me that pole over there," she whispered.

She poked tentatively at the most probable hump. The

"Cordelia . . . Good luck. Stuben out."

Cordelia sat back and stared at the little communicator. "Whew. What a peculiar business."

Ensign Dubauer snorted. "That's an understatement."

"It's an exact statement. I don't know if you noticed—"

A movement in the mottled shade caught her eye. She started to her feet, hand moving toward her stunner. The tall, hatchet-faced Barrayaran soldier in the green and grey splotched camouflage fatigues moved even faster. Dubauer moved faster still, shoving her blindly behind him. She heard the crackle of a nerve disruptor as she pitched backward into the ravine, stunner and comm link flying from her hands. Forest, earth, stream, and sky spun wildly around her, her head struck something with a sickening, starry crack, and darkness swallowed her.

The forest mold pressed against Cordelia's cheek. The damp earthy smell tickled her nostrils. She breathed deeper, filling her mouth and lungs, and then the odor of decay wrung her stomach. She turned her face from the muck. Pain exploded through her head in radiating lines.

She groaned inarticulately. Dark sparkling whorls curtained her vision, then cleared. She forced her eyes to focus on the nearest object, about half a meter to the right of her head.

Heavy black boots, sunk in the mud and topped by green and grey splotched camouflage trousers, encased legs spread apart in a patient parade rest. She suppressed a weary whimper. Very gently she laid her head back in the black ooze, and rolled cautiously onto her side for a better view of the Barrayaran officer.

Her stunner! She stared into the little rectangle of its business end, held steadily in a broad and heavy hand. Her eyes searched anxiously for his nerve disruptor. The officer's belt hung heavy with equipment, but the disruptor holster on his right hip was empty, as was the plasma arc holster on his left.

He was barely taller than herself, but stocky and powerful. Untidy dark hair touched with grey, cold intent grey eyes—in fact, his whole appearance was untidy by the strict Barrayaran military standards. His fatigues were almost as rumpled and muddy and stained with plant juices as her own, and he had a raw contusion across his right cheekbone. Looks like he's had a rotten day too, she thought muzzily. Then the sparkly black whirlpools expanded and drowned her again.

When her vision cleared again the boots were gone—no. There he was, seated comfortably on a log. She tried to focus on something other than her rebellious belly, but her belly won control in a wrenching rush.

The enemy captain stirred involuntarily as she vomited, but remained sitting. She crawled the few meters to the little stream at the bottom of the ravine, and washed out her mouth and face in its icy water. Feeling relatively better, she sat up and croaked, "Well?"

The officer inclined his head in a shadow of courtesy. "I am Captain Aral Vorkosigan, commanding the Barrayaran Imperial war cruiser *General Vorkraft.* Identify yourself, please." His voice was baritone, his speech barely accented.

"Commander Cordelia Naismith. Betan Astronomical Survey. We are a scientific party," she emphasized accusingly. "Non-combatants."

"So I noticed," he said dryly. "What happened to your party?"

Cordelia's eyes narrowed. "Weren't you there? I was up on the mountain, assisting my team botanist." And more urgently, "Have you seen my botanist—my ensign? He pushed me into the ravine when we were ambushed—"

He glanced up to the rim of the gorge at the point where she had toppled in—how long ago? "Was he a brown-haired boy?"

Her heart sank in sick anticipation. "Yes."

"There's nothing you can do for him now."

"That was murder! All he had was a stunner!" Her eyes burned the Barrayaran. "Why were my people attacked?"

He tapped her stunner thoughtfully in his palm. "Your expedition," he said carefully, "was to be interned, preferably peacefully, for violation of Barrayaran space. There was an altercation. I was hit in the back with a stun beam. When I came to, I found your camp as you did."

"Good." Bitter bile soured her mouth. "I'm glad Reg got one of you, before you murdered him too."

"If you are referring to that misguided but admittedly courageous blond boy in the clearing, he couldn't have hit the side of a house. I don't know why you Betans put on soldiers' uniforms. You're no better trained than children on a picnic. If your ranks denote anything but pay scale, it's not apparent to me."

"He was a geologist, not a hired killer," she snapped. "As for my 'children,' your soldiers couldn't even capture them."

His brows drew together. Cordelia shut her mouth abruptly. Oh, great, she thought. He hasn't even started to wrench my arms off, and already I'm giving away free intelligence.

"Didn't they now," Vorkosigan mused. He pointed upstream with the stunner to where the comm link lay cracked open in the brook. A little sputtering of steam rose from the ruin. "What orders did you give your ship when they informed you of their escape?"

"I told them to use their initiative," she murmured vaguely, groping for inspiration in a throbbing fog.

He snorted. "A safe order to give a Betan. At least you're sure to be obeyed."

Oh, no. My turn. "Hey, I know why my people left me behind—why did yours leave you? Isn't one's commanding officer, even a Barrayaran one, too important to mislay?" She sat up straighter. "If Reg couldn't hit the side of a house, who shot you?"

That's fetched him, she thought, as the stunner with which he had been absently gesturing was swiveled back to aim on her. But he said only, "That is not your concern. Have you another comm link?"

Oh ho—was this stern Barrayaran commander dealing with a mutiny? Well, confusion to the enemy! "No. Your soldiers trashed everything."

"No matter," muttered Vorkosigan. "I know where to get another. Are you able to walk yet?"

"I'm not sure." She pushed herself to her feet, then pressed her hand to her head to contain the shooting pains.

"It's only a concussion," Vorkosigan said unsympathetically. "A walk will do you good."

"How far?" she gasped.

"About two hundred kilometers."

She fell back to her knees. "Have a nice trip."

"By myself, two days. I suppose you will take longer, being a geologist, or whatever."

"Astrocartographer."

"Get up, please." He unbent so far as to help her with a hand under her elbow. He seemed curiously reluctant to touch her. She was chilled and stiff; she could feel the heat from his hand through the heavy cloth of her sleeve. Vorkosigan pushed her determinedly up the side of the ravine.

"You're stone serious," she said. "What are you going to do with a prisoner on a forced march? Suppose I bash in your head with a rock while you sleep?"

"I'll take my chances."

They cleared the top. Cordelia draped herself around one of the little trees, winded. Vorkosigan wasn't even breathing hard, she noticed enviously. "Well, I'm not going anywhere till I've buried my officers."

He looked irritated. "It's a waste of time and energy."

"I won't leave them to the scavengers like dead animals. Your Barrayaran thugs may know more about killing, but not one of them could have died a more soldierly death."

He stared at her a moment, face unreadable, then shrugged. "Very well."

Cordelia began to make her way along the side of the ravine. "I thought it was here," she said, puzzled. "Did you move him?"

"No. But he can't have crawled far, in his condition."

"You said he was dead!"

"So he is. His body, however, was still animate. The disruptor must have missed his cerebellum."

Cordelia traced the trail of broken vegetation over a small rise, Vorkosigan following silently.

"Dubauer!" She ran to the tan-clad figure curled up in the bracken. As she knelt beside him he turned and stretched out stiffly, then began to shake all over in slow waves, his lips drawn back in a strange grin. Cold? she thought wildly, then realized what she was seeing. She yanked her handkerchief from her pocket, folded it, and forced it between his teeth. His mouth was already bloody from a previous convulsion. After about three minutes he sighed and went limp.

She blew out her breath in distress and examined him anxiously. He opened his eyes, and seemed to focus on her face. He clutched ineffectually at her arm and made noises, all moans and clotted vowels. She tried to soothe his animal agitation by gently stroking his head, and wiping the bloody spittle from his mouth; he quieted.

She turned to Vorkosigan, tears of fury and pain blurring her vision. "Not dead! Liar! Only injured. He must have medical help."

"You are being unrealistic, Commander Naismith. One does not recover from disruptor injuries."

"So? You can't tell the extent of the damage your filthy weapon has done from the outside. He can still see and hear and feel—you can't demote him to the status of a corpse for your convenience!"

His face seemed a mask. "If you wish," he said carefully. "I can put him out of his suffering. My combat knife is quite sharp. Used quickly, it would cut his throat almost painlessly. Or should you feel it is your duty as his commander, I'll lend you the knife and you may use it."

"Is that what you'd do for one of your men?"

"Certainly. And they'd do the same for me. No man could wish to live on like that."

She stood and looked at him very steadily. "It must be like living among cannibals, to be a Barrayaran."

A long silence fell between them. Dubauer broke it with a moan. Vorkosigan stirred. "What, then, do you propose to do with him?"

She rubbed her temples tiredly, ransacking for an appeal that would penetrate that expressionless front. Her stomach undulated, her tongue was woolly, her legs trembled with exhaustion, low blood sugar, and reaction to pain. "Just where is it you're planning to go?" she asked finally.

"There is a supply cache located—in a place I know. Hidden. It contains communications equipment, weapons, food—possession of it would put me in a position to, ah, correct the problems in my command."

"Does it have medical supplies?"

"Yes," he admitted reluctantly.

"All right." Here goes nothing. "I will cooperate with you—give you my parole, as a prisoner—assist you in any way I can that does not actually endanger my ship—if I can take Ensign Dubauer with us."

"That's impossible. He can't even walk."

"I think he can, if he's helped."

He stared at her in baffled irritation. "And if I refuse?"

"Then you can either leave us both or kill us both." She glanced away from his knife, lifted her chin, and waited.

"I do not kill prisoners."

She was relieved to hear the plural. Dubauer was evidently promoted back to humanity in her strange captor's mind. She knelt down to try to help Dubauer to his feet, praying this Vorkosigan would not decide to end the argument by stunning her and killing her botanist outright.

"Very well," he capitulated, giving her an odd intent look. "Bring him along. But we must travel quickly."

She managed to get the ensign up. With his arm draped heavily over her shoulder, she guided him on a shambling walk. It seemed he could hear, but not decode meaning from the noises of speech. "You see," she defended him desperately, "he can walk. He just needs a little help."

They reached the edge of the glade as the last level light of early evening was striping it with long black shadows, like a tiger's skin. Vorkosigan paused.

"If I were by myself," he said, "I'd travel to the cache on the emergency rations in my belt. With you two along, we'll have to risk scavenging your camp for more food. You can bury your other officer while I'm looking around."

Cordelia nodded. "Look for something to dig with, too. I've got to tend to Dubauer first."

He acknowledged this with a wave of his hand and started toward the wasted ring. Cordelia was able to excavate a couple of half-burned bedrolls from the remains of the women's tent, but no clothes, medicine, soap, or even a bucket to carry or heat water. She finally coaxed the ensign over to the spring and washed him, his wounds, and his trousers as best she could in the plain cold water, dried him with one bedroll, put his undershirt and fatigue jacket back on him, and wrapped the other bedroll around him sarong style. He shivered and moaned, but did not resist her makeshift ministrations.

Vorkosigan in the meanwhile had found two cases of ration packs, with the labels burned off but otherwise scarcely damaged. Cordelia tore open one silvery pouch, added spring water, and found that it was soya-fortified oatmeal.

"That's lucky," she commented. "He's sure to be able to eat that. What's the other case?"

Vorkosigan was conducting his own experiment. He added water to his pouch, mixed it by squeezing, and sniffed the result.

"I'm not really sure," he said, handing it to her. "It smells rather strange. Could it be spoiled?"

It was a white paste with a pungent aroma. "It's all right," Cordelia assured him. "It's artificial blue cheese salad dressing." She sat back and contemplated the menu. "At least it's high in calories," she encouraged herself. "We'll need calories. I don't suppose you have a spoon in that utility belt of yours?"

Vorkosigan unhooked an object from his belt and handed it to her without comment. It turned out to be several small useful utensils folded into a handle, including a spoon.

"Thanks," Cordelia said, absurdly pleased, as if granting her mumbled wish had been a conjuror's trick.

Vorkosigan shrugged and wandered away to continue his search in the gathering darkness, and she began to feed Dubauer. He seemed voraciously hungry, but unable to manage for himself.

Vorkosigan returned to the spring. "I found this." He handed her a small geologist's shovel about a meter long, used for digging soil samples. "It's a poor tool for the purpose, but I've found nothing better yet."

"It was Reg's," Cordelia said, taking it. "It will do."

She led Dubauer to a spot near her next job and settled him. She wondered if some bracken from the forest might provide some insulation for him, and resolved to get some later. She marked out the dimensions of a grave near the place where Rosemont had fallen, and began hacking away at the heavy turf with the little shovel. The sod was tough, wiry, and resistant, and she ran out of breath quickly.

Vorkosigan appeared out of the night. "I found some cold lights." He cracked one pencil-sized tube and laid it on the ground beside the grave, where it gave off an eerie but bright blue-green glow. He watched her critically as she worked.

She stabbed away at the dirt, resentful of his scrutiny. Go away, you, she thought, and let me bury my friend in peace. She grew self-conscious as a new thought struck her—maybe he won't let me finish—I'm taking too long. . . . She dug harder.

"At this rate, we'll be here until next week."

If she moved fast enough, she wondered irritably, could she succeed in hitting him with the shovel? Just once . . .

"Go sit down with your botanist." He was holding out his hand; it dawned on her at last that he was volunteering to help dig.

"Oh . . ." She relinquished the tool. He drew his combat knife and cut through the grasses' roots where she had marked her rectangle, and began to dig, far more efficiently than she had.

"What kind of scavengers have you found around here?" he asked between tosses. "How deep does this have to be?"

"I'm not sure," she replied. "We'd only been downside three days. It's a pretty complex ecosystem, though, and most imaginable niches seem to be filled."

"Hm."

"Lieutenant Stuben, my chief zoologist, found a couple of those browser hexapeds killed and pretty well consumed. He caught a glimpse of something he called a fuzzy crab at one of the kills."

"How big were they?" asked Vorkosigan curiously.

"He didn't say. I've seen pictures of crabs from Earth, and they don't seem very large—as big as your hand, perhaps."

"A meter may be enough." He continued the excavation with short powerful bites of the inadequate shovel. The cold light illuminated his face from below, casting shadows upward from heavy jaw, straight broad nose, and thick brows. He had an old faded L-shaped scar, Cordelia noticed, on the left side of his chin. He reminded her of a dwarf king in some northern saga, digging in a fathomless deep.

"There's a pole over by the tents," she offered. "I could fix that light up in the air so it shines on your work."

"That would help."

She returned to the tents, beyond the circle of cold light, and found her pole where she had dropped it that morning. Returning to the gravesite, she spliced the light to the pole with a few tough grass stems and fixed it upright in the dirt, flinging the circle of light wider. She remembered her plan to collect bracken for Dubauer, and turned to make for the forest, then stopped.

"Did you hear that?" she asked Vorkosigan.

"What?" Even he was beginning to breathe heavily. He paused, up to his knees in the hole, and listened with her.

"A sort of scuttling noise, coming from the forest."

He waited a minute, then shook his head and continued his work.

"How many cold lights are there?"

"Six."

So few. She hated to waste them by running two at once. She was about to ask him if he would mind digging in the dark for a while, when she heard the noise again, more distinctly.

"There *is* something out there."

"You know that," said Vorkosigan. "The question is—"

The three creatures made a concerted rush into the ring of light. Cordelia caught a glimpse of fast low bodies, entirely too many hairy black legs, four beady black eyes set in neckless faces, and razor-sharp yellow beaks that clacked and hissed. They were the size of pigs.

Vorkosigan reacted instantly, smashing the nearest accurately across its face with the blade of the shovel. A second one flung itself across Rosemont's body, biting deep into the flesh and cloth of one arm, and attempting to drag it away from the light. Cordelia grabbed her pole and ran full tilt upon it, getting in a hard blow between its eyes. Its beak snapped the end off the aluminum rod. It hissed and retreated before her.

By this time Vorkosigan had his combat knife out. He vigorously attacked the third, shouting, stabbing, and kicking with his heavy boots. Blood spattered as claws plowed his leg, but he got in a blow with his knife that sent the creature shrieking and hissing back to the shelter of the forest along with its pack mates. With a moment to breathe, he dug out her stun gun from the bottom of the too-large disruptor holster where, judging from his muttered swearing, it had slipped down and stuck, and peered into the night.

"Fuzzy crabs, huh?" Cordelia panted. "Stuben, I'm going to scrag you." Her voice squeaked upward and she clamped her teeth.

Vorkosigan wiped the dark blood from his blade in the grass and returned it to its sheath. "I think your grave had better be a full two meters," he said seriously. "Maybe a little more."

Cordelia sighed in agreement, and returned the shortened pole to its original position. "How's your leg?"

"I can take care of it. You'd better see to your ensign."

Dubauer, drowsing, had been aroused by the uproar and was attempting to crawl away again. Cordelia tried to soothe him, then found herself having to deal with another seizure, after which, to her relief, he went to sleep.

Vorkosigan, in the meanwhile, had patched his scratch using the small emergency medical kit on his belt, and returned to digging, slowing down only a little. Getting down to shoulder depth, he pressed her into hauling dirt up out of the grave using the emptied-out botanical specimen box as a makeshift bucket. It was near midnight before he called from the dark pit, "That should be the last," and clambered out. "Could have done that in five seconds with a plasma arc," he panted, recovering his wind. He was dirty and sweating in the cold night air. Tendrils of fog writhed up from the ravine and the spring.

Together they dragged Rosemont's body to the lip of the grave. Vorkosigan hesitated.

"Do you want his clothes for your ensign?"

It was an unavoidably practical suggestion. Cordelia loathed the indignity of lowering Rosemont naked into the earth, but wished at the same time she had thought of it earlier, when Dubauer was so cold. She horsed the uniform off over the stiffened limbs with the macabre sensation of undressing a giant doll, and they tipped him into the grave. He landed on his back with a muffled thump.

"Just a minute." She dug out Rosemont's handkerchief from his uniform pocket and jumped down into the grave, slipping on the body. She spread the handkerchief over his face. It was a small, reality-defying gesture, but she felt better for it. Vorkosigan grasped her hand and pulled her up.

"All right." They shoveled and pushed the dirt back into the hole far more quickly than it had been excavated, and packed it down as best they could by walking on it.

"Is there some ceremony you wish to perform?" Vorkosigan asked.

Cordelia shook her head, not feeling up to reciting the

vague, official funeral service. But she knelt by the grave for a few minutes making a more serious, less certain inward prayer for her dead. It seemed to fly upward and vanish in the void, echoless as a feather.

Vorkosigan waited patiently until she arose. "It's rather late," he said, "and we have just seen three good reasons not to go stumbling around in the dark. We may as well rest here until dawn. I'll take the first watch. Do you still want to bash my head in with a rock?"

"Not at the moment," she said sincerely.

"Very well. I'll wake you later."

Vorkosigan began his watch with a patrol of the perimeter of the glade, taking the cold light with him. It wavered through the black distance like a captive firefly. Cordelia lay down on her back beside Dubauer. The stars glimmered faintly through the gathering mist. Could one be her ship yet, or Vorkosigan's? Not likely, at the range they undoubtedly were by now.

She felt hollow. Energy, will, desire, slipped through her fingers like shining liquid, sucked away through some infinite sand. She glanced at Dubauer beside her, and jerked her mind from the easy vortex of despair. I'm still a commander, she told herself sharply; I have a command. You serve me still, ensign, although you cannot now serve even yourself. . . .

The thought seemed a thread to some great insight, but it melted in her grasp, and she slept.

CHAPTER TWO

They divided the meager spoils from the camp in makeshift backpacks and started down the mountain in the grey mist of morning. Cordelia led Dubauer by the hand and helped him when he stumbled. She was not sure how clearly he recognized her, but he clung to her and avoided Vorkosigan.

The forest grew thicker and the trees taller as they went down. Vorkosigan hacked through the undergrowth with his knife for a while, then they took to the stream bed. Splashes of sunlight began to filter through the canopy, picking out fiery green velvet humps of moss, sparkling rills of water, and stones on the stream bed like a layer of bronze coins.

Radial symmetry was popular among the tiny creatures occupying the ecological niches held by insects on Earth. Some aerial varieties like gas-filled jellyfishes floated in iridescent clouds above the stream like flocks of delicate soap bubbles, delighting Cordelia's eye. They seemed to have a mellowing effect on Vorkosigan, too, for he called for a break from what seemed to her a killing pace.

They drank from the stream and sat a while watching the little radials dart and puff in the spray from a waterfall. Vorkosigan closed his eyes and leaned against a tree. He was running on the ragged edge of exhaustion too, Cordelia realized. Temporarily unwatched, she studied him curiously. He had behaved throughout with curt but dignified military professionalism. Still she was bothered by a subliminal alarm, a persistent sense of something of importance forgotten. It popped out of her memory suddenly, like a ball held underwater breaking the surface on release and arcing into the air.

"I know who you are. Vorkosigan, the Butcher of Komarr." She immediately wished she had not spoken, for he opened his eyes and stared at her, a peculiar play of expressions passing across his face.

"What do you know about Komarr?" His tone added, *An ignorant Betan.*

"Just what everyone knows. It was a worthless ball of rock your people annexed by military force for command of its wormhole clusters. The ruling senate surrendered on terms, and were murdered immediately after. You commanded the expedition, or . . ." Surely the Vorkosigan of Komarr had been an admiral. "Was it you? I thought you said you didn't kill prisoners."

"It was."

"Did they demote you for it?" she asked, surprised. She had thought that sort of conduct to be Barrayaran standard.

"Not for that. For the sequel." He seemed reluctant to say more, but he surprised her again by going on. "The sequel was more effectively suppressed. I had given my word—*my* word, as Vorkosigan—they were to be spared. My Political Officer countermanded my order, and had them killed behind my back. I executed him for it."

"Good God."

"I broke his neck with my own hands, on the bridge of my ship. It was a personal matter, you see, touching my honor. I couldn't order a firing squad—they were all afraid of the Ministry of Political Education."

That was the official euphemism for the secret police, Cordelia recalled, of which Political Officers were the military branch. "And you aren't?"

"They're afraid of me." He smiled sourly. "Like those scavengers last night, they'll run from a bold attack. But one must not turn one's back."

"I'm surprised they didn't have you hanged."

"There was a great uproar, behind closed doors," he admitted reminiscently, fingering his collar tabs. "But a Vorkosigan can't be made to disappear in the night, not yet. I did make some powerful enemies."

"I'll bet." This bald story, told without adornment or apology, had the ring of truth to her inner ear, although she had no logical reason to trust him. "Did you, uh, happen to turn your back on one of those enemies yesterday?"

He glanced at her sharply. "Possibly," he said slowly. "There are some problems with that theory, however."

"Like what?"

"I'm still alive. I wouldn't have thought they'd risk starting the job without finishing it. To be sure, they'd be tempted by the opportunity to blame my death on you Betans."

"Whew. And I thought I had command troubles just keeping a bunch of Betan intellectual prima donnas working together for months on end. God keep me from politics."

Vorkosigan smiled slightly. "From what I've heard of Betans, that's no easy task either. I don't think I should care to trade commands. It would irritate me to have every order argued over."

"They don't argue *every* order." She grinned, as his crack ferreted up some particular memories. "You learn how to coax them along."

"Where do you suppose your ship is now?"

Wariness dropped across her amusement like a portcullis. "I suppose that depends on where your ship is."

Vorkosigan shrugged and stood, hitching his pack more securely to his shoulders. "Then perhaps we should waste no more time finding out." He gave her a hand to pull her up, the soldier-mask repossessing his features.

It took all the long day to descend the great mountain to the red-soiled plains. A closer view found them cut and channeled by watercourses running turbid from the recent rains, and confused by outcrops of rocky badlands. They caught glimpses of groups of hexapedal grazers. Cordelia deduced from their wary herd behavior that associated predators must lurk nearby.

Vorkosigan would have pushed on, but Dubauer was seized by a serious and prolonged convulsion followed by lethargy and sleepiness. Cordelia insisted adamantly on a halt for the night. They made camp, if one could so describe stopping and sitting down, in an open gap in the trees perhaps three hundred meters above the levels. They shared their simple supper of oatmeal and blue cheese dressing in a beaten-down silence. Vorkosigan cracked another cold light as the last colors of a gaudy sunset drained from the sky, and seated himself on a large flat boulder. Cordelia lay down and watched the Barrayaran watching until sleep relieved her of her aching legs and head.

He woke her past the middle of the night. Her muscles seemed to screech and creak as she rose stiffly to take her watch. This time Vorkosigan gave her the stunner.

"I haven't seen anything close," he commented, "but something out there makes a hellish racket from time to time." It seemed an adequate explanation for the gesture of trust.

She checked Dubauer, then took her place on the boulder, leaning back and staring up at the dark bulk of the mountain. Up there Rosemont lay in his deep grave, safe from the beaks and bellies of the carrion eaters, but still doomed to slow decomposition. She bent her night-wandering thoughts instead to Vorkosigan, lying nearly invisible in his camouflage fatigues in the border of the blue-green light.

A puzzle within a puzzle, he was. Clearly, he must be one of the Barrayaran warrior aristocrats of the old school, at odds with the rising new men of the bureaucracy. The militarists of both parties maintained a bastard, uneasy alliance that controlled both government policy and the armed forces, but at heart they were natural enemies. The Emperor subtly stabilized the delicate balance of power between them, but there was not much doubt that on the clever old man's death Barrayar was destined for a period of political cannibalism, if not outright civil war, unless his successor showed more strength than was currently expected. She wished she knew more about the matrix of blood relationships and power on Barrayar. She could give the Emperor's family name, Vorbarra, it being associated with the name of the planet, but beyond that she was quite vague.

She absently fingered the little stunner, and tantalized herself: who now was the captive, and who the captor? But it would be nearly impossible to care for Dubauer in this wilderness by herself. She had to have supplies for him, and since Vorkosigan had been careful not to say exactly where his cache lay, she needed the Barrayaran to take her there. Besides, she had given her parole. It was a curious insight into Vorkosigan that he should so automatically accept her bare word as binding; he evidently thought along the same lines himself.

The east began to grow grey at last, then peach, green, and gold in a pastel repeat of last night's spectacular sunset. Vorkosigan stirred and sat up, and helped her take Dubauer down to the stream to wash. They had another breakfast of oatmeal and blue cheese dressing. Vorkosigan tried mixing his together this time, for variety. Cordelia tried alternating bites, to see if that would help. Neither commented aloud on the menu.

Vorkosigan led northwest across the sandy, brick-colored plain. In the dry season it would have been near-desert. Now it was brightly decorated with fresh green and yellow growth, and dozens of varieties of low-growing wildflowers. Dubauer did not seem to notice them, Cordelia saw sadly.

After about three hours at a brisk pace they came to their first check of the day, a steep rocky valley with a coffee-and-cream-colored river rushing through it. They walked along the edge of the escarpment looking for a ford.

"That rock down there moved," Cordelia observed suddenly.

Vorkosigan pulled his field scope from his belt and took a closer look. "You're right."

Half a dozen coffee-and-cream-colored lumps that looked like rocks on a sandbar proved to be low-slung, thick-limbed hexapeds, basking in the morning sun.

"They seem to be some sort of amphibian. I wonder if they're carnivores?" said Vorkosigan.

"I wish you hadn't interrupted my survey so soon," Cordelia complained. "Then I could have answered all those questions. There go some more of those soap-bubble things—goodness, I wouldn't have thought they could grow so big and still fly."

A flock of a dozen or so large radials, transparent as wineglasses and fully a foot across, came floating like a flight of lost balloons above the river. A few of them drifted over to the hexapeds and settled gently on their backs, flattening over their withers like weird berets. Cordelia borrowed the scope for a closer look.

"Do you suppose they could be like those birds from Earth, that pick the parasites off the cattle? Oh. No, I guess not."

The hexapeds roused themselves with hisses and whistles, humping their bodies in a kind of obese bucking, and slid into the river. The radials, colored now like wineglasses filled with burgundy, inflated themselves and retreated into the air.

"Vampire balloons?" asked Vorkosigan.

"Apparently."

"What appalling creatures."

Cordelia almost laughed at his revolted look. "As a carnivore yourself, you can't really condemn them."

"Condemn, no; avoid, yes."

"I'll go along with that."

They continued upstream past a frothing, opaque tan waterfall. After about a kilometer and a half they came to a place where two tributaries joined, and stumbled across at the shallowest place they could find. Crossing the second branch, Dubauer lost his footing as a rock turned under him, and went down with a wordless cry.

Cordelia tightened her grip on his arm convulsively, and perforce went with him, slipping into a deeper area. Terror shook her, that he might be swept downstream beyond her reach—those amphibious hexapeds, sharp rocks—the waterfall! Careless of the water filling her mouth, she grabbed him with both hands. Here they went—no.

Something pulled her bodily with a tremendous counter-surge against the rush of waters. Vorkosigan had grabbed her by the back of the belt, and was hauling them both toward the shallows with the strength and style of a stevedore.

Feeling undignified, but grateful, she scrambled to her feet and pushed the coughing Dubauer up the far bank.

"Thanks," she gasped to Vorkosigan.

"What, did you think I'd let you drown?" he inquired wryly, emptying his boots.

Cordelia shrugged, embarrassed. "Well—at least we wouldn't be delaying you."

"Hm." He cleared his throat, but said no more. They found a rocky place to sit, eat their cereal and salad dressing, and dry awhile before moving on.

Kilometers fell behind them, while their view of the great mountain to their right scarcely seemed to change. At some point Vorkosigan took a bearing known only to himself, and led them more westerly, with the mountain at their backs and the sun beginning to slant into their eyes.

They crossed another watercourse. Coming up over the lip of its valley, Cordelia nearly stumbled over a red-coated hexaped, lying quite still in a depression and blending perfectly with its background. It was a delicately formed thing, as big as a middle-sized dog, and it rippled over the red plains in graceful bounds.

Cordelia woke up abruptly. "That thing's edible!"

"The stunner, the stunner!" cried Vorkosigan. She pressed it hastily into his hand. He fell to one knee, took aim, and dropped the creature in one burst.

"Oh, good shot!" cried Cordelia ecstatically.

Vorkosigan grinned like a boy over his shoulder at her, and jogged after his prize.

"Oh," she murmured, stunned herself by the effect of the grin. It had lit his face like the sun for that brief instant. Oh, do that again, she thought; then shook off the thought. Duty. Stick to duty.

She followed him to where the animal lay. Vorkosigan had his knife out, puzzling over where to begin. He could not cut its throat, for it had no neck.

"The brain is located right behind the eyes. Maybe you could pith it going in between the first set of shoulder blades," Cordelia suggested.

"That would be quick enough," Vorkosigan agreed, and did so. The creature shivered, sighed, and died. "It's early to make camp, but there's water here, and driftwood from the river for a fire. It will mean extra kilometers tomorrow, though," he warned.

Cordelia eyed the carcass, thinking of roast meat. "That's all right."

Vorkosigan hoisted it to his shoulder, and stood. "Where's your ensign?"

Cordelia looked around. Dubauer was not in sight. "Oh, lord," she inhaled, and ran back to the spot where they had been standing when Vorkosigan had shot dinner. No Dubauer. She approached the rim of the watercourse.

Dubauer was standing by the stream, arms hanging by his sides, gazing upward blank and entranced. Floating softly down toward his upturned face was a large transparent radial.

"Dubauer, no!" shrieked Cordelia, and scrambled down the bank toward him. Vorkosigan passed her with a bound, and they raced for the waterside. The radial settled over Dubauer's face and began to flatten, and he flung up his hands with a cry.

Vorkosigan arrived first. He grabbed the half-limp thing with his bare hand and pulled it away from Dubauer's face. A dozen dark, tendril-like appendages were hooked into Dubauer's flesh, and they stretched and snapped as the creature was ripped off its prey. Vorkosigan flung it to the sand and stamped on it as Dubauer fell to the ground and curled up on his side. Cordelia tried to pull his hands away from his face. He was making strange, hoarse noises, and his body shook. Another seizure, she thought—but then realized with a shock that he was weeping.

She held his head on her lap to stop the wild rocking. The spots where the tendrils had penetrated his skin were black in the center, surrounded by rings of red flesh that were beginning to swell alarmingly. There was a particularly nasty one at the corner of his eye. She plucked one of the remaining embedded tendrils out of his skin, and found it burned her fingers acidly. Apparently the creature had been coated all over with a similar poison, for Vorkosigan was kneeling with his hand in the stream. She quickly pulled the rest of them, and called the Barrayaran over to her side.

"Have you got anything in your kit that will help this?"

"Only the antibiotic." He handed her a tube, and she smeared some on Dubauer's face. It was not really a proper burn ointment, but it would have to do. Vorkosigan stared at Dubauer a moment, then reluctantly produced a small white pill.

"This is a powerful analgesic. I have only four. It should carry him through the evening."

Cordelia placed it on the back of Dubauer's tongue. It evidently tasted bitter, for he tried to spit it out, but she caught it and forced him to swallow it. In a few minutes she was able to get him to his feet and take him to the campsite Vorkosigan chose overlooking the sandy channel.

Vorkosigan meanwhile made a handsome collection of driftwood for a fire.

"How are you going to light it?" inquired Cordelia.

"When I was a small boy, I had to learn to start a fire by friction," Vorkosigan reminisced. "Military school summer camp. It wasn't easy. Took all afternoon. Come to think of it, I never did get it started that way. I lit it by dissecting a communicator for the power pack."

He was searching through his belt and pockets. "The instructor was furious. I think it must have been his communicator."

"No chemical starters?" Cordelia asked, with a nod to his ongoing inventory of his utility belt.

"It's assumed if you want heat, you can fire your plasma arc." He tapped his fingers on the empty holster. "I have another idea. A bit drastic, but I think it will be effective. You'd better go sit with your botanist. This is going to be loud."

He removed a useless plasma arc power cartridge from a row on the back of his belt.

"Uh, oh," said Cordelia, moving away. "Won't that be overkill? And what are you going to do with the crater? It'll be visible from the air for kilometers."

"Do you want to sit there and rub two sticks together? I suppose I had better do something about the crater, though."

He thought a moment, then trotted away over the edge of the little valley. Cordelia sat down beside Dubauer, putting an arm around his shoulders and hunching in anticipation.

Vorkosigan shot back over the rim at a dead run, and hit the ground rolling. There was a brilliant blue-white flash, and a boom that shook the ground. A large column of smoke, dust, and steam rose into the air, and pebbles, dirt, and bits of melted sand began to patter down like rain all around. Vorkosigan disappeared over the edge again, and returned shortly with a fine flaming torch.

Cordelia went for a peek at the damage. Vorkosigan had placed the short-circuited cartridge upstream about a hundred meters, at the outer edge of a bend where the swift little river curved away to the east. The explosion had left a spectacular glass-lined crater some fifteen meters wide and five deep that was still smoking. As she watched, the stream eroded its edge and poured in, billowing steam. In an hour it would be scoured into a natural-looking backwater.

"Not bad," she murmured approvingly.

By the time the fire burned down to a bed of coals they had cubes of dark red meat on sticks ready to broil.

"How do you like yours?" Vorkosigan asked. "Rare? Medium?"

"I think it had better be well done," suggested Cordelia. "We hadn't completed the parasite survey yet."

Vorkosigan glanced at his cube with a new dubiousness. "Ah. Quite," he said faintly.

They cooked it thoroughly, then sat by the fire and tore into the smoking meat with happy savagery. Even Dubauer managed to feed himself with small chunks. It was gamey and tough, burned on the outside and with a bitter undertaste, but no one suggested a side dish of either oatmeal or blue cheese dressing.

Cordelia's humor was touched. Vorkosigan's fatigues were filthy, damp, and splashed with dried blood from hacking up their dinner, as were her own. He had a three-day growth of beard, his face glistened in the firelight with hexaped grease, and he reeked with dried sweat. Barring the beard, she suspected she looked no better, and she knew she smelled no better. She found herself disquietingly aware of his body, muscular, compact, wholly masculine, stirring senses she thought she had suppressed. Best think of something else . . .

"From spaceman to caveman in three days," she meditated aloud. "How we imagine our civilization is in ourselves, when it's really in our things."

Vorkosigan glanced with a twisted smile at the carefully tended Dubauer. "You seem able to carry your civilization on the inside."

Cordelia flushed uncomfortably, glad for the camouflaging firelight. "One does one's duty."

"Some people find their duty more elastic. Or—were you in love with him?"

"With Dubauer? Heavens, no! I'm no cradle snatcher. He was a good kid, though. I'd like to get him home to his family."

"Do you have a family?"

"Sure. My mom and brother, back home on Beta Colony. My dad used to be in the Survey too."

"Was he one of those who never came back?"

"No, he died in a shuttleport accident, not ten kilometers from home. He'd been home on leave, and was just reporting back."

"My condolences."

"Oh, that was years and years ago." Getting a little personal, isn't he? she thought. But it was better than trying to deflect military interrogation. She hoped fervently that the subject, say, of the latest Betan equipment would not come up. "How about you? Do you have a family?" It suddenly occurred to her that this phrase was also a polite way of asking, *Are you married?*

"My father lives. He is Count Vorkosigan. My mother was half Betan, you know," he offered hesitantly.

Cordelia decided that if Vorkosigan, full of military curtness, was formidable, Vorkosigan trying to make himself pleasant was truly terrifying. But curiosity overcame the urge to cut the conversation short. "That's unusual. How did that happen?"

"My maternal grandfather was Prince Xav Vorbarra, the diplomat. He held the post of ambassador to Beta Colony for a time, in his youth, before the First Cetagandan War. I believe my grandmother was in your Bureau for Interstellar Trade."

"Did you know her well?"

"After my mother—died, and Yuri Vorbarra's Civil War was brought to an end, I spent some school vacations at the Prince's home in the capital. He was at odds with my father, though, before and after that war, being of different political parties. Xav was the leading light of the progressives in his day, and of course my father was—is—part of the last stand of the old military aristocracy."

"Was your grandmother happy on Barrayar?" Cordelia estimated Vorkosigan's school days were perhaps thirty years ago.

"I don't think she ever adjusted completely to our society. And of course, Yuri's War . . ." He trailed off, then began again. "Outsiders—you Betans particularly—have this odd vision of Barrayar as some monolith, but we are a fundamentally divided society. My government is always fighting these centrifugal tendencies."

Vorkosigan leaned forward and tossed another piece of wood onto the fire. Sparks cascaded upward like a stream of little orange stars flowing home to the sky. Cordelia felt a sharp longing to fly away with them.

"What party has your allegiance?" she asked, hoping to keep the conversation on a less unnervingly personal plane. "Do you stand with your father?"

"While he lives. I always wanted to be a soldier, and avoid all parties. I have an aversion to politics; they've been death on my family. But it's past time someone took on those damned bureaucrats and their pet spies. They imagine they're the wave of the future, but it's only sewage flowing downhill."

"If you express those opinions that forcibly at home, it's no wonder politics come looking for you." She poked at the fire with a stick, freeing more sparks for their journey.

Dubauer, sedated by the painkiller, fell asleep quickly, but Cordelia lay long awake, replaying the disturbing conversation in her mind. Still, what did she care if this Barrayaran chose to run his head into nooses? No reason for her to get involved. None at all. Surely not. Even if the shape of his square strong hands was a dream of power in form . . .

She awakened deep in the night with a start. But it was only the fire flaring up as Vorkosigan added an unusually large armload of wood. She sat up, and he came over to her.

"I'm glad you're awake. I need you." He pressed his combat knife into her hand. "That carcass seems to be attracting something. I'm going to pitch it into the river. Will you hold a torch?"

"Sure." She stretched, got up, and selected a suitable brand. She followed him down into the watercourse, rubbing her eyes. The flickering orange light made jumpy

black shadows that were almost harder to see into than
plain starlight. As they reached the water's edge she caught
movement out of the corner of her eye, and heard a
scrambling among the rocks and a familiar hiss.

"Uh, oh. There's a group of those scavengers just
upstream to the left."

"Right." Vorkosigan flung the remains of their dinner
to the middle of the river, where they vanished with a
dim gurgle. There was an extra splash, a loud one, not
an echo. Aha! Cordelia thought—I saw you jump too,
Barrayaran. But whatever had splashed didn't show above
the surface, and its ripples were lost in the current. There
came some more hisses, and a shattering shriek, from
downstream. Vorkosigan drew the stunner.

"There's a whole herd of them out there," Cordelia
commented nervously. They stood back to back, trying to
penetrate the blackness. Vorkosigan rested the stunner
across one wrist, and let off a carefully aimed burst. It
buzzed quietly, and one of the dark shapes slumped to
the ground. Its comrades sniffed it curiously, and moved
in closer.

"I wish your gun had more of a bang." He aimed again
and dropped two more, without any effect on the rest.
He cleared his throat. "You know, your stunner's almost
out of charge."

"Not enough to flatten the rest of them, eh?"

"No."

One of the scavengers, bolder than the rest, darted
forward. Vorkosigan met its charge with a shout and a rush
of his own. It retreated temporarily. The breed of scavengers that ranged the plains was slightly larger than its
mountain cousins, and if possible, uglier. Obviously, it also
traveled in larger groups. The ring of beasts closed tighter
as they attempted to retreat toward the valley rim.

"Oh, hell," said Vorkosigan. "That does it." A dozen
silent, ghostly globes were drifting in from above. "What
a foul way to die. Well, let's take as many with us as
possible." He glanced at her, seemed about to say more,
but then only shook his head and braced for the rush.

Cordelia, heart lurching, gazed up at the descending radials and was illuminated by an idea of awesome brilliance.

"Oh, no," she breathed. "That's not the last straw. That's the home fleet, coming to the rescue. Come, my pretties," she coaxed. "Come to Mama."

"Have you lost your mind?" asked Vorkosigan.

"You wanted a bang? I'll give you a bang. What do you think holds those things up?"

"Hadn't thought about it. But of course it would almost have to be—"

"Hydrogen! Bet you anything those darling little chemistry sets are electrolyzing water. Notice how they hang around rivers and streams? Wish I had some gloves."

"Allow me." His grin winked out of the fire-streaked dark at her. He jumped up and hooked a radial out of the air by its writhing maroon tendrils, and flung it to earth before the approaching scavengers. Cordelia, holding her torch like a fencer's foil, thrust toward it at full extension. Sparks scattered as she jabbed two, then three times.

The radial exploded in a ball of blinding flame that singed her eyebrows, with a great bass whoom and an astonishing stench. Orange and green afterimages danced across her retinas. She repeated the trick at Vorkosigan's next snatch. One of the scavengers' fur caught fire, and it led a general retreat, screeching and hissing. She poked again at a radial in the air. It went off with a flash that illuminated the whole reach of the river valley and the humping backs of the fleeing pack of scavengers.

Vorkosigan was frantically patting her on the back; it wasn't until the smell caught her that she realized she'd set her own hair on fire. He got it out. The rest of the radials sailed high into the air and away, except for one Vorkosigan captured and held by standing on its tendrils.

"Ha!" Cordelia war danced around him in triumph, the adrenaline rush giving her a silly urge to giggle. She drew a deep breath. "Is your hand all right?"

"It's a little burned," he admitted. He took off his shirt and bundled the radial into it. It pulsated and stank. "We might want this later." He rinsed his hand briefly in the stream, and they jogged quickly back to their campsite. Dubauer lay undisturbed, although a few minutes later one stray scavenger turned up at the edge of the firelight, sniffing and hissing. Vorkosigan put it to flight with torch, knife, and swearing—whispered, so as not to wake the ensign.

"I think we'd better live on field rations for the rest of the trip," he said, returning.

Cordelia nodded heartfelt agreement.

She roused the men at the first grey light of dawn, as anxious now as Vorkosigan to complete the trip to the safety of the supply cache as quickly as possible. The radial held captive in Vorkosigan's shirt had died and deflated during the night, turning into a horrible gelid blob. Vorkosigan of necessity took a few minutes to wash it out in the stream, but the stinks and stains it left made him the unquestioned front-runner in the filth-collection contest Cordelia felt they were having. They had a quick snack of their dull but safe oatmeal and blue cheese dressing, and started on their way as the sun rose, sending their long shadows racing ahead of them across the rusty, flower-strewn levels.

Near their noon halt Vorkosigan took a break and disappeared behind a bush for biological necessity. In a few moments a string of curses came floating around it, followed shortly by the speaker himself, hopping from foot to foot and shaking out the legs of his trousers. Cordelia gave him a look of innocent inquiry.

"You know those light yellow cones of sand we've been seeing?" Vorkosigan said, unbuckling his pants.

"Yes . . ."

"Don't stand on one to piss."

Cordelia failed to strangle a giggle. "What did you find? Or should I say, what found you?"

Vorkosigan turned his trousers inside out and began picking the little round white creatures running among their folds on cilia-like legs. Cordelia appropriated one and held it on the palm of her hand for a closer look. It was yet another model of the radials, an underground form.

"Ow!" She brushed it away hastily.

"Stings, doesn't it?" snarled Vorkosigan.

A burble of laughter welled up within her. But she was saved from a lapse of control when she noticed a more sobering feature of his appearance.

"Hey, that scratch doesn't look too good, does it?"

The claw mark of the scavenger on his right leg that Vorkosigan had collected the night they buried Rosemont was swollen and bluish, with ugly red streaks radiating from it up as far as his knee.

"It's all right," he said firmly, beginning to put on his de-radialed pants.

"It doesn't look all right. Let me see."

"There's nothing you can do about it here," he protested, but submitted to a brief examination. "Satisfied?" he inquired sarcastically, and finished dressing.

"I wish your micro people had been a little more thorough when they concocted that salve," Cordelia shrugged. "But you're right. Nothing to be done now."

They trudged on. Cordelia watched him more closely now. From time to time he would begin to favor the leg, then notice her scrutiny and march forward with a determinedly even stride. But by the end of the day he had abandoned subterfuge and was frankly limping. In spite of it he led on into the sunset, the afterglow of the sunset, and the gathering night, until the cratered mountain toward which they had been angling was a black bulk on the horizon. At last, stumbling in the dark, he gave up and called a halt. She was glad, for Dubauer was flagging, leaning on her heavily and trying to lie down. They slept where they stopped on the red sandy soil. Vorkosigan cracked a cold light and took his usual watch, as Cordelia lay in the dirt and watched the unreachable stars wheel overhead.

Vorkosigan had asked to be waked before dawn, but she let him sleep until full light. She didn't like the way

he looked, alternately pale and flushed, or his shallow
rapid breathing.

"Think you'd better take one of your painkillers?" she
asked him when he rose, for he seemed barely able to
put weight on the leg, which was much more swollen.

"Not yet. I have to save some for the end." He cut a
long stick instead, and the three of them began the day's
task of walking down their shadows.

"How far to the end?" Cordelia asked.

"I estimate a day, day and a half, depending on what
kind of time we can make." He grimaced. "Don't worry.
You're not going to have to carry me. I'm one of the fittest
men in my command." He limped on. "Over forty."

"How many men over forty are there in your command?"

"Four."

Cordelia snorted.

"Anyway, if it becomes necessary, I have a stimulant
in my medkit that would animate a corpse. But I want
to save it for the end too."

"What kind of trouble are you anticipating?"

"It all depends on who picks up my call. I know
Radnov—my Political Officer—has at least two agents in
my communications section." He pursed his lips, measuring her again. "You see, I don't think it was a general
mutiny. I think it was a spur-of-the-moment assassination
attempt on the part of Radnov and a very few others.
Using you Betans, they thought they could get rid of me
without implicating themselves. If I'm right, everyone
aboard ship thinks I'm dead. All but one."

"Which one?"

"Wouldn't I like to know. The one who hit me on the
head and hid me in the bracken, instead of cutting my
throat and dumping me in the nearest hole. Lieutenant
Radnov seems to have a ringer in his group. And yet—
if this ringer were loyal to me, all he'd have to do is tell
Gottyan, my first officer, and he'd have had a loyal patrol
down to pick me up before now. Now who in my command is so confused in his thinking as to betray both sides
at once? Or am I missing something?"

"Maybe they're all still chasing my ship," suggested Cordelia.

"Where is your ship?"

Honesty should be safely academic by now, Cordelia calculated. "Well on its way back to Beta Colony."

"Unless they've been captured."

"No. They were out of your range when I talked to them. They may not be armed, but they can run rings around your battle cruiser."

"Hm. Well, it's possible."

He doesn't sound surprised, Cordelia noted. I'd bet his secret reports on our stuff would give our counter-intelligence people colonic spasms. "How far will they pursue?"

"That's up to Gottyan. If he judges he can't possibly catch them, he'll return to the picket station. If he thinks he can, he's bound to make maximum effort."

"Why?"

He glanced sidelong at her. "I can't discuss that."

"I don't see why not. I'm not going anywhere but a Barrayaran prison cell, for a while. Funny how one's standards change. After this trek, it will seem like the lap of luxury."

"I'll try to see it doesn't come to that," he smiled.

His eyes bothered her, and his smile. His curtness she could meet and match with her own flippancy, guarding herself as with a fencer's foil. His kindness was like fencing with the sea, her strokes going soft and losing all volition. She flinched from the smile, and his face fell, then became closed and grave again.

CHAPTER THREE

They walked in silence for a time after breakfast. Vorkosigan broke it first. His fever seemed to be eating away at his original taciturnity.

"Converse with me. It will take my mind off my leg."

"What about?"

"Anything."

She considered, walking. "Do you find commanding a warship very different from ordinary vessels?"

He thought it over. "It's not the ship that's different. It's the men. Leadership is mostly a power over imagination, and never more so than in combat. The bravest man alone can only be an armed lunatic. The real strength lies in the ability to get others to do your work. Don't you find it so even in the fleets of Beta Colony?"

Cordelia smiled. "If anything, even more so. If it ever came down to exerting power by force, it would mean I'd already lost it. I prefer to maintain a light touch. Then I have the advantage, because I find I can always keep my temper, or whatever, just a little longer than the next man." She glanced around at the spring desert. "I think civilization must have been invented for the benefit of women, certainly of mothers. I can't imagine how my cavewoman ancestors cared for families under primitive conditions."

"I suspect they worked together in groups," said Vorkosigan. "I'll wager you could have handled it, had you been born in those days. You have the competence one would look for in a mother of warriors."

Cordelia wondered if Vorkosigan was pulling her leg. He did seem to have a streak of dry humor. "Save me from that! To pour your life into sons for eighteen or twenty years, and then have the government take them away and waste them cleaning up after some failure of politics—no thanks."

"I never really looked at it that way," allowed Vorkosigan. He was quiet for a time, stumping along with his stick. "Suppose they volunteered? Do your people have no ideal of service?"

"Noblesse oblige?" But it was her turn to be silent, a little embarrassed. "I suppose, if they volunteered, it would be different. However, I have no children, so fortunately I won't have to face those decisions."

"Are you glad, or sorry?"

"About children?" She glanced at his face. He seemed to have no awareness of having hit a sore point dead on. "They just haven't come my way, I guess."

The thread of their talk was broken as they negotiated a rocky stretch of badlands, full of sudden clefts opening at their feet. It involved some tricky climbing, and shoving Dubauer through safely took all her attention. On the far side they took a break by unspoken mutual agreement, sitting leaning against a rock in exhaustion. Vorkosigan rolled up his pants leg and loosened his boot top for a look at the festering wound that was threatening to slow him to a halt.

"You seem a fair nurse. Do you think it would help to open and drain it?" he asked Cordelia.

"I don't know. I'd be afraid messing around with it would just make it dirtier." She deduced the injury must be feeling very much worse for him to have mentioned it, confirmed when he took half a painkiller from his precious and limited store.

They pressed on, and Vorkosigan began to talk again. He told some sardonic anecdotes from his cadet days, and described his father, who had been a general commanding ground forces in his day, and a contemporary and friend of the wily old man who was now Emperor. Cordelia caught a faint, faraway impression of a cold father whom a young son could never quite please, even with his best efforts, yet who shared with him a bond of underlying loyalty. She described her mother, a tough-minded medical professional resisting retirement, and her brother, who had just purchased his second child permit.

"Do you remember your mother well?" Cordelia asked. "She died when you were quite young, I gather. An accident, like my father?"

"No accident. Politics." His face became sober, and distant. "Had you not heard of Yuri Vorbarra's Massacre?"

"I—don't know much about Barrayar."

"Ah. Well, Emperor Yuri, in the later days of his madness, became extremely paranoid about his relations. It became a self-fulfilling prophecy, in the end. He sent his death squads out, all in one night. The squad sent for Prince Xav never got past his liveried men. And for some obscure reason, he didn't send one for my father, presumably because he wasn't a descendant of Emperor Dorca Vorbarra. I can't imagine what old Yuri thought he was about, to kill my mother and leave my father alive. That was when my father threw his corps behind Ezar Vorbarra, in the civil war that followed."

"Oh." Her throat seemed dry and thick in the dusty afternoon. She had evoked a coldness in him, so that the film of sweat on his forehead seemed suddenly like a condensation.

"It's been on my mind. . . . You were talking about the peculiar things people do in a panic, earlier, and I remembered it. Hadn't thought of it in years. When Yuri's men blew in the door—"

"My God, you weren't *present*?"

"Oh, yes. I was on the list too, of course. Each assassin was assigned a particular target. The one assigned to my mother—I grabbed this knife, a table knife, by my plate, and struck at him. But right in front of me on the table there had been a good carving knife. If only I had grabbed it instead . . . I might as well have struck him with a spoon. He just picked me up, and threw me across the room—"

"How old were you?"

"Eleven. Small for my age. I was always small for my age. He cornered her against the far wall. He fired a . . ." He sucked his lower lip between his teeth and chewed it, just short of breaking the skin to bleed. "Odd how many details come back when you talk about something. I thought I had forgotten more."

He glanced at her white face, and grew suddenly contrite. "I've disturbed you, with this babble. I'm sorry. It was all very long ago. I don't know why I'm talking so much."

I do, thought Cordelia. He was pale and no longer sweating, in spite of the heat. Half-unconsciously, he fastened the top of his shirt. He feels cold, she thought; fever going up. How far up? Plus whatever effect those pills have. This could get very scary.

An obscure impulse made her say, "I know what you mean, though, about talking bringing it back. First there was the shuttle going up, like a bullet as usual, and my brother waving, which was silly, because he couldn't possibly see us—and then there was this smear of light across the sky, like a second sun, and a rain of fire. And this *stupid* feeling of total comprehension. You wait for the shock to set in, and relieve you—and it never does. Then the blank vision. Not blackness, but this silver-purple glow, for days after. I had almost forgotten about being blinded, till just now."

He stared at her. "That's exactly—I was about to say, he fired a sonic grenade into her stomach. I couldn't hear anything after that for quite some time. As if all sound had gone off the scale of human reception. Total noise, emptier of meaning than silence."

"Yes . . ." How strange, that he should know exactly what I felt—he says it better, though. . . .

"I suppose my determination to be a soldier stems from that date. I mean the real thing, not the parades and the uniforms and the glamour, but the logistics, the offensive advantage, the speed and surprise—the power. A better-prepared, stronger, tougher, faster, meaner son-of-a-bitch than any who came through that door. My first combat experience. Not very successful."

He was shivering, now. But then, so was she. They walked on, and she sought to turn the subject.

"I've never been in combat. What's it like?"

He paused thoughtfully. *Measuring me again,* thought Cordelia. *And sweating; fever must be topping out, for the moment, thank heavens.*

"At a distance, in space, there's the illusion of a clean and glorious fight. Almost abstract. It might be a simulation, or a game. Reality doesn't break in unless your ship is hit." He gazed at the ground in front of him, as if choosing his path, but the ground was very level there. "Murder—murder is different. That day at Komarr, when I killed my Political Officer—I was angrier that day than the day I—than another time. But close up, feeling the life pass out under your hands, seeing that blank unoccupied corpse, you see your own death in the face of your victim. Yet he had betrayed my honor."

"I'm not sure I quite understand that."

"Yes. Anger seems to make you stronger, not weaker like me. I wish I understood how you do that."

It was another one of his weird unmanageable compliments. She fell silent, looking at her feet, the mountain ahead, the sky, anywhere but his unreadable face. So she was the first to notice the contrail glowing in the westering sun.

"Hey, does that look like a shuttle up there to you?"

"Indeed it does. Let's watch from the shade of that big bush," directed Vorkosigan.

"Don't you want to try and attract their attention?"

"No." He turned his hand palm up in response to her look of inquiry. "My best friends and my deadliest enemies all wear the same uniform. I prefer to make my presence known as selectively as possible."

They could hear the distant roar of the shuttle's engines

now as it vanished behind the grey-green wooded mountain to the west.

"They seem to be headed for the cache," commented Vorkosigan. "That complicates things." He compressed his lips. "What are they doing back there, I wonder? Could Gottyan have found the sealed orders?"

"Surely he'd inherit all your orders."

"Yes, but I didn't have my files in the standard location, not wishing to share all my affairs with the Council of Ministers. I don't think Korabik Gottyan could find what eludes Radnov. Radnov's a clever spy."

"Is Radnov a tall, broad-shouldered man with a face like an axeblade?"

"No, that sounds like Sergeant Bothari. Where did you see him?"

"He was the man who shot Dubauer, in the woods by the ravine."

"Oh, really?" Vorkosigan's eyes lit, and he smiled wolfishly. "Much becomes clear."

"Not to me," Cordelia prodded.

"Sergeant Bothari is a very strange man. I had to discipline him rather severely last month."

"Severely enough to make him a candidate for Radnov's conspiracy?"

"I'll wager Radnov thought so. I'm not sure I can make you understand about Bothari. Nobody else seems to. He's a superb ground combat soldier. He also hates my guts, as you Betans would phrase it. He *enjoys* hating my guts. It seems to be necessary for his ego, somehow."

"Would he shoot you in the back?"

"Never. Strike me in the face, yes. In fact, it was for decking me that he was disciplined last time." Vorkosigan rubbed his jaw thoughtfully. "But arming him to the teeth and leading him into battle at my back is perfectly safe."

"He sounds like an absolute looney."

"Odd, a number of people have said that. I like him."

"And you accuse us Betans of running a circus."

Vorkosigan shrugged, amused. "Well, it's useful for me to have someone to work out with who doesn't pull his punches. Surviving hand-to-hand combat practice with Bothari gives me a real edge. I prefer to keep that phase of our relationship confined to the practice ring, however. I can imagine how Radnov might be misled into including Bothari without examining his politics too closely. He acts like just the sort of fellow one might stick with the dirty work—by God, I'll bet that's just what Radnov did! Good old Bothari."

Cordelia glanced at Dubauer, standing blankly beside her. "I'm afraid I can't share your enthusiasm. He nearly killed me."

"I can't pretend he's a moral or intellectual giant. He's a very complex man with a very limited range of expression, who's had some very bad experiences. But in his own twisty way, he's honorable."

The ground rose almost imperceptibly as they approached the mountain's base. The change was marked by the gradual encroachment of vegetation, thin woods watered by a multitude of small springs from the mountain's secret sources. They struck south around the base of the dusty green cone that rose steeply some 1500 meters above the more gradually sloping shoulderland.

Pulling the stumbling Dubauer along, Cordelia mentally cursed, for what seemed the thousandth time, Vorkosigan's choice of weapons. When the ensign fell, cutting his forehead, her grief and irritation erupted into words.

"Why can't you people use civilized weapons, anyway? I'd as soon give a disruptor to a chimpanzee as a Barrayaran. Trigger-happy goons." Dubauer sat dizzily, and she mopped at the blood with her dirty handkerchief, then sat too.

Vorkosigan lowered himself awkwardly to the ground beside them, bad leg out straight, silently endorsing the break. He gazed at her tense unhappy face, and offered her a serious answer.

"I have an aversion to stunners, in that sort of situation," he said slowly. "Nobody hesitates to rush one, and if there are enough of them they can always get it away from you in the end. I've seen men killed, relying on stunners, who could have walked right through with a disruptor or plasma arc. A disruptor has real authority."

"On the other hand, nobody hesitates to *fire* a stunner," said Cordelia suggestively. "And it gives you a margin for error."

"What, would you hesitate to fire a disruptor?"

"Yes. I might as well not have it at all."

"Ah."

Curiosity prodded her, mulling on his words. "How in the world did they kill him with a stunner, the man you saw?"

"They didn't kill him with the stunner. After they took it away from him they kicked him to death."

"Oh." Cordelia's stomach tightened. "Not—not a friend of yours, I hope."

"As it happens, he was. He shared something of your attitude toward weaponry. Soft." He frowned into the distance.

They struggled up, and trudged on through the woods. The Barrayaran tried to help her more with Dubauer, for a time. But Dubauer recoiled from him, and between the ensign's resistance and his own bad leg, the awkward attempt failed.

Vorkosigan withdrew into himself, and became less talkative, after that. All his concentration seemed focused on pushing himself ahead just one more step, but he muttered to himself alarmingly. Cordelia had a nasty vision of collapse and fevered delirium, and no faith at all in her ability to take over his role of identifying and contacting a loyal member of his crew. It was plain that an error in judgment could be lethal, and while she could not say that all Barrayarans looked alike to her, she was forcibly reminded of the old conundrum that starts, "All Cretans are liars."

Near sunset, threading their way through a patch of denser woods, they came suddenly on a little glade of astonishing beauty. A waterfall foamed down over a bed of black rocks that glistened like obsidian, a cascade of lace alive with light. The grass that bordered the streambed was backlit by the sun in a translucent gold glow. The surrounding trees, tall, dark green, and shady, set it like a gem.

Vorkosigan leaned on his stick and gazed at it a while. Cordelia thought she had never seen a tireder looking human being, but then, she had no mirror.

"We have about fifteen kilometers to go," he said. "I don't wish to approach the cache in the dark. We'll stop here tonight, rest, and take it in the morning."

They flopped down in the soft grass and watched the glorious flaming sunset in silence, like an old married couple too tired to get up and turn it off. At last the failing light forced them into action. They washed hands and faces in the stream, and Vorkosigan shared his Barrayaran field rations at last. Even after four days of oatmeal and blue cheese dressing, they were a disappointment.

"Are you sure this isn't instant boots?" asked Cordelia sadly, for in color, taste, and smell they closely resembled pulverized shoe leather pressed into wafers.

Vorkosigan grinned sardonically. "They're organic, nutritious, and they'll keep for years—in fact, they probably have."

Cordelia smiled around a dry and chewy mouthful. She hand-fed Dubauer his—he was inclined to spit them out—then washed and settled him for the night. He had had no seizures this day, which she hoped might be a sign of partial improvement in his condition.

The earth still breathed a comfortable warmth from the heat of the day, and the stream purled softly in the stillness. She wished she could sleep for a hundred years, like an enchanted princess. Instead she rose and volunteered for the first watch.

"I think you'd better have the extra sleep tonight," she told Vorkosigan. "I've had the short watch two nights out of three. It's your turn."

"There's no need—" he began.

"If you don't make it, I don't make it," she pointed out bluntly. "And neither does he." She jerked her thumb at the quiescent Dubauer. "I intend to see that you make it tomorrow."

Vorkosigan took another half painkiller and lay back where he sat, conceding the argument. Still he remained restless, sleep evading him, and he watched her through the dimness. His eyes seemed to gleam feverishly. He finally propped himself up on one elbow, as she finished a patrol around the edge of the glade and sat down cross-legged on the ground beside him.

"I . . ." he began, and trailed off. "You're not what I expected a female officer to be."

"Oh? Well, you're not what I expected a Barrayaran officer to be, either, so I guess that makes two of us." She added curiously, "What did you expect?"

"I'm—not sure. You're as professional as any officer I've ever served with, without once trying to be an, an imitation man. It's extraordinary."

"There's nothing extraordinary about me," she denied.

"Beta Colony must be a very unusual place, then."

"It's just home. Nothing special. Lousy climate."

"So I've heard." He picked up a twig and dug little furrows into the soil with it, until it snapped. "They don't have arranged marriages on Beta Colony, do they?"

She stared. "Certainly not! What a bizarre concept. Sounds almost like a civil rights violation. Heavens—you don't mean to say they do, on Barrayar?"

"In my caste, almost always."

"Doesn't anybody object?"

"They're not *forced*. Arranged, by the parents usually. It—seems to work. For many people."

"Well, I suppose it's possible."

"How, ah—how do you arrange yourselves? With no go-betweens it must be very awkward. I mean, to refuse someone, to their face."

"I don't know. It's something lovers work out after they've known each other quite a time, usually, and wish to apply for a child permit. This contractual thing you describe must be like marrying a total stranger. Naturally it would be awkward."

"Hm." He found another twig. "In the Time of Isolation, on Barrayar, for a man to take a woman of the soldier caste for a lover was regarded as stealing her honor, and he was supposed to die a thief's death for it. A custom more honored in the breach, I'm sure, although it's a favorite subject for drama. Today we are betwixt and between. The old customs are dead, and we keep trying on new ones, like badly fitting clothes. It's hard to know what's right, anymore." After a moment he added, "What had you expected?"

"From a Barrayaran? I don't know. Something criminal, I suppose. I wasn't too crazy about being taken prisoner."

His eyes fell. "I've—seen what you're talking about, of course. I can't deny it exists. It's an infection of the imagination, that spreads from man to man. It's worst when it goes from the top down. Bad for discipline, bad for morale . . . I hate most how it affects the younger officers, when they encounter it in the men they should be molding themselves on. They haven't the weight of experience, to fight it in their own minds, nor distinguish when a man is stealing the Emperor's authority to cloak his own appetites. And so they are corrupted almost before they know what's happening." His voice was intense in the darkness.

"I'd actually only thought about it from the prisoner's point of view, myself. I take it I am fortunate in my choice of captors."

"They're the scum of the service. But you must believe, a small minority. Although I've no use for those who pretend not to see, either, and they are not such a minority as . . . Make no mistake. It's not an easy infection to fight off. But you have nothing to fear from me. I promise you."

"I'd—already figured that out."

They sat in silence for a time, until the night crept up out of the low places to drain the last turquoise from the sky, and the waterfall ran pearly in the starlight. She thought he had fallen asleep, but he stirred, and spoke again. She could barely see his face, but for a little glint from the whites of his eyes, and his teeth.

"Your customs seem so free, and calm, to me. As innocent as sunlight. No grief, no pain, no irrevocable mistakes.

No boys turned criminal by fear. No stupid jealousy. No honor ever lost."

"That's an illusion. You can still lose your honor. It just doesn't happen in a night. It can take years, to drain away in bits and dribbles." She paused, in the friendly dark. "I knew this woman, once—a very good friend of mine. In Survey. She was rather—socially inept. Everyone around her seemed to be finding their soul-mates, and the older she grew, the more panicky she got about being left out. Quite pathetically anxious.

"She finally fell in with a man with the most astonishing talent for turning gold into lead. She couldn't use a word like love, or trust, or honor in his presence without eliciting clever mockery. Pornography was permitted; poetry, never.

"They were, as it happened, of equal rank when the captaincy of their ship fell open. She'd sweated blood for this command, worked her tail off—well, I'm sure you know what it's like. Commands are few, and everybody wants one. Her lover persuaded her, partly by promise that turned out to be lies, later—children, in fact—to stand down in his favor, and he got the command. Quite the strategist. It ended soon after. Thoroughly dry.

"She had no stomach for another lover, after that. So you see, I think your old Barrayarans may have been on to something, after all. The inept—need rules, for their own protection."

The waterfall whispered in the silence. "I—knew a man once," his voice came out of the darkness. "He was married, at twenty, to a girl of high rank of eighteen. Arranged, of course, but he was very happy with it.

"He was away most of the time, on duty. She found herself free, rich, alone in the capital in the society of people—not altogether vicious, but older than herself. Rich parasites, their parasites, users. She was courted, and it went to her head. Not her heart, I think. She took lovers, as those around her did. Looking back, I don't think she felt any more emotion for them than vanity and pride of conquest, but at the time . . . He had built up a false picture of her in his mind, and having it suddenly shattered . . . This boy had a very bad temper. It was his particular curse. He resolved on a duel with her lovers.

"She had two on her string, or her on theirs, I can't say which. He didn't care who survived, or if he were arrested. He imagined he was dishonored, you see. He arranged to have each meet him at a deserted place, about half an hour apart."

He paused for a long time. Cordelia waited, barely breathing, uncertain whether to encourage him to go on or not. He continued eventually, but his voice went flatter and he spoke in a rush.

"The first was another pigheaded young aristocrat like himself, and he played out the game by the rules. He knew the use of the two swords, fought with flair, and almost killed m—my friend. The last thing he said was that he'd always wanted to be killed by a jealous husband, only at age eighty."

By this time, the little slip was no surprise to Cordelia, and she wondered if her story had been as transparent to him. It certainly seemed so.

"The second was a high government minister, an older man. He wouldn't fight, although he knocked him down and stood him up several times. After—after the other, who had died with a joke in his mouth, he could hardly bear it. He finally slew him outright in the middle of his begging, and left them there.

"He stopped at his wife's apartment, to tell her what he'd done, and returned to his ship, to wait for arrest. This all happened in one afternoon. She was enraged, full of wounded pride—she would have dueled with him, if she could—and she killed herself. Shot herself in the head, with his service plasma arc. I wouldn't have thought it a woman's weapon. Poison, or cutting the wrists, or something. But she was true Vor. It burned her face entirely away. She'd had the most beautiful imaginable face. . . .

"Things worked out very strangely. It was assumed the two lovers had killed each other—I swear, he never planned it that way—and that she'd killed herself in despondency. No one ever asked him the first question about it."

His voice slowed, and intensified. "He went through that whole afternoon like a sleepwalker, or an actor, saying the expected lines, going through the expected motions, and at the end his honor was no better for it. Nothing was served, no point was proved. It was all as false as her love affairs, except for the deaths. They were real." He paused. "So you see, you Betans have one advantage. You at least permit each other to learn from your mistakes."

"I'm—grieved, for your friend. Does it seem very long ago?"

"Sometimes. Over twenty years. They say that senile people remember things from their youth more clearly than those of last week. Maybe he's getting senile."

"I see." She took the story in like some strange, spiked gift, too fragile to drop, too painful to hold. He lay back, silent again, and she took another turn around the glade, listening at the wood's edge to a silence so profound the roaring of the blood in her ears seemed to drown it out. When she'd completed the round, Vorkosigan was asleep, restless and shivering in his fever. She filched one of the half-burned bedrolls from Dubauer, and covered him up.

CHAPTER FOUR

Vorkosigan woke about three hours before dawn, and made her lie down to snatch a couple hours sleep. In the grey before sunup he roused her again. He had evidently bathed in the stream, and used the single-application packet of depilitory he had been saving in his belt to wipe away the itchy four-day growth on his face.

"I need some help with this leg. I want to open and drain it and cover it back up. That will hold until this afternoon, and after that it won't matter."

"Right."

Vorkosigan stripped off boot and sock, and Cordelia had him hold his leg under a rushing spout at the edge of the waterfall. She rinsed his combat knife, then laid open the grossly swollen wound in a deep, quick stroke. Vorkosigan went white around the lips, but said nothing. It was Cordelia who winced. The cut squirted blood and pus and odd-smelling clotted matter which the stream washed away. She tried not to think about what new microbes they might be introducing by the procedure. It only needed to be a temporary palliative.

She packed the wound with the last of the tube of his

rather ineffective antibiotic, and stripped out the tube of plastic bandage to cover it.

"It feels better." But Vorkosigan stumbled and almost fell when he attempted to walk normally. "Right," he muttered. "The time has come." Ceremoniously, he removed the last painkiller and a small blue pill from his first-aid kit, swallowed them, and threw the empty case away. Cordelia somewhat absently picked it up, found herself with no place to put it, and surreptitiously dropped it again.

"These things work great," he told her, "until they give out, when you fall down like a marionette with the strings cut. I'm good for about sixteen hours now."

Indeed, by the time they'd finished the field rations and readied Dubauer for the day's march, he looked not merely normal, but fresh and rested and full of energy. Neither referred to the previous night's conversation.

He led them in a wide arc around the mountain's base, so that by noon they were approaching the cratered side from nearly due west. They made their way through woods and glades to a spur opposite a great bowl that was all that remained of the lower mountainside from the days before an ancient volcanic cataclysm. Vorkosigan crawled out on a treeless promontory, taking care not to show himself above the tall grass. Dubauer, wan and exhausted, curled up on his side in their place of concealment and fell asleep. Cordelia watched him until his breathing was slow and steady, then crept out beside Vorkosigan. The Barrayaran captain had his field scope out, sweeping over the hazy green amphitheater.

"There's the shuttle. They're camped in the cache caves. See that dark streak beside the long waterfall? That's the entrance." He lent her the scope for a closer look.

"Oh, there's somebody coming out. You can see their faces on high magnification."

Vorkosigan took back the scope. "Koudelka. He's all right. But the thin man with him is Darobey, one of Radnov's spies in my communications section. Remember his face—you'll need to know when to keep your head down."

Cordelia wondered if Vorkosigan's air of enjoyment was an artifact of the stimulant, or a primitive anticipation of the clash to come. His eyes seemed to gleam as he watched, counted, and calculated.

He hissed through his teeth, sounding a bit like one of the local carnivores himself. "There's Radnov, by God! Wouldn't I like to get my hands on him. But this time I can take the Ministry men to trial. I'd like to see them try to get one of their pets out from under a bona fide charge of mutiny. The high command and the Council of Counts will be with me this time. No, Radnov, you're going to live—and regret it." He settled on stomach and elbows and devoured the scene.

He stiffened suddenly, and grinned. "It's time my luck changed. There's Gottyan, armed, so he must be in charge. We're nearly home. Come on."

They crept back to the cloaking shelter of the trees. Dubauer was not where they'd left him.

"Oh, lord," breathed Cordelia, turning and peering into the brush in all directions. "Which way did he go?"

"He can't have gone far," reassured Vorkosigan, although he too looked worried. They each made a circle of a hundred meters or so through the woods. Idiot! Cordelia castigated herself furiously in her panic. You just had to go peek. . . . They met back at the original spot without seeing any mark made by the wandering ensign.

"Look, we haven't the time to search for him now," said Vorkosigan. "As soon as I've regained command, I'll send a patrol out to look for him. With proper search-scopes, they could find him faster than we can."

Cordelia thought of carnivores, cliffs, deep pools, Barrayaran patrols with twitchy trigger fingers. "We've come so far," she began.

"And if I don't regain command soon, neither of you will survive anyway."

Torn, but obedient to reason, she allowed Vorkosigan to take her by the arm. Only leaning on her slightly, he picked a way down through the woods. As they neared the Barrayaran camp, he put a thick finger to his lips.

"Go as quietly as you can. I haven't come this far to be shot by one of my own pickets. Ah. Lie down here." He placed her in a spot behind some fallen logs and knee-high vegetation overlooking a faint new path beaten through the brush.

"You're not just going to knock on the front door?"

"No."

"Why not, if your Gottyan is all right?"

"Because there's something else wrong. I don't know why this landing party is here." He meditated a moment, then handed her back the stunner. "If you have to use a weapon, it had better be one you can handle. It still has a bit of charge—one or two shots. This path runs between sentry points, and sooner or later someone's going to come down it. Keep your head down until I call you."

He loosed his knife in its sheath and took a concealed position on the other side of the path. They waited a quarter of an hour, then another. The woodland drowsed in the warm, soft, white air.

Then down the path came the sound of boots scuffing through the leaf litter. Cordelia went rigidly still, trying to peer through the weeds without raising her head. A tall form in the wonderfully effective Barrayaran camouflage fatigues resolved itself as a grey-haired officer. As he passed Vorkosigan rose from his hiding place as if resurrected.

"Korabik," he said softly, but with genuine warmth in his voice. He stood grinning, arms folded, waiting.

Gottyan spun about, one hand drawing the nerve disruptor at his hip. After a beat, a look of surprise came over his face. "Aral! The landing party reported the Betans had killed you," and he stepped, not forward as Cordelia had expected from the tone of Vorkosigan's voice, but back. The disruptor was still in his hand as if he had forgotten to put it away, but gripped firmly, not dangling. Cordelia's stomach sank.

Vorkosigan looked faintly puzzled, as if disappointed

by the cool, controlled reception. "I'm glad to know you're
not superstitious," he joked.

"I should have known better than to think you dead
until I'd seen you buried with a stake through your heart,"
said Gottyan, sadly ironic.

"What's wrong, Korabik?" asked Vorkosigan quietly.
"You're no Minister's lickspittle."

At these words Gottyan brought the disruptor up to
undisguised aim. Vorkosigan stood very still.

"No," he answered frankly. "I thought the story Radnov
told about you and the Betans smelled. And I was going
to make damn sure it went through a board of inquiry
when we got home." He paused. "But then—I would have
been in command. After being acting captain for six
months, I'd be sure to be confirmed. What do you think
the chances of command are at my age? Five percent?
Two? Zero?"

"They're not as bad as you think," said Vorkosigan, still
quietly. "There are some things coming up that very few
people have heard about. More ships, more openings."

"The usual rumors," Gottyan dismissed this.

"So you didn't believe I was dead?" probed Vorkosigan.

"I was sure you were. I took over—where did you put
the sealed orders, by the way? We turned your cabin
inside out looking for them."

Vorkosigan smiled dryly and shook his head. "I shall
not increase your temptations."

"No matter." Gottyan's aim did not waver. "Then day
before yesterday that psychopathic idiot Bothari came to
see me in my cabin. He gave me the real story of what
happened at the Betans' camp. Surprised the hell out of
me—I'd have thought he'd be delighted at a chance to
slit your throat. So we came back here to practice ground
training. I was sure you'd turn up sooner or later—I
expected you before this."

"I was delayed." Vorkosigan shifted position slightly,
away from Cordelia's line of fire toward Gottyan. "Where's
Bothari now?"

"Solitary confinement."

Vorkosigan winced. "That's very bad for him. I take it you didn't spread the news of my narrow escape?"

"Not even Radnov knows. He still thinks Bothari gutted you."

"Smug, is he?"

"Smug as a cat. I'd have taken great pleasure in wiping his face at the board, if only you'd had the good grace to meet with an accident on your hike."

Vorkosigan grimaced wryly. "It seems to me you haven't quite made up your mind what you really want to do. May I suggest it is not too late, even now, to change course?"

"You could never overlook this," stated Gottyan uncertainly.

"In my younger and more stiff-necked days, perhaps not. But to tell you the truth, I'm getting a little tired of slaying my enemies to teach them a lesson." Vorkosigan raised his chin and held Gottyan's eyes. "If you like, you can have my word. You know the worth of it."

The disruptor trembled slightly in Gottyan's hand, as he wavered on the edge of his decision. Cordelia, barely breathing, saw water standing in his eyes. One does not weep for the living, she thought, but for the dead; in that moment, while Vorkosigan still doubted, she knew he intended to fire.

She brought her stunner up, took careful aim, and squeezed off a burst. It buzzed weakly, but it was enough to bring Gottyan, head turning at the sudden movement, to his knees. Vorkosigan pounced on the disruptor, then relieved him of his plasma arc and knocked him to the ground.

"Damn you," croaked Gottyan, half-paralyzed. "Haven't you ever been out-maneuvered?"

"If I had I wouldn't be here," shrugged Vorkosigan. He subjected Gottyan to a rapid search, confiscating his knife and a number of other objects. "Who do you have posted as pickets?"

"Sens to the north, Koudelka to the south."

Vorkosigan removed Gottyan's belt and bound his hands behind his back. "You really did have trouble making up your mind, didn't you?" In an aside to Cordelia he explained, "Sens is one of Radnov's. Koudelka's mine. Rather like flipping a coin."

"And this was your friend?" Cordelia raised her eyebrows. "Seems to me the only difference between your friends and your enemies is how long they stand around chatting before they shoot you."

"Yes," Vorkosigan agreed, "I could take over the universe with this army if I could ever get all their weapons pointed in the same direction. Since your pants will stay up without it, Commander Naismith, may I please borrow your belt?" He finished securing Gottyan's legs with it, gagged him, then stood a moment looking up, then down the path.

"All Cretans are liars," murmured Cordelia, then more loudly, "North or south?"

"An interesting question. How would you answer it?"

"I had a teacher who used to reflect back my questions that way. I thought it was the Socratic method, and it impressed me immensely, until I found out he used it whenever he didn't know the answer." Cordelia stared at Gottyan, whom they had placed in the spot that had so effectively concealed her, wondering whether his directions marked a return to loyalty or a last-ditch effort to complete Vorkosigan's botched assassination. He stared back in puzzlement and hostility.

"North," she said reluctantly at last. She and Vorkosigan exchanged a look of understanding, and he nodded briefly.

"Come on then."

They started quietly up the path, over a rise and through a hollow dense with grey-green thickets. "Have you known Gottyan long?"

"We served together for the last four years, since my demotion. He was a good career officer, I thought. Apolitical, thorough. He has a family."

"Do you think you could—get him back, later?"

"Forgive and forget? I gave him a chance at that. He turned me down. Twice, if you're right in your choice of directions." They were climbing another slope. "The sentry post is at the top. Whoever's there will be able to scope us in a moment. Drop back here and cover me. If you hear firing—" he paused, "use your initiative."

Cordelia smothered a short laugh. Vorkosigan loosed his disruptor in its holster and walked openly up the path, making plenty of noise.

"Sentry, report," she heard his voice call firmly.

"Nothing new since—good God, it's the *Captain*!" followed by the most honestly delighted laugh she felt she'd heard in centuries. She leaned against a tree, suddenly weak. And just when was it, she asked herself, that you stopped being afraid of him and started being afraid for him? And why is this new fear so much more gut-wrenching than the first? You don't seem to have come out ahead on the trade, have you?

"You can come out now, Commander Naismith," Vorkosigan's voice carried back to her. She rounded the last stand of underbrush and climbed a grassy knoll. Camped upon it were two young men looking very neat and military in their clean fatigues. One, taller than Vorkosigan by a head, with a boy's face on a man's body, she recognized from her view through the scope as Koudelka. He was shaking his Captain's hand with unabashed enthusiasm, assuring himself of its unghostly reality. The other man's hand went to his disruptor when he saw her uniform.

"We were told the Betans killed you, sir," he said suspiciously.

"Yes, it's a rumor I've had difficulty living down," said Vorkosigan. "As you can see, it's not true."

"Your funeral was splendid," said Koudelka. "You should have been there."

"Next time, perhaps," Vorkosigan grinned.

"Oh. You know I didn't mean it that way, sir. Lieutenant Radnov made the best speech."

"I'm sure. He'd probably been working on it for months."

Koudelka, a little quicker on the uptake than his companion, said "Oh." His fellow merely looked puzzled.

Vorkosigan went on. "Permit me to introduce Commander Cordelia Naismith, of the Betan Astronomical

Survey. She is . . ." he paused, and Cordelia waited interestedly to hear what status she was to be assigned, "ah . . ."

"Sounds like?" she murmured helpfully.

Vorkosigan closed his lips firmly, pressing a smile out straight. "My prisoner," he chose finally. "On parole. Except for access to classified areas, she is to be extended every courtesy."

The two young men looked impressed, and wildly curious. "She's armed," Koudelka's companion pointed out.

"And a good thing, too." Vorkosigan did not enlarge on this, but went on to more urgent affairs. "Who is in the landing party?"

Koudelka rattled off a list of names, his memory jogged occasionally by his cohort.

"All right," Vorkosigan sighed. "Radnov, Darobey, Sens, and Tafas are to be disarmed, as quietly and cleanly as possible, and placed under arrest on a charge of mutiny. There will be some others later. I don't want any communication with the *General Vorkraft* until they're under lock and key. Do you know where Lieutenant Buffa is?"

"In the caverns. Sir?" Koudelka was starting to look a little miserable, as he began to deduce what was happening.

"Yes?"

"Are you sure about Tafas?"

"Nearly." Vorkosigan gentled his voice. "They'll be tried. That's the purpose of a trial, to separate the guilty from the innocent."

"Yes, sir." Koudelka accepted this limited guarantee for the welfare of a man Cordelia guessed must be his friend with a little bow of his head.

"Do you begin to see why I said the statistics about civil war conceal the most reality?" said Vorkosigan.

"Yes, sir." Koudelka met his eye squarely, and Vorkosigan nodded, sure of his man.

"All right. You two come with me."

They started off, Vorkosigan taking her arm again and scarcely limping, neatly concealing how much weight he was putting on her. They followed another path through the woodlands, up and down uneven ground, coming out within sight of the camouflaged door to the cache caverns.

The waterfall that spun down beside it ended in a little pool, spilling over into a pretty stream which ran off into the woods. A strange group was assembled beside it. Cordelia could not at first make out what they were doing. Two Barrayarans stood watching while two more knelt by the water. As they approached the two kneelers stood, hauling a dripping, tan-clad figure, hands tied behind his back, from a prone position to his feet. He coughed, struggling for breath in sobbing gasps.

"It's Dubauer!" cried Cordelia. "What are they doing to him?"

Vorkosigan, who seemed to know instantly just what they were doing to him, muttered "Oh, hell," and started forward at a jerky jog. "That's my prisoner!" he roared out as they neared the group. "Hands off him!"

The Barrayarans braced so fast it looked like a spinal reflex. Dubauer, released, fell to his knees, still drawing breath in long sobs. Cordelia, running past them to Dubauer, thought she had never seen a more astonished-looking array of men. Dubauer's hair, swollen face, scanty new beard, and collar were soaking wet, his eyes were red, and he continued to cough and sneeze. Horrified, she finally realized the Barrayarans had been holding his head underwater by way of torture.

"What is this, Lieutenant Buffa?" Vorkosigan pinned the senior of the group with a thunderous frown.

"I thought the Betans killed you, sir!" said Buffa.

"They didn't," Vorkosigan said shortly. "What are you doing with this Betan?"

"Tafas captured him in the woods, sir. We've been trying to question him—find out if there's any more around—" he glanced at Cordelia, "but he refuses to talk. Hasn't said a word. And I always thought Betans were soft."

Vorkosigan rubbed his hand over his face for a moment, as if praying for strength.

"Buffa," he said patiently, "this man was hit by disruptor

fire five days ago. He can't talk, and if he could he wouldn't know anything anyway."

"Barbarians!" cried Cordelia, kneeling on the ground. Dubauer had recognized her, and was clutching her. "You Barrayarans are nothing but barbarians, scoundrels, and assassins!"

"And fools. Don't leave out fools." Vorkosigan withered Buffa with a glare. A couple of the men had the good grace to look rather ill, as well as ill at ease. Vorkosigan let out his breath with a sigh. "Is he all right?"

"Seems to be," she admitted reluctantly. "But he's pretty shaken up." She was shaking herself in her outrage.

"Commander Naismith, I apologize for my men," said Vorkosigan formally, and loudly, so that no one there could mistake that their Captain humbled himself before his prisoner because of them.

"Don't click your heels at me," muttered Cordelia savagely, for his ear alone. At his bleak look she relented a little, and said more loudly, "It was an error in interpretation." Her eye fell on Lieutenant Buffa, attempting to make his considerable height appear to melt into the ground. "Any blind man could have made it. Oh, hell," she added, for Dubauer's terror and distress were triggering another convulsion. Most of the Barrayarans looked away, variously embarrassed. Vorkosigan, who was getting practiced, knelt to give her what aid she needed. When the seizure subsided he stood.

"Tafas, give your weapons to Koudelka," he ordered. Tafas hesitated, glancing around, then slowly complied.

"I didn't want any part of it, sir," he said desperately. "But Lieutenant Radnov said it was too late."

"You'll get a chance to speak for yourself later on," said Vorkosigan wearily.

"What's going on?" asked the bewildered Buffa. "Have you seen Commander Gottyan, sir?"

"I've given Commander Gottyan—separate orders. Buffa, you are now in charge of the landing party." Vorkosigan repeated his orders for the arrest of his short list, and detached a group to carry out the task.

"Ensign Koudelka, take *my* prisoners to the cave, and see that they're given proper food, and whatever else Commander Naismith requires. Then see that the shuttle is ready to go. We'll be leaving for the ship as soon as the—other prisoners are secured." He avoided the word "mutineers," as though it were too strong, like blasphemy.

"Where are you going?" asked Cordelia.

"I'm going to have a talk with Commander Gottyan. Alone."

"Hm. Well, don't make me regret my own advice." Which was as close as she could come at the moment to saying, *Be careful.*

Vorkosigan acknowledged all her meanings with a wave of his hand, and turned back for the woods. He was limping more noticeably now.

She helped Dubauer to his feet, and Koudelka led them to the cave's mouth. The young man seemed so much like Dubauer's opposite number, she found it hard to maintain her hostility.

"What happened to the old man's leg?" Koudelka asked her, glancing back over his shoulder.

"He's got an infected scratch," she understated, inclined to endorse his evident policy of keeping up a good show for the benefit of his unreliable crew. "It should get some high grade medical attention, as soon as you can get him to slow down for it."

"That's the old man for you. I've never seen anybody that age with that much energy."

"That age?" Cordelia raised an eyebrow.

"Well, of course he wouldn't seem old to you," Koudelka allowed, and looked puzzled when she burst out laughing. "Energy isn't quite what I wanted to say, though."

"How about power," she suggested, curiously glad that Vorkosigan had at least one admirer. "Energy applied to work."

"That's very good," he applauded, gratified. Cordelia decided not to mention the little blue pill, either.

"He seems an interesting person," she said, angling for

another view of Vorkosigan. "How did he ever get in this fix?"

"You mean, Radnov?"

She nodded.

"Well, I don't want to criticize the old man, but—I don't know of anyone else who'd tell a *Political* Officer when he came on board to stay out of his sight if he wanted to live to the end of the voyage." Koudelka was hushed in his awe.

Cordelia, making the second turning behind him in the halls of the cave, was jerked alert by her surroundings. *Most* peculiar, she thought. Vorkosigan misled me. The labyrinthine series of caverns was partly natural but mostly carved out by plasma arc: cool, moist, and dimly lit. The huge spaces were stuffed with supplies. This was no cache; it was a full-scale fleet depot. She pursed her lips soundlessly, staring around, suddenly awake to a whole new range of unpleasant possibilities.

In one corner of the caverns stood a standard Barrayaran field shelter, a semicircular ribbed vault covered with a fabric like the Betans' tents. This one was given over to a field kitchen and mess hall, crude and bleak. A lone yeoman was cleaning up after lunch.

"The old man just turned up, alive!" Koudelka greeted him.

"Huh! I thought the Betans had cut his throat," said the yeoman, surprised. "And we did the funeral dinner up so nice."

"These two are the old man's *personal* prisoners," Koudelka introduced them to the cook, whom Cordelia suspected was more combat soldier than gourmet chef, "and you know what he's like on that subject. The guy's got disruptor damage. He said they're to have proper food, so don't try to poison them with the usual swill."

"Everyone's a critic," muttered the yeoman-cook, as Koudelka vanished about his other chores. "What'll you have?"

"Anything. Anything but oatmeal or blue cheese," she amended hastily.

The yeoman disappeared into the back room, and returned a few minutes later with two steaming bowls of a stew-like substance, and real bread with genuine vegetable oil spread. Cordelia fell to it wolfishly.

"How is it?" asked the yeoman tonelessly, hunching down into his shoulders.

"S'delishoush," she said around a large mouthful. "S'wonderful."

"Really?" He straightened up. "You really like it?"

"Really." She stopped to shove a few spoonfuls into the dazed Dubauer. The taste of the warm food cut across his post-seizure sleepiness, and he chewed away with something like her enthusiasm.

"Here—can I help you feed him?" the yeoman offered.

Cordelia beamed upon him like the sun. "You certainly may."

In less than an hour she had learned that the yeoman's name was Nilesa, heard most of his life's history, and been offered the complete, if severely limited, range of dainties a Barrayaran field kitchen had to offer. The yeoman was evidently as starved for praise as his fellows were for home cooking, for he followed her around racking his brain for small personal services to offer her.

Vorkosigan came in by himself, and sat wearily down beside Cordelia.

"Welcome back, sir," the yeoman greeted him. "We thought the Betans had killed you."

"Yes, I know," Vorkosigan waved away this by-now-familiar greeting. "How about some food?"

"What'll you have, sir?"

"Anything but oatmeal."

He too was served with bread and stew, which he ate without Cordelia's appetite, for the fever and stimulant combined to kill it.

"How did things work out with Commander Gottyan?" Cordelia asked him quietly.

"Not bad. He's back on the job."

"How did you do it?"

"Untied him, and gave him my plasma arc. I told him

I couldn't work with a man who made my shoulder blades itch, and this was the last chance I was going to give him for instant promotion. Then I sat down with my back to him. Sat there for about ten minutes. We didn't say a word. Then he gave the arc back, and we walked back to camp."

"I wondered if something like that might work. Although I'm not sure I could have done it, if I were you."

"I don't think I could have done it either, if I wasn't so damn tired. It felt good to sit down." His tone became slightly more animated. "As soon as they get the arrests made, we'll lift off for the *General*. It's a fine ship. I'm assigning you the visiting officer's cabin—Admiral's Quarters, they call it, although it's no different from the others." Vorkosigan pushed the last bites of stew around in the bottom of his dish. "How was your food?"

"Wonderful."

"That's not what most people say."

"Yeoman Nilesa has been most kind and thoughtful."

"Are we talking about the same man?"

"I think he just needs a little appreciation for his work. You might try it."

Vorkosigan, elbows on the table, propped his chin on his hands and smiled. "I'll take it under advisement."

They both sat silent, tired and digesting, at the simple metal table. Vorkosigan leaned back in his chair with his eyes closed. Cordelia leaned on the table with her head pillowed on one arm. In about half an hour Koudelka entered.

"We've got Sens, sir," he reported. "But we had—are having—a little trouble with Radnov and Darobey. They tumbled on to it, somehow, and escaped into the woods. I have a patrol out searching now."

Vorkosigan looked like he wanted to swear. "Should have gone myself," he muttered. "Did they have any weapons?"

"They both had their disruptors. We got their plasma arcs."

"All right. I don't want to waste any more time down here. Recall your patrol and seal all the cavern entrances. They can find out how they like spending a few nights in the woods." His eyes glinted at the vision. "We can pick them up later. They've nowhere to go."

Cordelia pushed Dubauer ahead of her into the shuttle, a bare and rather decrepit troop transport, and settled him in a free seat. With the arrival of the last patrol the shuttle seemed crammed with Barrayarans, including the huddled and subdued prisoners, hapless subordinates of the escaped ringleaders, bound in back. They all seemed such large and muscular young men. Indeed, Vorkosigan was the shortest one she'd seen so far.

They stared at her curiously, and she caught snatches of conversation in two or three languages. It wasn't hard to guess their content, and she smiled a bit grimly. Youth, it appeared, was full of illusions as to how much sexual energy two people might have to spare while hiking forty or so kilometers a day, concussed, stunned, diseased, on poor food and little sleep, alternating caring for a wounded man with avoiding becoming dinner for every carnivore within range—and with a coup to plan for at the end. Old folks, too, of thirty-three and forty plus. She laughed to herself, and closed her eyes, shutting them out.

Vorkosigan returned from the forward pilot's compartment, and slid in beside her. "Are you doing all right?"

She gave him a nod. "Yes. Rather overwhelmed by all these herds of boys. I think you Barrayarans are the only ones who don't carry mixed crews. Why is that, I wonder?"

"Partly tradition, partly to maintain an aggressive outlook. They haven't been annoying you?"

"No, amusing me only. I wonder if they realize how they are used?"

"Not a bit. They think they are the emperors of creation."

"Poor lambs."

"That's not how I'd describe them."

"I was thinking of animal sacrifice."

"Ah. That's closer."

The shuttle's engines began to whine, and they rose into

the air. They circled the cratered mountain once, then struck east and upward to the sky. Cordelia watched out the window as the land they had so painfully traversed on foot swept under them in as many minutes as they had taken days. They soared over the great mountain where Rosemont lay rotting, close enough to see the snowcap and glaciers gleaming orange in the setting sun. They passed on east through nightrise, and dead of night, the horizon curved away, and they broke into the perpetual day of space.

As they approached the *General Vorkraft*'s parking orbit Vorkosigan left her again to go forward and supervise. He seemed to be receding from her, absorbed back into the matrix of men and duty from which he had been torn. Well, surely they would have some quiet times together in the months ahead. Quite a few months, by what Gottyan had said. Pretend you're an anthropologist, she told herself, studying the savage Barrayarans. Think of it as a vacation— you wanted a long vacation after this Survey tour anyway. Well, here it is. Her fingers were picking loose threads from the seat, and she stilled them with a slight frown.

They made their docking very cleanly, and the mob of hulking soldiers rose, gathered their equipment, and clattered out. Koudelka appeared at her elbow, and informed her he was assigned as her guide. Guard, more likely—or babysitter—she did not feel very dangerous this moment. She gathered Dubauer and followed him aboard Vorkosigan's ship.

It smelled different from her Survey ship, colder, full of bare unpainted metal and cost-effective shortcuts taken out of comfort and decor, like the difference between a living room and a locker room. Their first destination was sickbay, to drop off Dubauer. It was a clean, austere series of rooms, much larger even proportionally than her Survey ship's, prepared to handle plenty of company. It was nearly deserted now, but for the chief surgeon and a couple of corpsmen whiling away their duty hours doing inventory, and a lone soldier with a broken arm kicking his heels and kibitzing. Dubauer was examined by the doctor, whom Cordelia suspected was more expert at disruptor injuries

than her own surgeon, and turned over to the corpsmen
to be washed and bedded down.

"You're going to have another customer shortly,"
Cordelia told the surgeon, who was one of Vorkosigan's
four men over forty. "Your captain has a really filthy infection going on his shin. It's gone systemic. Also, I don't
know what those little blue pills are you fellows have in
your medkits, but by what he said the one he took this
morning ought to be running out just about now."

"That damned poison," the doctor bitched. "Sure, it's
effective, but they could find something less wearing. Not
to mention the trouble we have hanging on to them."

Cordelia suspected this last was the crux of the matter. The doctor busied himself setting up the antibiotic
synthesizer and preparing it for programming. Cordelia
watched the expressionless Dubauer put to bed, the start,
she saw, of an endless series of hospital days as straight
and same as a tunnel to the end of his life. The cold
whispering doubt of whether she had done him a service
would be forever added to her inventory of night thoughts.
She dawdled around him for a while, covertly waiting for
the arrival of her other ex-charge.

Vorkosigan came in at last, accompanied, in fact supported, by a couple of other officers she had not yet met,
and giving orders. He had obviously cut his timing too fine,
for he looked frighteningly bad. He was white, sweating,
and trembling, and Cordelia thought she could see where
the lines on his face would be when he was seventy.

"Haven't you been taken care of yet?" he asked when
he saw her. "Where's Koudelka? I thought I told him—
oh, there you are. She's to have the Admiral's cabin. Did
I say that? And stop by stores and get her some clothes.
And dinner. And a new charge for her stunner."

"I'm fine. Hadn't you better lie down yourself?" said
Cordelia anxiously.

Vorkosigan, still on his feet, was wandering around in
circles like a wind-up toy with a damaged mainspring.
"Got to let Bothari out," he muttered. "He'll be halluci-
nating by now."

"You just did that, sir," reminded one of the officers. The surgeon caught his eye, and jerked his head meaningfully toward the examining table. Together they intercepted Vorkosigan in his orbit, propelled him semi-forcibly to it, and made him lie down.

"It's those damned pills," the surgeon explained to Cordelia, taking pity on her alarmed look. "He'll be all right in the morning, except for lethargy and a hell of a headache."

The surgeon turned back to his task, to cut the taut trouser away from the swollen leg, and swear under his breath at what he found beneath. Koudelka glanced over the surgeon's shoulder, and turned back to Cordelia with a false smile pinned over a green face.

Cordelia nodded and reluctantly withdrew, leaving Vorkosigan in the hands of his professionals. Koudelka, seeming to enjoy his role as courier even though it had caused him to miss the show of his captain's return on board, led her off to stores for clothing, disappeared with her stunner, and dutifully returned it fully charged. It seemed to go against his grain.

"There's not a whole lot I could do with it anyway," she said at the dubious look on his face.

"No, no, the old man said you were to have it. I'm not going to argue with him about prisoners. It's a sensitive subject with him."

"So I understand. I might point out, if it will help your perspective, that our two governments are not at war as far as I know, and that I am being unlawfully detained."

Koudelka puzzled over this attempted readjustment of his point of view, then let it bounce harmlessly off his impermeable habits of thought. Carrying her new kit, he led her to her quarters.

CHAPTER FIVE

Stepping out of her cabin door next morning she found a guard posted. The top of her head was level with his broad shoulders, and his face reminded her of an overbred borzoi, narrow, hook-nosed, with his eyes too close together. She realized at once where she had seen him before, at a distance in a dappled wood, and had a moment of residual fear.

"Sergeant Bothari?" she hazarded.

He saluted her, the first Barrayaran to have done so. "Ma'am," he said, and fell silent.

"I want to go to sickbay," she said uncertainly.

"Yes, ma'am." His voice was a deep bass, monotonous in its cadence. He executed a neat turn and led off. Guessing that he had relieved Koudelka as her guide and keeper, she pattered after him. She was not quite ready to attempt light conversation with him, so asked him no questions en route. He offered her only silence. Watching him, it occurred to her that a guard on her door might be as much to keep others out as her in. Her stunner seemed suddenly heavy on her hip.

At sickbay she found Dubauer sitting up and dressed in insignialess black fatigues like the ones she had been

issued. His hair had been cut and he had been shaved.
There was certainly nothing wrong with the physical care
he was receiving. She spoke to him a while, until her own
voice began to sound inane in her ears. He looked at her,
but gave little other reaction.

She caught a glimpse of Vorkosigan in a private chamber off the main ward, and he motioned her to enter.
He was dressed in plain green pajamas of the standard
design, and was sitting up in bed stabbing away with
a light pen at a computer interface swung over it.
Curiously, although he was clothed almost civilian style,
bootless and weaponless, her impression of him was
unchanged. He seemed a man who could carry on stark
naked, and only make those around him feel overdressed.
She smiled a little at this private image, and greeted
him with a sketchy wave. One of the officers who had
escorted him to sickbay last night was standing by the
bed.

"Commander Naismith, this is Lieutenant Commander
Vorkalloner, my second officer. Excuse me a moment;
captains may come and captains may go, but the administration goes on forever."

"Amen."

Vorkalloner looked very much the professional
Barrayaran soldier; he might have stepped out of a
recruiting advertisement. Yet there was a certain underlying humor in his expression that made her think him
a tolerable preview of Ensign Koudelka in ten or twelve
years time.

"Captain Vorkosigan speaks highly of you," said
Vorkalloner, making small talk. A slight frown from his
captain at this opening escaped his notice. "I guess if we
could only catch one Betan, you were the best choice."

Vorkosigan winced. Cordelia gave him a slight shake
of her head, signaling to let the gaffe pass. He shrugged,
and began tapping out something on his keyboard.

"As long as all my people are safely on their way home,
I'll take it as a fair trade. Almost all of them, anyway."
Rosemont's ghost breathed coldly in her ear, and

Vorkalloner seemed suddenly less amusing. "Why were you all so anxious to put us in a bottle, anyway?"

"Why, orders," said Vorkalloner simply, like an ancient fundamentalist who answers every question with the tautology, "Because God made it that way." Then a little agnostic doubt began to creep over his face. "Actually, I thought we might have been sent out here on guard duty as some kind of punishment," he joked.

The remark caught Vorkosigan's humor. "For your sins? Your cosmology is too egocentric, Aristede." Leaving Vorkalloner to unravel that, he went on to Cordelia, "Your detention was intended to be free of bloodshed. It would have been, too, but for that other little matter cropping up in the middle of it. It is a worthless apology for some," and she knew he shared the memory of Rosemont's burial in the cold black fog, "but it is the only truth I can offer you. The responsibility is no less mine for that. As I am sure someone in the high command will point out when this arrives." He smiled sourly and continued typing.

"Well, I can't say I'm sorry to have messed up their invasion plans," she said daringly. There, let's see what that stirs up. . . .

"What invasion?" asked Vorkalloner, waking up.

"I was afraid you'd figure that out, once you saw the cache caverns," said Vorkosigan to her. "It was still being hotly debated when we left, and the expansionists were waving the advantage of surprise as a big stick to beat the peace party. Speaking as a private person—well, I have not that right while in uniform. Let it go."

"What invasion?" probed Vorkalloner hopefully.

"With luck, none," answered Vorkosigan, allowing himself to be persuaded to partial frankness. "One of those was enough for a lifetime." He seemed to look inward on private, unpleasant memories.

Vorkalloner plainly found this a baffling attitude from the Hero of Komarr. "It was a great victory, sir. With very little loss of life."

"On our side." Vorkosigan finished typing his report

and signed it off, then entered a request for another form and began fencing at it with the light pen.

"That's the idea, isn't it?"

"It depends on whether you mean to stay or are just passing through. A very messy political legacy was left at Komarr. Not the sort of thing I care to leave in trust for the next generation. How did we get onto this subject?" He finished the last form.

"Who were they thinking of invading?" asked Cordelia doggedly.

"Why haven't I heard anything about it?" asked Vorkalloner.

"In order, that is classified information, and it is not being discussed below the level of the General Staff, the central committee of the two Councils, and the Emperor. That means this conversation is to go no farther, Aristede."

Vorkalloner glanced at Cordelia pointedly. "*She's* not on the General Staff. Come to think of it—"

"Neither am I, anymore," Vorkosigan conceded. "As for our guest, I've told her nothing she couldn't deduce for herself. As for myself, my opinion was requested on—certain aspects. They didn't like it, once they'd got it, but they did ask for it." His smile was not at all nice.

"Is that why you were shipped out of town?" asked Cordelia perceptively, feeling she was beginning to get the hang of how things were done on Barrayar. "So Lieutenant Commander Vorkalloner was right about pulling guard duty. Was your opinion requested by, uh, a certain old friend of your father's?"

"It certainly wasn't requested by the Council of Ministers," said Vorkosigan, but refused to be drawn any further, and changed the subject firmly. "Have my men been treating you properly?"

"Quite well, yes."

"My surgeon swears he will release me this afternoon, if I am good and stay in bed this morning. May I stop by your cabin to speak with you privately later? There are some things I need to make clear."

"Sure," she responded, thinking the request was phrased rather ominously.

The surgeon came in, aggrieved. "You're supposed to be resting, sir." He glared pointedly at Cordelia and Vorkalloner.

"Oh, very well. Send these off with the next courier, Aristede," he pointed to the screen, "along with the verbals and the formal charges."

The doctor herded them out, as Vorkosigan began typing again.

She wandered around the ship for the rest of the morning, exploring the limits of her parole. Vorkosigan's ship was a confusing warren of corridors, sealable levels, tubes, and narrow doors designed, she realized at last, to be defensible from boarding parties in hand-to-hand combat. Sergeant Bothari kept pace with slow strides, looming silently as the shadow of death at her shoulder, except when she would begin to make a turn into some forbidden door or corridor, when he would halt abruptly and say, "No, ma'am." She was not permitted to touch anything, though, as she found when she ran a hand casually over a control panel, eliciting another monotonous "No, ma'am," from Bothari. It made her feel like a two-year-old being taken on a toddle.

She made one attempt to draw him out.

"Have you served Captain Vorkosigan long?" she inquired brightly.

"Yes, ma'am."

Silence. She tried again. "Do you like him?"

"No, ma'am."

Silence.

"Why not?" This at least could not have a yes-or-no answer. For a while she thought he wasn't going to answer at all, but he finally came up with, "He's a Vor."

"Class conflict?" she hazarded.

"I don't like Vors."

"I'm not a Vor," she suggested.

He stared through her glumly. "You're like a Vor. Ma'am."

Unnerved, she gave up.

✧ ✧ ✧

That afternoon she made herself comfortable on her narrow bunk and began to explore the menu the library computer had to offer her. She picked out a vid with the unalarming grade school title of "People and Places of Barrayar" and punched it up.

Its narration was as banal as the title had promised, but the pictures were utterly fascinating. It seemed a green, delicious, sunlit world to her Betan eyes. People went about without nose filters or rebreathers, or heat shields in the summer. The climate and terrain were immensely varied, and it had real oceans, with moon-raised tides, in contrast to the flat saline puddles that passed for lakes at home.

A knock sounded at her door. "Enter," she called, and Vorkosigan appeared around it, greeting her with a nod. Odd hour of the day for him to be in dress uniform, she thought—but my word, he cleans up good. Nice, very nice. Sergeant Bothari accompanied him; he remained standing stolidly outside the half-opened door. Vorkosigan walked around the room for a moment as if searching for something. He finally emptied her lunch tray and used it to prop the door open a narrow crack. Cordelia raised her eyebrows at this.

"Is that really necessary?"

"I think so. At the current rate of gossip I'm bound to encounter some joke soon about the privileges of rank that I can't pretend not to hear, and I'll have to quash the unlucky, er, humorist. I have an aversion to closed doors anyway. You never know what's on the other side."

Cordelia laughed outright. "It reminds me of that old joke, where the girl says, 'Let's not, and tell everybody we have.'"

Vorkosigan grimaced agreement and seated himself on the bolted-down swivel chair by the metal desk built into the wall, and swung to face her. He leaned back with his legs stretched out before him, and his face became serious. Cordelia cocked her head, half-smiling. He began obliquely, nodding toward the screen swung over her bed. "What have you been viewing?"

"Barrayaran geography. It's a beautiful place. Have you ever been to the oceans?"

"When I was a small boy, my mother used to take me to Bonsanklar every summer. It was a sort of upper-class resort town with a lot of virgin forest backing up to the mountains behind it. My father was away mostly, at the capital or with his corps. Midsummer's Day was the old Emperor's birthday, and they used to have the most fantastic fireworks—at least, they seemed so to me at the time—out over the ocean. The whole town would turn out on the esplanade, nobody even armed. No duels were permitted on the Emperor's birthday, and I was allowed to run all over the place freely." He looked at the floor, beyond the toes of his boots. "I haven't been back there for years. I should like to take you there someday, for the Midsummer's festival, should the opportunity present itself."

"I'd like that very much. Will your ship be returning to Barrayar soon?"

"Not for some time, I'm afraid. You're in for a long period as a prisoner. But when we return, in view of the escape of your ship, there should be no reason to continue your internment. You should be freed to present yourself at the Betan embassy, and go home. If you wish."

"If I wish!" She laughed a little, uncertainly, and sat back against her hard pillow. He was watching her face intently. His posture was a fair simulation of a man at his ease, but one boot was tapping unconsciously. His eye fell on it, he frowned, and it stopped. "Why shouldn't I wish?"

"I thought, perhaps, when we arrive on Barrayar, and you are free, you might consider staying."

"To visit—where you said, Bonsanklar, and so on? I don't know how much leave I'll have, but—sure, I like to see new places. I'd like to see your planet."

"Not a visit. Permanently. As—as Lady Vorkosigan." His face brightened with a wry smile. "I'm making a hash of this. I promise, I'll never think of Betans as cowards again. I swear your customs take more bravery than the most suicidal of our boys' contests of skill."

She let her breath trickle out through pursed lips. "You

don't—deal in small change, do you?" She wondered where the phrase about hearts leaping up came from. It felt far more like the bottom dropping out of her stomach. Her consciousness of her own body shot up with a lurch; she was already overwhelmingly conscious of his.

He shook his head. "That's not what I want, for you, with you. You should have the best. I'm hardly that, you must know by now. But at least I can offer you the best that I have. Dear C—Commander, am I too sudden, by Betan standards? I've been waiting for days, for the right opportunity, but there never seemed to be one."

"Days! How long have you been thinking along these lines?"

"It first occurred to me when I saw you in the ravine."

"What, throwing up in the mud?"

He grinned at that. "With great composure. By the time we finished burying your officer, I knew."

She rubbed her lips. "Anybody ever tell you you're a lunatic?"

"Not in this context."

"I—you've confused me."

"Not offended you?"

"No, of course not."

He relaxed just slightly. "You needn't say yes or no right now, of course. It will be months before we're home. But I didn't want you to think—it makes things awkward, your being a prisoner. I didn't want you to think I was offering you an insult."

"Not at all," she said faintly.

"There are some other things I should tell you," he went on, his attention seemingly caught by his boots again. "It wouldn't be an easy life. I have been thinking, since I met you, that a career cleaning up after the failures of politics, as you phrased it, might not be the highest honor after all. Maybe I should be trying to prevent the failures at their source. It would be more dangerous than soldiering—chances of betrayal, false charges, assassination, maybe exile, poverty, death. Evil compromises with bad men for a little good result, and that not guaranteed.

Not a good life, but if one had children—better me than them."

"You sure know how to show a girl a good time," she said helplessly, rubbing her chin and smiling.

Vorkosigan looked up, uncertain of his hope.

"How does one set about a political career, on Barrayar?" she asked, feeling her way. "I presume you're thinking of following in your grandfather Prince Xav's steps, but without the advantage of being an Imperial prince, how do you get an office?"

"Three ways. Imperial appointment, inheritance, and rising through the ranks. The Council of Ministers gets its best men through the last method. It's their great strength, but closed to me. The Council of Counts, by inheritance. That's my surest route, but it waits on my father's death. It can just go on waiting. It's a moribund body anyway, afflicted with the narrowest conservatism, and stuffed with old relics only concerned with protecting their privileges. I'm not sure anything can be done with the Counts in the long run. Perhaps they should finally be allowed to dodder over the brink of extinction. Don't quote that," he added as an afterthought.

"It's the weirdest design for a government."

"It wasn't designed. It grew."

"Maybe what you need is a constitutional convention."

"Spoken like a true Betan. Well, perhaps we do, although it sounds like a prescription for civil war, in our context. That leaves Imperial appointment. It's quick, but my fall could be as sudden and spectacular as my rise, if I should offend the old man, or he dies." The light of battle was in his eyes as he spoke, planning. "My one advantage with him is that he enjoys plain speaking. I don't know how he acquired the taste for it, because he doesn't get much of it.

"Do you know, I think you'd like politics, at least on Barrayar. Maybe because it's so similar to what we call war, elsewhere.

"There is a more immediate political problem, though, with respect to your ship, and some other things . . ."

He paused, losing momentum. "Maybe—maybe an insoluble one. It really may be premature for me to be discussing marriage until I know which way it's going to fall out. But I couldn't let you go on thinking—what *were* you thinking, anyway?"

She shook her head. "I don't think I want to say, just now. I'll tell you someday. It's nothing you'll dislike, I don't believe."

He accepted that with a little hopeful nod, and went on. "Your ship—"

She frowned uneasily. "You won't be getting into any trouble over my ship getting away, will you?"

"It *was* just the situation we were on our way out here to prevent. The fact that I was unconscious at the time should be a mitigating factor. Balancing that are the views I aired at the Emperor's council. There's bound to be suspicion I let it escape on purpose, to sabotage an adventure I deeply disapprove."

"Another demotion?"

He laughed. "I was the youngest admiral in the history of our fleet—I might end up the oldest ensign, too. But no," he sobered. "There will almost certainly be a charge of treason laid, by the war party in the Ministries. Until that's settled, one way or another," he met her eyes, "it may be difficult to settle any personal affairs either."

"Is treason a capital crime on Barrayar?" she asked, morbidly curious.

"Oh, yes. Public exposure and death by starvation." He raised a quizzical eyebrow at her appalled look. "If it's any consolation, high-born traitors always seem to be smuggled some neat means to private suicide, before the event. It saves stirring up any unnecessary public sympathy. I think I should not give them the satisfaction, though. Let it be public, and messy, and tedious, and embarrassing as all hell." He looked alarmingly fey.

"Would you sabotage the invasion, if you could?"

He shook his head, eyes going distant. "No. I am a man under authority. That's what the syllable in front of my name means. While the question is still being debated,

I'll continue to argue my case. But if the Emperor puts his word to the order, I'll go without question. The alternative is civil chaos, and we've had enough of that."

"What's different about this invasion? You must have favored Komarr, or they wouldn't have put you in charge of it."

"Komarr was a unique opportunity, almost a textbook case. When I was designing the strategy for its conquest, I made maximum use of those chances." He ticked off the points on his thick fingers. "A small population, all concentrated in climate-controlled cities. No place for guerillas to fall back and regroup. No allies—we weren't the only ones whose trade was being strangled by their greedy tariffs. All I had to do was let it leak out that we were going to drop their twenty-five percent cut of everything that passed through their nexus points to fifteen, and the neighbors that should have supported them fell into our pockets. No heavy industry. Fat and lazy from living off unearned income—they didn't even want to do their own fighting, until those scraggly mercenaries they'd hired found out what they were up against, and turned tail. If I'd had a free hand, and a little more time, I think it could have been taken without a shot being fired. A perfect war, it should have been, if the Council of Ministers hadn't been so impatient." Remembered frustrations played themselves out before his eyes, and he frowned into the past. "This other plan—well, I think you'll understand if I tell you it's Escobar."

Cordelia sat up, shocked. "You found a jump through here to Escobar?" No wonder, then, the Barrayarans had not announced their discovery of this place. Of all the possibilities she had revolved in her mind, that was the last. Escobar was one of the major planetary hubs in the network of wormhole exits that strung scattered humanity together. Large, old, rich, temperate, it counted among its many neighbors Beta Colony itself. "They're out of their minds!"

"Do you know, that's almost exactly what I said, before the Minister of the West started shouting, and Count

Vortala threatened—well, became very rude to him. Vortala can be more obnoxious without actually swearing than any man I know."

"Beta Colony would be drawn in for sure. Why, half our interstellar trade passes through Escobar. And Tau Ceti Five. And Jackson's Whole."

"At the very least, I should think," Vorkosigan nodded agreement. "The idea was to make it a quick operation, and present the potential allies with a fait accompli. Being intimately familiar with everything that went wrong with my 'perfect' plan for Komarr, I told them they were dreaming, or words to that effect." He shook his head. "I wish I'd kept my temper better. I could still be back there, arguing against it. Instead, for all I know, the fleet is being readied even now. And the further preparations go, the harder they will be to stop." He sighed.

"War," Cordelia mused, immensely disturbed. "You realize, if your fleet goes—if Barrayar goes to war with Escobar—they'll be wanting navigators at home. Even if Beta Colony doesn't get directly involved in the fight, we're sure to be selling them weapons, technical assistance, shiploads of supplies—"

Vorkosigan started to speak, then stopped himself. "I suppose you would," he said bleakly. "And we would be trying to blockade you."

She could feel the blood beating in her ears in the silence that followed. The little noises and vibrations of Vorkosigan's ship still drifted through the walls, Bothari stirred in the corridor, and footsteps passed by.

She shook her head. "I'm going to have to think about this. It's not as easy as it looked, at first."

"No, it's not." He turned his hand palm-outward, a gesture of completion, and rose stiffly, his leg still bothering him. "That's all I wanted to say. You need not say anything."

She nodded, grateful for the release, and he withdrew, collecting Bothari and shutting the door firmly behind him. She sighed distress and deep uncertainty, and lay back staring at the ceiling until Yeoman Nilesa brought dinner.

CHAPTER SIX

Next morning, ship time, she remained quietly in her cabin reading. She wanted time to assimilate yesterday's conversation before she saw Vorkosigan again. She was as unsettled as if all her star maps had been randomized, leaving her lost; but at least knowing she was lost. A step backwards toward truth, she supposed, better than mistaken certainties. She hungered forlornly for certainties, even as they receded beyond reach.

The ship's library offered a wide range of Barrayaran material. A gentleman named Abell had produced a turgid general history, full of names, dates, and detailed descriptions of forgotten battles all of whose participants were irrelevantly dead by now. A scholar named Aczith had done better, with a vivid biography of Emperor Dorca Vorbarra the Just, the ambiguous figure whom Cordelia calculated was Vorkosigan's great-grandfather, and whose reign had straddled the end of the Time of Isolation. Deeply involved in the multitude of personalities and convoluted politics of his day, she did not even look up at the knock on her door, but called, "Enter."

A pair of soldiers wearing green-and-grey planetside camouflage fatigues fell through the door and shut it hastily behind them. What a ratty-looking pair, she thought; finally, a Barrayaran soldier shorter than Vorkosigan. It was only on the third thought that she recognized them, as from the corridor outside, muffled by the door, an alarm klaxon began to hoot rhythmically. *Looks like I'm not going to make it to the B's. . . .*

"Captain!" cried Lieutenant Stuben. "Are you all right?"

All the crushing weight of old responsibility descended on her at the sight of his face. His shoulder-length brown hair had been sacrificed to an imitation Barrayaran military burr that looked as though it had been grazed over by some herbivore, and his head seemed small, naked, and strange without it. Lieutenant Lai, beside him, slight and thin with a scholarly stoop, made an even less likely looking warrior, the too-large uniform he wore folded up at the wrists and ankles, with one ankle coming unfolded and getting under the heel of his boot.

She opened her mouth once to speak, closed it, then finally ripped out, "Why aren't you on your way home? I gave you an order, Lieutenant!"

Stuben, anticipating a warmer reception, was momentarily nonplussed. "We took a vote," he said simply, as though it explained everything.

Cordelia shook her head helplessly. "You would. A vote. Right." She buried her face in her hands a moment, and sobbed a laugh. "Why?" she asked through her fingers.

"We identified the Barrayaran ship as the *General Vorkraft*—looked it up and found out who was in command. We just couldn't leave you in the hands of the Butcher of Komarr. It was unanimous."

She was momentarily diverted. "How the devil did you get a unanimous vote out of—no, never mind," she cut him off as he began to answer, a self-satisfied gleam starting in his eye. *I shall beat my head against the wall— no. Got to have more information. And so does he.*

"Do you realize," she said carefully, "that the Barrayarans were planning to bring an invasion fleet through here, to attack Escobar by surprise? If you had reached home and reported this planet's existence, their

chance of surprise would have been destroyed. Now all
bets are off. Where is the *Rene Magritte* now, and how
did you *ever* get in here?"

Lieutenant Stuben looked astonished. "How did you
find all that out?"

"Time, time," Lieutenant Lai reminded him anxiously,
tapping his wrist chronometer.

Stuben went on. "Let me tell you on the way to the
shuttle. Do you know where Dubauer is? He wasn't in
the brig."

"Yes, what shuttle? No—begin at the beginning. I've
got to know everything before we set foot in the corridor. I take it they know you're aboard?" The beat of the
klaxon still sounded outside, and she cringed in expec-
tation of her door bursting inward at any moment.

"No, they don't. That's the beauty of it," said Stuben
proudly. "We had the greatest piece of luck.

"They pursued us for two days when we first ran off.
I didn't put on full power—just enough to stay out of their
range and keep them trailing us. I thought we might still
get a chance to circle back and pick you up, somehow.
Then all of a sudden they stopped, turned around, and
started back here.

"We waited until they were well away, then turned around
ourselves. We hoped you were still hiding in the woods."

"No, I was captured the first night. Go on."

"We got everything lined up, put on max boost, then
cut everything we could think of that made electromag-
netic noise. The projector worked fine as a muffler, by
the way, just like Ross's simulation last month. We waltzed
right past 'em and they never blinked—"

"For God's sake, Stu, stick to the point," muttered Lai.
"We haven't got all day." He bounced on his heels in
impatience.

"If that projector falls into Barrayaran hands—" began
Cordelia in rising tones.

"It won't, I tell you. Anyway, the *Rene Magritte*'s
making a parabola around the sun—as soon as they get
close enough to be masked by its noise, they're supposed

to brake and boost, then shoot back through here for a pickup. We'll have a two-hour time window to match velocities starting—well, starting about ten minutes ago."

"Too chancey," criticized Cordelia, all the possible disasters inherent in this scenario parading through her imagination.

"It worked," defended Stuben. "—at least, it's going to work. Then we struck it lucky. We found these two Barrayarans wandering in the woods while we were looking for you and Dubauer—"

Cordelia's stomach tightened. "Radnov and Darobey, by chance?"

Stuben stared. "How did you know?"

"Go on, just go on."

"They were the ringleaders of a conspiracy to unseat that homicidal maniac Vorkosigan. Vorkosigan was after them, so they were glad to see us."

"I'll bet. Just like manna from heaven."

"A Barrayaran patrol shuttled down after them. We set up an ambush—stunned them all, except for one Radnov shot with a nerve disruptor. Those guys really play for keeps."

"Do you happen to know which—no, never mind. Go on." Her stomach churned.

"We took their uniforms, took their shuttle, and slid on up to the *General* as neat as you please. Radnov and Darobey between 'em knew all the countersigns. We made it to the brig—that was easy, it was where they were expecting their patrol to go anyway—we thought you and Dubauer would be there. Radnov and Darobey let all their buddies out, and went to take over the engine room. They can cut off any system from there, weapons, life support, anything. They're supposed to cut weapons when we make our break with the shuttle."

"I wouldn't count on that," Cordelia warned.

"No matter," said Stuben cheerfully. "The Barrayarans will be so busy fighting each other we can walk right through. Think of the splendid irony! The Butcher of Komarr, shot by his own men! Now I know how judo is supposed to work."

"Splendid," she echoed hollowly. His head, she thought—I'm going to beat his head against the wall, not mine. "How many of us are aboard?"

"Six. Two at the shuttle, two looking for Dubauer, and we two to get you."

"Nobody left planetside?"

"No."

"All right." She rubbed her face tensely, ravenous for inspiration that would not come. "What a mess. Dubauer's in sickbay, by the way. Disruptor damage." She decided not to detail his condition just then.

"Filthy killers," said Lai. "I hope they choke each other."

She turned to the library interface by her bed, and dialed up the crude schematic map of the *General Vorkraft*, minus technical data, that the library was programmed to allow her. "Study this, and figure out your route to sickbay and the shuttle hatch. I'm going to find something out. Stay here and don't answer the door. Who are the other two wandering around out there?"

"McIntyre and Big Pete."

"Well, at least they have a better chance of passing for Barrayarans close up than you two do."

"Captain, where are you going? Why can't we just go?"

"I'll explain it when I have a week to spare. This time follow your damned orders. Stay here!"

She slipped out the door and dog-trotted toward the bridge. Her nerves screamed to run, but it would draw too much attention. She passed a group of four Barrayarans hurrying somewhere; they barely spared her a glance. She had never been more glad to be a wallflower.

She found Vorkosigan on the bridge with his officers, clustered intently around the intercom from engineering. Bothari was there too, looming like Vorkosigan's sad shadow.

"Who's that guy on the comm?" she whispered to Vorkalloner. "Radnov?"

"Yes. Sh."

The face was speaking. "Vorkosigan, Gottyan, and Vorkalloner, one by one, at two-minute intervals. Unarmed, or all life support systems will be cut off throughout the ship. You have fifteen minutes before we start letting in the vacuum. Ah. Have you patched it in? Good. Better not waste time, *Captain*." His inflection made the rank a deadly insult.

The face vanished, but the voice returned ghost-like over the loudspeaker system. "Soldiers of Barrayar," it blared. "Your Captain has betrayed the Emperor and the Council of Ministers. Don't let him betray you too. Turn him over to the proper authority, your Political Officer, or we will be forced to slay the innocent with the guilty. In fifteen minutes we will cut life support—"

"Cut that off," said Vorkosigan irritably.

"Can't sir," said a technician. Bothari, more direct, unslung his plasma arc and with a negligent gesture fired from the hip. The speaker exploded off the wall and several men ducked the molten fragments.

"Hey, we might need that ourselves," began Vorkalloner indignantly.

"Never mind," Vorkosigan waved him down. "Thank you, Sergeant." A distant echo of the voice continued from loudspeakers all over the ship.

"There's no time for anything more elaborate, I'm afraid," Vorkosigan said, apparently winding up a planning session. "Go ahead with your engineering idea, Lieutenant Saint Simon; if you can get it in place in time, so much the better. I'm sure we'd all rather be clever than brave."

The lieutenant nodded and hurried out.

"If he can't, I'm afraid we'll have to rush them," Vorkosigan went on. "They are perfectly capable of killing everyone aboard and rerecording the log to prove anything they please. Between Darobey and Tafas they have the technical know-how. I want volunteers. Myself and Bothari, of course."

A unanimous chorus put themselves forward.

"Gottyan and Vorkalloner are both out. I need somebody who can explain things, afterward. Now the battle

order. First me, then Bothari, then Siegel's patrol, then
Kush's. Stunners only, I don't want stray shots smashing
up engineering." A number of men glanced at the hole
in the wall where the speaker had been.

"Sir," said Vorkalloner desperately, "I question that
battle order. They'll be using disruptors for sure. The first
men through the door haven't got a chance."

Vorkosigan took a few seconds and stared him down.
He dropped his eyes miserably. "Yes, sir."

"Lieutenant Commander Vorkalloner is right, sir," an
unexpected bass voice put in. Cordelia realized with a start
it was Bothari. "The first place is mine, by right. I've
earned it." He faced his captain, narrow jaw working. "It's
mine."

Their eyes met in a weird understanding. "Very well,
Sergeant," conceded Vorkosigan. "You first, then me, then
the rest as ordered. Let's go."

Vorkosigan paused before her as they herded out. "I'm
afraid I'm not going to make that walk on the esplanade
in the summer, after all."

Cordelia shook her head helplessly, the glimmer of a
terrifying idea beginning in the back of her brain. "I—
I—I have to withdraw my parole now."

Vorkosigan looked puzzled, then waved it aside for a
more immediate concern. "If I should chance to end up
like your Ensign Dubauer—remember my preferences.
If you can bring yourself to it, I would like it to be by
your hand. I'll tell Vorkalloner. Can I have your word?"

"Yes."

"You'd better stay in your cabin until this is over."

He reached out to her shoulder, to touch one curl of
red hair resting there, then turned away. Cordelia fled
down the corridor, Radnov's propaganda droning sense-
lessly in her ears. Her plan blossomed furiously in her
mind. Her reason yammered protest, like a rider on a
runaway horse; you have no duty to these Barrayarans,
your duty is to Beta Colony, to Stuben, to the *Rene
Magritte*—your duty is to escape, and warn . . .

She swung into her cabin. Wonder of wonders, Stuben

and Lai were still there. They looked up, alarmed by her wild appearance.

"Go to sickbay now. Pick up Dubauer and take him to the shuttle. When were Pete and Mac supposed to report back there if they couldn't find him?"

"In—" Lai checked his time, "ten minutes."

"Thank God. When you get to sickbay, tell the surgeon that Captain Vorkosigan ordered you to bring Dubauer to me. Lai, you wait in the corridor. You'd never fool the surgeon. Dubauer can't talk. Don't act surprised by his condition. When you get to the shuttle, wait—let me see your chrono, Lai—till 0620 our ship time, then take off. If I'm not back by then I'm not coming. Full power and don't look back. Exactly how many men did Radnov and Darobey have with them?"

"Ten or eleven, I guess," Stuben said.

"All right. Give me your stunner. Go. Go. Go."

"Captain, we came here to rescue you!" cried Stuben, bewildered.

Words failed her utterly. She put a hand on his shoulder instead. "I know. Thank you." She ran.

Approaching engineering from one deck above, she came to an intersection of two corridors. Down the larger was a group of men assembling and checking weapons. Down the smaller were two men covering an entry port to the next deck, a last checkpoint before territory covered by Radnov's fire. One of them was Yeoman Nilesa. She pounced on him.

"Captain Vorkosigan sent me down," she lied. "He wants me to try one last effort at negotiation, as a neutral in the affair."

"That's a waste of time," observed Nilesa.

"So he hopes," she improvised. "It'll keep them tied up while he's getting ready. Can you get me in without alarming anybody?"

"I can try, I guess." Nilesa went forward and undogged a circular hatch in the floor at the end of the corridor.

"How many guards on this entrance?" she whispered.

"Two or three, I think."

The hatch swung up, revealing a man-width access tube with a ladder up one side and a pole down the middle.

"Hey, Wentz!" he shouted down it.

"Who's that?" a voice floated up.

"Me, Nilesa. Captain Vorkosigan wants to send that Betan frill down to talk to Radnov."

"What for?"

"How the hell should I know? You're the ones who're supposed to have comm pickups in everybody's bunks. Maybe she's not such a good lay after all." Nilesa shrugged an apology toward her, and she accepted it with a nod.

There was a whispered debate below.

"Is she armed?"

Cordelia, readying both stunners, shook her head.

"Would you give a weapon to a Betan frill?" Nilesa called back rhetorically, watching her preparations in puzzlement.

"All right. Put her in, dog the hatch, and let her drop. If you don't close the hatch before she drops, we'll shoot her. Got that?"

"Yo."

"What'll I be looking at when I get to the bottom?" she quizzed Nilesa.

"Nasty spot. You'll be standing in a sort of niche in the storeroom off the main control room. You can only get one man at a time through it, and you're pinned in there like a target, with the wall on three sides. It's designed that way on purpose."

"No way to rush them through it? I mean, you're not planning to?"

"No way in hell."

"Good. Thanks."

Cordelia climbed down into the tube, and Nilesa closed the hatch over her with a sound like the lid of a coffin.

"All right," came the voice from below, "drop."

"It's a long way down," she called back, having no trouble sounding tremulous. "I'm afraid."

"Screw it. I'll catch you."

"All right." She wrapped her legs and one arm around the pole. Her hand shook as she jammed the second

stunner into her holster. Her stomach pumped sour bile
into the back of her throat. She swallowed, took a deep
breath to keep it there, held her stunner pointed ready,
and dropped.

She landed face-to-face with the man below, his nerve
disruptor held casually at the level of her waist. His eyes
widened as he saw her stunner. Here the Barrayaran
custom of all-male crews on warships paid her, for he
hesitated just a fraction of a second to shoot a woman.
In that fraction she fired first. He slumped heavily over
her, head lolling on her shoulder. Bracing, she held him
as a shield before her.

Her second shot laid out the next guard as he was
bringing his disruptor to aim. The third guard got off
a hasty burst that was absorbed by the back of the man
she held, although the nimbus of it seared the outer
edge of her left thigh. The pain of it flared screamingly,
but no sound escaped her clenched teeth. With a wild
berserker accuracy that seemed no part of herself, she
felled him too, then looked frantically around for a place
of concealment.

Some conduits ran overhead; people entering a room
usually look down and around before thinking to look up.
She stuck the stunner in her belt, and with a leap she
could never have duplicated in cold blood, pulled herself up between the conduits and the armored ceiling.
Breathing silently through her open mouth, she drew her
stunner again and prepared for whatever might come
through the oval door to the main engineering bay.

"What was that noise? What's going on in there?"

"Throw in a grenade and seal the door."

"We can't, our men are in there."

"Wentz, report!"

Silence.

"You go in, Tafas."

"Why me?"

"Because I order you."

Tafas crept cautiously around the door, stepping over
the threshold almost on tiptoe. He turned around and

around, staring. Afraid that they would close and lock the door at another firing, she waited until he at last looked up.

She smiled winningly at him, and gave a little wave of her fingers. "Close the door," she mouthed silently, pointing.

He stared at her with a very odd expression on his face, baffled, hopeful, and angry all at once. The bell of his disruptor seemed large as a searchlight, pointed quite accurately at her head. It was like looking into the eye of judgment. A standoff, of sorts. Vorkosigan is right, she thought; a disruptor *does* have real authority. . . .

Then Tafas called, "I think there may be some kind of gas leak or something. Better close the door a second while I check." It swung closed obediently behind him.

Cordelia smiled down from the ceiling, eyes narrowed. "Hi. Want to get out of this mess?"

"What are you doing here—Betan?"

Excellent question, she thought ruefully. "Trying to save a few lives. Don't worry—your friends over there are only stunned." I won't mention the one hit by friendly fire— dead, perhaps, because of a moment's mercy for me. . . . "Come on over to our side," she coaxed, madly echoing a child's game. "Captain Vorkosigan will forgive you— expunge the record. Give you a medal," she promised recklessly.

"What medal?"

"How should I know? Any medal you want. You don't even have to kill anybody. I have another stunner."

"What guarantee do I have?"

Desperation made her daring. "Vorkosigan's word. You tell him I pledged it to you."

"Who are you to pledge his word?"

"Lady Vorkosigan, if we both live." A lie? Truth? Hopeless fantasy?

Tafas gave a whistle, staring up at her. Belief began to illuminate his face.

"You really want to be responsible for letting a hundred fifty of your friends breathe vacuum just to save that Ministerial spy's career?" she added cogently.

"No," he said firmly at last. "Give me the stunner."

Now shall trust be tested. . . . She dropped it down to him. "Three down and seven to go. What's the best approach?"

"I can lure a couple more in here. The others are at the main entrance. We can rush them from behind, if we're lucky."

"Go ahead."

Tafas opened the door. "It was a gas leak," he coughed convincingly. "Help me drag these guys out and we'll seal the door."

"I could swear I heard a stunner go off a while ago," said his companion, entering.

"Maybe they were trying to attract attention."

The mutineer's face flared with suspicion as the stupidity of this suggestion sank in. "They didn't have stunners," he began. Fortunately, the second man entered at this point. Cordelia and Tafas fired in unison.

"Five down, five to go," Cordelia said, dropping to the floor. Her left leg buckled; it wasn't moving quite right. "Odds are getting better all the time."

"It had better be quick, if it's going to work at all," warned Tafas.

"Suits me."

They slid out the door and ran lightly across the engineering bay, which continued its automatic tasks, indifferent to its masters' identity. Some black-uniformed bodies were piled carelessly to one side. Tafas held up his hand for caution as they rounded the corner, jabbing a finger significantly. Cordelia nodded. Tafas walked around the corner quietly, and Cordelia pinned herself to its very edge, waiting. As Tafas raised his stunner she oozed around, searching for a target. The chamber narrowed in this L, ending in the main entrance to the deck above. Five men stood with their attention riveted to the clanks and hisses penetrating dimly through a hatch at the top of some metal stairs.

"They're getting ready to storm," said one. "It's time to let their air out."

Famous last words, she thought, and fired, once and twice. Tafas fired too, rapidly fanning the group, and it was over. And I will never, she pledged silently, call one of Stuben's stunts harebrained again. She wanted to throw down her stunner and howl and roll in reaction, but her own job was not finished.

"Tafas," she called. "I've got to do one more thing."

He came to her side, looking shaky himself.

"I've gotten you out of this, and I need a favor in return. How can I cut control to the long-range plasma weapons so you can't get it back for an hour and a half?"

"Why do you want to do that? Did the Captain order it?"

"No," she said honestly. "The Captain didn't order any of this, but he'll like it when he sees it, don't you think?"

Tafas, confused, agreed. "If you short this panel," he suggested, "it should slow things down quite a bit."

"Give me your plasma arc."

Need I? she wondered, looking over the section. Yes. He would fire on us, just as surely as I'm cutting for home. Trust is one thing; treason another. I have no wish to test him to destruction.

Now, if Tafas isn't fooling me by pointing out the controls to the toilets or something . . . She blasted the panel, and stared with a moment's primitive fascination as it popped and sparked.

"Now," she said, handing the plasma arc back, "I want a couple of minutes head start. Then you can open the door and be a hero. I suggest you call first and warn them; Sergeant Bothari's in front."

"Right. Thanks."

She glanced up at the main entry hatch. About three meters away, he is now, she thought. An uncrossable gulf. So in the physics of the heart, distance is relative; it's time that's absolute. The seconds spun like spiders down her spine.

She chewed her lip, eyes devouring Tafas. Last chance to leave a message for Vorkosigan—no. The absurdity of transmitting the words, "I love you" through Tafas's mouth shook her with painful inward laughter. "My compliments" sounded rather swelled-headed, under the circumstances: "my regards," too cold; as for the simplest of all, "yes" . . .

She shook her head silently and smiled at the puzzled soldier, then ran back to the storeroom and scrambled back up the ladder. She beat a rhythmic tattoo upon the hatch. In a moment it opened. She found herself nose to nose with a plasma arc held by Yeoman Nilesa.

"I've got some new terms to carry back to your Captain," she said glibly. "They're a little screwy, but I think he'll like them."

Nilesa, surprised, let her out and resealed the hatch. She walked away from him, glancing down the main corridor as she passed. Several dozen men were assembled in it. A technical team had half the panels off the walls; sparks flared from a tool. She could just see Sergeant Bothari's head on the far side of the crowd, and knew him to be standing next to Vorkosigan. She reached the ladder at the end of the corridor, ascended it, and began to run, threading her way level by level through the maze of the ship.

Laughing, crying, out of breath and shaking violently, she arrived at the shuttle hatch corridor. Dr. McIntyre stood guard, trying to appear grim and Barrayaran.

"Is everybody here?"

He nodded, looking at her with delight.

"Pile in, let's go."

They sealed the doors behind them and fell into their seats as the shuttle pulled away at maximum acceleration with a crunch and a jerk. Pete Lightner was piloting manually, for his Betan pilot's neurological implant would not interface to the Barrayaran control system without an interpreter coupler, and Cordelia braced herself for a terrifying ride.

She lay back in her seat, still gasping, lungs raw from her mad dash. Stuben joined her, seething, and staring worriedly at her uncontrollable trembling.

"It's a crime what they did to Dubauer," he said. "I wish we could blow up their whole damn ship. Is Radnov still covering us, do you know?"

"Their long-range weapons will be out for a while," she reported, not volunteering details. Could she ever make him understand? "Oh. I meant to ask—who was the Barrayaran hit by disruptor fire, planet-side?"

"I don't know. Doc Mac got his uniform. Hey, Mac—what's the name on your pocket?"

"Uh, let me see if I can sound out their alphabet." His lips moved silently. "Kou—Koudelka."

Cordelia bowed her head. "Was he killed?"

"He wasn't dead when we left, but he sure didn't look very healthy."

"What were you doing all that time aboard the *General*?" asked Stuben.

"Paying off a debt. Of honor."

"All right, be like that. I'll get the story later." He was silent, then added with a short nod, "I hope you got the bastard good, whoever he was."

"Look, Stu—I appreciate all you've done. But I've really got to be alone for a few minutes."

"Sure, Captain." He gave her a look of concern, and moved off muttering, "Damned monsters," under his breath.

Cordelia leaned her forehead against the cold window, and wept silently for her enemies.

CHAPTER SEVEN

Captain Cordelia Naismith, Betan Expeditionary Force, fed the last normal space navigational observations into her ship's computer. Beside her, Pilot Officer Parnell adjusted the leads and cannulae to his headset and settled more comfortably into his padded chair, ready for the neurological control of the upcoming wormhole jump.

Her new command was a slow bulk freighter, unarmed, a steady workhorse of the Beta Colony–Escobar trade run. But there had been no direct communication with Escobar for over sixty days now, since the Barrayaran invasion fleet had plugged the Escobaran side of the exit as effectively as a cork in a bottle. At last word the Barrayaran and Escobaran fleets were still maneuvering in a deadly gavotte for tactical position, with little actual engagement. The Barrayarans were not expected to commit their ground forces until their control of Escobaran space was secure.

Cordelia intercomed engineering. "Naismith here. You about ready down there?"

The face of her engineer, a man she had first met but two days ago, appeared on the screen. He was young, and pulled from Survey like herself. No point in wasting

experienced and knowledgeable military personnel on this
excursion. Like Cordelia he wore Survey fatigues. The
Expeditionary Force uniforms were rumored to be in the
works, but no one had seen them yet.

"All set, Captain."

No fear trembled his voice. Well, she reflected, perhaps he was not old enough yet to have really come to
believe in death after life. She took one last look around,
settled herself, and drew a breath. "Pilot, the ship is
yours."

"Ship accepted, ma'am," he replied formally.

A few seconds ticked by. An unpleasant wave of nausea passed over her, and she had the gluey, unsettling
sensation of just waking up from a bad dream she could
not remember. The jump was over.

"Ship is yours, ma'am," muttered the pilot wearily. The
few seconds she had experienced translated to several
subjective hours for him.

"Ship accepted, Pilot." She grabbed for the comconsole
and began punching up a look at the tactical situation into
which they had popped. There had been nothing through
this passage for a month; she hoped fervently the
Barrayaran crews would be bored and slow on the uptake.

There they were. Six ships, two of them starting to
move already. So much for slow on the uptake.

"Right through the middle of 'em, Pilot," she ordered,
keying data to him. "It's best if we can draw 'em all off
their stations."

The two moving ships neared rapidly, and began firing with leisurely accuracy. They were taking their time,
and making every shot count. Just a little target practice,
that's all we are, she thought. I'll give you target practice. All non-shield power systems dimmed, and the ship
seemed to groan as the plasma fire engulfed it. Then they
cut across the tickling limit of the Barrayarans' range.

She called engineering. "Projection ready?"

"Ready and steady."

"Go."

Twelve thousand kilometers behind them, as if just

emerged from the wormhole, a Betan dreadnought sprang into being. It accelerated astonishingly for so large a craft; indeed, its speed matched their own. It followed them like an arrow.

"Aha!" She clapped her hands in delight, and cried into the intercom, "We've fetched 'em! They're all moving now. Oh, better and better!"

Their pursuit ships slowed, preparing to turn and attack this much bigger prize. The four ships that had previously remained properly on station began to wheel away also. Minutes sped by as they jockeyed for position. The last Barrayaran ships wasted little fire on them, scarcely more than a salute, their attention all drawn to big brother behind them. The Barrayaran commanders undoubtedly felt themselves to be in a fine tactical position, spread out in a gauntlet and beginning a withering fire. The little ship preceding the warship was on the far side of them from Escobar, with nowhere to go. They could pick it off at their leisure.

Her own shields were down now, and acceleration failing as the ghastly power drain of the projector took its toll. But minute by precious minute the Barrayaran blockaders were being drawn farther from their assigned mousehole.

"We can keep this up for about ten more minutes," the engineer called up.

"All right. Save enough power to slag it when you're done. If we're captured Command doesn't want one molecule left connected to another for the Barrayarans to puzzle back together."

"What a crime. It's such a beautiful machine. I'm dying for a look inside."

You might, too, if the Barrayarans capture us, she thought. She directed all her ship's eyes back along their route. Far, far back at the wormhole exit, the first real Betan freighter winked into existence and began to boost for Escobar, unopposed. It was the newest addition to the merchant fleet, stripped of weapons and shields, rebuilt to do two things only now; carry a heavy payload and go like hell. Then the second, and the third. That was it. They were away, and with a start the Barrayarans could never hope to close.

The Betan dreadnought exploded with a spectacular radioactive light show. Unfortunately, there was no way to fake debris. *I wonder how long it will take the Barrayarans to figure out they've been had?* she thought. *I sincerely hope they have a sense of humor. . . .*

Her ship drifted dead in space now, its power nearly depleted. She felt light in the head, and realized it wasn't psychosomatic. The artificial gravity was failing.

They rendezvoused with the engineer and his two assistants at the shuttle hatch, traveling with gazelle-like leaps that turned into bird-like swoops as the gravity gave up the ghost. The shuttle which was to be their lifeboat was a stripped-down model, cramped and comfortless. Into it they floated and sealed the hatch. The pilot slid into the control chair and lowered his headset, and the shuttle kicked away from the side of their dying ship.

The engineer floated to her and handed her a little black box. "I thought you ought to do the honors, Captain."

"Ha. I bet you wouldn't kill your own dinner, either," she replied, trying to lighten the mood. They had served their ship together for barely five hours, but it still hurt. "Are we out of range, Parnell?"

"Yes, Captain."

"Gentlemen," she said, and paused, gathering them in by eye, "I thank you all. Look away from the left port, please."

She pulled the lever on the box. There was a soundless flash of brilliant blue light, and a general rush for the tiny port immediately after to see the last red glow as the ship folded into itself, carrying its military secrets to a wandering grave.

They shook hands solemnly all around, some right side up, some upside down, some floating at other angles, then secured themselves. Cordelia pulled herself into the navigation station beside Parnell, strapped in, and ran a quick check of its systems.

"Now comes the tricky part," murmured Parnell. "I'd still be happier with a straight max boost and try to outrun 'em."

"We could get away from those fat battlewagons, maybe," Cordelia conceded. "But their fast couriers would eat us alive. At least we look like a rock," she added, thinking of the artistic, probe-reflective camouflage that encased the lifeboat like a shell.

Several minutes of silence followed, as she concentrated on her work. "All right," she spoke at last, "let's sneak out of this neighborhood. It's going to be overcrowded very soon."

She did not fight the acceleration, but let it press her back into her seat. Tired. She hadn't thought it possible to be more tired than she was afraid. This war nonsense was a great psychological education. That chronometer had to be wrong. Surely it had been a year, and not an hour. . . .

A small light blinked on her control panel. Fear washed the weariness back out of her body with a rush.

"Kill everything," she ordered, tapping controls herself, and was instantly plunged into weightless darkness. "Parnell, give us a little realistic tumble." Her inner ear and a greasy queasiness in her belly told her she was obeyed.

Now her sense of time began to be truly disordered. Darkness and silence reigned, but for an occasional whisper of movement, fabric on plastic, as someone stirred in his seat. In her imagination she felt the Barrayaran probes touching her ship, touching her, icy fingers up her back. I am a rock. I am a void. I am a silence. . . . In the rear the silence was broken by the noise of someone vomiting, and some muffled swearing. Blast this tumble. Hope he had time to grab a bag. . . .

There came a jerk and a pressure of weight at an odd angle. Parnell spat an oath like a sob. "Tractor tow! That's it."

She sighed without relief, and reached out to key the shuttle back to life, wincing at the blinding brightness of the little lights. "Well, let's see what's caught us."

Her hands flicked over the panels. She took a glance at her exterior monitors, and hastily pressed the red button that crashed the lifeboat's computer memory and recognition codes.

"What the hell have we got out there?" asked the engineer anxiously, noting the gesture as he made his way to her shoulder.

"Two cruisers and a fast courier," she informed him. "We appear to be slightly outnumbered."

He snorted unhappily.

A disembodied voice blared from the comm, at too great a volume; she turned it down quickly.

". . . not acknowledge surrender, we will destroy you."

"This is Lifeboat Shuttle A5A," she responded, modulating her voice carefully. "Captain Cordelia Naismith, Betan Expeditionary Force, commanding. We are an unarmed lifeboat."

The comm emitted a surprised "Peh!" and the voice added, "Another damned woman! You people are slow learners."

There was an unintelligible murmur in the background, and the voice returned to its original official tone. "You will be taken in tow. At the first sign of resistance, you will be obliterated. Understood?"

"Acknowledged," Cordelia responded. "We surrender."

Parnell shook his head angrily. She killed the comm and raised an eyebrow.

"I think we should try and make a break," he said.

"No. These guys are professional paranoids. The sanest one I ever met didn't like being in a room with a closed door—claimed you never knew what was on the other side. If they say they'll shoot, you'd better believe 'em."

Parnell and the engineer exchanged a look. "Go ahead, 'Nell," said the engineer. "Tell her."

Parnell cleared his throat, and moistened dry lips. "We wanted to let you know, Captain—that if you think, uh, blowing up the lifeboat might be the best thing for all concerned, we're with you. Nobody else is looking forward to being taken prisoner either."

Cordelia blinked at this offer. "That's—very courageous of you, Pilot Officer, but totally unnecessary. Don't flatter yourself. We were handpicked for our ignorance, not our knowledge. You all only have guesses about what was aboard that convoy, and even I don't know any technical details. If we cooperate on the surface, we've at least some chance of getting through this alive."

"It—wasn't spilling intelligence we were thinking about, ma'am. It's their other habits."

A sticky silence fell. Cordelia sighed, spiraling in a vortex of grieving doubt. "It's all right," she said at last. "Their reputation is way overblown. Quite decent fellows, some of them." Especially one, her mind mocked. And even assuming he's still alive, do you really think you could find him in all this mess? Or finding him, save him from the gifts you yourself have brought from hell's hardware store without betraying your duty? Or is this a secret suicide pact? Do you even know yourself? Know thyself.

Parnell, watching her face, shook his head grimly. "You sure?"

"I've never killed anybody in my life. I'm not going to start with people on my own side, for pity's sake."

Parnell acknowledged the justice of this with a little quizzical shrug, not quite concealing an underlying relief.

"Anyway, I've got things to live for. This war can't last forever."

"Somebody back home?" he asked, and as her eyes turned to the probe readouts, added wisely, "Or out there?"

"Uh, yeah. Out there somewhere."

He shook his head in sympathy. "That's a tough one." He studied her still profile, and added encouragingly, "But you're right. The big boys will blast those bastards out of the sky sooner or later."

She gave vent to a small, mechanical, "Ha," and massaged her face with her fingertips, trying to rub out the tension. She had a sudden waking vision of a great warship cracked open, spilling its living guts like some monstrous seedpod. Frozen, sterile seeds, adrift on no wind, bloated from decompression and turning forever. Could one recognize a face, after that? she wondered. She turned her chair half away from Parnell, signifying an end to the conversation.

A Barrayaran fast courier took them in tow within an hour.

It was the familiar smell that hit her first, the metal-and-machine-oil, ozone-redolent, locker-room smell of a Barrayaran warship. The two tall soldiers in black who escorted her, each keeping a hand firmly on her elbow, maneuvered her through one last narrow oval doorway to what she guessed must be the main prison area of the great flagship. She and her four men were stripped ruthlessly, searched in minute and paranoid detail, medically examined, holographed, retinaprinted, identified, and issued shapeless orange pajamas. Her men were led away separately. In spite of her words to Parnell, she was sickened by dread of them being peeled, layer by layer, for information they did not hold. Gently now, reason argued; surely the Barrayarans would save them for prisoner exchange.

The guards snapped to attention. Turning, she saw a high-ranking Barrayaran officer enter the processing chamber. The bright yellow of the collar tabs on his dark green dress uniform marked a rank she had not seen before, and with a shock she identified it as the color for a vice-admiral. Knowing what he was, she knew at once who he was, and studied him with grave interest.

Vorrutyer, that was his name. Co-commander of the Barrayaran armada, along with Crown Prince Serg Vorbarra. She supposed he was the one who did the real work; she'd heard he was slated to be the Barrayarans' next Minister of War. So that was what a rising star looked like.

In a way he was a little like Vorkosigan, a bit taller, about the same weight but less of it in bone and muscle and more of it in fat. He had dark hair too, curlier than Vorkosigan's and with less grey in it, was a similar age, and rather more handsome. His eyes were quite different, a deep velvet brown fringed by long black lashes, by far the most beautiful eyes she had ever seen in a man's face. They triggered a small subliminal wailing deep in her mind, crying, *you thought you had faced fear earlier today, but you were mistaken; here is the real thing, fear without exhilaration or hope;* which was strange, for they ought to have attracted her. She broke eye contact, telling herself firmly the unease and instant dislike were mere nerves, and waited.

"Identify yourself, Betan," he growled. It gave her a disjointed sense of deja vu.

She fought for equilibrium, giving him a snappy salute and saying smartly, "Captain Cordelia Naismith, Betan Expeditionary. We are a military party. Combatants." This private joke of course passed by him.

"Hah. Strip her, and turn her about."

He stepped back, watching. The two grinning soldiers guarding her obeyed. *I don't like the way this is starting out. . . .* She forced her face to blandness, holding on to all her secret sources of serenity. *Calm. Calm. This one wants to rattle you. You can see it in his eyes, his hungry eyes. Calm.*

"A little old, but she'll do. I'll send for her later."

The guard shoved the pajamas back at her. She dressed slowly, to annoy them, like a striptease in reverse, with precise controlled motions of the sort suitable for a Japanese tea ceremony. One growled, and the other shoved her roughly in the back toward her cell. She smiled sourly at her success, thinking, *well, at least I have that much control over my destiny. Should I award myself points if I can goad them into beating me up?*

They bundled her into a bare metal room, and left her. She continued the ploy, for her own thin amusement, by kneeling gracefully on the floor with the same sort of movements, right toe crossed correctly over the left, hands resting motionless upon her thighs. The touch reminded her of the patch on her left leg that was devoid of all sensation, heat, cold, pain, pressure, legacy of her last encounter with the armies of Barrayar. She half-closed her eyes and let her mind drift, hoping to give her captors an unsettling impression of deep and possibly dangerous psychic meditations. Pretend aggression was better than nothing.

After an hour or so of stillness, by which time her unaccustomed muscles were protesting the kneeling position most painfully, the guard returned.

"Admiral wants you," he said laconically. "Come along."

She had a guard at each elbow again for the trip through the ship. One grinned and undressed her with his eyes. The other looked at her with pity, far more disturbing. She began to wonder just how much her time with Vorkosigan had led her to discount the risks of capture. They came to officer's country, and stopped before an oval metal door in a row of identical ones. The grinning guard knocked, and was bidden to enter.

This admiral's quarters were very different from her austere cabin aboard the *General Vorkraft*. For one thing, the bulkheads had been knocked out of the two adjoining chambers, giving a triple share of space. It was full of personal furnishings of a most luxurious order. Admiral Vorrutyer rose from a velvet-covered seat as she entered, but she did not mistake it for a gesture of courtesy.

He walked slyly around her as she stood silent, watching her gaze travel around the room. "A step up from that cell, eh?" he probed.

For the guards' benefit she replied, "Looks like a whore's boudoir."

The grinning guard choked, and the other one laughed outright, but cut it off quickly at a glare from Vorrutyer. Didn't think it was *that* funny, she puzzled. Some of the details of the decor began to penetrate, and she realized she'd spoken more truly than she knew. What an extremely odd little statuette in that corner, for instance. Although it had a certain redeeming artistic merit, she supposed. "One with very unusual customers," she added.

"Buckle her in," ordered Vorrutyer, "and return to your posts. I'll call you when I'm done."

She was placed on her back across his wide, non-regulation bed, arms and legs stretched to the four corners and tautly attached by soft bracelets to short chains, attached in turn to the bedframe. Simple, chilling, quite beyond her strength to break.

The guard who pitied whispered to her under his breath as he buckled a wrist strap, hidden almost inaudibly in a sigh, "Sorry."

"It's all right," she breathed back. Their eyes passed over each other, hiding the secret transaction from the watching Vorrutyer.

"Ha. That's what you think now," murmured the other through his grin, fastening the other strap.

"Shut up," muttered the first, and shot him a fierce look. An unclean silence filled the room until the guards withdrew.

"Looks like a permanent installation," she observed to Vorrutyer, horribly fascinated. It was like a sick joke come to life. "What do you do when you can't catch Betans? Call for volunteers?"

A frown appeared between his eyes briefly, then smoothed. "Keep it up," he encouraged. "It amuses me. It will make the ultimate denouement so much more piquant."

He loosened his uniform collar, poured himself a glass of wine from a very non-regulation portable bar in one corner, and seated himself on the bed beside her with the chatty air of a man visiting a sick friend. He looked her over minutely, beautiful brown eyes liquid with anticipation.

She tried to string herself along; maybe he's only a rapist. It might be possible to handle a simple rapist. Such direct, childlike souls, hardly offensive at all. Even vileness has a relative range. . . .

"I don't know any military secrets worth a thing," she fenced. "This isn't really worth your time."

"I didn't think you did," he replied easily. "Although you will undoubtedly insist on telling me everything you know over the next few weeks. Quite tedious, I'm not in the least interested. If I want your information, my medical staff can have it out of you in a trice." He sipped his wine. "Although it's curious you should bring up the subject—perhaps I will send you to sickbay, later today."

Her stomach knotted. Fool, she shrieked silently at herself, did you just blow a chance of ducking interrogation? But no, it had to be standard operating procedure—he's just working you over. Subtle. Calm . . .

He drank again. "Do you know, I think I shall enjoy having an older woman for a change. The young ones may look pretty, but they're too easy. No sport. I can tell already, you're going to be great sport. A very great fall requires a very great height, to fall from, not so?"

She sighed, and gazed up at the ceiling. "Well, I'm sure it will be educational." She tried to remember how she'd occupied her mind during sex with her old lover, in the bad times before she'd finally shed him. This might well be no worse. . . .

Vorrutyer, smiling, put his wine down on a bedside table and took from its drawer a small knife, sharp as an old-fashioned scalpel, with a jeweled handle that glittered before his hand eclipsed it. Rather desultorily, he began slicing away at the orange pajamas, peeling them away from her like the skin of a fruit.

"Isn't that government property?" she inquired, but was sorry she'd spoken, for a tremble made the word "property" squeaky. It was like throwing a tidbit to a hungry dog, likely to make him jump higher.

He chuckled, pleased. "Oops." Deliberately, he let the knife slip. It sliced half an inch into her thigh. He watched her face avidly for her reaction. It was in the area without sensation; she could not even feel the wet trickle of blood that welled from the wound. His eyes narrowed in disappointment. She even kept from glancing down. She wished she'd studied more about trance states.

"I'm not going to rape you today," he offered conversationally, "if that's what you've been thinking."

"It had crossed my mind. I can't imagine what suggested it."

"There's scarcely time," he explained. "Today is but the, as it were, hors d'ouevre of the banquet, or a simple clear soup, very pristine. All the complicated things will be saved for dessert, in a few weeks."

"I never eat dessert. Weight, you know."

He chuckled again. "You are a delight." He put the knife down and took another sip of wine. "You know, officers always delegate their work. Now, I am an aficionado of Earth history. My favorite century is the eighteenth."

"I'd have guessed the fourteenth. Or the twentieth."

"In a day or two, I shall teach you not to interrupt. Where was I? Ah, yes. Well, in my reading, I came upon the loveliest scene, where a certain great lady," he raised the wineglass to her in a toast, "was raped by a diseased servant, on the orders of his master. Very piquant. Venereal disease is, alas, a thing of the past. But I am able to command a diseased servant, although his disease is mental rather than physical. A real, bona fide, paranoid schizophrenic."

"Like master, like man," she shot at random. I cannot keep this up much longer; my heart shall fail me soon. . . .

This won a rather sour smile. "He hears voices, you know, like Joan of Arc, except that he tells me they are demons, not saints. He has visual hallucinations, too, on occasion. And he's a very large man. I've used him before, many times. He's not the sort of fellow who finds it easy to, er, attract women."

There was a timely knock on the door, and Vorrutyer went to it. "Ah, come in, Sergeant. I was just talking about you."

"*Bothari,*" she breathed. Ducking his head through the door came the tall frame and familiar borzoi face of Vorkosigan's soldier. How, how *could* he have hit on her personal nightmare? A kaleidoscope of images spun through her memory: a dappled wood, the crackle of disruptors, the faces of the dead and the half-dead, a looming shape like the shadow of death.

She focused on the present reality. Would he recognize her? His eyes had not yet touched her; they were fixed on Vorrutyer. Too close together, those eyes, and not quite on the same level. They gave his face an unusual degree of asymmetry that added much to his remarkable ugliness.

Her boiling imagination lurched to his body. His body—it was all wrong, somehow, hunched in his black uniform, not like the straight figure she had last seen demanding pride of place from Vorkosigan. Wrong, wrong, terribly wrong. A head taller than Vorrutyer, yet he seemed almost to creep before his master. His spine was coiled with tension as he glowered down at his—torturer? What, she wondered, might a mind molester like Vorrutyer do with the material presented by Bothari? God, Vorrutyer, do you imagine, in your amoral flashy freakiness, in your monstrous vanity, that you *control* this elemental? And you dare play games with that sullen madness in his eyes? Her thoughts kept time with her racing pulse. There are two victims in this room. There are two victims in this room. There are two . . .

"There you go, Sergeant." Vorrutyer hooked a thumb over his shoulder at Cordelia, spread-eagled on the bed. "Rape me this woman." He pulled up a chair and prepared to watch, closely and gleefully. "Go on, go on."

Bothari, face as unreadable as ever, unfastened his trousers and approached the foot of the bed. He looked at her for the first time.

"Any last words, 'Captain' Naismith?" Vorrutyer inquired sarcastically. "Or have you finally run out of words?"

She stared at Bothari, shaken by a pity almost like love. He seemed nearly in a trance, lust without pleasure, anticipation without hope. Poor sod, she thought, what a mess they've made of you. No longer fencing for points, she searched her heart for words not for Vorrutyer but for Bothari. Some healing words—I would not add to his madness. . . . The air of the room seemed clammy cold, and she shivered, feeling unutterably weary, resistless, and sad. He crouched over her, heavy and dark as lead, making the bed creak.

"I believe," she said slowly at last, "that the tormented are very close to God. I'm sorry, Sergeant."

He stared at her, his face a foot from hers, for so long she wondered if he'd heard her. His breath was not good, but she did not flinch. Then, to her astonishment, he stood up and refastened his pants, trembling slightly.

"No, sir," he said in his bass monotone.

"What?" Vorrutyer sat up, amazed. "Why not?" he demanded.

The Sergeant groped for words. "She's Commodore Vorkosigan's prisoner. Sir."

Vorrutyer stared, first puzzled, then illuminated. "So *you're* Vorkosigan's Betan!" His cool amusement evaporated at the name, with a hiss like a drop of water on a red-hot coil.

Vorkosigan's Betan? A brief hope flared within her, that Vorkosigan's name might be a password to safety, but it died. The chance of this creature being any kind of a friend of his was surely something well under zero. He was looking now not at her, but through her, like a window on some more wonderful view. *Vorkosigan's Betan?*

"I've got that stiff-necked puritan son-of-a-bitch by the balls now," he breathed fiercely. "This could be even better than the day I told him about his wife." The expression on his face was strange and startling, the mask of suavity seeming to melt, and run off in patches. It was like stumbling suddenly over the center of a caldera. He seemed to remember the mask, and clutched its pieces around him, half-effectually.

"Do you know, you have quite overwhelmed me. The possibilities you present—eighteen years were not too long to wait for so ideal a revenge. A woman soldier. Ha! He probably thought you the ideal solution to our mutual—difficulty. My perfect warrior, my dear hypocrite, Aral. You have much to learn of him, I wager. But do you know, I somehow feel quite certain he hasn't mentioned me to you."

"Not by name," she agreed. "Possibly by category."

"And what category was that?"

"I believe the term he used was 'scum of the service.'"

He grinned sourly. "I shouldn't recommend name-calling to a woman in your position."

"Oh, you embrace the category, then?" Her response was automatic, but her heart was shrinking within her, leaving an echoing hollowness. What is Vorkosigan doing in the center of this one's madness? His eyes look like Bothari's, now. . . .

His smile tightened. "I've embraced a number of things in my time. Not least of which was your puritan lover. Let your imagination dwell on that a while, my dear, my sweet, my pet. You'd scarcely believe it to meet him now, but he was quite a merry widower, before he gave himself over so irritatingly to these random outbreaks of righteousness." He laughed.

"Your skin is very white. Has he touched it—so?" He ran one fingernail up the inside of her arm, and she shuddered. "And your hair. I am quite certain he must be fascinated by that twining hair. So fine, and such an unusual color." He twisted a strand gently between his fingers. "I must think what can be done with that hair. One might remove the scalp entirely, of course, but there must be something more creative yet. Perhaps I'll take a bit with me, and take it out and play with it, quite casually, at the Staff meeting. Let it slip silkily through my fingers—see how long it takes to lock his attention on it. Feed the doubt, and the growing fear, with, oh, one or two casual remarks. I wonder how much it would take to start him scrambling those annoyingly perfect reports of his—ha! Then send him off for about a week of detached duty, still wondering, still in doubt. . . ."

He picked up the jeweled knife and sawed off a thick strand, to coil up and place carefully in his breast pocket, smiling down at her the while. "One must be careful, of course, not to goad him quite into violence—he becomes so tediously unmanageable—" he ran one finger in an L-shaped motion across the left side of his chin in the exact position of Vorkosigan's scar. "Much easier to start than stop. Although he's become remarkably temperate of late. Your influence, my pet? Or is he simply growing old?"

He tossed the knife carelessly back on the bedside table, then rubbed his hands together, laughed out loud, and draped himself beside her to murmur lovingly in her ear. "And after Escobar, when we need no longer regard the Emperor's watchdog, there will be no limit to what I can do. So many choices . . ." He gave vent to a stream of plans for torturing Vorkosigan through her, glistening with obscene detail. He was taut with his vision, his face pale and moist.

"You can't possibly get away with anything like that," she said faintly. There was fear in her face now, and tears, running down from the corners of her eyes in iridescent trails to wet the tendrils of hair around her ears, but he was scarcely interested. She had believed she had fallen into the deepest possible pit of fear, but now that floor opened beneath her and she fell again, endlessly, turning in the air.

Some measure of control seemed to return to him, and he walked around the foot of the bed, looking at her. "Well. How very refreshing. Do you know, I am quite energized. I believe I shall do it myself, after all. You should be glad. I'm much better looking than Bothari."

"Not to me."

He dropped his trousers and prepared to climb on her. "Do you forgive me too, sweetheart?"

She felt cold, and dry, and vanishingly small. "I'm afraid I'll have to leave that to the Infinitely Merciful. You exceed my capacity."

"Later in the week," he promised, mistaking her defeat for flippancy, and clearly excited by what he took for a continued show of resistance.

Sergeant Bothari had been mooning around the room, head moving from side to side and narrow jaw working, as Cordelia had seen it once before, a sign of agitation. Vorrutyer, intent on Cordelia, paid no attention to the movements behind him. So his moment of utter astonishment was very brief when the Sergeant grabbed him by his curly hair, yanked his head back, and drew the jeweled knife most expertly around his neck, slicing through all four of the major vessels in a swift double movement. The blood spurted over Cordelia in a fountain, horribly hot and flowing.

Vorrutyer gave one convulsive twist and lost consciousness as the blood pressure in his brain fell to nothing. Sergeant Bothari let go of the hair, and Vorrutyer dropped between her legs and slithered down out of sight over the end of the bed.

The Sergeant stood hulkingly, breathing heavily, by the end of the bed. Cordelia could not remember if she'd screamed. No matter, odds were no one paid much attention to screams coming out of this room anyway. She felt frozen and bloodless in her hands, face, feet; her heart hammered.

She cleared her throat. "Uh, thank you, Sergeant Bothari. That was a very, uh, knightly deed. Do you suppose you could unbuckle me, too?" Her voice squeaked uncontrollably, and she swallowed, irritated at it.

She regarded Bothari with terrorized fascination. There was absolutely no way of predicting what he might do next. Muttering to himself, with a look of bewilderment on his face, he fumbled apart the buckle on her left wrist. Swiftly, stiffly, she rolled over and loosed the right wrist, then sat up and undid the ankles. She sat cross-legged a moment in the center of the bed, stark naked and dripping with blood, rubbing ankles and wrists and trying to get her paralyzed brain into motion.

"Clothes. Clothes," she muttered to herself. She peeked over the end of the bed at the crumpled form of the late Admiral Vorrutyer, pants about his ankles and his last look of surprise frozen on his face. The great brown eyes had lost their liquid glow, and were already beginning to film over.

She slipped out of the side of the bed away from Bothari and began searching frantically through the metal drawers and cupboards that lined the room. A couple of the drawers contained his toy collection, and she shut them hastily, nauseated, finally understanding what he'd meant by his last words. The man's taste in perversions had certainly had remarkable scope. Some uniforms, all with too much yellow insignia. At last she found a set of plain black fatigues. She wiped the blood from her body with a soft dressing gown, and flung them on.

Sergeant Bothari meanwhile had sat on the floor, curled up with his head resting on his knees, talking under his breath. She knelt beside him. Was he starting to hallucinate? She had to get him to his feet, and out of here. They could not count on being undiscovered much longer. Yet where could they hide? Or was it adrenaline, not reason, that demanded flight? Was there a better option?

As she hesitated, the door slammed suddenly open. She cried out for the first time. But the man standing white-faced in the aperture with the plasma arc in his hand was Vorkosigan.

CHAPTER EIGHT

She sighed shakily at the sight of him, and the paralyzing panic streamed out of her in that long breath. "My God, you almost gave me heart failure," she managed in a small tight voice. "Come in, and close the door."

His lips moved silently around the shape of her name, and he entered, a sudden panic in his face almost matching her own. Then she saw he was followed by another officer, a lieutenant with brown hair and a bland puppy face. So she did not fling herself upon him and shriek into his shoulder, as she passionately wished, but said instead cautiously, "There's been an accident."

"Close the door, Illyan," said Vorkosigan to the lieutenant. His features became tightly controlled as the young man came even with him. "You're going to have to witness this with the greatest attention."

His lips pressed to a white slit, Vorkosigan walked slowly around the room, noting the details, some of which he pointed out silently to his companion. The lieutenant said, "Er, ah," at the first gesture, which was with the plasma arc. Vorkosigan stopped before the body, looked at the weapon in his hand as though seeing it for the first time, and put it in its holster.

119

"Been reading the Marquis again, have you?" he addressed the corpse with a sigh. He turned it over with the toe of his boot, and a little more blood ran out of the meaty slice in its neck. "A little learning is a dangerous thing." He glanced up at Cordelia. "Which of you should I congratulate?"

She moistened her lips. "I'm not sure. How annoyed is everyone going to be about this?"

The lieutenant was going through Vorrutyer's drawers and cupboards also, using a handkerchief to open them, and from his expression finding that his cosmopolitan education was not so complete as he had supposed. He remained staring for a long time into the drawer that Cordelia had shut so hastily.

"The Emperor, for one, will be delighted," said Vorkosigan. "But—strictly in private."

"In fact, I was tied up at the time. Sergeant Bothari, uh, did the honors."

Vorkosigan glanced at Bothari, still sitting curled up on the floor. "Hm." He gazed around the room one last time. "There's something about this that reminds me forcibly of that remarkable scene when we broke into my engine room. It has your personal signature. My grandmother had a phrase for it—something about late, and a dollar . . ."

"A day late and a dollar short?" suggested Cordelia involuntarily.

"Yes, that was it." He bit an ironic twist from his lips. "A very Betan remark—I begin to see why." His face maintained a mask of cool neutrality, but his eyes searched her in secret agony. "Was I, ah, short?"

"Not at all," she reassured him. "You're, um, very timely. I was just dithering around in a panic, wondering what to do next."

He was facing away from Illyan, and a quickly suppressed grin crinkled his eyes briefly. "It seems I am rescuing my fleet from you, then," he murmured between his teeth. "Not exactly what I had in mind when I came up here, but I'm glad to rescue *something*." He raised his voice. "As soon as you're done, Illyan, I suggest we adjourn to my cabin for further discussion."

Vorkosigan knelt by Bothari, studying him. "That bloody bastard has about ruined him again," he growled. "He was almost well, after his time with me. Sergeant Bothari," he said more gently, "can you walk a little way with me?"

Bothari muttered something unintelligible into his knees.

"Come here, Cordelia," said Vorkosigan. It was the first time she had heard her first name in his mouth. "See if you can get him up. I don't think I'd better touch him, just now."

She got down into the line of his sight. "Bothari. Bothari, look at me. You've got to get up, and walk a little way." She took his blood-coated hand, and tried to think of a line of reason, or more likely unreason, that might reach him. She tried a smile. "Look. See? You're washed in blood. Blood washes away sin, right? You're going to be all right now. Uh, the bad man is gone, and in a little while the bad voices will go away too. So you come along with me, and I'll take you where you can rest."

During this speech he gradually focused on her, and at the end he nodded, and stood. Still holding his hand, she followed Vorkosigan out, Illyan bringing up the rear. She hoped her psychological band-aid would hold; an alarm of any sort might touch him off like a bomb.

She was astonished when Vorkosigan's cabin proved to be just one door down, across the corridor.

"Are you captain of this ship?" she asked. His collar tabs, now that she got a better look at them, proclaimed him a commodore now. "Were you here all the time?"

"No, I'm on the Staff. My courier just got in from the front a few hours ago. I've been in conference with Admiral Vorhalas and the Prince ever since. It just broke up. I came up straight away when the guard told me about Vorrutyer's new prisoner. You—in my foulest nightmare, I never dreamed it might be you."

Vorkosigan's cabin seemed tranquil as a monk's cell compared to the carnage they had left across the hall. Everything regulation, a proper soldier's room. Vorkosigan

locked the door behind them. He rubbed his face and
sighed, drinking her in. "Are you sure you're all right?"

"Just shaken up. I knew I was running risks, when I
was selected, but I wasn't expecting anything quite like
that man. He was a classic. I'm surprised you served him."

His face became shuttered. "I serve the Emperor."

She became conscious of Illyan, standing silent and
watchful. What would she say if Vorkosigan asked her
about the convoy? He was a greater danger to her duty
than torture. She had begun to think, in the past months,
that their separation must eventually diminish her heart-
hunger for him, but seeing him live and intense before
her made it ravenous. No telling what he felt, though.
Right now he looked tired, uncertain, and strained. Wrong,
all wrong . . .

"Ah, permit me to introduce Lieutenant Simon Illyan,
of the Emperor's personal security staff. He's my spy.
Lieutenant Illyan, Commander Naismith."

"It's Captain Naismith now," she put in automatically.
The lieutenant shook her hand with a bland calm inno-
cence wholly at odds with the bizarre scene they had just
left. He might have been at an embassy reception. Her
touch left a streak of blood on his palm. "Who do you
spy on?"

"I prefer the term, 'surveillance,' " he said.

"Bureaucratic weaselwording," put in Vorkosigan. He
added to Cordelia, "The lieutenant spies on me. He represents a compromise between the Emperor, the Ministry of Political Education, and myself."

"The phrase the Emperor used," said Illyan distantly,
"was 'cease-fire.' "

"Yes. Lieutenant Illyan also has an eidetic memory
biochip. You may think of him as a recording device with
legs, which the Emperor may play back at will."

Cordelia stared covertly at him. "It's too bad we
couldn't meet again under more auspicious circumstances,"
she said carefully to Vorkosigan.

"There are no auspicious circumstances here."

Lieutenant Illyan cleared his throat, glancing at Bothari,

who stood twining and untwining his fingers and staring at the wall. "What now, sir?"

"Hm. There is entirely too much physical evidence in that room, not to mention witnesses as to who went in and when, to attempt to monkey with the scenario. Personally, I should prefer for Bothari not to have been there at all. The fact that he is clearly *non compos mentis* will carry no weight with the Prince when he gets wind of this." He stood, thinking furiously. "You will simply have to have escaped, before Illyan and I arrived on the scene. I don't know how long it will be possible to hide Bothari in here—maybe I can get some sedatives for him." His eye fell on Illyan. "How about the Emperor's staff agent in the medical section?"

Illyan looked noncommittal. "It's possible something might be arranged."

"Good man." He turned to Cordelia. "You're going to have to stay in here and keep Bothari under control. Illyan and I must go at once, or there will be too many unaccounted minutes between the time we left Vorhalas and the time we sound the alarm. The Prince's security men will be going over that room thoroughly, and everyone's movements as well."

"Were Vorrutyer and the Prince in the same party?" she asked, feeling for footing in the riptides of Barrayaran politics.

Vorkosigan smiled bitterly. "They were just good friends."

And he was gone, leaving her alone with Bothari and utter confusion.

She had Bothari sit down in Vorkosigan's desk chair, where he fidgeted silently and incessantly. She sat cross-legged on the bed, trying to radiate an air of calm control and good cheer. Not easy, from a spirit filled with panic frenzied for expression.

Bothari stood and began to pace about the room, talking to himself. No, not to himself, she realized. And most certainly not to her. The choppy whispered flow of words made no sense to her at all. Time flowed by slowly, viscous with fear.

Both she and Bothari jumped when the door clicked open, but it was only Illyan. Bothari fell into a knife-fighter's crouch as he slipped in.

"Servants of the beast are the beast's hands," he said. "He feeds them on the wife's blood. Bad servants."

Illyan eyed him nervously, and pressed some ampules into her hand. "Here. You give it to him. One of these would knock out a charging elephant. Can't stay." He slipped back out again.

"Coward," she muttered after him. But he was probably right. She might well have a better chance than he of getting it into the Sergeant. Bothari's agitation was approaching an explosive level.

She set the bulk of the ampules aside, and approached him with a sunny smile. Its effect was diminished by her eyes, large with fear. Bothari's eyes were flickering slits. "Commodore Vorkosigan wants you to rest now. He sent some medicine to help you."

He backed warily before her, and she stopped, cautious of forcing him into a corner. "It's just a sedative, see?"

"The beast's drugs made the demons drunk. They sang and shouted. Bad medicine."

"No, no. This is good medicine. It will make the demons go to sleep," she promised. This was walking a tightrope in the dark. She tried another tack.

"Come to attention, soldier," she said sharply. "Inspection."

It was a wrong move. He batted the ampule nearly out of her hand as she tried to stick it in his arm, and his hand closed around her wrist like a hot iron band. Her breath hissed inward at the pain, but she just managed to twist her fingers around and press the administrative spray end of the ampule against the inside of his wrist, before he picked her up bodily and flung her across the room.

She landed on her back, skidding across the friction matting with what seemed to her a dreadful amount of noise, fetching up with a bang against the door. Bothari lunged after her. *Can he kill me before the stuff cuts in?* she wondered wildly, and forced herself to go limp, as if unconscious. Surely unconscious people were very non-threatening.

Evidently not to Bothari, for his hands closed around her neck. One knee pressed into her rib cage, and she felt something go painfully wrong in the region. She popped her eyes open in time to see his eyes roll back. His hands slackened in their twisting, and he rolled off her to his hands and knees, head wagging dizzily, then slumped to the deck.

She sat up, leaning against the wall. "I want to go home," she muttered. "This wasn't in my job description." The feeble joke did nothing to dissolve the clot of hysteria rising in her throat, so she fell back on an older and more serious discipline, whispering its words aloud. By the time she finished self-control had returned.

She could not lift Bothari to the bunk. She raised his heavy head and slipped the pillow under it, and pulled his arms and legs into a more comfortable-looking position. When Vorkosigan and his shadow returned they could have a go at it.

The door opened at last, and Vorkosigan and Illyan entered, closing it quickly and walking carefully around Bothari.

"Well?" said Cordelia. "How did it go?"

"With machine-like precision, like a wormhole jump to hell," Vorkosigan replied. He turned his hand palm upward in a familiar gesture that caught her heart like a hook.

She looked her puzzlement at him. "You're as baffling as Bothari. How did they take the murder?"

"It went just fine. I'm under arrest and confined to quarters, for suspicion of conspiracy. The Prince thinks I put Bothari up to it," he explained. "God knows how."

"Uh, I know I'm very tired," she said, "and not thinking too clearly. But you did say, 'Just fine?' "

"Commodore Vorkosigan, sir," interrupted Illyan. "Keep in mind that I'm going to have to report this conversation."

"What conversation?" said Vorkosigan. "You and I are alone in here, remember? You're not required to observe me when I'm alone, as everyone knows. They'll start wondering why you're lingering in here before long."

Lieutenant Illyan frowned over this jesuitry. "The Emperor's intention—"

"Yes? Tell me all about the Emperor's intention." Vorkosigan looked savage.

"The Emperor's intention, as communicated to *me*, was that you be discouraged from incriminating yourself. I cannot edit my report, you know."

"That was your argument four weeks ago. You saw the result."

Illyan looked perturbed.

Vorkosigan spoke low and controlled. "Everything the Emperor requires of me will be accomplished. He's a great choreographer, and he shall have his dance of dreamers down to the last step." Vorkosigan's hand closed in a fist, and opened again. "I have withheld nothing that is mine from his service. Not my life. Not even my honor. Grant me this." He pointed at Cordelia. "You gave me your word on it then. Do you intend to take it back?"

"Will someone please tell me what you are talking about?" interrupted Cordelia.

"Lieutenant Illyan is having a little conflict at the moment between duty and conscience," said Vorkosigan, folding his arms and staring at the far wall. "It is not solvable without redefining one or the other, and he must now choose which."

"You see, there was another incident," Illyan jerked his thumb in the direction of Vorrutyer's quarters, "like that, with a prisoner, a few weeks ago. Commodore Vorkosigan wanted to, er, do something about it then. I talked him out of it. After—afterwards, I agreed that I would not interfere with any action he chose to take, should the situation come up again."

"Did Vorrutyer kill her?" asked Cordelia morbidly.

"No," said Illyan. He stared moodily at his boots.

"Come on, Illyan," said Vorkosigan wearily. "If they

aren't discovered, you can give the Emperor your true report, and let him edit it. If they are found here—the public integrity of your reports is not going to be your most pressing worry, believe me."

"Damn! Captain Negri was right," said Illyan.

"He usually is—what was the instance?"

"He said that permitting private judgments to turn my duty in the smallest matter would be just like getting a little bit pregnant—that the consequences would very soon get beyond me."

Vorkosigan laughed. "Captain Negri is a very experienced man. But I can tell you that—very rarely—even he has been known to make a private judgment."

"But Security is tearing the place apart out there. They're going to arrive back here eventually just by process of elimination. The moment it occurs to someone to suspect my integrity, it's all over."

"In time," agreed Vorkosigan. "How much time, do you estimate?"

"They'll complete the search sweep of the ship in a few hours."

"Then you'll just have to re-direct their efforts. Widen their search area—didn't any ships depart the flag during the time window after Vorrutyer's death and before the security cordon was started?"

"Yes, two, but . . ."

"Good. Use your Imperial influence there. Volunteer all the assistance that you, as Captain Negri's most trusted aide, can supply. Mention Negri frequently. Suggest. Recommend. Doubt. Better not bribe or threaten, that's too obvious, although it may come to that. Slander their inspection procedures, make records evaporate—whatever is necessary to muddy the waters. Buy me forty-eight hours, Illyan. That's all I ask."

"All?" choked Illyan.

"Ah. Try to be sure it's you and no one else who brings meals and so on. And try to slip in some extra rations when you do."

❖   ❖   ❖

Vorkosigan relaxed measurably when he had gone, and turned to her with a sad and awkward smile that was good as a touch. "Well met, lady."

She sketched him a salute, and returned the smile. "I hope I haven't messed things up for you too much. Personally, that is."

"By no means. In fact, you have simplified them enormously."

"East is west, up is down, and being falsely arrested for getting your C.O.'s throat cut is a simplification. I must be on Barrayar. I don't suppose you'd care to explain what's going on around here?"

"No. But at last I understand why there have been so many madmen in Barrayaran history. They are not its cause, they are its effect." He sighed, and spoke so low it was almost a whisper. "Oh, Cordelia. You have no idea how much I need one sane clean person near me. You are water in the desert."

"You look pretty, uh—you look like you've lost weight." He looked, she thought, ten years older than six months ago.

"Oh, me." He ran his hand over his face. "I'm not thinking. You must be exhausted. Do you want to go to sleep, or something?"

"I'm not sure I can, yet. But I'd like to wash up. Didn't think I ought to run the shower when you weren't here, in case it's monitored."

"Good thinking. Go ahead."

She rubbed her hand over her nerveless thigh, black cloth sticky with blood. "Uh, have you got a change of clothes for me? These are messed up. Besides, they were Vorrutyer's. They have a psychic stink."

"Right." His face darkened. "Is that your blood?"

"Yeah, Vorrutyer was playing surgeon. It doesn't hurt. I've got no nerves there."

"Hm." Vorkosigan fingered his scar, and smiled a little. "Yes, I think I have just the thing for you."

He unlocked one of his drawers with an eight-digit number code, sorted down to the bottom layer, and to

Cordelia's astonishment pulled out the Survey fatigues she had left behind on the *General Vorkraft*, now cleaned, mended, pressed, and neatly folded. "I haven't got the boots with me, and the insignia are obsolete, but I rather imagine these will fit," Vorkosigan remarked blandly, handing them over.

"You—saved my clothes?"

"As you see."

"Good heavens. Uh—why?"

His mouth crimped ruefully. "Well—it was all you left. Except for the shuttle your people abandoned downside, which would have made a rather awkward memento."

She ran her hand over the tan cloth, feeling suddenly shy. But just before disappearing into the bathroom with the clothes and a first-aid kit, she said abruptly, "I've still got my Barrayaran uniform at home. Wrapped in paper, in a drawer." She gave him a firm nod; his eyes lit.

When she came out again the room was dim and night-quiet, but for a light over the desk where Vorkosigan was studying a disk at his computer interface. She hopped onto his bed and sat cross-legged again, wriggling her bare toes. "What's all that?"

"Homework. It's my official function on Vorrutyer's—the late Admiral Vorrutyer's—Staff." He smiled a little as he corrected himself, like the famous tiger of the limerick when he returned from the ride with the lady inside. "I'm charged with planning and keeping the contingency orders up to date, in case we are forced to fall back. As the Emperor said in the Council meeting, since I was so convinced it was going to be a disaster, I could bloody well do the planning for it. I'm regarded as a bit of a fifth wheel around here at the moment."

"Things going well for your side, are they?" she asked, oppressed.

"We're becoming nicely overextended. Some people regard that as progress." He entered some new data, then shut down the interface.

She sought to turn the subject from the dangerous present. "I take it you didn't get charged with treason after all?" she asked, thinking back to their last conversation, long ago and far away above another world.

"Ah, that turned out something of a draw. I was recalled back to Barrayar after you escaped. Minister Grishnov—he's head of Political Education, and third in real power after the Emperor and Captain Negri—was practically drooling on himself, he was so convinced he'd got me at last. But my case against Radnov was air-tight.

"The Emperor stepped in before we could draw blood, and forced a compromise, or more correctly, an abeyance. I haven't actually been cleared, the charges are still pending in some legal limbo."

"How'd he do it?"

"Sleight of hand. He was giving Grishnov and the whole war party everything they'd asked for, the entire Escobar scheme on a platter, and more. He gave them the Prince. And all the credit. After the conquest of Escobar, Grishnov and the Prince each think they're going to be the de facto ruler of Barrayar.

"He even made Vorrutyer swallow my promotion. Pointed out he'd have me directly under his command. Vorrutyer saw the light at once." Vorkosigan's teeth set at some searing memory, his hand opening and closing once, unconsciously.

"How long have you known him?" she asked cautiously, thinking of the bottomless well of hatred she had fallen down.

His eyes slid away from her. "We were in school, and lieutenants together, back when he was only a common voyeur. He grew worse, I understand, in recent years, since he started associating with Prince Serg, and thinking he could get away with anything. God help us, he was nearly right. Bothari has done a great public service."

You knew him better than that, my breath, thought Cordelia. Was that your infection of the imagination, so hard to fight off? Bothari has done a great private service, too, it seems. . . . "Speaking of Bothari—next time, you sedate him. He went wild when I came at him with the ampule."

"Ah. Yes. I think I understand why. It was in one of Captain Negri's reports. Vorrutyer was in the habit of drugging his, uh, players, with a variety of concoctions, when he wanted a better show. I'm fairly certain Bothari was one of his victims that way."

"Vile." She felt sick. Her muscles cramped around the ache in her side. "Who's this Captain Negri you keep talking about?"

"Negri? He does keep a low profile, but he's hardly secret. He heads the Emperor's personal security staff. Illyan's boss. They call him Ezar Vorbarra's familiar.

"If you think of the Ministry of Political Education as the Emperor's right hand, then Negri is his left, the one the right is not permitted to know. He watches internal security on the highest levels—the Ministry heads, the Counts, the Emperor's family—the Prince . . ." Vorkosigan frowned introspectively. "I came to know him rather well during the preparations for this strategist's nightmare. Curious fellow. He could have any rank he wanted. But forms are meaningless to him. He's only interested in substance."

"Is he a good guy or bad guy?"

"What an absurd question!"

"I just thought he might be the power behind the throne."

"Hardly. If Ezar Vorbarra said, 'You're a frog,' he'd hop and croak. No. There is only one Emperor on Barrayar, and he permits no one to get behind him. He still remembers how he came to power."

She stretched, and winced at the pain in her side.

"Something wrong?" he asked, instantly concerned.

"Oh, Bothari got me with his knee, when we had that go-round about the sedative. I thought for sure they'd hear us. Scared me to death."

"May I see?" His fingers slid gently along her ribs. It was only in her imagination that they left a trail of rainbow light.

"Ow."

"Yes. You have two cracked ribs."

"Thought so. I'm lucky it wasn't my neck." She lay back, and he made shift to tape them with strips of cloth, then sat beside her on his bunk. "Have you ever considered chucking it all, and moving someplace nobody ever bothers with?" Cordelia asked. "Earth, for example."

He smiled. "Often. I even had a little fantasy about emigrating to Beta Colony, and turning up on your doorstep. Do you have a doorstep?"

"Not as such, but go on."

"I can't imagine what I'd do for a living there. I'm a strategist, not a technician or navigator or pilot, so I couldn't go into your merchant fleet. They would scarcely take me in your military, and I can't see myself being elected to office."

Cordelia snorted. "Wouldn't that startle Steady Freddy?"

"Is that what you call your President?"

"I didn't vote for him."

"The only employment I can think of would be as a teacher of martial arts, for sport. Would you marry a judo instructor, dear Captain? But no," he sighed. "Barrayar is bred in my bones. I cannot shake it, no matter how far I travel. This struggle, God knows, has no honor in it. But exile, for no other motive than ease—that would be to give up all hope of honor. The last defeat, with no seed of future victory in it."

She thought of the deadly cargo she had convoyed, now safe on Escobar. Compared to all the lives that hung on it, her own and Vorkosigan's weighed less than a feather. He misread the grief in her face, she thought, for fear.

"It isn't exactly like waking from the nightmare, to see your face." He touched it gently, fingertips on the curve of her jaw, thumb laid a moment across her lips, lighter than a kiss. "More like, knowing, while dreaming still, that beyond the dream there is a waking world. I mean to join you in that waking world, someday. You'll see. You'll see." He squeezed her hand and smiled reassuringly.

On the floor Bothari stirred, and groaned.

"I'll take care of him," Vorkosigan said. "Get some sleep, while you can."

CHAPTER NINE

She woke to movement, and voices. Vorkosigan was rising from his chair, and Illyan was standing before him taut as a bowstring, saying "Vorhalas and the Prince! Here! Now!"

"Son-of-a . . ." Vorkosigan turned on his heel, eyes raking the little room. "It'll have to be the bathroom. Fold him into the shower."

Swiftly, Vorkosigan took Bothari's shoulders and Illyan his feet, bumping through the narrow door and dumping him pell-mell into the fixture.

"Should he have more sedative?" asked Illyan.

"Maybe he'd better. Cordelia, give him another ampule. It's too early, but it's death for you both if he makes a noise now." He bundled her into the closet-sized room, shoving the drug into her hand and killing the light. "No noise, no movement."

"Door shut?" asked Illyan.

"Partway. Lean on the frame, look casual, and don't let the Prince's bodyguard wander into your psychological space."

Cordelia, feeling her way in the dimness, knelt and pressed another shot of sedative into the unconscious

Sergeant's arm. Seating herself in the logical spot, she found she could just see a slice of Vorkosigan's cabin in the mirror, reversed and disorienting. She heard the cabin door open, and new voices.

"—unless you mean to officially relieve him of his duties as well, I will continue to follow standard procedure. I saw that room. Your charge is nonsensical."

"We will see," replied the second voice, tight and angry.

"Hello, Aral." The owner of the first voice, an officer of perhaps fifty in dress greens, shook Vorkosigan's hand and presented him with a packet of data disks. "We're off to Escobar within the hour. Courier just brought these—the latest hard-copy updates. I've ordered you to be kept up on events. The Escos are falling back through the whole volume. They've even abandoned that slugging match for the wormhole jump to Tau Ceti. We've got them on the run."

The owner of the second voice also wore dress greens, more heavily encrusted with gilt than any she had ever seen. Jeweled decorations on his breast glinted and winked like lizards' eyes in the light from Vorkosigan's desk lamp. He was about thirty, black haired, with a rectangular tense face, hooded eyes, and thin lips compressed now with annoyance.

"You're not both going, are you?" said Vorkosigan. "The senior officer ought properly to stay with the flag. Now that Vorrutyer is dead, his duties devolve on the Prince. That dog-and-pony show you had planned was based on the assumption that he would still be at his post."

Prince Serg went stiff with outrage. "I *will* lead my troops on Escobar! Let my father and his cronies try to say I am no soldier now!"

"You will," said Vorkosigan wearily, "sit in that fortified palace that half the engineers are going to be tied up constructing, and party in it, and let your men do your dying for you, until you've bought your ground by the sheer weight of the corpses piled on it, because that's the kind of soldiering your mentor has taught you. And then send bulletins home about your great victory. Maybe you can have the casualty lists declared top secret."

"Aral, careful," warned Vorhalas, shocked.

"You go too far," the Prince snarled. "Especially for a man who will get no closer to the fighting than clinging to the wormhole exit for home. If you want to talk of—undue caution." His tone clearly made the phrase a euphemism for an uglier term.

"You can hardly order me confined to quarters and then accuse me of cowardice for not being at the front. Sir. Even Minister Grishnov's propaganda has to simulate logic better than that."

"You'd just love that, wouldn't you, Vorkosigan," hissed the Prince. "Stick me back here, and grab all the glory for yourself and that wrinkled clown Vortala and his phoney progressives. Over my dead body! You're going to sit in here till you grow mold."

Vorkosigan's teeth were clenched, his eyes narrowed and unreadable. His lips curled back on a white smile, but closed again instantly. "I must formally protest. By landing with the ground troops on Escobar you are leaving your proper post."

"Protest away." The Prince approached him closely, leaning into his face and dropping his voice. "But even my father can't live forever. And when that day comes, your father won't be able to protect you anymore. You, and Vortala, and all his cronies will be first against the wall, I promise you." He looked up, remembering Illyan leaning silently against the doorjamb. "Or perhaps you'll find yourself back on the Leper Colony, for another five years of patrol duty."

In the bathroom, Bothari stirred uncomfortably in his semi-coma and, to Cordelia's horror, began to snore.

Lieutenant Illyan was seized by a spasmodic coughing fit. "Excuse me," he gasped, and retreated into the bathroom, shutting the door firmly.

He hit the light and traded a silent look of panic with Cordelia for an equally silent grimace of despair. With difficulty, they turned Bothari's deadweight to one side in the constricted space, until he breathed quietly again. Cordelia gave Illyan the thumbs-up signal, and he nodded and squeezed back out the door.

The Prince had left. Admiral Vorhalas lingered a moment, to exchange a last word with his subordinate.

"—put it in writing. I'll sign it before we go."

"At least don't travel in the same ship," begged Vorkosigan seriously.

Vorhalas sighed. "I appreciate your trying to get him out of my hair. But somebody has to clean his cage for the Emperor, with Vorrutyer out, thank God. He won't have you, so it looks like I'm elected. Why can't you just lose your temper with subordinates, like normal men, instead of with superiors, like a lunatic? I thought you were cured of that, after what I saw you take from Vorrutyer."

"That's dead and buried now."

"Aye." Vorhalas made a superstitious sign, automatically, evidently a gestural relic from childhood, empty of belief but full of habit.

"By the by—what's the Leper Colony?" asked Vorkosigan curiously.

"You never heard that? Well—maybe I can see why not. Did you never wonder why you received such a remarkable percentage of screw-ups, incorrigibles, and near-discharges among your crew?"

"I hadn't expected to get the cream of the Service."

"They used to call it Vorkosigan's Leper Colony, at headquarters."

"With myself as leper-in-chief, eh?" Vorkosigan seemed more amused than offended. "Well, if they were the worst the Service has to offer, perhaps we shall not do so badly after all. Take care of yourself. I don't fancy being his second-in-command."

Vorhalas chuckled, and they shook hands. He started for the door, then paused. "Do you think they'll counterattack?"

"My God, of course they'll counterattack. This isn't some trade outpost. These people are fighting for their homes."

"When?"

Vorkosigan hesitated. "Sometime after you've started disembarking ground troops, but well before it's completed. Wouldn't you? Worst time to have to start a retreat. Shuttles not knowing whether to go up or down, their mother ships scattering to hell and gone under fire, supplies needed not landed, supplies landed not needed, the chain of command disrupted—an inexperienced commander in absolute control . . ."

"You give me the shivers."

"Yes, well—try to hold the start for as long as possible. And make sure your troopship commanders have their contingency orders crystal clear."

"The Prince doesn't see it your way."

"Yes, he's itching to lead a parade."

"What do you advise?"

"I'm not your commander this time, Rulf."

"Not my fault. I recommended you to the Emperor."

"I know. I wouldn't take it. I recommended you instead."

"So we ended up with that sodomizing son-of-a-bitch Vorrutyer." Vorhalas shook his head bleakly. "Something wrong there . . ."

Vorkosigan chivvied him gently out the door, blew out his breath with a sigh, and remained standing, caught up in his vision of the future. He looked up, and met Cordelia's eyes with unhappy irony. "Wasn't there some character, when the old Romans held their triumphs, who rode along whispering in the honored party's ear that he was mortal, and death waited for him? The old Romans probably thought he was a pain in the neck, too."

She held her peace.

Vorkosigan and Illyan went to retrieve Sergeant Bothari from his makeshift and uncomfortable hiding place. They were halfway through the door with him when Vorkosigan swore. "He's stopped breathing."

Illyan hissed explosively, and they laid Bothari out quickly on the friction matting on his back. Vorkosigan laid his ear to his chest, and felt his neck for a pulse.

"Son-of-a-bitch." He doubled his fists, and brought them down sharply against the Sergeant's sternum, then listened again. "Nothing."

He rolled back on his heels, looking fierce. "Illyan. Whoever you got that lizard's piss from, go find him and get a shot of the antidote. Quickly. And quietly. Very quietly."

"How did you—what if—shouldn't you—is it worth—" began Illyan. He threw up his hands helplessly, and fled out the door.

Vorkosigan looked at Cordelia. "Do you want to push, or blow?"

"Push, I guess."

She knelt by Bothari's side, and Vorkosigan went to his head, tilted it back, and gave him his first breath of air. Cordelia pressed the heels of her hands on his sternum and pushed with all her strength, setting up the rhythm. Push, push, push, blow, over and over, don't stop. After a short time her arms were shaking, and sweat beaded on her hairline. She could feel her own ribs grind with each push, screamingly, and her chest muscles knotted spasmodically.

"Got to switch."

"Good. I'm hyperventilating."

They changed places, Vorkosigan taking over the heart massage, Cordelia pinching Bothari's nostrils shut and closing her mouth over his. His mouth was wet from Vorkosigan's saliva. The parody of a kiss was horrible, but to shrink from it beneath contempt. They went on, and on.

Lieutenant Illyan returned at last, breathless. He knelt and pressed the new ampule against Bothari's corded neck over the carotid artery. Nothing happened. Vorkosigan kept pumping.

Suddenly, Bothari shuddered, then stiffened, arching his back. He took an irregular, gasping gulp of air, then stopped again.

"Come on," urged Cordelia, half to herself.

With a sharp spasmodic intake he began to breathe again, raggedly, but persistently. Cordelia slumped from her knees to a sitting position on the floor and gazed at him in joyless triumph. "Suffering bastard."

"I thought you saw meaning in that sort of thing," said Vorkosigan.

"In the abstract. Most days it's just stumbling around

in the dark with the rest of creation, smashing into things and wondering why it hurts."

Vorkosigan gazed at Bothari too, sweat runneling down his face. Then he jumped to his feet and hurried to his desk.

"The protest. Have to get it written and filed before Vorhalas leaves, or it will be no damned good." He slid into his chair and began rapidly keying his console.

"What's so important about it?" asked Cordelia.

"Sh. Later." He typed furiously for ten minutes, then set it electronically in pursuit of his commander.

Bothari in the meanwhile continued to breathe, although his face retained a deathly greenish pallor.

"What do we do now?" asked Cordelia.

"Wait. Pray that the dosage is right," he glanced irritably at Illyan, "and that it won't send him into some kind of manic state."

"Shouldn't we be thinking of some way to get them both out of here?" protested Illyan.

"Think away." Vorkosigan began plugging the new data disks into his console and viewing the tactical readouts. "But as a hiding place it has two advantages not shared by any other spot on the ship. If you're as good as you claim, it's not monitored by either the Chief Political Officer or the Prince's men—"

"I'm quite sure I got them all. I'd stake my reputation on it."

"Right now you're staking your life on it, so you'd better be correct. Second, there are two armed guards in the corridor to keep everybody out. You could scarcely ask for more. I admit it's a bit crowded."

Illyan rolled his eyes in exasperation. "I've diddled the Security search to the limit I dare. I can't do any more without drawing more attention than I divert."

"Will it hold twenty-six more hours?"

"Maybe." Illyan frowned at his charge, baffled and bothered. "You have something planned, don't you, sir." It was not a question.

"I?" His fingers worked the keys of his console, and reflections of colored light from the readouts played over his impassive face. "I'm merely waiting in hope of some reasonable opportunity. When the Prince leaves for Escobar most of his own security people will go with him. Patience, Illyan."

He keyed his console again. "Vorkosigan to Tactics Room."

"Commander Venne here, sir."

"Oh, good. Venne, I'd like hourly updates piped down here from the time the Prince and Admiral Vorhalas leave. And let me know immediately, regardless of time, if you start getting anything unusual, anything not in the plans."

"Yes, sir. The Prince and Admiral Vorhalas are leaving now, sir."

"Very good. Carry on. Vorkosigan out."

He sat back and drummed his fingers on the desk. "Now we wait. It will be about twelve hours before the Prince reaches Escobar orbit. They'll be starting landings soon after that. An hour for signals to reach us from Escobar. An hour for signals to return. So much lag. A battle can be over in two hours. We could cut the lag by three-quarters if the Prince would let us move off station."

His casual tone barely masked his tension, in spite of his advice to Illyan. The room in which he sat scarcely seemed to exist for him. His mind moved with the armada wheeling in a tightening constellation around Escobar, fast glittering couriers, grim cruisers, sluggish troop carriers, bellies crammed with men. A light pen turned, forgotten, in his fingers, around and over, around and over.

"Hadn't you better eat, sir?" suggested Illyan.

"What? Oh, yes, I suppose. And you, Cordelia—you must be hungry. Go ahead, Illyan."

Illyan left to forage. Vorkosigan worked at his desk console for a few more minutes before shutting it down with a sigh. "I suppose I'd better think about sleep, too. Last time I slept was on board the *General Vorhartung*, closing on Escobar—a day and a half ago, I guess. About the time you were being captured."

"We were captured a bit before that. We were in tow for almost a day."

"Yes. Congratulations, by the way, on a very successful maneuver. That wasn't a real battle cruiser, I take it?"

"I really can't say."

"Somebody wants to claim it as a kill."

Cordelia suppressed a grin. "Fine by me." She braced herself for more questioning, but, strangely, he turned the subject.

"Poor Bothari. I wish the Emperor might give him a medal. I'm afraid the best I'll be able to do for him is get him properly hospitalized."

"If the Emperor disliked Vorrutyer so, why did he put him in charge?"

"Because he was Grishnov's man, and widely famous as such, and the Prince's favorite. Putting all the bad eggs in one basket, so to speak." He cut himself off with a fist-closing gesture.

"He made me feel like I'd met the ultimate in evil. I don't think anything will really scare me, after him."

"Ges Vorrutyer? He was just a little villain. An old-fashioned craftsman, making crimes one-off. The really unforgivable acts are committed by calm men in beautiful green silk rooms, who deal death wholesale, by the shipload, without lust, or anger, or desire, or any redeeming emotion to excuse them but cold fear of some pretended future. But the crimes they hope to prevent in that future are imaginary. The ones they commit in the present—they are real." His voice fell, as he spoke, so that by the end he was almost whispering.

"Commodore Vorkosigan—Aral—what's eating you? You're so keyed up I expect you to start pacing the ceiling any minute." Hag-ridden, she thought.

He laughed a little. "I feel like it. It's the waiting, I expect. I'm bad at waiting. Not a good thing, in a soldier. I envy your ability to wait in patience. You seem calm as moonlight on the water."

"Is that pretty?"

"Very."

"It sounds nice. We don't have either one at home."
She was absurdly pleased by the implied compliment.

Illyan returned with a tray, and she got no more out
of Vorkosigan. They ate, and Vorkosigan took a turn at
sleeping, or at least lying on the bed with his eyes shut,
but getting up every hour to view the new tacticals.

Lieutenant Illyan watched over his shoulder, and
Vorkosigan pointed out salient features of the strategy to
him as they came up.

"It looks pretty good to me," Illyan commented once.
"I don't see why you're so anxious. We really could carry
it off, in spite of the Esco's superior command of resources
in the long run. Won't do them any good if it's all over in
the short run."

Afraid to put Bothari back into a deep coma, they let
him return to near-consciousness. He sat in the corner
in a miserable knot, drifting in and out of sleep with bad
dreams in both states.

Eventually Illyan took himself off to his own cabin to
sleep, and Cordelia had another nap herself. She slept
a long time, not waking until Illyan returned with another
tray of food. She was becoming disoriented with respect
to time, locked in this changeless room. Vorkosigan, however, was tracking time by the minute now. After they ate
he vanished into the bathroom to wash and shave, and
returned in fresh dress greens, as neat as though ready
for a conference with the Emperor.

He checked through the last tactical update for the
second time.

"Have they started landing troops yet?" Cordelia asked.

He checked his chronometer. "Almost an hour ago. We
should be getting the first reports through any minute."
He sat now without fidgeting, like a man in deep meditation, face like stone.

That hour's tactical update arrived, and he began sorting through its reports, apparently checking key items. In
the middle of it his screen was overridden by the face
of Commander Venne.

"Commodore Vorkosigan? We're getting something very

strange here. Do you want me to shunt a copy of raw incoming straight down there?"

"Yes, please. Immediately."

Vorkosigan searched through an assortment of chatter of all kinds, and picked out a verbal from a ship commander, a dark and heavy-set man who spoke into his log with a guttural accent tinged by fear.

Here it comes, moaned Cordelia inwardly.

"—attacking with *shuttles!* They're returning our fire shot by shot. Plasma shields at maximum now—we can't put more power into them and still keep firing. We must either drop shields and try to increase our firepower, or give up the attack. . . ." The transmission was interrupted by static. "—don't know how they're doing it. They can't possibly have packed enough engine in those shuttles to generate this. . . ." More static. The transmission abruptly broke off.

Vorkosigan selected another. Illyan leaned over his shoulder anxiously. Cordelia sat on the bed, silent, head bowed, listening. The cup of victory; bitter on the tongue, heavy in the stomach, sad as defeat . . .

"—the flagship is under heavy fire," reported another commander. Cordelia recognized the voice with a start, and craned her neck for a view of his face. It was Gottyan; evidently he had his captaincy at last. "I'm going to drop shields altogether and attempt to knock one out with a maximum burst."

"Don't do it, Korabik!" Vorkosigan shouted hopelessly. The decision, whatever it was, had been made an hour ago, its consequences ineradicably fixed in time.

Gottyan turned his head to one side. "Ready, Commander Vorkalloner? We are attempting—" he began, and was drowned by static, then silence.

Vorkosigan struck his fist on the desk, hard. "Damn! How the hell long is it going to take them to figure . . ." He stared into the snow, then reran the transmission, transfixing it with a frightening expression, grief and rage and nausea mixed. He then selected another band, this time a computer graphic of the space around Escobar, and the ships as little colored lights winking and diving through it. It looked tiny, and bright, and simple, like a child's game. He shook his head at it, lips tight and bloodless.

Venne's face interrupted again. He was pale, with peculiar lines of tension running down to the corners of his mouth.

"Sir, I think you'd better come to the Tactics Room."

"I can't, Venne, without breaking arrest. Where's Commodore Helski, or Commodore Couer?"

"Helski went forward with the Prince and Admiral Vorhalas, sir. Commodore Couer is here now. You're the ranking flag officer aboard now."

"The Prince was quite explicit."

"The Prince—I believe the Prince is dead, sir."

Vorkosigan closed his eyes, and a sigh went out of him, joylessly. He opened them again, and leaned forward. "Is that confirmed? Do you have any new orders from Admiral Vorhalas?"

"It's—Admiral Vorhalas was with the Prince, sir. Their ship was hit." Venne turned away to view something over his shoulder, then turned back. "It's," he had to clear his throat, "it's confirmed. The Prince's flagship has been— obliterated. There's nothing left but debris. You're in command now, sir."

Vorkosigan's face was cold and unhappy. "Then transmit Contingency Blue orders at once. All ships cease firing immediately. Put all power into shields. This ship to make course for Escobar now at maximum boost. We've got to cut down on our transmission time lag."

"Contingency Blue, sir? That's full retreat!"

"I know, Commander. I wrote it."

"But full retreat . . ."

"Commander Venne, the Escobarans have a new weapon system. It's called a plasma mirror field. It's a new Betan development. It turns the attacker's burst back on itself. Our ships are shooting themselves down with their own firepower."

"My God! What can we do?"

"Not a damn thing, unless we want to start boarding

their ships and strangling the bastards by hand, one at a time. Attractive, but impractical. Transmit those orders! And order the Commander of Engineers and the Chief Pilot Officer to the Tactics Room. And get the guard commander down here to relieve his men. I don't care to be stunned on the way out the door."

"Yes, sir!" Venne broke off.

"Got to get those troopships turned around first," muttered Vorkosigan, rising from his swivel chair. He turned to find both Cordelia and Illyan staring at him.

"How did you know—" began Illyan.

"—about the plasma mirrors?" finished Cordelia.

Vorkosigan was quite expressionless. "You told me, Cordelia, in your sleep, while Illyan was out. Under the influence of one of the surgeon's potions, of course. You'll suffer no ill effects from it."

She stood upright, aghast. "That—you miserable—torture would have been more honorable!"

"Oh, smooth, sir!" congratulated Illyan. "I knew you were all right!"

Vorkosigan shot him a look of dislike. "It doesn't matter. The information was confirmed too late to do us any good."

There was a knock on the door.

"Come on, Illyan. It's time to take my soldiers home."

CHAPTER TEN

Illyan came back promptly for Bothari, barely an hour later. This was followed for Cordelia by twelve hours alone. She considered escaping the room, as her soldierly duty, and engaging in a little one-woman sabotage. But if Vorkosigan was indeed directing a full retreat, it would hardly do to interfere.

She lay on his bed in a black weariness. He had betrayed her; he was no better than the rest of them. "My perfect warrior, my dear hypocrite"—and it appeared Vorrutyer had known him better than she, after all—no. That was unjust. He had done his duty, in extracting that information; she had done the same, in concealing it for as long as possible. And as one soldier to another, even if an ersatz one—five hours active service, was it?—she had to agree with Illyan, it had been smooth. She could detect no aftereffects at all in herself from whatever he had used for the secret invasion of her mind.

Whatever he had used . . . What, indeed, could he have used? Where had he cadged it, and when? Illyan hadn't brought it to him. He had been as surprised as she when Vorkosigan dropped that bit of intelligence. One must either believe he kept a secret stash of interrogation drugs hidden in his quarters, or . . .

"Dear God," she whispered, not a curse, but a prayer. "What have I stumbled into now?" She paced the room, the connections clicking unstoppably into place.

Heart-certainty. Vorkosigan had never questioned her; he had known about the plasma mirrors in advance.

It appeared, further, that he was the only man in the Barrayaran command who knew. Vorhalas had not. The Prince certainly had not. Nor Illyan.

"Put all the bad eggs in one basket," she muttered. "And—drop the basket? Oh, it couldn't have been his own plan! Surely not . . ."

She had a sudden horrific vision of it, all complete; the most wasteful political assassination plot in Barrayaran history, and the most subtle, the corpses hidden in a mountain of corpses, forever inextricable.

But he must have had the information from somewhere. Somewhere between the time she had left him with no worse troubles than an engine room full of mutineers, and now, struggling to pull a disarmed armada back to safety before the destruction they had unleashed crashed back on them. Somewhere in a quiet, green silk room, where a great choreographer designed a dance of death, and the honor of a man of honor was broken on the wheel of his service.

Vorrutyer of the demonic vanity shrank, and shrank, before the swelling vision, to a mouse, to a flea, to a pinprick.

"My God, I thought Aral seemed twitchy. He must be half-mad. And the Emperor—the Prince was his *son*. Can this be real? Or have I gone as crazy as Bothari?"

She forced herself to sit, then lie down, but the plots and counterplots still turned in her brain, an orrery of betrayal within betrayal lining up abruptly at one point in space and time to accomplish its end. The blood beat in her brain, thick and sick.

"Maybe it's not true," she consoled herself at last. "I'll ask him, and that's what he'll say. He just questioned me

in my sleep. We got the drop on them, and I'm the heroine who saved Escobar. He's just a simple soldier, doing
his job." She turned on her side, and stared into the dimness. "Pigs have wings, and I can fly home on one."

Illyan relieved her at last, and took her to the brig.

The atmosphere there was somewhat changed, she
noticed. The guards did not look at her in the same way;
in fact, they seemed to try to avoid looking at her. The
procedures were still stark and efficient, but subdued, very
subdued. She recognized a face; the guard who had
escorted her to Vorrutyer's quarters, the one who'd pitied her, seemed to be in charge now, a pair of new red
lieutenant's tabs pinned hastily and crookedly to his collar. She had donned Vorrutyer's fatigues again for the trip
down. This time she was permitted to change in to the
orange pajamas in physical privacy. She was then escorted
to a permanent cell, not a holding area.

The cell had another occupant, a young Escobaran
woman of extraordinary beauty who lay on her bunk
staring at the wall. She did not look up at Cordelia's
entrance, nor respond to her greeting. After a time, a
Barrayaran medical team arrived and took her away. She
went wordlessly, but at the door she started to struggle
with them. At a sign from the doctor a corpsman sedated
her with an ampule which Cordelia thought she recognized, and after another moment she was carried out
unconscious.

The doctor, who from his age and rank Cordelia
guessed might be the chief surgeon, stayed a short time
to attend to her ribs. After that she was left alone, with
nothing but the periodic delivery of rations to mark the
time, and occasional changes in the slight noises and
vibrations from the walls around her on which to base
guesses about what was happening outside.

About eight ration packs later, as she was lying on her
bunk bored and depressed, the lights dimmed. They came
back, but dimmed again almost immediately.

"Awk," she muttered, as the bottom dropped out of

her stomach and she began to float upward. She made a hasty grab and held on to her bunk firmly. Her foresight was rewarded a moment later when she was crushed back into it at about three gees. The lights flickered on and off again, and she was weightless once more.

"Plasma attack," she murmured to herself. "Shields must be overloaded."

A tremendous shock rattled the ship. She was flung from her bunk across the cell into total blackness, weightlessness, silence. Direct hit! She ricocheted off the far wall, flailing for a handhold, banging an elbow painfully on—a wall? the floor, the ceiling? She spun in midair, crying out. Friendly fire, she thought hysterically—I'm going to be killed by friendly fire. The perfect end to my military career . . . She clamped her jaw and listened with fierce concentration.

Too much silence. Had they lost air? She had a nasty vision of herself as the only one left alive, trapped in this black box and doomed to float until either slow suffocation or slow freezing squeezed out her life. The cell would be her coffin, to be unsealed months later by some salvage crew.

And, more horribly: could the hit have been on the bridge? The nerve center where Vorkosigan would surely be, on which the Escobarans would surely concentrate their fire—was he smashed by flying debris, flash frozen in vacuum, burned up in plasma fire, pinned somewhere between crushed decks?

Her fingers found a surface at last, and scrabbled for a hold. A corner: good. She braced herself in it, curled up on the floor, breath firing in and out of her lungs in uneven gasps.

An unknowable time passed in the stygian dark. Her arms and legs trembled with the effort of bracing herself in place. Then the ship groaned about her, and the lights came back on.

Oh hell, she thought, this is the *ceiling*.

The gravity returned and smashed her to the floor. Pain flashed up her left arm, and numbness. She scrambled back to the bunk, taking a white-knuckle grip on its rigid bars with her right hand, sticking one foot through as well, bracing herself again.

Nothing. She waited. There was a wetness soaking her orange shirt. She looked down to see a shard of pinkish-yellow bone poking through the skin of her left forearm, and blood welling around it. She slipped awkwardly out of her smock top, wrapping it around one arm and trying to stanch the flow. The pressure woke the pain. She tried, rather experimentally, calling out for help. Surely the cell was monitored.

No one came. Over the next three hours she varied the experiment with screaming, speaking reasonably, banging on the door and walls endlessly with her good hand, or simply sitting on the bunk crying in pain. The gravity and lights flip-flopped several more times. Finally she had the familiar sensation of being pulled inside-out through a pot of glue, marking a wormhole jump, and the environment steadied.

When the door of the cell opened at last, it startled her so she recoiled into the wall, banging her head. But it was the lieutenant in charge of the brig, with a medical corpsman. The lieutenant had an interesting reddish-purple bruise the size of an egg on his forehead; the corpsman looked harried.

"This is the next worst one," said the lieutenant to the corpsman. "After that you can just go down the row in order."

White-faced and exhausted into silence, she unwrapped her arm for examination and repair. The corpsman was competent, but lacked the delicacy of touch of the chief surgeon. She nearly fainted before the plastic cast was at last applied.

There were no more signs of attack. A clean prisoner's uniform was delivered through a wall slot. Two ration packs later she felt another wormhole jump. Her thought revolved endlessly on the wheel of her fears; her sleep was all dreams and her dreams were all nightmares.

It was Lieutenant Illyan who came to escort her at last, along with an ordinary guard. She nearly kissed him, in her joy at seeing a familiar face. Instead she cleared her throat diffidently, and asked with what she hoped would pass for nonchalance, "Was Commodore Vorkosigan all right, after that attack?"

His eyebrows rose, and he shot her a look of bemused study from beneath them. "Of course."

Of course. Of course. That "of course" even suggested, uninjured. Her eyes puddled with relief, which she attempted to mask with an expression of cool professional interest. "Where are you taking me?" she asked him, as they left the brig and started down the corridor.

"Shuttle. You're to be transferred to the POW camp planetside, until the exchange arrangements are made, and they begin shipping you all home."

"Home! What about the war?"

"It's over."

"Over!" She assimilated that. "Over. That was quick. Why aren't the Escobarans pursuing their advantage?"

"They can't. We've blocked the wormhole exit."

"Blocked? Not blockaded?"

He nodded.

"How the devil do you block a wormhole?"

"In a way, it's a very old idea. Fireships."

"Huh?"

"Send a ship in, set up a major matter-antimatter explosion at a midpoint between nodes. It sets up a resonance—nothing else can get through for weeks, until it dies down."

Cordelia whistled. "Clever—why didn't we think of that? How do you get the pilot out?"

"Maybe that's why you didn't think of it. We don't."

"God—what a death." Her vision of it was clear and instant.

"They were volunteers."

She shook her head numbly. "Only a Barrayaran . . ." She probed for some less horrifying subject. "Did you take many prisoners?"

"Not very. Maybe a thousand in all. We left over eleven thousand ground troops behind on Escobar. It makes you rather valuable, if we have to try to trade you more than ten for one."

The prisoners' shuttle was a windowless craft, and she shared it with only two others, one of her own engineer's assistants, and the dark-haired Escobaran girl who had been in her cell. Her tech was eager to exchange stories, although he didn't have much to trade. He had spent the whole time locked in one cell with his other three shipmates, who had been taken downside yesterday.

The beautiful Escobaran, a young ensign who had been captured when her ship was disabled in the fighting for the wormhole jump to Beta Colony over two months ago, had even less to tell. "I must have lost track of time, somewhere," she said uneasily. "Not hard to do in that cell, seeing no one. Except that I woke up in their sickbay, yesterday, and couldn't remember how I'd come there."

And if that surgeon's as good as he looked, you never will, thought Cordelia. "Do you remember Admiral Vorrutyer?"

"Who?"

"Never mind."

The shuttle landed at last, and the hatch was opened. A shaft of sunlight and a breath of summer-scented air fell through it, sweet green air that made them suddenly realize they had been breathing reek for days.

"Wow, where is this place?" said the technician, awed, as he stepped through the hatch, prodded by the guards. "It's beautiful."

Cordelia followed him, and laughed out loud, although not happily, in instant recognition.

The prison camp was a triple row of Barrayaran field shelters, ugly grey half-cylinders surrounded by a force screen, set at the bottom of a kilometers-wide amphitheater of dry woodland and waterfall, beneath a turquoise sky. It was a hazy, warm, quiet afternoon that made Cordelia feel she had never left.

Yes, there was even the entrance to the underground depot, not camouflaged anymore, but widened, with a great paved area for landing and loading gouged out before it, alive with shuttles and activity. The waterfall and pool were gone. She turned about, as they walked, gazing at her planet. Now that she thought about it, it seemed inevitable that they should end up here, quite logical really. She shook her head helplessly.

She and her young Escobaran companion were signed in by a neat and expressionless guard and directed to a shelter halfway down one row. They entered, to find it occupied by eleven women in a space meant for fifty. They had their choice of bunks.

They were pounced upon by the older prisoners, frantic for news. A plump woman of about forty restored order, and introduced herself.

"I'm Lieutenant Marsha Alfredi. I'm ranking officer in this shelter. Insofar as there is order in this cess pit. Do you know what the hell is going on?"

"I'm Captain Cordelia Naismith. Betan Expeditionary."

"Thank God. I can dump it on you."

"Oh, my." Cordelia braced herself. "Fill me in."

"It's been hell. The guards are pigs. Then, all of a sudden yesterday afternoon, this bunch of high-ranking Barrayaran officers came trooping through. At first we thought they were shopping for rapees, like the last bunch. But this morning about half the guards had disappeared— the worst of the lot—and been replaced by a crew that look like they're on parade. And the Barrayaran camp commandant—I couldn't believe it. They paraded him out on the shuttle tarmac this morning and *shot* him! In full view of everyone!"

"I see," said Cordelia, rather tonelessly. She cleared her throat. "Uh—have you heard yet? The Barrayarans have been run completely out of Escobaran local space. They're probably sending around the long way for a formal truce and some sort of negotiated settlement by now."

There was a stunned silence, then jubilation. Some laughed, some cried, some hugged each other, and some sat alone. Some broke away to spread the news to neighboring shelters and from there up and down the whole camp. Cordelia was pressed for details. She gave a brief precis of the fighting, leaving out her own exploits and the source of her information. Their joy made her a little happier, for the first time in days.

"Well, that explains why the Barrayarans have straightened up all of a sudden," said Lieutenant Alfredi. "I guess they didn't expect to be held accountable, before."

"They've got a new commander," explained Cordelia. "He's got a thing about prisoners. Win or lose, there'd have been changes with him in charge."

Alfredi didn't look convinced. "Oh? Who is he?"

"A Commodore Vorkosigan," Cordelia said neutrally.

"Vorkosigan, the Butcher of Komarr? My God, we're in for it now." Alfredi looked genuinely afraid.

"I should think you had an adequate pledge of good faith on the shuttle pad this morning."

"I should think it just proves he's a lunatic," said Alfredi. "The commandant didn't even participate in those abuses. He wasn't the worst by a long shot."

"He was the man in charge. If he knew about them, he should have stopped them. If he didn't know, he was incompetent. Either way, he was responsible." Cordelia, hearing herself defending a Barrayaran execution, stopped abruptly. "I don't know." She shook her head. "I'm not Vorkosigan's keeper."

The noise of near-riot penetrated from outside, and their shelter was invaded by a deputation of fellow prisoners, all eager to hear the rumors of peace confirmed. The guards withdrew to the perimeter and let the excitement play itself out. She had to repeat her precis, twice. Her own crew members, led by Parnell, came over from the men's side.

Parnell jumped up on a bunk to address the orange-clad crowd, shouting over the glad babble. "This lady isn't telling you everything. I had the real story from one of the Barrayaran guards. After we were taken aboard the flagship, she escaped and personally assassinated the Barrayaran commander, Admiral Vorrutyer. That's why their advance collapsed. Let's *hear* it for Captain Naismith!"

"That's not the real story," she objected, but was drowned out by shouts and cheers. "I didn't kill Vorrutyer. Here! Put me down!" Her crew, ring-led by Parnell, hoisted her to their shoulders for an impromptu parade around the camp. "It's not true! Stop this! Awk!"

It was like trying to turn back the tide with a teacup. The story had too much innate appeal to the battered prisoners, too much wish-fulfillment come to life. They took it in like balm for their wounded spirits, and made it their own vicarious revenge. The story was passed around, elaborated, built up, sea-changed, until within twenty-four hours it was as rich and unkillable as legend. After a few days she gave up trying.

The truth was too complicated and ambiguous to appeal to them, and she herself, suppressing everything in it that had to do with Vorkosigan, was unable to make it sound convincing. Her duty seemed drained of meaning, dull and discolored. She longed for home, and her sensible mother and brother, and quiet, and one thought that would connect to another without making a chain of secret horror.

CHAPTER ELEVEN

Camp returned to routine soon, or what routine should always have been. There followed weeks of waiting for the slow negotiations for prisoner exchange to be completed, with everyone honing elaborate plans for what they would do when they got home. Cordelia gradually came to a nearly normal relationship with her shelter mates, although they still tried to give her special privileges and services. She heard nothing from Vorkosigan.

She was lying on her bunk one afternoon, pretending to sleep, when Lieutenant Alfredi roused her.

"There's a Barrayaran officer out here who says he wants to talk to you." Alfredi trailed her to the door, suspicion and hostility in her face. "I don't think we should let them take you away by yourself. We're so close to going home. They've surely got it in for you."

"Oh. It's all right, Marsha."

Vorkosigan stood outside the shelter, in the dress greens worn daily by the Staff, accompanied as usual by Illyan. He seemed tense, deferential, weary, and closed.

"Captain Naismith," he said formally, "may I speak with you?"

"Yes, but—not here." She was acutely conscious of the

eyes of her fellows upon her. "Can we take a walk or something?"

He nodded, and they started off in shared silence. He clasped his hands behind his back. She shoved hers into the pockets of her orange smock top. Illyan trailed them, dog-like, impossible to shake. They left the prison compound, and headed into the woods.

"I'm glad you came," said Cordelia. "There are some things I've been meaning to ask you."

"Yes. I wanted to see you sooner, but winding this thing up properly has been keeping me rather busy."

She nodded toward his yellow collar tabs. "Congratulations on your promotion."

"Oh, that." He touched one briefly. "It's meaningless. Just a formality, to expedite the work I'm doing now."

"Which is what?"

"Dismantling the armada, guarding the local space around this planet, shuffling politicians back and forth between Barrayar and Escobar. General housecleaning, now the party's over. Supervising prisoner exchange."

They were following a wide beaten path through the grey-green woods, up the slope out of the crater's bowl.

"I wanted to apologize for questioning you under drugs. I know it offended you deeply. Need drove me. It was a military necessity."

"You have nothing to apologize for." She glanced back at Illyan. I must know. . . . "Quite literally nothing, I eventually realized."

He was silent. "I see," he said at last. "You are very acute."

"On the contrary, I am very baffled."

He swung to face Illyan. "Lieutenant, I crave a boon from you. I wish a few minutes alone with this lady to discuss a very personal matter."

"I shouldn't, sir. You know that."

"I once asked her to marry me. She never gave me her answer. If I give you my word that we will discuss nothing but what touches on that, *may* we have a few moments' privacy?"

"Oh . . ." Illyan frowned. "Your word, sir?"

"My word. As Vorkosigan."

"Well—I guess it's all right then." Illyan seated himself glumly on a fallen log to wait, and they walked on up the path.

They came out, at the top, on a familiar promontory overlooking the crater, the very spot where Vorkosigan had planned the repossession of his ship, so long ago. They seated themselves on the ground, watching the activity of the camp made silent by distance.

"Time was you would never have done that," Cordelia observed. "Pledged your word falsely."

"Times change."

"Nor lied to me."

"That is so."

"Nor shot a man out of hand for crimes he didn't participate in."

"It wasn't out of hand. He had a summary court-martial first. And it did get things straightened around in a hurry. Anyway, it will satisfy the Interstellar Judiciary's commission. I'll have them on my hands too, come tomorrow. Investigating prisoner abuses."

"I think you're getting blood-glutted. Individual lives are losing their meaning for you."

"Yes. There have been so many. It's nearly time to quit." Expression was deadened in his face and words.

"How did the Emperor buy you for that—extraordinary assassination? You of all men. Was it your idea? Or his?"

He did not evade, or deny. "His idea, and Negri's. I am but his agent."

His fingers pulled gently on the grass stems, breaking them off delicately one by one. "He didn't come out with it directly. First he asked me to take command of the Escobar invasion. He started with a bribe—the viceroyalty of this planet, in fact, when it's colonized. I turned him down. Then he tried a threat, said he'd throw me to Grishnov, let him have me up for treason, and no Imperial pardon. I told him to go to hell, not in so many words. That was a bad moment, between us. Then he apologized. Called me Lord Vorkosigan. He called me Captain when he wished to be offensive. Then he called in Captain Negri, with a file that didn't even have a name, and the playacting stopped.

"Reason. Logic. Argument. Evidence. We sat in that green silk room in the Imperial Residence at Vorbarr Sultana one whole mortal week, the Emperor and Negri and I, going over it, while Illyan kicked his heels in the hall, studying the Emperor's art collection. You are correct in your deduction about Illyan, by the way. He knows nothing about the real purpose of the invasion.

"You saw the Prince, briefly. I may add that you saw him at his best. Vorrutyer may have been his teacher once, but the Prince surpassed him some time ago. But if only he had had some saving notion of political service, I think his father would have forgiven him even his vilest personal vices.

"He was not balanced, and he surrounded himself with men whose interests lay in making him even less balanced. A true nephew of his Uncle Yuri. Grishnov meant to rule Barrayar through him when he came to the throne. On his own—Grishnov would have been willing to wait, I think—the Prince had engineered two assassination attempts on his father in the last eighteen months."

Cordelia whistled soundlessly. "I almost begin to see. But why not just put him out of the way quietly? Surely the Emperor and your Captain Negri could have managed it between them, if anyone could."

"The idea was discussed. God help me, I even volunteered to lend myself to it, as an alternative to this—bloodbath."

He paused. "The Emperor is dying. He has run out of time to wait for the problem to solve itself. It's become an obsession with him, to try to leave his house in order.

"The problem is the Prince's son. He's only four. Sixteen years is a long time for a Regency government. With the Prince dead Grishnov and the whole Ministerial party would just slide right into the power vacuum, if they were left intact.

"It was not enough to kill the Prince. The Emperor felt he had to destroy the whole war party, so effectively that it would not rise again for another generation. So first there was me, bitching about the strategic problems with Escobar. Then the information about the plasma mirrors came through Negri's own intelligence network. Military intelligence didn't have it. Then me again, with the news that surprise had been lost. Do you know, he suppressed part of that, too? It could only be a disaster. And then there was Grishnov, and the war party, and the Prince, all crying for glory. He had only to step aside and let them rush to their doom." Grass was being pulled up in bunches now.

"It all fit so well, there was a hypnotizing fascination to it. But chancy. There was even a possibility, leaving events to themselves, that everyone might be killed *but* the Prince. I was placed where I was to see the script was followed. Goading the Prince, making sure he got to the front lines at the right time. Hence that little scene you witnessed in my cabin. I never lost my temper. I was just putting another nail in the coffin."

"I suppose I can see why the other agent was—the chief surgeon?"

"Quite."

"Lovely."

"Isn't it, though." He lay back on the grass, looking through the turquoise sky. "I couldn't even be an honest assassin. Do you recall me saying I wanted to go into politics? I believe I'm cured of that ambition."

"What about Vorrutyer? Were you supposed to get him killed, too?"

"No. In the original script he was cast as the scapegoat. It would have been his part, after the disaster, to apologize to the Emperor for the mess, in the full old Japanese sense of the phrase, as part of the general collapse of the war party. For all he was the Prince's spiritual advisor, I did not envy him his future. All the while he was riding me, I could see the ground crumbling away beneath his feet. It baffled him. He always used to be able to make me lose my temper. It was great sport for him, when we were younger. He couldn't understand why he'd lost his touch." His eyes remained focused somewhere in the high blue emptiness, not meeting hers.

"For what it's worth to you, his death just then saved a great many lives. He would have tried to continue the fight much longer, to save his political skin. That was the price that bought me, in the end. I thought, if only I were in the right place at the right time, I could do a better job of running the pullout than anyone else on the General Staff."

"So we are, all of us, just Ezar Vorbarra's tools," said Cordelia slowly, belly-sick. "Me and my convoy, you, the Escobarans—even old Vorrutyer. So much for patriotic hoopla and righteous wrath. All a charade."

"That's right."

"It makes me feel very cold. Was the Prince really that bad?"

"There was no doubt of it. I shall not sicken you with the details of Negri's reports. . . . But the Emperor said if it wasn't done now, we would all be trying to do it ourselves, five or ten years down the road, and probably botching the job and getting all our friends killed, in a full-scale planet-wide civil war. He's seen two, in his lifetime. That was the nightmare that haunted him. A Caligula, or a Yuri Vorbarra, can rule a long time, while the best men hesitate to do what is necessary to stop him, and the worst ones take advantage.

"The Emperor spares himself nothing. Reads the reports over and over—he had them all nearly word-perfect. This wasn't something undertaken lightly, or casually. Wrongly, perhaps, but not lightly. He didn't want him to die in shame, you see. It was the last gift he could give him."

She sat numbly hugging her knees, memorizing his profile, as the soft airs of the afternoon rustled in the woods and stirred the golden grasses.

He turned his face toward her. "Was I wrong, Cordelia, to give myself to this thing? If I had not gone, he would simply have had another. I've always tried to walk the path of honor. But what do you do when all choices are evil? Shameful action, shameful inaction, every path leading to a thicket of death."

"You're asking me to judge you?"

"Someone must."

"I'm sorry. I can love you. I can grieve for you, or with you. I can share your pain. But I cannot judge you."

"Ah." He turned on his stomach, and stared down at the camp. "I talk too much to you. If my brain would ever grant me release from reality, I believe I would be the babbling sort of madman."

"You don't talk to anyone else like that, do you?" she asked, alarmed.

"Good God, no. You are—you are—I don't know what you are. But I need it. Will you marry me?"

She sighed, and laid her head upon her knees, twisting a grass stem around her fingers. "I love you. You know that, I hope. But I can't take Barrayar. Barrayar eats its children."

"It isn't all these damnable politics. Some people get through their whole lives practically unconscious of them."

"Yes, but you're not one of them."

He sat up. "I don't know if I could get a visa for Beta Colony."

"Not this year, I suspect. Nor next. All Barrayarans are considered war criminals there at the moment. Politically speaking, we haven't had this much excitement in years. They're all a little drunk on it just now. And then there is Komarr."

"I see. I should have trouble getting a job as a judo instructor, then. And I could hardly write my memoirs, all things considered."

"Right now I should think you'd have trouble avoiding lynch mobs." She looked up at his bleak face. A mistake; it wrenched her heart. "I've—got to go home for a while, anyway. See my family, and think things through in peace and quiet. Maybe we can come up with some alternate solution. We can write, anyway."

"Yes, I suppose." He stood, and helped her up.

"Where will you be, after this?" she asked. "You have your rank back."

"Well, I'm going to finish up all this dirty work," a wave of his arm indicated the prison camp, and by implication the whole Escobaran adventure, "—and then I believe I too shall go home. And get drunk. I cannot serve him anymore. He's used me up on this. The death of his son, and the five thousand men who escorted him to hell, will always hang between us now. Vorhalas, Gottyan . . ."

"Don't forget the Escobarans. And a few Betans, too."

"I shall remember them." He walked beside her down the path. "Is there anything you need, in camp? I've tried to see that everything was provided generally, within the limits of our supplies, but I may have missed something."

"Camp seems to be all right, now. I don't need anything special. All we really need is to go home. No—come to think of it, I do want a favor."

"Name it," he said eagerly.

"Lieutenant Rosemont's grave. It was never marked. I may never get back here. While it's still possible to find the remains of our camp, could you have your people mark it? I have all his numbers and dates. I handled his personnel forms often enough, I still have them memorized."

"I'll see to it personally."

"Wait." He paused, and she held out a hand to him. His thick fingers engulfed her tapering ones; his skin was warm and dry, and scorched her. "Before we go pick up poor Lieutenant Illyan again . . ."

He took her in his arms, and they kissed, for the first time, for a long time.

"Oh," she muttered after. "Perhaps that was a mistake. It hurts so much when you stop."

"Well, let me . . ." His hand stroked her hair gently, then desperately wrapped itself in a shimmering coil; they kissed again.

"Uh, sir?" Lieutenant Illyan, coming up the path, cleared his throat noisily. "Had you forgotten the Staff conference?"

Vorkosigan put her from him with a sigh. "No, Lieutenant. I haven't forgotten."

"May I congratulate you, sir?" he smiled.

"No, Lieutenant."

He unsmiled. "I—don't understand, sir."

"That's quite all right, Lieutenant."

They walked on, Cordelia with her hands in her pockets, Vorkosigan with his clasped behind his back.

Most of the Escobaran women had already gone up by shuttle to the ship that had arrived to transport them home, late next afternoon, when a spruce Barrayaran guard appeared at the door of their shelter requesting Captain Naismith.

"Admiral's compliments, ma'am, and he wishes to know if you'd care to check the data on the marker he had made for your officer. It's in his office."

"Yes, certainly."

"Cordelia, for God's sake," hissed Lieutenant Alfredi, "don't go in there alone."

"It's *all right*," she murmured back impatiently. "Vorkosigan's all right."

"Oh? So what did he want yesterday?"

"I told you, to arrange for the marker."

"That didn't take two solid hours. Do you realize that's how long you were gone? I saw how he looked at you. And you—you came back looking like death warmed over."

Cordelia irritably waved away her concerned protests, and followed the extremely polite guard to the cache caverns. The planetside administrative offices of the Barrayaran force were set up in one of the side chambers. They had a carefully busy air that suggested the nearby presence of Staff officers, and indeed when they entered Vorkosigan's office, his name and rank emblazoned over the smudge that had been his predecessor's, they found him within.

Illyan, a captain, and a commodore were grouped around a computer interface with him, evidently undergoing some kind of briefing. He broke off to greet her with a careful nod, which she acknowledged in kind. *I wonder if my eyes look as hungry as his,* she thought. *This minuet of manners we go through to conceal our private selves from the mob will be for nothing, if we don't hide our eyes better.*

"It's on the clerk's desk, Cor—Captain Naismith," he directed her with a wave of his hand. "Go ahead and look it over." He returned his attention to his waiting officers.

It was a simple steel tablet, standard Barrayaran military issue, and the spelling, numbers, and dates were all in order. She fingered it briefly. It certainly looked like it ought to last. Vorkosigan finished his business and came to her side.

"Is it all right?"

"Fine." She gave him a smile. "Could you find the grave?"

"Yes, your camp's still visible from the air at low altitude, although another rainy season will obliterate it—"

The duty guard's voice floated in over a commotion at the door. "So *you* say. For all I know they could be bombs. You can't take that in there," followed by another voice replying, "He has to sign it personally. Those are *my* orders. You guys act like you won the damn war."

The second speaker, a man in the dark red uniform of an Escobaran medical technician, backed through the door followed by a float-pallet on a control lead, looking like some bizarre balloon. It was loaded with large canisters, each about half a meter high, studded with control panels and access apertures. Cordelia recognized them at once, and stiffened, feeling sick. Vorkosigan looked blank.

The technician stared around. "I have a receipt for these that requires Admiral Vorkosigan's personal signature. Is he here?"

Vorkosigan stepped forward. "I'm Vorkosigan. What are these, um . . ."

"Medtech," Cordelia whispered in cue.

"Medtech?" Vorkosigan finished smoothly, although the exasperated glance he gave her suggested that was not the cue he'd wanted.

The medtech smiled sourly. "We're returning these to the senders."

Vorkosigan walked around the pallet. "Yes, but what *are* they?"

"All your bastards," said the medtech.

Cordelia, catching the genuine puzzlement in Vorkosigan's voice, added, "They're uterine replicators, um, Admiral. Self-contained, independently powered—they need servicing, though—"

"Every week," agreed the medtech, viciously cordial. He held up a data disk. "They sent you instructions with them."

Vorkosigan looked appalled. "What the hell am I supposed to do with them?"

"Thought you were going to make our women answer that question, did you?" replied the medtech, taut and sarcastic. "Personally, I'd suggest you hang them around their fathers' necks. The paternal gene complements are marked on each one, so you should have no trouble telling who they belong to. Sign here."

Vorkosigan took the receipt panel, and read it through twice. He walked around the pallet again, counting, looking deeply troubled. He came up beside Cordelia in his circuit, and murmured, "I didn't realize they could do things like that."

"They use them all the time at home."

"They must be fantastically complex."

"And expensive, too. I'm surprised—maybe they just didn't want to argue about taking them home with any of the mothers. A couple of them were pretty emotionally divided about abortions. This puts the blood guilt on you." Her words seemed to enter him like bullets, and she wished she'd phrased herself differently.

"They're all alive in there?"

"Sure. See all the green lights? Placentas and all. They float right in their amniotic sacs, just like home."

"Moving?"

"I suppose so."

He rubbed his face, staring hauntedly at the canisters.

"Seventeen. God, Cordelia, what do I do with them? Surgeon, of course, but . . ." He turned to the fascinated clerk. "Get the chief surgeon down here, on the double." He turned back to Cordelia, keeping his voice down. "How long will those things keep working?"

"The whole nine months, if necessary."

"May I have my receipt, Admiral?" said the medtech loudly. "I have other duties waiting." He stared curiously at Cordelia in her orange pajamas.

Vorkosigan scribbled his name absently on the bottom of the receipt panel with a light pen, thumbprinted it, and handed it back, still slightly hypnotized by the pallet load of canisters. Cordelia, morbidly curious, walked around them too, inspecting the readouts. "The youngest one seems to be about seven weeks old. The oldest is over four months. Must have been right after the war started."

"But what do *I* do with them?" he muttered again. She had never seen him more at a loss.

"What do you usually do with soldier's by-blows? Surely the situation has come up before, not on this scale, maybe."

"We usually abort bastards. In this case, it seems to have already been done, in a sense. So much trouble—do they expect us to keep them alive? Floating fetuses—babies in cans . . ."

"I don't know." Cordelia sighed thoughtfully. "What a thoroughly rejected little group of humanity they are. Except—but for the grace of God and Sergeant Bothari, one of those canned kids might have been mine, and Vorrutyer's. Or mine and Bothari's, for that matter."

He looked quite ill at the thought. He lowered his voice almost to a whisper, and began again. "But what do I—what would *you* have me do with them?"

"You're asking me for orders?"

"I've never—Cordelia, please—what honorable . . ."

It must be quite a shock to suddenly find out you're pregnant, seventeen times over—at your age, too, she thought. She squelched the black humor—he was so clearly out of his depth—and took pity on his real confusion. "Take care of them, I suppose. I have no idea what that will entail, but—you did sign for them."

He sighed. "Quite. Pledged my word, in a sense." He set the problem up in familiar terms, and found his balance therein. "My word as Vorkosigan, in fact. Right. Good. Objective defined, plan of attack proposed—we're in business."

The surgeon entered, and was taken aback at the sight of the float pallet. "What the hell—oh, I know what they are. I never thought I'd see one. . . ." He ran his fingers over one canister in a sort of technical lust. "Are they ours?"

"All ours, it seems," replied Vorkosigan. "The Escobarans sent them down."

The surgeon chuckled. "What an obscene gesture. One can see why, I suppose. But why not just flush them?"

"Some unmilitary notion about the value of human life, perhaps," said Cordelia hotly. "Some cultures have it."

The surgeon raised an eyebrow, but was quelled, as much by the total lack of amusement on his commander's face as by her words.

"There are the instructions." Vorkosigan handed him the disk.

"Oh, good. Can I empty one out and take it apart?"

"No, you may not," said Vorkosigan coldly. "I pledged my word—as Vorkosigan—that they would be cared for. All of them."

"How the devil did they maneuver you into that? Oh, well, I'll get one later, maybe. . . ." He returned to his examination of the glittering machinery.

"Have you the facilities here to handle any problems that may arise?" asked Vorkosigan.

"Hell, no. Imp Mil would be the only place. And they don't even have an obstetrics department. But I bet Research would love to get hold of these babies. . . ."

It took Cordelia a dizzy moment to realize he was referring to the uterine replicators, and not their contents.

"They have to be serviced in a week. Can you do it here?"

"I don't think . . ." The surgeon set the disk into the monitor at the clerk's station, and began flashing through it. "There must be ten written kilometers of instructions— ah. No. We don't have—no. Too bad, Admiral. I'm afraid you'll have to eat your word this time."

Vorkosigan grinned, wolfishly and without humor. "Do you recall what happened to the last man who called me on my word?"

The surgeon's smile faded into uncertainty.

"These are your orders, then," Vorkosigan went on, clipped. "In thirty minutes you, personally, will lift off with these—things, for the fast courier. And it will arrive in Vorbarr Sultana in less than a week. You will go to the Imperial Military Hospital and requisition, by whatever means necessary, the men and equipment needed to— complete the project. Get an Imperial order if you have to. Directly, not through channels. I'm sure our friend Negri will put you in touch. See them set up, serviced, and report back to me."

"We can't possibly make it in under a week! Not even in the courier!"

"You'll make it in five days, boosting six points past emergency max the whole way. If the engineer's been doing his job, the engines won't blow until you hit eight. Quite safe." He glanced over his shoulder. "Couer, scramble the courier crew, please. And get their captain on the line, I want to give him his orders personally."

Commodore Couer's eyebrows rose, but he moved to obey.

The surgeon lowered his voice, glancing at Cordelia. "Is this Betan sentimentality at work, sir? A little odd in the Emperor's service, don't you think?"

Vorkosigan smiled, narrow-eyed, and matched his tone. "Betan insubordination, Doctor? You will oblige me by directing your energies to carrying out your orders instead of evolving excuses why you can't."

"Hell of a lot easier just to open the stopcocks. And what are you going to do with them once they're—completed, born, whatever you call it? Who's going to take

responsibility for them then? I can sympathize with your
wish to impress your girlfriend, but think ahead, sir!"

Vorkosigan's eyebrows snapped together, and he
growled, down in his throat. The surgeon recoiled.
Vorkosigan buried the growl in a throat-clearing noise, and
took a breath.

"That will be my problem. My word. Your responsibility will end there. Twenty-five minutes, Doctor. If you're
on time I may let you ride up on the inside of the
shuttle." He grinned a small white grin, eloquently
aggressive. "You can have three days home leave after
they're in place at ImpMil, if you wish."

The surgeon shrugged wry defeat, and vanished to
collect his things.

Cordelia looked after him doubtfully. "Will he be all
right?"

"Oh, yes, it just takes him a while to turn his thinking around. By the time they get to Vorbarr Sultana, he'll
be acting like he invented the project, and the—uterine
replicators." Vorkosigan's gaze returned to the float pallet. "Those are the damnedest things. . . ."

A guard entered. "Pardon me, sir, but the Escobaran
shuttle pilot is asking for Captain Naismith. They're ready
to lift."

Couer spoke from the communications monitor. "Sir,
I have the courier captain on line."

Cordelia gave Vorkosigan a look of helpless frustration,
acknowledged by a small shake of his head, and each
turned wordlessly to the demands of duty. She left meditating on the doctor's parting shot. And we thought we
were being so careful. We really must do something about
our eyes.

CHAPTER TWELVE

She traveled home with about 200 others, mostly Escobarans, on a Tau Cetan passenger liner hastily converted for the purpose. There was a lot of time spent exchanging stories and sharing memories among the ex-prisoners, sessions subtly guided, she realized shortly, by the heavy sprinkling of psych officers the Escobarans had sent with the ship. After a while her silence about her own experiences began to stand out, and she learned to spot the casual-looking roundup techniques for the only-apparently-impromptu group therapy, and make herself scarce.

It wasn't enough. She found herself quietly but implacably pursued by a bright-faced young woman named Irene, whom she deduced must be assigned to her case. She popped up at meals, in the corridors, in the lounges, always with a novel excuse for starting a conversation. Cordelia avoided her when she could, and turned the conversation deftly, or sometimes bluntly, to other topics when she couldn't.

After another week the girl disappeared back into the mob, but Cordelia returned to her cabin one day to discover her roommate gone and replaced by another, a steady-eyed, easygoing older woman in civilian dress who was not one of the ex-prisoners. Cordelia lay on her bed glumly and watched her unpacking.

"Hi, I'm Joan Sprague," the woman introduced herself sunnily.

Time to get explicit. "Good afternoon, Dr. Sprague. I am correct, I think, in identifying you as Irene's boss?"

Sprague paused. "You're quite right. But I prefer to keep things on a casual basis."

"No, you don't. You prefer to keep things *looking* like they're on a casual basis. I appreciate the difference."

"You are a very interesting person, Captain Naismith."

"Yes, well, there's more of you than there are of me. Suppose I agree to talk to you. Will you call off the rest of your dogs?"

"I'm here for you to talk to—but when you are ready."

"So, ask me what you want to know. Let's get this over with, so we can both relax." I could use a little therapy, at that, Cordelia thought wistfully. I feel so lousy. . . .

Sprague seated herself on the bed, a mild smile on her face and the utmost attention in her eyes. "I want to try and help you remember what happened during the time you were a prisoner aboard the Barrayaran flagship. Getting it into your consciousness, however horrible it was, is your first step to healing."

"Um, I think we may be at cross-purposes. I remember everything that happened during that time with the utmost clarity. I have no trouble getting it into my consciousness. What I would like is to get it out, at least long enough to sleep now and then."

"I see. Go on. Why don't you describe what happened?"

Cordelia gave an account of events, from the time of the wormhole jump from Beta Colony until after the murder of Vorrutyer, but ended it before Vorkosigan's entrance, saying vaguely, "I moved around to different hiding places on the ship for a couple of days, but they caught me in the end and put me back in the brig."

"So. You don't remember being tortured or raped by

Admiral Vorrutyer, and you don't remember killing him."

"I *wasn't*. And I *didn't*. I thought I made that clear."

The doctor shook her head sorrowfully. "It's reported you were taken away from camp twice by the Barrayarans. Do you remember what happened during those times?"

"Yes, of course."

"Can you describe it?"

She balked. "No." The secret of the Prince's assassination would be nothing to the Escobarans—they could hardly dislike the Barrayarans any more than they did already—but the mere rumor of the truth could be devastating to civil order on Barrayar. Riots, military mutiny, the downfall of Vorkosigan's Emperor—those were just the beginnings of the possible consequences. If there was a civil war on Barrayar, could Vorkosigan be killed in it? God, please, thought Cordelia wearily, no more death . . .

Sprague looked tremendously interested. Cordelia felt pounced on. She amended herself. "There was an officer of mine, who was killed during the Betan survey of that planet—you know about that, I hope?" The doctor nodded. "They made arrangements to put a marker on his grave, at my request. That's all."

"I understand," Sprague sighed. "We had another case like yours. The girl had also been raped by Vorrutyer, or some of his men, and had it covered up by the Barrayaran medical people. I suppose they were trying to protect his reputation."

"Oh, I believe I met her, aboard the flagship. She was in my shelter, too, right?"

Sprague's surprised look confirmed it, although she made a little vague gesture indicating professional confidence.

"You're right about her," Cordelia went on. "I'm glad she's getting what she needs. But you're wrong about me. You're wrong about Vorrutyer's reputation, too. The whole reason they put out this stupid story about me was because they thought it would look worse for him to be killed by a weak woman than by one of his own combat soldiers."

"The physical evidence from your medical examination alone is enough to make me question that," said Sprague.

"What physical evidence?" asked Cordelia, momentarily bewildered.

"The evidence of torture," the doctor replied, looking grim, even a little angry. Not angry at her, Cordelia realized.

"What? I was never tortured!"

"Yes. An excellent cover-up. Outrageous—but they couldn't hide the physical traces. Are you aware that you had a broken arm, two broken ribs, numerous contusions on your neck, head, hands, arms—your whole body, in fact? And your biochemistry—evidence of extreme stress, sensory deprivation, considerable weight loss, sleep disorders, adrenal excess—shall I go on?"

"Oh," said Cordelia. "That."

"Oh, that?" echoed the doctor, raising an eyebrow.

"I can explain that," said Cordelia eagerly. She laughed a little. "In a way, I suppose I can blame it on you Escobarans. I was in a cell on the flagship during the retreat. It took a hit—shook everything around like gravel in a can, including me. That's where I got the broken bones and so on."

The doctor made a note. "Very good. Very good indeed. Subtle. But not subtle enough—your bones were broken on two different occasions."

"Oh," said Cordelia. And how am I going to explain Bothari, without mentioning Vorkosigan's cabin? *A friend tried to strangle me. . . .*

"I would like you to think," said Dr. Sprague carefully, "about the possibility of drug therapy. The Barrayarans have done an excellent cover-up on you, even better than the other, and it took very deep probing indeed for her. I think it's going to be even more necessary in your case. But we must have your voluntary cooperation."

"Thank God for that." Cordelia lay back on her bed and pulled her pillow over her face, thinking of drug therapy. It made her blood run cold. She wondered how long she could take deep probing for memories that weren't there before she started manufacturing them to meet the demand. And worse: the very first effect of probing must be to bring up those secret agonies that were uppermost on her mind—Vorkosigan's secret wounds. . . . She sighed, removed the pillow from her head and hugged it to her chest, and looked up to find Sprague regarding her with deep concern. "You still here?"

"I'll always be here, Cordelia."

"That's—what I was afraid of."

Sprague got no more from her after that. She was afraid to sleep, now, for fear of talking or even being questioned in her sleep. She took little catnaps, waking with a start whenever there was movement in the cabin, such as her roommate getting up to go to the bathroom in the night. Cordelia did not admire Ezar Vorbarra's secret purposes in the late war, but at least they had been accomplished. The thought of all that pain and death being made vain as smoke haunted her, and she resolved that all Vorkosigan's soldiers, yes, even Vorrutyer and the camp commandant, would not be made to have died for nothing through her.

She ended the trip far more frayed than she had begun it, floating on the edge of real breakdown, plagued by pounding headaches, insomnia, a mysterious left-hand tremula, and the beginnings of a stutter.

The trip from Escobar to Beta Colony was much easier. It only took four days, in a Betan fast courier sent, she was surprised to find, especially for her. She viewed the news reports on her cabin holovid. She was deathly tired of the war, but she caught by chance a mention of Vorkosigan's name, and could not resist following it up to find out what the public view of his part was.

Horrified, she discovered that his work with the Judiciary's investigative commission led the Betan and Escobaran press to blame him for the way the prisoners had been treated, as if he had been in charge of them from the beginning. The old false Komarr story was dragged out on parade, and his name was reviled everywhere. The injustice of it all made her furious, and she gave up the news in disgust.

At last they orbited Beta Colony, and she haunted Nav and Com for a glimpse of home.

"There's the old sandbox at last." The captain cheerfully keyed her a view. "They're sending a shuttle up for you, but there's a storm over the capital, and it's a bit delayed, till it subsides enough for them to drop screens at the port."

"I may as well wait till I get down to call my mom," Cordelia commented. "She's probably at work now. No point bothering her there. Hospital's not far from the shuttleport. I can get a nice relaxing drink while I wait for her to get off shift and pick me up."

The captain gave her a peculiar look. "Uh, yeah."

The shuttle arrived eventually. Cordelia shook hands all around, thanking the courier crew for the ride, and went aboard. The shuttle stewardess greeted her with a pile of new clothes.

"What's all this? By heavens, the Expeditionary Force uniforms at last! Better late than never, I guess."

"Why don't you go ahead and put them on," urged the stewardess, smiling extraordinarily.

"Why not." She had been wearing the same borrowed Escobaran uniform for quite some time now, and was thoroughly tired of it. She took the sky blue cloth and the shiny black boots, amused. "Why jackboots, in God's name? There's scarcely a horse on Beta Colony, except in the zoos. I admit, they do look wicked."

Finding she was the sole passenger on the shuttle, she changed on the spot. The stewardess had to help her with the boots.

"Whoever designed these should be forced to wear them to bed," Cordelia muttered. "Or perhaps he does."

The shuttle descended, and she went to the window, eager for the first look at her hometown. The ochre haze parted at last, and they spiraled neatly down to the shuttleport and taxied to the docking bay.

"Seems to be a lot of people out there today."

"Yes, the President's going to make a speech," said the stewardess. "It's very exciting. Even if I didn't vote for him."

"Steady Freddy got that many people to show up for one of his speeches? Just as well. I can blend with the crowd. This thing is a bit bright. I think I'd rather be invisible, today."

She could feel the letdown beginning, and wondered how far down it would end. The Escobaran doctor had been right in her principles, if not in her facts; there was an emotional debt yet to be paid, knotted somewhere under her stomach.

The shuttle's engines whined to silence, and she rose to thank the grinning stewardess, uneasy. "There's not going to be a r-reception committee out there for me, is there? I really don't think I could handle it today."

"You'll have some help," the stewardess assured her. "Here he comes now."

A man in a civilian sarong entered the shuttle, smiling broadly. "How do you do, Captain Naismith," he introduced himself. "I'm Philip Gould, the President's Press Secretary." Cordelia was shocked. Press Secretary was a cabinet-level post. "It's an honor to meet you."

She was tumbling fast. "You're not p-planning some kind of, of d-dog and pony show out there, are you? I r-really just want to go home."

"Well, the President is planning a speech. And he has a little something for you," he said soothingly. "In fact, he was hoping he might make several speeches with you, but we can discuss that later. Now, we hardly expect the Heroine of Escobar to suffer from stage fright, but we have prepared some remarks for you. I'll be with you all the time, and help you with the cues, and the press." He passed her a hand viewer. "Do try and look surprised, when you first step out of the shuttle."

"I am surprised." She scanned the script rapidly. "Th-this is a p-pack of lies!"

He looked worried. "Have you always had that little speech impediment?" he asked cautiously.

"N-no, it's my souvenir from the Escobaran psych service,

and the l-late war. Who came up with this g-garbage, anyway?" The line that particularly caught her eye referred to
"the cowardly Admiral Vorkosigan and his pack of ruffians."
"Vorkosigan's the bravest man I ever met."

Gould took her firmly by the upper arm, and guided
her to the shuttle hatch. "We have to go, now, to make
the holovid timing. Maybe you can just leave that line
out, all right? Now, smile."

"I want to see my mother."

"She's with the President. Here we go."

They exited the tube from the shuttle hatch into a
milling mob of men, women, and equipment. They all
began shouting questions at once. Cordelia began to shake,
all over, in waves that began in the pit of her stomach
and radiated outward. "I don't know any of these people,"
she hissed to Gould.

"Keep walking," he hissed back through a fixed smile.
They mounted a reviewing stand set up on the balcony
overlooking the shuttleport concourse. The concourse was
packed solidly with a colorful crowd in a holiday mood.
They blurred before Cordelia's eyes. She saw a familiar face
at last, her mother, smiling and crying, and she fell into her
arms, to the delight of the press who recorded it copiously.

"Get me out of this as fast as you can," she whispered
fiercely into her mother's ear. "I'm about to lose it."

Her mother held her at arm's length, not understanding, still smiling. Her place was taken by Cordelia's
brother, his family clustered nervously and proudly behind
him, looking at her, she felt, with eyes that devoured her.

She spotted her crew, also dressed in the new uniforms,
standing with some government officials. Parnell gave her
a thumbs-up, grinning dementedly. She was bundled over
to stand behind a rostrum with the President of Beta
Colony.

Steady Freddy seemed larger than life to her confused
eyes, big and booming. Perhaps that was why he projected
over the holovid so well. He grasped her hand and held
it up in his, to the cheers of the crowd. It made her feel
like an idiot.

The President gave a fine performance with his speech, not even using the prompter. It was full of the jingoistic patriotism that had so intoxicated the place when she'd left, and not one word in a dozen touched the real truth even from the Betan point of view. He worked up gradually and with perfect showmanship to the medal. Cordelia's heart began to pound lumpishly as she caught the drift of it. She tried desperately to evade the knowledge, turning to the Press Secretary.

"Is this on behalf of m-my crew, for the plasma mirrors?"

"They have theirs already." Was he ever going to stop smiling? "This is your very own."

"I s-see."

The medal, it appeared, was to be awarded for her brave, one-woman assassination of Admiral Vorrutyer. Steady Freddy actually avoided the word assassination, along with blunt terms like murder and killing, favoring more liquid phrases like "freeing the universe of a viper of iniquity."

The speech lumbered to its close, and the glittering medal on its colorful ribbon, Beta Colony's highest honor, was lowered over her head by the President's own hand. Gould positioned her in front of the rostrum, and pointed out the glowing green words of the prompter marching across thin air before her eyes. "Start reading," he whispered.

"Am I on? Oh, Uh . . . People of Beta Colony, my beloved home," that was all right so far, "when I left you to meet the m-menace of Barrayaran tyranny, s-succoring our friend and ally Escobar, it was with no idea that fate was to bring me face-to-face with a n-nobler d-destiny."

It was here she departed from the script, watching herself go helplessly, like a doomed sea ship sinking beneath the waves. "I don't see what's so n-noble about b-butchering that sadistic ass Vorrutyer. And I wouldn't take a medal for m-murdering an unarmed m-man even if I had done it."

She pulled it off over her head. The ribbon caught in

her hair, and she yanked it free, painfully, angrily. "For the last time. I did *not* kill Vorrutyer. One of his own men killed Vorrutyer. He c-caught him from behind and cut his throat from ear to ear. I was *there*, damn it. He bled all over me. The press from both sides are stuffing you with lies about that s-stupid war. D-damn voyeurs! Vorkosigan was *not* in charge of the prison camp when the atrocities took place. As s-soon as he was in charge he stopped them. Sh-sh-shot one of his own officers just to feed your l-lust for vengeance, and it cost him in his honor, too, I can tell you."

The sound going out from the rostrum was cut off suddenly. She turned to Steady Freddy, tears of fury blurring her view of his astonished face, and flung the medal back at him with all the force of her arm. It missed his head and glittered down over the balcony into the crowd.

Her arms were pinned from behind. It triggered some buried reflex, and she kicked out frantically.

If only the President hadn't tried to dodge, he would have been all right. As it was, the toe of her jackboot caught him in the groin with perfect unplanned accuracy. His mouth made a soundless "O" and he went down behind the rostrum.

Cordelia, hyperventilating uncontrollably, began to cry as a dozen more hands grabbed her arms, waist, legs. "*P-please* don't lock me up again! I couldn't take it. I just wanted to go home! Get that goddamn ampule away from me! No! No! No drugs, please, please! I'm *sorry!*"

She was hustled out, and the media event of the year collapsed just like Steady Freddy.

She was taken to a quiet room, one of the shuttleport's administrative offices, immediately afterwards. The President's personal physician arrived after a time and took charge, had everyone removed but himself and her mother, and gave her some breathing space to regain her self-control. It took her almost an hour to stop crying, once she had started. The embarrassment and outrage stopped seesawing at last, and she was able to sit up and talk in a voice like a bad cold.

"Please apologize to the President for me. If only someone had warned me, or asked me about it first. I'm—n-not in very good shape right now."

"We should have realized it ourselves," said the physician sorrowfully. "Your ordeal, after all, was much more personal than the usual soldier's experience. It is we who must apologize, for subjecting you to an unnecessary strain."

"We thought it would be a nice surprise," added her mother.

"It was a surprise, all right. I only hope I don't get myself locked in a padded cell. I'm a bit off cells at the moment." The thought tightened her throat, and she breathed carefully to calm back down.

She wondered where Vorkosigan was now, what he was doing. Getting drunk sounded better all the time, and she wished she were with him, doing so. She pressed thumb and forefinger to the bridge of her nose, rubbing out the tension. "May I be permitted to go home now?"

"Is there still a crowd out there?" asked her mother.

"I'm afraid so. We'll try to keep them back."

With the doctor on one side and her mother on the other, she dwelt in Vorkosigan's kiss all during the long walk to her mother's groundcar. The crowd still pressed upon her, but in a hushed, respectful, almost frightened way, a great contrast to their earlier holiday mood. She felt sorry to have taken away their party.

There was a crowd at her mother's apartment shaft too, in the foyer by the lift tubes, and even in the hallway to her door. Cordelia smiled and waved a little, cautiously, but just shook her head at questions, not trusting herself to speak coherently. They made their way through and closed the door at last.

"Whew! I suppose they meant well, but my Lord—I felt like they wanted to eat me alive."

"There was so much excitement about the war, and the

Expeditionary Force—anyone in a blue uniform is getting star treatment. And when the prisoners got home, and your story came out—I'm glad I knew you were safe by then. My poor darling!" Cordelia got another hug, and welcomed it.

"Well, that explains where they got the nonsense. It was the wildest rumor. The Barrayarans started it, and everyone just ate it up. I couldn't stop it."

"What did they do to you?"

"They kept following me around, pestering me with these offers of therapy—they thought the Barrayarans had been messing with my memory. . . . Oh, I see. You mean, what did the *Barrayarans* do to me. Nothing much. V-vorrutyer might have liked to, but he met with his accident before he'd got half started." She decided not to disturb her mother with the details. "Something important did happen, though." She hesitated. "I ran into Aral Vorkosigan again."

"That horrible man? I wondered, when I heard the name in the news, if it was the same fellow who killed your Lieutenant Rosemont last year."

"No. Yes. I mean, he didn't kill Rosemont, one of his people did. But he's the same one."

"I don't understand why you're so sympathetic to him."

"You ought to appreciate him now. He saved my life. Hid me in his cabin, during those missing two days after Vorrutyer was killed. I'd have been executed for it, if they'd caught me before the change in command."

Her mother looked more disturbed than appreciative. "Did he—do anything to you?"

The question was filled with unanswerable irony. Cordelia dared not tell even her mother about the intolerable burden of truth he had laid on her. Her mother misunderstood the haunted look on her face.

"Oh, dear. I'm so sorry."

"Huh? No, damn it. Vorkosigan's no rapist. He's got this thing about prisoners. Wouldn't touch one with a stick. He asked me . . ." she trailed off, looking into the kind, concerned, and loving wall of her mother's face. "We talked a lot. He's all right."

"He doesn't have a very good reputation."

"Yeah, I've seen some of it. It's all lies."

"He's—not a murderer, then?"

"Well . . ." Cordelia foundered on the truth. "He has k-killed a lot of people, I suppose. He's a soldier, you know. It's his job. It can't help spilling over a bit. I only know about three that weren't in the line of duty, though."

"*Only* three?" repeated her mother faintly. There was a pause. "He's not a, a sex criminal, then?"

"Certainly not! Although I gather he went through a rather strange phase, after his wife committed suicide— I don't think he realizes how much I know about it, not that that maniac Vorrutyer should be trusted as a source of information, even if he was there. I suspect it's partly true, at least about their relationship. Vorrutyer was clearly obsessed with him. And Aral went awfully vague when I asked him about it."

Looking at her mother's appalled face, Cordelia thought, it's a good thing I never wanted to be a defense lawyer. All my clients would be in therapy *forever*. "It all makes a lot more sense if you meet him in person," she offered hopefully.

Cordelia's mother laughed uncertainly. "He surely seems to have charmed you. What does he have, then? Conversation? Good looks?"

"I'm not sure. He mostly talks Barrayaran politics. He claims to have an aversion to them, but it sounds more like an obsession to me. He can't leave them alone for five minutes. It's like they're in him."

"Is that—a very interesting subject?"

"It's awful," said Cordelia frankly. "His bedtime stories can keep you awake for weeks."

"It can't be his looks," sighed her mother. "I've seen a holovid of him in the news."

"Oh, did you save it?" asked Cordelia, instantly interested. "Where is it?"

"I'm sure there's something in the vid files," her mother allowed, staring. "But really, Cordelia—your Reg Rosemont was ten times better looking."

"I suppose he was," Cordelia agreed, "by any objective standard."

"So what does the man have, anyway?"

"I don't know. The virtues of his vices, perhaps. Courage. Strength. Energy. He could run me into the ground any day. He has power over people. Not leadership, exactly, although there's that too. They either worship him or hate his guts. The strangest man I ever met did both at the same time. But nobody falls asleep when he's around."

"And which category do you fall in, Cordelia?" asked her mother, bemused.

"Well, I don't hate him. Can't say as I worship him, either." She paused a long time, and looked up to meet her mother's eyes squarely. "But when he's cut, I bleed."

"Oh," said her mother, whitely. Her mouth smiled, her eyes flinched, and she busied herself with unnecessary vigor in getting Cordelia's meager belongings settled.

On the fourth afternoon of her leave, Cordelia's commanding officer brought a disturbing visitor.

"Captain Naismith, this is Dr. Mehta, from the Expeditionary Force Medical Service," Commodore Tailor introduced them. Dr. Mehta was a slim, tan-skinned woman about Cordelia's age, with dark hair drawn back, cool and antiseptic in her blue uniform.

"Not another psychiatrist," Cordelia sighed. Her muscles knotted up the back of her neck. More interrogations—more twisting, more evasions, ever-shakier webs of lies to cover the gaps in her story where Vorkosigan's bitter truths dwelt . . .

"Commodore Sprague's reports finally caught up with your file, a little late, it seems." Tailor's lips thinned sympathetically. "Ghastly. I'm sorry. If we'd had them earlier, we might have been able to spare you last week. And everybody else."

Cordelia flushed. "I didn't mean to kick him. He kind of ran into me. It won't happen again."

Commodore Tailor suppressed a smile. "Well, I didn't vote for him. Steady Freddy is not my main concern. Although," he cleared his throat, "he has taken a personal interest in your case. You're a public figure now, like it or not."

"Oh, nonsense."

"It's not nonsense. You have an obligation."

Who are you quoting, Bill? thought Cordelia. That's not your voice. She rubbed the back of her neck. "I thought I'd discharged all my obligations. What more do they want from me?"

Tailor shrugged. "It was thought—I was given to understand—that you could have a future as a spokesman for—for the government. Due to your war experience. Once you're well."

Cordelia snorted. "They've got some awfully strange illusions about my soldierly career. Look—as far as I'm concerned, Steady Freddy can put on falsies and go woo the hermaphrodite vote in Quartz. But I'm n-not going to play the part of a, a propaganda cow, to be milked by any party. I've an aversion to politics, to quote a friend."

"Well . . ." He shrugged, as though he too had discharged a duty, and went on more firmly. "Be that as it may, getting you fit for work again *is* my concern."

"I'm—I'll be all right, after m-my month's leave. I just need a rest. I want to go back to Survey."

"And so you can. Just as soon as you're medically cleared."

"Oh." The implications of that took a moment to sink in. "Oh, no—wait a minute. I had a little p-problem with Dr. Sprague. Very nice lady, her reasoning was sound, but her premises were wrong."

Commodore Tailor gazed at her sadly. "I think I'd better turn you over to Dr. Mehta, now. She'll explain everything. You will cooperate with her, won't you, Cordelia?"

Cordelia pursed her lips, chilled. "Let me get this straight. What you're saying is, if I can't make your shrink happy, I'll never set foot on a Survey ship again. No c-command—no job, in fact."

"That's—a very harsh way of putting it. But you know yourself, for Survey, with small groups of people isolated together for extended periods of time, the psych profiles are of the utmost importance."

"Yes, I know. . . ." She twitched her mouth into a smile. "I'll c-cooperate. S-sure."

CHAPTER THIRTEEN

"Now," said Dr. Mehta cheerfully, setting up her box on a table in the Naismiths' apartment next afternoon, "this is a completely non-invasive method of monitoring. You won't feel a thing, it won't do a thing to you, except give me clues as to which subjects are of subconscious importance to you." She paused to swallow a capsule, remarking, "Allergy. Excuse me. Think of it as an emotional dowsing rod, looking for those buried streams of experience."

"Telling you where to drill the well, eh?"

"Exactly. Do you mind if I smoke?"

"Go ahead."

Mehta lit an aromatic cigarette and set it casually in an ashtray she had brought with her. The smoke drifted toward Cordelia. She squinted at its acridity. Odd perversion for a doctor; well, we all have our weaknesses. She eyed the box, suppressing irritation.

"Now for a baseline," said Mehta. "July."

"Am I supposed to say August, or something?"

"No, it's not a free-association test—the machine will do the work. But you may, if you wish."

"That's all right."

"Twelve."

Apostles, thought Cordelia. Eggs. Days of Christmas.

"Death."

Birth, thought Cordelia. Those upper-class Barrayarans put everything into their children. Name, property, culture, even their government's continuity. A huge burden, no wonder the children bend and twist under the strain.

"Birth."

Death, thought Cordelia. A man without a son is a walking ghost there, with no part in their future. And when their government fails, they pay the price in their children's lives. Five thousand.

Mehta moved her ashtray a little to the left. It didn't help; made it worse, in fact.

"Sex."

Not likely, with me here and him there . . .

"Seventeen."

Canisters, thought Cordelia. Wonder how those poor desperate little scraps of life are doing?

Dr. Mehta frowned uncertainly at her readouts. "Seventeen?" she repeated.

Eighteen, Cordelia thought firmly. Dr. Mehta made a note.

"Admiral Vorrutyer."

Poor butchered toad. You know, I think you spoke the truth—you must have loved Aral once, to have hated him so. What did he do to you, I wonder? Rejected you, most likely. I could understand that pain. We have some common ground after all, perhaps. . . .

Mehta adjusted another dial, frowned again, turned it back. "Admiral Vorkosigan."

Ah love, let us be true to one another. . . . Cordelia focused wearily on Mehta's blue uniform. She'll get a geyser if she drills her well there—probably knows it already, she's making another note. . . .

Mehta glanced at her chronometer, and leaned forward with increased attention. "Let's talk about Admiral Vorkosigan."

Let's not, thought Cordelia, "What about him?"

"Does he work much in their Intelligence section, do you know?"

"I don't think so. His main line seems to be Staff tactician, when—when he isn't on patrol duty."

"The Butcher of Komarr."

"That's a damned lie," said Cordelia automatically, then wished she hadn't spoken.

"Who told you that?" asked Mehta.

"He did."

"He did. Ah."

I'll get you for that "Ah"—no. Cooperation. Calm. I do feel calm. . . . Wish that woman would either finish smoking that thing or put it out. Stings my eyes.

"What proof did he offer you?"

None, Cordelia realized. "His word, I guess. His honor."

"Rather intangible." She made another note. "And you believed him?"

"Yes."

"Why?"

"It—seemed consistent, with what I saw of his character."

"You were his prisoner for six days, were you not, on that Survey mission?"

"That's right."

Mehta tapped her light pen and said "hm," absently, looking through her. "You seem quite convinced of this Vorkosigan's veracity. You don't think he ever lied to you, then?"

"Well—yes, but after all, I was an enemy officer."

"Yet you seem to accept his statements unquestioningly."

Cordelia tried to explain. "A man's word is something more to a Barrayaran than a vague promise, at least for the old-fashioned types. Heavens, it's even the basis for their government, oaths of fealty and all that."

Mehta whistled soundlessly. "You approve of their form of government now, do you?"

Cordelia stirred uncomfortably. "Not exactly. I'm just

starting to understand it a little, is all. It could be made
to work, I suppose."

"So this word of honor business—you believe he never
breaks it?"

"Well . . ."

"He does, then."

"I have seen him do so. But the cost was huge."

"He breaks it for a price, then."

"Not for a price. At a cost."

"I fail to see the distinction."

"A price is something you get. A cost is something you
lose. He lost—much, at Escobar."

The talk was drifting onto dangerous ground. Got to
change the subject, Cordelia thought drowsily. Or take
a nap . . . Mehta glanced at the time again, and studied
Cordelia's face intently.

"Escobar," said Mehta.

"Aral lost his honor at Escobar, you know. He said he
was going to go home and get drunk, afterwards. Escobar
broke his heart, I think."

"Aral . . . You call him by his first name?"

"He calls me 'dear Captain.' I always thought that was
funny. Very revealing, in a way. He really does think of
me as a lady soldier. Vorrutyer was right again—I think
I am the solution to a difficulty for him. I'm glad. . . ."
The room was getting warm. She yawned. The wisps of
smoke wound tendril-like about her.

"Soldier."

"He loves his soldiers, you know. He really does. He's
stuffed with this peculiar Barrayaran patriotism. All honor
to the Emperor. The Emperor hardly seems worthy of
it. . . ."

"Emperor."

"Poor sod. Tormented as Bothari. May be as mad."

"Bothari? Who is Bothari?"

"He talks to demons. The demons talk back. You'd like
Bothari. Aral does. I do. Good guy to have with you on
your next trip to hell. He speaks the language."

Mehta frowned, twiddled her dials again, and tapped

her readout screen with a long fingernail. She backtracked. "Emperor."

Cordelia could hardly keep her eyes open. Mehta lit another cigarette and set it beside the stub of the first.

"Prince," said Cordelia. Mustn't talk about the Prince. . . .

"Prince," repeated Mehta.

"Mustn't talk about the Prince. That mountain of corpses . . ." Cordelia squinted in the smoke. The smoke—the odd, acrid smoke from cigarettes, once lit, never again lifted to the mouth . . .

"You're—drugging—*me*. . . ." Her voice broke in a strangled howl, and she staggered to her feet. The air was like glue. Mehta leaned forward, lips parted in concentration. She then jumped from her chair and back in surprise as Cordelia lurched toward her.

Cordelia swept the recorder from the table and fell upon it as it smashed to the floor, beating on it with her good hand, her right hand. "Never talk! No more death! You can't make me! Blew it—you can't get away with it, I'm sorry, watchdog, remembers every word, I'm sorry, shot him, please, talk to me, please, let me out, please let me out pleaseletmeout . . ."

Mehta was trying to lift her from the floor, speaking soothingly. Cordelia caught pieces in the outwash of her own babble. "—not supposed to do that—idiosyncratic reaction—*most* unusual. Please, Captain Naismith, come lie down. . . ."

Something glittered at Mehta's fingertips. An ampule.

"No!" screamed Cordelia, rolling on her back and kicking at her. She connected. The ampule arced away to roll under a low table. "No drugs no drugs no no no . . ."

Mehta was pale olive. "All right! All right! But come lie down—that's it, like that . . ." She darted away to turn up the air-conditioning full blast, and stub out the second cigarette. The air cleared quickly.

Cordelia lay on the couch, regaining her breath and trembling. So close—she had come so close to betraying him—and this was only the first session. Gradually she began to feel cooler and clearer.

She sat up, her face buried in her hands. "That was a dirty trick," she observed in a flat voice.

Mehta smiled, thin as plastic over an underlying excitement. "Well, it was, a little. But it's been an enormously productive session. Far more than I ever expected."

I'll bet, thought Cordelia. Enjoyed my performance, did you? Mehta was kneeling on the floor, picking up pieces of the recorder.

"Sorry about your machine. Can't imagine what came over me. Did I—destroy your results?"

"Yes, you should have just fallen asleep. Strange. And no." Rather triumphantly, she pulled a data cartridge from the wreck, and set it carefully on the table. "You won't have to go through that again. It's all right here. Very good."

"What do you make of it?" asked Cordelia dryly, through her fingers.

Mehta regarded her with professional fascination. "You are without doubt the most challenging case I've ever handled. But this should relieve your mind of any lingering doubts about whether the Barrayarans have, ah, violently rearranged your thinking. Your readouts practically went off the scales." She nodded firmly.

"You know," said Cordelia, "I'm not too crazy about your methods. I have a—particular aversion to being drugged against my will. I thought that sort of thing was illegal."

"But necessary, sometimes. The data are much purer if the subject is not aware of the observation. It's considered sufficiently ethical if permission is obtained post facto."

"Post facto permission, eh?" Cordelia purred. Fear and fury wound a double helix up her spine, coiling tighter and tighter. With an effort, she kept her smile straight, not letting it turn into a snarl. "That's a legal concept I'd never thought of. It sounds—almost Barrayaran. I don't want you on my case," she added abruptly.

Mehta made a note, and looked up, smiling.

"That's not a statement of emotion," Cordelia

emphasized. "That's a legal demand. I refuse any further treatment from you."

Mehta nodded understandingly. Was the woman deaf?

"Enormous progress," said Mehta happily. "I wouldn't have expected to uncover the aversion defense for another week yet."

"What?"

"You didn't expect the Barrayarans would put that much work into you and not plant defenses around it, did you? Of course you feel hostile. Just remember, those are not your own feelings. Tomorrow, we will work on them."

"Oh no we won't!" The muscles up her scalp were tense as wire. Her head ached fiercely. "You're fired!"

Mehta looked eager. "Oh, excellent!"

"Did you hear me?" demanded Cordelia. Where did that shrieky whine in my voice come from? Calm, calm . . .

"Captain Naismith, I remind you that we are not civilians. I am not in the ordinary legal physician-patient relationship with you; we are both under military discipline, pursuing, I have reason to believe, a military—never mind. Suffice it to say, you did not hire me and you can't fire me. Tomorrow, then."

Cordelia remained seated for hours after she left, staring at the wall and swinging her leg in absent thumps against the side of the couch, until her mother came home with supper. The next day she left the apartment early in the morning on a random tour of the city, and didn't return until late at night.

That night, in her weariness and loneliness, she sat down to write her first letter to Vorkosigan. She threw away her original attempt halfway through, when she realized his mail was probably read by other eyes, perhaps Illyan's. Her second was more neutrally worded. She made it handwritten, on paper, and being alone kissed it before she sealed it, then smiled wryly at herself for doing so. A paper letter was far more expensive to ship to Barrayar than an electronic one, but he would handle it, as she had. It was as close to a touch as they could come.

The next morning Mehta called early on the comconsole, to tell Cordelia cheerily she could relax; something had come up, and their session that afternoon was canceled. She did not refer to Cordelia's absence the previous afternoon.

Cordelia was relieved at first, until she began thinking about it. Just to be sure, she absented herself from home again. The day might have been pleasant, but for a dust-up with some journalists lurking around the apartment shaft, and the discovery about mid-afternoon that she was being followed by two men in very inconspicuous civilian sarongs. Sarongs were last year's fashion; this year it was exotic and whimsical body paint, at least for the brave. Cordelia, wearing her old tan Survey fatigues, lost them by trailing them through a pornographic feelie-show. But they turned up again later in the afternoon as she puttered through the Silica Zoo.

At Mehta's appointed hour the next afternoon the door chimed. Cordelia slouched reluctantly to answer it. How am I going to handle her today? she wondered. I'm running low on inspiration. So tired . . .

Her stomach sank. *Now what?* Framed in the doorway were Mehta, Commodore Tailor, and a husky medtech. That one, Cordelia thought, staring up at him, looks like he could handle *Bothari*. Backing up a bit, she led them into her mother's living room. Her mother retreated to the kitchen, ostensibly to prepare coffee.

Commodore Tailor seated himself and cleared his throat nervously. "Cordelia, I have something to say that will be a little painful, I'm afraid."

Cordelia perched on the arm of a chair and swung her leg back and forth, baring her teeth in what she hoped was a bland smile. "S-sticking you with the dirty work, eh? One of the joys of command. Go ahead."

"We're going to have to ask you to agree to hospitalization for further therapy."

Dear God, here we go. The muscles of her belly trembled beneath her shirt; it was a loose shirt, maybe they wouldn't notice. "Oh? Why?" she inquired casually.

"We're afraid—we're very much afraid that the Barrayaran mind programming you underwent was a lot more extensive than anyone realized. We think, in fact . . ." he paused, taking a deep breath, "that they've tried to make you an agent."

Is that an editorial or an imperial "we," Bill? "Tried, or succeeded?"

Tailor's gaze wavered. Mehta fixed him with a cold stare. "Our opinion is divided on that—"

Note, class, how sedulously he avoids the "I" of personal responsibility—it suggests the worst "we" of all, the guilty "we"—what the hell are they planning?

"—but that letter you sent day before yesterday to the Barrayaran admiral, Vorkosigan—we thought you should have a chance to explain it, first."

"I s-see." You dared! "Not an official l-letter. How could it be? You know Vorkosigan's retired now. But perhaps," her eye nailed Tailor, "you would care to explain by what right you are intercepting and reading my private mail?"

"Emergency security. For the war."

"War's over."

He looked uncomfortable at that. "But the espionage goes on."

Probably true. She had often wondered how Ezar Vorbarra came by the knowledge of the plasma mirrors, until the war the most closely guarded new weapon in the Betan arsenal. Her foot was tapping nervously. She stilled it. "My letter." My heart, on paper—paper wraps stone. . . . She kept her voice cool. "And what did you learn from my letter, Bill?"

"Well, that's a problem. We've had our best cryptographers, our most advanced computer programs, working on it for the better part of two days. Analyzed it right down to the molecular structure of the paper. Frankly," he glanced rather irritably at Mehta, "I'm not convinced they found anything."

No, Cordelia thought, you wouldn't. The secret was in the kiss. Not subject to molecular analysis. She sighed glumly. "Did you send it on, after you were done?"

"Well—I'm afraid there wasn't anything left, by then."

Scissors cut paper. . . . "I'm no agent. I g-give you my word."

Mehta looked up alertly.

"I find it hard to believe, myself," Tailor said.

Cordelia tried to hold his eyes; he looked away. You do believe it, she thought. "What happens if I refuse to have myself committed?"

"Then as your commanding officer, I must order you to do so."

I'll see you in hell first—no. Calm. Must stay calm, keep them taking, maybe I can talk my way out of this yet. "Even if it's against your private judgment?"

"This is a serious security matter. I'm afraid it doesn't admit private judgments."

"Oh, come on. Even Captain Negri has been known to make a private judgment, they say."

She'd said something wrong. The temperature in the room seemed to drop suddenly.

"How do you know about Captain Negri?" said Tailor frozenly.

"Everybody knows about Negri." They were staring at her. "Oh, c-come on! If I were an agent of Negri's, you'd never know it. He's not so inept!"

"On the contrary," said Mehta in a clipped tone, "we think he's so good that *you'd* never know it."

"Garbage!" said Cordelia, disgusted. "How *do* you figure that?"

Mehta answered literally. "My hypothesis is that you are being controlled—unconsciously, perhaps—by this rather sinister and enigmatic Admiral Vorkosigan. That your programming began during your first captivity and was completed, probably, during the late war. You were destined to be the linchpin of a new Barrayaran intelligence network here, to replace the one that was just rooted out. A mole, perhaps, put in place and not activated for years, until some critical moment—"

"Sinister?" Cordelia interrupted. "Enigmatic? Aral? I could laugh." I could weep. . . .

"He is obviously your control," said Mehta complacently. "You have apparently been programmed to obey him unquestioningly."

"I am not a computer." Thump, thump, went her foot. "And Aral is the one person who has *never* constrained me. A point of honor, I believe."

"You see?" said Mehta. To Tailor; she didn't look at Cordelia. "All the evidence points one way."

"Only if you're s-standing on your head!" cried Cordelia, furious. She glared at Tailor. "That's not an order I have to take. I can resign my commission."

"We need not have your permission," said Mehta calmly, "even as a civilian. If your next of kin will agree to it."

"My mother'd never do that to me!"

"We've already discussed it with her, at length. She's very concerned for you."

"I s-see." Cordelia subsided abruptly, glancing toward the kitchen. "I wondered why that coffee was taking so long. Guilty conscience, eh?" She hummed a snatch of tune under her breath, then stopped. "You people have really done your homework. Covered all the exits."

Tailor summoned up a smile and offered it to her, placatingly. "You don't have anything to be afraid of, Cordelia. You'll have our very best people working for—with—"

On, thought Cordelia.

"—you. And when you're done, you'll be able to return to your old life as if none of this had ever happened."

Erase me, will you? Erase *him* . . . Analyze me to death, like my poor timid love letter. She smiled back at him, ruefully. "Sorry, Bill. I just have this awful vision of being p-peeled like an onion, looking for the seeds."

He grinned. "Onions don't have seeds, Cordelia."

"I stand corrected," she said dryly.

"And frankly," he went on, "if you are right and, uh, we are wrong—the fastest way you can prove it is to come along." He smiled the smile of reason.

"Yes, true . . ." But for that little matter of a civil war on Barrayar—that tiny stumbling block—that stone—paper wraps stone . . .

"Sorry, Cordelia." He really was.

"It's all right."

"Remarkable ploy of the Barrayarans," Mehta expounded thoughtfully. "Concealing an espionage ring under the cover of a love affair. I might even have bought it, if the principals had been more likely."

"Yes," Cordelia agreed cordially, writhing within. "One doesn't expect a thirty-four-year-old to fall in love like an adolescent. Quite an unexpected—gift, at my age. Even more unexpected at forty-four, I gather."

"Exactly," said Mehta, pleased by Cordelia's ready understanding. "A middle-aged career officer is hardly the stuff of romance."

Tailor, behind her, opened his mouth as if to speak, then shut it again. He stared meditatively at his hands.

"Think you can cure me of it?" asked Cordelia.

"Oh, yes."

"Ah." Sergeant Bothari, where are you now? Too late. "You leave me no choice. Curious." Delay, whispered her mind. Look for an opportunity. If you can't find one, make one. Pretend this is Barrayar, where anything is possible. "Is it all right if I g-get a shower—change clothes, pack? I assume this is going to be a lengthy business."

"Of course." Tailor and Mehta exchanged a relieved look. Cordelia smiled pleasantly.

Dr. Mehta, without the medtech, accompanied her to her bedroom. Opportunity, thought Cordelia dizzily. "Ah, good," she said, closing the door behind the doctor. "We can chat while I pack."

Sergeant Bothari—there is a time for words, and there is a time when even the very best words fail. You were a man of very few words, but you didn't fail. I wish I'd understood you better. Too late . . .

Mehta seated herself on the bed, watching her specimen, perhaps, as it wriggled on its pin. Her triumph of logical deduction. Are you planning to write a paper on me, Mehta? wondered Cordelia dourly. Paper wraps stone. . . .

She puttered around the room, opening drawers, slamming cabinets. There was a belt—two belts—and a chain belt. There were her identity cards, bank cards, money. She pretended not to see them. As she moved, she talked. Her brain seethed. Stone smashes scissors. . . .

"You know you remind me a bit of the late Admiral Vorrutyer. You both want to take me apart, see what makes me tick. Vorrutyer was more like a little kid, though. Had no intention of picking up his mess afterwards.

"You, on the other hand, will take me apart and not even get a giggle out of it. Of course, you fully intend to put the pieces back together afterwards, but from my point of view that scarcely makes any difference. Aral was right about people in green silk rooms. . . ."

Mehta looked puzzled. "You've stopped stuttering," she noted.

"Yes . . ." Cordelia paused before her aquarium, considering it curiously. "So I have. How strange." Stone smashes scissors. . . .

She removed the top. The old familiar nausea of funk and fear wrung her stomach. She wandered aimlessly behind Mehta, the chain belt and a shirt in her hands. I must choose now. I must choose now. I choose—now!

She lunged, wrapping the belt around the doctor's throat, yanking her arms up behind her back, securing them painfully with the other end of the belt. Mehta emitted a strangled squeak.

Cordelia held her from behind, and whispered in her ear.

"In a moment I'll give you your air back. How long depends on you. You're about to get a short course in the real Barrayaran interrogation techniques. I never used to approve of them, but lately I've come to see they have their uses—when you're in a tearing hurry, for instance—"

Can't let her guess I'm playacting. Playacting. "How many men does Tailor have planted around this building, and what are their positions?"

She loosened the chain slightly. Mehta, eyes stunned with fear, choked, "None!"

"All Cretans are liars," Cordelia muttered. "Bill's not inept either." She dragged the doctor over to the aquarium and pushed her face into the water. She struggled wildly, but Cordelia, larger, stronger, in better training, held her under with a furious strength that astonished herself.

Mehta showed signs of passing out. Cordelia pulled her up and allowed her a couple of breaths.

"Care to revise your estimate yet?" *God help me, what if this doesn't work? They'll never believe I'm not an agent now.*

"Oh, please," Mehta gasped.

"All right, back you go." She held her down again.

The water roiled, splashing over the sides of the aquarium. Cordelia could see Mehta's face through the glass, strangely magnified, deathly yellow in the odd re-flected light from the gravel. Silver bubbles broke around her mouth and flowed up over her face. Cordelia was temporarily fascinated by them. *Air flows like water, underwater,* she thought; *is there an aesthetic of death?*

"Now. How many? Where?"

"No, really!"

"Have another drink."

At her next breath Mehta gasped, "You wouldn't kill me!"

"Diagnosis, Doctor," hissed Cordelia. "Am I a sane woman, pretending to be mad, or a madwoman, pretend-ing to be sane? Grow gills!" Her voice rose uncontrolla-bly. She shoved Mehta back under, and found she was holding her own breath. *And what if she's right and I'm wrong? What if I am an agent, and don't know it? How do you tell a copy from the original? Stone smashes scissors. . . .*

She had a vision, trembling to her fingers, of holding the woman's head under, and under, until her resistance drained away, until unconsciousness took her, and a full count beyond that to assure brain death. Power, opportunity, will—she lacked nothing. So this is what Aral felt at Komarr, she thought. Now I understand—no. Now I *know*.

"How many? Where?"

"Four," Mehta croaked. Cordelia melted with relief. "Two outside the foyer. Two in the garage."

"Thank you," said Cordelia, automatically courteous; but her throat was tightened to a slit and squeezed her words to a smear of sound. "I'm sorry. . . ." She could not tell if Mehta, livid, heard or understood. Paper wraps stone. . . .

She bound and gagged her as she had once seen Vorkosigan do Gottyan. She shoved her down behind the bed, out of sight from the door. She stuffed bank cards, IDs, money, into her pockets. She turned on the shower.

She tiptoed out the bedroom door, breathing raggedly through her mouth. She ached for a minute, just one minute, to collect her shattered balance, but Tailor and the medtech were gone—to the kitchen for coffee, probably. She dared not risk the opening even to pause for boots.

No, God—! Tailor was standing in the archway to the kitchen, just raising a cup of coffee to his lips. She froze, he went still, and they stared at each other.

Her eyes, Cordelia realized, must be huge as some nocturnal animal's. She never could control her eyes.

Tailor's mouth twisted oddly, watching her. Then, slowly, he raised his left hand and saluted her. The incorrect hand, but the other was holding the coffee. He took a sip of his drink, gaze steady over the rim of his cup.

Cordelia came gravely to attention, returned the salute, and slipped quietly out the apartment door.

To her temporary terror, she found a journalist and his vidman in the hallway, one of the most persistent and obnoxious, the one she'd had thrown out of the building yesterday. She smiled at him, dizzy with exhilaration, like a sky diver just stepping into air.

"Still want to do that interview?"

He jumped at the bait.

"Slow down, now. Not here. I'm being watched, you know." She dropped her voice conspiratorially. "The government's doing a cover-up. What I know could blow the administration sky-high. Things about the prisoners. You could—make your reputation."

"Where, then?" He was avid.

"How about the shuttleport? Their bar's quiet. I'll buy you a drink, and we can—plan our campaign." Time ticked in her brain. She expected her mother's apartment door to slam open any second. "It's dangerous, though. There are two government agents up in the foyer and two in the garage. I'd have to get past them without being seen. If it were known I was talking to you, you might not get a chance at a second interview. No rough stuff—just a little quiet disappearance in the night, and the ripple of a rumor about 'gone for medical tests.' Know what I mean?" She was fairly sure he didn't—his media service dealt mainly in sex fantasies—but she could see a vision of journalistic glory growing in his face.

He turned to his vidman. "Jon, give her your jacket, your hat, and your holovid."

She tucked her hair up in the broad-brimmed hat, concealed her fatigues under the jacket, and carried the vid ostentatiously. They took the lift tube up to the garage. There were two men in blue uniforms waiting by its exit. She placed the vid casually on her shoulder, her arm half-concealing her face, as they walked past them to the journalist's groundcar.

At the shuttleport bar she ordered drinks, and took a large gulp of her own. "I'll be right back," she promised, and left him sitting there with the unpaid-for liquor in front of him.

The next stop was the ticket computer. She punched up the schedule. No passenger ships leaving for Escobar for at least six hours. Far too long. The shuttleport would surely be one of the first places searched. A woman in shuttleport uniform walked past. Cordelia collared her.

"Pardon me. Could you help me find out something

about private freighter schedules, or any other private ships leaving soon?"

The woman frowned, then smiled in sudden recognition. "You're Captain Naismith!"

Her heart lurched, and pounded drunkenly. No—steady on . . . "Yes. Um . . . The press have been giving me a rather hard time. I'm sure *you* understand." Cordelia gave the woman a look that raised her to an inner circle. "I want to do this quietly. Maybe we could go to an office? I know *you're* not like *them*. You have a respect for privacy. I can see it in your face."

"You can?" The woman was flattered and excited, and led Cordelia away. In her office she had access to the full traffic control schedules, and Cordelia keyed through them rapidly. "Hm. This looks good. Starts for Escobar within the hour. Has the pilot gone up yet, do you know?"

"That freighter isn't certified for passengers."

"That's all right. I just want to talk to the pilot. Personally. And privately. Can you catch him for me?"

"I'll try." She succeeded. "He'll meet you in Docking Bay 27. But you'll have to hurry."

"Thanks. Um . . . You know, the journalists have been making my life miserable. They'll stop at nothing. There's even a pair who've gone so far as to put on Expeditionary Force uniforms to try and get in. Call themselves Captain Mehta and Commodore Tailor. A real pain. If any of them come sniffing around, do you suppose you could sort of forget you saw me?"

"Why, sure, Captain Naismith."

"Call me Cordelia. You're first-rate! Thanks!"

The pilot was a very young one, getting his first experience on freighters before taking on the larger responsibilities of passenger ships. He too recognized her, and promptly asked for her autograph.

"I suppose you're wondering why you were chosen," she began as she wrote it out for him, without the faintest idea of where she was going, but only with the thought that he looked the sort of person who had never won a contest in his life.

"Me, ma'am?"

"Believe me, the security people went over your life from end to end. You're trustworthy. That's what you are. Really trustworthy."

"Oh—they can't have found out about the cordolite!" Alarm struggled with response to flattery.

"Resourceful, too," Cordelia extemporized, wondering what cordolite was. She'd never heard of it. "Just the man for this mission."

"What mission!"

"Sh, not so loud. I'm on a secret mission for the President. Personally. It's so delicate, even the Department of War doesn't know about it. There'd be heavy political repercussions if it ever got out. I have to deliver a secret ultimatum to the Emperor of Barrayar. But no one must know I've left Beta Colony."

"Am I supposed to take you there?" he asked, amazed. "My freight run—"

I believe I could talk this kid into running me all the way to Barrayar on his employer's fuel, she thought. But it would be the end of his career. Conscience controlled soaring ambition.

"No, no. Your freight run must appear to be exactly the same as usual. I'm to meet a secret contact on Escobar. You'll simply be carrying one article of freight that isn't on the manifest. Me."

"I'm not cleared for passengers, ma'am."

"Good heavens, don't you think we know that? Why do you suppose you were picked over all the other candidates, by the President himself?"

"Wow. And I didn't even vote for him."

He took her aboard the freighter shuttle, and made her a seat among the last-minute cargo. "You know all the big names in Survey, don't you, ma'am? Lightner, Parnell . . . Do you suppose you could ever introduce me?"

"I don't know. But—you will get to meet a lot of the big names from the Expeditionary Force, and Security, when you get back from Escobar. I promise." Will you ever . . .

"May I ask you a personal question, ma'am?"

"Why not? Everyone else does."

"Why are you wearing slippers?"

She stared down at her feet. "I'm—sorry, Pilot Officer Mayhew. That's classified."

"Oh." He went forward to lift ship.

Alone at last, she leaned her forehead against the cool smooth plastic side of a packing case, and wept silently for herself.

CHAPTER FOURTEEN

It was about noon, local time, when the lightflyer she had rented in Vorbarr Sultana brought her over the long lake. The shore was bordered by vine-garlanded slopes backed in turn by steep, scrub-covered hills. The population here was thinly scattered, except around the lake, which had a village at its foot. A cliffed headland at the water's edge was crowned by the ruins of an old fortification. She circled it, rechecking her map on which it was a principle landmark. Counting northward from it past three large properties, she brought her flyer down on a driveway that wound up the slope to a fourth.

A rambling old house built of native stone blended with the vegetation into the side of the hill. She retracted the wings, killed the engine, pocketed the keys, and sat staring uncertainly at its sun-warmed front.

A tall figure in a strange brown and silver uniform ambled around the corner. He bore a weapon in a holster on his hip, and his hand rested on it caressingly. She knew then that Vorkosigan must be nearby, for it was Sergeant Bothari. He looked to be in good health, at least physically.

She hopped out of the lightflyer. "Uh, good afternoon, Sergeant. Is Admiral Vorkosigan at home?"

He stared at her, narrow-eyed, then his face seemed to clear, and he saluted her. "Captain Naismith. Ma'am. Yes."

"You're looking a lot better than when we last met."

"Ma'am?"

"On the flagship. At Escobar."

He looked troubled. "I—can't remember Escobar. Admiral Vorkosigan says I was there."

"I see." Took away your memory, did they? Or did you do it yourself? No telling now. "I'm sorry to hear that. You served bravely."

"Did I? I was discharged, after."

"Oh? What's the uniform?"

"Count Vorkosigan's livery, ma'am. He took me into his personal guard."

"I'm—sure you'll serve him well. May I see Admiral Vorkosigan?"

"He's around back, ma'am. You can go up." He wandered away, evidently making some kind of patrol circuit.

She trudged around the house, the sun warm on her back, kicking at the unaccustomed skirts of her dress and making them swirl about her knees. She had bought it yesterday in Vorbarr Sultana, partly for fun, mostly because her old tan Survey fatigues with the insignia taken off collected stares in the streets. Its dark floral pattern pleased her eye. Her hair hung loose, parted in the middle and held back from her face by two enameled combs, also purchased yesterday.

A little farther up the hill was a garden, surrounded by a low grey stone wall. No, not a garden, she realized as she approached: a graveyard. An old man in old coveralls was working in it, kneeling in the dirt planting young flowers from a flat. He squinted up at her as she pushed through the little gate. She did not mistake his identity. He was a little taller than his son, and his musculature had gone thin and stringy with age, but she saw Vorkosigan in the bones of his face.

"General Count Vorkosigan, sir?" She saluted him

automatically, then realized how peculiar it must look in the dress. He rose stiffly to his feet. "My name is Cap— my name is Cordelia Naismith. I'm a friend of Aral's. I— don't know if he mentioned me to you. Is he here?"

"How do you do, madam." He came more or less to attention, and gave her a courteous half-nod that was achingly familiar. "He said very little, and it did not lead me to think I might meet you." A smile creaked across his face, as if those muscles were stiff from long disuse. "You have no idea how pleased I am to be wrong." He gestured over his shoulder up the hill. "There is a little pavilion at the top of our property, overlooking the lake. He, ah, sits up there most of the time."

"I see." She spotted the path, winding up past the graveyard. "Um. I'm not sure how to put this . . . is he sober?"

He glanced at the sun, and pursed leathery lips. "Probably not, by this hour. When he first came home he only drank after dinner, but the time has been creeping up, gradually. Very disturbing, but there isn't much I can do about it. Although if that gut of his starts bleeding again I may . . ." He broke off, looking her over with intense, uncertain speculation. "He has taken this Escobar failure unnecessarily personally, I think. His resignation was not in the least called for."

She deduced the old Count was not in the Emperor's confidence on this matter, and thought, *it wasn't its failure that slew his spirit, sir; it was its success.* Aloud, she said, "Loyalty to your Emperor was a very great point of honor for him, I know." *Almost its last bastion, and your Emperor chose to flatten it to its foundations in the service of his great need. . . .*

"Why don't you go on up," suggested the old man. "Although, this isn't a very good day for him, I—had better warn you."

"Thank you. I understand."

He stood looking after her as she left the walled enclosure and went on up the winding walk. It was shaded by trees, most of them Earth imports, and some other vegetation that had to be local. The hedge of bush-like things with flowers—she assumed they were flowers, Dubauer would have known—that looked like pink ostrich feathers was particularly striking.

The pavilion was a faintly oriental structure of weathered wood, commanding a fine view of the sparkling lake. Vines climbed it, seeming to claim it for the rocky soil. It was open on all four sides, and furnished with a couple of shabby chaises, a large faded armchair and footstool, and a small table holding two decanters, some glasses, and a bottle of a thick white liquid.

Vorkosigan lay back in the chair, eyes closed, bare feet on the stool, a pair of sandals kicked carelessly over the side. Cordelia paused at the pavilion's edge to study him with a sort of delicate enjoyment. He wore an old pair of black uniform trousers and a very civilian shirt, a loud and unexpected floral print. He obviously had not shaved that morning. His toes, she noticed, had a little wiry black hair on them like the backs of his fingers and hands. She decided she definitely liked his feet; indeed could easily become quite foolishly fond of every part of him. His generally seedy air was less amusing. Tired, and more than tired. Ill.

He opened his eyes to slits and reached for a crystal tumbler filled with an amber liquid, then appeared to change his mind and picked up the white bottle instead. A small measuring cup stood beside it, which he ignored, knocking back a slug of the white liquid directly from its source instead. He sneered briefly at the bottle, then traded it for the crystal tumbler and took a drink, rinsing it around in his mouth and swallowing. He hunched back down in the armchair, at a slightly lower level than before.

"Liquid breakfast?" Cordelia inquired. "Is it as tasty as oatmeal and blue cheese dressing?"

His eyes snapped open. "You," he said hoarsely after a moment, "are not a hallucination." He started to get up, then appeared to think better of it and sank back in frozen self-consciousness. "I never wanted you to see . . ."

She mounted the steps to the shade, pushed a chaise closer to him, and seated herself. Blast, she thought, I've embarrassed him, catching him all awry like this. Off balance. How to put him at his ease? I would have him at his ease, always. . . . "I tried to call ahead, when I first landed yesterday, but I kept missing you. If hallucinations are what you expect, that must be remarkable stuff. Pour me one too, please."

"I think you'd prefer the other." He poured from the second decanter, looking shaken. Curious, she tasted from his glass.

"Faugh! That's not wine."

"Brandy."

"At this hour?"

"If I start after breakfast," he explained, "I can generally achieve total unconsciousness by lunch."

Pretty close to lunch now, she thought. His speech had misled her at first, being perfectly clear, only slower and more hesitant than usual. "There must be less poisonous general anesthetics." The straw-pale wine he had poured her was excellent, although dry for her taste. "You do this every day?"

"God, no." He shuddered. "Two or three times a week at most. One day drinking, the next day being ill—a hangover is quite as good as being drunk for taking your mind off other things—the next day running errands and such for my father. He's slowed down a great deal in the last few years."

He was gradually pulling himself into better focus, as his initial awkward terror of being repellant to her ebbed. He sat up and rubbed his hand over his face in the familiar gesture, as if to scrub away the numbness, and made a stab at light conversation. "That's a pretty dress. A great improvement over those orange things."

"Thanks," she said, falling in immediately with his lead. "I'm sorry I can't say the same for your shirt—does that represent your own taste, by chance?"

"No, it was a gift."

"I'm relieved."

"Something of a joke. Some of my officers got together and purchased it on the occasion of my first promotion to admiral, before Komarr. I always think of them, when I wear it."

"Well, that's nice. In that case I guess I can get used to it."

"Three of the four are dead, now. Two died at Escobar."

"I see." So much for light chitchat. She swirled her wine around in the bottom of her glass. "You look like hell, you know. Pasty."

"Yes, I stopped exercising. Bothari's quite offended."

"I'm glad Bothari didn't get in too much trouble over Vorrutyer."

"It was touch and go, but I got him off. Illyan's testimony helped."

"Yet they discharged him."

"Honorably. On a medical."

"Did you put your father up to hiring him?"

"Yes. It seemed like the right thing to do. He'll never be normal, as we think of it, but at least he has a uniform, and a weapon, and regulations of a sort to follow. It seems to give him an anchor." He ran a finger slowly around the rim of the brandy tumbler. "He was Vorrutyer's batman for four years, you see. He was not too well, when he was first assigned to the *General Vorkraft*. On the verge of a split personality—separating memories, the works. Rather scary. Being a soldier seems to be about the only human role he can meet the demands of. It allows him a kind of self-respect." He smiled at her. "You, on the other hand, look like heaven. Can you, ah—stay long?"

There was a hesitant hunger in his face, soundless desire suppressed by uncertainty. *We have hesitated so long,* she thought, *it's become a habit.* Then it dawned on her that he feared she might only be visiting. *Hell of a long trip for a chat, my love. You* are *drunk.*

"As long as you like. I discovered, when I went home— it was changed. Or I was changed. Nothing fit anymore.

I offended nearly everybody, and left one step ahead of, um, a whole lot of trouble. I can't go back. I resigned my commission—mailed it in from Escobar—and everything I own is in the back of that flyer down there."

She savored the delight that ignited his eyes during this speech, as it finally penetrated that she was here to stay. It contented her.

"I would get up," he said, sliding to the side of his chair, "but for some reason my legs go first and my tongue last. I'd rather fall at your feet in some more controlled fashion. I'll improve shortly. Meantime, will you come sit here?"

"Gladly." She changed chairs. "But won't I squash you? I'm kind of tall."

"Not a bit. I loathe tiny women. Ah, that's better."

"Yes." She nestled down with him, arms around his chest, resting her head on his shoulder, and hooking one leg over him as well, to emphatically complete his capture. The captive emitted something between a sigh and a laugh. She wished they might sit like that forever.

"You'll have to give up this suicide-by-alcohol thing, you know."

He cocked his head. "I thought I was being subtle."

"Not noticeably."

"Well, it suits me. It's extraordinarily uncomfortable."

"Yes, you've worried your father. He gave me the funniest look."

"Not his glare, I hope. He has a very withering glare. Perfected over a lifetime."

"Not at all. He smiled."

"Good God." A grin crinkled the corners of his eyes. She laughed, and craned her neck for a look at his face. That *was* better. . . .

"I'll shave, too," he promised in a burst of enthusiasm.

"Don't go overboard on my account. I came to retire, too. A separate peace, as they say."

"Peace, indeed." He nuzzled her hair, breathing its scent. His muscles unwound beneath her like an overtaut bow unstrung.

❖   ❖   ❖

A few weeks after their marriage they took their first trip together, Cordelia accompanying Vorkosigan on his periodic pilgrimmage to the Imperial Military Hospital in Vorbarr Sultana. They traveled in a groundcar borrowed from the Count, Bothari taking what was evidently his usual role as combination driver and bodyguard. To Cordelia, who was just beginning to know him well enough to see through his taciturn facade, he seemed on edge. He glanced uncertainly over her head, seated between him and Vorkosigan.

"Did you tell her, sir?"

"Yes, everything. It's all right, Sergeant."

Cordelia added encouragingly, "I think you're doing the right thing, Sergeant. I'm, um, very pleased."

He relaxed a little, and almost smiled. "Thank you, Milady."

She studied his profile covertly, her mind ranging over the array of difficulties he would be taking back to the hired village woman at Vorkosigan Surleau this day, gravely doubtful of his ability to handle them. She risked probing a little.

"Have you thought about—what you're going to tell her about her mother, as she grows older? She's bound to want to know eventually."

He nodded, was silent, then spoke. "Going to tell her she's dead. Tell her we were married. It's not a good thing to be a bastard here." His hand tightened on the controls. "So she won't be. No one must call her that."

"I see." Good luck, she thought. She turned to a lighter question. "Do you know what you're going to name her?"

"Elena."

"That's pretty. Elena Bothari."

"It was her mother's name."

Cordelia was surprised into an unguarded remark. "I thought you couldn't remember Escobar!"

A little time went by, and he said, "You can beat the memory drugs, some, if you know how."

Vorkosigan raised his eyebrows. Evidently this was new to him, too. "How do you do that, Sergeant?" he asked, carefully neutral.

"Someone I knew once told me . . . You write down what you want to remember, and think about it. Then hide it—the way we used to hide your secret files from Radnov, sir—they never figured it out either. Then first thing when you get back, before your stomach even settles, take it out and look at it. If you can remember one thing on the list, you can usually get the rest, before they come back again. Then do the same thing again. And again. It helps if you have an, an object, too."

"Did you have, ah, an object?" asked Vorkosigan, clearly fascinated.

"Piece of hair." He fell silent again for a long time, then volunteered, "She had long black hair. It smelled nice."

Cordelia, boggled and bemused by the implications of his story, settled back and found something to look at out the canopy. Vorkosigan looked faintly illuminated, like a man who'd found a key piece in a difficult puzzle. She watched the varied scenery, enjoying the clear sunlight, summer air so cool one needed no protective devices, and the little glimpses of green and water in the hollows of the hills. She also noticed something else. Vorkosigan saw the direction of her glance.

"Ah, you spotted them, did you?"

Bothari smiled slightly.

"The flyer that doesn't outpace us?" said Cordelia. "Do you know who it is?"

"Imperial Security."

"Do they always follow you to the capital?"

"They always follow me all the time. It hasn't been easy to convince people I was serious about retiring. Before you came I used to amuse myself flushing them out. Do things like go drunk driving in my flyer in those canyons to the south on the moonlit nights. It's new. Very fast. That used to drive them to distraction."

"Heavens, that sounds positively lethal. Did you really do that?"

He looked mildly ashamed of himself. "I'm afraid so. I didn't think you'd be coming here, then. It was a thrill.

I hadn't gone adrenaline-tripping on purpose since I was a teenager. The Service rather supplied that need."

"I'm surprised you didn't have a wreck."

"I did, once," he admitted. "Just a minor crack-up. That reminds me, I must check on the repairs. They seem to be taking forever at it. The alcohol made me limp as a rag, I suppose, and I never quite had the nerve to do without the shoulder harness. No harm done, except to the flyer and Captain Negri's agent's nerves."

"Twice," commented Bothari unexpectedly.

"I beg your pardon, Sergeant?"

"You wrecked it twice." The Sergeant's lips twitched. "You don't remember the second time. Your father said he wasn't surprised. We helped, um, pour you out of the safety cage. You were unconscious for a day."

Vorkosigan looked startled. "Are you pulling my leg, Sergeant?"

"No, sir. You can go look at the pieces of the flyer. They're scattered for a kilometer and a half down Dendarii Gorge."

Vorkosigan cleared his throat, and shrunk down in his seat. "I see." He was quiet, then added, "How—unpleasant, to have a blank like that in one's memory."

"Yes, sir," agreed Bothari blandly.

Cordelia glanced up at the following flyer through a gap in the hills. "Have they been watching us all this time? Me, too?"

Vorkosigan smiled at the look on her face. "From the moment you set foot in the Vorbarr Sultana shuttleport, I should imagine. I happen to be politically hot, after Escobar. The press, which is Ezar Vorbarra's third hand here, has me set up as a kind of hero-in-retreat, snatching victory spontaneously from the jaws of defeat and so on—absolute tripe. Makes my stomach hurt, even without the brandy. I should have been able to do a better job, knowing what I knew in advance. Sacrificed too many cruisers, covering the troopships—it had to be traded off that way, sheer arithmetic demanded it, though. . . ."

She could mark by his face as his thoughts wandered

into a well-trodden labyrinth of military might-have-beens. Damn Escobar, she thought, and damn your Emperor, damn Serg Vorbarra and Ges Vorrutyer, damn all the chances of time and place that combined to squeeze a boy's dream of heroism into a man's nightmare of murder, crime, and deceit. Her presence was a great palliative for him, but it was not enough; still something remained unwell in him, out of tune.

As they approached Vorbarr Sultana from the south, the hill country flattened out into a fertile plain, and the population grew more concentrated. The city straddled a broad silver river, with the oldest government buildings, ancient converted fortresses most of them, hugging the bluffs and high points commanding the river's edge. The modern city spilled back from them to the north and south.

The newer government offices, efficient blocky monoliths, were concentrated between. They passed through this complex, making for one of the city's famous bridges to cross the river to the north.

"My God, what happened there?" asked Cordelia, as they passed one whole block of burnt-out buildings, blackened and skeletal.

Vorkosigan smiled sourly. "That *was* the Ministry of Political Education, before the riots two months ago."

"I heard a little about those, at Escobar, on my way here. I had no idea they were so extensive."

"They weren't, really. Quite carefully orchestrated. Personally, I thought it was a damn dangerous way to get the job done. Although I suppose it was a step up in subtlety from Yuri Vorbarra's Defenestration of the Privy Council. A generation of progress, of sorts . . . I didn't think Ezar was going to get that genie back in the bottle, but he seems to have managed it. As soon as Grishnov was killed all the troops they'd called for, which for some reason all seemed to have been diverted to guard the Imperial Residence—" he snorted, "turned up and cleared the streets, and the riot just melted away, except for a few fanatics, and some wounded spirits who'd lost kin at Escobar. That got ugly, but it was suppressed in the news."

They crossed the river and came at length to the large and famous hospital, almost a city within a city, spread out in its walled park. They found Ensign Koudelka alone in his room, lying glumly on his bed in the green uniform pajamas. Cordelia thought at first that he waved to them, but abandoned the idea as his left arm continued to move up and down from the elbow in slow rhythm.

He did sit up and smile as his ex-commander entered, and exchange nods with Bothari. The smile broadened to a grin as he saw her in Vorkosigan's wake. His face was much older than it used to be.

"Captain Naismith, ma'am! Lady Vorkosigan, I should say. I never thought I'd see you again."

"I thought the same. Glad to be mistaken," she smiled back.

"And congratulations, sir. Thanks for sending the note. I sort of missed you the past few weeks, but—I can see you had better things to do." His grin made this comment stingless.

"Thank you, Ensign. Ah—what happened to your arm?"

Koudelka grimaced. "I had a fall this morning. Something's shorted out. Doc should be coming around to fix it in a few minutes. It could have been worse."

The skin on his arms, Cordelia noted, was covered with a network of fine red scars, marking the lines of the prosthetic nerve implants.

"You're walking, then. That's good to hear," Vorkosigan encouraged.

"Yeah, sort of." He brightened. "And at least they've got my guts under control now. I don't care that I can't feel anything from that department, now that I've finally got rid of that damned colostomy."

"Are you in very much pain?" asked Cordelia diffidently.

"Not much," Koudelka tossed off. She felt he was lying. "—but the worst part, besides being so clumsy and out-of-balance, are the sensations. Not pain, but weird things. False intelligence reports. Like tasting colors with your left foot, or feeling things that aren't there, like bugs crawling all over you, or not feeling things that *are* there, like heat . . ." His gaze fell on his bandaged right ankle.

A doctor entered, and conversation stopped while Koudelka removed his shirt. The doctor attached a 'scope to his shoulder, and went fishing for the short circuit with a delicate surgical hand tractor. Koudelka went pale and stared fixedly at his knees, but at last the arm stopped its slow oscillation and lay limply at his side.

"I'm afraid I'm going to have to leave it out of commission for the rest of the day," apologized the doctor. "We'll get it tomorrow when you go in for the work on that adductor group on your right leg."

"Yeah, yeah." Koudelka waved him away with his working right hand, and he gathered his tools and moved on.

"I know it must seem to you to be taking forever," said Vorkosigan, looking at Koudelka's frustrated face, "but it seems to me every time I come in here you've made more progress. You are going to get out of here," he said confidently.

"Yeah, the surgeon says they're going to kick me out in about two months." He smiled. "But they say I'll never be fit for combat again." The smile slid away, and his face crumpled. "Oh, sir! They're going to *discharge* me! All this endless hacking around for *nothing!*" He turned his face away from them, rigid and embarrassed, until his features were under control again.

Vorkosigan too looked away, not inflicting his sympathy, until the ensign looked back again with his smile carefully re-attached. "I can see why," Koudelka said brightly, nodding to the silent Bothari propping up the wall and apparently content just to listen. "A few good body blows like the ones you used to give me in the practice ring, and I'd be flopping around like a fish. *Not* a good example to set my men. I guess I'll just have to find—some kind of desk work." He glanced at Cordelia. "Whatever happened to your ensign, the one that got hit in the head?"

"The last time I saw him, after Escobar—I visited him just two days before I left home, I guess. He's the same.

He did get out of the hospital. His mother quit her job, and stays home to take care of him, now."

Koudelka's eyes fell, and Cordelia was wrenched by the shame in his face. "And I bitch my head off about a few twitches. Sorry."

She shook her head, not trusting herself to speak.

Later, alone with Vorkosigan in the corridor a moment, Cordelia leaned her head against his shoulder, and was taken in his arms. "I can see why you started drinking after breakfast, on the days after this. I could use a stiff one myself, just now."

"I'll take you to lunch after the next stop, and we can all have one," he promised.

The research wing was their next destination. The military doctor in charge greeted Vorkosigan cordially, and only looked a little blank when Cordelia was introduced, without explanation, as Lady Vorkosigan.

"I hadn't realized you were married, sir."

"Recently."

"Oh? Congratulations. I'm glad you decided to come see one of these, sir, before they're all done. It's really almost the most interesting part. Would Milady wish to wait here while we take care of this little business?" He looked embarrassed.

"Lady Vorkosigan has been fully briefed."

"Besides," added Cordelia brightly, "I have a personal interest."

The doctor looked puzzled, but led on to the monitoring room. Cordelia stared doubtfully at the half dozen remaining canisters lined up in a row. The technician on duty joined them trundling some equipment obviously borrowed from some other hospital's obstetrics department.

"Good morning, sir," he said cheerfully. "Going to watch us hatch this chick today?"

"I wish you'd find some other term for it," said the doctor.

"Yes, but you can't call it being born," he pointed out

reasonably. "Technically, they've all been born once already. You tell me what it is, then."

"They call it cracking the bottle at home," suggested Cordelia helpfully, watching the preparations with interest.

The technician, laying out measuring devices and placing a bassinet under a warming light, shot her a look of great curiosity. "You're Betan, aren't you, Milady? My wife caught the Admiral's marriage announcement in the news, way down in the fine print. I never read the vital statistics section, myself."

The doctor looked up, startled, then returned to his checklist. Bothari pretended to lean against the wall, eyes half closed, concealing his sharp attention. The doctor and the technician finished their preparations and motioned them closer.

"Got the soup ready, sir?" muttered the technician to the doctor.

"Right here. Inject into feed line C . . ."

The correct hormone mixture was inserted into the right aperture, the doctor rechecking the instruction disk on his monitor repeatedly.

"Five minute wait, mark—now." The doctor turned to Vorkosigan. "Fantastic machine, sir. Have you heard any more about getting funding and engineering personnel to try and duplicate them?"

"No," replied Vorkosigan. "I'm out of this project officially as soon as the last live child is—released, finished, whatever you call it. You're going to have to work on your own regular superiors for it, and you'll have to think up a military application to justify it, or at least something that sounds like one, to camouflage it."

The doctor smiled thoughtfully. "It's worth pursuing, I think. It might be a nice change from thinking up novel ways of killing people."

"Time mark, sir," said the technician, and he turned back to the current project.

"Placental separation looks good—tightening up just like it's supposed to. You know, the more I study this, the more impressed I am with the surgeons who did the sections on the mothers. We've got to get more medical students off planet, somehow. Getting those placentas out undamaged must be the most—there. There. And there. Break seal." He completed the adjustments and lifted the top. "Cut the membrane—and out she comes. Suction, quickly, please."

Cordelia realized that Bothari, still pinned to the wall, was holding his breath.

The wet and squirming infant took a breath and coughed as the cold air hit her. Bothari breathed too. She looked rather pretty to Cordelia, unbloodied, and much less red and squashed-looking than the vids of vivo newborns she had seen. The infant cried, loud and strong. Vorkosigan jumped, and Cordelia laughed out loud.

"Why, she looks quite perfect." Cordelia hovered at the shoulders of the two medical men, who were making their measurements and taking their samples from their tiny, astonished, bewildered and blinking charge.

"Why is she crying so loudly?" asked Vorkosigan nervously, like Bothari still in his original spot.

Because she knows she's been born on Barrayar, was the comment Cordelia suppressed on her lips. Instead she said, "What, you'd cry too if a bunch of giants hooked you out of a nice warm doze and tossed you around like a bag of beans." Cordelia and the technician exchanged a look half-amused, half-glowering.

"All *right*, Milady," surrendered the technician, as the doctor turned back to his precious machine.

"My sister-in-law says you're supposed to hold them close, like this. Not out at arm's length. I'd squall too if I thought I was being held over a pit about to be dropped. There, baby. Smile or something for Auntie Cordelia. That's it, nice and calm. Were you old enough to remember your mother's heartbeat, I wonder?" She hummed at the infant, who smacked her lips and yawned, and tucked the receiving blanket around her more firmly. "What a long, strange journey you've had."

"Want a look at the inside of this, sir?" the doctor went on. "You, too, Sergeant—you were asking so many questions the last time you were here. . . ."

Bothari shook his head, but Vorkosigan went over for the technical exposition the doctor was obviously itching to supply. Cordelia carried the baby over to the Sergeant.

"Want to hold her?"

"Is it all right, Milady?"

"Heavens, you don't have to ask me for permission. If anything, the other way around."

Bothari picked her up gingerly, his large hands seeming almost to engulf her, and stared into her face. "Are they sure it's the right one? I thought she'd have a bigger nose."

"They've been checked and rechecked," Cordelia reassured him, hoping he wouldn't ask her how she knew. But it seemed a safe assumption. "All babies have little noses. You don't know what kids are going to look like till they're eighteen."

"Maybe she'll look like her mother," he said hopefully. Cordelia seconded the hope, silently.

The doctor finished dragging Vorkosigan through the guts of his dream machine, Vorkosigan politely managing to look only a little unsettled.

"Want to hold her too, Aral?" Cordelia offered.

"Quite all right," he excused himself hastily.

"Get some practice. Maybe you'll need it someday." They exchanged a look of their private hope, and he loosened up and permitted himself to be talked into it.

"Hm. I've held cats with more heft. This isn't really my line." He looked relieved when the medical men repossessed her to complete their technical log.

"Um, let's see," said the doctor. "This is the one we don't take to the Imperial Orphanage, right? Where do we take her, after the observation period?"

"I've been asked to take care of that personally," said Vorkosigan smoothly. "For the sake of her family's privacy. I—Lady Vorkosigan and I, will be delivering her to her legal guardian."

The doctor looked extremely thoughtful. "Oh. I see, sir." He didn't look at Cordelia. "You're the man in charge of the project. You can do what you like with them. No one will ask any questions, I—I assure you, sir," he said earnestly.

"Fine, fine. How long is the observation period?"

"Four hours, sir."

"Good, we can go to lunch. Cordelia, Sergeant?"

"Uh, may I stay here, sir? I'm—not hungry."

Vorkosigan smiled. "Certainly, Sergeant. Captain Negri's men can use the exercise."

On the way to the groundcar, Vorkosigan asked her, "What are you laughing about?"

"I'm not laughing."

"Your eyes are laughing. Twinkling madly, in fact."

"It was the doctor. I'm afraid we combined to mislead him, quite unintentionally. Didn't you catch it?"

"Apparently not."

"He thinks that kid we uncorked today is mine. Or maybe yours. Or perhaps both. I could practically see the wheels turning. He thinks he's finally figured out why you didn't open the stopcocks."

"Good God." He almost turned around.

"No, no, let it go," said Cordelia. "You'll only make it worse if you try to deny it. I know. I've been blamed for Bothari's sins before. Just let him go on wondering." She fell silent. Vorkosigan studied her profile.

"Now what are you thinking? You've lost your twinkle."

"Just wondering what happened to her mother. I'm certain I met her. Long black hair, named Elena, on the flagship—there could only have been one. Incredibly beautiful. I can see how she caught Vorrutyer's eye. But so young, to deal with that sort of horror . . ."

"Women shouldn't be in combat," said Vorkosigan, grimly glum.

"Neither should men, in my opinion. Why did your people try to cover up her memories? Did you order it?"

"No, it was the surgeon's idea. He felt sorry for her." His face was tense and his eyes, distant.

"It was the damnedest thing. I didn't understand it at the time. I do now, I think. When Vorrutyer was done with her—and he outdid himself on her, even by his standards—

she was catatonic. I—it was too late for her, but that's when I decided to kill him, if it happened again, and to hell with the Emperor's script. First Vorrutyer, then the Prince, then myself. Should have left Vorhalas in the clear . . .

"Anyway, Bothari—begged the body from him, so to speak. Took her off to his own cabin. Vorrutyer assumed, to continue torturing her, presumably in imitation of his sweet self. He was flattered, and left them alone. Bothari fuzzed his monitors, somehow. Nobody had the foggiest idea what he was doing in there, every minute of his off duty time. But he came to me with this list of medical supplies he wanted me to sneak to him. Anesthetic salves, some things for treatment of shock, really a well-thought-out list. He was good at first aid, from his combat experience. It occurred to me then that he wasn't torturing her, he just wanted Vorrutyer to think so. He was insane, not stupid. He was in love, in some weird way, and had the mother-wit not to let Vorrutyer guess."

"That doesn't sound altogether insane, under the circumstances," she commented, remembering the plans Vorrutyer had had for Vorkosigan.

"No, but the way he went about it—I caught a glimpse or two." Vorkosigan blew out his breath. "He took care of her in his cabin—fed her, dressed her, washed her—all the while keeping up this whispered dialogue. He supplied both halves. He had apparently worked out this elaborate fantasy in which she was in love with him, married in fact— a normal sane happy couple. Why shouldn't a madman dream of being sane? It must have terrified the hell out of her during her periods of consciousness."

"Lord. I feel almost as sorry for him as I do for her."

"Not quite. He slept with her, too, and I have every reason to believe he didn't limit that marriage fantasy thing to just words. I can see why, I suppose. Can you imagine Bothari getting within a hundred kilometers of such a girl under any normal circumstances?"

"Mm, hardly. The Escobarans fielded their best against you."

"But that, I believe, is what he chose to try and

remember from Escobar. It must have taken incredible strength of will. He was in therapy for months."

"Whew," breathed Cordelia, haunted by the visions his words conjured. She was glad she would have a few hours to settle before seeing Bothari again. "Let's go get that drink now, all right?"

CHAPTER FIFTEEN

Summer was waning when Vorkosigan proposed a trip to Bonsanklar. They were about half packed on the morning selected when Cordelia looked out of their front bedroom window, and said in a constricted voice, "Aral? A flyer just landed out front and there are six armed men getting out of it. They're spreading out all over your property."

Vorkosigan, instantly alert, came to her side to look, then relaxed. "It's all right. Those are Count Vortala's men. He must be coming to visit my father. I'm surprised he found time to break away from the capital just now. I heard the Emperor's been keeping him jumping."

A few minutes later a second flyer landed beside the first, and Cordelia had her first view of Barrayar's new Prime Minister. Prince Serg's description of him as a wrinkled clown was an exaggeration, but a just one; he was a lean man, shrunken with age but still moving briskly. He carried a stick, but from the way he swung it around Cordelia guessed it was an affectation. Clipped white hair fringed a bald and liver-spotted head that shone in the sunshine as he and a pair of aides, or bodyguards, Cordelia was not sure which, passed under her line of sight to the front door.

The two Counts were standing chatting in the front hall as Cordelia and Vorkosigan came down the stairs, the General saying, "Ah, here he comes now."

Vortala looked them over with a bright and penetrating twinkle. "Aral, my boy. Good to see you looking so well. And is this your Betan Penthesileia? Congratulations on a remarkable capture. Milady." He bent over her hand and kissed it with a sort of manic savoir faire.

Cordelia blinked at this description of herself, but managed a "How do you do, sir?" in return. Vortala met her eyes calculatingly.

"Nice that you could get away for a visit, sir," said Vorkosigan. "My wife and I," the phrase was emphasized in his mouth, like a sip of wine with a superior bouquet, "very nearly missed you. I'm promised to take her to the ocean today."

"Just so . . . This isn't a social call, as it happens. I'm playing messenger boy for my master. And my time is unfortunately tight."

Vorkosigan gave a nod. "I'll leave you gentlemen to it, then."

"Ha. Don't try to weasel off on me, boy. The message is for you."

Vorkosigan looked wary. "I didn't think the Emperor and I had anything further to say to each other. I thought I made that clear when I resigned."

"Yes, well, he was perfectly content to have you out of the capital while that dirty work on the Ministry of Political Education was in progress. But I am charged to inform you," he gave a little bow, "that you are requested and required to attend him. This afternoon. Your wife, too," he added as an afterthought.

"Why?" asked Vorkosigan bluntly. "Frankly, Ezar Vorbarra was not in my plans for the day—or any other day."

Vortala grew serious. "He's run out of time to wait for you to get bored in the country. He's dying, Aral."

Vorkosigan blew out his breath. "He's been dying for the last eleven months. Can't he die a little longer?"

Vortala chuckled. "Five months," he corrected absently, then frowned speculation at Vorkosigan. "Hm. Well, it has been very convenient for him. He's flushed more rats out of the wainscotting in the last five months than the past twenty years. You could practically mark the shakedowns in the Ministries by his medical bulletins. One week: condition very grave. Next week: another deputy minister caught out on charges of peculation, or whatever." He became serious again. "But it's the real thing, this time. You must see him today. Tomorrow could be too late. Two weeks from now will definitely be too late."

Vorkosigan's lips tightened. "What does he want me for? Did he say?"

"Ah . . . I believe he has a post in mind for you in the upcoming Regency government. The one you didn't want to hear about at your last meeting."

Vorkosigan shook his head. "I don't think there's a post in the government that would tempt me to step back into that arena. Well, maybe—no. Not even the Ministry of War. It's too damn dangerous. I have a nice quiet life here." His arm circled Cordelia's waist protectively. "We're going to have a family. I'll not risk them in those gladiator politics."

"Yes, I can just picture you, whiling away your twilight years—at age forty-four. Ha! Picking grapes, sailing your boat—your father told me about your sailboat. I hear they're going to rename the village Vorkosigan Sousleau in your honor, by the way—"

Vorkosigan snorted, and they exchanged an ironic bow.

"Anyway, you will have to tell him so yourself."

"I'd be—curious, to see the man," murmured Cordelia. "If it's really the last chance."

Vortala smiled at her, and Vorkosigan yielded, reluctantly. They returned to his bedroom to dress, Cordelia in her most formal afternoon wear, Vorkosigan in the dress greens he had not worn since their wedding.

"Why so jumpy?" asked Cordelia. "Maybe he just wants to bid you farewell or something."

"We're talking about a man who can make even his

own death serve his political purposes, remember? And if there's some way to govern Barrayar from beyond the grave, you can bet he's figured it out. I've never come out ahead on any dealing I've ever had with him."

On that ambiguous note they joined the Prime Minister for the flight back to Vorbarr Sultana.

The Imperial Residence was an old building, almost a museum piece, thought Cordelia, as they climbed the worn granite steps to its east portico. The long facade was heavy with stone carving, each figure an individual work of art, the aesthetic opposite of the modern, faceless Ministry buildings rising a kilometer or two to the east.

They were ushered into a room half hospital, half antique display. Tall windows looked out on the formal gardens and lawns to the north of the Residence. The room's principal inhabitant lay in a huge carved bed inherited from some splendor-minded ancestor, his body pierced in a dozen places by the utilitarian plastic tubes that kept him alive this day.

Ezar Vorbarra was the whitest man Cordelia had ever seen, as white as his sheets, as white as his hair. His skin was white and wrinkled over his sunken cheeks. His eyelids were white, heavy and hooded over hazel eyes whose like she had seen once before, dimly in a mirror. His hands were white, with blue veins standing up on their backs. His teeth, when he spoke, were ivory yellow against their bloodless backdrop.

Vortala and Vorkosigan, and after an uncertain beat Cordelia, went down on one knee beside the bed. The Emperor waved his attendant physician out of the room with a little effortful jerk of one finger. The man bowed and left. They stood, Vortala rather stiffly.

"So, Aral," said the Emperor. "Tell me how I look."

"Very ill, sir."

Vorbarra chuckled, and coughed. "You refresh me. First honest opinion I've heard from anyone in weeks. Even Vortala beats around the bush." His voice cracked, and he cleared his throat of phlegm. "Pissed away the last of my melanin last week. That damned doctor won't let me out into my garden anymore during daylight." He snorted, for disapproval or breath. "So this is your Betan, eh? Come here, girl."

Cordelia approached the bed, and the white old man stared into her face, hazel eyes intent. "Commander Illyan has told me of you. Captain Negri, too. I've seen all your Survey records, you know. And that astonishing flight of fancy of your psychiatrist's. Negri wanted to hire her, just to generate ideas for his section. Vorkosigan, being Vorkosigan, has told me much less." He paused, as if for breath. "Tell me quite truly, now—what do you see in him, a broken-down, ah, what was that phrase? hired killer?"

"Aral has told you something, it seems," she said, startled to hear her own words in his mouth. She stared back at him with equal curiosity. The question seemed to demand an honest answer, and she struggled to frame it.

"I suppose—I see myself. Or someone like myself. We're both looking for the same thing. We call it by different names, and look in different places. I believe he calls it honor. I guess I'd call it the grace of God. We both come up empty, mostly."

"Ah, yes. I recall from your file that you are some sort of theist," said the Emperor. "I am an atheist, myself. A simple faith, but a great comfort to me, in these last days."

"Yes, I have often felt the pull of it myself."

"Hm." He smiled at that. "A very interesting answer, in light of what Vorkosigan said about you."

"What was that, sir?" asked Cordelia, her curiosity piqued.

"You must get him to tell you. It was in confidence. Very poetic, too. I was surprised." He waved her away, as if satisfied, and motioned Vorkosigan closer. Vorkosigan stood in a kind of aggressive parade rest. His mouth was sardonic but his eyes, Cordelia saw, were moved.

"How long have you served me, Aral?" asked the Emperor.

"Since my commission, twenty-six years. Or do you mean body and blood?"

"Body and blood. I always counted it from the day old Yuri's death squad slew your mother and uncle. The night your father and Prince Xav came to me at Green Army Headquarters with their peculiar proposition. Day One of Yuri Vorbarra's Civil War. Why is it never called Piotr Vorkosigan's Civil War, I wonder? Ah, well. How old were you?"

"Eleven, sir."

"Eleven. I was just the age you are now. Strange. So body and blood you have served me—damn, you know this thing is starting to affect my brain, now . . ."

"Thirty-three years, sir."

"God. Thank you. Not much time left."

From the cynical expression on his face Cordelia gathered that Vorkosigan was not in the least convinced of the Emperor's self-proclaimed senility.

The old man cleared his throat again. "I always meant to ask what you and old Yuri said to each other, that day two years later when we finally butchered him in that old castle. I've developed a particular interest in Emperors' last words, lately. Count Vorhalas thought you were playing with him."

Vorkosigan's eyes closed briefly, in pain or memory. "Hardly. Oh, I thought I was eager for the first cut, until he was stripped and held before me. Then—I had this impulse to strike suddenly at his throat, and end it cleanly, just be done with it."

The Emperor smiled sourly, eyes closed. "What a riot that would have started."

"Mm. I think he knew by my face I was funking out. He leered at me. 'Strike, little boy. If you dare while you wear *my* uniform. My uniform on a child.' That was all he said. I said, 'You killed all the children in that room,' which was fatuous, but it was the best I could come up with at the time, then took my cut out of his stomach. I often wished I'd said—said something else, later. But mostly I wished I'd had the guts to follow my first impulse."

"You looked pretty green, out on the parapet in the rain."

"He'd started screaming by then. I was sorry my hearing had come back."

The Emperor sighed. "Yes, I remember."

"You stage-managed it."

"Somebody had to." He paused, resting, then added, "Well, I didn't call you here to chat over old times. Did my Prime Minister tell you my purpose?"

"Something about a post. I told him I wasn't interested, but he refused to convey the message."

Vorbarra closed his eyes wearily and addressed, apparently, the ceiling. "Tell me—Lord Vorkosigan—who should be Regent of Barrayar?"

Vorkosigan looked as if he'd just bitten into something vile, but was too polite to spit it out. "Vortala."

"Too old. He'd never last sixteen years."

"The Princess, then."

"The General Staff would eat her alive."

"Vordarian?"

The Emperor's eyes snapped open. "Oh, for God's sake! Gather your wits, boy."

"He does have some military background."

"We will discuss his drawbacks at length—if the doctors give me another week to live. Have you any other jokes, before we get down to business?"

"Quintillan of the Interior. And that is not a joke."

The Emperor grinned yellowly. "So you do have something good to say for my Ministers after all. I may die now; I've heard everything."

"You'd never get a vote of consent out of the Counts for anyone without a Vor in front of his name," said Vortala. "Not even if he walked on water."

"So, make him one. Give him a rank to go with the job."

"Vorkosigan," said Vortala, aghast, "he's not of the warrior caste!"

"Neither are many of our best soldiers. We're only Vor because some dead Emperor declared one of our dead ancestors so. Why not start the custom up again, as a reward for merit? Better yet, declare everybody a Vor and be done with the whole bloody nonsense forever."

The Emperor laughed, then choked and coughed, sputtering. "Wouldn't that pull the rug out from under the People's Defense League? What an attractive counterproposal to assassinating the aristocracy! I don't believe the most wild-eyed of them could come up with a more radical proposal. You're a dangerous man, Lord Vorkosigan."

"You asked for my opinion."

"Yes, indeed. And you always give it to me. Strange." The Emperor sighed. "You can quit wriggling, Aral. You shall not wriggle out of this.

"Allow me to put it in a capsule. What the Regency requires is a man of impeccable rank, no more than middle-aged, with a strong military background. He should be popular with his officers and men, well-known to the public, and above all respected by the General Staff. Ruthless enough to hold near-absolute power in this madhouse for sixteen years, and honest enough to hand over that power at the end of those sixteen years to a boy who will no doubt be an idiot—I was, at that age, and as I recall, so were you—and, oh yes, happily married. Reduces the temptation of becoming bedroom Emperor via the Princess. In short, yourself."

Vortala grinned. Vorkosigan frowned. Cordelia's stomach sank.

"Oh, no," said Vorkosigan whitely. "You're not going to lay that thing on me. It's grotesque. Me, of all men, to step into his father's shoes, speak to him with his father's voice, become his mother's advisor—it's worse than grotesque. It's obscene. No."

Vortala looked puzzled at his vehemence. "A little decent reticence is one thing, Aral, but let's not go overboard. If you're worried about the vote, it's already bagged. Everyone can see you're the man of the hour."

"Everyone most certainly will not. Vordarian will become my instant enemy, and so will the Minister of the West. And as for absolute power, you sir, know what a false chimera that notion is. A shaky illusion, based on—God knows what. Magic. Sleight of hand. Believing your own propaganda."

The Emperor shrugged, carefully, cautious of dislodging his tubing. "Well, it won't be my problem. It will be Prince Gregor's, and his mother's. And that of—whatever individual can be persuaded to stand by them, in their hour of need. How long do you think they could last, without help? One year? Two?"

"Six months," muttered Vortala.

Vorkosigan shook his head. "You pinned me with that 'what if' argument before Escobar. It was false then—although it took me some time to realize it—and it's false now."

"Not false," the Emperor denied. "Either then or now. I must so believe."

Vorkosigan yielded a little. "Yes. I can see that you must." His face tensed in frustration, as he contemplated the man in the bed. "Why must it be me? Vortala has more political acuity. The Princess has a better right. Quintillan has a better grasp of internal affairs. You even have better military strategists. Vorlakial. Or Kanzian."

"You can't name a third, though," murmured the Emperor.

"Well—perhaps not. But you must see my point. I am not the irreplaceable man which for some reason you choose to imagine me."

"On the contrary. You have two unique advantages, from my point of view. I have kept them in mind from the day we killed old Yuri. I always knew I wouldn't live forever—too many latent poisons in my chromosomes, absorbed when I was fighting the Cetagandans as your father's military apprentice, and careless about my clean techniques, not expecting to live to grow old." The Emperor smiled again, and focused on Cordelia's intent, uncertain face. "Of the five men with a better right by blood and law to the Imperium of Barrayar than mine, your name heads the list. Ha—" he added, "I was right. Didn't think you'd told her that. Tricky, Aral."

Cordelia, faint, turned wide grey eyes to Vorkosigan. He shook his head irritably, "Not true. Salic descent."

"A debate we shall not continue here. Be that as it may,

anyone who wishes to dislodge Prince Gregor using argument based on blood and law must first either get rid of you, or offer you the Imperium. We all know how hard you are to kill. And you are the one man—the only man on that list who I am absolutely certain, by the scattered remains of Yuri Vorbarra, *truly* does not wish to be Emperor. Others may believe you coy. I know better."

"Thank you for that, sir." Vorkosigan looked extremely saturnine.

"As an inducement, I point out that you can be no better placed to prevent that eventuality than as Regent. Gregor is your lifeline, boy. Gregor is all that stands between you, and being targeted. Your hope of heaven."

Count Vortala turned to Cordelia. "Lady Vorkosigan. Won't you lend us your vote? You seem to have come to know him very well. Tell him he's the man for the job."

"When we came up here," said Cordelia slowly, "with this vague talk of a post, I thought I might urge him to take it up. He needs work. He's made for it. I confess I wasn't anticipating that offer." She stared at the Emperor's embroidered bedspread, caught by its intricate patterns and colors. "But I've always thought—tests are a gift. And great tests are a great gift. To fail the test is a misfortune. But to refuse the test is to refuse the gift, and something worse, more irrevocable, than misfortune. Do you understand what I'm saying?"

"No," said Vortala.

"Yes," said Vorkosigan.

"I've always felt that theists were more ruthless than atheists," said Ezar Vorbarra.

"If you think it's really wrong," said Cordelia to Vorkosigan, "that's one thing. Maybe that's the test. But if it's only fear of failure—you have not the right to refuse the gift for that."

"It's an impossible job."

"That happens, sometimes."

He took her aside, quietly, to the tall windows. "Cordelia—you have not the first conception of what kind of life it would be. Did you think our public men

surrounded themselves with liveried retainers for decoration? If they have a moment's ease, it is at the cost of
twenty men's vigilance. No separate peace permitted.
Three generations of Emperors have spent themselves
trying to untangle the violence in our affairs, and we're
still not come to the end of it. I haven't the hubris to
think I can succeed where *he* failed." His eyes flicked in
the direction of the great bed.

Cordelia shook her head. "Failure doesn't frighten me
as much as it used to. But I'll quote you a quote, if you
like. 'Exile, for no other motive than ease, would be the
last defeat, with no seed of future victory in it.' I thought
the man who said that was on to something."

Vorkosigan turned his head, to some unfocused distance. "It's not the desire for ease I'm talking about now.
It's fear. Simple, squalid terror." He smiled ruefully at her.
"You know, I fancied myself quite a bravo once, until I
met you and rediscovered funk. I'd forgotten what it was
to have my heart in the future."

"Yeah, me too."

"I don't have to take it. I can turn it down."

"Can you?" Their eyes met.

"It's not the life you were anticipating, when you left
Beta Colony."

"I didn't come for a life. I came for you. Do you want
it?"

He laughed, shakily. "God, what a question. It's the
chance of a lifetime. Yes. I want it. But it's poison,
Cordelia. Power is a bad drug. Look what it did to *him*.
He was sane too, once, and happy. I think I could turn
down almost any other offer without a blink."

Vortala leaned on his stick ostentatiously, and called
across the room, "Make up your mind, Aral. My legs are
beginning to ache. But for your delicacy—it's a job any
number of men I know would kill for. And you're getting it offered free and clear."

Only Cordelia and the Emperor knew why Vorkosigan
barked a short laugh at this. He sighed, gazed at his
master, and nodded.

"Well, old man. I thought you might find a way to rule from your grave."

"Yes. I propose to haunt you continually." A little silence fell while the Emperor digested his victory. "You'll need to start assembling your personal staff immediately. I'm willing Captain Negri to my grandson and the Princess, for Security. But I thought perhaps you might like to have Commander Illyan, for yourself."

"Yes. I think he and I might deal very well together." A pleasant thought seemed to strike a light in Vorkosigan's dark face. "And I know just the man for the job of personal secretary. He'll need a promotion for it—a lieutenancy."

"Vortala will take care of it for you." The Emperor lay back wearily, and cleared his throat of phlegm again, lips leaden. "Take care of it all. I suppose you'd better send that doctor back in." He waved them out with a tired twitch of one hand.

Vorkosigan and Cordelia emerged from the Imperial Residence into the warm air of the late summer evening, soft and grey with humidity from the nearby river. They were trailed by their new bodyguards, trim in the familiar black uniforms. There had been a lengthy conference with Vortala, Negri, and Illyan. Cordelia's head swam with the number and detail of subjects covered. Vorkosigan, she'd noticed enviously, seemed to have no trouble keeping up; indeed, he'd set the pace.

His face seemed focused, more electric than she'd seen it since she'd come to Barrayar, filled with an eager tension. *He's alive again,* she thought. *Looking out, not in; forward, not back. Like when I first met him. I'm glad. Whatever the risks.*

Vorkosigan snapped his fingers and said "Tabs," out loud, cryptically. "First stop Vorkosigan House."

They had driven past the Count's official residence on their last trip to Vorbarr Sultana, but this was the first time Cordelia had been in it. Vorkosigan took the wide circular staircase two steps at a time to his own room. It was a large chamber, simply furnished, overlooking the back garden. It had the same feel as Cordelia's own room in her mother's apartment, of frequent and prolonged disoccupation, with archeological layers of past passions stuffed into drawers and closets.

Not surprisingly, there was evidence of interest in all kinds of strategy games, and civil and military history. More surprising was a portfolio of yellowing pen-and-ink drawings, run across as he sorted through a drawer full of medals, mementos, and pure junk.

"Did you do these?" Cordelia asked curiously. "They're pretty good."

"When I was a teenager," he explained, still sorting. "Some later. I gave it up in my twenties. Too busy."

His medal and campaign ribbon collection showed a peculiar history. The early, lesser ones were carefully arranged and displayed on velvet-covered cards, with notes attached. The later, greater ones were piled haphazardly in a jar. One, which Cordelia recognized as a high Barrayaran award for valor, was shoved loose in the back of the drawer, its ribbon crumpled and tangled.

She sat on his bed and sorted through the portfolio. They were mostly meticulous architectural studies, but also a few figure studies and portraits done in a less certain style. There were several of a striking young woman with short dark curls, both clothed and nude, and Cordelia realized with a shock from the notes on them that she was looking at Vorkosigan's first wife. She had seen no other pictures of her anywhere in his things. There were also three studies of a laughing young man labeled "Ges" that seemed hauntingly familiar. She mentally added forty pounds and twenty years to him, and the room seemed to tilt as she recognized Admiral Vorrutyer. She closed the portfolio back up quietly.

Vorkosigan finally found what he was looking for; a couple of sets of old red lieutenant's tabs. "Good. It was quicker than going by headquarters."

At the Imperial Military Hospital they were stopped by a male nurse. "Sir? Visiting hours are over, sir."

"Did no one call from headquarters? Where's that surgeon?"

Koudelka's surgeon, the man who had worked on, or over, him with the hand tractor during Cordelia's first visit, was routed out at last.

"Admiral Vorkosigan, sir. No, of course visiting hours don't apply to him. Thank you, corpsman, dismissed."

"I'm not visiting this time, Doctor. Official business. I mean to relieve you of your patient tonight, if it's physically possible. Koudelka's been reassigned."

"Reassigned? He was to be discharged in a week! Reassigned to what? Hasn't anybody read my reports? He can barely walk."

"He won't need to. His new assignment is all desk work. I trust you have his hands working?"

"Pretty well."

"Any medical work left to be done?"

"Nothing important. A few last tests. I was just holding him to the end of the month, so he would have completed his fourth year. Thought it would help his pension a bit, such as it is."

Vorkosigan sorted through the papers and disks, and handed the pertinent ones to the doctor. "Here. Cram this in your computer and get his release signed. Come on, Cordelia, let's go surprise him." He looked happier than he had all day.

They entered Koudelka's room to find him still dressed for the day in black fatigues, struggling with a therapeutic hand coordination exercise and cursing under his breath.

"Hello, sir," he greeted Vorkosigan absently. "The trouble with this damn tin-foil nervous system is that you can't *teach* it anything. Practice only helps the organic parts. I swear some days I could beat my head on the wall." He gave up the exercise with a sigh.

"Don't do that. You're going to need it in the days to come."

"I suppose so. It was never my best part, though." He stared, abstracted and downcast, at the board, then remembered to be cheerful for his commander. Looking up, he noticed the time. "What are you doing here at this hour, sir?"

"Business. Just what are your plans for the next few weeks, Ensign?"

"Well, they're discharging me next week, you know. I'll go home for a while. Then start looking for work, I guess. I don't know what kind."

"Too bad," said Vorkosigan, keeping his face straight. "I hate to make you alter your plans, Lieutenant Koudelka, but you've been reassigned." And laid on his bedside tray, in order, like a fine hand of cards, Koudelka's newly cut orders, his promotion, and a pair of red collar tabs.

Cordelia had never enjoyed Koudelka's expressive face more. It was a study in bewilderment and rising hope. He picked up the orders carefully and read them through.

"Oh, sir! I know this isn't a joke, but it's got to be a mistake! Personal secretary to the Regent-elect—I don't know anything about the work. It's an impossible job."

"Do you know, that's almost exactly what the Regent-elect said about his job, when he was first offered it," said Cordelia. "I guess you'll both have to learn them together."

"How did he come to pick me? Did you recommend me, sir? Come to think of it . . ." He turned the orders over, reading them through again, "who is the Regent going to be, anyway?" He raised his eyes to Vorkosigan, and made the connection at last. "My God," he whispered. He did not, as Cordelia thought he might, grin and congratulate, but instead looked quite serious. "It's—a hell of a job, sir. But I think the government's finally done something right. I'd be proud to serve you again. Thank you."

Vorkosigan nodded, in agreement and acceptance.

Koudelka did grin, when he picked up the promotion order. "Thanks for this, too, sir."

"Don't thank me too soon. I intend to sweat blood out of you in return."

Koudelka's grin widened. "Nothing new about that." He fumbled clumsily with the collar tabs.

"May I do that, Lieutenant?" asked Cordelia. He looked up defensively. "For my pleasure," she added.

"It would be an honor, Milady."

Cordelia fastened them to his collar straightly, with the greatest care, and stepped back to admire her work. "Congratulations, Lieutenant."

"You can get shiny new ones tomorrow," Vorkosigan said. "But I thought these would do for tonight. I'm springing you out of here now. We'll put you up at the Count my father's Residence tonight, because work starts tomorrow at dawn."

Koudelka fingered the red rectangles. "Were they yours, sir?"

"Once. I hope they don't bring you my luck, which was always vile, but—wear them in good health."

Koudelka gave him a nod, and a smile. He clearly found Vorkosigan's gesture profoundly meaningful, exceeding his capacity for words. But the two men understood each other perfectly well without them. "Don't think I want new ones, sir. People would just think I'd been an ensign yesterday."

Later, lying warm in the darkness in Vorkosigan's room in the Count's town house, Cordelia remembered a curiosity. "What did you say to the Emperor, about me?"

He stirred beside her, and pulled the sheet tenderly up over her bare shoulder, tenting them together. "Hm? Oh, that." He hesitated. "Ezar had been questioning me about you, in our argument about Escobar. Implied that you had affected my nerve, for the worse. I didn't know then if I'd ever see you again. He wanted to know what I saw in you. I told him . . ." he paused again, and then continued almost shyly, "that you poured out honor like a fountain, all around you."

"That's weird. I don't feel full of honor, or anything else, except maybe confusion."

"Naturally not. Fountains keep nothing for themselves."

AFTERMATHS

The shattered ship hung in space, a black bulk in the darkness. It still turned, imperceptibly slowly; one edge eclipsed and swallowed the bright point of a star. The lights of the salvage crew arced over the skeleton. Ants, ripping up a dead moth, Ferrell thought. Scavengers . . .

He sighed dismay into his forward observation screen, and pictured the ship as it had been, scant weeks before. The wreckage untwisted in his mind—a cruiser, alive with patterns of gaudy lights that always made him think of a party seen across night waters. Responsive as a mirror to the mind under its Pilot's headset, where man and machine penetrated the interface and became one. Swift, gleaming, functional . . . no more. He glanced to his right, and cleared his throat self-consciously.

"Well, Medtech," he spoke to the woman who stood beside his station, staring into the screen as silently and long as he had. "There's our starting point. Might as well go ahead and begin the pattern sweep now, I suppose.

"Yes, please do, Pilot Officer." She had a gravelly alto voice, suitable for her age, which Ferrell judged to be about forty-five. The collection of thin silver five-year service chevrons on her left sleeve made an impressive glitter against the dark red uniform of the Escobaran military medical service. Dark hair shot with grey, cut short for ease of maintenance, not style; a matronly heaviness to her hips. A veteran, it appeared. Ferrell's sleeve had yet to sprout even his first-year stripe, and his hips, and the rest of his body, still maintained an unfilled adolescent stringiness.

But she was only a tech, he reminded himself, not even a physician. He was a full-fledged Pilot Officer. His neurological implants and biofeedback training were all complete. He was certified, licensed, and graduated— just three frustrating days too late to participate in what was now being dubbed the 120 Day War. Although in fact it had only been 118 days and part of an hour between the time the spearhead of the Barrayaran invasion fleet penetrated Escobaran local space, and the time the last survivors fled the counterattack, piling through the wormhole exit for home as though scuttling for a burrow.

"Do you wish to stand by?" he asked her.

She shook her head. "Not yet. This inner area has been pretty well worked over in the last three weeks. I wouldn't expect to find anything on the first four turns, although it's good to be thorough. I've a few things to arrange yet in my work area, and then I think I'll get a catnap. My department has been awfully busy the last few months," she added apologetically. "Understaffed, you know. Please call me if you do spot anything, though—I prefer to handle the tractor myself, whenever possible."

"Fine by me." He swung about in his chair to his comconsole. "What minimum mass do you want a bleep for? About forty kilos, say?"

"One kilo is the standard I prefer."

"One kilo!" He stared. "Are you joking?"

"Joking?" She stared back, then seemed to arrive at enlightenment. "Oh, I see. You were thinking in terms of whole—I can make positive identification with quite small pieces, you see. I wouldn't even mind picking up smaller bits than that, but if you go much under a kilo you spend too much time on false alarms from micrometeors and other rubbish. One kilo seems to be the best practical compromise."

"Bleh." But he obediently set his probes for a mass of one kilo, minimum, and finished programming the search sweep.

She gave him a brief nod and withdrew from the closet-sized Navigation and Control Room. The obsolete courier ship had been pulled from junkyard orbit and hastily overhauled with some notion first of converting it into a personnel carrier for middle brass—top brass in a hurry having a monopoly on the new ships—but like Ferrell himself, it had graduated too late to participate. So they both had been re-routed together, he and his first command, to the dull duties he privately thought on a par with sanitation engineering, or worse.

He gazed one last moment at the relic of battle in the forward screen, its structural girdering poking up like bones through sloughing skin, and shook his head at the waste of it all. Then, with a little sigh of pleasure, he pulled his headset down into contact with the silvery circles on his temples and midforehead, closed his eyes, and slid into control of his own ship.

Space seemed to spread itself all around him, buoyant as a sea. He was the ship, he was a fish, he was a merman; unbreathing, limitless, and without pain. He fired his engines as though flame leapt from his fingertips, and began the slow rolling spiral of the search pattern.

"Medtech Boni?" he keyed the intercom to her cabin. "I believe I have something for you here."

She rubbed sleep from her face, framed in the intercom screen. "Already? What time—oh. I must have been tireder than I realized. I'll be right up, Pilot Officer."

Ferrell stretched, and began an automatic series of isometrics in his chair. It had been a long and uneventful watch. He would have been hungry, but what he contemplated now through the viewscreens subdued his appetite.

Boni appeared promptly, and slid into the seat beside him. "Oh, quite right, Pilot Officer." She unshipped the controls to the exterior tractor beam, and flexed her fingers before taking a delicate hold.

"Yeah, there wasn't much doubt about that one," he agreed, leaning back and watching her work. "Why so tender with the tractors?" he asked curiously, noting the low power level she was using.

"Well, they're frozen right through, you know," she replied, not taking her eyes from her readouts. "Brittle. If you play hotshot and bang them around, they can shatter. Let's stop that nasty spin, first," she added, half to herself. "A slow spin is all right. Seemly. But that fast spinning you get sometimes—it must be very unrestful for them, don't you think?"

His attention was pulled from the thing in the screen, and he stared at her. "They're *dead*, lady!"

She smiled slowly as the corpse, bloated from decompression, limbs twisted as though frozen in a strobe-flash of convulsion, was drawn gently toward the cargo bay. "Well, that's not their fault, is it?—one of our fellows, I see by the uniform."

"Bleh!" he repeated himself, then gave vent to an embarrassed laugh. "You act like you enjoy it."

"Enjoy? No . . . But I've been in Personnel Retrieval and Identification for nine years, now. I don't mind. And of course, vacuum work is always a little nicer than planetary work."

"Nicer? With that godawful decompression?"

"Yes, but there are the temperature effects to consider. No decomposition."

He took a breath, and let it out carefully. "I see. I guess you would get—pretty hardened, after a while. Is it true you guys call them corpse-sicles?"

"Some do," she admitted. "I don't."

She maneuvered the twisted thing carefully through the cargo bay doors and keyed them shut. "Temperature set for a slow thaw and he'll be ready to handle in a few hours," she murmured.

"What do you call them?" he asked as she rose.

"People."

She awarded his bewilderment a small smile, like a

salute, and withdrew to the temporary mortuary set up next to the cargo bay.

On his next scheduled break he went down himself, drawn by morbid curiosity. He poked his nose around the doorframe. She was seated at her desk. The table in the center of the room was yet unoccupied.

"Uh—hello."

She looked up with her quick smile. "Hello, Pilot Officer. Come on in."

"Uh, thank you. You know, you don't really have to be so formal. Call me Falco, if you want," he said, entering.

"Certainly, if you wish. My first name is Tersa."

"Oh, yeah? I have a cousin named Tersa."

"It's a popular name. There were always at least three in my classes at school." She rose, and checked a gauge by the door to the cargo bay. "He should be just about ready to take care of, now. Pulled to shore, so to speak."

Ferrell sniffed, and cleared his throat, wondering whether to stay or excuse himself. "Grotesque sort of fishing." *Excuse myself, I think.*

She picked up the control lead to the float pallet, and trailed it after her into the cargo bay. There were some thumping noises, and she returned, the pallet drifting behind her. The corpse was in the dark blue of a deck officer, and covered thickly with frost, which flaked and dripped upon the floor as the medtech slid it onto the examining table. Ferrell shivered with disgust.

Definitely excuse myself. But he lingered, leaning against the doorframe at a safe distance.

She pulled an instrument, trailing its lead to the computers, from the crowded rack above the table. It was the size of a pencil, and emitted a thin blue beam of light when aligned with the corpse's eyes.

"Retinal identification," Tersa explained. She pulled down a pad-like object, similarly connected, and pressed it to each of the monstrosity's hands. "And fingerprints," she went on. "I always do both, and cross-match. The eyes can get awfully distorted. Errors in identification can be brutal for the families. Hm. Hm." She checked her read-out screen. "Lieutenant Marco Deleo. Age twenty-nine. Well, Lieutenant," she went on chattily, "let's see what I can do for you."

She applied an instrument to its joints, which loosened them, and began removing its clothes.

"Do you often talk to—them?" inquired Ferrell, unnerved.

"Always. It's a courtesy, you see. Some of the things I have to do for them are rather undignified, but they can still be done with courtesy."

Ferrell shook his head. "I think it's obscene, myself."

"Obscene?"

"All this horsing around with dead bodies. All the trouble and expense we go to collecting them. I mean, what do they care? Fifty or a hundred kilos of rotting meat. It'd be cleaner to leave them in space."

She shrugged, unoffended, undiverted from her task. She folded the clothes and inventoried the pockets, laying out their contents in a row.

"I rather like going through the pockets," she remarked. "It reminds me of when I was a little girl, visiting in someone else's home. When I went upstairs by myself, to go to the bathroom or whatever, it was always a kind of pleasure to peek into the other rooms, and see what kind of things they had, and how they kept them. If they were very neat, I was always very impressed—I've never been able to keep my own things neat. If it was a mess, I felt I'd found a secret kindred spirit. A person's things can be a kind of exterior morphology of their mind—like a snail's shell, or something. I like to imagine what kind of person they were, from what's in the pockets. Neat, or messy. Very regulation, or full of personal things . . . Take Lieutenant Deleo, here. He must have been very conscientious. Everything regulation, except this little vid disc from home. From his wife, I'd imagine. I think he must have been a very nice person to know."

She placed the collection of objects carefully into its labeled bag.

"Aren't you going to listen to it?" asked Ferrell.

"Oh, no. That would be prying."

He barked a laugh. "I fail to see the distinction."

"Ah." She completed the medical examination, readied the plastic body bag, and began to wash the corpse. When she worked her way down to the careful cleaning around the genital area, necessary because of sphincter relaxation, Ferrell fled at last.

That woman is nuts, he thought. I wonder if it's the cause of her choice of work, or the effect?

It was another full day before they hooked their next fish. Ferrell had a dream, during his sleep cycle, about being on a deep-sea boat, and hauling up nets full of corpses to be dumped, wet and shining as though with iridescent scales, in a huge pile in the hold. He awoke from it sweating, but with very cold feet. It was with profound relief that he returned to the pilot's station, and slid into the skin of his ship. The ship was clean, mechanical and pure, immortal as a god; one could forget one had ever owned a sphincter muscle.

"Odd trajectory," he remarked, as the medtech again took her place at the tractor controls.

"Yes . . . Oh, I see. He's a Barrayaran. He's a long way from home."

"Oh, bleh. Throw him back."

"Oh, no. We have identification files for all their missing. Part of the peace settlement, you know, along with prisoner exchange."

"Considering what they did to our people as prisoners, I don't think we owe them a thing."

She shrugged.

The Barrayaran officer had been a tall, broadshouldered man, a commander by the rank on his collar tabs. The medtech treated him with the same care she had expended on Lieutenant Deleo, and more. She went to considerable trouble to smooth and straighten him, and massage the mottled face back into some semblance of manhood with her fingertips, a process Ferrell watched with a rising gorge.

"I wish his lips wouldn't curl back *quite* so much," she remarked, while at this task. "Gives him what I imagine to be an uncharacteristically snarly look. I think he must have been rather handsome."

One of the objects in his pockets was a little locket. It held a tiny glass bubble filled with a clear liquid. The inside of its gold cover was densely engraved with the elaborate curlicues of the Barrayaran alphabet.

"What is it?" asked Ferrell curiously.

She held it pensively to the light. "It's a sort of charm, or memento. I've learned a lot about the Barrayarans in the last three months. Turn ten of them upside down and you'll find some kind of good luck charm or amulet or medallion or something in the pockets of nine of them. The high-ranking officers are just as bad as the enlisted people."

"Silly superstition."

"I'm not sure if it's superstition or just custom. We treated an injured prisoner once—he claimed it was just custom. People gave them to the soldiers as presents, and that nobody really believes in them. But when we took his away from him, when we were undressing him for surgery, he tried to fight us for it. It took three of us to hold him down for the anesthetic. I thought it a rather remarkable performance for a man whose legs had been blown away. He wept. . . . Of course, he was in shock."

Ferrell dangled the locket on the end of its short chain, intrigued in spite of himself. It hung with a companion piece, a curl of hair embedded in a plastic pendant.

"Some sort of holy water, is it?" he inquired.

"Almost. It's a very common design. It's called a mother's tears charm. Let me see if I can make out— he's had it a while, it seems. From the inscription—I think that says 'ensign,' and the date—it must have been given him on the occasion of his commission."

"It's not really his mother's tears, is it?"

"Oh, yes. That's what's supposed to make it work, as a protection."

"Doesn't seem to be very effective."

"No, well . . . no."

Ferrell snorted ironically. "I hate those guys—but I do guess I feel sort of sorry for his mother."

Boni retrieved the chain and its pendants, holding the curl in plastic to the light and reading its inscription. "No, not at all. She's a fortunate woman."

"How so?"

"This is her death lock. She died three years ago, by this."

"Is that supposed to be lucky, too?"

"No, not necessarily. Just a remembrance, as far as I know. Kind of a nice one, really. The nastiest charm I ever ran across, and the most unique, was this little leather bag hung around a fellow's neck. It was filled with dirt and leaves, and what I took at first to be some sort of little frog-like animal skeleton, about ten centimeters long. But when I looked at it more closely, it turned out to be the skeleton of a human fetus. Very strange. I suppose it was some sort of black magic. Seemed an odd thing to find on an engineering officer."

"Doesn't seem to work for any of them, does it?"

She smiled wryly. "Well, if there are any that work, I wouldn't see them, would I?"

She took the processing one step further, by cleaning the Barrayaran's clothes and carefully re-dressing him, before bagging him and returning him to the freeze.

"The Barrayarans are all so army-mad," she explained. "I always like to put them back in their uniforms. They mean so much to them, I'm sure they're more comfortable with them on."

Ferrell frowned uneasily. "I still think he ought to be dumped with the rest of the garbage."

"Not at all," said the medtech. "Think of all the work he represents on somebody's part. Nine months of pregnancy, childbirth, two years of diapering, and that's just the beginning. Tens of thousands of meals, thousands of bedtime stories, years of school. Dozens of teachers. And all that military training, too. A lot of people went into making him."

She smoothed a strand of the corpse's hair into place. "That head held the universe, once. He had a good rank for his age," she added, rechecking her monitor. "Thirty-two. Commander Aristede Vorkalloner. It has a kind of nice ethnic ring. Very Barrayaranish, that name. Vor, too, one of those warrior-class fellows."

"Homicidal-class loonies. Or worse," Ferrell said automatically. But his vehemence had lost momentum, somehow.

Boni shrugged, "Well, he's joined the great democracy now. And he had nice pockets."

Three full days went by with no further alarms but a rare scattering of mechanical debris. Ferrell began to hope the Barrayaran was the last pickup they would have to make. They were nearing the end of their search pattern. Besides, he thought resentfully, this duty was sabotaging the efficiency of his sleep cycle. But the medtech made a request.

"If you don't mind, Falco," she said, "I'd greatly appreciate it if we could run the pattern out just a few extra turns. The original orders are based on this average estimated trajectory speed, you see, and if someone just happened to get a bit of extra kick when the ship split, they could well be beyond it by now."

Ferrell was less than thrilled, but the prospect of an extra day of piloting had its attractions, and he gave a grudging consent. Her reasoning proved itself; before the day was half done, they turned up another gruesome relic.

"Oh," muttered Ferrell, when they got a close look. It had been a female officer. Boni reeled her in with enormous tenderness. He didn't really want to go watch, this time, but the medtech seemed to have come to expect him.

"I—don't really want to look at a woman blown up," he tried to excuse himself.

"Mm," said Tersa. "Is it fair, though, to reject a person just because they're dead? You wouldn't have minded her body a bit when she was alive."

He laughed a little, macabrely. "Equal rights for the dead?"

Her smile twisted. "Why not? Some of my best friends are corpses."

He snorted.

She grew more serious. "I'd—sort of like the company, on this one." So he took up his usual station by the door.

The medtech laid out the thing that had been a woman upon her table, undressed, inventoried, washed, and straightened it. When she finished, she kissed the dead lips.

"Oh, God," cried Ferrell, shocked and nauseated. "You *are* crazy! You're a damn, damn necrophiliac! A *lesbian* necrophiliac, at that!" He turned to go.

"Is that what it looks like, to you?" Her voice was soft, and still unoffended. It stopped him, and he looked over his shoulder. She was looking at him as gently as if he had been one of her precious corpses. "What a strange world you must live in, inside your head."

She opened a suitcase, and shook out a dress, fine underwear, and a pair of white embroidered slippers. A wedding dress, Ferrell realized. This woman is a bona fide *psychopath.* . . .

She dressed the corpse, and arranged its soft dark hair with great delicacy, before bagging it.

"I believe I shall place her next to that nice tall Barrayaran," she said. "I think they would have liked each other very well, if they could have met in another place and time. And Lieutenant Deleo was married, after all."

She completed the label. Ferrell's battered mind was sending him little subliminal messages; he struggled to overcome his shock and bemusement, and pay attention. It tumbled into the open day of his consciousness with a start.

She had not run an identification check on this one.

Out the door, he told himself, is the way you want to walk. I guarantee it. Instead, timorously, he went over to the corpse and checked its label.

Ensign Sylva Boni, it said. *Age twenty.* His own age . . .

He was trembling, as if with cold. It *was* cold, in that room. Tersa Boni finished packing up the suitcase, and turned back with the float pallet.

"Daughter?" he asked. It was all he could ask.

She pursed her lips, and nodded.

"It's—a helluva coincidence."

"No coincidence at all. I asked for this sector."

"Oh." He swallowed, turned away, turned back, face flaming. "I'm sorry I said—"

She smiled her slow sad smile. "Never mind."

They found yet one more bit of mechanical debris, so agreed to run another cycle of the search spiral, to be sure that all possible trajectories had been outdistanced. And yes, they found another; a nasty one, spinning fiercely, guts split open from some great blow and hanging out in a frozen cascade.

The acolyte of death did her dirty work without once so much as wrinkling her nose. When it came to the washing, the least technical of the tasks, Ferrell said suddenly, "May I help?"

"Certainly," said the medtech, moving aside. "An honor is not diminished for being shared."

And so he did, as shy as an apprentice saint washing his first leper.

"Don't be afraid," she said. "The dead cannot hurt you. They give you no pain, except that of seeing your own death in their faces. And one can face that, I find."

Yes, he thought, the good face pain. But the great—they embrace it.

BARRAYAR

For Anne and Paul

CHAPTER ONE

I am afraid. Cordelia's hand pushed aside the drape in the third-floor parlor window of Vorkosigan House. She stared down into the sunlit street below. A long silver groundcar was pulling into the half-circular drive that serviced the front portico, braking past the spiked iron fence and the Earth-imported shrubbery. A government car. The door of the rear passenger compartment swung up, and a man in a green uniform emerged. Despite her foreshortened view Cordelia recognized Commander Illyan, brown-haired and hatless as usual. He strode out of sight under the portico. *Guess I don't really need to worry till Imperial Security comes for us in the middle of the night.* But a residue of dread remained, burrowed in her belly. *Why did I ever come here to Barrayar? What have I done to myself, to my life?*

Booted footsteps sounded in the corridor, and the door of the parlor creaked inward. Sergeant Bothari stuck his head in, and grunted with satisfaction at finding her. "Milady. Time to go."

"Thank you, Sergeant." She let the drape fall, and turned to inspect herself one last time in a wall-mounted mirror above the archaic fireplace. Hard to believe people here still burned vegetable matter just for the release of its chemically-bound heat.

She lifted her chin, above the stiff white lace collar of her blouse, adjusted the sleeves of her tan jacket, and kicked her knee absently against the long swirling skirt of a Vor-class woman, tan to match the jacket. The color comforted her, almost the same tan as her old Betan Astronomical Survey fatigues. She ran her hands over her red hair, parted in the middle and held away from her face by two enameled combs, and flopped it over her shoulders to curl loosely halfway down her back. Her grey eyes stared back at her from the pale face in the mirror. Nose a little too bony, chin a shade too long, but certainly a servicable face, good for all practical purposes.

Well, if she wanted to look dainty, all she had to do was stand next to Sergeant Bothari. He loomed mournfully beside her, all two meters of him. Cordelia considered herself a tall woman, but the top of her head was only level with his shoulder. He had a gargoyle's face, closed, wary, beak-nosed, its lumpiness exaggerated to criminality by his military-burr haircut. Even Count Vorkosigan's elegant livery, dark brown with the symbols of the house embroidered in silver, failed to save Bothari from his astonishing ugliness. *But a very good face indeed, for practical purposes.*

A liveried retainer. What a concept. What did he retain? *Our lives, our fortunes, and our sacred honors, for starters.* She nodded cordially to him, in the mirror, and about-faced to follow him through the warren of Vorkosigan House.

She must learn her way around this great pile of a residence as soon as possible. Embarrassing, to be lost in one's own home, and have to ask some passing guard or servant to de-tangle one. In the middle of the night, wearing only a towel. *I used to be a jumpship navigator. Really.* If she could handle five dimensions upside, surely she ought to be able to manage a mere three downside.

They came to the head of a large circular staircase, curving gracefully down three flights to a black-and-white stone-paved foyer. Her light steps followed Bothari's measured tread. Her skirts made her feel she was floating, parachuting inexorably down the spiral.

A tall young man, leaning on a cane at the foot of the stairs, looked up at the echo of their feet. Lieutenant Koudelka's face was as regular and pleasant as Bothari's was narrow and strange, and he smiled openly at Cordelia. Even the pain lines at the corners of his eyes and mouth failed to age that face. He wore Imperial undress greens, identical but for the insignia to Security Commander Illyan's. The long sleeves and high neck of his jacket concealed the tracery of thin red scars that netted half his body, but Cordelia mapped them in her mind's eye. Nude, Koudelka could pose as a visual aid for a lecture on the structure of the human nervous system, each scar representing a dead nerve excised and replaced with artificial silver threads. Lieutenant Koudelka was not quite used to his new nervous system yet. *Speak truth. The surgeons here are ignorant clumsy butchers.* The work was certainly not up to Betan standards. Cordelia permitted no hint of this private judgment to escape onto her face.

Koudelka turned jerkily, and nodded to Bothari. "Hello, Sergeant. Good morning, Lady Vorkosigan."

Her new name still seemed strange in her ear, ill-fitting. She smiled back. "Good morning, Kou. Where's Aral?"

"He and Commander Illyan went into the library, to check out where the new secured comconsole will be installed. They should be right along. Ah." He nodded, as footsteps sounded through an archway. Cordelia followed his gaze. Illyan, slight and bland and polite, flanked—was eclipsed by—a man in his mid-forties resplendent in Imperial dress greens. The reason she'd come to Barrayar.

Admiral Lord Aral Vorkosigan, retired. Formerly retired, till yesterday. Their lives had surely been turned upside down, yesterday. *We'll land on our feet somehow, you bet*. Vorkosigan's body was stocky and powerful, his dark hair salted with grey. His heavy jaw was marred by an old L-shaped scar. He moved with compressed energy, his grey eyes intense and inward, until they lighted on Cordelia.

"I give you good morrow, my lady," he sang out to her, reaching for her hand. The syntax was self-conscious but the sentiment naked-sincere in his mirror-bright eyes. *In those mirrors, I am altogether beautiful*, Cordelia realized warmly. *Much more flattering than that one on the wall upstairs. I shall use them to see myself from now on*. His thick hand was dry and hot, welcome heat, live heat, closing around her cool tapering fingers. *My husband*. That fit, as smoothly and tightly as her hand fit in his, even though her new name, *Lady Vorkosigan*, still seemed to slither off her shoulders.

She watched Bothari, Koudelka, and Vorkosigan standing together for that brief moment. *The walking wounded, one, two, three. And me, the lady auxiliary*. The survivors. Kou in body, Bothari in mind, Vorkosigan in spirit, all had taken near-mortal wounds in the late war at Escobar. *Life goes on. March or die. Do we all begin to recover at last?* She hoped so.

"Ready to go, dear Captain?" Vorkosigan asked her. His voice was a baritone, his Barrayaran accent guttural-warm.

"Ready as I'll ever be, I guess."

Illyan and Lieutenant Koudelka led the way out. Koudelka's walk was a loose-kneed shamble beside Illyan's brisk march, and Cordelia frowned doubtfully. She took Vorkosigan's arm, and they followed, leaving Bothari to his Household duties.

"What's the timetable for the next few days?" she asked.

"Well, this audience first, of course," Vorkosigan replied. "After which I see men. Count Vortala will be choreographing that. In a few days comes the vote of consent from the full Councils Assembled, and my swearing-in. We haven't had a Regent in a hundred and twenty years, God knows what protocol they'll dig out and dust off."

Koudelka sat in the front compartment of the

groundcar with the uniformed driver. Commander Illyan slid in opposite Cordelia and Vorkosigan, facing rearward, in the back compartment. *This car is armored,* Cordelia realized from the thickness of the transparent canopy as it closed over them. At a signal from Illyan to the driver, they pulled away smoothly into the street. Almost no sound penetrated from the outside.

"Regent-consort," Cordelia tasted the phrase. "Is that my official title?"

"Yes, Milady," said Illyan.

"Does it have any official duties to go with it?"

Illyan looked to Vorkosigan, who said, "Hm. Yes and no. There will be a lot of ceremonies to attend—grace, in your case. Beginning with the emperor's funeral, which will be grueling for all concerned—except, perhaps, for Emperor Ezar. All that waits on his last breath. I don't know if he has a timetable for that, but I wouldn't put it past him.

"The social side of your duties can be as much as you wish. Speeches and ceremonies, important weddings and name-days and funerals, greeting deputations from the Districts—public relations, in short. The sort of thing Princess-dowager Kareen does with such flair." Vorkosigan paused, taking in her appalled look, and added hastily, "Or, if you choose, you can live a completely private life. You have the perfect excuse to do so right now—" his hand, around her waist, secretly caressed her still-flat belly, "—and in fact I'd rather you didn't spend yourself too freely.

"More importantly, on the political side . . . I'd like it very much if you could be my liaison with the Princess-dowager, and the . . . child emperor. Make friends with her, if you can; she's an extremely reserved woman. The boy's upbringing is vital. We must not repeat Ezar Vorbarra's mistakes."

"I can give it a try," she sighed. "I can see it's going to be quite a job, passing for a Barrayaran Vor."

"Don't bend yourself painfully. I shouldn't like to see you so constricted. Besides, there's another angle."

"Why doesn't that surprise me? Go ahead."

He paused, choosing his words. "When the late Crown Prince Serg called Count Vortala a phoney progressive, it wasn't altogether nonsense. Insults that sting always have some truth in them. Count Vortala has been trying to form his progressive party in the upper classes only. Among the people who matter, as he would say. You see the little discontinuity in his thinking?"

"About the size of Hogarth Canyon back home? Yes."

"You are a Betan, a woman of galactic-wide reputation."

"Oh, come on now."

"You are seen so here. I don't think you quite realize how you are perceived. Very flattering for me, as it happens."

"I hoped I was invisible. But I shouldn't think I'd be too popular, after what we did to your side at Escobar."

"It's our culture. My people will forgive a brave soldier almost anything. And you, in your person, unite two of the opposing factions—the aristocratic military, and the pro-galactic plebians. I really think I could pull the whole middle out of the People's Defense League through you, if you're willing to play my cards for me."

"Good heavens. How long have you been thinking about this?"

"The problem, long. You as part of the solution, just today."

"What, casting me as figurehead for some sort of constitutional party?"

"No, no. That is just the sort of thing I will be sworn, on my honor, to prevent. It would not fulfill the spirit of my oath to hand over to Prince Gregor an emperor-ship gutted of power. What I want . . . what I want is to find some way of pulling the best men, from every class and language group and party, into the Emperor's service. The Vor have simply too small a pool of talent. Make the government more like the military at its best, with ability promoted regardless of background. Emperor Ezar tried to do something like that, by strengthening the Ministries at the expense of the Counts, but it swung too far.

The Counts are eviscerated and the Ministries are corrupt. There must be some way to strike a balance."

Cordelia sighed. "I guess we'll just have to agree to disagree, about constitutions. Nobody appointed me Regent of Barrayar. I warn you, though—I'll keep trying to change your mind."

Illyan raised his brow at this. Cordelia sat back wanly, and watched the Barrayaran capital city of Vorbarr Sultana pass by through the thick canopy. She hadn't married the Regent of Barrayar, four months back. She'd married a simple retired soldier. Yes, men were supposed to change after marriage, usually for the worse, but—this much? This fast? *This isn't the duty I signed up for, sir*.

"That's quite a gesture of trust Emperor Ezar placed in you yesterday, appointing you Regent. I don't think he's such a ruthless pragmatist as you'd have me believe," she remarked.

"Well, it is a gesture of trust, but driven by necessity. You didn't catch the significance of Captain Negri's assignment to the Princess's household, then."

"No. Was there one?"

"Oh, yes, a very clear message. Negri is to continue right on in his old job as Chief of Imperial Security. He will not, of course, be making his reports to a four-year-old boy, but to me. Commander Illyan will in fact merely be his assistant." Vorkosigan and Illyan exchanged mildly ironic nods. "But there is no question where Negri's loyalties will lie, in case I should, um, run mad and make a bid for Imperial power in name as well as fact. He unquestionably has secret orders to dispose of me, in that event."

"Oh. Well, I guarantee I have no desire whatsoever to be Empress of Barrayar. Just in case you were wondering."

"I didn't think so."

The groundcar paused at a gate in a stone wall. Four guards inspected them thoroughly, checked Illyan's passes, and waved them through. All those guards, here, at Vorkosigan House—what did they guard against? Other

Barrayarans, presumably, in the faction-fractured political landscape. A very Barrayaran phrase the old Count had used that tickled her humor now ran, disquieting, through her memory. *With all this manure around, there's got to be a pony someplace.* Horses were practically unknown on Beta Colony, except for a few specimens in zoos. *With all these guards around . . . But if I'm not anyone's enemy, how can anyone be my enemy?*

Illyan, who had been shifting in his seat, now spoke up. "I would suggest, sir," he said tentatively to Vorkosigan, "even beg, that you re-consider and take up quarters here at the Imperial Residence. Security problems—my problems," he smiled slightly, bad for his image, with his snub features it made him look puppyish, "will be very much easier to control here."

"What suite did you have in mind?" asked Vorkosigan.

"Well, when . . . Gregor succeeds, he and his mother will be moving into the Emperor's suite. Kareen's rooms will then be vacant."

"Prince Serg's, you mean." Vorkosigan looked grim. "I . . . think I would prefer to take official residence at Vorkosigan House. My father spends more and more time in the country at Vorkosigan Surleau these days, I don't think he'll mind being shifted."

"I can't really endorse that idea, sir. Strictly from a security standpoint. It's in the old part of town. The streets are warrens. There are at least three sets of old tunnels under the area, from old sewage and transport systems, and there are too many new tall buildings overlooking that have, er, commanding views. It will take at least six full-time patrols for the most cursory protection."

"Do you have the men?"

"Well, yes."

"Vorkosigan House, then." Vorkosigan consoled Illyan's disappointed look. "It may be bad security, but it's very good public relations. It will give an excellent air of, ah, soldierly humility to the new Regency. Should help reduce palace coup paranoia."

And here they were at the very palace in question. As

an architectural pile, the Imperial Residence made
Vorkosigan House look small. Sprawling wings rose two
to four stories high, accented with sporadic towers. Additions of different ages crisscrossed each other to create
both vast and intimate courts, some justly proportioned,
some rather accidental-looking. The east façade was of
the most uniform style, heavy with stone carving. The
north side was more cut-up, interlocking with elaborate
formal gardens. The west was the oldest, the south the
newest construction.

The groundcar pulled up to a two-story porch on the
south side, and Illyan led them past more guards and up
wide stone stairs to an extensive second-floor suite. They
climbed slowly, matching steps to Lieutenant Koudelka's
awkward pace. Koudelka glanced up with a self-conscious
apologetic frown, then bent his head again in concentration—or shame? *Doesn't this place have a lift tube?*
Cordelia wondered irritably. On the other side of this
stone labyrinth, in a room with a northern view of the
gardens, a white old man lay drained and dying on his
enormous ancestral bed. . . .

In the spacious upper corridor, softly carpeted and
decorated with paintings and side tables cluttered with
knickknacks—objets d'art, Cordelia supposed—they found
Captain Negri talking in low tones with a woman who
stood with her arms folded. Cordelia had met the famous,
or infamous, Chief of Barrayaran Imperial Security for the
first time yesterday, after Vorkosigan's historic job interview
in the northern wing with the soon-to-be-late Ezar
Vorbarra. Negri was a hard-faced, hard-bodied, bullet-
headed man who had served his emperor, body and blood,
for the better part of forty years, a sinister legend with
unreadable eyes.

Now he bowed over her hand and called her "Milady"
as if he meant it, or at least no more tinged with irony
than any of his other statements. The alert blonde
woman—girl?—wore an ordinary civilian dress. She was
tall and heavily muscled, and she looked back at Cordelia
with even greater interest.

Vorkosigan and Negri exchanged curt greetings in the telegraphic style of two men who had been communicating for so long all of the amenities had been compressed into some kind of tight-burst code. "And this is Miss Droushnakovi." Negri did not so much introduce as label the woman for Cordelia's benefit, with a wave of his hand.

"And what's a Droushnakovi?" asked Cordelia lightly and somewhat desperately. Everybody always seemed to get briefed around here but her, though Negri had also failed to introduce Lieutenant Koudelka; Koudelka and Droushnakovi glanced covertly at each other.

"I'm a Servant of the Inner Chamber, Milady." Droushnakovi gave her a ducking nod, half a curtsey.

"And what do you serve? Besides the chamber."

"Princess Kareen, Milady. That's just my official title. I'm listed on Captain Negri's staff budget as Bodyguard, Class One." It was hard to tell which title gave her the more pride and pleasure, but Cordelia suspected it was the latter.

"I'm sure you must be good, to be so ranked by him."

This won a smile, and a "Thank you, Milady. I try."

They all followed Negri through a nearby door to a long, sunny yellow room with lots of south-facing windows. Cordelia wondered if the eclectic mix of furnishings were priceless antiques, or merely shabby seconds. She couldn't tell. A woman waited on a yellow silk settee at the far end, watching them gravely as they trooped toward her en masse.

Princess-dowager Kareen was a thin, strained-looking woman of thirty with elaborately dressed, beautiful dark hair, though her grey gown was of a simple cut. Simple but perfect. A dark-haired boy of four or so was sprawled on the floor on his stomach muttering to his cat-sized toy stegosaurus, which muttered back. She made him get up and turn off the robot toy, and sit beside her, though his hands still clutched the leathery stuffed beast in his lap. Cordelia was relieved to see the boy prince was sensibly dressed for his age in comfortable-looking play clothes.

In formal phrases, Negri introduced Cordelia to the princess and Prince Gregor. Cordelia wasn't sure whether to bow, curtsey, or salute, and ended up ducking her head rather like Droushnakovi. Gregor, solemn, stared at her most doubtfully, and she tried to smile back in what she hoped was a reassuring way.

Vorkosigan went down on one knee in front of the boy—only Cordelia saw Aral swallow—and said, "Do you know who I am, Prince Gregor?"

Gregor shrank a little against his mother's side, and glanced up at her. She nodded encouragement. "Lord Aral Vorkosigan," Gregor said in a thin voice.

Vorkosigan gentled his tone, relaxed his hands, self-consciously trying to dampen his usual intensity. "Your grandfather has asked me to be your Regent. Has anybody explained to you what that means?"

Gregor shook his head mutely; Vorkosigan quirked a brow at Negri, a whiff of censure. Negri did not change expression.

"That means I will do your grandfather's job until you are old enough to do it yourself, when you turn twenty. The next sixteen years. I will look after you and your mother in your grandfather's place, and see that you get the education and training to do a good job, like your grandfather did. Good government."

Did the kid even know yet what a government was? Vorkosigan had been careful not to say, *in your father's place*, Cordelia noted dryly. Careful not to mention Crown Prince Serg at all. Serg was well on his way to being disappeared from Barrayaran history, it seemed, as thoroughly as he had been vaporized in orbital battle.

"For now," Vorkosigan continued, "your job is to study hard with your tutors and do what your mother tells you. Can you do that?"

Gregor swallowed, nodded.

"I think you can do well." Vorkosigan gave him a firm nod, identical to the ones he gave his staff officers, and rose.

I think you can do well too, Aral, Cordelia thought.

"While you are here, sir," Negri began after a short wait to be certain he wasn't stepping on some further word, "I wish you would come down to Ops. There are two or three reports I'd like to present. The latest from Darkoi seems to indicate that Count Vorlakail was dead before his Residence was burned, which throws a new light—or shadow—on that matter. And then there is the problem of revamping the Ministry of Political Education—"

"Dismantling, surely," Vorkosigan muttered.

"As may be. And, as ever, the latest sabotage from Komarr . . ."

"I get the picture. Let's go. Cordelia, ah . . ."

"Perhaps Lady Vorkosigan would care to stay and visit a while," Princess Kareen murmured on cue, with only a faint trace of irony.

Vorkosigan shot her a look of gratitude. "Thank you, Milady."

She absently stroked her fine lips with one finger, as all the men trooped out, relaxing slightly as they exited. "Good. I'd hoped to have you all to myself." Her expression grew more animated, as she regarded Cordelia. At a wordless touch, the boy slid off the bench and returned, with backward glances, to his play.

Droushnakovi frowned down the room. "What was the matter with that lieutenant?" she asked Cordelia.

"Lieutenant Koudelka was hit by nerve disruptor fire," Cordelia said stiffly, uncertain if the girl's odd tone concealed some kind of disapproval. "A year ago, when he was serving Aral aboard the *General Vorkraft*. The neural repairs do not seem to be quite up to galactic standard." She shut her mouth, afraid of seeming to criticize her hostess. Not that Princess Kareen was responsible for Barrayar's dubious standards of medical practice.

"Oh. Not during the Escobar war?" said Droushnakovi.

"Actually, in a weird sense, it was the opening shot of the Escobar war. Though I suppose you would call it friendly fire." Mind-boggling oxymoron, that phrase.

"Lady Vorkosigan—or should I say, Captain

Naismith—was there," remarked Princess Kareen. "She should know."

Cordelia found her expression hard to read. How many of Negri's famous reports was the princess privy to?

"How terrible for him! He looks as though he had been very athletic," said the bodyguard.

"He was." Cordelia smiled more favorably at the girl, relaxing her defensive hackles. "Nerve disruptors are filthy weapons, in my opinion." She scrubbed absently at the sense-dead spot on her thigh, disruptor-burned by no more than the nimbus of a blast that had fortunately not penetrated subcutaneous fat to damage muscle function. Clearly, she should have had it fixed before she'd left home.

"Sit, Lady Vorkosigan." Princess Kareen patted the settee beside her, just vacated by the emperor-to-be. "Drou, will you please take Gregor to his lunch?"

Droushnakovi nodded understandingly, as if she had received some coded underlayer to this simple request, gathered up the boy, and walked out hand in hand with him. His child-voice drifted back, "Droushie, can I have a cream cake? And one for Steggie?"

Cordelia sat gingerly, thinking about Negri's reports, and Barrayaran disinformation about their recent aborted campaign to invade the planet Escobar. Escobar, Beta Colony's good neighbor and ally . . . the weapons that had disintegrated Crown Prince Serg and his ship high above Escobar had been bravely convoyed through the Barrayaran blockade by one Captain Cordelia Naismith, Betan Expeditionary Force. That much truth was plain and public and not to be apologized for. It was the secret history, behind the scenes in the Barrayaran high command, that was so . . . treacherous, Cordelia decided, was the precise word. Dangerous, like ill-stored toxic waste.

To Cordelia's astonishment, Princess Kareen leaned over, took her right hand, lifted it to her lips, and kissed it hard.

"I swore," said Kareen thickly, "that I would kiss the hand that slew Ges Vorrutyer. Thank you. Thank you." Her voice was breathy, earnest, tear-caught, grateful emotion naked in her face. She sat up, her face growing reserved again, and nodded. "Thank you. Bless you."

"Uh . . ." Cordelia rubbed at the kissed spot. "Um . . . I . . . this honor belongs to another, Milady. I was present, when Admiral Vorrutyer's throat was cut, but it was not by my hand."

Kareen's hands clenched in her lap, and her eyes glowed. "Then it *was* Lord Vorkosigan!"

"No!" Cordelia's lips compressed in exasperation. "Negri should have given you the true report. It was Sergeant Bothari. Saved my life, at the time."

"Bothari?" Kareen sat bolt upright in astonishment. "Bothari the monster, Bothari, Vorrutyer's mad batman?"

"I don't mind getting blamed in his place, ma'am, because if it had become public they'd have been forced to execute him for murder and mutiny, and this gets him off and out. But I . . . but I should not steal his praise. I'll pass it on to him if you wish, but I'm not sure he remembers the incident. He went through some draconian mind-therapy after the war, before they discharged him—what you Barrayarans call therapy"—on a par with their neurosurgery, Cordelia feared, "and I gather he wasn't exactly, uh, normal before that, either."

"No," said Kareen. "He was not. I thought he was Vorrutyer's creature."

"He chose . . . he chose to be otherwise. I think it was the most heroic act I've ever witnessed. Out of the middle of that swamp of evil and insanity, to reach for . . ." Cordelia trailed off, embarrassed to say, *reach for redemption.* After a pause she asked, "Do you blame Admiral Vorrutyer for Prince Serg's, uh, corruption?" As long as they were clearing the air . . . *Nobody mentions Prince Serg. He thought to take a bloody shortcut to the Imperium, and now he's just . . . disappeared.*

"Ges Vorrutyer . . ." Kareen's hands twisted, "found a like-minded friend in Serg. A fertile follower, in his vile amusements. Maybe not . . . all Vorrutyer's fault. I don't know."

An honest answer, Cordelia sensed. Kareen added lowly, "Ezar protected me from Serg, after I became pregnant.

I had not even seen my husband for over a year, when
he was killed at Escobar."

Perhaps I will not mention Prince Serg again either.
"Ezar was a powerful protector. I hope Aral may do as
well," Cordelia offered. Ought she to refer to Emperor
Ezar in the past tense already? Everybody else seemed to.

Kareen came back from some absence, and shook herself to focus. "Tea, Lady Vorkosigan?" She smiled. She
touched a comm link, concealed in a jeweled pin on her
shoulder, and gave domestic orders. Apparently the private
interview was over. Captain Naismith must now try to figure
out how Lady Vorkosigan should take tea with a princess.

Gregor and the bodyguard reappeared about the time
the cream cakes were being served, and Gregor set about
successfully charming the ladies for a second helping.
Kareen drew the line firmly at thirds. Prince Serg's son
seemed an utterly normal boy, if quiet around strangers.
Cordelia watched him with Kareen with deep personal
interest. Motherhood. Everybody did it. How hard could
it be?

"How do you like your new home so far, Lady
Vorkosigan?" the princess inquired, making polite conversation. Tea-table stuff; no naked faces now. Not in front
of the children.

Cordelia thought it over. "The country place, south at
Vorkosigan Surleau, is just beautiful. That wonderful
lake—it's bigger than any open body of water on the whole
of Beta Colony, yet Aral just takes it for granted. Your
planet is beautiful beyond measure." *Your planet. Not my
planet?* In a free-association test, "home" still triggered
"Beta Colony" in Cordelia's mind. Yet she could have
rested in Vorkosigan's arms by the lake forever.

"The capital here—well, it's certainly more varied than
anything we have at ho—on Beta Colony. Although," she
laughed self-consciously, "there seem to be so many soldiers. Last time I was surrounded by that many green
uniforms, I was in a POW camp."

"Do we still look like the enemy to you?" asked the
princess curiously.

"Oh—you all stopped looking like the enemy to me even before the war was over. Just assorted victims, variously blind."

"You have penetrating eyes, Lady Vorkosigan." The princess sipped tea, smiling into her cup. Cordelia blinked.

"Vorkosigan House does tend to a barracks atmosphere, when Count Piotr is in residence," Cordelia commented. "All his liveried men. I think I've seen a couple of women servants so far, whisking around corners, but I haven't caught one yet. A Barrayaran barracks, that is. My Betan service was a different sort of thing."

"Mixed," said Droushnakovi. Was that the light of envy in her eyes? "Women and men both serving."

"Assignment by aptitude test," Cordelia agreed. "Strictly. Of course the more physical jobs are skewed to the men, but there doesn't seem to be that strange obsessive status-thing attached to them."

"Respect," sighed Droushnakovi.

"Well, if people are laying their lives on the line for their community, they ought certainly to get its respect," Cordelia said equably. "I do miss my—my sister-officers, I guess. The bright women, the techs, like my pool of friends at home." There was that tricky word again, home. "There have to be bright women around here somewhere, with all these bright men. Where are they hiding?" Cordelia shut her mouth, as it suddenly occurred to her that Kareen might mistakenly construe this remark as a slur on herself. Adding *present company excepted* would put her foot in it for sure, though.

But if Kareen so construed, she kept it to herself, and Cordelia was rescued from further potential social embarrassment by the return of Aral and Illyan. They all made polite farewells, and returned to Vorkosigan House.

That evening Commander Illyan popped in to Vorkosigan House with Droushnakovi in tow. She clutched a large valise, and gazed about her with starry-eyed interest.

"Captain Negri is assigning Miss Droushnakovi to the Regent-consort for her personal security," Illyan explained briefly. Aral nodded approval.

Later, Droushnakovi handed Cordelia a sealed note, on thick cream paper. Brows rising, Cordelia broke it open. The handwriting was small and neat, the signature legible and without flourishes.

With my compliments, it read. *She will suit you well. Kareen.*

CHAPTER TWO

The next morning Cordelia awoke to find Vorkosigan already gone, and herself facing her first day on Barrayar without his supportive company. She decided to devote it to the shopping project that had occurred to her while watching Koudelka negotiate the spiral staircase last night. She suspected Droushnakovi would be the ideal native guide for what she had in mind.

She dressed and went hunting for her bodyguard. Finding her was not difficult; Droushnakovi was seated in the hall, just outside the bedroom door, and popped to attention at Cordelia's appearance. The girl really ought to be wearing a uniform, Cordelia reflected. The dress she wore made her near-six-foot frame and excellent musculature look heavy. Cordelia wondered if, as Regent-consort, she might be permitted her own livery, and bemused herself through breakfast mentally designing one that would set off the girl's Valkyrie good looks.

"Do you know, you're the first female Barrayaran guard I've met," Cordelia commented to her over her egg and coffee, and a kind of steamed native groats with butter, evidently a morning staple here. "How did you get into this line of work?"

"Well, I'm not a real guard, like the liveried men—"

Ah, the magic of uniforms again.

"—but my father and all three of my brothers are in the Service. It's as close as I can come to being a real soldier, like you."

Army-mad, like the rest of Barrayar. "Yes?"

"I used to study judo, for sport, when I was younger. But I was too big for the women's classes. Nobody could give me any real practice, and besides, doing all katas was so dull. My brothers used to sneak me into the men's classes with them. One thing led to another. I was all-Barrayar women's champion two years running, when I was in school. Then three years ago a man from Captain Negri's staff approached my father with a job offer for me. That's when I had weapons training. It seemed the Princess had been asking for female guards for years, but they had a lot of trouble getting anyone who could pass all the tests. Although," she smiled self-depreciatingly, "the lady who assassinated Admiral Vorrutyer could scarcely be supposed to need my poor services."

Cordelia bit her tongue. "Um. I was lucky. Besides, I'd rather stay out of the physical end of things just now. Pregnant, you know."

"Yes, Milady. It was in one of Captain—"

"Negri's reports," Cordelia finished in unison with her. "I'm sure it was. He probably knew before I did."

"Yes, Milady."

"Were you much encouraged in your interests, as a child?"

"Not . . . really. Everyone thought I was just odd." She frowned deeply, and Cordelia had the sense of stirring up a painful memory.

She regarded the girl thoughtfully. "Older brothers?"

Droushnakovi returned a wide blue gaze. "Why, yes."

"Figured." *And I feared Barrayar for what it did to its sons. No wonder they have trouble getting anyone to pass the tests.* "So, you've had weapons training. Excellent. You can guide me on my shopping trip today."

A slightly glazed look crept over Droushnakovi's face.

"Yes, Milady. What sort of clothing do you wish to look at?" she asked politely, not quite concealing a glum disappointment with the interests of her "real" lady soldier.

"Where in this town would you go to buy a really good swordstick?"

The glazed look vanished. "Oh, I know just the place, where the Vor officers go, and the counts, to supply their liveried men. That is—I've never been inside. My family's not Vor, so of course we're not permitted to own personal weapons. Just Service issue. But it's supposed to be the best."

One of Count Vorkosigan's liveried guards chauffeured them to the shop. Cordelia relaxed and enjoyed the view of the passing city. Droushnakovi, on duty, kept alert, eyes constantly checking the crowds all around. Cordelia had the feeling she didn't miss much. From time to time her hand wandered to check the stunner worn concealed on the inside of her embroidered bolero.

They turned into a clean narrow street of older buildings with cut stone fronts. The weapons shop was marked only by its name, *Siegling's,* in discreet gold letters. Evidently if you didn't know where you were you shouldn't be there. The liveried man waited outside when Cordelia and Droushnakovi entered the shop, a thick-carpeted, wood-grained place with a little of the aroma of the armory Cordelia remembered from her Survey ship, an odd whiff of home in an alien place. She stared covertly at the wood paneling, and mentally translated its value into Betan dollars. A great many Betan dollars. Yet wood seemed almost as common as plastic, here, and as little regarded. Those personal weapons which were legal for the upper classes to own were elegantly displayed in cases and on the walls. Besides stunners and hunting weapons, there was an impressive array of swords and knives; evidently the Emperor's ferocious edicts against dueling only forbade their use, not their possession.

The clerk, a narrow-eyed, soft-treading older man,

came up to them. "What may I do for you ladies?" He
was cordial enough. Cordelia supposed Vor-class women
must sometimes enter here, to buy presents for their masculine relations. But he might have said, *What may I do
for you children?* in the same tone of voice.
Diminutization by body language? Let it go.

"I'm looking for a swordstick, for a man about six-foot-
four. Should be about, oh, yea long," she estimated, calling
up Koudelka's arm and leg length in her mind's eye, and
gesturing to the height of her hip. "Spring-sheathed,
probably."

"Yes, madam." The clerk disappeared, and returned
with a sample, in an elaborately carved light wood.

"Looks a bit . . . I don't know." *Flashy.* "How does it
work?"

The clerk demonstrated the spring mechanism. The
wooden sheathing dropped off, revealing a long thin blade.
Cordelia held out her hand, and the clerk, rather reluctantly, handed it over for inspection.

She wriggled it a little, sighted down the blade, and
handed it to her bodyguard. "What do you think?"

Droushnakovi smiled first, then frowned doubtfully. "It's
not very well balanced." She glanced uncertainly at the
clerk.

"Remember, you're working for me, not him," said
Cordelia, correctly identifying class-consciousness in action.

"I don't think it's a very good blade."

"That's excellent Darkoi workmanship, madam," the
clerk defended coolly.

Smiling, Cordelia took it back. "Let us test your
hypothesis."

She raised the blade suddenly to the salute, and lunged
at the wall in a neat extension. The tip penetrated and
caught in the wood, and Cordelia leaned on it. The blade
snapped. Blandly, she handed the pieces back to the clerk.
"How do you stay in business if your customers don't survive long enough for repeat sales? Siegling's certainly didn't
acquire its reputation selling toys like that. Bring me something a decent soldier can carry, not a pimp's plaything."

"Madam," said the clerk stiffly, "I must insist the damaged merchandise be paid for."

Cordelia, thoroughly irritated, said, "Very well. Send the bill to my husband. Admiral Aral Vorkosigan, Vorkosigan House. While you're about it you can explain why you tried to pass off sleaze on his wife—Yeoman." This last was a guess, based on his age and walk, but she could tell from his eyes she'd struck home.

The clerk bowed profoundly. "I beg pardon, Milady. I believe I have something more suitable, if Milady will be pleased to wait."

He vanished again, and Cordelia sighed. "Buying from machines is so much easier. But at least the Appeal to the Irrelevant Authorities at Headquarters works just as well here as at home."

The next sample was a plain dark wood, with a finish like satin. The clerk handed it to her unopened, with another little bow. "You press the handle there, Milady."

It was much heavier than the first swordstick. The sheathing sprang away at velocity, landing against the wall on the other side of the room with a satisfying thunk, almost a weapon in itself. Cordelia sighted down the blade again. A strange watermark pattern down its length shifted in the light. She saluted the wall once more, and caught the clerk's eye. "Do these come out of your salary?"

"Go ahead, Milady." There was a little gleam of satisfaction in his eye. "You can't break that one."

She gave it the same test as she had the other. The tip went much further into the wood, and leaning against it with all her strength, she could barely bend it. Even so, there was more bend left in it; she could feel she was nowhere near the limit of its tensile strength. She handed it to Droushnakovi, who examined it lovingly.

"That's *fine*, Milady. That's worthy."

"I'm sure it will be used more as a stick than as a sword. Nevertheless . . . it should indeed be worthy. We'll take this one."

As the clerk wrapped it, Cordelia lingered over a case of enamel-decorated stunners.

"Thinking of buying one for yourself, Milady?" asked Droushnakovi.

"I . . . don't think so. Barrayar has enough soldiers, without importing them from Beta Colony. Whatever I'm here for, it isn't soldiering. See anything you want?"

Droushnakovi looked wistful, but shook her head, her hand going to her bolero. "Captain Negri's equipment is the best. Even Siegling's doesn't have anything better, just prettier."

They sat down three to dinner that night, late, Vorkosigan, Cordelia, and Lieutenant Koudelka. Vorkosigan's new personal secretary looked a little tired.

"What did you two do all day?" asked Cordelia.

"Herded men, mostly," answered Vorkosigan. "Prime Minister Vortala had a few votes that weren't as much in the bag as he claimed, and we worked them over, one or two at a time, behind closed doors. What you'll see tomorrow in the Council chambers isn't Barrayaran politics at work, just their result. Were you all right today?"

"Fine. Went shopping. Wait'll you see." She produced the swordstick, and stripped off the wrapping. "Just to help keep you from running Kou completely into the ground."

Koudelka looked politely grateful, over a more fundamental irritation. His look changed to one of surprise as he took the stick and nearly dropped it from the unexpected weight. "Hey! This isn't—"

"You press the handle there. Don't point it—!"
Thwack!

"—at the window." Fortunately, the sheath struck the frame, and bounced back with a clatter. Kou and Aral both jumped.

Koudelka's eyes lit up as he examined the blade, while Cordelia retrieved the sheath. "Oh, Milady!" Then his face fell. He carefully resheathed it, and handed it back sadly. "I guess you didn't realize. I'm not Vor. It's not legal for me to own a private sword."

"Oh." Cordelia was crestfallen.

Vorkosigan raised an eyebrow. "May I see that,

Cordelia?" He looked it over, unsheathing it more cautiously. "Hm. Am I right in guessing I paid for this?"

"Well, you will, I suppose, when the bill arrives. Although I don't think you should pay for the one I broke. I might as well take it back, though."

"I see." He smiled a little. "Lieutenant Koudelka, as your commanding officer and a vassal secundus to Ezar Vorbarra, I am officially issuing you this weapon of mine, to carry in the service of the Emperor, long may he rule." The unavoidable irony of the formal phrase tightened his mouth, but he shook off the blackness, and handed the stick back to Koudelka, who bloomed again.

"Thank you, sir!"

Cordelia just shook her head. "I don't believe I'll ever understand this place."

"I'll have Kou find you some legal histories. Not tonight, though. He has barely time to put his notes from today in order before Vortala's due here with a couple more of his strays. You can take over part of the Count my father's library, Kou; we'll meet in there."

Dinner broke up. Koudelka retreated to the library to work, while Vorkosigan and Cordelia retired to the drawing room next to it to read, before Vorkosigan's evening meeting. He had yet more reports, which he ran rapidly through a hand viewer. Cordelia divided her time between a Barrayaran Russian phrase earbug, and an even more intimidating disk on child care. The silence was broken by an occasional mutter from Vorkosigan, more to himself than her, of phrases like, "Ah ha! So that's what the bastard was really up to," or "Damn, those figures are strange. Got to check it out. . . ." Or from Cordelia, "Oh, my, I wonder if all babies do that," and a periodic *thwack!* penetrating the wall from the library, which caused them to look up at each other and burst out laughing.

"Oh, dear," said Cordelia, after the third or fourth of these. "I hope I haven't distracted him unduly from his duties."

"He'll do all right, when he settles down. Vorbarra's personal secretary has taken him in hand, and is showing

him how to organize himself. After Kou follows him
through the funeral protocol, he should be able to tackle
anything. That swordstick was a stroke of genius, by the
way; thank you."

"Yes, I noticed he was pretty touchy about his handi-
caps. I thought it might unruffle his feathers a little."

"It's our society. It tends to be . . . rather hard on
anyone who can't keep up."

"I see. Strange . . . now that you mention it, I don't
recall seeing any but healthy-looking people, on the streets
and so on, except at the hospital. No float chairs, none
of those vacuous faces in the tow of their parents . . ."

"Nor will you." Vorkosigan looked grim. "Any problems
that are detectable are eliminated before birth."

"Well, we do that, too. Though usually before conception."

"Also at birth. And after, in the backcountry."

"Oh."

"As for the maimed adults . . ."

"Good heavens, you don't practice euthanasia on them,
do you?"

"Your Ensign Dubauer would not have lived, here."

Dubauer had taken disruptor fire to the head, and
survived. Sort of.

"As for injuries like Koudelka's, or worse . . . the social
stigma is very great. Watch him in a larger group sometime, not his close friends. It's no accident that the suicide rate among medically discharged soldiers is high."

"That's horrible."

"I took it for granted, once. Now . . . not anymore.
But many people still do."

"What about problems like Bothari's?"

"It depends. He was a usable madman. For the
unusable . . ." he trailed off, staring at his boots.

Cordelia felt cold. "I keep thinking I'm beginning to
adjust to this place. Then I go around another corner and
run headlong into something like that."

"It's only been eighty years since Barrayar made contact with the wider galactic civilization again. It wasn't

just technology we lost, in the Time of Isolation. That we put back on again quickly, like a borrowed coat. But underneath it . . . we're still pretty damned naked in places. In forty-four years, I've only begun to see how naked."

Count Vortala and his "strays" came in soon after, and Vorkosigan vanished into the library. The old Count Piotr Vorkosigan, Aral's father, arrived from his District later that evening, come up to attend the full Council vote.

"Well, that's one vote he's assured of tomorrow," Cordelia joked to her father-in-law, helping him get stiffly out of his jacket in the stone-paved foyer.

"Ha. He's lucky to get it. He's picked up some damned peculiar radical notions in the last few years. If he wasn't my son, he could whistle for it." But Piotr's seamed face looked proud.

Cordelia blinked at this description of Aral Vorkosigan's political views. "I confess, I've never thought of him as a revolutionary. Radical must be a more elastic term than I thought."

"Oh, he doesn't see himself that way. He thinks he can go halfway, and then stop. I think he'll find himself riding a tiger, a few years down the road." The count shook his head grimly. "But come, my girl, and sit down and tell me that you're well. You look well—is everything all right?"

The old count was passionately interested in the development of his grandson-to-be. Cordelia sensed her pregnancy had raised her status with him enormously, from a tolerated caprice of Aral's to something bordering perilously on the semi-divine. He fairly blasted her with approval. It was nearly irresistible, and she never laughed at him, although she had no illusions about it.

Cordelia had found Aral's earlier sketch of his father's reaction to her pregnancy, the day she'd brought home the confirming news, to be right on target. She'd returned to the estate at Vorkosigan Surleau that summer day to search Aral out down by the boat dock. He was puttering around with his sailboat, and had the sails laid out, drying in the sun, as he squished around them in wet shoes.

He looked up to meet her smile, unsuccessful at concealing the eagerness in his eyes. "Well?" He bounced a little, on his heels.

"Well." She attempted a sad and disappointed look, to tease him, but the grin escaped and took over her whole face. "Your doctor says it's a boy."

"Ah." A long and eloquent sigh escaped him, and he scooped her up and twirled her around.

"Aral! Awk! Don't drop me." He was no taller than herself, if, um, thicker.

"Never." He let her slide down against him, and they shared a long kiss, ending in laughter.

"My father will be ecstatic."

"You look pretty ecstatic yourself."

"Yes, but you haven't seen anything until you've seen an old-fashioned Barrayaran paterfamilias in a trance over the growth of his family tree. I've had the poor old man convinced for years that his line was ending with me."

"Will he forgive me for being an offworlder plebe?"

"No insult intended, but by this time I don't think he'd have cared what *species* of wife I dragged home, as long as she was fertile. You think I'm exaggerating?" he added at her trill of laughter. "You'll see."

"Is it too early to think of names?" she asked, slightly wistful.

"No thinking to it. Firstborn son. It's a strict custom here. He gets named after his two grandfathers. Paternal for the first, maternal for the second."

"Ah, that's why your history is so confusing to read. I was always having to put dates next to those duplicate names, to try and keep track. Piotr Miles. Hm. Well, I guess I can get used to it. I'd been thinking of . . . something else."

"Another time, perhaps."

"Ooh, ambitious."

A short wrestling match ensued, Cordelia having previously made the useful discovery that in certain moods he was more ticklish than she. She extracted a reasonable amount of revenge, and they ended laughing on the grass in the sun.

"This is very undignified," Aral complained as she let him up.

"Afraid I'll shock Negri's fisher of men out there?"

"They're beyond shock, I guarantee."

Cordelia waved at the distant hoverboat, whose occupant steadfastly ignored the gesture. She had been at first angered, then resigned to learn that Aral was being kept under continuous observation by Imperial Security. The price, she'd supposed, of his involvement in the secret and lethal politics of the Escobar War, and the penalty for some of his less welcome outspoken opinions.

"I can see why you took up baiting them for a hobby. Maybe we ought to unbend and invite them to lunch or something. I feel they must know me so well by now, I'd like to know them." Had Negri's man recorded the domestic conversation she'd just had? Were there bugs in their bedroom? Their bathroom?

Aral grinned, but replied, "They wouldn't be permitted to accept. They don't eat or drink anything but what they bring themselves."

"Heavens, how paranoid. Is that really necessary?"

"Sometimes. Theirs is a dangerous trade. I don't envy them."

"I'd think sitting around down here watching you would constitute a nice little vacation. He's got to have a great suntan."

"The sitting around is the hardest part. They may sit for a year, and then be called to five minutes of all-out action of deadly importance. But they have to be instantly ready for that five minutes the whole year. Quite a strain. I much prefer attack to defense."

"I still don't understand why anybody would want to bother you. I mean, you're just a retired officer, living in obscurity. There must be hundreds like you, even of high Vor blood."

"Hm." He'd rested his gaze on the distant boat, avoiding answer, then jumped to his feet. "Come on. Let's go spring the good news on Father."

Well, she understood it now. Count Piotr drew her hand through his arm, and carried her off to the dining room, where he ate a late supper between demands for the latest obstetrical report, and pressed fresh garden dainties upon her that he'd brought with him from the country. She ate grapes obediently.

After the Count's supper, walking arm in arm with him into the foyer, Cordelia's ear was caught by the sound of raised voices coming from the library. The words were muffled but the tones were sharp, chop-cadenced. Cordelia paused, disturbed.

After a moment the—argument?—stopped, the library door swung open, and a man stalked out. Cordelia could see Aral and Count Vortala through the aperture. Aral's face was set, his eyes burning. Vortala, an age-shrunken man with a balding liver-spotted head fringed with white, was brick-pink to the top of his naked scalp. With a curt gesture the man collected his waiting liveried retainer, who followed smartly, blank-faced.

The curt man was about forty years old, Cordelia guessed, dressed expensively in the upper-class style, dark-haired. He was rendered a bit dish-faced by a prominent forehead and jaw that his nose and moustache had trouble overpowering. Neither handsome nor ugly, in another mood one might call him strong-featured. Now he just looked sour. He paused, coming upon Count Piotr in the foyer, and managed—just barely—a polite nod of greeting. "Vorkosigan," he said thickly. A reluctant *good evening* was encoded in his jerky half-bow.

The old count tilted his head in return, eyebrows up. "Vordarian." His tone made the name an inquiry.

Vordarian's lips were tight, his hands clenching in unconscious rhythm with his jaw. "Mark my words," he ground out, "you, and I, and every other man of worth on Barrayar will live to regret tomorrow."

Piotr pursed his lips, wariness in the crow's-feet corners of his eyes. "My son will not betray his class, Vordarian."

"You blind yourself." His stare cut across Cordelia, not

lingering long enough to be construed as insult, but cold, very cold, repelling introduction. With effort, he made the minimum courtesy of a farewell nod, turned, and exited the front door with his retainer-shadow.

Aral and Vortala emerged from the library. Aral drifted to the foyer to stare moodily into the darkness through the etched glass panels flanking the door. Vortala placed a placating hand on his sleeve.

"Let him go," said Vortala. "We can live without his vote tomorrow."

"I don't plan to go running down the street after him," Aral snapped. "Nevertheless . . . next time, save your wit for those with the brains to appreciate it, eh?"

"Who was that irate fellow?" asked Cordelia lightly, trying to lift the black mood.

"Count Vidal Vordarian." Aral turned from the glass panel back to her, and managed a smile for her benefit. "Commodore Count Vordarian. I used to work with him from time to time when I was on the General Staff. He is now a leader in what you might call the next-to-most conservative party on Barrayar; not the back-to-the-Time-of-Isolation loonies, but, shall we say, those honestly fearing all change is change for the worse." He glanced covertly at Count Piotr.

"His name was mentioned frequently, in speculation about the upcoming Regency," Vortala commented. "I rather fear he may have been counting on it for himself. He's made great efforts to cultivate Kareen."

"He should have been cultivating Ezar," said Aral dryly. "Well . . . maybe he'll come down out of the air overnight. Try him again in the morning, Vortala—a little more humbly this time, eh?"

"Coddling Vordarian's ego could be a full-time task," grumbled Vortala. "He spends too damn much time studying his family tree."

Aral grimaced agreement. "He's not the only one."

"He is to hear him tell it," growled Vortala.

CHAPTER THREE

The next day Cordelia had an official escort to the full Joint Council session in the person of Captain Lord Padma Xav Vorpatril. He turned out to be not only a member of her husband's new staff, but also his first cousin, son of Aral's long-dead mother's younger sister. Lord Vorpatril was the first close relative of Aral's Cordelia had encountered besides Count Piotr. It wasn't that Aral's relatives were avoiding her, as she might have feared; he had a real dearth of them. He and Vorpatril were the only surviving children of the previous generation, of whom Count Piotr was himself the last living representative. Vorpatril was a big cheerful man of about thirty-five, clean-cut in his dress greens. He had also, she discovered shortly, been one of her husband's junior officers during his first captaincy, before Vorkosigan's military successes of the Komarr campaign and its politically ruinous aftermath.

She sat with Vorpatril on one side and Droushnakovi on the other, in an ornate-railed gallery overlooking the Council chamber. The chamber itself was a surprisingly plain room, though heavy with what still seemed to Cordelia's Betan eye to be incredibly luxurious wood paneling. Wooden benches and desks ringed the room. Morning light poured through stained-glass windows high in the east wall. The colorful ceremonies were played out below with great punctilio.

The ministers wore archaic-looking black and purple robes set off by gold chains of office. They were outnumbered by the nearly sixty District counts, even more splendid in scarlet and silver. A sprinkling of men young enough to be on active service in the military wore the red and blue parade uniform. Vorkosigan had been right in describing the parade uniform as gaudy, Cordelia reflected, but in the wonderful setting of this ancient room the gaud seemed most appropriate. Vorkosigan looked quite good in his set, she thought.

Prince Gregor and his mother were seated on a dais to one side of the chamber. The princess wore a black gown shot with silver decoration, high-necked and long-sleeved. Her dark-haired son looked rather like an elf in his red and blue uniform. Cordelia thought he fidgeted remarkably little, under the circumstances.

The Emperor too had a ghostly presence, over closed circuit commlink from the Imperial Residence. Ezar was shown in the holovid seated, in full uniform, at what physical cost Cordelia could not guess, the tubes and monitor leads piercing his body concealed at least from the vid pickup. His face was paper-white, his skin almost transparent, as if he were literally fading from the stage he had dominated for so long.

The gallery was crammed with wives, staff, and guards. The women were elegantly dressed and decorated with jewelry, and Cordelia studied them with interest, then turned her attention back to pumping Vorpatril for information.

"Was Aral's appointment as Regent a surprise to you?" she asked.

"Not really. A few people took that resignation-and-retirement business after the Escobar mess seriously, but I never did."

"He meant it seriously, I thought."

"Oh, I don't doubt it. The first person Aral fools with that prosey-stone-soldier routine is himself. It's the sort of man he always wanted to be, I think. Like his father."

"Hm. Yes, I had noticed a certain political bent to his conversations. In the middle of the most extraordinary circumstances, too. Marriage proposals, for instance."

Vorpatril laughed. "I can just picture it. When he was young he was a real conservative—if you wanted to know what Aral thought about anything, all you had to do was ask Count Piotr, and multiply by two. But by the time we served together, he was getting . . . um . . . strange. If you could get him going . . ." There was a certain wicked reminiscence in his eye, which Cordelia promptly encouraged.

"How did you get him going? I thought political discussion was forbidden to officers."

He snorted. "I suppose they could forbid breathing with about as much chance of success. The dictum is, shall we say, sporadically enforced. Aral stuck to it, though, unless Rulf Vorhalas and I took him out and got him really relaxed."

"Aral? Relaxed?"

"Oh, yes. Now, Aral's drinking was notable—"

"I thought he was a terrible drinker. No stomach for it."

"Oh, that's what was notable. He seldom drank. Although he went through a bad period after his first wife died, when he used to run around with Ges Vorrutyer a lot . . . um . . ." He glanced sideways, and took another tack. "Anyway, it was dangerous to get him too relaxed, because then he'd go all depressed and serious, and then it didn't take a thing to get him on to whatever current injustice or incompetence or insanity was rousing his ire. God, the man could talk. By the time he'd had his fifth drink—just before he slid under the table for the night—he'd be declaiming revolution in iambic pentameter. I always thought he'd end up on the political side someday." He chuckled, and looked rather lovingly at the stocky red-and-blue-clad figure seated with the Counts on the far side of the chamber.

The Joint Council vote of confirmation for Vorkosigan's

Imperial appointment was a curious affair, to Cordelia's mind. She hadn't imagined it possible to get seventy-five Barrayarans to agree on which direction their sun rose in the morning, but the tally was nearly unanimous in favor of Emperor Ezar's choice. The exceptions were five set-jawed men who abstained, four loudly, one so weakly the Lord Guardian of the Speaker's Circle had to ask him to repeat himself. Even Count Vordarian voted yea, Cordelia noticed—perhaps Vortala had managed to repair last night's breach in some early-morning meeting after all. It all seemed a very auspicious and encouraging start to Vorkosigan's new job, anyway, and she said as much to Lord Vorpatril.

"Uh . . . yes, Milady," said Lord Vorpatril after a sideways smile at her. "Emperor Ezar made it clear he wanted united approval."

His tone made it clear she was missing cues, again. "Are you trying to tell me some of those men would rather have voted no?"

"That would be imprudent of them, at this juncture."

"Then the men who abstained . . . must have some courage of conscience." She studied the little group with new interest.

"Oh, *they're* all right," said Vorpatril.

"What do you mean? They are the opposition, surely."

"Yes, but they're the open opposition. No one plotting serious treason would mark himself so publicly. The fellows Aral will need to guard his back from are in the other mob, among the yes-men."

"Which ones?" Cordelia's brow wrinkled in worry.

"Who knows?" Lord Vorpatril shrugged, then answered his own question. "Negri, probably."

They were surrounded by a ring of empty seats. Cordelia hadn't been sure if it was for security or courtesy. Evidently the second, for two latecomers, a man in commander's dress greens and a younger one in rich-looking civilian clothes, arrived and apologetically sat in front of them. Cordelia thought they looked like brothers, and had the guess confirmed when the younger said,

"Look, there's Father, three seats behind old Vortala.
Which one's the new Regent?"

"The bandy-legged character in the red-and-blues, just
sitting down to Vortala's right."

Cordelia and Vorpatril exchanged a look behind their
backs, and Cordelia put a finger to her lips. Vorpatril
grinned and shrugged.

"What's the word on him in the Service?"

"Depends on who you ask," said the commander. "Sardi
thinks he's a strategic genius, and dotes on his commu-
niques. He's been all over the place. Every brushfire in
the last twenty-five years seems to have his name in it
someplace. Uncle Rulf used to think the world of him.
On the other hand, Niels, who was at Escobar, said he
was the most cold-blooded bastard he'd ever met."

"I hear he has a reputation as a secret progressive."

"There's nothing secret about it. Some of the senior
Vor officers are scared to death of him. He's been trying to get Father with him and Vortala on that new tax
ruling."

"Oh, yawn."

"It's the direct Imperial tax on inheritances."

"Ouch! Well, that wouldn't hit *him*, would it? The
Vorkosigans are so damn poor. Let Komarr pay. That's why
we conquered it, isn't it?"

"Not exactly, my fraternal ignoramus. Have any of you
town clowns met his Betan frill yet?"

"Men of fashion, sirrah," corrected his brother. "Not
to be confused with you Service grubs."

"No danger of that. No, really. There are the
damnedest rumors circulating about her, Vorkosigan, and
Vorrutyer at Escobar, most of which contradict each other.
I thought Mother might have a line on it."

"She keeps a low profile, for somebody who's supposed
to be three meters tall and eat battle cruisers for breakfast.
Scarcely anybody's seen her. Maybe she's ugly."

"They'll make a pair, then. Vorkosigan's no beauty
either."

Cordelia, vastly amused, hid a grin behind her hand,

until the commander said, "I don't know who that three-legged spastic is he has trailing him, though. Staff, do you suppose?"

"You'd think he could do better than that. What a mutant. Surely Vorkosigan has the pick of the Service, as Regent."

She felt she'd received a body blow, so great was the unexpected pain of the careless remark. Captain Lord Vorpatril scarcely seemed to notice it. He had heard it, but his attention was on the floor below, where oaths were being made. Droushnakovi, surprisingly, blushed, and turned her head away.

Cordelia leaned forward. Words boiled up within her, but she chose only a few, and fired them off in her coldest Captain's voice.

"Commander. And you, whoever you are." They looked back at her, surprised at the interruption. "For your information, the gentleman in question is Lieutenant Koudelka. And there are no better officers. Not in anybody's service."

They stared at her, irritated and baffled, unable to place her in their scheme of things. "I believe this was a private conversation, madam," said the commander stiffly.

"Quite so," she returned, equally stiffly, still boiling. "For eavesdropping, unavoidable as it was, I beg your pardon. But for that shameful remark upon Admiral Vorkosigan's secretary, *you* must apologize. It was a disgrace to the uniform you both wear and the service to your Emperor you both share." She kept her voice very low, almost hissing. She was trembling. *An overdose of Barrayar. Get hold of yourself.*

Vorpatril's wandering attention was drawn, startled, back to her by this speech. "Here, here," he remonstrated. "What is this—"

The commander turned around further. "Oh, Captain Vorpatril, sir. I didn't recognize you at first. Um . . ." He gestured helplessly at his red-haired attacker, as if to say, Is this lady with you? And if so, can't you keep her under control? He added coldly, "We have not met, madam."

"No, but I don't go 'round flipping over rocks to see what's living underneath." She was instantly conscious of having been lured into going too far. With difficulty, she put a lid on her temper. It wouldn't do to be making new enemies for Vorkosigan at the very moment he was taking up his duties.

Vorpatril, waking up to his responsibilities as escort, began, "Commander, you don't know who—"

"*Don't* . . . introduce us, Lord Vorpatril," Cordelia interrupted him. "We should only embarrass each other further." She pressed thumb and forefinger to the bridge of her nose, closing her eyes and gathering more conciliating words. *And I used to pride myself on keeping my temper.* She looked up at their furious faces.

"Commander. My lord." She correctly deduced the young man's title from his reference to his father, sitting among the counts. "My words were hasty and rude, and I take them back. I had no right to comment on a private conversation. I apologize. Most humbly."

"As well you should," snapped the young lord.

His brother had more self-control, and replied reluctantly, "I accept your apology, madam. I presume the lieutenant is some relative of yours. I apologize for whatever insult you felt was implied."

"And I accept your apology, Commander. Although Lieutenant Koudelka is not a relation, but only my second-dearest . . . enemy." She paused, and they exchanged frowns, hers of irony, his of puzzlement. "I would ask a favor of you, however, sir. Don't let a comment like that fall in Admiral Vorkosigan's hearing. Koudelka was one of his officers aboard the *General Vorkraft,* and was wounded in his defense during that political mutiny last year. He loves him as a son."

The commander was calming down, although Droushnakovi still looked as if she had a bad taste in her mouth. He smiled a little. "Are you implying I'd find myself doing guard duty on Kyril Island?"

What was Kyril Island? Some distant and unpleasant outpost, apparently. "I . . . doubt it. He wouldn't use his office to carry out a personal grudge. But it would cause him unnecessary pain."

"Madam." She had puzzled him thoroughly now, this plain-looking woman, so out-of-place in the glittering gallery. He turned back with his brother to watch the show below, and all maintained a sticky silence for another twenty minutes, until the ceremonies stopped for lunch. The crowds in both gallery and floor broke away to meet in the corridors of power.

She found Vorkosigan, Koudelka at his side, speaking with his father Count Piotr and another older man in count's robes. Vorpatril delivered her and vanished, and Aral greeted her with a tired smile.

"Dear Captain, are you holding up all right? I want you to meet Count Vorhalas. Admiral Rulf Vorhalas was his younger brother. We must go shortly, we're scheduled for a private lunch with the Princess and Prince Gregor."

Count Vorhalas bowed profoundly over her hand. "Milady. I'm honored."

"Count. I . . . only saw your brother briefly. But Admiral Vorhalas struck me as a man of outstanding worth." *And my side blew him away.* She felt queasy, with her hand in his, but he seemed to hold no personal animosity.

"Thank you, Milady. We all thought so. Ah, there are the boys. I promised them an introduction. Evon is itching for a place on the Staff, but I told him he'd have to earn it. I wish Carl had as much interest in the Service. My daughter will be mad with jealousy. You've stirred up all the girls, you know, Milady."

The count darted away to round up his sons. *Oh, God,* thought Cordelia. *It would have to be them.* The two men who had sat before her in the gallery were presented to her. They both blanched, and bowed nervously over her hand.

"But you've met," said Vorkosigan. "I saw you talking in the gallery. What did you find to discuss so animatedly, Cordelia?"

"Oh . . . geology. Zoology. Courtesy. Much on courtesy. We had quite a wide-ranging discussion. We each of us taught the other something, I think." She smiled, and did not flick an eyelid.

Commander Evon Vorhalas, looking rather ill, said, "Yes. I've . . . had a lesson I'll never forget, Milady."

Vorkosigan was continuing the introductions. "Commander Vorhalas, Lord Carl; Lieutenant Koudelka."

Koudelka, loaded with plastic flimsys, disks, the baton of the commander-in-chief of the armed forces that had just been presented to Vorkosigan as Regent-elect, and his own stick, and uncertain whether to shake hands or salute, managed to drop them all and do neither. There was a general scramble to retrieve the load, and Koudelka went red, bending awkwardly after it. Droushnakovi and he put a hand on his stick at the same time.

"I don't need your help, miss," Koudelka snarled at her in a low voice, and she recoiled to go stand rigidly behind Cordelia.

Commander Vorhalas handed him back some disks. "Pardon me, sir," said Koudelka. "Thank you."

"Not at all, Lieutenant. I was almost hit by disruptor fire myself once. Scared the hell out of me. You are an example to us all."

"It . . . didn't hurt, sir."

Cordelia, who knew from personal experience that this was a lie, held her peace, satisfied. The group broke up for its separate destinations. Cordelia paused before Evon Vorhalas.

"Nice to meet you, Commander. I predict you will go far, in your future career—and *not* in the direction of Kyril Island."

Vorhalas smiled tightly. "I believe you will, too, Milady." They exchanged wary and respectful nods, and Cordelia turned to take Vorkosigan's arm, and follow him to his next task, trailed by Koudelka and Droushnakovi.

The Barrayaran Emperor slipped into his final coma a week later, but lingered on another week beyond that. Aral and Cordelia were routed out of bed at Vorkosigan House in the early hours of the morning by a special messenger from the Imperial Residence, with the simple words, "The doctor thinks it's time, sir." They dressed hastily, and accompanied the messenger back to the beautiful chamber Ezar had chosen for the last month of his life, its priceless antiques cluttered over with off-worlder medical equipment.

The room was crowded, with the old man's personal physicians, Vortala, Count Piotr and themselves, the Princess and Prince Gregor, several ministers, and some men from the General Staff. They kept a quiet, standing death-watch for almost an hour before the still, decayed figure on the bed took on, almost imperceptibly, an added stillness. Cordelia thought it a gruesome scene to which to subject the boy, but his presence seemed ceremonially necessary. Very quietly, beginning with Vorkosigan, they turned to kneel and place their hands between Gregor's, to renew their oaths of fealty.

Cordelia too was guided by Vorkosigan to kneel before the boy. The prince—Emperor—had his mother's hair, but hazel eyes like Ezar and Serg, and Cordelia found herself wondering how much of his father, or his grandfather, was latent in him, its expression waiting on the power that would come with age. *Do you bear curses in your chromosomes, child?* she wondered as her hands were placed between his. Cursed or blessed, regardless, she gave him her oath. The words seemed to cut her last tie to Beta Colony; it parted with a *ping!* audible only to her.

I am a Barrayaran now. It had been a long strange journey, that began with a view of a pair of boots in the mud, and ended in these clean child's hands. *Do you know I helped kill your father, boy? Will you ever know? Pray not.* She wondered if it was delicacy or oversight, that she had never been required to give oath to Ezar Vorbarra.

Of all present, only Captain Negri wept. Cordelia only knew this because she was standing next to him, in the darkest corner of the room, and saw him twice brush his face with the back of his hand. His face grew suffused, and more lined, for a time; when he stepped forward to take his oath, it had returned to its normal blank hardness.

The five days of funeral ceremonies that followed were grueling for Cordelia, but not, she was led to understand, so grueling as the ones had been for Crown Prince Serg, which had run for two weeks, despite the absence of a body for a centerpiece. The public view was that Prince Serg had died the death of a heroic soldier. By Cordelia's count, only five human beings knew the whole truth of that subtle assassination. No, four, now that Ezar was no more. Perhaps the grave was the safest repository of Ezar's secrets. Well, the old man's torment was over now, his time done, his era passing.

There was no coronation as such for the boy Emperor, but instead a surprisingly business-like, if elegantly garbed, several days spent back in the Council chambers collecting personal oaths from ministers, counts, a host of their relatives, and anybody else who had not already made their vows in Ezar's death chamber. Vorkosigan too received oaths, seeming to grow burdened with their accumulation as if each had a physical weight.

The boy, closely supported by his mother, held up well. Kareen made sure Gregor's hourly breaks to rest were respected by the busy, impatient men who had thronged to the capital to discharge their obligation. The strangeness of the Barrayaran government system, with all its unwritten customs, pressed on Cordelia not so much at first glance, but gradually. And yet it seemed to work for them, somehow. They made it work. Pretending a government into existence. Perhaps all governments were such consensus fictions, at their hearts.

After the spate of ceremonies had died down, Cordelia began at last to establish her domestic routine at Vorkosigan House. Not that there was that much to do. Most days Vorkosigan left at dawn, Koudelka in tow, and returned after dark, to snatch a cold supper and lock himself in the library, or see men there, until bedtime. His long hours were a start-up cost, Cordelia told herself. He would settle in, become more efficient, when everything wasn't all for the first time. She remembered her first ship command in the Betan Astronomical Survey—not so very long ago—and her first few months of nervous hyper-preparedness. Later, the painfully studied tasks had become automatic, then nearly unconscious, and her personal life had re-emerged. Aral's would, too. She waited patiently, and smiled when she did see him.

Besides, she had a job. Gestating. It was a task of no little status, judging from the cosseting she received from everyone from Count Piotr down to the kitchen maid who brought her nutritious little snacks at odd hours. She hadn't received this much approval even when she'd returned from a yearlong survey mission with a zero-accident record. Reproduction seemed far more enthusiastically encouraged here than on Beta Colony.

After lunch one afternoon she lay with her feet up on a sofa in a shaded patio between the house and its back garden—gestating assiduously—and reflected upon the assorted reproductive customs of Barrayar versus Beta Colony. Gestation in uterine replicators, artifical wombs, seemed unknown here. On Beta Colony replicators were the most popular choice by three to one, but a large minority stood by claimed psycho-social advantages to the old-fashioned natural method. Cordelia had never been able to detect any difference between vitro and vivo babies, certainly not by the time they reached adulthood at twenty-two. Her brother had been vivo, herself vitro; her brother's co-parent had chosen vivo for both her children, and bragged about it rather a lot.

Cordelia had always assumed that when her turn came, she'd have her own kid cooked up in a replicator bank at the start of a Survey mission, to be ready and waiting for her arms upon her return. If she returned—there was always that possible catch, exploring the blind unknown. And assuming, also, that she could nail down an interested co-parent with whom to pool, willing and able to pass the physical, psychological, and economic tests and take the course to qualify for a parent's license.

Aral was going to be a suberb co-parent, she was certain. If he ever touched down again, from his new high place. Surely the first rush must be over soon. It was a long fall from that high place, with nowhere to land. Aral was her safe haven, if he fell first . . . she wrenched her meditations firmly into more positive channels.

Now, family *size;* that was the real, secret, wicked fascination of Barrayar. There were no legal limits here, no certificates to be earned, no third-child variances to be scrimped for; no rules, in fact, at all. She'd seen a woman on the street with not three but four children in tow, and no one had even stared. Cordelia had upped her own imagined brood from two to three, and felt deliciously sinful, till she'd met a woman with ten. Four, maybe? Six? Vorkosigan could afford it. Cordelia wriggled her toes and cuddled into the cushions, afloat on an atavistic cloud of genetic greed.

Barrayar's economy was wide open now, Aral said, despite the losses of the recent war. No wounds had touched the surface of the planet this time. The terraforming of the second continent opened new frontiers every day, and when the new planet Sergyar was cleared for colonization, the effect would triple. Labor was short everywhere, wages rising. Barrayar perceived itself to be severely underpopulated. Vorkosigan called the economic situation his gift from the gods, politically. So did Cordelia, for more personal, secret reasons; *herds* of little Vorkosigans. . . .

She could have a daughter. Not just one, but two—sisters! Cordelia had never had a sister. Captain Vorpatril's wife had two, she'd said.

Cordelia had meet Lady Vorpatril at one of the rare evening political-social events at Vorkosigan House. The affair was managed smoothly by the Vorkosigan House staff. All Cordelia had to do was show up appropriately dressed (she had acquired more clothes), smile a lot, and keep her mouth shut. She listened with fascination, trying to puzzle out yet more about How Things Were Done Here.

Alys Vorpatril too was pregnant. Lord Vorpatril had sort of stuck them together and ducked out. Naturally, they talked shop. Lady Vorpatril mourned much at her personal discomforts. Cordelia decided she herself must be fortunate; the anti-nausea med, the same chemical formulation that they used at home, worked, and she was only naturally tired, not from the weight of the still-tiny baby but from the surprising metabolic load. *Peeing for two* was how Cordelia thought of it. Well, after five-space navigational math, how hard could motherhood be?

Leaving aside Alys's whispered obstetrical horror stories, of course. Hemorrhages, strokes, kidney failure, birth injuries, oxygen interruption to fetal brains, infant heads grown larger than pelvic diameters and a spasming uterus laboring both mother and child to death . . . Medical complications were only a problem if one was somehow caught alone and isolated at term, and with these mobs of guards about that wasn't likely to happen to her. Bothari as a midwife? Bemusing thought. She shuddered.

She rolled over again on the lawn sofa, her brow creasing. Ah, Barrayar's primitive medicine. True, moms had popped kids for hundreds of thousands of years, pre-spaceflight, with less help than what was available here. Yet the niggling worry gnawed still, *Maybe I ought to go home for the birth.*

No. She was Barrayaran now, oath-sworn like the rest of the lunatics. It was a two-month journey. And besides, as far as she knew there was still an arrest warrant outstanding for her, charging military desertion, suspicion of espionage, fraud, anti-social violence—she probably shouldn't have tried to drown that idiot army psychiatrist in her aquarium, Cordelia supposed, sighing in memory of her harried and disordered departure from Beta Colony. Would her name ever be cleared? Not while Ezar's secrets stayed chambered in four skulls, surely.

No. Beta Colony was closed to her, had driven her out. Barrayar held no monopoly on political idiocy, that much was certain.

I can handle Barrayar. Aral and I. You bet.

It was time to go in. The sun was giving her a slight headache.

CHAPTER FOUR

One aspect of her new life as Regent-consort that Cordelia found easier to deal with than she'd anticipated was the influx of personal guards into their home. Her experience in the Betan Survey, and Vorkosigan's in the Barrayaran military service, had given them both practice with life in close quarters. It didn't take Cordelia long to start to know the persons in the uniforms, and take them on their own terms. The guards were a lively young group, hand-picked for their service and proud of it. Although when Piotr was also in residence, with all his liveried men including Bothari, the sense it gave Cordelia of living in a barracks became acute.

It was the Count who first suggested the informal hand-to-hand combat tournament between Illyan's men and his own. In spite of a vague mutter from the security commander about free training at the Emperor's expense, a ring was set up in the back garden, and the contest quickly became a weekly tradition. Even Koudelka was roped in, as referee and expert judge, with Piotr and Cordelia as cheering sections. Vorkosigan attended whenever time permitted, to Cordelia's gratification; she felt he needed the break in the grinding routine of government business to which he subjected himself daily.

Cordelia was settling down on the upholstered lawn sofa to watch the show one sunny autumn morning, attended by her handmaiden, when she suddenly remarked, "Why aren't you playing, Drou? Surely you need the practice as much as any of them. The excuse for this thing in the first place—not that you Barrayarans seem to need an excuse to practice mayhem—was that it was supposed to keep everybody on their toes."

Droushnakovi looked longingly at the ring, but said, "I wasn't invited, Milady."

"A rude oversight on somebody's part. Hm. Tell you what—go change your clothes. You can be my team. Aral can root for his own today. A proper Barrayaran contest should have at least three sides anyway, it's traditional."

"Do you think it will be all right?" she said doubtfully. "They might not like it."

The *they* in question were what Droushnakovi called the "real" guards, the liveried men.

"Aral won't mind. Anyone else who objects can argue with him. If they dare." Cordelia grinned, and Droushnakovi grinned back, then dashed off.

Aral arrived to settle comfortably beside her, and she told him of her plan. He raised an eyebrow. "Betan innovations? Well, why not? Brace yourself for chaff, though."

"I'm braced. They won't be as inclined to make jokes if she can pound a few of them. I think she can—on Beta Colony that girl would be a commando officer by now. All that natural talent is wasted toddling around after me all day. If she can't—well, then she shouldn't be guarding me anyway, eh?" She met his eyes.

"Point taken . . . I'll make sure Koudelka puts her in the first round against someone of her own height and weight class. In absolute terms she's a bit on the small side."

"She's bigger than you are."

"In height. I imagine I have a few kilos on her in weight. Nevertheless, your wish is my command. Oof." He climbed

back to his feet, and went to enter Droushnakovi on
Koudelka's list for the lists. Cordelia could not hear what
they said to each other, across the garden, but supplied her
own dialogue from gesture and expression, murmuring,
"Aral: Cordelia wants Drou to play. Kou: Aw! Who wants
gurls? Aral: Tough. Kou: They mess everything up, and
besides, they cry a lot. Sergeant Bothari will squash her—
hm, I do hope that's what that gesture means, otherwise
you're getting obscene, Kou—wipe that smirk off your face,
Vorkosigan—Aral: The little woman insists. You know how
henpecked I am. Kou: Oh, all right. Phooey. Transaction
complete: the rest is up to you, Drou."

Vorkosigan rejoined her. "All set. She'll start against
one of father's men."

Droushnakovi returned, attired in loose slacks and a
knit shirt, as close to the men's workout suits as her wardrobe could provide. The Count came out to consult with
Sergeant Bothari, his team leader, and find a place to
warm his bones in the sun beside them.

"What's this?" Piotr asked, as Koudelka called
Droushnakovi's name for the second pair up. "Are we
importing Betan customs now?"

"The girl has a lot of natural talent," Vorkosigan
explained. "Besides, she needs the practice as much as
any of them—more; she has the most important job of
any of them."

"You'll be wanting women in the Service, next," complained Piotr. "Where will it end? That's what I'd like to
know."

"What's wrong with women in the Service?" Cordelia
asked, baiting him a little.

"It's unmilitary," snapped the old man.

"'Military' is whatever wins the war, I should think."
She smiled blandly. A small friendly warning pinch from
Vorkosigan restrained her from rubbing in the point any
harder.

In any case it wasn't necessary. Piotr turned to watch
his player, saying only, "Humph."

The Count's player carelessly underestimated his

opponent, and took the first fall for his error. It woke him up considerably. The onlookers shouted raucous comments. He pinned her on the next fall.

"Koudelka counted a bit fast there, didn't he?" asked Cordelia, as the Count's player let Droushnakovi up after the decision.

"Mm. Maybe," said Vorkosigan in a non-committal tone.

"She pulls her punches a bit, too, I notice. She'll never make it to the next round if she keeps doing that in this company."

On the next encounter, the deciding one for the two-out-of-three, Droushnakovi applied a successful arm-bar, but let it slip away from her.

"Oh, too bad," murmured the Count cheerfully.

"You should have let him break it!" cried Cordelia, getting more and more involved. The Count's player took a soft and sloppy fall. "Call it, Kou!" But the referee, leaning on his stick, let it pass. In any case, Droushnakovi spotted an opportunity for a choke, and grabbed it.

"Why doesn't he tap out?" asked Cordelia.

"He'd rather pass out," replied Aral. "That way he won't have to listen to his friends."

Droushnakovi was beginning to look doubtful, as the face clamped under her arm turned a dusky purple. Cordelia could see release coming, and leaped up to shout, "Hang on, Drou! Don't let him fake you out!" Droushnakovi took a firmer hold, and the figure stopped struggling.

"Go ahead and call it, Koudelka," called Piotr, shaking his head ruefully. "He has to be on duty tonight." And so the round went to Droushnakovi.

"Good work, Drou!" said Cordelia as Droushnakovi returned to them. "But you've got to be more aggressive. Release your killer instincts."

"I agree," said Vorkosigan unexpectedly. "That little hesitation you display could be deadly—and not just for yourself." He held her eye. "You're practicing for the real thing here, although we all pray that no such situation occurs. The kind of all-out effort it takes should be absolutely automatic."

"Yes, sir. I'll try, sir."

The next round featured Sergeant Bothari, who flattened his opponent twice in rapid succession. The defeated crawled out of the ring. Several more rounds went by, and it was Droushnakovi's turn again, this time with one of Illyan's men.

They connected, and in the struggle he goosed her effectively, loosing catcalls from the audience. In her angry distraction, he pulled her off-balance for a fairly clean fall.

"Did you see that!" cried Cordelia to Aral. "That was a dirty trick!"

"Mm. It wasn't one of the eight forbidden blows, though. You couldn't disqualify him on it. Nevertheless . . ." he motioned Koudelka for a time-out, and called Droushnakovi over for a quiet word.

"We saw the blow," he murmured. Her lips were tight and her face red. "Now, as Milady's champion, an insult to you is in some measure an insult to her. Also a very bad precedent. It is my desire that your opponent not leave the ring conscious. How, is your problem. You may take that as an order, if you like. And don't worry needlessly about breaking bones, either," he added blandly.

Droushnakovi returned to the ring with a slight smile on her face, eyes narrowed and glittering. She followed a feint with a lightning kick to her opponent's jaw, a punch to his belly, and a low body blow to his knees that brought him down with a boom on the matting. He did not get up. There was a slightly shocked silence.

"You're right," said Vorkosigan. "She was pulling her punches."

Cordelia smiled smugly, and settled herself more comfortably. "Thought so."

The next round to come up for Droushnakovi was the semi-final, and it was the luck of the draw that her opponent was Sergeant Bothari.

"Hm," murmured Cordelia to Vorkosigan. "I'm not sure about the psychodynamics of this. Is it safe? I mean for both of them, not just for her. And not just physically."

"I think so," he replied, equally quietly. "Life in the

Count's service has been a nice, quiet routine for Bothari.
He's been taking his medication. I think he's in pretty
good shape at the moment. And the atmosphere of the
practice ring is a safe, familiar one for him. It would take
more tension than Drou can provide to unhinge him."

Cordelia nodded, satisfied, and settled back to watch
the slaughter. Droushnakovi looked nervous.

The start was slow, with Droushnakovi mainly concentrating on staying out of reach. Swinging around to watch,
Lieutenant Koudelka accidently pressed the release of his
swordstick, and the cover shot off into the bushes. Bothari
was distracted for an instant, and Drou struck, low and
fast. Bothari landed clean with a firm impact, although
he rolled immediately to his feet with scarcely a pause.

"Oh, good throw!" cried Cordelia ecstatically. Drou
looked quite as amazed as everyone else. "Call it, Kou!"

Lieutenant Koudelka frowned. "It wasn't a fair throw,
Milady." One of the Count's men retrieved the cover, and
Koudelka resheathed the weapon. "It was my fault. Un-
fair distraction."

"You didn't call it unfair distraction a while ago,"
Cordelia objected.

"Let it go, Cordelia," said Vorkosigan quietly.

"But he's cheating her out of her point!" she whispered
back furiously. "And what a point! Bothari's been tops in
every round to date."

"Yes. It took six months practice on the old *General
Vorkraft* before Koudelka ever threw him."

"Oh. Hm." That gave her pause. "Jealousy?"

"Haven't you seen it? She has everything he lost."

"I have seen he's been blasted rude to her on occasion. It's a shame. She's obviously—"

Vorkosigan held up a restraining finger. "Talk about it
later. Not here."

She paused, then nodded in agreement. "Right."

The round went on, with Sergeant Bothari putting
Droushnakovi practically through the mat, twice, quickly,
and then dispatching his final challenger with almost equal
ease.

A conference of players on the other side of the garden sent Koudelka limping over as an emissary.

"Sir? We were wondering if you would go a demonstration round. With Sergeant Bothari. None of the fellows here have ever seen that."

Vorkosigan waved down the idea, not very convincingly. "I'm not in shape for it, Lieutenant. Besides, how did they ever find out about that? Been telling tales?"

Koudelka grinned. "A few. I think it would enlighten them. About what kind of game this can really be."

"A bad example, I'm afraid."

"I've never seen this," murmured Cordelia. "Is it really that good a show?"

"I don't know. Have I offended you lately? Would watching Bothari pound me be a catharsis?"

"I think it would be for you," said Cordelia, falling in with his obvious desire to be persuaded. "I think you've missed that sort of thing, in this headquarters life you've been leading lately."

"Yes. . . ." He rose, to a bit of clapping, and removed uniform jacket, shoes, rings, and the contents of his pockets, and stepped to the ring to do some stretching and warm-up exercises.

"You'd better referee, Kou," he called back. "Just to prevent undue alarm."

"Yes, sir." Koudelka turned to Cordelia before limping back to the arena. "Um. Just remember, Milady. They never killed each other in four years of this."

"Why do I find that more ominous than reassuring? Still, Bothari's done six rounds this morning. Maybe he's getting tired."

The two men faced off in the arena and bowed formally. Koudelka backed hastily out of the way. The raucous good humor died away among the watchers, as the icy cold and concentrated stillness of the two players drew all eyes. They began to circle, lightly, then met in a blur. Cordelia did not quite see what happened, but when they parted Vorkosigan was spitting blood from a lacerated mouth, and Bothari was hunched over his belly.

In the next contact Bothari landed a kick to
Vorkosigan's back that echoed off the garden walls and
propelled him completely out of the arena, to land rolling and running back in spite of disrupted breathing. The
men in whose protection the Regent's life was supposed
to lie began to look worriedly at one another. At the next
grappling Vorkosigan underwent a vicious fall, with Bothari
landing atop him instantly for a follow-up choke. Cordelia
thought she could see his ribs bend from the knees on
his chest. A couple of the guards started forward, but
Koudelka waved them back, and Vorkosigan, face dark and
suffused, tapped out.

"First point to Sergeant Bothari," called Koudelka.
"Best two out of three, sir?"

Sergeant Bothari stood, smiling a little, and Vorkosigan
sat on the mat a minute, regaining his wind. "One more,
anyway. Got to get my revenge. Out of shape."

"Told you so," murmured Bothari.

They circled again. They met, parted, met again, and
suddenly Bothari was doing a spectacular cartwheel, while
Vorkosigan rolled beneath to grab an arm-bar that nearly
dislocated his shoulder in his twisting fall. Bothari
struggled briefly against the lock, then tapped out. This
time it was Bothari who sat on the mat a minute before
getting up.

"That's amazing," Droushnakovi commented, eyes avid.
"Especially considering how much smaller he is."

"Small but vicious," agreed Cordelia, fascinated. "Keep
that in mind."

The third round was brief. A blur of grappling and blows
and messy joint fall resolved suddenly in an armlock, with
Bothari in charge. Vorkosigan unwisely attempted a break,
and Bothari, quite expressionlessly, dislocated his elbow
with an audible pop. Vorkosigan yelled and tapped out.
Once again Koudelka suppressed a rush of uninvited aid.

"Put it back, Sergeant," Vorkosigan groaned from his
seat on the ground, and Bothari braced one foot on his
former captain and gave the arm an accurately aligned
yank.

"Must remember," gasped Vorkosigan, "not to do that."

"At least he didn't break it this time," said Koudelka encouragingly, and helped him up, with Bothari's assistance. Vorkosigan limped back to the lawn chair, and seated himself, very cautiously, at Cordelia's feet. Bothari, too, was moving a lot more slowly and stiffly.

"And that," said Vorkosigan, still catching his breath, "is how . . . we used to play the game . . . aboard the old *General Vorkraft*."

"All that effort," remarked Cordelia. "And how often did you ever get into a real hand-to-hand combat situation?"

"Very, very seldom. But when we did, we won."

The party broke up, with a murmuring undercurrent of comment from the other players. Cordelia accompanied Aral off to help with first-aid to his elbow and mouth, a hot soak and rubdown, and a change of clothes.

During the rubdown she brought up the personnel problem that had been growing in her notice.

"Do you suppose you could say something to Kou about the way he treats Drou? It's not like his usual self at all. She about does flips trying to be nice to him. And he doesn't even treat her with the courtesy he'd give one of his men. She's practically a fellow officer. And, unless I'm totally wide of the mark, madly in love with him. Why doesn't he see it?"

"What makes you think he doesn't?" asked Aral slowly.

"His behavior, of course. A shame. They'd make quite a pair. Don't you think she's attractive?"

"Marvelously. But then, I like tall amazons," he grinned over his shoulder at her, "as everyone knows. It's not every man's taste. But if that's a matchmaking gleam I detect in your eye—do you suppose it could be maternal hormones, by the way?"

"Shall I dislocate your other elbow?"

"Ugh. No thanks. I'd forgotten how painful a workout with Bothari could be. Ah, that's better. Down a bit . . ."

"You're going to have some astonishing bruises there tomorrow."

"Don't I know it. But before you get carried away over Drou's love life . . . have you thought carefully about Koudelka's injuries?"

"Oh." Cordelia was struck silent. "I'd assumed . . . that his sexual functions were as well repaired as the rest of him."

"Or as poorly. It's a very delicate bit of surgery."

Cordelia pursed her lips. "Do you know this for a fact?"

"No, I don't. I do know that in all our conversations the subject was never once brought up. Ever."

"Hm. Wish I knew how to interpret that. It sounds a little ominous. Do you think you could ask . . . ?"

"Good God, Cordelia, of course not! What a question to ask the man. Particularly if the answer is no. I've got to work with him, remember."

"Well, I've got to work with Drou. She's no use to me if she pines away and dies of a broken heart. He has reduced her to tears, more than once. She goes off where she thinks nobody's looking."

"Really? That's hard to imagine."

"You can hardly expect me to tell her he's not worth it, all things considered. But does he really dislike her? Or is it just self-defense?"

"Good question . . . For what it's worth, my driver made a joke about her the other day—not even a very offensive one—and Kou got rather frosty with him. I don't think he dislikes her. But I do think he envies her."

Cordelia left the subject on that ambiguous note. She longed to help the pair, but had no answer to offer for their dilemma. Her own mind had no trouble generating creative solutions to the practical problems of physical intimacy posed by the lieutenant's injuries, but shrank from the violation of their shy reserve that offering them would entail. She suspected wryly that she would merely shock them. Sex therapy appeared to be unheard of, here.

True Betan, she had always considered a double standard of sexual behavior to be a logical impossibility. Dabbling now on the fringes of Barrayaran high society in Vorkosigan's wake, she began to finally see how it could be done. It all seemed to come down to impeding the free flow of information to certain persons, preselected by an unspoken code somehow known to and agreed upon by all present but her. One could not mention sex to or in front of unmarried women or children. Young men, it appeared, were exempt from all rules when talking to each other, but not if a woman of any age or degree were present. The rules also changed bewilderingly with variations of the social status of those present. And married women, in groups free of male eavesdroppers, sometimes underwent the most astonishing transformations in apparent databases. Some subjects could be joked about but not discussed seriously. And some variations could not be mentioned at all. She had blighted more than one conversation beyond hope of recovery by what seemed to her a perfectly obvious and casual remark, and been taken aside by Aral for a quick debriefing.

She tried writing out a list of the rules she thought she had deduced, but found them so illogical and conflicting, especially in the area of what certain people were supposed to pretend not to know in front of certain other people, she gave up the effort. She did show the list to Aral, who read it in bed one night and nearly doubled over laughing.

"Is that what we really look like to you? I like your Rule Seven. Must keep it in mind . . . I wish I'd known it in my youth. I could have skipped all those godawful Service training vids."

"If you snicker any harder, you're going to get a nosebleed," she said tartly. "These are your rules, not mine. You people play by them. I just try to figure them out."

"My sweet scientist. Hm. You certainly call things by their correct names. We've never tried . . . would you like to violate Rule Eleven with me, dear Captain?"

"Let me, see, which one—oh, yes! Certainly. Now? And while we're about it, let's knock off Thirteen. My hormones are up. I remember my brother's co-parent told me about this effect, but I didn't really believe her at the time. She says you make up for it later, post-partum."

"Thirteen? I'd never have guessed. . . ."

"That's because, being Barrayaran, you spend so much time following Rule Two."

Anthropology was forgotten, for a time. But she found she could crack him up, later, with a properly timed mutter of "Rule Nine, sir."

The season was turning. There had been a hint of winter in the air that morning, a frost that had wilted some of the plants in Count Piotr's back garden. Cordelia anticipated her first real winter with fascination. Vorkosigan promised her snow, frozen water, something she'd experienced on only two Survey missions. *Before spring, I shall bear a son. Huh.*

But the afternoon had basked in the autumn light, warming again. The flat roof of Vorkosigan House above the front wing now breathed back that heat around Cordelia's ankles as she picked her way across it, though the air on her cheeks was cooling to crispness as the sun slanted to the city's horizon.

"Good evening, boys." Cordelia nodded to the two guards posted to this rooftop duty station.

They nodded back, the senior touching his forehead in a hesitant semi-salute. "Milady."

Cordelia had taken to regular sunset-watching up here. The view of the cityscape from this four-floors-up vantage was very fine. She could catch a gleam of the river that divided the town, beyond trees and buildings. Although the excavation of a large hole a few blocks away along the line of sight suggested that the riverine scene would be occluded soon by new architecture. The tallest turret of Vorhartung Castle, where she'd attended all those ceremonies in the Council of Counts' chamber, peaked from a bluff overlooking the water.

Beyond Vorhartung Castle lay the oldest parts of the capital. She'd not yet seen that area, its kinked one-horse-wide streets impassable to groundcars, though she'd flown over the strange, low, dark blots in the heart of the city. The newer parts, glittering out toward the horizon, were more like galactic standard, patterned around the modern transportation systems.

None of it was like Beta Colony. Vorbarr Sultana was all spread out on the surface, or climbed skyward, strangely two-dimensional and exposed. Beta Colony's cities plunged down into shafts and tunnels, many-layered and complex, cozy and safe. Indeed, Beta Colony did not have architecture so much as it had interior design. It was amazing, the variety of schemes people came up with to vary dwellings that had *outsides*.

The guards twitched and sighed, as she leaned on the stonework, gazing out. They really didn't like it when she strayed nearer than three meters to the edge, though the space was only six meters wide. But she should be able to spot Vorkosigan's groundcar turning into the street soon. Sunsets were all very well, but her eyes turned downward.

She inhaled the complex odors, from vegetation, water vapor, industrial waste gases. Barrayar permitted an amazing amount of air dumping, as if . . . well, air *was* free, here. Nobody measured it, there were no air processing and filtration fees. . . . Did these people even realize how rich they were? All the air they could breathe, just by stepping outdoors, taken for granted as casually as they took frozen water falling from the sky. She took an extra breath, as if she could somehow greedily hoard it, and smiled—

A distant, crackling, hard-edged *boom* shattered her thoughts and stopped her breath. Both guards jumped. *So, you heard a bang. It doesn't necessarily have anything to do with Aral.* And, icily, *It sounded like a sonic grenade. Not a little one. Dear God.* There was a column of smoke and dust rising from a street-canyon several blocks over, she couldn't see the source—she craned outward—

"Milady." The younger guard grasped her upper arm. "Please go inside." His face was tense, eyes wide. The senior man had his hand clamped to his ear, sucking info off his comm channel—*she* had no comm link.

"What's coming on?" she asked.

"Milady, please go below!" He hustled her toward the trapdoor to the attic, from which stairs led down to the fourth floor. "I'm sure it was nothing," he soothed as he pushed.

"It was a Class Four sonic grenade, probably air-tube launched," she informed his appalling ignorance. "Unless the thrower was suicidal. Haven't you ever heard one go off?"

Droushnakovi shot out the trapdoor, a buttered roll squashed in one hand and her stunner clutched in the other. "Milady?" The guard, looking relieved, shoved Cordelia at her and returned to his senior. Cordelia, screaming inside, grinned through clenched teeth and allowed herself to be guarded, climbing dutifully down the trap.

"What happened?" she hissed to Droushnakovi.

"Don't know yet. The red alert went off in the basement refectory, and everybody ran for their posts," panted Drou. She must have practically teleported up the six flights.

"*Ngh.*" Cordelia galloped down the stairs, wishing for a drop tube. The comconsole in the library would surely be manned—somebody must have a comm link—she spun down the circular staircase and pelted across the black and white stones.

The house guard commander was indeed at the post, channeling orders. Count Piotr's senior liveried man jittered at his shoulder. "They're coming straight here," the ImpSec man said over his shoulder. "You fetch that doctor." The brown-uniformed man dashed out.

"What happened?" Cordelia demanded. Her heart was hammering now, and not just from the dash downstairs.

He glanced up at her, started to say something calming and meaningless, and changed his mind in mid-breath. "Somebody took a potshot at the Regent's groundcar. They missed. They're continuing on here."

"How near a miss?"

"I don't know, Milady."

He probably didn't. But if the groundcar still functioned . . . Helplessly, she gestured him back to his work, and wheeled

to return to the foyer, now manned by a couple of Count
Piotr's men, who discouraged her from standing too near
the door. She hung on the stair railing three steps up and
bit her lip.

"Was Lieutenant Koudelka with him, do you think?"
asked Droushnakovi faintly.

"Probably. He usually is," Cordelia answered absently,
her eyes on the door, waiting, waiting. . . .

She heard the car pull up. One of Count Piotr's men
opened the house door. Security men swarmed over the
silver shape of the vehicle in the portico—God, where
did they all *come* from? The car's shiny finish was scored
and smoked, but not deeply dented; the rear canopy was
not cracked, though the front was scarred. The rear doors
swung up, and Cordelia stretched for a view of Vorkosigan,
maddeningly obstructed by the green backs of the ImpSec
men. They parted. Lieutenant Koudelka sat in the aperture, blinking dizzily, blood dripping down his chin, then
was levered to his feet by a guard. Vorkosigan emerged
at last, refusing to be hustled, waving back help. Even
the most worried guards did not dare to touch him without an invitation. Vorkosigan strode inside, grim-faced and
pale. Koudelka, propped by his stick and an ImpSec
corporal, followed, looking wilder. The blood issued from
his nose. Piotr's man swung closed the front door of
Vorkosigan House, shutting out three-fourths of the chaos.

Aral met her eyes, above the heads of the men, and
the saturnine look fixed on his face slipped just a little.
He offered her a fractional nod, *I'm all right.* Her lips
tightened in return, *You'd by-God better be. . . .*

Kou was saying in a shaken voice, "—bloody great hole
in the street! Could've swallowed a freight shuttle. That
driver has amazing reflexes—what?" He shook his head
at a questioner. "Sorry, my ears are ringing—come again?"
He stood openmouthed, as if he could drink in sound
orally, touched his face and stared in surprise at his crim-
son-smeared hand.

"Your ears are only stunned, Kou," said Vorkosigan. His
voice was calm, but much too loud. "They'll be back to

normal by tomorrow morning." Only Cordelia realized the raised tone wasn't for Koudelka's benefit—Vorkosigan couldn't hear himself, either. His eyes shifted too quickly, the only hint that he was trying to read lips.

Simon Illyan and a physician arrived at almost the same moment. Vorkosigan and Koudelka were taken to a quiet back parlor, shedding all the—to Cordelia's mind—rather useless guards. Cordelia and Droushnakovi followed. The physician began an immediate examination, starting, at Vorkosigan's command, with the gory Koudelka.

"One shot?" asked Illyan.

"Only one," confirmed Vorkosigan, watching his face. "If they'd lingered for a second try, they could have bracketed me."

"If he'd lingered, we could have bracketed *him*. A forensic team's on the firing site now. The assassin's long gone, of course. A clever spot, he had a dozen escape routes."

"We vary our route daily," Lieutenant Koudelka, following this with difficulty, said around the cloth he pressed to his face. "How did he know where to set up his ambush?"

"Inside information?" Illyan shrugged, his teeth clenching at the thought.

"Not necessarily," said Vorkosigan. "There are only so many routes, this close to home. He could have been set up waiting for days."

"Precisely at the limit of our close-search perimeter?" said Illyan. "I don't like it."

"It bothers me more that he missed," said Vorkosigan. "Why? Could it have been some sort of warning shot? An attempt, not on my life, but on my balance of mind?"

"It was old ordnance," said Illyan. "There could have been something wrong with its tracker—nobody detected a laser rangefinder pulse." He paused, taking in Cordelia's white face. "I'm sure it was a lone lunatic, Milady. At least, it was certainly only one man."

"How does a lone maniac get hold of military-grade weaponry?" she inquired tartly.

Illyan looked uncomfortable. "We will be investigating that. It was definitely old issue."

"Don't you destroy obsolete stockpiles?"

"There's so much of it. . . ."

Cordelia glared at this wit-scattered utterance. "He only needed one shot. If he'd managed a direct hit on that sealed car, Aral'd have been emulsified. Your forensic team would be trying right now to sort out which molecules were his and which were Kou's."

Droushnakovi turned faintly green; Vorkosigan's saturnine look was now firmly back in place.

"You want me to give you a precise resonance reflection amplitude calculation for that sealed passenger cabin, Simon?" Cordelia went on hotly. "Whoever chose that weapon was a competent military tech—if, fortunately, a poorish shot." She bit back further words, recognizing, even if no one else did, the suppressed hysteria driving the speed of her speech.

"My apologies. Captain Naismith." Illyan's tone grew more clipped. "You are quite correct." His nod was a shade more respectful.

Aral tracked this interplay, his face lightening, for the first time, with some hidden amusement.

Illyan took himself off, conspiracy theories no doubt dancing in his head. The doctor confirmed Aral's combat-experienced diagnosis of aural stun, issued powerful anti-headache pills—Aral hung on to his firmly—and made an appointment to re-check both men in the morning.

When Illyan stopped back by Vorkosigan House in the late evening to confer with his guard commander, it was all Cordelia could do not to grab him by the jacket and pin him to the nearest wall to shake out his information. She confined herself to simply asking, "Who tried to kill Aral? Who *wants* to kill Aral? Whatever benefit do they imagine they'll gain?"

Illyan sighed. "Do you want the short list, or the long one, Milady?"

"How long is the short list?" she asked in morbid fascination.

"Too long. But I can name you the top layer, if you like." He ticked them off on his fingers. "The Cetagandans, always. They had counted on political chaos here, following Ezar's death. They're not above prodding it along. An assassination is cheap interference, compared to an invasion fleet. The Komarrans, for old revenge or new revolt. Some there still call the Admiral the Butcher of Komarr—"

Cordelia, knowing the whole story behind that loathed sobriquet, winced.

"The anti-Vor, because my lord Regent is too conservative for their tastes. The military right, who fear he is too progressive for theirs. Leftover members of Prince Serg and Vorrutyer's old war party. Former operatives of the now-suppressed Ministry of Political Education, though I doubt one of them would have missed. Negri's department used to train them. Some disgruntled Vor who thinks he came out short in the recent power-shift. Any lunatic with access to weapons and a desire for instant fame as a big-game hunter—shall I go on?"

"Please don't. But what about today? If motive yields too broad a field of suspects, what about method and opportunity?"

"We have a little to work with there, though too much of it is negative. As I noted, it was a very clean attempt. Whoever set it up had to have access to certain kinds of knowledge. We'll work those angles first."

It was the anonymity of the assassination attempt that bothered her most, Cordelia decided. When the killer could be anyone, the impulse to suspect everyone became overwhelming. Paranoia was a contagious disease here, it seemed; Barrayarans gave it to each other. Well, Negri and Illyan's combined forces must winkle out some concrete facts soon. She packed all her fears down hard into a little tiny compartment in the pit of her stomach, and locked them there. Next to her child.

Vorkosigan held her tight that night, curled into the

curve of his stocky body, though he made no sexual
advances. He just held her. He didn't fall asleep for hours,
despite the painkillers that glazed his eyes. She didn't fall
asleep till he did. His snores lulled her at last. There
wasn't that much to say. *They missed; we go on.*

Till the next try.

CHAPTER FIVE

The Emperor's Birthday was a traditional Barrayaran holiday, celebrated with feasting, dancing, drinking, veterans' parades, and an incredible amount of apparently totally unregulated fireworks. It would make a great day for a surprise attack on the capital, Cordelia decided; an artillery barrage could be well under way before anybody noticed it in the general din. The uproar began at dawn.

The duty guards, who had a natural tendency to jump at sudden noises anyway, were twitchy and miserable, except for a couple more youthful types who attempted to celebrate with a few crackers let off inside the walls. They were taken aside by the guard commander, and emerged much later, pale and shrunken, to slink off. Cordelia later saw them hauling rubbish under the command of a sardonic housemaid, while a scullery girl and the second cook galloped happily out of the house for a surprise day off. The Emperor's Birthday was a moveable feast. The Barrayarans' enthusiasm for the holiday seemed undaunted by the fact that, due to Ezar's death and Gregor's ascension, this was the second time they would celebrate it this year.

Cordelia passed up an invitation to attend a major

military review that gobbled Aral's morning in favor of
staying fresh for the event of the evening—the event
of the year, she was given to understand—personal
attendence upon the Emperor's birthday dinner at the
Imperial Residence. She looked forward to seeing
Kareen and Gregor again, however briefly. At least she
was certain that her clothing was all right. Lady
Vorpatril, who had both excellent taste and an advance
line on Barrayaran-style maternity wear, had taken pity
on Cordelia's cultural bafflement and offered herself as
an expert native guide.

As a result, Cordelia confidently wore an impeccably
cut forest green silk dress that swirled from shoulder to
floor, with an open overvest of thick ivory velvet. Live
flowers in matching colors were arranged in her copper
hair by the live human hairdresser Alys also sent on. Like
their public events, the Barrayarans made of their clothes
a sort of folk-art, as elaborate as Betan body paint.
Cordelia couldn't be sure from Aral—his face always lit
when he saw her—but judging from the delighted "Oohs"
of Count Piotr's female staff, Cordelia's sartorial art team
had outdone themselves.

Waiting at the foot of the spiral stairs in the front hall,
she smoothed the panel of green silk surreptitiously down
over her belly. A little over three months of metabolic
overdrive, and all she had to show for it was this grape-
fruit-sized lump—so much had happened since midsummer, it seemed like her pregnancy ought to be
progressing faster to keep up. She purred an encouraging mental mantra bellywards, *Grow, grow, grow. . . .* At
least she was actually beginning to look pregnant, instead
of just feel exhausted. Aral shared her nightly fascination
with their progress, gently feeling with spread fingers, so
far without success, for the butterfly-wing flutters of movement through her skin.

Aral himself now appeared, with Lieutenant Koudelka.
They were both thoroughly scrubbed, shaved, cut,
combed, and chromatically blinding in their formal red-
and-blue Imperial parade uniforms. Count Piotr joined

them wearing the uniform Cordelia had seen him in at the Joint Council sessions, brown and silver, a more glittery version of his armsmen's livery. All twenty of Piotr's armsmen had some sort of formal function tonight, and had been driven to meticulous preparation all week by their frenzied commander. Droushnakovi, accompanying Cordelia, wore a simplified garment in Cordelia's colors, carefully cut to facilitate rapid movement and conceal weaponry and comm links.

After a moment for everyone to admire each other, they herded through the front doors to the waiting groundcars. Aral handed Cordelia into her vehicle personally, then stepped back. "See you there, love."

"What?" Her head swiveled. "Oh. Then that second car . . . isn't just for the size of the group?"

Aral's mouth tightened fractionally. "No. It seems . . . prudent, to me, that we should travel in separate vehicles from now on."

"Yes," she said faintly. "Quite."

He nodded, and turned away. *Damn* this place. Taking yet another bite out of their lives, out of her heart. They had so little time together anymore, losing even a little more hurt.

Count Piotr, apparently, was to be Aral's stand-in, at least for tonight; he slid in beside her. Droushnakovi sat across from them, and the canopy was sealed. The car turned smoothly into the street. Cordelia craned over her shoulder, trying to see Aral's car, but it followed too far back for her even to catch a glimpse. She straightened, sighing.

The sun was sinking yellowly in a grey bank of clouds, and lights were beginning to glow in the cool damp autumn evening, giving the city a somber, melancholy atmosphere. Maybe a raucous street party—they drove around several—wasn't such a bad idea. The celebrators reminded Cordelia of primitive Earth men banging pots and firing guns to drive off the dragon that was eating the eclipsing moon. This strange autumn sadness could consume an unwary soul. Gregor's birthday was well timed.

Piotr's knobby hands fiddled with a brown silk bag embroidered with the Vorkosigan crest in silver. Cordelia eyed it with interest. "What's that?"

Piotr smiled slightly, and handed it to her. "Gold coins."

More folk-art; the bag and its contents were a tactile treat. She caressed the silk, admired the needlework, and shook a few gleaming sculptured disks out into her hand. "Pretty." Prior to the end of the Time of Isolation, gold had had great value on Barrayar, Cordelia recalled reading. *Gold* to her Betan mind called up something like, *Sometimes-useful metal to the electronics industry,* but ancient peoples had waxed mystical about it. "Does this mean something?"

"Ha! Indeed. It's the Emperor's birthday present."

Cordelia pictured five-year-old Gregor playing with a bag of gold. Besides building towers and maybe practicing counting, it was hard to figure what the boy could do with it. She hoped he was past the age of putting everything in his mouth; those disks were just the right size for a child to swallow or choke on. "I'm sure he'll like it," she said a little doubtfully.

Piotr chuckled. "You don't know what's going on, do you?"

Cordelia sighed. "I almost never do. Cue me." She settled back, smiling. Piotr had gradually become an enthusiast in explaining Barrayar to her, always seeming pleased to discover some new pocket of her ignorance and fill it with information and opinion. She had the feeling he could be lecturing her for the next twenty years and not run out of baffling topics.

"The Emperor's birthday is the traditional end of the fiscal year, for each count's district in relation to the Imperial government. In other words, it's tax day, except— the Vor are not taxed. That would imply too subordinate a relationship to the Imperium. Instead, we give the Emperor a present."

"Ah . . ." said Cordelia. "You don't run this place for a year on sixty little bags of gold, sir."

"Of course not. The real funds went from Hassadar to Vorbarr Sultana by comm link transfer earlier today. The gold is merely symbolic."

Cordelia frowned. "Wait. Haven't you done this once this year?"

"In the spring for Ezar, yes. So we've just changed the date of our fiscal year."

"Isn't that disruptive to your banking system?"

He shrugged. "We manage." He grinned suddenly. "Where do you think the term 'Count' came from, anyway?"

"Earth, I thought. A pre-atomic—late Roman, actually—term for a nobleman who ran a county. Or maybe the district was named after the rank."

"On Barrayar, it is in fact a contraction of the term 'accountant.' The first 'counts were Varadar Tau's—an amazing bandit, you should read up on him sometime—Varadar Tau's tax collectors."

"All this time I thought it was a military rank! Aping medieval history."

"Oh, the military part came immediately thereafter, the first time the old goons tried to shake down somebody who didn't want to contribute. The rank acquired more glamour later."

"I never knew." She regarded him with sudden suspicion. "You're not pulling my leg, sir, are you?"

He spread his hands in denial.

Check your assumptions, Cordelia thought to herself in amusement. *In fact, check your assumptions at the door.*

They arrived at the Imperial Residence's great gate. The ambiance was much changed tonight from some of Cordelia's earlier, more morbid visits to the dying Ezar and to the funeral ceremonies. Colored lights picked out architectural details on the stone pile. The gardens glowed, fountains glittered. Beautifully dressed people warmed the landscape, spilling out from the formal rooms of the north wing onto the terraces. The guard checks, however, were no less meticulous, and the guards' numbers were vastly multiplied. Cordelia had the feeling this was going to be a much less rowdy party than some they'd passed in the city streets.

Aral's car pulled up behind theirs as they disembarked at a western portico, and Cordelia reattached herself gratefully to his arm. He smiled proudly at her, and in a relatively unobserved moment sneaked a kiss onto the back of her neck while stealing a whiff of the flowers perfuming her hair. She squeezed his hand secretly in return. They passed through the doors, and a corridor. A majordomo in Vorbarra House livery loudly announced them, and then they were pinned by the gaze of what to Cordelia for a moment seemed several thousand pairs of critical Barrayaran Vor-class eyes. Actually there were only a couple hundred people in the room. Better than, say, looking down the throat of a fully charged nerve disruptor any day. Really.

They circulated, exchanging greetings, making courtesies. *Why can't these people wear nametags?* Cordelia thought hopelessly. As usual, everyone but her seemed to know everyone else. She pictured herself opening a conversation, *Hey you, Vor-guy*—. She clutched Aral more firmly, and tried to look mysterious and exotic rather than tongue-tied and mislaid.

They found the little ceremony with the bags of coins going on in another chamber, the counts or their representatives lining up to discharge their obligation with a few formal words each. Emperor Gregor, whom Cordelia suspected was up past his bedtime, sat on a raised bench with his mother, looking small and trapped, manfully trying to suppress his yawns. It occurred to Cordelia to wonder if he even got to keep the bags of coins, or if they were simply re-circulated to present again next year. Hell of a birthday party. There wasn't another child in sight. But they were running the counts through pretty efficiently, maybe the kid could escape soon.

An offerer in red-and-blues knelt before Gregor and Kareen, and presented his bag of maroon and gold silk. Cordelia recognized Count Vidal Vordarian, the dish-faced man whom Aral had politely described as of the "next-most-conservative party," i.e., of roughly the same political views as Count Piotr, in a tone of voice that had made

Cordelia wonder if it was a code-phrase for "Isolationist
fanatic." He did not look a fanatic. Freed of its distort-
ing anger, his face was much more attractive; he turned
it now to Princess Kareen, and said something which made
her lift her chin and laugh. His hand rested a moment
familiarly upon her robed knee, and her hand briefly
covered his, before he clambered back to his feet and
bowed, and made way for the next man. Kareen's smile
faded as Vordarian turned his back.

Gregor's sad glance crossed Aral, Cordelia, and
Droushnakovi; he spoke earnestly up to his mother.
Kareen motioned a guard over, and a few minutes later
a guard commander approached them, for permission to
carry off Drou. She was replaced by an unobtrusive
young man who trailed them out of earshot, a mere
flicker at the corner of the eye, a neat trick for a fellow that large.

Happily, Cordelia and Aral soon ran across Lord and
Lady Vorpatril, someone Cordelia dared talk to without
a politico-social pre-briefing. Captain Lord Vorpatril's
parade red-and-blues set off his dark-haired good looks
to perfection. Lady Vorpatril barely outshone him in a
carnelian dress with matching roses woven into her cloud
of black hair, stunning against her velvety white skin. They
made, Cordelia thought, an archetypal Vor couple, sophis-
ticated and serene, the effect only slightly spoiled by the
gradual awareness from his disjointed conversation that
Captain Vorpatril was drunk. He was a cheerful drunk,
though, his personality merely stretched a bit, not unpleas-
antly transformed.

Vorkosigan, drawn away by some men who bore down
on him with Purpose in their eyes, handed Cordelia off
to Lady Vorpatril. The two women cruised the elegant
hors d'oeuvre trays being offered around by yet more
human servants, and compared obstetrical reports. Lord
Vorpatril hastily excused himself to pursue a tray bearing wine. Alys plotted the colors and cut of Cordelia's next
gown. "Black and white, for you, for Winterfair," she
asserted with authority. Cordelia nodded meekly,

wondering if they were actually going to sit down for a meal soon, or if they were expected to keep grazing off the passing trays.

Alys guided her to the ladies' lavatory, an object of hourly interest to their pregnancy-crowded bladders, and introduced her on the return journey to several more women of her rarified social circle. Alys then fell into an animated discussion with a longstanding crony regarding an upcoming party for the woman's daughter, and Cordelia drifted to the edge of the group.

She stepped back quietly, separating herself (she tried not to think, *from the herd*) for a moment of quiet contemplation. What a strange mix Barrayar was, at one moment homey and familiar, in the next terrifying and alien . . . they put on a good show, though . . . ah! That's what was missing from the scene, Cordelia realized. On Beta Colony a ceremony of this magnitude would be fully covered by holovid, to be shared real-time planet-wide. Every move would be a carefully choreographed dance around the vid angles and commentators' timing, almost to the point of annihilating the event being recorded. Here, there wasn't a holovid in sight. The only recordings were made by ImpSec, for their own purposes, which did not include choreography. The people in this room danced only for each other, all their glittering show tossed blithely away in time, which carried it off forever; the event would exist tomorrow only in their memories.

"Lady Vorkosigan?"

Cordelia started from her meditations at the urbane voice at her elbow. She turned to find Commodore Count Vordarian. His wearing of red-and-blues, rather than his personal House livery colors, marked him as being on active service, ornamenting Imperial Headquarters no doubt—in what department? Yes, Ops, Aral had said. He had a drink in his hand, and smiled cordially.

"Count Vordarian," she offered in return, smiling, too. They'd seen each other in passing often enough, Cordelia decided to take him as introduced. This Regency business wasn't going to go away, however much she might

wish it to; it was time and past time for her to start
making connections of her own, and quit pestering Aral
for guidance at every new step.

"Are you enjoying the party?" he inquired.

"Oh, yes." She tried to think of something more to say.
"It's extremely beautiful."

"As are you, Milady." He raised his glass to her in a
gesture of toast, and sipped.

Her heart lurched, but she identified the reason why
before her eyes did more than widen slightly. The last
Barrayaran officer to toast her had been the late Admi-
ral Vorrutyer, under rather different social circumstances.
Vordarian had accidently mimicked his precise gesture.
This was no time for torture-flashbacks. Cordelia blinked.
"Lady Vorpatril helped me a lot. She's very generous."

Vordarian nodded delicately toward her torso. "I understand you also are to be congratulated. Is it a boy or a girl?"

"Uh? Oh. Yes, a boy, thank you. He's to be named Piotr
Miles, I'm told."

"I'm surprised. I should have thought the Lord Regent
would have sought a daughter first."

Cordelia cocked her head, puzzled by his ironic tone.
"We started this before Aral became Regent."

"But you knew he was to receive the appointment, surely."

"I didn't. But I thought all you Barrayaran militarists
were mad after sons. Why did you think a daughter?" *I
want a daughter. . . .*

"I assumed Lord Vorkosigan would be thinking ahead
to his long-term, ah, employment, of course. What better way to maintain the continuity of his power after the
Regency is over than to slip neatly into position as the
Emperor's father-in-law?"

Cordelia boggled. "You think he'd bet the continuity
of a planetary government on the chance of a couple of
teenagers falling in love, a decade and a half from now?"

"Love?" Now he looked baffled.

"You Barrayarans are—" she bit her tongue on the
crazy. Impolite. "Aral is certainly more . . . practical."
Though she could hardly call him unromantic.

"That's extremely interesting," he breathed. His eyes flicked to and away from her abdomen. "Do you fancy he contemplates something more direct?"

Her mind was running tangential to this twisting conversation, somehow. "Beg pardon?"

He smiled and shrugged.

Cordelia frowned. "Do you mean to say, if we were having a girl, that's what everyone would be thinking?"

"Certainly."

She blew out her breath. "God. That's . . . I can't imagine anyone in their right mind wanting to get near the Barrayaran Imperium. It just makes you a target for every maniac with a grievance, as far as I can see." An image of Lieutenant Koudelka, bloody-faced and deafened, flashed in her mind. "Also hard on the poor fellow who's unlucky enough to be standing next to you."

His attention sharpened. "Ah, yes, that unfortunate incident the other day. Has anything come of the investigation, do you know?"

"Nothing that I've heard. Negri and Illyan are talking Cetagandans, mostly. But the guy who launched the grenade got away clean."

"Too bad." He drained his glass, and exchanged it for a freshly charged one presented immediately by a passing Vorbarra-liveried servant. Cordelia eyed the wineglasses wistfully. But she was off metabolic poisons for the duration. Yet another advantage of Betan-style gestation in uterine replicators, none of this blasted enforced clean living. At home she could have poisoned and endangered herself freely, while her child grew, fully monitored round-the-clock by sober techs, safe and protected in the replicator banks. Suppose *she* had been under that sonic grenade . . . She longed for a drink.

Well, she did not need the mind-numbing buzz of ethanol; conversation with Barrayarans was mind-numbing enough. Her eyes sought Aral in the crowd—there he was, Kou at his shoulder, talking with Piotr and two other grizzled old men in counts' liveries. As Aral had predicted, his hearing had returned to normal within a couple of days. Yet still his eyes shifted from face to face, drinking in cues of gesture and inflection, his glass a mere untasted ornament in his hand. On duty, no question. Was he ever off-duty, anymore?

"Was he much disturbed by the attack?" Vordarian inquired, following her gaze to Aral.

"Wouldn't you be?" said Cordelia. "I don't know . . . he's seen so much violence in his life, almost more than I can imagine. It may be almost like . . . white noise. Tuned out." *I wish I could tune it out.*

"You have not known him that long, though. Just since Escobar."

"We met once before the war. Briefly."

"Oh?" His brows rose. "I didn't know that. How little one truly knows of people." He paused, watching Aral, watching her watch Aral. One corner of his mouth crooked up, then the quirk vanished in a thoughtful pursing of his lips. "He's bisexual, you know." He took a delicate sip of his wine.

"Was bisexual," she corrected absently, looking fondly across the room. "Now he's monogamous."

Vordarian choked, sputtering. Cordelia watched him with concern, wondering if she ought to pat him on the back or something, but he regained his breath and balance. "He *told* you that?" he wheezed in astonishment.

"No, Vorrutyer did. Just before he met his, um, fatal accident." Vordarian was standing frozen; she felt a certain malicious glee at having at last baffled a Barrayaran as much as they sometimes baffled her. Now, if she could just figure out what she'd said that had thrown him . . . She went on seriously, "The more I look back on Vorrutyer, the more he seems a tragic figure. Still obsessed with a love affair that was over eighteen years ago. Yet I sometimes wonder, if he could have had what he wanted then—kept Aral—if Aral might have kept that sadistic streak that ultimately consumed Vorrutyer's sanity under control. It's as if the two of them were on some kind of weird see-saw, each one's survival entailing the other's destruction."

"A Betan." His stunned look was gradually fading to one Cordelia mentally dubbed as Awful Realization. "I should have guessed. You are, after all, the people who bioengineered hermaphrodites. . . ." He paused. "How long did you know Vorrutyer?"

"About twenty minutes. But it was a very *intense* twenty minutes." She decided to let him wonder what the hell *that* meant.

"Their, ah, affair, as you call it, was a great secret scandal, at the time."

She wrinkled her nose. "Great secret scandal? Isn't that an oxymoron? Like 'military intelligence,' or 'friendly fire.' Also typical Barrayaranisms, now that I think on it."

Vordarian had the strangest look on his face. He looked, she realized, exactly like a man who had thrown a bomb, had it go *fizz* instead of *BOOM!* and was now trying to decide whether to stick his hand in and tap the firing mechanism to test it.

Then it was her turn for Awful Realization. *This man just tried to blow up my marriage.* No—*Aral's* marriage. She fixed a bright, sunny, innocent smile on her face, her brain kicking—at last!—into overdrive. Vordarian couldn't be of Vorrutyer's old war party; their leaders had all met with their fatal accidents before Ezar had bowed out, and the rest were scattered and lying low. What did he want? She fiddled with a flower from her hair, and considered simpering. "I didn't imagine I was marrying a forty-four-year-old virgin, Count Vordarian."

"So it seems." He knocked back another gulp of wine. "You galactics are all degenerate . . . what perversions does he tolerate in return, I wonder?" His eyes glinted in sudden open malice. "Do you know how Lord Vorkosigan's first wife died?"

"Suicide. Plasma arc to the head," she replied promptly.

"It was rumored he'd murdered her. For adultery. Betan, beware." His smile had turned wholly acid.

"Yes, I knew that, too. In this case, an untrue rumor." All pretense of cordiality had evaporated from their exchange. Cordelia had a bad sense of all control escaping with it. She leaned forward, and lowered her voice. "Do you know why Vorrutyer died?"

He couldn't help it; he tilted toward her, drawn in. "No . . ."

"He tried to hurt Aral through me. I found that . . . annoying. I wish you would cease trying to annoy me, Count Vordarian, I'm afraid you might succeed." Her voice fell further, almost to a whisper. "You should fear it, too."

His initial patronizing tone had certainly given way to wariness. He made a smooth, openhanded gesture that seemed to symbolize a bow of farewell, and backed away. "Milady." The glance over his shoulder as he moved off was thoroughly spooked.

She frowned after him. *Whew*. What an *odd* exchange. What had the man expected, dropping that obsolete datum on her as if it were some shocking surprise? Did Vordarian actually imagine she would go off and tax her husband with his poor taste in companions two decades ago? Would a naive young Barrayaran bride have gone into hysterics? Not Lady Vorpatril, whose social enthusiasms concealed an acid judgment; not Princess Kareen, whose naivete had surely been burned out long ago by that expert sadist Serg. *He fired, but he missed.*

And, more coldly, *Has he fired and missed once before?* That had not been a normal social interaction, not even by Barrayaran standards of one-upsmanship. *Or maybe he was just drunk.* She suddenly wanted to talk to Illyan. She closed her eyes, trying to clear her fogged head.

"Are you well, love?" Aral's concerned voice murmured in her ear. "Do you need your nausea medication?"

Her eyes flew open. There he was, safe and sound beside her. "Oh, I'm fine." She attached herself to his arm, lightly, not a panicked limpet-like clamp. "Just thinking."

"They're seating us for dinner."

"Good. It will be nice to sit down, my feet are swelling."

He looked as if he wanted to pick her up and carry her, but they paraded in normally, joining the other formal pairs. They sat at a raised table set a little apart from the others, with Gregor, Kareen, Piotr, the Lord Guardian of the

Speaker's Circle and his wife, and Prime Minister Vortala. At Gregor's insistence, Droushnakovi was seated with them; the boy seemed painfully glad to see his old bodyguard. *Did I take away your playmate, child?* Cordelia wondered apologetically. It seemed so; Gregor engaged in a negotiation with Kareen for Drou's weekly return "for judo lessons." Drou, used to the Residence atmosphere, was not so overawed as Koudelka, who was stiff with exaggerated care against betrayal by his own clumsiness.

Cordelia found herself seated between Vortala and the Speaker, and carried on conversations with reasonable ease; Vortala was charming, in his blunt way. Cordelia managed nibbles of all the elegantly served food except a slice off the carcass of a roast bovine, carried in whole. Usually she was able to put out of her mind the fact that Barrayaran protein was not grown in vats, but taken from the bodies of real dead animals. She'd known about their primitive culinary practices before she'd chosen to come here, after all, and had tasted animal muscle before on Survey missions, in the interests of science, survival, or potential new product development for the homeworld. The Barrayarans applauded the fruit- and flower-decked beast, seeming to actually find it attractive and not horrific, and the cook, who'd followed it anxiously out, took a bow. The primitive olfactory circuits of her brain had to agree, it smelled great. Vorkosigan had his portion bloody-rare. Cordelia sipped water.

After dessert, and some brief formal toasts offered by Vortala and Vorkosigan, the boy Gregor was at last taken off to bed by his mother. Kareen motioned Cordelia and Droushnakovi to join her. The tension eased in Cordelia's shoulders as they left the big public assembly and climbed to the Emperor's quiet, private quarters.

Gregor was peeled out of his little uniform and dove into pajamas, becoming boy and not icon once again. Drou supervised his teeth-brushing, and was inveigled into "just one round" of some game they'd used to play with a board and pieces, as a bedtime treat. This Kareen indulgently permitted, and after a kiss for and from her son, she and

Cordelia withdrew to a softly lit sitting room nearby. A night breeze from the open windows cooled the upper chamber. Both women sat with a sigh, unwinding; Cordelia kicked off her shoes immediately after Kareen did so. Distance-muffled voices and laughter drifted through the windows from the gardens below.

"How long does this party go on?" Cordelia asked.

"Dawn, for those with more endurance than myself. I shall retire at midnight, after which the serious drinkers will take over."

"Some of them looked pretty serious already."

"Unfortunately." Kareen smiled. "You will be able to see the Vor class at both its best and its worst, before the night is over."

"I can imagine. I'm surprised you don't import less lethal mood-altering drugs."

Kareen's smile sharpened. "But drunken brawls are *traditional*." She allowed the cutting edge of her voice to soften. "In fact, such things are coming in, at least in the shuttleport cities. As usual, we seem to be adding to rather than replacing our own customs."

"Perhaps that's the best way." Cordelia frowned. How best to probe delicately . . . ? "Is Count Vidal Vordarian one of those in the habit of getting publicly potted?"

"No." Kareen glanced up, narrowing her eyes. "Why do you ask?"

"I had a peculiar conversation with him. I thought an overdose of ethanol might account for it." She remembered Vordarian's hand resting lightly upon the Princess's knee, just short of an intimate caress. "Do you know him well? How would you estimate him?"

Kareen said judiciously, "He's rich . . . proud . . . He was loyal to Ezar during Serg's late machinations against his father. Loyal to the Imperium, to the Vor class. There are four major manufacturing cities in Vordarian's District, plus military bases, supply depots, the biggest military shuttleport. . . . Vidal's is certainly the most economically important area on Barrayar today. The war barely touched the Vordarians' District; it's one of the few the

Cetagandans pulled out of by treaty. We sited our first space bases there because we took over facilities the Cetagandans had built and abandoned, and a good deal of economic development followed from that."

"That's . . . interesting," said Cordelia, "but I was wondering about the man personally. His, ah, likes and dislikes, for example. Do you like him?"

"At one time," said Kareen slowly, "I wondered if Vidal might be powerful enough to protect me from Serg. After Ezar died. As Ezar grew more ill, I was thinking, I had better look to my own defense. Nothing appeared to be happening, and no one told me anything."

"If Serg had become emperor, how could a mere count have protected you?" asked Cordelia.

"He would have had to become . . . more. Vidal had ambition, if it were properly encouraged—and patriotism, God knows if Serg had lived he might have destroyed Barrayar—Vidal might have saved us all. But Ezar promised I'd have nothing to fear, and Ezar delivered. Serg died before Ezar and . . . and I have been trying to let things cool, with Vidal, since."

Cordelia abstractedly rubbed her lower lip. "Oh. But do you, personally—I mean, do you like him? Would becoming Countess Vordarian be a nice retirement from the dowager-princess business, someday?"

"Oh! Not now. The Emperor's stepfather would be too powerful a man, to set up opposite the Regent. A dangerous polarity, if they were not allied or exactly balanced. Or were not combined in one person."

"Like being the Emperor's father-in-law?"

"Yes, exactly."

"I'm having trouble understanding this . . . venereal transmission of power. Do you have some claim to the Imperium in your own right, or not?"

"That would be for the military to decide," she shrugged. Her voice lowered. "It is like a disease, isn't it? I'm too close, I'm touched, infected. . . . Gregor is my hope of survival. And my prison."

"Don't you want a life of your own?"

"No. I just want to live."

Cordelia sat back, disturbed. *Did Serg teach you not to give offense?* "Does Vordarian see it that way? I mean, power isn't the only thing you have to offer. I think you underestimate your personal attractiveness."

"On Barrayar . . . power is the only thing." Her expression grew distant. "I admit . . . I did once ask Captain Negri to get me a report on Vidal. He uses his courtesans normally."

This wistful approval was not exactly Cordelia's idea of a declaration of boundless love. Yet that hadn't been just desire for power she'd seen in Vordarian's eyes at the ceremony, she would swear. Had Aral's appointment as Regent accidently messed up the man's courtship? Might that very well account for the sex-tinged animosity in his speech to her . . . ?

Droushnakovi returned on tiptoe. "He fell asleep," she whispered fondly. Kareen nodded, and tilted her head back in an unguarded moment of rest, until a Vorbarra-liveried messenger arrived and addressed her: "Will you open the dancing with my lord Regent, Milady? They're waiting."

Request, or order? It sounded more sinister-mandatory than fun, in the servant's flat voice.

"Last duty for the night," Kareen assured Cordelia, as they both shoved their shoes back on. Cordelia's footgear seemed to have shrunk two sizes since the start of the evening. She hobbled after Kareen, Drou trailing.

A large downstairs room was floored in multi-toned wood marquetry in patterns of flowers, vines, and animals. The polished surface would have been put on a museum wall on Beta Colony; these incredible people danced across it. A live orchestra—selected by cutthroat competition from the Imperial Service Band, Cordelia was informed—provided music, in the Barrayaran style. Even the waltzes sounded faintly like marches. Aral and the princess were presented to each other, and he led her off for a couple of good-natured turns around the room, a formal dance that involved each mirroring the other's steps and slides, hands raised but never quite touching. Cordelia was fascinated. She'd never guessed that Aral could dance. This seemed to complete the social requirements, and other couples filtered out onto the floor. Aral returned to her side, looking stimulated. "Dance, Milady?"

After that dinner, more like a nap. How did he keep up that alarming hyperactivity? Secret terror, probably. She shook her head, smiling. "I don't know how."

"Ah." They strolled, instead. "I could show you how," he offered as they exited the room onto a bank of terraces that wound off into the gardens, pleasantly cool and dark but for a few colored lights to prevent stumbles on the pathways.

"Mm," she said doubtfully. "If you can find a private spot." If they could find a private spot, she could think of better things to do than dance, though.

"Well, here we—shh." His scimitar grin winked in the dark, and his grip tightened warningly on her hand. They both stood still, at the entrance to a little open space screened from eyes above by yews and some pink feathery non-Earth plant. The music floated clearly down.

"Try, Kou," urged Droushnakovi's voice. Drou and Kou stood facing each other on the far side of the terrace-nook. Doubtfully, Koudelka set his stick down on the stone balustrade, and held up his hands to hers. They began to step, slide, and dip, Drou counting earnestly, "*One*-two-three, one-two-three . . ."

Koudelka tripped, and she caught him; his grip found her waist. "It's no damned good, Drou." He shook his head in frustration.

"Sh . . ." Her hand touched his lips. "Try again. I'm for it. You said you had to practice that hand-coordination thing, how long, before you got it? More than once, I bet."

"The old man wouldn't let me give up."

"Well, maybe I won't let you give up either."

"I'm tired," complained Koudelka.

So, switch to kissing, Cordelia urged silently, muffling a laugh. *That you can do sitting down.* Droushnakovi was determined, however, and they began again. "*One*-two-three, one-two-three . . ." Once again the effort ended in what seemed to Cordelia a very good start on a clinch, if only one party or the other would gather the wit and nerve to follow through.

Aral shook his head, and they backed silently away around the shrubbery. Apparently a little inspired, his lips found hers to muffle his own chuckle. Alas, their delicacy was futile; an anonymous Vor lord wandered blindly past them, stumbled across the terrace nook, freezing Kou and Drou in mid-step, and hung over the stone balustrade to be very traditionally sick into the defenseless bushes below. Sudden swearing, in new voices, one male, one female, rose up from the dark and shaded target zone. Koudelka retrieved his stick, and the two would-be dancers hastily retreated. The Vor lord was sick again, and his male victim started climbing up after him, slipping on the beslimed stonework and promising violent retribution. Vorkosigan guided Cordelia prudently away.

Later, while waiting by one of the Residence's entrances for the groundcars to be brought round, Cordelia found herself standing next to the lieutenant. Koudelka gazed pensively back over his shoulder at the Residence, from which music and party-noises wafted almost unabated.

"Good party, Kou?" she inquired genially.

"What? Oh, yes, astonishing. When I joined the Service, I never dreamed I'd end up here." He blinked. "Time was, I never thought I'd end up anywhere." And then he added, giving Cordelia a slight case of mental whiplash, "I sure wish women came with operating manuals."

Cordelia laughed aloud. "I could say the same for men."

"But you and Admiral Vorkosigan—you're different."

"Not . . . really. We've learned from experience, maybe. A lot of people fail to."

"Do you think I have a chance at a normal life?" He gazed, not at her, but into the dark.

"You make your own chances, Kou. And your own dances."

"You sound just like the Admiral."

Cordelia cornered Illyan the next morning, when he stopped in to Vorkosigan House for the daily report from his guard commander.

"Tell me, Simon. Is Vidal Vordarian on your short list, or your long list?"

"Everybody's on my long list," Illyan sighed.

"I want you to move him to your short list."

His head cocked. "Why?"

She hesitated. She wasn't about to reply, *Intuition*, though that was exactly what those subliminal cues added up to. "He seems to me to have an assassin's mind. The sort that fires from cover into the back of his enemy."

Illyan smiled quizzically. "Beg pardon, Milady, but that doesn't sound like the Vordarian I know. I've always found him more the openly bullheaded type."

How badly must he hurt, how ardently desire, for a bullheaded man to turn subtle? She was unsure. Perhaps, not knowing how deeply Aral's happiness with her ran, Vordarian did not recognize how vicious his attack upon it was? And did personal and political animosity necessarily run together? *No*. The man's hatred had been profound, his blow precisely, if mistakenly, aimed.

"Move him to your short list," she said.

Illyan opened his hand; not mere placation, by his expression some chain of thought was engaged. "Very well, Milady."

CHAPTER SIX

Cordelia watched the shadow of the lightflyer flow over the ground below, a slim blot arrowing south. The arrow wavered across farm fields, creeks, rivers, and dusty roads—the road net was rudimentary, stunted, its development leapfrogged by the personal air transport that had arrived in the blast of galactic technology at the end of the Time of Isolation. Coils of tension unwound in her neck with each kilometer they put between themselves and the hectic hothouse atmosphere of the capital. A day in the country was an excellent idea, overdue. She only wished Aral could have shared it with her.

Sergeant Bothari, cued by some landmark below, banked the lightflyer gently to its new course. Droushnakovi, sharing the back seat with Cordelia, stiffened, trying not to lean into her. Dr. Henri, in front with the Sergeant, stared out the canopy with an interest almost equal to Cordelia's.

Dr. Henri turned half around, to speak over his shoulder to Cordelia. "I do thank you for the luncheon invitation, Lady Vorkosigan. It's a rare privilege to visit the Vorkosigans' private estate."

"Is it?" said Cordelia. "I know they don't have crowds, but Count Piotr's horse friends drop in fairly often.

Fascinating animals." Cordelia thought that over a second, then decided Dr. Henri would realize without being told that the "fascinating animals" applied to the horses, and not Count Piotr's friends. "Drop the least little hint that you're interested, and Count Piotr will probably show you personally around the stable."

"I've never met the General." Dr. Henri looked daunted by the prospect, and fingered the collar of his undress greens. A research scientist from the Imperial Military Hospital, Henri dealt with high rankers often enough not to be awed; it had to be all that Barrayaran history clinging to Piotr that made the difference.

Piotr had acquired his present rank at the age of twenty-two, fighting the Cetagandans in the fierce guerilla war that had raged through the Dendarii Mountains, just now showing blue on the southern horizon. Rank was all then-emperor Dorca Vorbarra could give him at the time; more tangible assets such as reinforcements, supplies, and pay were out of the question in that desperate hour. Twenty years later Piotr had changed Barrayaran history again, playing kingmaker to Ezar Vorbarra in the civil war that had brought down Mad Emperor Yuri. Not your average HQ staffer, General Piotr Vorkosigan, not by anybody's standards.

"He's easy to get along with," Cordelia assured Dr. Henri. "Just admire the horses, and ask a few leading questions about the wars, and you can relax and spend the rest of your time listening."

Henri's brows went up, as he searched her face for irony. Henri was a sharp man. Cordelia smiled cheerfully.

Bothari was silently watching her in the mirror set over his control interface, Cordelia noticed. Again. The sergeant seemed tense today. It was the position of his hands, the cording of the muscles in his neck, that gave him away. Bothari's flat yellow eyes were always unreadable; set deep, too close together, and not quite on the same level, above his sharp cheekbones and long narrow jaw. Anxiety over the doctor's visit? Understandable.

The land below was rolling, but soon rucked up into the rugged ridges that channeled the lake district. The mountains rose beyond, and Cordelia thought she caught a distant glint of early snow on the highest peaks. Bothari hopped the flyer over three running ridges, and banked again, zooming up a narrow valley. A few more minutes, a swoop over another ridge, and the long lake was in sight. An enormous maze of burnt-out fortifications made a black crown on a headland, and a village nestled below it. Bothari brought the flyer down neatly on a circle painted on the pavement of the village's widest street.

Dr. Henri gathered up his bag of medical equipment. "The examination will only take a few minutes," he assured Cordelia, "then we can go on."

Don't tell me, tell Bothari. Cordelia sensed Dr. Henri was a little unnerved by Bothari. He kept addressing her instead of the Sergeant, as if she were some translator who would put it all into terms that Bothari would understand. Bothari was formidable, true, but talking past him wouldn't make him magically disappear.

Bothari led them to a little house set in a narrow side street that went down to the glimmering water. At his knock, a heavyset woman with greying hair opened the door and smiled. "Good morning, Sergeant. Come in, everything's all ready. Milady." She favored Cordelia with an awkward curtsey.

Cordelia returned a nod, gazing around with interest. "Good morning, Mistress Hysopi. How nice your house looks today." The place was painfully scrubbed and straightened—as a military widow, Mistress Hysopi understood all about inspections. Cordelia trusted the everyday atmosphere in the hired fosterer's house was a trifle more relaxed.

"Your little girl's been very good this morning," Mistress Hysopi assured the Sergeant. "Took her bottle right down—she's just had her bath. Right this way, Doctor. I hope you'll find everything's all right. . . ."

She guided the way up narrow stairs. One bedroom was clearly her own; the other, with a bright window looking down over rooftops to the lake, had recently been made over into a nursery. A dark-haired infant with big brown eyes cooed to herself in a crib. "There's a girl," Mistress Hysopi smiled, picking her up. "Say hi to your daddy, eh, Elena? Pretty-pretty."

Bothari entered no further than the door, watching the infant warily. "Her head has grown a lot," he offered after a moment.

"They usually do, between three and four months," Mistress Hysopi agreed.

Dr. Henri laid out his instruments on the crib sheet, and Mistress Hysopi carried the baby back over and began undressing her. The two began a technical discussion about formulae and feces, and Bothari walked around the little room, looking but not touching. He did look terribly huge and out-of-place among the colorful, delicate infant furnishings, dark and dangerous in his brown and silver uniform. His head brushed the slanting ceiling, and he backed cautiously to the door.

Cordelia hung curiously over Henri and Hysopi's shoulders, watching the little girl wriggle and attempt to roll. Infants. Soon enough she would have one of those. As if in response her belly fluttered. Piotr Miles was not, fortunately, strong enough to fight his way out of a paper bag yet, but if his development continued at this rate, the last couple of months were going to be sleepless. She wished she'd taken the parents' training course back on Beta Colony even if she hadn't been ready to apply for a license. Yet Barrayaran parents seemed to manage to ad lib. Mistress Hysopi had learned on the job, and she had three grown children now.

"Amazing," said Dr. Henri, shaking his head and recording his data. "Absolutely normal development, as far as I can tell. Nothing to even show she came out of a uterine replicator."

"*I* came out of a uterine replicator," Cordelia noted with amusement. Henri glanced involuntarily up and down at her, as if suddenly expecting to find antennae sprouting from her head. "Betan experience suggests it doesn't matter so much how you got here, as what you do after you arrive."

"Really." He frowned thoughtfully. "And you are free of genetic defects?"

"Certified," Cordelia agreed.

"We *need* this technology." He sighed, and began packing his things back up. "She's fine, you can dress her again," he added to Mistress Hysopi.

Bothari loomed over the crib at last, to stare down, the lines creased deep between his eyes. He touched the infant only once, a finger to her cheek, then rubbed thumb and finger together as if checking his neural function. Mistress Hysopi studied him sideways, but said nothing.

While Bothari lingered to settle up the month's expenses with Mistress Hysopi, Cordelia and Dr. Henri strolled down to the lake, Droushnakovi following.

"When those seventeen Escobaran uterine replicators first arrived at Imp Mil," said Henri, "sent from the war zone, I was frankly appalled. Why save those unwanted fetuses, and at such a cost? Why land them on *my* department? Since then I've become a believer, Milady. I've even thought of an application, spin-off technology, for burn patients. I'm working on it now, the project approval came down just a week ago." His eyes were eager, as he detailed his theory, which was sound as far as Cordelia understood the principles.

"My mother is a medical equipment and maintenance engineer at Silica Hospital," she explained to Henri, when he paused for breath and approval. "She works on these sorts of applications all the time." Henri redoubled his technical exposition.

Cordelia greeted two women in the street by name, and politely introduced them to Dr. Henri.

"They're wives of some of Count Piotr's sworn armsmen," she explained as they passed on.

"I should have thought they'd choose to live in the capital."

"Some do, some stay here. It seems to depend on taste.

The cost of living is much lower out here, and these fellows aren't paid as much as I'd imagined. Some of the backcountry men are suspicious of city life, they seem to think it's purer here." She grinned briefly. "One fellow has a wife in each location. None of his brother-armsmen have ratted on him yet. A solid bunch."

Henri's brows rose. "How jolly for him."

"Not really. He's chronically short of cash, and always looks worried. But he can't decide which wife to give up. Apparently, he actually loves them both."

When Dr. Henri stepped aside to talk to an old man they saw pottering around the docks about possible boat rentals, Droushnakovi came up to Cordelia, and lowered her voice. She looked disturbed.

"Milady . . . how in the world did Sergeant Bothari come by a baby? He's not married, is he?"

"Would you believe the stork brought her?" said Cordelia lightly.

"No."

From her frown, Drou did not approve this levity. Cordelia hardly blamed her. She sighed. *How do I wriggle out of this one?* "Very nearly. Her uterine replicator was sent on a fast courier from Escobar, after the war. She finished her gestation in a laboratory in Imp Mil, under Dr. Henri's supervision."

"Is she really Bothari's?"

"Oh, yes. Genetically certified. That's how they identified—" Cordelia snapped that last sentence off midway. Carefully, now . . .

"But what was all that about seventeen replicators? And how did the baby get in the replicator? Was—was she an experiment?"

"Placental transfer. A delicate operation, even by galactic standards, but hardly experimental. Look." Cordelia paused, thinking fast. "I'll tell you the truth." *Just not all of it.* "Little Elena is the daughter of Bothari and a young Escobaran officer named Elena Visconti. Bothari . . . loved her . . . very much. But after the war, she would not return with him to Barrayar. The child was conceived, er . . .

Barrayaran-style, then transferred to the replicator when they parted. There were some similar cases. The replicators were all sent to Imp Mil, which was interested in learning more about the technology. Bothari was in . . . medical therapy, for quite a long time, after the war. But when he got out, and she got out, he took custody of her."

"Did the others take their babies, too?"

"Most of the other fathers were dead by then. The children went to the Imperial Service orphanage." There. The official version, all right and tight.

"Oh." Drou frowned at her feet. "That's not at all . . . it's hard to picture Bothari . . . To tell the truth," she said in a burst of candor, "I'm not sure I'd want to give custody of a pet cat to Bothari. Doesn't he strike you as a bit strange?"

"Aral and I are keeping an eye on things. Bothari's doing very well so far, I think. He found Mistress Hysopi on his own, and is making sure she gets everything she needs. Has Bothari—that is, does Bothari bother you?"

Droushnakovi gave Cordelia an are-you-kidding? look. "He's so big. And ugly. And he . . . mutters to himself, some days. And he's sick so much, days in a row when he won't get out of bed, but he doesn't have a fever or anything. Count Piotr's Armsman-commander thinks he's malingering."

"He's not malingering. But I'm glad you mentioned it, I'll have Aral talk to the commander and straighten him out."

"But aren't you at all afraid of him? On the bad days, at least?"

"I could weep for Bothari," said Cordelia slowly, "but I don't fear him. On the bad days or any days. You shouldn't either. It's . . . it's a profound insult."

"Sorry." Droushnakovi scuffed her shoe across the gravel. "It's a sad story. No wonder he doesn't talk about the Escobar war."

"Yes, I'd . . . appreciate it if you'd refrain from bringing it up. It's very painful for him."

❖   ❖   ❖

A short hop in the lightflyer from the village across a tongue of the lake brought them to the Vorkosigans' country estate. A century ago the house had been an outlying guard post to the headland's fort. Modern weaponry had rendered aboveground fortifications obsolete, and the old stone barracks had been converted to more peaceful uses. Dr. Henri had evidently been expecting more grandeur, for he said, "It's smaller than I expected."

Piotr's housekeeper had a pleasant luncheon set up for them on a flower-decked terrace off the south end of the house by the kitchen. While she was escorting the party out, Cordelia fell back beside Count Piotr.

"Thank you, sir, for letting us invade you."

"Invade me indeed! This is your house, dear. You are free to entertain any friends you choose in it. This is the first time you've done so, do you realize?" He stopped, standing with her in the doorway. "You know, when my mother married my father, she completely re-decorated Vorkosigan House. My wife did the same in her day. Aral married so late, I'm afraid an updating is sadly overdue. Wouldn't you . . . like to?"

But it's *your* house, thought Cordelia helplessly. Not even Aral's, really . . .

"You've touched down so lightly on us, one almost fears you'll fly away again." Piotr chuckled, but his eyes were concerned.

Cordelia patted her rounding belly. "Oh, I'm thoroughly weighted down now, sir." She hesitated. "To tell the truth, I have thought it would be nice to have a lift tube in Vorkosigan House. Counting the basement, sub-basement, attic, and roof, there are eight floors in the main section. It can make quite a hike."

"A lift tube? We've never—" He bit his tongue. "Where?"

"You could put it in the back hallway next to the plumbing stack, without disrupting the internal architecture."

"So you could. Very well. Find a builder. Do it."

"I'll look into it tomorrow, then. Thank you, sir." Her brows rose, behind his back.

Count Piotr, evidently with the same idea in mind of encouraging her, was studiously cordial to Dr. Henri over lunch, New Man though Henri clearly was. Henri, following Cordelia's advice, hit it off well with Piotr in turn. Piotr told Henri all about the new foal, born in his stables over the back ridge. The creature was a genetically certified pureblood that Piotr called a *quarter horse*, though it looked like an entire horse to Cordelia. The stud-colt had been imported at great cost as a frozen embryo from Earth, and implanted in a grade mare, the gestation supervised anxiously by Piotr. The biologically trained Henri expressed technical interest, and after lunch was done Piotr carried him off for a personal inspection of the big beasts.

Cordelia begged off. "I think I'd like to rest a bit. You can go, Drou. Sergeant Bothari will stay with me." In fact, Cordelia was worried about Bothari. He hadn't eaten a single bite of lunch, nor said a word for over an hour.

Doubtful, but madly interested in the horses, Drou allowed herself to be persuaded. The three trudged off up the hill. Cordelia watched them away, then turned her face back to catch Bothari watching her again. He gave her a strange approving nod.

"Thank you, Milady."

"Ahem. Yes. I wondered if you felt ill."

"No . . . yes. I don't know. I wanted . . . I've wanted to talk to you, Milady. For—for some weeks. But there never seemed to be a good time. Lately it's been getting worse. I can't wait anymore. I'd hoped today . . ."

"Seize the moment." The housekeeper was rattling about in Piotr's kitchen. "Would you care to take a walk, or something?"

"Please, Milady."

They walked together, around the old stone house. The pavilion on the crest of the hill, overlooking the lake, would be a great place to sit and talk, but Cordelia felt too full and pregnant to make the climb. She led left, instead, on the path parallel to the slope, till they came to what appeared to be a little walled garden.

The Vorkosigan family plot was crowded with an odd assortment of graves, of core family, distant relatives, retainers of special merit. The cemetery had originally been part of the ruined fort complex, the oldest graves of guards and officers going back centuries. The Vorkosigan intrusion dated only from the atomic destruction of the old district capital of Vorkosigan Vashnoi during the Cetagandan invasion. The dead had been melted down with the living there, then eight generations of family history obliterated. It was interesting to note the clusters of more recent dates, and key them to their current events: the Cetagandan invasion, Mad Yuri's War. Aral's mother's grave dated exactly to the start of Yuri's War. A space was reserved beside her for Piotr, and had been for thirty-three years. She waited patiently for her husband. *And men accuse us women of being slow.* Her eldest son, Aral's brother, lay buried at her other hand.

"Let's sit over there." She nodded toward a stone bench set round with small orange flowers, and shaded by an Earth-import oak at least a century old. "These people are all good listeners, now. And they don't pass on gossip."

Cordelia sat on the warm stone, and studied Bothari. He sat as far from her as the bench permitted. The lines on his face were deep-cut today, harsh despite the muting of the afternoon light by the warm autumn haze. One hand, wrapped around the rough stone edge of the bench, flexed arrhythmically. His breathing was too careful.

Cordelia softened her voice. "So, what's the trouble, Sergeant? You seem a little . . . stretched, today. Is it something about Elena?"

He breathed a humorless laugh. "*Stretched.* Yes. I guess so. It's not about the baby . . . it's . . . well, not directly." His eyes met hers squarely for almost the first time today. "You remember Escobar, milady. You were there. Right?"

"Right." *This man is in pain,* Cordelia realized. What sort of pain?

"I can't remember Escobar."

"So I understand. I believe your military therapists went to a great deal of trouble to make sure you did not remember Escobar."

"Oh yes."

"I don't approve of Barrayaran notions of therapy. Particularly when colored by political expediency."

"I've come to realize that, Milady." Cautious hope flickered in his eyes.

"How did they work it? Burn out selected neurons? Chemical erasure?"

"No . . . they used drugs, but nothing was destroyed. They tell me. The doctors called it suppression-therapy. We just called it hell. Every day we went to hell, till we didn't want to go there anymore." Bothari shifted in his seat, his brow wrinkling. "Trying to remember—to talk about Escobar at all—gives me these headaches. Sounds stupid, doesn't it? Big man like me whining about headaches like some old woman. Certain special parts, memories, they give me these really bad headaches that make red rings around everything I see, and I start vomiting. When I stop trying to think about it, the pain goes away. Simple."

Cordelia swallowed. "I see. I'm sorry. I knew it was bad, but I didn't know it was . . . that bad."

"The worst part is the dreams. I dream of . . . it . . . and if I wake up too slowly, I remember the dream. I remember too much, all at once, and my head—all I can do is roll over and cry, until I can start thinking about something else. Count Piotr's other armsmen—they think I'm crazy, they think I'm stupid, they don't know what I'm doing in there with them. *I* don't know what I'm doing in there with them." He rubbed his big hands over his burr-scalp in a harried swipe. "To be a count's sworn Armsman—it's an honor. Only twenty places to fill. They take the best, they take the bloody heroes, the men with medals, the twenty-year men with perfect records. If what I did—at Escobar—was so bad, why did the Admiral make Count Piotr make a place for me? And if I was such a bloody hero, why did they take away my memory of it?" His breath was coming faster, whistling through his long yellow teeth.

"How much pain are you in now? Trying to talk about this?"

"Some. More to come." He stared at her, frowning deeply. "I've got to talk about this. To you. It's driving me . . ."

She took a calming breath, trying to listen with her whole mind, body, and soul. And carefully. So carefully. "Go on."

"I have . . . four pictures . . . in my head, from Escobar. Four pictures, and I cannot explain them. To myself. A few minutes, out of—three months? Four? They all of them bother me, but one bothers me the most. You're in it," he added abruptly, and stared at the ground. Both hands clenched the bench now, white-knuckled.

"I see. Go on."

"One—the least-bad one—it was an argument. Prince Serg was there, and Admiral Vorrutyer, Lord Vorkosigan, and Admiral Rulf Vorhalas. And I was there. Except I didn't have any clothes on."

"Are you sure this isn't a dream?"

"No. I'm not sure. Admiral Vorrutyer said . . . something very insulting, to Lord Vorkosigan. He had Lord Vorkosigan backed up against the wall. Prince Serg laughed. Then Vorrutyer kissed him, full on the mouth, and Vorhalas tried to knock Vorrutyer's head off, but Lord Vorkosigan wouldn't let him. And I don't remember after that."

"Um . . . yeah," said Cordelia. "I wasn't there for that part, but I know there was some really weird stuff going on in the high command at that point, as Vorrutyer and Serg pushed their limits. So it's probably a true memory. I could ask Aral, if you wish."

"No! No. That one doesn't feel as important, anyway. As the others."

"Tell me about the others, then."

His voice fell to a whisper. "I remember Elena. So pretty. I only have two pictures in my head, of Elena. One, I remember Vorrutyer making me . . . no, I don't want to talk about that one." He stopped for a full minute, rocking gently, forward and back. "The other . . . we were in my cabin. She and I. She was my wife. . . ." His voice faltered. "She wasn't my wife, was she." It wasn't even a question.

"No. But you know that."

"But I remember *believing* she was." His hands pressed his forehead, and rubbed his neck, hard and futilely.

"She was a prisoner of war," said Cordelia. "Her beauty drew Vorrutyer's and Serg's attention, and they made a project of tormenting her, for no reason—not for her military intelligence, not even for political terrorism—just for their gratification. She was raped. But you know that, too. On some level."

"Yes," he whispered.

"Taking away her contraceptive implant and allowing— or compelling—you to impregnate her was part of their idea of sadism. The first part. They did not, thank God, live long enough to get to the second part."

His legs had drawn up, his long arms wrapped around them in a tight, tight ball. His breathing was fast and shallow, panting. His face was freezer-burn white, sheened with cold sweat.

"Do I have red rings around me now?" Cordelia asked curiously.

"It's all . . . kind of pink."

"And the last picture?"

"Oh, Milady." He swallowed. "Whatever it was . . . I know it must be very close to whatever it is they most don't want me to remember." He swallowed again. Cordelia began to understand why he hadn't touched his lunch.

"Do you want to go on? *Can* you go on?"

"I must go on. Milady. Captain Naismith. Because I remember you. Remember seeing you. Stretched out on Vorrutyer's bed, all your clothes cut away, naked. You were bleeding. I was looking up your . . . What I want to know. Must know." His arms were wrapped around his head, now, tilted toward her on his knees, his face hollow, haunted, hungry.

His blood pressure must be fantastically high, to drive

that monstrous migraine. If they went too far, pressed this through to the last truth, might he be in danger of a stroke? An incredible piece of psychoengineering, to program his own body to punish him for his forbidden thoughts . . .

"Did I rape *you*, Milady?"

"Huh? *No!*" She sat bolt upright, fiercely indignant. They had taken *that* knowledge away from him? They'd *dared* take that away from him?

He began to cry, if that's what that ragged breathing, tight-screwed face, and tears leaking from his eyes meant. Equal parts agony and joy. "Oh. Thank God." And, "Are you *sure* . . . ?"

"Vorrutyer ordered you to. You refused. Out of your own will, without hope of rescue or reward. It got you in a hell of a lot of trouble, for a little while." She longed to tell him the rest, but the state he was in now was so terrifying, it was impossible to guess the consequences. "How long have you been remembering this? Wondering this?"

"Since I first saw you again. This summer. When you came to marry Lord Vorkosigan."

"You've been walking around for over *six months*, with this in your head, not daring to ask—?"

"Yes, Milady."

She sat back, horrified, her breath trickling out between pursed lips. "Next time, don't wait so long."

Swallowing hard, he stumbled to his feet, a big hand waving in a desperate wait-for-me gesture. He swung his legs over the low stone wall, and found some bushes. Anxiously, she listened to him dry-vomiting his empty stomach for several minutes. An extremely bad attack, she judged, but finally the violent paroxysms slowed, then stopped. He returned, wiping his lips, looking very white and not much better, except for his eyes. A little life flickered in those eyes now, a half-suppressed light of overwhelming relief.

The light faded, as he sat in thought. He rubbed his palms on his trouser knees, and stared at his boots. "But

I'm not less a rapist, just because *you* were not my victim."

"That is correct."

"I can't . . . trust myself. How can you trust me? . . . Do you know what's better than sex?"

She wondered if she could take one more sharp turn in this conversation without running off screaming. *You encouraged him to uncork, now you're stuck with it.* "Go on."

"Killing. It feels even better, afterwards. It shouldn't be . . . such a pleasure. Lord Vorkosigan doesn't kill like that." His eyes were narrowed, brows creased, but he was uncurled from his ball of agony; he must be speaking generally, Vorrutyer no longer on his mind.

"It's a release of rage, I'd guess," said Cordelia cautiously. "How did you get so much rage, balled up inside of you? The density is palpable. People can sense it."

His hand curled, in front of his solar plexus. "It goes back a long way. But I don't feel angry, most of the time. It snaps out suddenly."

"Even Bothari fears Bothari," she murmured in wonder.

"Yet you don't. You're less afraid even than Lord Vorkosigan."

"I see you as bound up with him, somehow. And he's my own heart. How can I fear my own heart?"

"Milady. A bargain."

"Hm?"

"You tell me . . . when it's all right. To kill. And then I'll know."

"I can't—look, suppose I'm not there? When that sort of thing lands on you, there's not usually time to stop and analyze. You have to be allowed self-defense, but you also have to be able to discern when you're really being attacked." She sat up, eyes widening in sudden insight. "That's why your uniform is so important to you, isn't it? It tells you when it's all right. When you can't tell yourself. All those rigid routines you keep to, they're to tell you you're all right, on track."

"Yes. I'm sworn to the defense of House Vorkosigan,

now. So *that's* all right." He nodded, apparently reassured. By what, for God's sake?

"You're asking me to be your conscience. Make your judgments for you. But you are a whole man. I've seen you make right choices, under the most absolute stress."

His hands pressed to his skull again, his narrow jaw clenching, and he grated out, "But I can't *remember* them. Can't remember how I did it."

"Oh." She felt very small. "Well . . . whatever you think I can do for you, you've got a blood-right to it. We owe you, Aral and I. We remember why, even if you can't."

"Remember it for me, then, Milady," he said lowly, "and I'll be all right."

"Believe it."

CHAPTER SEVEN

Cordelia shared breakfast one morning the following week with Aral and Piotr in a private parlor overlooking the back garden. Aral motioned to the Count's footman, who was serving.

"Would you please rout out Lieutenant Koudelka for me? Tell him to bring that agenda for this morning that we were discussing."

"Uh, I guess you hadn't heard, my lord?" murmured the man. Cordelia had the impression that his eyes were searching the room for an escape route.

"Heard what? We just came down."

"Lieutenant Koudelka is in hospital this morning."

"Hospital! Good God, why wasn't I told at once? What happened?"

"We were told Commander Illyan would be bringing a full report, my lord. The guard commander . . . thought he'd wait for him."

Alarm struggled with annoyance on Vorkosigan's face. "How bad is he? It's not some . . . delayed aftereffect of the sonic grenade, is it? What happened to him?"

"He was beaten up, my lord," said the footman woodenly.

Vorkosigan sat back with a little hiss. A muscle jumped in his jaw. "You get that guard commander in here," he growled.

The footman evaporated instantly, leaving Vorkosigan tapping a spoon nervously and impatiently on the table. He met Cordelia's horrified eyes and produced a small false smile of reassurance for her. Even Piotr looked startled.

"Who could possibly want to beat up Kou?" asked Cordelia wonderingly. "That's sickening. He couldn't fight back worth a damn."

Vorkosigan shook his head. "Someone looking for a safe target, I suppose. We'll find out. Oh, we will find out."

The green-uniformed ImpSec guard commander appeared, to stand at attention. "Sir."

"For your future information, and you may pass it on, should any accident occur to any of my key staff members, I wish to be informed at once. Understood?"

"Yes, sir. It was quite late when word got back here, sir. And since we knew by then that they were both going to live, Commander Illyan said I might let you sleep. Sir."

"I see." Vorkosigan rubbed his face. "Both?"

"Lieutenant Koudelka and Sergeant Bothari, sir."

"They didn't get into a fight, did they?" asked Cordelia, now thoroughly alarmed.

"Yes. Oh—not with each other, Milady. They were set upon."

Vorkosigan's face was darkening. "You had better begin at the beginning."

"Yes, sir. Um. Lieutenant Koudelka and Sergeant Bothari went out last night. Not in uniform. Down to that area in back of the old caravanserai."

"My God, what for?"

"Um." The guard commander glanced uncertainly at Cordelia. "Entertainment, I believe, sir."

"Entertainment?"

"Yes, sir. Sergeant Bothari goes down there about once a month, on his duty-free day, when my lord Count is in town. It's apparently some place he's been going to for years."

"In the caravanserai?" said Count Piotr in an unbelieving tone.

"Um." The guard commander eyed the footman in appeal.

"Sergeant Bothari isn't very particular about his entertainment, sir," the footman volunteered uneasily.

"Evidently not!" said Piotr.

Cordelia questioned Vorkosigan with her eyebrows.

"It's a very rough area," he explained. "I wouldn't go down there myself without a patrol at my back. Two patrols, at night. And I'd definitely wear my uniform, though not my rank insignia . . . but I believe Bothari grew up there. I imagine it looks different to his eyes."

"Why so rough?"

"It's very poor. It was the town center during the Time of Isolation, and it hasn't been touched by renovation yet. Minimal water, no electricity, choked with refuse . . ."

"Mostly human," added Piotr tartly.

"Poor?" said Cordelia, bewildered. "No electricity? How can it be on the comm network?"

"It's not, of course," answered Vorkosigan.

"Then how can anybody get their schooling?"

"They don't."

Cordelia stared. "I don't understand. How do they get their jobs?"

"A few escape to the Service. The rest prey on each other, mostly." Vorkosigan regarded her face uneasily. "Have you no poverty on Beta Colony?"

"Poverty? Well, some people have more money than others, of course, but . . . no comconsoles?"

Vorkosigan was diverted from his interrogation. "Is not owning a comconsole the lowest standard of living you can imagine?" he said in wonder.

"It's the first article in the constitution. 'Access to information shall not be abridged.' "

"Cordelia . . . these people barely have access to food, clothing, and shelter. They have a few rags and cooking pots, and squat in buildings that aren't economical to repair or tear down yet, with the wind whistling through the cracks in the walls."

"No air-conditioning?"

"No heat in the winter is a bigger problem, here."

"I suppose so. You people don't really have summer. . . . How do they call for help when they're sick or hurt?"

"What help?" Vorkosigan was growing grim. "If they're sick, they either get well or die."

"Die, if we're lucky," muttered Piotr. "Vermin."

"You're not joking." She stared back and forth between the pair of them. "That's horrible . . . why, think of all the geniuses you must be missing!"

"I doubt we're missing very many, from the caravanserai," said Piotr dryly.

"Why not? They have the same genetic complement as you," Cordelia pointed out the, to her, obvious.

The Count went rigid. "My dear girl! They most certainly do not! My family have been Vor for nine generations."

Cordelia raised her eyebrows. "How do you know, if you didn't have gene typing till eighty years ago?"

Both the guard commander and the footman were acquiring peculiar stuffed expressions. The footman bit his lip.

"Besides," she went on reasonably, "if you Vor got around half as much as those histories I've been reading imply, ninety percent of the people on this planet must have Vor blood by now. Who knows who your relatives are on your father's side?"

Vorkosigan bit his linen napkin absently, his eyes gone crinkly with much the same expression as the footman, and murmured, "Cordelia, you can't . . . you really *can't* sit at the breakfast table and imply my ancestors were bastards. It's a mortal insult here."

Where should I sit? "Oh. I'll never understand that, I guess. Oh, never mind. Koudelka, and Bothari."

"Quite. Go on, duty officer."

"Yes, sir. Well, sir, they were coming back, I was told,

about an hour after midnight, when they were set on by a gang of area toughs. Evidently Lieutenant Koudelka was too well dressed, and besides there's that walk of his, and the stick . . . anyway, he attracted attention. I don't know the details, sir, but there were four deaths and three in the hospital this morning, in addition to the ones that got away."

Vorkosigan whistled, very faintly, through his teeth. "What was the extent of Bothari's and Koudelka's injuries?"

"They . . . I don't have an official report, sir. Just hearsay."

"Say, then."

The duty officer swallowed a little. "Sergeant Bothari has a broken arm, some broken ribs, internal injuries, and a concussion. Lieutenant Koudelka, both legs broken, and a lot of, uh . . . shock burns." His voice trailed off.

"What?"

"Evidently—I heard—their assailants had a couple of high-voltage shock sticks, and they discovered they could get some . . . peculiar effects on his prosthetic nerves with them. After they'd broken his legs they spent . . . quite a long time working him over. That's how it was Commander Illyan's men caught up with them. They didn't clear off in time."

Cordelia pushed her plate away and sat trembling.

"Hearsay, eh? Very well. Dismissed. See that Commander Illyan is sent to me immediately he arrives." Vorkosigan's expression was introspective and grim.

Piotr's was sourly triumphant. "Vermin," he asserted. "You ought to burn them all out."

Vorkosigan sighed. "Easier to start a war than finish it. Not this week, sir."

Illyan attended on Vorkosigan within the hour, in the library, with his informal verbal report. Cordelia trailed in after them, to sit and listen.

"Sure you want to hear this?" Vorkosigan asked her quietly.

She shook her head. "Next to you, they are my best friends here. I'd rather know than wonder."

The duty officer's synopsis proved tolerably accurate, but Illyan, who had talked to both Bothari and Koudelka at the Imperial Military Hospital where they had been taken, had a number of details to add, in blunt terms. His puppy-dog face looked unusually old this morning.

"Your secretary was apparently seized with a desire to get laid," he began. "Why he picked Bothari as a native guide, I can't imagine."

"We three are the sole survivors of the *General Vorkraft*," Vorkosigan replied. "It's a bond, I suppose. Kou and Bothari always got on well, though. He appeals to Bothari's latent fatherly instincts, maybe. And Kou's a clean-minded boy—don't tell him I said that, he'd take it as an insult. It's good to be reminded such people still exist. Wish he'd come to me, though."

"Well, Bothari did his best," said Illyan. "Took him to this dismal dive, which I gather has a number of points in its favor from Bothari's point of view. It's cheap, it's quick, and nobody talks to him. It's also far removed from Admiral Vorrutyer's old circles. No unpleasant associations. He has a strict routine. According to Kou, Bothari's regular woman is almost as ugly as he is. Bothari likes her, it appears, because she never makes any noise. I don't think I want to think about that.

"Be that as it may, Kou got mismatched with one of the other employees, who terrified him. Bothari says he asked for the best girl for him—hardly a girl, woman, whatever—and apparently Kou's needs were misinterpreted. Anyway, Bothari was done and kicking his heels waiting while Kou was still trying to make polite conversation and being offered an assortment of delights for jaded appetites he'd never heard of before. He gave up and fled back downstairs at last, where Bothari was by this time pretty thoroughly tanked. He usually has one drink and leaves, it seems.

"Kou, Bothari, and this whore then got into an argument over payment, on the grounds that he'd burned up enough time for four customers versus—most of this won't be in the official report, all right?—she couldn't get his circuits working. Kou forked over a partial payment— Bothari's still grumbling over how much, insofar as he can talk at all through that mouth of his this morning—and they retreated in disorder, a lousy time having been had by all."

"The first obvious question that arises," said Vorkosigan, "is, was the attack ordered by anyone from that establishment?"

"To the best of my knowledge, no. I threw a cordon around the place, once we'd found it, and questioned everyone inside under fast-penta. Scared the shit out of them all, I'm glad to say. They're used to Count Vorbohn's municipal guards, whom they bribe, or who blackmail them, and vice versa. We turned up a lot of information on petty crimes, none of which was of the least interest to us—do you want me to pass it on to the municipals, by the way?"

"Hm. If they're innocent of the attack, just file it. Bothari may want to go back there someday. Do they know why they were questioned?"

"Certainly not! I insist my men work clean. We're here to gather information, not pass it out."

"My apologies, Commander. I should have known. Carry on."

"Well, they left the place about an hour after midnight, on foot, and took a wrong turn somewhere. Bothari's pretty upset about that. Thinks it's his fault, for getting so drunk. Bothari and Koudelka both say they saw movements in the shadows for about ten minutes before the attack. So they were stalked, apparently, until they were manuevered into a high walled alley, and found themselves with six in front and six behind.

"Bothari pulled his stunner and fired—got three, before he was jumped. Someone down there is richer by a good service stunner this morning. Kou had his swordstick, but nothing else.

"They ganged up on Bothari first. He took out two

more, after he'd lost the stunner. They stunned him, then
tried to beat him to death after he was down. Kou had
been using his stick as a quarterstaff up till then, but at
that point he popped the cover off. He says now he
wished he hadn't, because this murmur of 'Vor!' went up
all around, and things got really ugly.

"He stabbed two, until somebody struck the sword with
a shock stick, and his hand went into spasms. The five
that were left sat on him and broke both his legs backwards at the knees. He asked me to tell you it wasn't as
painful as it sounds. He says they broke so many circuits
he had hardly any sensation. I don't know if that's true."

"It's hard to tell with Kou," said Vorkosigan. "He's been
concealing pain for so long, it's almost second nature. Go on."

"I have to jump back a bit now. My man who was
assigned to Kou followed them down into that warren by
himself. He wasn't one of the men who are familiar with
the place, supposedly, and he wasn't dressed for it—Kou
had two reservations for some live musical performance
last night, and until three hours before midnight that's
where we thought he was going. My man went in there
and vanished, between the first and second hourly checks.
That's what has me going this morning. Was he murdered?
Or kidnapped? Rolled and raped? Or was he a plant, a
setup, a double agent? We won't know till we find the
body, or whatever.

"Thirty minutes after the missed check my people sent
in another tail. But he was looking for the first man. Kou
was uncovered for three solid bloody hours last night
before my night shift supervisor came on duty and woke
to the fact. Fortunately, Kou'd spent most of that time
in Bothari's old whore's retirement home.

"My night shift man, whom I commend, redirected the
field agent, and put a patrol in the air to boot. So when
the field agent finally got to that revolting scene, he was
able to call a flyer down on top of it almost immediately,
and drop half a dozen of my uniformed bruisers in to
break up the party. That business with the shock sticks—
it was bad, but not as bad as it might have been. Kou's

assailants evidently lacked the sort of, hm, imaginative approach that, say, the late Admiral Vorrutyer might have had in the same situation. Or maybe they just didn't have time to get really refined."

"Thank God," murmured Vorkosigan. "And the deaths?"

"Two were Bothari's work, clean blows, one was Kou's—cut him across the neck—and one, I'm afraid, was mine. The kid went into anaphylactic shock in an allergic reaction to fast-penta. We zipped him over to ImpMil, but they couldn't get him going again. I don't like it. They're autopsying him now, trying to find out if it was natural or a planted defense against questioning."

"And the gang?"

"Appears to be a perfectly legitimate—if that's the word—caravanserai mutual benefit society. According to the survivors we captured, they decided to pick on Kou because he 'walked funny.' Charming. Although Bothari wasn't exactly walking in a straight line, either. None of the ones we captured is an agent for anybody but themselves. I cannot speak for the dead. I supervised the questioning personally, and will swear to it. They were quite shocked to find themselves of interest to Imperial Security."

"Anything else?" said Vorkosigan.

Illyan yawned behind his hand, and apologized. "It's been a long night. My night shift man got me out of bed after midnight. Good man, good judgment. No, that about wraps it up, except for Kou's motivation for going down there in the first place. He went all vague, and started asking for pain medication, when we came to that subject. I was hoping you might have a suggestion, to ease my paranoias. Being suspicious of Kou gives me a crick in the neck." He yawned again.

"I do," said Cordelia, "but for your paranoia, not for your report, all right?"

He nodded.

"I think he's in love with someone. After all, you don't test something unless you're planning to use it. Unfortunately his test was a major disaster. I expect he'll be pretty depressed and touchy for quite some time."

Vorkosigan nodded understanding.

"Any idea who?" asked Illyan automatically.

"Yes, but I don't think it's your business. Especially if it's not going to happen."

Illyan shrugged acceptance, and left to pursue his lost sheep, the missing man who'd first been assigned to follow Koudelka.

Sergeant Bothari was back at Vorkosigan House, though not yet back on duty, within five days, a plastic casing on the broken arm. He volunteered no information on the brutal affair, and discouraged curious questioners with a sour glower and noncommittal grunts.

Droushnakovi asked no questions and offered no comments. But Cordelia saw her occasionally cast a haunted look at the empty comconsole in the library, with its double-scrambled links to the Imperial Residence and the General Staff Headquarters, where Koudelka usually sat to work while at Vorkosigan House. Cordelia wondered just how much detail of that night's events had been poured, searing as lead, into her ears.

Lieutenant Koudelka returned to curtailed light duties the following month, apparently quite cheerful and unaffected by his ordeal. But in his own way he was as uninformative as Bothari. Questioning Bothari had been like questioning a wall. Questioning Koudelka was like talking to a stream; one got back babble, or little eddies of jokes, or anecdotes that pulled the current of the discussion inexorably away from the original subject. Cordelia responded to his sunniness with automatic good grace, playing along with his obvious desire to slide over the affair as lightly as possible. Inwardly she was far more doubtful.

Her own mood was not the best. Her imagination returned again and again to the assassination scare of six weeks ago, dwelling uncomfortably on the chances that had almost taken Vorkosigan from her. Only when he was with her was she completely at ease, and he was gone more and more now. Something was brewing at Imperial

HQ; he had been gone four times to all-night sessions, and had taken a trip without her, some flying inspection of military affairs, of which he gave her no details and from which he returned white-tired around the eyes. He came in and out at odd hours. The flow of military and political gossip and chitchat with which he was wont to entertain her at meals, or undressing for bed, dried up to an uncommunicative silence, though he seemed to need her presence no less.

Where would she be without him? A pregnant widow, without family or friends, bearing a child already a focal point of dynastic paranoias, inheritor of a legacy of violence. Could she get off-planet? And where would she go if she could? Would Beta Colony ever let her come back?

Even the autumn rain, and the fat lingering greenness of the city parks, began to fail to please her. Oh, for a breath of really dry desert air, the familiar alkali tang, the endless flat distances. Would her son ever know what a real desert was? The horizons here, crowded close with buildings and vegetation, seemed almost to rise around her like a huge wall at times. On really bad days the wall seemed to topple inward.

She was holed up in the library one rainy afternoon, curled on an old high-backed sofa, reading, for the third time, a page in an old volume from the Count's shelves. The book was a relic of the printer's art from the Time of Isolation. The English in which it was written was printed in a mutant variation of the cyrillic alphabet, all forty-six characters of it, once used for all tongues on Barrayar. Her mind seemed unusually mushy and unresponsive to it today. She turned out the light and rested her eyes a few minutes. With relief, she observed Lieutenant Koudelka enter the library and seat himself, stiffly and carefully, at the comconsole. *I shan't interrupt him; he at least has real work to do,* she thought, not yet returning to her page, but still comforted by his unconscious company.

He worked only for a moment or two, then shut down the machine with a sigh, staring abstractedly into the empty carved fireplace that was the room's original centerpiece, still not noticing her. *So, I'm not the only one who can't concentrate. Maybe it's this strange grey weather. It does seem to have a depressing effect on people. . . .*

Picking up his swordstick, he ran a hand down the smooth length of its casing. He clicked it open, holding it firmly and releasing the spring silently and slowly. He sighted along the length of the gleaming blade, which almost seemed to glow with a light of its own in the shadowed room, and angled it, as if meditating on its pattern and fine workmanship. He then turned it end for end, point over his left shoulder and hilt away from him. He wrapped a handkerchief around the blade for a hold, and pressed it, very lightly, against the side of his neck over the area of the carotid artery. The expression on his face was distant and thoughtful, his grip on the blade as light as a lover's. His hand tightened suddenly.

Her indrawn breath, the first half of a sob, startled him from his reverie. He looked up to see her for the first time; his lips thinned and his face turned a dusky red. He swung the sword down. It left a white line on his neck, like part of a necklace, with a few ruby drops of blood welling along it.

"I . . . didn't see you, Milady," he said hoarsely. "I . . . don't mind me. Just fooling around, you know."

They stared at each other in silence. Her own words broke from her lips against her will. "I hate this place! I'm afraid all the time, now."

She turned her face into the high side of the sofa, and, to her own horror, began to cry. *Stop it! Not in front of Kou of all people! The man has enough real troubles without you dumping your imaginary ones on him.* But she couldn't stop.

He levered himself up and limped over to her couch, looking worried. Tentatively, he seated himself beside her.

"Um . . ." he began. "Don't cry, Milady. I was just fooling around, really." He patted her clumsily on the shoulder.

"Garbage," she choked back at him. "You scare the hell

out of me." On impulse she transferred her tear-smeared face from the cold silken fabric of the sofa to the warm roughness of the shoulder of his green uniform. It tore a like honesty from him.

"You can't imagine what it's like," he whispered fiercely. "They pity me, you know? Even *he* does." A jerk of his head in no particular direction indicated Vorkosigan. "It's a hundred times worse than the scorn. And it's going to go on *forever*."

She shook her head, devoid of answer in the face of this undoubted truth.

"I hate this place, too," he continued. "Just as much as it hates me. More, some days. So you see, you're not alone."

"So many people trying to kill him," she whispered back, despising herself for her weakness. "Total strangers . . . one of them is bound to succeed in the end. I think about it all the time, now." Would it be a bomb? Some poison? Plasma arc, burning away Aral's face, leaving no lips even to kiss goodbye?

Koudelka's attention was drawn achingly from his pain to hers, brows drawing quizzically together.

"Oh, Kou," she went on, looking down blindly into his lap and stroking his sleeve. "No matter how much it hurts, don't do it to him. He loves you . . . you're like a son to him, just the sort of son he always wanted. That," she nodded toward the sword laid on the couch, shinier than silk, "would cut out his heart. This place pours craziness on him every day, and demands he give back justice. He can't do it except with a whole heart. Or he must eventually start giving back the craziness, like every one of his predecessors. And," she added in a burst of uncontrollable illogic, "it's so damn *wet* here! It won't be my fault if my son is born with *gills*!"

His arms encircled her in a kindly hug. "Are you . . . afraid of the childbirth?" he inquired, with a gentle and unexpected perceptiveness.

Cordelia went still, suddenly face-to-face with her

tightly suppressed fears. "I don't trust your doctors," she admitted shakily.

He smiled in deep irony. "I can't blame you."

A laugh puffed from her, and she hugged him back, around the chest, and raised her hand to wipe away the tiny drops of blood from the side of his neck. "When you love someone, it's like your skin covers theirs. Every hurt is doubled. And I do love you so, Kou. I wish you'd let me help you."

"Therapy, Cordelia?" Vorkosigan's voice was cold, and cut like a stinging spray of rattling hail. She looked up, surprised, to see him standing before them, his face frozen as his voice. "I realize you have a great deal of Betan . . . expertise, in such matters, but I beg you will leave the project to someone else."

Koudelka turned red, and recoiled from her. "Sir," he began, and trailed off, as startled as Cordelia by the icy anger in Vorkosigan's eyes. Vorkosigan's gaze flicked over him, and they both clamped their jaws shut.

Cordelia drew in a very deep breath for a retort, but released it only as a furious "Oh!" at Vorkosigan's back as he wheeled and stalked out, spine stiff as Kou's swordblade.

Koudelka, still red, folded into himself, and using his sword as a prop levered himself to his feet, his breath too rapid. "Milady. I beg your pardon." The words seemed quite without meaning.

"Kou," said Cordelia, "you know he didn't mean that hateful thing. He spoke without thinking. I'm sure he doesn't, doesn't . . ."

"Yes, I realize," returned Koudelka, his eyes blank and hard. "I am universally known to be quite harmless to any man's marriage, I believe. But if you will excuse me— Milady—I do have some work to do. Of a sort."

"Oh!" Cordelia didn't know if she was more furious with Vorkosigan, Koudelka, or herself. She steamed to her feet and left the room, throwing her words back over her shoulder. "Damn all Barrayarans to hell anyway!"

Droushnakovi appeared in her path, with a timid, "Milady?"

"And you, you useless . . . frill," snarled Cordelia, her rage escaping helplessly in all directions now. "Why can't you manage your own affairs? You Barrayaran women seem to expect your lives to be handed to you on a platter. It doesn't work that way!"

The girl stepped back a pace, bewildered. Cordelia contained her seething outrage, and asked more sensibly, "Which way did Aral go?"

"Why . . . upstairs, I believe, Milady."

A little of her old and battered humor came to her rescue then. "Two steps at a time, by chance?"

"Um . . . three, actually," Drou replied faintly.

"I suppose I'd better go talk to him," said Cordelia, running her hands through her hair and wondering if tearing it out would have any practical benefit. "Son of a bitch." She did not know herself if that was expletive or description. *And to think I never used to swear.*

She trudged after him, her anger draining with her energy as she climbed the stairs. *This pregnancy business sure slows you down.* She passed a duty guard in the corridor. "Lord Vorkosigan go this way?" she asked him.

"To his rooms, Milady," he replied, and stared curiously after her. *Great. Love it,* she thought savagely. *The old newlyweds' first real fight will have plenty of built-in audience. These old walls are not soundproof. I wonder if I can keep my voice down? Aral's no problem; when he gets mad he whispers.*

She entered their bedroom, to find him seated on the side of the bed, removing uniform jacket and boots with violent, jerky gestures. He looked up, and they glared at each other. Cordelia opened fire first, thinking, *Let's get this over with.*

"That remark you made in front of Kou was totally out of line."

"What, I walk in to find my wife . . . cuddling, with one of my officers, and you expect me to make polite conversation about the weather?" he bit back.

"You know it was nothing of the sort."

"Fine. Suppose it hadn't been me? Suppose it had been

one of the duty guards, or my father. How would you have explained it then? You know what they think of Betans. They'd jump on it, and the rumors would never be stopped. Next thing I knew, it would be coming back at me as political chaff. Every enemy I have out there is just waiting for a weak spot to pounce on. They'd love one like that."

"How the devil did we get onto your damned politics? I'm talking about a friend. I doubt you could have come up with a more wounding remark if you'd funded a study project. That was foul, Aral! What's the matter with you, anyway?"

"I don't know." He slowed, and rubbed his face tiredly. "It's the damn job, I expect. I don't mean to spill it on you."

Cordelia suspected that was as near as she could expect of an admission of his being in the wrong, and accepted it with a little nod, letting her own rage evaporate. She then remembered why the rage had felt so good, for the vacuum it left filled back up with fear.

"Yes, well . . . just how much do you fancy having to break down his door one of these mornings?"

Vorkosigan frowned at her, going still. "Do you . . . have some reason to believe's he's thinking along suicidal lines? He seemed quite content to me."

"He would—to you." Cordelia let the words hang in the air a moment, for emphasis. "I think he's about that close." She held up thumb and forefinger a bare millimeter apart. The finger still had a smear of blood on it, and it caught her eye in unhappy fascination. "He was playing around with that blasted swordstick. I wish I'd never given it to him. I don't think I could bear it if he used it to cut his own throat. That—seemed to be what he had in mind."

"Oh." Vorkosigan looked smaller, somehow, without his glittering military jacket, without his anger. He held out his hand to her, and she took it and sat beside him.

"So if you're having visions of, of playing King Arthur to our Lancelot and Guinevere in that—pig-head of yours, forget it. It won't wash."

He laughed a little at that. "My visions were closer to home, I'm afraid, and considerably more sordid. Just an old bad dream."

"Yeah, I . . . guess it would hit a nerve, at that." She wondered if the ghost of his first wife ever hovered by him, breathing cold death in his ear, as Vorrutyer's ghost sometimes did by her. He looked deathly enough. "But I'm Cordelia, remember? Not . . . anybody else."

He leaned his forehead against hers. "Forgive me, dear Captain. I'm just an ugly scared old man, and growing older and uglier and more paranoid every day."

"You, too?" She rested in his arms. "I take exception to the old and ugly part, though. Pigheaded did *not* refer to your exterior appearance."

"Thank you—I think."

It pleased her to amuse him even that little. "It is the job, isn't it?" she said. "Can you talk about it at all?"

His lips compressed. "In confidence—although that seems to be your natural state, I don't know why I bother to emphasize it—it looks like we could have another war on our hands before the end of the year. And we're not nearly well enough recovered for it, after Escobar."

"What! I thought the war party was half-paralyzed."

"Ours is. The Cetagandans' is still in good working order, however. Intelligence indicates they were planning to use the political chaos here following Ezar Vorbarra's death to cover a move on those disputed wormhole jump points. Instead they got me, and—well, I can hardly call it stability. Dynamic equilibrium, at best. Anyway, not the kind of disruption they were counting on. Hence that little incident with the sonic grenade. Negri and Illyan are now seventy percent sure it was Cetagandan work."

"Will they . . . try again?"

"Almost certainly. But with or without me, consensus in the Staff is that they'll be probing in force before the end of the year. And if we're weak—they'll just keep right on moving until they're stopped."

"No wonder you've been . . . abstracted."

"Is that the polite term for it? But no. I've known about

the Cetagandans for some time. Something else came up today, after the Council session. A private audience. Count Vorhalas came to see me, to beg a favor."

"I'd think it would be your pleasure, to do a favor for Rulf Vorhalas's brother. I gather not?"

He shook his head unhappily. "The Count's youngest son, who is a hotheaded young idiot of eighteen who should have been sent to military school—you met him at the Council confirmation, as I recall—"

"Lord Carl?"

"Yes. He got into a drunken fight at a party last night."

"A universal tradition. Such things happen even on Beta Colony."

"Quite. But they stepped outside to settle their affair armed, each one, with a pair of dull swords that had been part of a wall decoration, and a couple of kitchen knives. That made it, technically, a duel with the two swords."

"Uh-oh. Was anyone hurt?"

"Unfortunately, yes. More or less by accident, I gather, in a scrambling fall, the Count's son managed to put his sword through his friend's stomach and sever his abdominal aorta. He bled to death almost immediately. By the time the bystanders had gathered their wits sufficiently to get a medical team up there it was much too late."

"Dear God."

"It was a duel. It began as a mockery, but it ended as . . . And the penalties for dueling are . . . an Imperial pardon. Or, if I could not grant . . . if I could get the charges changed to simple . . . er. If it were tried as a simple murder, the boy could . . . ead self-defense, and possibly end up with a mere prison term." He paced the room, stopping by the window, staring out into the rain. "His father came begging me if I could . . .

"That seems . . . fair enough, I suppose."

"Yes." He paced again. "A favor for a friend. Or . . . the first crack in the door to let that hell-bred custom back into our society. What happens when the next case is brought before me, and the next, and the next? Where do I begin drawing the line? What if the next case involves some political enemy of mine, and not a member of my own party? Shall all the deaths that went into stamping this thing out be made void? I remember dueling, and what things were like back then. And worse—an entry point for government by friends, then cliques. Say what you will about Ezar Vorbarra, in thirty years of ruthless labor he transformed the government from a Vor-class club into some semblance, however shaky, of a rule of law, one law for everyone."

"I begin to see the problem."

"And me—me, of all men, to have to make that decision! Who should have been publicly executed twenty-two years ago for the selfsame crime!" He paused before her. "The story about last night is all over town, in various forms, this morning. It will be all over everywhere in a few days. I had the news service kill it, temporarily, but that was mere spitting in the wind. It's too late for a coverup, even if I wanted to do one. So what shall I betray this day? A friend? Or Ezar Vorbarra's trust? There is no doubt which decision *he* would have made."

He sat back beside her, and took her in his arms. "And this is only the beginning. Every month, every week, there will be some other impossible thing. What's going to be left of me after fiftee_ thing we buried three mars of this? A husk, like that breath that there may be no _go, praying with his last monstrosity, like his son, so in__r a power-corrupted ilized by plasma arc? Or someth__r a power-corrupted

His naked agony terrified her. Sh_ld only be ster-return. "I don't know. I don't know. B__rse?" somebody has been making these kinds of ___htly in along, while we went along blissfully unconsc__ the world as given. And they were only human, _ better, no worse than you."

"Frightening thought."

She sighed. "You can't choose between evil and evil, in the dark, by logic. You can only cling to some safety line of principle. I can't make your decision. But whatever

principles you choose now are going to be your safety
lines, to carry you forward. And for the sake of your
people, they're going to have to be consistent ones."

He rested in her arms. "I know. There wasn't really
a question, about the decision. I was just . . . kicking a
bit, going down." He disengaged himself, and stood again.
"Dear Captain. If I'm still sane, fifteen years from now,
I believe it will be your doing."

She looked up at him. "So what decision is it?"

The pain in his eyes gave her the answer. "Oh, no,"
she said involuntarily, then bit off further words. *And I
was trying to speak so wisely. I didn't mean* this.

"Don't you know?" he said gently, resigned. "Ezar's way
is the only way that can work, here. It's true after all. He
does rule from his grave." He headed for their bathroom,
to wash and change clothes.

"But you're not him," she whispered to the empty
room. "Can't you find a way of your own?"

CHAPTER EIGHT

Vorkosigan attended Carl Vorhalas's public execution three weeks later.

"Are you required to go?" Cordelia asked him that morning, as he dressed, cold and withdrawn. "I don't have to go, do I?"

"God, no, of course not. I don't have to go, officially, except . . . I have to go. You can see why, surely."

"Not . . . really, except as a form of self-punishment. I'm not sure that's a luxury you can afford, in your line of work."

"I must go. A dog returns to its vomit, doesn't it? His parents will be there, do you know? And his brother."

"What a barbaric custom."

"Well, we could treat crime as a disease, like you Betans. You know what that's like. At least we kill a man cleanly, all at once, instead of in bits over years. . . . I don't know."

"How will they . . . do it?"

"Beheading. It's supposed to be almost painless."

"How do they know?"

His laugh was totally without humor. "A very cogent question."

He did not embrace her when he left. He returned

376

a bare two hours later, silent, to shake his head at a tentative offer of lunch, cancel an afternoon appointment, and withdraw to Count Piotr's library and sit, not-reading a book-viewer. Cordelia joined him there after a while, resting on the couch, and waited patiently for him to come back to her from whatever distant country of the mind he dwelt in.

"The boy was going to be brave," he said after an hour's silence. "You could see that he had every gesture planned out in advance. But nobody else followed the script. His mother broke him down. . . . And to top it the damned executioner missed his stroke. Had to take three cuts, to get the head off."

"Sounds like Sergeant Bothari did better with a pocketknife." Vorrutyer had been haunting her more than usual that morning, scarletly.

"It lacked nothing for perfect hideousness. His mother cursed me, too. Until Evon and Count Vorhalas took her away." The dead-expressioned voice escaped him then. "Oh, Cordelia! It can't have been the right decision! And yet . . . and yet . . . no other one was possible. Was it?"

He came to her then, and held her in silence. He seemed very close to weeping, and it almost frightened her more that he did not. The tension eventually drained out of him.

"I suppose I'd better pull myself together and go change. Vortala has a meeting scheduled with the Minister of Agriculture that's too important to miss, and after that there's the general staff. . . ." By the time he left his usual self-possession had returned.

That night he lay long awake beside her. His eyes were closed, but she could tell from his breathing it was pretense. She could not dredge up one word of comfort that did not seem inane to her, so kept silence with him through the watches of the night. Rain began outside, a steady drizzle. He spoke once.

"I've watched men die before. Ordered executions, ordered men into battle, chosen this one over that one,

committed three sheer murders and but for the grace of God
and Sergeant Bothari would have committed a fourth . . . I
don't know why this one should hit like a wall. It's stopped
me, Cordelia. And I dare not stop, or we'll all fall together.
Got to keep it in the air somehow."

She awoke in the dark to a tinkling crash and a soft
report, and drew in her breath with a start. Acridity seared
her lungs, mouth, nostrils, eyes. A gut-wrenching
undertaste pumped her stomach into her throat. Beside
her, Vorkosigan snapped from sleep with an oath.

"Soltoxin gas grenade! Don't breathe, Cordelia!"
Emphasizing his shout, he shoved a pillow over her face,
his hot strong arms encircling her and dragging her from
the bed. She found her feet and lost her stomach at the
same moment, stumbling into the hall, and he slammed
the bedroom door shut behind them.

Running footsteps shook the floor. Vorkosigan cried,
"Get back! Soltoxin gas! Clear the floor! Call Illyan!"
before he too doubled over, coughing and retching. Other
hands bundled them both toward the stairs. She could
scarcely see through her madly watering eyes.

Between spasms Vorkosigan gasped, "They'll have the
antidote . . . Imperial Residence . . . closer than ImpMil
. . . get Illyan at once. He'll know. Into the shower—
where's Milady's woman? Get a maid. . . ."

Within moments she was dumped into a downstairs
shower, Vorkosigan with her. He was shaking and barely
able to stand, but still trying to help her. "Start washing
it off your skin, and keep washing. Don't stop. Keep the
water cool."

"You, too, then. What was that crap?" She coughed
again, in the spray of the water, and they exchanged help
with the soap.

"Wash out your mouth, too. . . . Soltoxin. It's been
fifteen, sixteen years since I last smelled that stink, but
you never forget it. It's a poison gas. Military. Should
be strictly controlled. How the hell anyone got hold of
some . . . Damn Security! They'll be flapping around

like headless chickens tomorrow . . . too late." His face was greenish-white beneath the night's beard stubble.

"I don't feel too bad now," said Cordelia. "Nausea's passing off. I take it we missed the full dose?"

"No. It just acts slowly. Doesn't take much at all to do you. It mostly affects soft tissue—lungs will be jelly in an hour, if the antidote doesn't get here soon."

The growing fear that pounded in her gut, heart, and mind half-clotted her words. "Does it cross the placental barrier?"

He was silent for too long before he said, "I'm not sure. Have to ask the doctor. I've only seen the effects on young men." Another spasm of deep coughing seized him, that went on and on.

One of Count Piotr's serving women arrived, disheveled and frightened, to help Cordelia and the terrified young guard who had been assisting them. Another guard came in to report, raising his voice over the running water. "We reached the Residence, sir. They have some people on the way."

Cordelia's own throat, bronchia, and lungs were beginning to secrete foul-tasting phlegm, and she coughed and spat. "Anyone see Drou?"

"I think she took out after the assassins, Milady."

"Not her job. When an alarm goes up, she's supposed to run to Cordelia," growled Vorkosigan. The talking triggered more coughing.

"She was downstairs, sir, at the time the attack took place, with Lieutenant Koudelka. They both went out the back door."

"Dammit," Vorkosigan muttered, "not his job either." His effort was punished by another coughing jag. "They catch anybody?"

"I think so, sir. There was some kind of uproar at the back of the garden, by the wall."

They stood under the water for a few more minutes, until the guard reported back. "The doctor from the Residence is here, sir."

The maid wrapped Cordelia in a robe, and Vorkosigan

put on a towel, growling to the guard, "Go find me some clothes, boy." His voice rattled like gravel.

A middle-aged man, his hair standing up stiffly, wearing trousers, pajama tops, and bedroom slippers, was off-loading equipment in the guest bedroom when they came out. He took a pressurized canister from his bag and fitted a breathing mask to it, glancing at Cordelia's rounding abdomen and then at Vorkosigan.

"My lord. Are you certain of the identification of the poison?"

"Unfortunately, yes. It was soltoxin."

The doctor bowed his head. "I am sorry, Milady."

"Is it going to hurt my . . ." She choked on the mucus.

"Just shut up and give it to her," snarled Vorkosigan.

The doctor fitted the mask over her nose and mouth. "Breathe deeply. Inhale . . . exhale. Keep exhaling. Now draw in. Hold it. . . ."

The antidote gas had a greenish taste, cooler, but nearly as nauseating as the original poison. Her stomach heaved, but had nothing left in it to reject. She watched Vorkosigan over the mask, watching her, and tried to smile reassuringly. It must be reaction catching up with him; he seemed greyer, more distressed, with each breath she took. She was certain he had taken in a larger dose than she, and pushed the mask away to say, "Isn't it about your turn?"

The doctor pressed it back, saying, "One more breath, Milady, to be sure." She inhaled deeply, and the doctor transferred the mask to Vorkosigan. He seemed to need no instruction in the procedure.

"How many minutes since the exposure?" asked the doctor anxiously.

"I'm not sure. Did anyone note the time? You, uh . . ." She had forgotten the young guard's name.

"About fifteen or twenty minutes, Milady, I think."

The doctor relaxed measurably. "It should be all right, then. You'll both be in hospital for a few days. I'll arrange for medical transport. Was anyone else exposed?" he asked the guard.

"Doctor, wait." He had repossessed canister and mask,

and was making for the door. "What will that . . . soltoxin do to my baby?"

He did not meet her eyes. "No one knows. No one has ever survived exposure without an immediate antidote treatment."

Cordelia could feel her heart beating. "But given the treatment . . ." She did not like his look of pity, and turned to Vorkosigan. "Is that—" but was stopped cold by his expression, a leaden greyness lit from beneath by pain and growing anger, a stranger's face with a lover's eyes, meeting her eyes at last.

"Tell her about it," he whispered to the doctor. "I can't."

"Need we distress—"

"*Now*. Get it over with." His voice cracked and croaked.

"The problem is the antidote, Milady," said the doctor reluctantly. "It's a violent teratogen. Destroys bone development in the growing fetus. Your bones are grown, so it won't affect you, except for an increased tendency to arthritic-type breakdowns, which can be treated . . . if and when they arise. . . ." He trailed off as she closed her eyes, shutting him out.

"I must see that hall guard," he added.

"Go, go," replied Vorkosigan, releasing him. He maneuvered out the door past the guard arriving with Vorkosigan's clothes.

She opened her eyes to Vorkosigan, and they stared at each other.

"The look on your face . . ." he whispered. "It's not . . . Weep. Rage! Do something!" His voice rose to hoarseness. "Hate me at least!"

"I can't," she whispered back, "feel anything yet. Tomorrow, maybe." Every breath was fire.

With a muttered curse, he flung on the clothes, a set of undress greens. "I can do something."

It was the stranger's face, possessing his. Words echoed hollowly in her memory, *If Death wore a dress uniform He would look just like that*.

"Where are you going?"

"Going to see what Koudelka caught." She followed him through the door. "You stay here," he ordered.

"No."

He glared back at her, and she brushed the glare away with an equally savage gesture, as if striking down a sword thrust. "I'm going with you."

"Come on, then." He turned jerkily, and made for the stairs to the first floor, rage rigid in his backbone.

"You will not," she murmured fiercely, for his ear alone, "murder anyone in front of me."

"Will I not?" he whispered back. "Will-I-not?" His steps were hard, bare feet jarring on the stone stairs.

The large entry hall was in chaos, filled with their guards, men in the Count's livery, medics. A man, or a body, Cordelia could not tell which, in the black fatigue uniform of the night guards, was laid out on the tessalated pavement, a medic at his head. Both were soaked from the rain, and smeared with mud. Bloodstained water pooled beneath them, and the medic's bootsoles squeaked in it.

Commander Illyan, beads of water gleaming in his hair from the foggy drizzle, was just coming in the front door with an aide, saying, "Let me know as soon as the techs get here with the kirilian detector. Meantime keep everyone off that wall and out of the alley. My lord!" he cried when he saw Vorkosigan. "Thank God you're all right!"

Vorkosigan growled in his throat, wordlessly. A knot of men surrounded the prisoner, who was leaning face to the wall, one hand over his head and the other held stiffly to his side at an odd angle. Droushnakovi stood near, wearing a wet shift. A wicked-looking metal crossbow dangled gleaming from her hand, evidently the weapon that had been used to fire the gas grenade through their window. She bore a livid mark on her face, and stanched a nosebleed with her other hand. Blood stained her nightgown here and there. Koudelka was there, too, leaning on his sword, one leg dragging. He wore a wet and muddy uniform and bedroom slippers, and a sour look on his face.

"I'd have had him," he was snapping, evidently

continuing an ongoing argument, "if you hadn't come running up and shouting at me—"

"Oh, really!" Droushnakovi snapped back. "Well, pardon me, but I don't see it that way. Seems to me he had you, laid out flat on the ground. If I hadn't seen his legs going up the wall—"

"Stuff it! It's Lord Vorkosigan!" hissed another guard. The knot of men turned, to step back before his face.

"How did he get in?" began Vorkosigan, and stopped. The man was wearing the black fatigues of the Service. "Surely not one of your men, Illyan!" His voice grated, metal on stone.

"My lord, we've got to have him alive, to question him," said Illyan uneasily at Vorkosigan's shoulder, half-hypnotized by the same look that had made the guards recoil. "There may be more to the conspiracy. You can't . . ."

The prisoner turned, then, to face his captors. A guard started forward to shove him back into position against the wall, but Vorkosigan motioned him away. Cordelia could not see Vorkosigan's face, standing behind him in that moment, but his shoulders lost their murderous tension, and the rage drained out of his backbone, leaving only a gutter-smear of pain. Above the insignialess black collar was the ravaged face of Evon Vorhalas.

"Oh, not *both* of them," breathed Cordelia.

Hatred hastened the rhythm of Vorhalas's breathing as he glared at his intended victim. "You bastard. You snake-cold bastard. Sitting there cold as stone while they hacked off his head. Did you feel a thing? Or did you enjoy it, my Lord Regent? I swore I'd get you then."

There was a long silence, then Vorkosigan leaned close to him, one arm extended past his head for support against the wall. He whispered hoarsely, "You missed me, Evon."

Vorhalas spat in his face, spittle bloody from his injured mouth. Vorkosigan made no move to wipe it away. "You missed my wife," he went on in a slow soft cadence. "But you got my son. Did you dream of sweet revenge? You have it. Look at her eyes, Evon. A man could drown in those sea-grey eyes. I'll be looking at them every day for the rest of my life. So eat vengeance, Evon. Drink it. Fondle it. Wrap it round you in the night watch. It's all yours. I will it all to you. For myself, I've gorged it to the gagging point, and have lost my stomach for it."

Vorhalas looked up, then, for the first time, past him to Cordelia. She thought of the child in her belly, his delicate girdering of new cartilagenous bones perhaps even now beginning to rot, twist, slough, but could not hate Vorhalas, although she tried to for a moment. She couldn't even find him baffling. She had a sense, as of a second sight, that she could see right through his wounded spirit the way doctors saw through a wounded body with their diagnostic viewers. Every twist and tear and emotional abrasion, every young cancer of resentment growing from them, and above all the great gash of his brother's death seemed red-lined in her mind's eye.

"He didn't enjoy it, Evon," she said. "What would you have had from him? Do you even know?"

"A little human pity," he snarled. "He could have saved Carl. Even then he could have. I thought at first that was why he had come."

"Oh, God," said Vorkosigan. He looked sick at the flashing vision of the rise and fall of hopes these words conjured. "I don't play theater with lives, Evon!"

Vorhalas held his hatred like a shield before him. "Go to hell."

Vorkosigan sighed, and pushed away from the wall. The doctor was lingering to chivvy them to the waiting vehicle for the trip to the Imperial Military Hospital. "Take him away, Illyan," said Vorkosigan wearily.

"Wait," said Cordelia. "I need to know—I need to ask him something."

Vorhalas eyed her sullenly.

"Was this the result you intended? I mean, when you chose that particular weapon? That specific poison?"

He looked away from her, speaking to the far wall. "It was what I could grab, going through the armory. I didn't think you could identify it, and get the antidote all the way from ImpMil in time. . . ."

"You relieve me of a burden," she whispered.

"The antidote came from the Imperial Residence," Vorkosigan explained. "A quarter of the distance. The Emperor's infirmary there has everything. As for identification . . . I was there, at the destruction of the Karian mutiny. Just about your age, I think, or a little younger. The smell brought it all back, just now. Boys coughing out their lungs in red blobs. . . ." He seemed to shrink into himself, into the past.

"I didn't intend your death particularly. You were just in the way, between me and him." Vorhalas gestured blindly at her swollen torso. "It wasn't the result I intended. I meant to kill him. I didn't even know for sure that you shared the same room at night." He was looking everywhere, now, except her face. "I never thought about killing your . . ."

"Look at me," she croaked, "and say the word out loud."

"Baby," he whispered, and burst into sudden, shocking sobs.

Vorkosigan stepped back, beside her. "Wish you hadn't done that," he whispered. "Reminds me of his brother. Why am I death to that family?"

"Still want him to eat vengeance?"

He leaned his forehead on her shoulder, briefly. "Not even that. You empty us all out, dear Captain. But, oh . . ." His hand reached out as if to cup her belly, then drew back in consciousness of their ring of silent watchers. He straightened. "Bring me a full report in the morning, Illyan," he said, "at the hospital."

He took her by the arm as they turned to follow the doctor. She could not tell if it was to support her or himself.

She was surrounded by helpers at the Imperial Military Hospital complex, carried along as on a river. Doctors, nurses, corpsmen, guards. Aral was separated from her at the door, and it made her uneasy and alone in the crowd. She said very little to them, empty courtesies, automatic as levers. She wished for shock to take her consciousness, numbness, reality-denying madness, hallucinations, anything. Instead she just felt tired.

The baby was moving within her, flutters, kneading turns; evidently the teratogenic antidote was a very slow-acting poison. They were still granted a little time together, it seemed, and she loved him through her skin, her fingertips moving in a slow massage over her abdomen. *Welcome, my son, to Barrayar, the abode of cannibals; this place didn't even wait the usual eighteen or twenty years to eat you.* Ravenous planet.

She was bedded down in a luxurious private room in a VIP wing, hastily cleared for their exclusive use. She was relieved to discover Vorkosigan had been ensconced just across the hall. Dressed already in green military-issue pajamas, he came promptly over to see her tucked into bed. She managed a small smile for him, but did not attempt to sit up. The force of gravity was pulling her down into the center of the world. Only the rigidity of the bed, the building, the planet's crust, held her up against it, not her will at all.

He was trailed by an anxious corpsman, saying, "Remember, sir, try not to talk so much, till after the doctor's had a chance to give your throat the irrigation treatment."

The grey light of dawn was making the windows pale. He sat on the edge of the bed and took her hand, rubbing it. "You're cold, dear Captain," he whispered hoarsely. She nodded. Her chest ached, her throat was raw, and her sinuses burned.

"I should never have let them talk me into taking the job," he went on. "So sorry . . ."

"I talked you into it, too. You tried to warn me. Not your fault. It seemed right for you. Is right."

He shook his head. "Don't talk. Makes scar tissue on the vocal cords."

She gave vent to a joyless "Ha!" and laid a finger across his lips as he started to speak again. He nodded, resigned, and they remained looking at each other for a time. He pushed her tangled hair back gently from her face, and she captured the broad hand to hold against her cheek for comfort, until he was hunted out by a posse of doctors and technicians and driven off for a treatment. "We'll be in to see you shortly, Milady," their chieftain promised ominously.

They returned after a while, to make her gargle a nasty pink fluid, and breathe into a machine, then rumbled out again. A female nurse brought her breakfast, which she did not touch.

Then a committee of grim-faced doctors entered her room. The one who had come from the Imperial Residence in the night was now smartly groomed and neatly dressed in civilian clothes. Her own personal physician was flanked by a younger, black-browed man in Service greens with captain's tabs on his collar. She gazed at their three faces and thought of Cerberus.

Her man introduced the stranger. "This is Captain Vaagen, of the Imperial Military Hospital's research facility. He's our resident expert on military poisons."

"Inventing them, or cleaning up after them, Captain?" Cordelia asked.

"Both, Milady." He stood at a sort of aggressive parade rest.

Her own man had the look about his eyes of someone who had drawn the short straw, although his lips smiled. "My Lord Regent has asked me to inform you of the schedule of treatments, and so on. I'm afraid," he cleared his throat, "that it would be best if we scheduled the abortion promptly. It is already unusually late in your pregnancy for it, and it would be as well for your recovery to relieve you of the physiological strain as soon as possible."

"Is there nothing that can be done?" she asked hopelessly, already knowing the answer from their faces.

"I'm afraid not," said her man sadly. The man from the Imperial Residence nodded confirmation.

"I ran a literature search," said the captain unexpectedly, staring out the window, "and there was that calcium experiment. True, the results they got weren't particularly heartening—"

"I thought we'd agreed not to bring that up," glared the Residence man.

"Vaagen, that's cruel," said her own man. "You're just raising false hopes. You can't make the Regent's wife into one of your hapless experimental animals for a lot of untried shots in the dark. You have your permission from the Regent for the autopsy—leave it at that."

Her world turned right-side-up again in a second, as she looked at the face of the man with ideas. She knew the type; half-right, half-cocked, half-successful, flitting from one monomania to another like a bee pollinating flowers, gathering little fruit but leaving seeds behind. She was nothing to him, personally, but the raw material for a monograph. The risks she took did not appall his imagination, she was not a person but a disease state. She smiled upon him, slowly, wildly, knowing him then for her ally in the enemy camp.

"How do you do, Dr. Vaagen? How would you like to write the paper of a lifetime?"

The Residence man barked a laugh. "She's got your number, Vaagen."

He smiled back, astonished to be so instantly understood. "You realize, I can't guarantee any results. . . ."

"Results!" interrupted her man. "My God, you'd better let her know what your idea of results is. Or show her the pictures—no, don't do that. Milady," he turned to her, "the treatment he's discussing was last tried twenty years ago. It did irreparable damage to the mothers. And the results—the very best results you could hope for would be a twisted cripple. Perhaps much worse. Indescribably worse."

"Jellyfish describes it pretty well," said Vaagen.

"You're inhuman, Vaagen!" snapped her man, with a glance her way to check the distress quotient.

"A viable jellyfish, Dr. Vaagen?" asked Cordelia, intent.

"Mm. Maybe," he replied, inhibited by his colleagues' angry glares. "But there is the difficulty of what happens to the mothers when the treatment is applied in vivo."

"So, can't you do it in vitro?" Cordelia asked the obvious question.

Vaagen shot a glance of triumph at her man. "It would certainly open up a number of possible lines of experiment, if it could be arranged," he murmured to the ceiling.

"In vitro?" said the Residence man, puzzled. "How?"

"What, how?" said Cordelia. "You've got seventeen Escobaran-manufactured uterine replicators stored in a closet around here somewhere, carried home from the war." She turned excitedly to Vaagen. "Do you happen to know a Dr. Henri?"

Vaagen nodded. "We've worked together."

"Then you know all about them!"

"Well—not exactly all. But, ah—in fact, he informs me that they are available. But you understand, I'm not an obstetrician."

"You certainly aren't," said her man. "Milady, this man isn't even a physician. He's only a biochemist."

"But you're an obstetrician," she pointed out. "So we have the whole team, then. Dr. Henri, and, um, Captain Vaagen here for Piotr Miles, and you, for the transfer."

His lips were compressed, and his eyes held a very strange expression. It took her a moment to identify it as fear. "I can't do the transfer, Milady," he said. "I don't know how. Nobody on Barrayar has ever done one."

"You don't advise it, then?"

"Definitely not. The possibility of permanent damage— you can, after all, begin again in a few months, if the soft-tissue scarring doesn't extend to testicular—ahem. You can begin again. I am your doctor, and that is my considered opinion."

"Yes, if somebody else doesn't knock Aral off in the meantime. I must remember this is Barrayar, where they are so in love with death they bury men who are still twitching. *Are* you willing to try the operation?"

He drew himself up in dignity. "No, Milady. And that's final."

"Very well." She pointed a finger at her doctor, "You're

out," and shifted it to Vaagen, "you're in. You are now in charge of this case. I rely on you to find me a surgeon—or a medical student, or a horse doctor, or *somebody* who's willing to try. And then you can experiment to your heart's content."

Vaagen looked mildly triumphant; her former man looked furious. "We had better see what my Lord Regent has to say, before you carry his wife off on this wave of criminally false optimism."

Vaagen looked a little less triumphant.

"You thinking of charging over there right now?" asked Cordelia.

"I'm sorry, Milady," said the Residence man, "but I think we'd do best to quash this thing right now. You don't know Captain Vaagen's reputation. Sorry to be so blunt, Vaagen, but you're an empire builder, and this time you've gone too far."

"Are you ambitious for a research wing, Captain Vaagen?" Cordelia inquired.

He shrugged, embarrassed rather than outraged, so she knew the Residence man's words to be at least half true. She gathered Vaagen in by eye, willing to possess him body, mind, and soul, but especially mind, and wondering how best to fire his imagination in her service.

"You shall have an institute, if you can bring this off. You tell him," she jerked her head in the direction of the hall, toward Aral's room, "*I* said so."

Variously discomfited, angry, and hopeful, they withdrew. Cordelia lay back on the bed and whistled a little soundless tune, her fingertips continuing their slow abdominal massage. Gravity had ceased to exist.

CHAPTER NINE

She slept at last, toward the middle of the day, and woke disoriented. She squinted at the afternoon light slanting through the hospital room's windows. The grey rain had gone away. She touched her belly, for grief and reassurance, and rolled over to find Count Piotr sitting at her bedside.

He was dressed in his country clothes, old uniform trousers, plain shirt, a jacket that he wore only at Vorkosigan Surleau. He must have come up directly to ImpMil. His thin lips smiled anxiously at her. His eyes looked tired and worried.

"Dear girl. You need not wake up for me."

"That's all right." She blinked away blear from her eyes, feeling older than the old man. "Is there something to drink?"

He hastily poured her cold water from the bedside basin spigot, and watched her swallow. "More?"

"That's enough. Have you seen Aral yet?"

He patted her hand. "I've talked to Aral already. He's resting now. I am so sorry, Cordelia."

"It may not be as bad as we feared at first. There's

still a chance. A hope. Did Aral tell you about the uterine replicator?"

"Something. But the damage has already been done, surely. Irrevocable damage."

"Damage, yes. How irrevocable it is, no one knows. Not even Captain Vaagen."

"Yes, I met Vaagen a little while ago." Piotr frowned. "A pushing sort of fellow. New Man type."

"Barrayar needs its new men. And women. Its technologically trained generation."

"Oh, yes. We fought and slaved to create them. They are absolutely necessary. They know it, too, some of them." A hint of self-aware irony softened his mouth. "But this operation you're proposing, this placental transfer . . . it doesn't sound too safe."

"On Beta Colony, it would be routine." Cordelia shrugged. *We are not, of course, on Beta Colony.*

"But something more straightforward, better understood—you would be ready to begin again much sooner. In the long run, you might actually lose less time."

"Time . . . isn't what I'm worried about losing." A meaningless concept, now she thought of it. She lost 26.7 hours every Barrayaran day. "Anyway, I'm never going through *that* again. I'm not a slow learner, sir."

A flicker of alarm crossed his face. "You'll change your mind, when you feel better. What does matter now—I've talked to Captain Vaagen. There seemed no question in his mind there is great damage."

"Well, yes. The unknown is whether there can be great repairs."

"Dear girl." His worried smile grew tenser. "Just so. If only the fetus were a girl . . . or even a second son . . . we could afford to indulge your understandable, even laudable, maternal emotions. But this thing, if it lived, would be *Count Vorkosigan* someday. We cannot afford to have a deformed *Count Vorkosigan*." He sat back, as if he had just made some cogent point.

Cordelia wrinkled her brow. "Who is we?"

"House Vorkosigan. We are one of the oldest great

houses on Barrayar. Never, perhaps, the richest, seldom
the strongest, but what we've lacked in wealth we've made
up in honor. Nine generations of Vor warriors. This would
be a horrible end to come to, after nine generations, don't
you see?"

"House Vorkosigan, at this point in time, consists of
two individuals, you and Aral," Cordelia observed, both
amused and disturbed. "And Counts Vorkosigan have come
to horrible ends throughout your history. You've been
blown up, shot, starved, drowned, burned alive, beheaded,
diseased, and demented. The only thing you've never done
is die in bed. I thought horrors were your stock in trade."

He returned her a pained smile. "But we've never been
mutants."

"I think you need to talk to Vaagen again. The fetal
damage he described was teratogenic, not genetic, if I
understand him correctly."

"But people will think it's a mutant."

"What the devil do you care what some ignorant prole
thinks?"

"Other Vor, dear."

"Vor, prole, they're equally ignorant, I assure you."

His hands twitched. He opened his mouth, closed it
again, frowned, and said more sharply, "A Count
Vorkosigan has never been an experimental laboratory
animal, either."

"There you go, then. He serves Barrayar even before
he's born. Not a bad start on a life of honor." Perhaps
some good would come of it, in the end, some knowledge gained; if not help for themselves, then for some
other parents' grief. The more she thought about it, the
more right her decision felt, on more than one level.

Piotr jerked his head back. "For all you Betans seem
soft, you have an appalling cold-blooded streak in you."

"Rational streak, sir. Rationality has its merits. You
Barrayarans ought to try it sometime." She bit her tongue.
"But we run ahead of ourselves, I think, sir. There are
lots of d—" *dangers,* "difficulties yet to come. A placental
transfer this late in pregnancy is tricky even for galactics.

I admit, I wish there were time to import a more experienced surgeon. But there's not."

"Yes . . . yes . . . it may yet die, you're right. No need to . . . but I'm afraid for you, too, girl. Is it worth it?"

Was what worth what? How could she know? Her lungs burned. She smiled wearily at him, and shook her head, which ached with tight pressure in her temples and neck.

"Father," came a raspy voice from the doorway. Aral leaned there, in his green pajamas, a portable oxygenator stuck up his nose. How long had he stood there? "I think Cordelia needs to rest."

Their eyes met, over Piotr. *Bless you, love. . . .*

"Yes, of course." Count Piotr gathered himself together, and creaked to his feet. "I'm sorry, you're quite correct." He pressed Cordelia's hand one more time, firmly, with his dry old-man's grip. "Sleep. You'll be able to think more clearly later."

"Father."

"You shouldn't be out of bed, should you?" said Piotr, drawn off. "Go back and lie down, boy. . . ." His voice drifted away, across the corridor.

Aral returned later, after Count Piotr had finally left. "Was Father bothering you?" he asked, looking grim. She held out her hand to him, and he sat beside her. She transferred her head from her pillow to his lap, her cheek on the firm-muscled leg beneath the thin pajama, and he stroked her hair.

"No more than usual," she sighed.

"I feared he was upsetting you."

"It's not that I'm not upset. It's just that I'm too tired to run up and down the corridor screaming."

"Ah. He did upset you."

"Yes." She hesitated. "In a way, he has a point. I was so afraid for so long, waiting for the blow to fall, from somewhere, nowhere, anywhere. Then came last night, and the worst was done, over . . . except it's not over. If the blow had been more complete, I could stop, quit now. But this is going to go on and on." She rubbed her cheek against the cloth. "Did Illyan come up with anything new? I thought I heard his voice out there, earlier."

His hand continued to stroke her hair, in even rhythm. "He'd finished the preliminary fast-penta interrogation of Evon Vorhalas. He's now investigating the old armory where Evon stole the soltoxin. It appears Evon might not have equipped himself so ad hoc unilaterally as he claimed. An ordnance major in charge there has disappeared, AWOL. Illyan's not certain yet if the man was eliminated, to clear Evon's path, or if he actually helped Evon, and has gone into hiding."

"He might just be afraid. If it was dereliction."

"He'd better be afraid. If he had any conscious connivance in this . . ." His hand clenched in her hair, he became aware of the pull, muttered, "Sorry," and continued petting. Cordelia, feeling very like an injured animal, crept deeper into his lap, her hand on his knee.

"About Father—if he upsets you again, send him to me. You shouldn't have to deal with him. I told him it was your decision."

"My decision?" Her hand rested, without moving. "Not our decision?"

He hesitated. "Whatever you want, I'll support you."

"But what do you want? Something you're not telling me?"

"I can't help understanding his fears. But . . . there's something I haven't discussed with him yet, nor am I going to. The next child may not be so easy to come by as the first."

Easy? You call this easy?

He went on, "One of the lesser-known side effects of soltoxin poisoning is testicular scarring, on the micro-level. It could reduce fertility below the point of no return. Or so my examining physician warns me."

"Nonsense," said Cordelia. "All you need is any two somatic cells and a replicator. Your little finger and my big toe, if that's all they can scrape off the walls after the next bomb, could go on reproducing little Vorkosigans into the next century. However many our survivors choose to afford."

"But not naturally. Not without leaving Barrayar."

"Or changing Barrayar. *Dammit.*" His hand jerked back at the bite in her tone. "If only I had *insisted* on using the replicator in the first place, the baby need never have been at risk. I knew it was safer, I knew it was there—" Her voice broke.

"Sh. Sh. If only I had . . . not taken the job. Kept you at Vorkosigan Surleau. Pardoned that murderous idiot Carl, for God's sake. If only we'd slept in separate rooms . . ."

"No!" Her hand tightened on his knee. "And I refuse to go live in some bomb shelter for the next fifteen years. Aral, this place has to change. This is unbearable." *If only I had never come here.*

If only. If only. If only.

The operating room seemed clean and bright, if not so copiously equipped as galactic standard. Cordelia, wafting on her float pallet, turned her head sideways to take in as much detail as she could. Lights, monitors, an operating table with a catch-basin set beneath it, a tech checking a bubbling tank of clear yellow fluid. This was not, she told herself sternly, the point of no return. This was simply the next logical step.

Captain Vaagen and Dr. Henri stood sterile-garbed and waiting, beyond the operating table. Next to them sat the portable uterine replicator, a metal and plastic canister half a meter tall, studded with control panels and access ports. The lights on its sides glowed green and amber. Cleaned, sterilized, its nutrient and oxygen tanks re-charged and ready . . . Cordelia eyed it with profound relief. The primitive Barrayaran back-to-the-apes style gestation was nothing but the utter failure of reason to triumph over emotion. She'd so wanted to please, to fit in, to try to become Barrayaran. . . . *And so my child pays the price. Never again.*

Dr. Ritter, the surgeon, was tall and dark-haired, with olive skin and long lean hands. Cordelia had liked his hands the first moment she saw them. Steady. Ritter and a medtech now positioned her over the operating table, and shifted the float pallet out from under her. Dr. Ritter smiled reassuringly. "You're doing fine."

Of course I'm fine, we haven't even started yet, Cordelia thought irritably. Dr. Ritter was palpably nervous, though the tension somehow stopped at his elbows. The surgeon was a friend of Vaagen's, whom Vaagen had strong-armed into this, after they'd spent a day running through a list of more experienced men who had refused to touch the case.

Vaagen had explained it to Cordelia. "What do you call four big bravos with clubs in a dark alley?"

"What?"

"A Vor lord's malpractice suit." He'd chuckled. Vaagen's sense of humor was acid-black. Cordelia could have hugged him for it. He'd been the only person to crack a joke in her presence in the last three days, possibly the most rational and honest person she'd met since she'd left Beta Colony. She was glad he was here.

They rolled her to her side, and touched her spine with the medical stun. A tingle, and her cold feet felt suddenly warm. Her legs went abruptly inert, like bags of lard.

"Can you feel that?" asked Dr. Ritter.

"Feel what?"

"Good." He nodded to the tech, and they straightened her out. The tech uncovered her stomach, and turned on the sterilizer-field. The surgeon palpated her, cross-checking the holovid monitors for the infant's exact position within her.

"Are you sure you wouldn't rather be asleep through this?" Dr. Ritter asked her for the last time.

"No. I want to watch. This is my first child being born." *Maybe my only child being born.*

He smiled wanly. "Brave girl."

Girl, hell, I'm older than you. Dr. Ritter, she sensed, would rather not be watched. Tough.

Dr. Ritter paused, taking one last glance around as if mentally checklisting the readiness of his tools and people. *And will and nerve,* Cordelia guessed.

"Come on, Ritter my man, let's get this over with," said Vaagen, tapping his fingers impatiently. His tone was a peculiar mix, a little sarcastic prodding lilt over an underlying warmth of genuine encouragement. "My scans show bone sloughing already under way. If the disintegration gets too far advanced, I'll have no matrix left to build from. Cut now, chew your nails later."

"Chew your own nails, Vaagen," said the surgeon genially. "Jog my elbow again and I'll have my medtech put a speculum down your throat."

Very old friends, Cordelia gauged. But the surgeon raised his hands, took a breath and a grip on his vibra-scalpel, and sliced her belly open in one perfectly controlled stroke. The medtech followed his motion smoothly with the surgical hand-tractor, clamping blood vessels; scarcely a cat-scratch of blood escaped. Cordelia felt pressure but no pain. Other cuts laid open her uterus.

A placental transfer was vastly more demanding than a straightforward cesarian section. The fragile placenta must be chemically and hormonally persuaded to release from the blood-vessel-enriched uterus, without damaging too many of its multitude of tiny villi, then floated free from the uterine wall in a running bath of highly oxygenated nutrient solution. The replicator sponge then had to be slipped into place between the placenta and the uterine wall, and the placenta's villi at least partially induced to re-interdigitate on its new matrix, before the whole mess could be lifted from the living body of the mother and placed in the replicator. The more advanced the pregnancy, the more difficult the transfer.

The umbilical cord between placenta and infant was monitored, and extra oxygen injected by hypospray as needed. On Beta Colony, a nifty little device would do this; here, an anxious tech hovered.

The tech began running the clear bright yellow solution-bath into her uterus. It filled her, and ran over, trickling pink-tinged down her sides and into the catch basin. The surgeon was now working, in effect, underwater. No question about it, a placental transfer was a messy operation.

"Sponge," called the surgeon softly, and Vaagen and Henri trundled the uterine replicator to her side, and strung out the matrix sponge from it on its feed lines. The surgeon fiddled interminably with a tiny hand-tractor, his hands out of Cordelia's line of sight as she peered down cross-eyed over her chest to her rounded—so-barely-rounded—belly. She shivered. Ritter was sweating.

"Doctor . . ." A tech pointed to something on a vid monitor.

"Mm," said Ritter, glancing up, then continuing fiddling. The techs murmured, Vaagen and Henri murmured, calm, professional, reassuring . . . she was so cold. . . .

The fluid trickling over the white dam of her skin changed abruptly from pink-tinged to bright, bright red, a splashing flow, much faster than the input feed was emitting.

"*Clamp* that," hissed the surgeon.

Cordelia caught just a glimpse, beneath a membrane, of tiny arms, legs, a wet dark head, wriggling on the surgeon's gloved hands, no larger than a half-drowned kitten. "Vaagen! Take this thing of yours *now* if you want it!" snapped Ritter. Vaagen plunged his gloved hands into her belly as dark whorls clouded Cordelia's vision, her head aching, exploding in sudden sparkling flashes. The blackness ballooned out, overwhelming her. The last thing she heard was the surgeon's despairing sibilant voice, "Oh, *shit* . . . !"

Her dreams were foggy with pain. The worst part was the choking. She choked and choked, and wept for lack of air. Her throat was full of obstructions, and she clawed at it, until her hands were bound. She dreamed of Vorrutyer's tortures, then, multiplied and extended into insane complications that went on for hours. A demented Bothari knelt on her chest, and she could get no air at all.

When she finally woke clear-headed, it was like breaking up out of some underground prison-hell into God's own light. Her relief was so profound she wept again, a muted whimper and a wetness in her eyes. She could breathe, although it pained her; she was bruised and aching and unable to move. But she could breathe. That was enough.

"Sh. Sh." A thick warm finger touched her eyelids, wiping away the moisture. "It's all right."

"Izzit?" She blinked and squinted. It was night, artificial light making warm pools in the room. Aral's face wavered over hers. "Izzit . . . tonight? Wha' happened?"

"Sh. You've been very, very sick. You had a violent hemorrhage during the placental transfer. Your heart stopped twice." He moistened his lips and went on. "The trauma, on top of the poisoning, flared into soltoxin pneumonia. You had a very bad day yesterday, but you're over the worst, off the respirator."

"How . . . long?"

"Three days."

"Ah. Baby, Aral. Diddit work? Details!"

"It went all right. Vaagen reports the transfer was successful. They lost about thirty percent of the placental function, but Henri compensated with an enriched and increased oxy-solution flow, and all seems to be well, or as well as can be expected. The baby's still alive, anyway. Vaagen has started his first calcium-treatment experiment, and promises us a baseline report soon." He caressed her forehead. "Vaagen has priority-access to any equipment, supplies, or techs he cares to requisition, including outside consultants. He has an advising civilian pediatrician, plus Henri. Vaagen himself knows more about our military poisons than any man, on Barrayar or off it. We can do no more, right now. So rest, love."

"Baby—where?"

"Ah—you can see where, if you wish." He helped her lift her head, and pointed out the window. "See that second building, with the red lights on the roof? That's the biochemistry research facility. Vaagen and Henri's lab is on the third floor."

"Oh, I recognize it now. Saw it from the other side, the day we collected Elena."

"That's right." His face softened. "Good to have you

back, dear Captain. Seeing you that sick . . . I haven't
felt that helpless and useless since I was eleven years old."

That was the year Mad Yuri's death squad had
murdered his mother and brother. "Sh," she said in turn.
"No, no . . . s'all right now."

They took away all the rest of the tubes piercing her
body the next morning, except for the oxygen. Days of
quiet routine followed. Her recovery was less interrupted
than Aral's. What seemed troops of men, headed by
Minister Vortala, came to see him at all hours. He had
a secured comconsole installed in his room, over medical protests. Koudelka joined him eight hours a day, in
the makeshift office.

Koudelka seemed very quiet, as depressed as everyone else in the wake of the disaster. Though not as morbid
as anyone who'd had to do with their failed Security. Even
Illyan shrank, when he saw her.

Aral walked her carefully up and down the corridor
a couple of times a day. The vibra-scalpel had made a
cleaner cut through her abdomen than, say, your average sabre-thrust, but it was no less deep. The healing
scar ached less than her lungs, though. Or her heart.
Her belly was not so much flat as flaccid, but definitely
no longer occupied. She was alone, uninhabited, she was
herself again, after five months of that strange doubled
existence.

Dr. Henri came with a float chair one day, and took
her on a short trip over to his laboratory, to see where
the replicator was safely installed. She watched her baby
moving in the vid scans, and studied the team's technical readouts and reports. Their subject's nerves, skin, and
eyes tested out encouragingly, though Henri was not so
sure about hearing, because of the tiny bones in the ear.
Henri and Vaagen were properly trained scientists, almost
Betan in their outlook, and she blessed them silently and
thanked them aloud, and returned to her room feeling
enormously better.

When Captain Vaagen burst into her room the next

afternoon, however, her heart sank. His face was thunderously dark, his lips tight and harsh.

"What's wrong, Captain?" she asked urgently. "That second calcium run—did it fail?"

"Too early to tell. No, your baby's the same, Milady. Our trouble is with your in-law."

"Beg pardon?"

"General Count Vorkosigan came to see us this morning."

"Oh! He came to see the baby? Oh, good. He's so disturbed by all this new life-technology. Maybe he's finally starting to work past those emotional blocks. He embraces the new death-technologies readily enough, old Vor warrior that he is. . . ."

"I wouldn't get too optimistic about him, if I were you, Milady." He took a deep breath, taking refuge in a formality of stance, just black, not black-humored this time. "Dr. Henri had the same idea you did. We showed the General all around the lab, went over the equipment, explained our treatment theories. We were absolutely honest, as we've been with you. Maybe too honest. He wanted to know what results we were going to get. Hell, we don't know. And so we said.

"After some beating around the bush, hinting . . . well, to cut it short, the General first asked, then ordered, then tried to bribe Dr. Henri to open the stopcock. To destroy the fetus. The mutation, he calls it. We threw him the hell out. He swore he'd be back."

She was shaking, down in her belly, though she kept her face blank. "I see."

"I want that old man kept *out* of my lab, Milady. And I don't care how you do it. I don't need this kind of crap coming down. Not from that high up."

"I'll see . . . wait here." She wrapped her robe around her own green pajamas more tightly, seated her oxygen tube more firmly, and walked carefully across the corridor. Aral, half-casual in uniform trousers and a shirt, sat at a small table by his window. The only sign of his continued patient-hood was the oxygen tube up his nose, treatment for his own lingering soltoxin pneumonia. He was conferring with a man while Koudelka took notes. The man was not, thank God, Piotr, but merely some ministerial secretary of Vortala's.

"Aral. I need you."

"Can it wait?"

"No."

He rose from his chair with a brief "Excuse me a moment, gentlemen," and trod across the hall in her wake. Cordelia closed the door behind them.

"Captain Vaagen, please tell Aral what you just told me."

Vaagen, looking a degree more nervous, repeated his tale. To his credit, he did not soften the details. A weight seemed to settle on Aral's shoulders as he listened, rounding and hunching them.

"Thank you, Captain. You were correct to report this. I will take care of it immediately."

"That's all?" Vaagen glanced at Cordelia in doubt.

She opened her palm to him. "You heard the man." Vaagen shrugged, and saluted himself out.

"You don't doubt his story?" asked Cordelia.

"I've been listening to the Count my father's thoughts on this subject for a week, love."

"You argued?"

"He argued. I just listened."

Aral returned to his own room, and asked Koudelka and the secretary to wait in the corridor. Cordelia sat on his bed and watched as he punched up codes on his comconsole.

"Lord Vorkosigan here. I wish to speak simultaneously to the Security chief, Imperial Military Hospital, and Commander Simon Illyan. Get them both on, please."

A brief wait, as each man was located. Judging from the fuzzy background in the vid, the ImpMil man was in his office somewhere in the hospital complex. They tracked Illyan down at a forensic laboratory in ImpSec HQ.

"Gentlemen." Aral's face was quite expressionless. "I wish to revoke a Security clearance." Each man attentively prepared to make notes on their respective comconsoles.

"General Count Piotr Vorkosigan is to be denied access to Building Six, Biochemical Research, Imperial Military Hospital, until further notice. Notice from me personally."

Illyan hesitated. "Sir—General Vorkosigan has absolute clearance, by Imperial order. He's had it for years. I need an Imperial order to countermand it."

"That's precisely what this is, Illyan." A trace of impatience rasped in Vorkosigan's voice. "By my order, Aral Vorkosigan, Regent to His Imperial Majesty Gregor Vorbarra. Is that official enough?"

Illyan whistled softly, but his face snapped to blankness at Vorkosigan's frown. "Yes, sir. Understood. Is there anything else?"

"That's all. Just that one building."

"Sir . . ." the hospital security commander said, "what if . . . General Vorkosigan refuses to halt when ordered?"

Cordelia could just picture it, some poor young guard being mowed down flat by all that history. . . .

"If your security people are indeed so overwhelmed by one old man, they may use force up to and including stunner fire," said Aral tiredly. "Dismissed. Thank you."

The ImpMil man nodded cautiously, and disconnected.

Illyan lingered in doubt a moment. "Is that a good idea, at his age? Stunning can be bad for the heart. And he's not going to like it one bit, when we tell him there's someplace he can't go. By the way, why—?" Aral merely stared coldly at him, till he gulped, "Yes, sir," saluted, and signed off.

Aral sat back, gazing pensively at the blank space where the vid images had glowed. He glanced up at Cordelia, and his lips twisted, a grimace of irony and pain. "He is an old man," he said at last.

"The old man just tried to kill your son. What's left of your son."

"I see his view. I see his fears."

"Do you see mine, too?"

"Yes. Both."

"When push comes to shove—if he tries to go back there—"

"He is my past." He met her eyes. "You are my future.

The rest of my life belongs to the future. I swear by my word as Vorkosigan."

Cordelia sighed, and rubbed her aching neck, her aching eyes.

Koudelka rattled at the door, and stuck his head surreptitiously within. "Sir? The minister's secretary wants to know—"

"In a minute, Lieutenant." Vorkosigan waved him back out.

"Let's blow out of this place," said Cordelia suddenly.

"Milady?"

"ImpMil, and ImpSec, and ImpEverything, is giving me a bad case of ImpClaustrophobia. Let's go down to Vorkosigan Surleau for a few days. You'll recover better there yourself, it will be harder for all your dedicated minions," she jerked her head at the corridor, "to get at you, there. Just you and me, boy." Would it work? Suppose they retired to the scene of their summer happiness, and it wasn't there anymore? Drowned in the autumn rains . . . She could feel the desperation in herself, seeking their lost balance, some solid center.

His brows rose in approval. "Outstanding idea, dear Captain. We'll take the old man along."

"Oh, must we—oh. Yes, I see. Quite. By all means."

CHAPTER TEN

Cordelia woke slowly, stretched, and clutched the magnificent silky feather-stuffed comforter to her. The other side of the bed was empty—she touched the dented pillow—cold and empty. Aral must have tiptoed out early. She luxuriated in the sensation of finally having enough sleep, not waking to that stunned exhaustion that had clotted her mind and body for so long. This made the third night in a row she'd slept well, warmed by her husband's body, both of them gladly rid of the irritating oxygen-fittings on their faces.

Their corner room, on the second floor of the old stone converted barracks, was cool this morning, and very quiet. The front window opened onto the bright green lawn, descending into mist that hid the lake and the village and hills of the farther shore. The damp morning felt comfortable, felt right, proper contrast to the feather comforter. When she sat up, the new pink scar on her abdomen only twinged.

Droushnakovi poked her head around the doorframe. "Milady?" she called softly, then saw Cordelia sitting up, bare feet hung out over the edge of the bed. Cordelia swung her feet back and forth, experimentally, encouraging circulation. "Oh, good, you're awake." Drou shouldered her way through the door, bearing a large and promising tray. She wore one of her more comfortable dresses, with a wide swinging skirt, and a warm padded vest with embroidery. Her footsteps sounded on the wide wooden floorboards, then were muffled on the handwoven rug as she crossed the room.

"I'm hungry," said Cordelia in wonder, as the aromas from the tray tickled her nose. "I think that's the first time in three weeks." Three weeks, since that night of horrors at Vorkosigan House.

Drou smiled, and set the tray down at the table by the front window. Cordelia found robe and slippers, and made for the coffeepot. Drou hovered, seeming ready to catch her if she fell over, but Cordelia did not feel nearly so shaky today. She seated herself and reached for steaming groats and butter, and a pitcher of hot syrup the Barrayarans made from boiled-down tree sap. Wonderful food.

"Have you eaten, Drou? Want some coffee? What time is it?"

The bodyguard shook her blonde head. "I'm fine, Milady. It's about elevenses."

Droushnakovi had been part of the assumed background, for the past several days here at Vorkosigan Surleau. Cordelia found herself really looking at the girl for almost the first time since she'd left ImpMil. Drou was attentive and alert as ever, but with an underlying tension, that same bad-guard-slink—perhaps it was only because she was feeling better herself, but Cordelia selfishly wanted the people around her to be feeling better, too, if only not to drag her back down.

"I'm feeling so much less thick, today. I talked to Captain Vaagen yesterday, on the vid. He thinks he's seen the first signs of molecular re-calcification in little Piotr Miles. Very encouraging, if you know how to interpret Vaagen. He doesn't offer false hopes, but what little he does say, you can rely on."

Drou glanced up from her lap, fixing a responding

smile on her downcast features. She shook her head. "Uterine replicators seem so strange to me. So alien."

"Not so strange as what evolution laid on us, ad lib empirical," Cordelia grinned back. "Thank God for technology and rational design. I know whereof I speak, now."

"Milady . . . how did you first know you were pregnant? Did you miss a monthly?"

"A menstrual period? No, actually." She thought back to last summer. This very room, that unmade bed in fact. She and Aral could begin sharing intimacies there again soon, though with some loss of piquancy without reproduction as a goal. "Aral and I thought we were all settled here, last summer. He was retired, I was retired . . . no impediments. I was on the verge of being old for the organic method, which seemed the only one available here on Barrayar; more to the point, he wanted to start soon. So a few weeks after we were married, I went and had my contraceptive implant removed. Made me feel very wicked; at home I couldn't have had it taken out without buying a license."

"Really?" Drou listened with openmouthed fascination.

"Yes, it's a Betan legal requirement. You have to qualify for a parent's license first. I've had my implant since I was fourteen. I had a menstrual period once then, I remember. We turn them off till they're needed. I got my implant, and my hymen cut, and my ears pierced, and had my coming-out party. . . ."

"You didn't . . . start doing sex when you were fourteen, did you?" Droushnakovi's voice was hushed.

"I could have. But it takes two, y'know. I didn't find a real lover till later." Cordelia was ashamed to admit how much later. She'd been so socially inept, back then. . . . *And you haven't changed much,* she admitted wryly to herself.

"I didn't think it would happen so fast," Cordelia went on. "I thought we'd be in for several months of earnest and delightful experiment. But we caught the baby first try. So I still haven't had a menstrual period, here on Barrayar."

"First try," echoed Drou. Her lip curled in introspective dismay. "How did you know you'd . . . caught? The nausea?"

"Fatigue, before nausea. But it was the little blue dots . . ." Her voice faltered, as she studied the girl's twisted-up features. "Drou, are all these questions academic, or do you have some more personal interest in the answers?"

Her face almost crumpled. "Personal," she choked out.

"Oh." Cordelia sat back. "D'you . . . want to talk about it?"

"No . . . I don't know. . . ."

"I presume that means yes," Cordelia sighed. Ah, yes. Just like playing Mama Captain to sixty Betan scientists back on Survey, though queries about pregnancy were perhaps the one interpersonal trouble they'd never laid in her lap. But given the Really Dumb Stuff that rational and select group had sprung on her from time to time, the feral Barrayaran version ought to be just . . . "You know I'll be glad to help you any way I can."

"It was the night of the soltoxin attack," she sniffled. "I couldn't sleep. I went down to the refectory kitchen to get something to eat. On the way back upstairs I noticed a light on in the library. Lieutenant Koudelka was in there. He couldn't sleep either."

Kou, eh? Oh, good, good. This might be all right after all. Cordelia smiled in genuine encouragement. "Yes?"

"We . . . I . . . he . . . kissed me."

"I trust you kissed him back?"

"You sound like you *approve*."

"I do. You are two of my favorite people, you and Kou. If only you'd get your heads straight . . . but go on, there has to be more." Unless Drou was more ignorant than Cordelia believed possible.

"We . . . we . . . we . . ."

"Screwed?" Cordelia suggested hopefully.

"Yes, Milady." Drou turned scarlet, and swallowed. "Kou seemed so happy . . . for a few minutes. I was so happy for him, so excited, I didn't care how much it hurt."

Ah, yes, the barbaric Barrayaran custom of introducing their women to sex with the pain of unanesthetized defloration. Though considering how much pain their reproductive methods later entailed, perhaps it constituted fair warning. But Kou, in the glimpses she'd had of him, hadn't seemed as happy as a new lover ought to be either. What were these two doing to each other? "Go on."

"I thought I saw a movement in the back garden, out the door from the library. Then came the crash upstairs— oh, Milady! I'm so sorry! If I'd been guarding you, instead of doing *that*—"

"Whoa, girl! You were off-duty. If you hadn't been doing *that*, you'd have been in bed asleep. No way is the soltoxin attack your fault, yours or Kou's. In fact, if you hadn't been up and, and more or less dressed, the would-be assassin might have gotten away." *And we wouldn't be anticipating yet another public beheading, or whatever, God help us.* One part of Cordelia wished they'd gone for seconds, and never looked out the damned window. But Droushnakovi had enough consequences to deal with right now without those mortal complications.

"But if only—"

"*If onlys* have been thick in the air around here, these last weeks. I think it's time to replace them with some *Now-we-go-ons*, frankly." Cordelia's mind caught up with herself at last. Drou was Barrayaran; Drou therefore didn't have a contraceptive implant. It didn't sound like that idiot Kou had offered an alternative, either. Drou had therefore spent the last three weeks wondering . . . "Would you like to try one of my little blue dots? I have lots left."

"Blue dots?"

"Yes, I started to tell you. I have a packet of these little diagnostic strips. Bought them in Vorbarr Sultana last summer at an import shop. You pee on one, and if the dot turns blue, you're in. I only used up three, last summer." Cordelia went to her dresser drawer, and rooted through it for the obsolete supplies. "Here." She handed one to Drou. "Go relieve yourself. And your mind."

"Do they work so soon?"

"After five days." Cordelia held up her hand. "Promise."

Staring worriedly at the little strip of paper, Droushnakovi vanished into Cordelia and Aral's bathroom, off the bedroom. She emerged in a few minutes. Her face was glum, her shoulders slumped.

What does this mean? Cordelia wondered in exasperation. "Well?"

"It stayed white."

"Then you aren't pregnant."

"Guess not."

"I can't tell if you're glad or sorry. Believe me, if you want to have a baby, you'd do much better to wait a couple years till they get a bit more medical technology on-line around here." Though the organic method had been fascinating, for a time. . . .

"I don't want . . . I want . . . I don't know . . . Kou's hardly spoken to me since that night. I didn't want to be pregnant, it would destroy me, and yet I thought maybe he would, would . . . be as excited and happy about it as he was about the sex, maybe. Maybe he'd come back and— oh, things were going so well, and now they're so spoiled!" Her hands were clenched, face white, teeth gritted.

Cry, so I can breathe, girl. But Droushnakovi regained her self-control. "I'm sorry, Milady. I didn't mean to spill all this stupidity on you."

Stupidity, yes, but not unilateral stupidity. Something this screwed up had to have taken a committee. "So what is the matter with Kou? I thought he was just suffering from soltoxin-guilt, like everyone else in the household." *From Aral and myself on down.*

"I don't know, Milady."

"Have you tried something really radical, like asking him?"

"He *hides*, when he sees me coming."

Cordelia sighed, and turned her attention to getting dressed. Real clothes, not patient robes, today. There in the back of Aral's closet were her tan trousers from her old Survey uniform, hung up. Curiously, she tried them on. Not only did they fasten, they were loose. She *had* been sick.

Rather aggressively, she left them on, and chose a long-sleeved flowered smock-top to go with them. Very comfortable. She smiled at her slim, if pale, profile in the mirror.

"Ah, dear Captain." Aral stuck his head in the bedroom door. "You're up." He glanced at Droushnakovi. "You're both here. Better still. I think I need your help, Cordelia. In fact, I'm certain of it." Aral's eyes were alight with the strangest expression. Amazement, bemusement, worry? He let himself in. He was wearing his standard gear for off-duty time at Vorkosigan Surleau, old uniform trousers and a civilian shirt. He was trailed by a tense and miserable Koudelka, dressed in neat black fatigues with his red lieutenant's tabs bright on the collar. He clutched his swordstick. Drou backed to the wall, and crossed her arms.

"Lieutenant Koudelka—he tells me—wishes to make a confession. He is also, I suspect, hoping for absolution," said Aral.

"I don't deserve that, sir," Koudelka muttered. "But I couldn't live with myself anymore. This has to come out." He stared at the floor, meeting no one's eyes. Droushnakovi watched him breathlessly. Aral eased over and sat on the edge of the bed beside Cordelia.

"Hold on to your hat," he murmured to her out of the corner of his mouth. "This one took *me* by surprise."

"I think I may be way ahead of you."

"That wouldn't be a first." He raised his voice. "Go ahead, Lieutenant. This won't be any easier for being dragged out."

"Drou—Miss Droushnakovi—I came to turn myself in. And to apologize. No, that sounds trivial, and believe me, I don't think it trivial. You deserve more than apology, I owe you expiation. Whatever you want. But I'm sorry, so *sorry* I raped you."

Droushnakovi's mouth fell open for a full three seconds, then shut so hard Cordelia could hear her teeth snap. *"What?!"*

Koudelka flinched, but never looked up. "Sorry . . . sorry," he mumbled.

"You. Think. You. What?!" gasped Droushnakovi, horrified and outraged. "You think you could—oh!" She stood rigid now, hands clenched, breathing fast. "Kou, you oaf! You idiot! You moron! You-you-you—" Her words sputtered off. Her whole body was shaking. Cordelia watched in utter fascination. Aral rubbed his lips thoughtfully.

Droushnakovi stalked over to Koudelka and kicked his swordstick out of his hand. He almost fell, with a startled "Huh?", clutching at it and missing as it clattered across the floor.

Drou slammed him expertly into the wall, and paralyzed him with a nerve thrust, her fingers jammed up into his solar plexus. His breath stopped.

"You *goon*. Do you think you could lay a hand on me without my permission? Oh! To be so, to be so, so, so—" Her baffled words dissolved into a scream of outrage, right next to his ear. He spasmed.

"Please don't break my secretary, Drou, the repairs are expensive," said Aral mildly.

"Oh!" She whirled away, releasing Koudelka. He staggered and fell to his knees. Hands over her face, biting her fingers, she stomped out the door, slamming it behind her. Only then did she sob, sharp breaths retreating up the hallway. Another door slammed. Silence.

"I'm sorry, Kou," said Aral into the long lull. "But it doesn't look as though your self-accusation stands up in court."

"I don't understand." Kou shook his head, crawled after his swordstick, and climbed very shakily to his feet.

"Do I gather you are both talking about what happened between you the night of the soltoxin attack?" Cordelia asked.

"Yes, Milady. I was sitting up in the library. Couldn't sleep, thought I'd run over some figures. She came in. We sat, talked. . . . Suddenly I found myself . . . well . . . it was the first time I'd been functional since I was hit by the nerve disruptor. I thought it might be another year, or *forever*—I panicked, I just panicked. I . . . took her . . . right there. Never asked, never said a word. And then came the crash from upstairs, and we both ran out into the back garden and . . . she never accused me, next day. I waited and waited."

"But if he didn't rape her, why did she get so angry just now?" asked Aral.

"But she's been mad," said Koudelka. "The looks she's given me, these last three weeks . . ."

"The looks were fear, Kou," Cordelia advised him.

"Yes, that's what I thought."

"Because she was afraid she was *pregnant*, not because she was afraid of *you*," Cordelia clarified.

"Oh." Koudelka's voice went small.

"She's not, as it happens." (Kou echoed himself with another small "Oh.") "But she's mad at you now, and I don't blame her."

"But if she doesn't think I—what reason?"

"You don't see it?" She frowned at Aral. "You either?"

"Well . . ."

"It's because you just insulted her, Kou. Not then, but right now, in this room. And not just in slighting her combat prowess. What you just said revealed to her, for the first time, that you were so intent on *yourself* that night, you never saw *her* at all. Bad, Kou. Very bad. You owe her a profound apology. Here she was, giving her Barrayaran all to you, and you so little appreciated what she was doing, you didn't even perceive it."

His head came up suddenly. "Gave me? Like some charity?"

"Gift of the gods, more like," murmured Aral, lost in some appreciation of his own.

"I'm not a—" Koudelka's head swiveled toward the door. "Are you saying I should run after her?"

"Crawl, actually, if I were you," recommended Aral. "Crawl fast. Slither under her door, go belly-up, let her stomp on you till she gets it out of her system. Then apologize some more. You may yet save the situation." Aral's eyes were openly alight with amusement now.

"What do you call that? Total surrender?" said Kou indignantly.

"No. I'd call it winning." His voice grew a shade cooler. "I've seen the war between men and women descend to scorched-earth heroics. Pyres of pride. You don't want to go down that road. I guarantee it."

"You're—Milady! You're laughing at me! Stop!"

"Then stop making yourself ridiculous," said Cordelia sharply. "Get your head out of your ass. Think for sixty consecutive seconds about somebody besides yourself."

"Milady. Milord." His teeth were gritted now with frozen dignity. He bowed himself out, well slapped. But he turned the wrong way in the hallway, the opposite direction to which Droushnakovi had fled, and clattered down the end stairs.

Aral shook his head helplessly, as Koudelka's footsteps faded. A splutter escaped him.

Cordelia punched him softly on the arm. "Stop that! It's not funny to them." Their eyes met; she sniggered, then caught her breath firmly. "Good heavens, I think he *wanted* to be a rapist. Odd ambition. Has he been hanging around with Bothari too much?"

This slightly sick joke sobered them both. Aral looked thoughtful. "I think . . . Kou was flattering his self-doubts. But his remorse was sincere."

"Sincere, but a trifle smug. I think we may have coddled his self-doubts long enough. It may be time to kick his tail."

Aral's shoulders slumped wearily. "He owes her, no doubt. Yet what should I order him to do? It's worthless, if he doesn't pay freely."

Cordelia growled agreement.

It wasn't until lunch that Cordelia noticed something missing from their little world.

"Where's the Count?" she asked Aral, as they found the table set only for two by Piotr's housekeeper, in a front dining room overlooking the lake. The day had failed to warm. The earlier mist had risen only to clot into low scudding grey clouds, windy and chilly. Cordelia had added an old black fatigue jacket of Aral's over her flowered blouse.

"I thought he went to the stables. For a training session with that new dressage prospect of his," said Aral, also regarding the table uneasily. "That's what he told me he was going to do."

The housekeeper, bringing in soup, volunteered, "No, m'lord. He went off in the groundcar early, with two of his men."

"Oh. Excuse me." Aral nodded to Cordelia and rose, and exited the dining room to the back hall. One of the storerooms on the back side of the house, wedged into the slope, had been converted into a secured comm center, with a double-scrambled comconsole and a full-time ImpSec guard outside its door. Aral's footsteps echoed down the hall in that direction.

Cordelia took one bite of soup, which went down like liquid lead, set her spoon aside, and waited. She could hear Aral's voice, in the quiet house, and electronically tinged responses in some stranger's tones, but too muffled for her to make out the words. After what seemed a small eternity, though in fact the soup was still hot, Aral returned, bleak-faced.

"Did he go up there?" Cordelia asked. "To ImpMil?"

"Yes. He's been and left. It's all right." His heavy jaw was set.

"Meaning, the baby's all right?"

"Yes. He was denied admittance, he argued awhile, he left. Nothing worse." He began glumly spooning soup.

The Count returned a few hours later. Cordelia heard the fine whine of his groundcar pass up the drive and around the north end of the house, pause, a canopy open and close, and the car continue on to the garages, sited over the crest of the hill near the stables. She was sitting with Aral in the front room with the new big windows. He had been engrossed in some government report on his handviewer, but at the sound of the closing canopy put it on "pause" and waited with her, listening, as hard footsteps passed rapidly around the house and up the front steps. Aral's mouth was taut with unpleased anticipation, his eyes grim. Cordelia shrank back in her chair, and steeled her nerves.

Count Piotr swung into their room, and stood, feet planted. He was formally dressed in his old uniform with his general's rank insignia. "There you are." The liveried man trailing him took one uneasy glance at Aral and Cordelia, and removed himself without waiting to be dismissed. Count Piotr didn't even notice him go.

Piotr focused on Aral first. "You. You *dared* to shame me in public. Entrap me."

"You shamed yourself, I fear, sir. If you had not gone down that path, you would not have found that trap."

Piotr's tight jaw worked this one over, the lines in his face grooved deep. Anger; embarrassment struggling with self-righteousness. Embarrassed as only one in the wrong can be. *He doubts himself,* Cordelia realized. A thread of hope. *Let us not lose that thread, it may be our only way out of this labyrinth.*

The self-righteousness took ascendance. "I shouldn't have to be doing this," snarled Piotr. "It's women's work. Guarding our genome."

"Was women's work, in the Time of Isolation," said Aral in level tones. "When the only answer to mutation was infanticide. Now there are other answers."

"How *strange* women must have felt about their pregnancies, never knowing if there was life or death at the end of them," Cordelia mused. One sip from that cup was all she desired for a lifetime, and yet Barrayaran women had drained it to the dregs over and over . . . the wonder was not that their descendants' culture was chaotic, but that it wasn't more completely insane.

"You fail all of us when you fail to control her," said Piotr. "How do you imagine you can run a planet when you cannot run your own household?"

One corner of Aral's mouth twisted up slightly. "Indeed, she is difficult to control. She escaped me twice. Her voluntary return still astounds me."

"Awake to your duties! To me as your Count if not as your father. You are liege-sworn to me. Do you choose to obey this off-worlder woman before me?"

"Yes." Aral looked him straight in the eye. His voice

fell to a whisper. "That is the proper order of things." Piotr flinched. Aral added dryly, "Attempting to switch the issue from infanticide to obedience will not help you, sir. You taught me specious-rhetoric-chopping yourself."

"In the old days, you could have been beheaded for less insolence."

"Yes, the present setup is a little peculiar. As a count's heir, my hands are between yours, but as your Regent, your hands are between mine. Oath-stalemate. In the old days we could have broken the deadlock with a nice little war." He grinned back, or at least bared his teeth. Cordelia's mind gyrated, *One day only: The Irresistible Force Meets the Immovable Object. Tickets, five marks.*

The door to the hallway swung open, and Lieutenant Koudelka peered nervously within. "Sir? Sorry to interrupt. I'm having trouble with the comconsole. It's down again."

"What sort of trouble, Lieutenant?" Vorkosigan asked, wrenching his attention around with an effort. "The intermittency?"

"It's just not working."

"It was fine a few hours ago. Check the power supply."

"Did that, sir."

"Call a tech."

"I can't, without the comconsole."

"Ah, yes. Get the guard commander to open it up for you, then, see if the trouble is anything obvious. Then send for a tech on his clear-link."

"Yes, sir." Koudelka backed out, after a wary glance at the three tense people still frozen in their places waiting for him to withdraw.

The Count wouldn't quit. "I swear, I will disown it. That thing in the can at ImpMil. Utterly disinherit it."

"Not an operative threat, sir. You can only directly disown me. By an Imperial order. Which you would have to humbly petition, ah . . . *me*, for." His edged smile gleamed. "I would, of course, grant it to you."

The muscles in Piotr's jaw jumped. Not the irresistible force and the immovable object after all, but the

irresistible force and some fluid sea; Piotr's blows kept
failing to land, splashing past helplessly. Mental judo. He
was off-balance, and flailed for his center, striking out
wildly now. "Think of Barrayar. Think of the example
you're setting."

"Oh," breathed Aral, "that I have." He paused. "We have
never led from the rear, you or I. Where a Vorkosigan goes,
maybe others might not find it so impossible to follow. A
little personal . . . social engineering."

"Maybe for galactics. But our society can't afford this
luxury. We barely hold our own as it is. We cannot carry
the deadweight of millions of dysfunctionals!"

"Millions?" Aral raised a brow. "Now you extrapolate
from one to infinity. A weak argument, sir, unworthy of you."

"And surely," said Cordelia quietly, "how much is bear-
able each individual, carrying his or her own burden, must
decide."

Piotr swung on her. "Yes, and who is paying for all this,
eh? The Imperium. Vaagen's laboratory is budgeted under
military research. All Barrayar is paying for prolonging the
life of your monster."

Discomfited, Cordelia replied, "Perhaps it will prove
a better investment than you think."

Piotr snorted, his head lowered mulishly, hunched
between his skinny shoulders. He stared through Cordelia
at Aral. "You are determined to lay this thing on me. On
my house. I cannot persuade you otherwise, I cannot
order you . . . very well. You're so set on change, here's
a change for you. I don't want my name on that thing.
I can deny you that, if nothing else."

Aral's lips were pinched, nostrils flaring. But he never
moved in his seat. The viewer glowed on, forgotten in
his still hands. He held his hands quiet and totally controlled, not permitting them to clench. "Very well, sir."

"Call him Miles Naismith Vorkosigan, then," said
Cordelia, feigning calm over a sick and trembling belly.
"My father will not begrudge it."

"Your father is dead," snapped Piotr.

Smeared to bright plasma in a shuttle accident more

than a decade ago . . . She sometimes fancied, when she closed her eyes, that she could still sense his death imprinted on her retina in magenta and teal. "Not wholly. Not while I live, and remember."

Piotr looked as if she'd just hit him in his Barrayaran stomach. Barrayaran ceremonies for the dead approached ancestor-worship, as if remembrance could keep the souls alive. Did his own mortality run chill in his veins today? He had gone too far, and knew it, but could not back down. "Nothing, nothing wakes you up! Try this, then." He straddled the floor, boots planted, and glared at Aral. "Get out of my house. Both houses, Vorkosigan House, too. Take your woman and remove yourself. Today!"

Aral's eyes flicked only once around his childhood home. He set the viewer carefully aside, and stood. "Very well, sir."

Piotr's anger was anguished. "You'd throw away your home for this?!"

"My home is not a place. It is a person, sir," Aral said gravely. Then added reluctantly, "People."

Meaning Piotr, as well as Cordelia. She sat bent over, aching with the tension. Was the old man stone? Even now Aral offered him gestures of courtesy that nearly stopped her heart.

"You will return your rents and revenues to the District purse," said Piotr desperately.

"As you wish, sir." Aral headed for the door.

Piotr's voice went smaller. "Where will you live?"

"Illyan has been urging me for some time to move to the Imperial Residence, for security reasons. Evon Vorhalas has persuaded me Illyan is right."

Cordelia had risen when Aral did. She went now to the window and stared out over the moody grey, green, and brown landscape. Whitecaps foamed on the pewter water of the lake. The Barrayaran winter was going to be so cold. . . .

"So, you set yourself up with Imperial airs after all, eh?" jibed Piotr. "Is that what this is, hubris?"

Aral grimaced in profound irritation. "On the contrary,

sir. If I'm to have no income but my admiral's half-pay, I cannot afford to pass up rent-free quarters."

A movement in the scudding clouds caught Cordelia's eye. She squinted uneasily. "What's wrong with that lightflyer?" she murmured half to herself.

The speck grew, jinking oddly. It trailed smoke. It stuttered over the lake, straight at them. "God, I wonder if it's full of bombs?"

"What?" said Aral and Piotr together, and stepped quickly to the window with her, Aral on her right hand, Piotr on her left.

"It has ImpSec markings," said Aral.

Piotr's old eyes narrowed. "Ah?"

Cordelia mentally planned a sprint down the back hall and out the end door. There was a bit of a ditch on the other side of the drive, if they went flat in it maybe . . . but the lightflyer was slowing at the end of its trajectory. It wobbled toward a landing on the front lawn. Men in Vorkosigan livery and ImpSec green and black cautiously surrounded it. The flyer's damage was clearly visible now, a plasma-slagged hole, black smears of soot, warped control surfaces—it was a miracle it flew at all.

"Who—?" said Aral.

Piotr's squint sharpened as a glimpse of the pilot winked through the damaged canopy. "Ye gods, it's Negri!"

"But who's that with—come on!" Aral flung over his shoulder, running out the door. They charged in his wake, around into the front hall, bursting out the door and churning down the green slope.

The guards had to pry open the warped canopy. Negri fell into their arms. They laid him on the grass. He had a grotesque burn a meter long on the left side of his body and thigh, his green uniform melted and charred away to reveal bleeding white bubbles, cracked-open flesh. He shivered uncontrollably.

The short figure strapped into the passenger seat was Emperor Gregor. The five-year-old boy was weeping in terror, not loudly, just muffled, gulping, suppressed whimpers. Such self-control in one so young seemed sinister to Cordelia. He should be screaming. She felt like screaming. He wore ordinary play-clothes, a soft shirt and pants in dark blue. He was missing one shoe. An ImpSec guard unhooked his seat belt and dragged him out of the flyer. He cringed from the man and stared at Negri in utter horror and confusion. *Did you think adults were indestructible, child?* Cordelia grieved.

Kou and Drou materialized from their separate holes in the house, to goggle along with the rest of the guards. Gregor spotted Droushnakovi, and flew to her like an arrow, to wind his hands tightly in her skirt. "Droushie, help!" His crying dared to become audible, then. She wrapped her arms around him and lifted him up.

Aral knelt by the injured ImpSec chief. "Negri, what happened?"

Negri reached up and grabbed his jacket with his working right hand. "He's trying for a coup—in the capital. His troops took ImpSec, took the comm center—why didn't you respond? HQ surrounded, infiltrated—bad fighting now at the Imperial Residence. We were on to him—about to arrest—he panicked. Struck too soon. I think he has Kareen—"

Piotr demanded, "Who has, Negri, who?"

"Vordarian."

Aral nodded grimly. "Yes . . ."

"You—take the boy," gasped Negri. "He's almost on top of us . . ." His shivers oscillated into convulsions, his eyes rolling back whitely. His breath stuttered in resonant chokes. His brown eyes refocused in sudden intensity. "Tell Ezar—" The convulsions took him again, racking his thick body. Then they stopped. *All stop.* He was no longer breathing.

CHAPTER ELEVEN

"Sir," said Koudelka urgently to Vorkosigan, "the secured comconsole was sabotaged." The ImpSec guard commander at his elbow nodded confirmation. "I was just coming to tell you. . . ." Koudelka glanced fearfully at Negri's body, laid out on the grass. Two ImpSec men now knelt beside it frantically applying first aid: heart massage, oxygen, and hypospray injections. But the body remained flaccid under their pummeling, the face waxy and inert. Cordelia had seen death before, and recognized the symptoms. *No good, fellows, you won't call this one back. Not this time. He's gone to deliver that last message to Ezar in person.* Negri's last report . . .

"What time-frame on the sabotage?" demanded Vorkosigan. "Delayed or immediate?"

"It looked like immediate," reported the guard commander. "No sign of a timer or device. Somebody just broke open the back and smashed it up inside."

Everyone's eyes went to the ImpSec man who had been assigned the guard post outside the comconsole room. He stood, dressed like most of the others in black fatigues, disarmed between two of his fellows. They had followed their commander out when the uproar began on the front lawn. The prisoner's face was about the same lead-grey color as Negri's, but animated by flickering fear.

"And?" Vorkosigan said to the guard commander.

"He denies doing it," shrugged the commander. "Naturally."

Vorkosigan looked at the arrestee. "Who went in after me?"

The guard stared around wildly. He pointed abruptly at Droushnakovi, still holding the whimpering Gregor. "Her."

"I never!" said Drou indignantly. Her clutch tightened.

Vorkosigan's teeth closed. "Well, I don't need fast-penta to know that one of you is lying. No time now. Commander, arrest them both. We'll sort it out later." Vorkosigan's eyes anxiously scanned the northern horizon. "You," he pointed to another ImpSec man, "assemble every piece of transport you can find. We evacuate immediately. You," this to one of Piotr's armsmen, "go warn them in the village. Kou, grab the files, take a plasma arc and finish melting down that comconsole, and get back to me."

Koudelka, with one anguished look back over his shoulder at Droushanakovi, stumped off toward the house. Drou stood stiffly, stunned and angry and frightened, the cold wind fluttering her skirts. Her brows drew down at Vorkosigan. She scarcely noticed Koudelka's departure.

"You going to Hassadar first?" said Piotr to his son in a strange mild tone.

"Right."

Hassadar, the Vorkosigan's District capital: Imperial troops were quartered there. A loyal garrison?

"Not planning to hold it, I trust," said Piotr.

"Of course not. Hassadar," Vorkosigan's wolf-grin winked on and off, "shall be my first gift to Commodore Vordarian."

Piotr nodded, as if satisfied. Cordelia's head spun. Despite Negri's surprise, neither Piotr nor Aral seemed at all panicked. No wasted motion; no wasted words.

"You," said Aral to Piotr in an undertone, "take the boy." Piotr nodded. "Meet us—no. Don't tell even me where. You contact us."

"Right."

"Take Cordelia."

Piotr's mouth opened; it closed saying only, "Ah."

"And Sergeant Bothari. For Cordelia. Drou being—temporarily—off duty."

"I must have Esterhazy, then," said Piotr.

"I'll want the rest of your men," said Aral.

"Right." Piotr took his Armsman Esterhazy aside, and spoke to him in low tones; Esterhazy departed upslope at a dead run. Men were scattering in every direction, as their orders proliferated down their command chain. Piotr called another liveried retainer to him, and told him to take his groundcar and start driving west.

"How far, m'lord?"

"As far as your ingenuity can take you. Then escape if you can, and rejoin m'lord Regent, eh?"

The man nodded, and galloped off like Esterhazy.

"Sergeant, you will obey Lady Vorkosigan's voice as my own," Aral told Bothari.

"Always, my lord."

"I want that lightflyer." Piotr nodded to Negri's damaged vehicle, which, while no longer smoking, did not look very airworthy to Cordelia. Not nearly ready for wild flight, jinking or diving to evade determined enemies . . . *It's in about as good a shape for this as I am,* she feared. "And Negri," Piotr continued.

"He would appreciate that," said Aral.

"I am certain of it." Piotr nodded shortly, and turned to the first-aid squad. "Leave off, boys, it's no damn good by now." He directed them instead to load the body into the lightflyer.

Aral turned to Cordelia last, at last, for the first time. "Dear Captain . . ." The same sere expression had been fixed on his face since Negri had fallen out of the lightflyer.

"Aral, was this a surprise to anyone but me?"

"I didn't want to worry you with it, when you were so sick." His lips thinned. "We'd found Vordarian was conspiring, at HQ and elsewhere. Illyan's investigation was inspired. Top security people must have that sort of intuition, I suppose. But to convict a man of Vordarian's magnitude and connections of treason, we needed the hardest of evidence. The Council of Counts as a body is highly intolerant of central Imperial interference with their members. We couldn't take a mere vaporplot before them.

"But Negri called me last night with the word he had his evidence in hand, enough to move on at last. He needed an Imperial order from me to arrest a ruling District Count. I was supposed to go up to Vorbarr Sultana tonight and oversee the operation. Clearly, Vordarian was warned. His original move wasn't planned for another month, preferably right after my successful assassination."

"But—"

"Go, now." He pushed her toward the lightflyer. "Vordarian's troops will be here in minutes. You must get away. No matter what else he holds, he can't make himself secure while Gregor stays free."

"Aral—" Her voice came out a stupid squeak; she swallowed what felt like freeze-dried chunks of spit. She wanted to gabble a thousand questions, ten thousand protests. "Take care."

"You, too." A last light flared in his eyes, but his face was already distant, lost to the driving internal rhythm of tactical calculation. No time.

Aral went to take Gregor from Drou's arms, whispering something to her; reluctantly, she released the boy to him. They piled into the lightflyer, Bothari at the controls, Cordelia jammed into the back beside Negri's corpse, Gregor dumped into her lap. The boy made no noise at all, but only shivered. His eyes were wide and shocky, turned up to hers. Her arms encircled him automatically. He did not cling back, but wrapped his arms around his own torso. Negri, lolling, feared nothing now, and she almost envied him.

"Did you see what happened to your mother, Gregor?" Cordelia murmured to him.

"The soldiers took her." His voice was thin and flat. The overloaded lightflyer hiccoughed into the air, and

Bothari aimed it generally upslope, wavering only meters from the ground. It whined and moaned and rattled. Cordelia did, too, internally. She twisted around to stare back through the distorted canopy for a look—a last look?—at Aral, who had turned away and was double-timing toward the driveway where his soldiers were assembling a motly collection of vehicles, personal and governmental. *Why aren't we taking one of those?*

"When you clear the second ridge—if you can—turn right, Sergeant," Piotr directed Bothari. "Follow the creek."

Branches slashed at the canopy, as Bothari flew less than a meter above the trickling water and sharp rocks.

"Land in that little space there and kill the power," ordered Piotr. "Everyone, strip off any powered items you may be carrying." He divested his chrono and a comm link. Cordelia shed her chrono.

Bothari, easing the flyer down beside the creek beneath some Earth-import trees that had only half-shed their leaves, asked, "Does that include weapons, m'lord?"

"Especially weapons, Sergeant. The charge unit on a stunner shows up on a scanner like a torch. A plasma arc power cell lights it up like a bloody bonfire."

Bothari fished two of each from his person, plus other useful gear; a hand-tractor, his comm link, his chrono, some kind of small medical diagnostic device. "My knife, too, m'lord?"

"Vibra-knife?"

"No, just steel."

"Keep that." Piotr hunched over the lightflyer's controls and began re-programming the automatic pilot. "Everyone out. Sergeant, jam the canopy half-open."

Bothari managed this task with a pebble crammed forcibly into the canopy's seating-groove, then whirled at a sound from the undergrowth.

"It's me," came Armsman Esterhazy's breathless voice. Esterhazy, age forty, a mere stripling beside some of Piotr's other grizzled veterans, kept himself in top shape; he'd been hustling indeed, to get so puffed. "I have them, my lord."

The "them" in question turned out to be four of Piotr's horses, tied together by lines attached to the metal bars in their mouths the Barrayarans called "bits." Cordelia thought it a very small control surface for such a large piece of transport. The big beasts twitched and stamped and shook their jingling heads, red nostrils round and flaring, ominous bulky shapes in the vegetation.

Piotr finished re-programming the autopilot. "Bothari, here," he said. Together, they manhandled Negri's corpse back to the pilot's seat and strapped it in. Bothari powered the lightflyer up and jumped out. It lurched into the air, nearly crashing into a tree, and lumbered back over the ridge. Piotr, standing watching it rise, muttered under his breath, "Salute him for me, Negri."

"Where are you sending him?" Cordelia asked. *Valhalla?*

"Bottom of the lake," said Piotr, with some satisfaction. "*That* will puzzle them."

"Won't whoever follows trace it? Hoist it back out?"

"Eventually. But it should go down in the two-hundred-meter-deep section. It will take them time. And they won't know at first when it went down, nor how many bodies are missing from it. They'll have to search that whole section of the lake bottom, to be sure that Gregor isn't stuck in it. And negative evidence is never quite conclusive, eh? They won't *know,* even then. Mount up, troops, we're on our way." He headed purposefully toward his animals.

Cordelia trailed doubtfully. Horses. Would one call them slaves, symbionts, or commensals? The one toward which Esterhazy aimed her stood five feet high at the top. He stuck its lines into her hands and turned away. Its saddle was at the level of her chin, and how was she supposed to levitate up there? The horse looked much larger, at this range, than when idling around decoratively at a distance in its pasture. The brown fur-covered skin of its shoulder shuddered suddenly. *Oh, God, they've given me a defective one, it's going into convulsions*—a small mew escaped her.

Bothari had climbed atop his, somehow. He at least was not overpowered by the size of the animal. Given his height he made the full-sized beast look like a pony. City-bred, Bothari was no horseman, and seemed all knees and elbows despite what cavalry training Piotr had managed to inflict on him in the months of his service. But he was clearly in control of his mount, however awkward and rough his motions.

"You're point-man, Sergeant," Piotr told him. "I want us strung out to the limit of mutual visibility. No bunching up. Start up the trails for the flat rock—you know the place—and wait for us."

Bothari jerked his horse's head around and kicked at its sides, and clattered off up the woodland path at the seat-thumping pace called a *canter*.

Supposedly-creaky Piotr swung up into his saddle in one fluid motion; Esterhazy handed Gregor up to him, and Piotr held the boy in front of him. Gregor had actually seemed to cheer up at the sight of the horses, Cordelia could not imagine why. Piotr appeared to do nothing at all, but his horse arranged itself neatly ready to start up the trail—*telepathy*, Cordelia decided wildly. *They've mutated into telepaths here and never told me . . .* or maybe it was the horse that was telepathic.

"Come on, woman, you're next," Piotr snapped impatiently.

Desperately, Cordelia stuck her foot through the whatchamacallit foot-holder, *stirrup*, grabbed, and heaved. The saddle slid slowly around the horse's belly, and Cordelia with it, till she was clinging underneath among a forest of horse legs. She fell to the ground with a thump, and scrambled out of the way. The horse twisted its neck around and peered at her, in a dismay much milder than her own, then stuck its rubbery lips to the ground and began nibbling up weeds.

"Oh, God," Piotr groaned in exasperation.

Esterhazy dismounted again, and hurried to her elbow to help her up. "Milady. Are you all right? Sorry, that was my fault, should have re-checked, uh—haven't you ever ridden before?"

"Never," Cordelia confessed. He hastily pulled off the saddle, straightened it back around, and fastened it more tightly. "Maybe I can walk. Or run." *Or slit my wrists. Aral, why did you send me off with these madmen?*

"It's not that hard, Milady," Esterhazy promised her. "Your horse will follow the others. Rose is the gentlest mare in the stables. Doesn't she have a sweet face?"

Malevolent brown eyes with purple centers ignored Cordelia. "I can't." Her breath caught in a sob, the first of this ungodly day.

Piotr glanced at the sky, and back over his shoulder. "Useless Betan frill," he snarled at her. "Don't tell *me* you've never ridden astride." His teeth bared. "Just pretend it's my son."

"Here, give me your knee," said Esterhazy after an anxious look at the Count, cupping his hands.

Take the whole damned leg. She was shaking with anger and fear. She glared at Piotr, and grabbed again at the saddle. Somehow, Esterhazy managed to boost her aboard. She clung like grim death, deciding after one glance not to look down.

Esterhazy tossed her reins to Piotr, who caught them with an easy wrist-flick and took her horse in tow. The trail became a kaleidoscope of trees, rocks, sucking mud puddles, whipping branches, all whirling and bumping past. Her belly began to ache, her new scar twinging. *If that bleeding starts again inside . . .* They went on, and on, and on.

They bumped down at last from a canter to a walk. She blinked, red-faced and wheezing and dizzy-sick. They had climbed, somehow, to a clearing overlooking the lake, having circled behind the broad shallow inlet that lay to the left of the Vorkosigan property. As her vision cleared, she could make out the little green patch in the general red-brown background that was the sloping lawn of the old stone house. Across the water lay the tiny village.

Bothari was there before them, waiting, hunkered down in the scrub out of sight, his blowing horse tied to a tree. He rose silently, and approached them, to stare worriedly at Cordelia. She half-fell, half-slid, off into his arms.

"You go too fast for her, m'lord. She's still sick."

Piotr snorted. "She'll be a lot sicker if Vordarian's squads overtake us."

"I'll manage," gasped Cordelia, bent over. "In a minute. Just. Give me. A minute." The breeze, chilling down as the autumn sun slanted toward evening, lapped her hot skin. The sky had greyed over to a solid shadowless milk-color. Gradually, she was able to straighten against the abdominal pain. Esterhazy arrived at the clearing, bringing up the rear at a less hectic pace.

Bothari nodded to the distant green patch. "There they are."

Piotr squinted; Cordelia stared. A couple of flyers were landing on the lawn. Not Aral's equipment. Men boiled out of them like black ants in their military fatigues, maybe one or two bright flecks of maroon and gold among them, and a few spots of officer's dark green. *Great. Our friends and our enemies are all wearing the same uniforms. What do we do, shoot them all and let God sort them out?*

Piotr looked sour indeed. Were they smashing his home, down there, tearing the place apart looking for the refugees?

"Won't they be able to tell, when they count the horses missing from the stable, where we've gone and how?" asked Cordelia.

"I let them all out, Milady," said Esterhazy. "At least they'll all have a chance, that way. I don't know how many we'll get back."

"Most of them will hang around, I'm afraid," said Piotr. "Hoping for their grain. I wish they had the sense to scatter. God knows what viciousness those vandals will come up with, if they're cheated of all their other prey."

A trio of flyers was landing around the perimeter of the little village. Armed men disembarked, and vanished among the houses.

"I hope Zai warned them all in time," muttered Esterhazy.

"Why would they bother those poor people?" asked Cordelia. "What do they want there?"

"Us, Milady," said Esterhazy grimly. At her confused look he went on, "Us armsmen. Our families. They're on a hostage-hunt down there."

Esterhazy had a wife and two children in the capital, Cordelia recalled. And what was happening to them right now? Had anyone passed them a warning? Esterhazy looked like he was wondering that, too.

"No doubt Vordarian will play the hostage game," said Piotr. "He's in for it now. He must win, or die."

Sergeant Bothari's narrow jaw worked, as he stared through the murky air. Had anyone remembered to warn Mistress Hysopi?

"They'll be starting their air-search shortly," said Piotr. "Time to get under cover. I'll go first. Sergeant, lead her."

He turned his horse and vanished into the undergrowth, following a path so faint Cordelia could not have recognized it as one. It took Bothari and Esterhazy together to lift her back aboard her transport. Piotr chose a walk for the pace, not for her sake, Cordelia suspected, but for his sweat-darkened animals. After that first hideous gallop, a walk was like a reprieve. At first.

They rode among trees and scrub, along a ravine, over a ridge, the horses' hooves scraping over stone. Her ears strained for the whine of flyers overhead. When one came, Bothari led her on a wild and head-spinning slide down into a ravine, where they dismounted and cowered under a rock ledge for minutes, until the whine faded. Getting back out of the ravine was even more difficult. They had to lead the horses up, Bothari practically seeming to hoist his along the precarious scrubby slope.

It grew darker, and colder, and windier. Two hours became three, four, five, and the smoky darkness turned pitchy. They bunched up with the horses nose to tail, trying not to lose Piotr. It began to rain, a sad black drizzle that made Cordelia's saddle even slipperier.

Around midnight they came to a clearing, hardly less black than the shadows, and Piotr at last called a halt. Cordelia sat against a tree, stunned with exhaustion, nerve-strung, holding Gregor. Bothari split a ration bar he'd been carrying in his pocket, their only food, between Cordelia and Gregor. With Bothari's uniform jacket wrapped around him, Gregor finally overcame the chill enough to sleep. Cordelia's legs went pins and needles, beneath him, but at least he was a lump of warmth.

Where was Aral, by now? For that matter, where were they? Cordelia hoped Piotr knew. They could not have made more than five kilometers an hour at most, with all that up and down and switch-back doubling. Did Piotr really imagine they were going to elude their pursuers this way?

Piotr, who had sat for a while under his own tree a few meters off, got up and went into the scrub to piss, then came back to peer at Gregor in the dimness. "Is he asleep?"

"Yes. Amazingly."

"Mm. Youth," Piotr grunted. Envy?

His tone was not so hostile as earlier, and Cordelia ventured, "Do you suppose Aral is in Hassadar by now?" She could not quite bring herself to say, *Do you suppose he ever made it to Hassadar?*

"He'll have been and gone by now."

"I thought he would raise its garrison."

"Raise and disperse, in a hundred different directions. And which squad has the Emperor? Vordarian won't know. But with luck, that traitor will be lured into occupying Hassadar."

"Luck?"

"A small but worthy diversion. Hassadar has no strategic value to speak of for either side. But Vordarian must divert a part of his—surely finite number of—loyal troops to hold it, deep in a hostile territory with a long guerilla tradition. We'll get good intelligence of everything they do there, but the population will be opaque to them.

"And it's my capital. He occupies a count's district capital with Imperial troops—all my brother counts must pause and think about that one. *Am I next?* Aral probably went on to Tanery Base Shuttleport. He must open an independent line of communication with the space-based forces, if Vordarian has truly choked off Imperial Headquarters. The spacers' choice of loyalties will be critical. I predict a severe outbreak of technical difficulties in their comm rooms, while the ship commanders scramble to figure out which is going to be the winning side." Piotr emitted a macabre chuckle, in the shadows. "Vordarian is too young to remember Mad Emperor Yuri's War. Too bad for him. He's gained sufficient advantage, with his quick start, I'd loathe to grant him more."

"How fast . . . did it all happen?"

"Fast. There was no hint of any trouble when I was up to the capital at noon. It must have broken out right after I left."

A chill that had nothing to do with the rain fell between them briefly, as both remembered why Piotr had made that journey this day.

"Does the capital . . . have great strategic value?" Cordelia asked, changing the subject, unwilling to break open that raw issue again.

"In some wars it would. Not this one. This is not a war for territory. I wonder if Vordarian realizes that? It's a war for loyalties, for the minds of men. No material object in it has more than a passing tactical importance. Vorbarr Sultana is a communications center, though, and communication is much. But not the only center. Collateral circulation will serve."

We have no communications at all, thought Cordelia dully. Out here in the woods in the rain. "But if Vordarian holds the Imperial Military Headquarters right now . . ."

"What he holds right now, unless I miss my guess, is a very large building full of chaos. I doubt a quarter of the men are at their posts, and half of them are plotting sabotage to benefit whatever side they secretly favor. The rest are out running for cover, or trying to get their families out of town."

"Will Captain Vorpatril be all—will Vordarian bother Lord and Lady Vorpatril, do you think?" Alys Vorpatril's pregnancy was very close to term. When she had visited

Cordelia at ImpMil—only ten days ago?—her gliding walk had become a heavy flatfooted waddle, her belly a swaying high arc. Her doctor promised her a big boy. Ivan, he was to be named. His nursery was completely equipped and fully decorated, she had groaned, shifting her stomach uncomfortably in her lap, and *now* would be a good time. . . .

Now was not a good time anymore.

"Padma Vorpatril will head the list. The hunt will be up for him, all right. He and Aral are the last descendants of Prince Xav, now, if anybody's fool enough to start up that damned succession-debate again. Or if anything does happen to Gregor." He bit down on this last line as if he might hold back fate with his teeth.

"Lady Vorpatril and the baby, too?"

"Perhaps not Alys Vorpatril. The boy, definitely."

Not exactly a separable matter, just at the moment.

The wind had died down at last. Cordelia could hear the horses' teeth tearing up plants, a steady *munch-munch-munch*.

"Won't the horses show up on thermal sensors? And us, too, despite dumping our power cells. I don't see how they can miss us for long." Were troops up there right now, eyes in the clouds?

"Oh, all the people and beasts in these hills will show up on their thermal sensors, once they start aiming them in the right direction."

"All? I hadn't seen any."

"We've passed about twenty little homesteads, so far tonight. All the people, and their cows, and their goats, and their red deer, and their horses, and their children. We're straws in a haystack. Still, it will be well for us to split up soon. If we can make it to the trail at the base of Amie Pass before mid-morning, I have an idea or two."

By the time Bothari shoved her back atop Rose, the deep blackness was greying. Pre-dawn light seeped into the woods as they began to move again. Tree branches were charcoal stokes in the dripping mist. She clung to her saddle in silent misery, towed along by Bothari. Gregor actually still slept, for the first twenty minutes of the ride, openmouthed and limp and pale in Piotr's grip.

The growing light revealed the night's ravages. Bothari and Esterhazy were both muddy and scuffed, beard-peppered, their brown-and-silver uniforms rumpled. Bothari, having given up his jacket to Gregor, went in shirtsleeves. The open round collar of his shirt made him look like a condemned criminal being led to the beheading-block. Piotr's general's dress greens had survived fairly well, but his stubbled red-eyed face above it was like a derelict's. Cordelia felt herself a hopeless tangle, with her wet tendrils of hair, mishmash of old clothing and house slippers.

It could be worse. I could still be pregnant. At least if I die, I die singly now. Was little Miles safer than she right now? Anonymous in his replicator on some shelf in Vaagen and Henri's restricted laboratory? She could pray so, even if she couldn't believe so. *You Barrayaran bastards had better leave my boy alone.*

They zigzagged up a long slope. The horses blew like bellows even though just walking: getting balky, stumbling over roots and rocks. They came to a halt at the bottom of a little hollow. Both horses and people drank from the murky stream. Esterhazy loosened girths again. He scratched under the horses' headbands, and they butted against him, nuzzling his empty pockets for tidbits. He murmured apologies and little encouragements to them. "It's all right, Rosie, you can rest at the end of the day. Just a few more hours." It was more briefing than anybody had bothered to give Cordelia.

Esterhazy left the horses to Bothari and accompanied Piotr into the woods, scrabbling up the slope. Gregor busied himself in an attempt to gather vegetation and hand-feed it to the animals. They lipped at the native Barrayaran plants and let them fall messily from their mouths, unpalatable. Gregor kept picking the wads up and offering them again, trying to shove them in around the horses' bits.

"What's the Count up to, do you know?" Cordelia asked Bothari.

He shrugged. "Gone to make contact with somebody. *This* won't do." A jerk of his head in no particular direction indicated their night of beating around in the brush.

Cordelia could only agree. She lay back and listened for lightflyers, but heard only the babble of water in the little stream, echoed by the gurgles of her empty stomach. She was galvanized into motion once, to keep the hungry Gregor from sampling some of the possibly-toxic plants himself.

"But the horses ate these ones," he protested.

"No!" Cordelia shuddered, detailed visions of unfavorable biochemical and histamine reactions dancing in a molecular crack-the-whip through her head. "It's one of the first habits you have to learn for Betan Astronomical Survey, you know. Never put strange things in your mouth till they've been cleared by the lab. In fact, avoid touching your eyes, mouth, and mucous membranes."

Gregor, unconsciously compelled, promptly rubbed his nose and eyes. Cordelia sighed, and sat back down. She sucked on her tongue, thinking about that stream water and hoping Gregor wouldn't point out her inconsistency. Gregor threw pebbles into the pools.

Fully an hour later, Esterhazy returned. "Come on." They merely led the horses this time, sure sign of a steep climb to come. Cordelia scrambled, and scraped her hands. The horses' haunches heaved. Over the crest, down, up again, and they came out on a muddy double trail carved through the forest.

"Where are we?" asked Cordelia.

"Aime Pass Road, Milady," supplied Esterhazy.

"This is a road?" Cordelia muttered in dismay, staring up and down it. Piotr stood a little way off, with another old man holding the reins of a sturdy little black-and-white horse.

The horse was considerably better groomed than the old man. Its white coat was bright and its black coat shiny. Its mane and tail were brushed to feather-softness. Its feet and fetlocks were wet and dark, though, and its belly flecked with fresh mud. In addition to an old cavalry saddle like Piotr's horse's, the pinto bore four large saddle-bags, a pair in front and a pair behind, and a bedroll.

The old man, as unshaven as Piotr, wore an Imperial Postal Service jacket so weatherworn its blue had turned grey. This was supplemented by odd bits of other old uniforms: a black fatigue shirt, an ancient pair of trousers from a set of dress greens, worn but well-oiled officer's knee-high riding boots on his bent bowlegs. He also wore a non-regulation felt hat with a few dried flowers stuck in its faded print headband. He smacked his black-stained lips and stared at Cordelia. He was missing several teeth; the rest were long and yellow-brown.

The old man's gaze fell on Gregor, holding Cordelia's hand. "So that's him, eh? Huh. Not much." He spat reflectively into the weeds by the side of the path.

"Might do in time," asserted Piotr. "If he gets time."

"I'll see what I can do, Gen'ral."

Piotr grinned, as if at some private joke. "You have any rations on you?"

" 'Course." The old man smirked, and turned to rummage in one of his saddlebags. He came up with a package of raisins in a discarded plastic flimsy, some little cakes of brownish crystals wrapped in leaves, and what looked like a handful of strips of leather, again in a twist made of a used plastic flimsy. Cordelia caught a heading, *Update of Postal Regluations C6.77a, modified 6/17. File Immediately In Permanent Files.*

Piotr looked the stores over judiciously. "Dried goat?" He nodded toward the leathery mess.

"Mostly," said the old man.

"We'll take half. And the raisins. Save the maple sugar for the children." Piotr popped one cube in his mouth, though. "I'll find you in maybe three days, maybe a week. You remember the drill from Yuri's War, eh?"

"Oh, yes," drawled the old man.

"Sergeant." Piotr waved Bothari to him. "You go with the Major, here. Take *her*, and the boy. He'll take you to ground. Lie low till I come get you."

"Yes, m'lord," Bothari intoned flatly. Only his flickering eyes betrayed his uneasiness.

"What we got here, Gen'ral?" inquired the old man, looking up at Bothari. "New one?"

"A city boy," said Piotr. "Belongs to my son. Doesn't talk much. He's good at throats, though. He'll do."

"Aye? Good."

Piotr was moving a lot more slowly. He waited for Esterhazy to give him a leg up on his horse. He settled into his saddle with a sigh, his back temporarily curved in an uncharacteristic slump. "Damn, but I'm getting old for this sort of thing."

Thoughtfully, the man Piotr had called the Major reached into a side pocket and pulled out a leather pouch. "Want my gum-leaf, Gen'ral? A better chew than goat, if not as long-lasting."

Piotr brightened. "Ah. I would be most grateful. But not your whole pouch, man." Piotr dug among the pressed dried leaves that filled the container, and crumbled himself off a generous half, which he stuffed in his breast pocket. He put a wad in his cheek, and returned the pouch with a sincere salute. Gum-leaf was a mild stimulant; Cordelia had never seen Piotr chew it in Vorbarr Sultana.

"Take care of m'lord's horses," called Esterhazy rather desperately to Bothari. "They're not machines, remember. "

Bothari grunted something noncommittal, as the Count and Esterhazy headed their animals back down the trail. They were out of sight in a few moments. A profound quiet descended.

CHAPTER TWELVE

The Major put Gregor, comfortably padded by the bed-roll and saddlebags, up behind him. Cordelia faced one more climb onto that torture-device for humans and horses called a saddle. She would never have made it without Bothari. The Major took her reins this time, and Rose and his horse walked side by side with a lot less jerking of the bridle. Bothari dropped back, trailing watchfully.

"So," said the old man after a time, with a sideways look at her, "you're the new Lady Vorkosigan."

Cordelia, rumpled and filthy, smiled back desperately. "Yes. Ah, Count Piotr didn't mention your name, Major . . . ?"

"Amor Klyeuvi, Milady. But folks up here just call me Kly."

"And, uh . . . what are you?" Besides some mountain kobold Piotr had conjured out of the ground.

He smiled, an expression more repellent than attractive given the state of his teeth. "I'm the Imperial Mail, Milady. I ride the circuit through these hills, out of Vorkosigan Surleau, every ten days. Been at it for eighteen years. There are grown kids up here with kids of their own who never knew me as anything but Kly the Mail."

"I thought mail went to these parts by lightflyer."

"They're phasing them in. But the flyers don't go to every house, just to these central drop-points. No courtesy to it, anymore." He spat disgust and gum-leaf. "But if the General'll hold 'em off another two years here, I'll make my last twenty, and be a triple-twenty-years Service man. I retired with my double-twenty, see."

"From what branch, Major Klyuevi?"

"Imperial Rangers." He watched slyly for her reaction; she rewarded him with impressed raised brows. "I was a throat-cutter, not a tech. 'S why I could never go higher than major. Got my start at age fourteen, in these mountains, running rings around the Cetagandans with the General and Ezar. Never did get back to school after that. Just training courses. The Service passed me by, in time."

"Not entirely, it seems," said Cordelia, staring around the apparently unpeopled wilderness.

"No . . ." His breath became a purse-lipped sigh, as he glanced back over his shoulder at Gregor in meditative unease.

"Did Piotr tell you what happened yesterday afternoon?"

"Yo. I left the lake day-before-yesterday morning. Missed all the excitement. I expect the news will catch up with me before noon."

"Is . . . anything else likely to catch up with us by then?"

"We'll just have to see." He added more hesitantly, "You'll have to get out of those clothes, Milady. The name VORKOSIGAN, A., in big block letters over your jacket-pocket isn't any too anonymous."

Cordelia glanced down at Aral's black fatigue shirt, quelled.

"My lord's livery sticks out like a flag, too," Kly added, looking back at Bothari. "But you'll pass well enough, in the right clothes. I'll see what I can do, in a bit here."

Cordelia sagged, her belly aching in anticipation of rest. Refuge. But at what price to those who gave her refuge? "Will helping us put you in danger?"

His tufted grey brow rose. "Belike." His tone did not invite further comment on the topic.

She had to bring her tired mind back on-line somehow, if she was to be asset and not hazard to everyone around her. "That gum-leaf of yours. Does it work anything like coffee?"

"Oh, better than coffee, Milady."

"Can I try some?" Shyness lowered her voice; it might be too intimate a request.

His cheeks creased in a dry grin. "Only backcountry sticks like me chew gum-leaf, Milady. Pretty Vor ladies from the capital wouldn't be caught dead with it in their pearly teeth."

"I'm not pretty, I'm not a lady, and I'm not from the capital. And I'd kill for coffee right now. I'll try it."

He let his reins drop to his steadily plodding horse's neck, rummaged in his blue-grey jacket pocket, and pulled out his pouch. He broke off a chunk, in none-too-clean fingers, and leaned across.

She regarded it a doubtful moment, dark and leafy in her palm. *Never put strange organics in your mouth till they've been cleared by the lab.* She lapped it up. The wad was made self-sticking by a bit of maple syrup, but after her saliva washed away the first startling sweetness, the flavor was pleasantly bitter and astringent. It seemed to peel away the night's film coating her teeth, a real improvement. She straightened.

Kly regarded her with bemusement. "So what are you, off-worlder not-a-lady?"

"I was an astrocartographer. Then a Survey captain. Then a soldier, then a POW, then a refugee. And then I was a wife, and then I was a mother. I don't know what I'm going to be next," she answered honestly, around the gum-leaf. *Pray not* widow.

"Mother? I'd heard you were pregnant, but . . . didn't you lose your baby to the soltoxin?" He eyed her waist in confusion.

"Not yet. He still has a fighting chance. Though it seems a little uneven, to match him against all of Barrayar just yet. . . . He was born prematurely. By surgical section." (She decided not to try to explain the uterine replicator.) "He's at the Imperial Military Hospital. In Vorbarr Sultana. Which for all I know has just been captured by Vordarian's rebel forces . . ." She shivered. Vaagen's lab was classified, nothing to draw anyone's attention. Miles was all right, all right, all right, and one crack in that thin shell of conviction would hatch out hysteria. . . . Aral, now, Aral could take care of himself if anyone could. So how had he been so caught-out, eh, eh? No question, ImpSec was riddled with treason. They couldn't trust anyone around here, and where was Illyan? Trapped in Vorbarr Sultana? Or was he Vordarian's quisling? No . . . Cut off, more likely. Like Kareen. Like Padma and Alys Vorpatril. Life racing death . . .

"No one will bother the hospital," said Kly, watching her face.

"I—yes. Right."

"Why did you come to Barrayar, off-worlder?"

"I wanted to have children." A humorless laugh puffed from her lips. "Do you have any children, Kly the Mail?"

"Not so far as I know."

"You were very wise."

"Oh . . ." His face grew distant. "I don't know. Since my old woman died, 's been pretty quiet. Some men I know, their children have been a great trouble to them. Ezar. Piotr. Don't know who will burn the offerings on my grave. M' niece, maybe."

Cordelia glanced at Gregor, riding along atop the saddlebags and listening. Gregor had lit the taper to Ezar's great funeral offering-pyre, his hand guided by Aral's.

They rode on up the road, climbing. Four times Kly ducked up side-trails, while Cordelia, Bothari, and Gregor waited out of sight. On the third of these delivery-runs Kly returned with a bundle including an old skirt, a pair of worn trousers, and some grain for the tired horses. Cordelia, still chilled, put the skirt on over her old Survey trousers. Bothari exchanged his conspicuous brown uniform pants with the silver stripe down the side for the hillman's cast-offs. The pants were too short, riding ankle-high, giving him the look of a sinister scarecrow. Bothari's uniform and Cordelia's black fatigue shirt were bundled out of sight in an empty mailbag. Kly solved the problem of Gregor's missing shoe by simply stripping off the remaining one and letting the boy go barefoot, and concealing his too-nice blue suit beneath a man's oversize shirt with the sleeves rolled up. Man, woman, child, they looked a haggard, ragged little hill family.

They made the top of Amie Pass and started back down. Occasionally folk waited by the roadside for Kly; he passed on verbal messages, rattling them off in what sounded to Cordelia to be verbatim style. He distributed letters on paper and cheap vocodisks, their self-playbacks tinny and thin. Twice he paused to read letters to apparently illiterate recipients, and once to a blind man guided by a small girl. Cordelia grew twitchier with each mild encounter, drained by nervous exhaustion. *Will that fellow betray us? What do we look like to that woman? At least the blind man can't describe us. . . .*

Toward dusk, Kly returned from one of his side-loops to gaze up and down the silent shadowed wilderness trail and declare, "This place is just too crowded." It was a measure of Cordelia's overstrain that she found herself mentally agreeing with him.

He looked her over, worry in his eyes. "Think you can go on for another four hours, Milady?"

What's the alternative? Sit by this mud puddle and weep till we're captured? She struggled to her feet, pushing up from the log she'd been perched on waiting their guide's return. "That depends on what's at the end of four more hours of this."

"My place. I usually spend this night at my niece's, near here. My route ends about another ten hours farther on, when I'm making my deliveries, but if we go straight up we can do it in four. I can double back to this point by tomorrow morning and keep my schedule as usual. Real quiet-like. Nothing to remark on."

What does "straight up" mean? But Kly was clearly right; their whole safety lay in their anonymity, their invisibility. The sooner they were out of sight, the better. "Lead on, Major."

It took six hours. Bothari's horse went lame, short of their goal. He dismounted and towed it. It limped and tossed its head. Cordelia walked, too, to ease her raw legs and to keep herself warm and awake in the chilling darkness. Gregor fell asleep and fell off, cried for his mother, then fell asleep again when Kly moved him around to his front to keep a better grip. The last climb stole Cordelia's breath and made her heart race, even though she hung on to Rose's stirrup for help. Both horses moved like old women with arthritis, stumping along jerkily; only the animals' innate gregariousness kept them following Kly's hardy pinto.

The climb became a drop, suddenly, over a ridge and into a great vale. The woods grew thin and ragged, interspersed with mountain meadows. Cordelia could feel the spaces stretching out around her, true mountain scale at last, vast gulfs of shadow, huge bulks of stone, silent as eternity. Three snowflakes melted on her staring, upturned face. At the edge of a vague patch of trees, Kly halted. "End of the line, folks."

Cordelia sleepwalked Gregor into the tiny shack, felt her way to a cot, and rolled him onto it. He whimpered in his sleep as she dragged the blankets over him. She stood swaying, numb-brained, then in a last burst of lucidity kicked off her slippers and climbed in with him. His feet were cold as a cryo-corpse's. As she warmed them against her body his shivering gradually relaxed into deeper sleep. Dimly, she was aware that Kly—Bothari—somebody, had started a fire in the fireplace. Poor Bothari, he'd been awake every bit as long as she had. In a quite military sense, he was her man; she should see that he ate, cared for his feet, slept . . . she should, she should. . . .

Cordelia snapped awake, to discover that the movement that had roused her was Gregor, sitting up beside her and rubbing his eyes in bleary disorientation. Light streamed in through two dirty windows on either side of the wooden front door. The shack, or cabin—two of the walls were made of whole logs stacked up—was only a single room. In the grey stone fireplace at one end a kettle and a covered pot sat on a grating over a bed of glowing coals. Cordelia reminded herself again that wood represented poverty, not wealth, here. They must have passed ten million trees yesterday.

She sat up, and gasped from the pain in her muscles. She straightened her legs. The bed was a rope net strung on a frame and supporting first a straw-stuffed mattress, then a feather-stuffed one. She and Gregor were warm, at least, in their nest. The air of the room was dusty-smelling, tinged with a pleasant edge of wood smoke.

Booted footsteps sounded on the boards of the porch outside, and Cordelia grasped Gregor's arm in sudden panic. She couldn't run—that black iron fireplace poker would make a pretty poor weapon against a stunner or nerve disruptor—but the steps were Bothari's. He slipped through the door along with a puff of outside air. His crudely sewn tan cloth jacket must be a borrowing from Kly, judging from the way his bony wrists stuck out beyond the turned-down sleeve cuffs. He'd pass for a hillman easily, as long as he kept his urban-accented mouth shut.

He nodded at them. "Milady. Sire." He knelt by the fireplace, glanced under the pot lid, and tested the kettle's temperature by cupping a big hand a few centimeters above it. "There's groats, and syrup," he said. "Hot water. Herb tea. Dried fruit. No butter."

"What's happening?" Cordelia rubbed her face awake, and swung her legs overboard, planning a stumble toward that herb tea.

"Not much. The Major rested his horse a while, and left before light, to keep his schedule. It's been real quiet, since."

"Did you get any sleep yet?"

"Couple of hours, I think."

The tea had to wait while Cordelia escorted the Emperor downslope to Kly's outhouse. Gregor wrinkled his nose, and eyed the adult-sized seat nervously. Back on the cabin porch Cordelia supervised hand and face washing over a dented metal basin.

The view from the porch, once she'd toweled her face dry and vision clear, was stunning. Half of Vorkosigan's District seemed spread out below, the brown foothills, the green- and yellow-specked peopled plains beyond. "Is that our lake?" Cordelia nodded to a glint of silver in the hills, near the limits of her vision.

"I think so," said Bothari, squinting.

So far, to have come this fast on foot. So fearfully near, in a lightflyer . . . Well, at least you could see whatever was coming.

The hot groats and syrup, served on a cracked white plate, tasted wonderful. Cordelia guzzled herb tea, and realized she'd become dangerously dehydrated. She tried to encourage Gregor to drink, but he didn't like the astringent taste of the tea. Bothari looked almost suffused with shame, that he couldn't produce milk out of the air at his Emperor's direct request. Cordelia solved the dilemma by sweetening the tea with syrup, rendering it acceptable.

By the time they finished breakfast, washed up the few utensils and dishes, and flung the bit of wash water over the porch rail, the porch had warmed enough in the morning sun to make sitting tolerable.

"Why don't you take over the bed, Sergeant. I'll keep watch. Ah . . . did Kly have any suggestions what we should do, if somebody hostile drops down on us here before he gets back? It kind of looks like we've run out of places to run to."

"Not quite, Milady. There's a set of caves, up in that patch of woods in back. An old guerilla cache. Kly took me back last night to see the entrance."

Cordelia sighed. "Right. Get some sleep, Sergeant, we'll surely need you later."

She sat in the sun in one of the wooden chairs, resting her body if not her mind. Her eyes and ears strained for the whine of a distant lightflyer or heavy aircar. She tied Gregor's feet up with makeshift rag shoes, and he wandered about examining things. She accompanied him on a visit to the shed to see the horses. The Sergeant's beast was still very lame, and Rose was moving as little as possible, but they had fodder in a rick and water from a little stream that ran across the end of their enclosure. Kly's other horse, a lean and fit-looking sorrel, seemed to tolerate the equine invasion, only nipping when Rose edged too close to its side of the hayrick.

Cordelia and Gregor sat on the porch steps as the sun passed zenith, comfortably warm now. The only sound in the vast vale besides a breeze in the branches was Bothari's snores, resonating through the cabin walls. Deciding this was as relaxed as they were likely to get, Cordelia at last dared quiz Gregor on his view—her only eyewitness report—of the coup in the capital. It wasn't much help; Gregor's five-year-old eyes saw the *what* well enough, it was the *whys* that escaped him. On a higher level, she had the same problem, Cordelia admitted ruefully to herself.

"The soldiers came. The colonel told Mama and me to come with him. One of our liveried men came in. The colonel shot him."

"Stunner, or nerve disruptor?"

"Nerve disruptor. Blue fire. He fell down. They took us to the Marble Courtyard. They had aircars. Then Captain Negri ran in, with some men. A soldier grabbed me, and Mama grabbed me back, and that's what happened to my shoe. It came off in her hand. I should have . . . fastened it tighter, in the morning. Then Captain Negri shot the soldier who was carrying me, and some soldiers shot Captain Negri—"

"Plasma arc? Is that when he got that horrible burn?" Cordelia asked. She tried to keep her tone very calm.

Gregor nodded mutely. "Some soldiers took Mama, those other ones, not Negri's ones. Captain Negri picked me up and ran. We went through the tunnels, under the Residence, and came out in a garage. We went in the lightflyer. They shot at us. Captain Negri kept telling me to shut up, to be quiet. We flew and flew, and he kept yelling at me to be quiet, but I *was*. And then we landed by the lake." Gregor was trembling again.

"Mm." Kareen spun in vivid detail in Cordelia's head, despite the simplicity of Gregor's account. That serene face, wrenched into screaming rage and terror as they tore the son she'd borne the Barrayaran hard way from her grip, leaving . . . nothing but a shoe, of all their precarious life and illusory possessions. So Vordarian's troops had Kareen. As hostage? Victim? Alive or dead?

"Do you think Mama's all right?"

"Sure." Cordelia shifted uncomfortably. "She's a very valuable lady. They won't hurt her." *Till it becomes expedient for them to do so.*

"She was crying."

"Yes." She could feel that same knot in her own belly. The mental flash she'd shied from all day yesterday burst in her brain. Boots, kicking open a secured laboratory door. Kicking over desks, tables. No faces, just boots. Gun butts sweeping delicate glassware and computerized monitors from benches into a tangled smash on the floor. A uterine replicator rudely jerked open, its sterile seals slashed, its contents dumped pell-mell wetly on the tiles . . . no need even for the traditional murderous swing by the heels of infant head against the nearest concrete wall, Miles was so little the boots could just *step* on him and smash him to jam. . . . She drew in her breath.

Miles is all right. Anonymous, just like us. We are very small, and very quiet, and safe. Shut up, keep quiet, kid. She hugged Gregor tightly. "My little boy is in the capital, too, same as your Mama. And you're with me. We'll look out for each other. You bet."

After supper, and still no sign of Kly, Cordelia said, "Show me that cave, Sergeant."

Kly kept a box of cold lights atop his mantel. Bothari cracked one, and led Cordelia and Gregor up into the woods on a faint stony path. He made a menacing will-o'-the-wisp, with the bright green-tinged light shining from the tube between his fingers.

The area near the cave mouth showed signs of having once been cleared, though recent overgrowth was closing back in. The entrance was by no means hidden, a yawning black hole twice the height of Bothari and wide enough to edge a lightflyer through. Immediately within, the roof rose and walls flared to create a dusty cavern. Whole patrols could camp therein, and had, in the distant past, judging from the antique litter. Bunk niches were carved in the rock, and names and initials and dates and crude comments covered the walls.

A cold fire-pit in the center was matched by a blackened vent-hole above, which had once provided exit for the smoke. A ghostly crowd of hillmen, guerilla soldiers, seemed to hover in Cordelia's mind's eye, eating, joking, spitting gum-leaf, cleaning their weapons and planning their next foray. Ranger spies came and went, ghosts among the ghosts, to place their precious blood-won information before their young general, who spread his maps out on that flat rock over there. . . . She shook the vision from her head, and took the light and explored the niches. At least five traversable exits led off from the cavern, three of which showed signs of having been heavily traveled.

"Did Kly say where these went, or where they came out, Sergeant?"

"Not exactly, Milady. He did say the passages went back for kilometers, into the hills. He was late, and in a hurry to get on."

"Is it a vertical or horizontal system, did he say?"

"Beg pardon, Milady?"

"All on one strata, or with unexpected big drops? Are there lots of blind alleys? Which path were we supposed to take? Are there underground streams?"

"I think he expected to be leading us, if we went in. He started to explain, then said it was too complicated."

She frowned, contemplating the possibilities. She'd done a bit of cave work in her Survey training, enough to grasp what the term *respect for the hazards* meant. Vents, drops, cracks, labyrinthine cross-passages . . . plus, here, the unexpected rise and fall of water, not a matter of much concern on Beta Colony. It had rained last night. Sensors were not much help in finding a lost cave explorer. And whose sensors? If the system was as extensive as Kly suggested, it could absorb hundreds of searchers. . . . Her frown changed to a slow smile.

"Sergeant, let's camp here tonight."

Gregor liked the cave, especially when Cordelia described the history of the place. He rattled around the cavern whispering military dialogue to himself like "Zap, zap, zap!", climbed in and out of all the niches, and tried to sound out the rude words carved in the walls. Bothari lit a small fire in the pit and spread a bedroll for Gregor and Cordelia, taking the night watch for himself. Cordelia set a second bedroll, wrapped around trail snacks and supplies, in a grabbable bundle near the entrance. She arranged the black fatigue jacket with the name VORKOSIGAN, A., artistically in a niche, as if used to sit upon and keep someone's haunches from the cold stone and then temporarily forgotten when the sitter rose. Last of all Bothari brought up their lame and useless horses, re-saddled and bridled, and tethered them just outside.

Cordelia emerged from the widest passage, where she'd dropped an almost-spent cold light a quarter kilometer along, over a rope-strung ten-meter cliff. The rope was natural fiber, and very old and brittle. She'd elected not to test it.

"I don't quite get it, Milady," said Bothari. "With the horses abandoned out there, if anyone comes looking they'll find us at once, and know exactly where we've gone."

"Find this, yes," said Cordelia. "Know where we've gone, no. Because without Kly, there is no way I'm taking Gregor down into this labyrinth. But the best way to look like we were here is to actually be here for a bit."

Bothari's flat eyes lit in understanding at last, as he gazed around at the five black entrances at their various levels. "Ah!"

"That means we also need to find a real bolt-hole.

Somewhere up in the woods, where we can cut across
to the trail Kly brought us up yesterday. Wish we'd done
this in daylight."

"I see what you mean, Milady. I'll scout."

"Please do, Sergeant."

Taking their trail bundle, he disappeared into the dim
woods. Cordelia tucked Gregor into the bedroll, then
perched outside among the rocks above the cave mouth
and kept watch. She could see the vale, stretched out
greyly below the tops of the trees, and make out Kly's
cabin roof. No smoke rose now from its chimney. Beneath
the stone, no remote thermal sensor would find their new
fire, though the smell of it hung in the chill air, detectable to nearby noses. She watched for moving lights in
the sky till the stars were a watery blur in her eyes.

Bothari returned after a very long time. "I have a spot.
Shall we move now?"

"Not yet. Kly might still show up." *First.*

"Your turn to sleep, then, Milady."

"Oh, yes." The evening's exertions had only partly
warmed the acid fatigue from her muscles. Leaving Bothari
on the limestone outcrop in the starlight like a guardian
gargoyle, she crawled in with Gregor. Eventually, she slept.

She woke with the grey light of dawn making the cavern entrance a luminous misty oval. Bothari made hot tea,
and they shared cold lumps of pan bread left from last
night, and nibbled dried fruit.

"I'll watch some more," Bothari volunteered. "I can't
sleep so good without my medication anyway."

"Medication?" said Cordelia.

"Yeah, I left my pills at Vorkosigan Surleau. I can feel
it clearing out of my system. Things seem sharper."

Cordelia chased a suddenly very lumpy bite of bread
with a swallow of hot tea. But were his psychoactive drugs
truly therapeutic, or merely political in their effect? "Let
me know if you are experiencing any kind of difficulty,
Sergeant," she said cautiously.

"Not so far. Except it's getting harder to sleep. They

suppress dreams." He took his tea and wandered back to his post.

Cordelia carefully refrained from cleaning up their campsite. She did escort Gregor to the nearest rivulet for a personal washup. They were certainly acquiring an authentic hill-folk aroma. They returned to the cavern, where Cordelia rested a while on the bedroll. She must insist on relieving Bothari soon. Come on, Kly. . . .

Bothari's tense low voice reverberated in the cavern. "Milady. Sire. Time to go."

"Kly?"

"No."

Cordelia rolled to her feet, kicked the pre-arranged pile of dirt over the last coals of their fire, grabbed Gregor, and hustled him out the cave mouth. He looked suddenly frightened and sickly. Bothari was pulling the bridles off the horses, loosing them and tossing the gear on the pile with the saddles. Cordelia pulled herself up beside the cave and snatched one quick glimpse over the treetops. A flyer had landed in front of Kly's cabin. Two black-uniformed soldiers were circling to the right and left. A third disappeared under the porch roof. Faint and delayed in the distance came the bang of Kly's front door being kicked open. Only soldiers, no hillman-guides or hillman-prisoners in that flyer. No sign of Kly.

They took to the woods at a jog, Bothari boosting up and carrying Gregor piggyback. Rose made to follow them, and Cordelia whirled to wave her arms and whisper frantically, "No! Go away, idiot beast!" to spook her off. Rose hesitated, then turned to stay by her lame companion.

Their run was steady, unpanicked. Bothari had his route all picked out, taking advantage of sheltering rocks and trees and water-carved steps. They scrambled up, down, up, but just when she thought her lungs would burst and their pursuers must spot them, Bothari vanished along a steep rock face.

"Over here, Milady!"

He'd found a thin, horizontal crack in the rocks, half a meter high and three meters deep. She rolled in beside

him to find the niche shielded by solid rock everywhere
but the front, and that almost blocked by fallen stone.
Their bedroll and supplies waited.

"No wonder," Cordelia gasped, "the Cetagandans had
trouble up here." A thermal sensor would have to be
aimed straight in, to pick them up, from a point twenty
meters in the air out over the ravine. The place was
riddled with hundreds of similar crannies.

"Even better." Bothari pulled a pair of antique field
glasses, looted from Kly's cabin, from their bedroll. "We
can see them."

The glasses were nothing but binocular tubes with sliding glass lenses, purely passive light-collectors. They must
have dated from the Time of Isolation. The magnification was poor by modern standards, no UV or infrared
boost, no rangefinder pulse . . . no power cell to leak
detectable energy traces. Flat on her belly, chin in the
rubble, Cordelia could glimpse the distant cavern entrance
on the slope rising beyond the ravine and a knife-backed
ridge. When she said, "Now we must be *very* quiet," pale
Gregor practically went fetal.

The black-clad scanner men found the horses at last,
though it seemed to take them forever. Then they found
the cave mouth. The tiny figures gesticulated excitedly
to each other, ran in and out, and called the flyer, which
landed outside the entrance with much crackling of shrubbery. Four men entered; eventually, one came back out.
In time, another flyer landed. Then a lift van arrived, and
disgorged a whole patrol. The mountain mouth ate them
all. Another lift van came, and men set up lights, a field
generator, comm links.

Cordelia made a nest of the bedroll for Gregor, and
fed him little snacks and sips from their water bottle.
Bothari stretched out in the back of the niche with the
thinnest blanket folded under his head, otherwise seeming
impervious to the stone. While Bothari dozed, Cordelia
kept careful count of the net flow of hunters. By mid-
afternoon, she calculated that some forty men had gone
below and not come up again.

Two men were brought out strapped to float pallets, loaded into a medical-evacuation lifter, and flown away. A lightflyer made a bad landing in the crowded area, toppled downslope, and crunched into a tree. Yet more men became involved in extracting, righting, and repairing it. By dusk over sixty men had been sucked down the drain. A whole company drawn away from the capital, not pursuing refugees, not available to root out the secrets of ImpMil . . . it wasn't enough to make a real difference, surely.

It's a start.

Cordelia and Bothari and Gregor slipped from the niche in the gloaming, cleared the ravines, and made their way silently through the woods. It was nearly full dark when they came to the edge of the trees and struck Kly's trail. As they crossed over the ridge edging the vale, Cordelia looked back. The area by the cave mouth was marked by searchlights, stabbing up through the mists. Lightflyers whined in and out of the site.

They dropped over the ridge and slithered down the slope that had so nearly killed her to climb, hanging on to Rose's stirrup two days ago. Fully five kilometers down the trail, in a rocky region of treeless scrub, Bothari came to an abrupt halt. "Sh. Milady, listen."

Voices. Men's voices, not far off, but strangely hollow. Cordelia stared into the darkness, but no lights moved. Nothing moved. They crouched beside the trail, senses straining.

Bothari crept off, head tilted, following his ears. After a few moments Cordelia and Gregor cautiously followed. She found Bothari kneeling by a striated outcrop. He motioned her closer.

"It's a vent," he announced in a whisper. "Listen."

The voices were much clearer now, sharp cadences, angry gutturals punctuated by swearing in two or three languages.

"Goddammit, I know we went left back at that third turn."

"That wasn't the third turn, that was the fourth."

"We re-crossed the stream."

"It wasn't the same friggin' stream, *sabaki!*"

"*Merde. Perdu!*"

"Lieutenant, you're an idiot!"

"Corporal, you're out of line!"

"This cold light's not going to last the hour. See, it's fading."

"Well, don't shake it up, you moron, when it glows brighter it goes faster."

"Give me that—!"

Bothari's teeth gleamed in the darkness. It was the first smile Cordelia had seen crack his face in months. Silently, he saluted her. They tiptoed softly away, into the chill of the Dendarii night.

Back on the trail, Bothari sighed deeply. "If only I'd had a grenade to drop down that vent. Their search parties would still be shooting at each other this time next week."

CHAPTER THIRTEEN

Four hours down the night trail, the distinctive black and white horse loomed out of the dark. Kly was a shadow aboard it, but his thick profile and battered hat were instantly recognizable.

"Bothari!" The name huffed from Kly's mouth. "We live. Grace of God."

Bothari's voice was flat. "What happened to you, Major?"

"I almost ran into one of Vordarian's squads at a cabin I was delivering mail to. They're actually trying to go over these hills house by house. Dosing everyone they meet with fast-penta. They must be bringing the drug in by the barrel."

"We expected you back last night," said Cordelia. She tried not to let her tone sound too accusing.

The felt hat bobbed as Kly gave her a weary nod of greeting. "Would've been, except for Vordarian's bloody patrol. I didn't dare let them question me. I spent a day and a night, dodging 'em. Sent my niece's husband to get you. But when he got to my place this morning, Vordarian's men were all over. I figured we'd lost everything. But when they were still all over by nightfall, I took heart. They wouldn't still be looking for you if they'd found you. Figured I'd better get my ass up here and do some scouting myself. This is beyond hope."

Kly turned his horse around, heading back down the trail. "Here, Sergeant, put the boy up."

"I can carry the boy. Think you'd better give m'lady a lift. She's about out."

Too true. It was a measure of Cordelia's exhaustion that she went willingly to Kly's horse. Between them, Bothari and Kly shoved her aboard, perched astraddle on the pinto's warm rump. They started off, Cordelia gripping the mailman's coat.

"What happened to you?" Kly asked in turn.

Cordelia let Bothari answer, in his short sentences made even shorter by his burdened stride, as he carried Gregor piggyback. When he got to a mention of the men heard down the vent, Kly barked a laugh, then clapped a hand over his mouth. "They'll be weeks getting out of there. Good work, Sergeant!"

"It was Lady Vorkosigan's idea."

"Oh?" Kly twisted around to glance back over his shoulder at Cordelia, clinging wanly.

"Aral and Piotr both seemed to think diversion worthwhile," Cordelia explained. "I gather Vordarian has limited reserves."

"You think like a soldier, m'lady." Kly sounded approving.

Cordelia wrinkled her brow in dismay. What an appalling compliment. The last thing she wanted was to start thinking like a soldier, playing their game by their rules. The hallucinatory military world-view was horribly infectious, though, immersed in it as she was now. *How long can I tread water?*

Kly led them on another two hours of night marching, striking out on unfamiliar trails. In deep pre-dawn dark they came to a shack, or house. It seemed to be of similar construction to Kly's place, but more extensive, with rooms built on and other rooms built on to the additions. A light from a tiny flame, some sort of greasy homemade candle, burned in a window.

An old woman in a nightgown and jacket, her grey hair in a braid down her back, came to the door and motioned them within. Another old man—but younger than Kly—took the horse out of sight toward a shed. Kly made to go with him.

"Is it safe here?" Cordelia asked dizzily. *Where is here?*

Kly shrugged. "They searched here day before yesterday. Before I sent for m' nephew-in-law. Checked it off clean."

The old woman snorted, surly memory in her eye.

"What with the caves, and all the unchecked homesteads, and the lake, it'll be a while before they get around to re-checking. They're still searching the lake bottom, I hear, they've flown in all kinds of equipment. It's as safe as any." He went off after his horse.

Meaning, as unsafe as any. Bothari was already taking his boots off. His feet must be bad. Her feet were a mess, her slippers walked to flinders, and Gregor's rag shoes utterly destroyed. She'd never felt so near the end of all endurance, bone-weary, blood-weary, though she'd done much longer hikes before. It was as if her truncated pregnancy had drained life itself out of her, to pass it on to another. She let herself be guided, fed bread and cheese and milk and put to bed in a little side room, herself on one narrow cot and drooping Gregor on another. She would believe in safety tonight the way Barrayaran children believed in Father Frost at Winterfair, true because she desperately wanted it to be.

The next day a raggedy boy of about ten appeared out of the woods, riding Kly's sorrel horse bareback with a rope halter. Kly made Cordelia, Gregor, and Bothari hide out of sight while he paid the boy off with a few coins, and Sonia, Kly's aged niece, packed him some sweet cakes to speed him on his way. Gregor peeked wistfully out the corner of one curtained window as the child vanished again.

"I didn't dare go myself," Kly explained to Cordelia. "Vordarian has three platoons of men up there now." A wheezing chuckle escaped him at some inner vision. "But the boy knows nothing but that the old mailman was sick and needed his re-mount."

"They didn't fast-penta that child, did they?"

"Oh, yes."

"They dared!"

Kly's black-stained lips compressed in sympathy with her outrage. "If he can't get hold of Gregor, Vordarian's coup is likely doomed. And he knows it. There's not much he wouldn't dare to do, at this point." He paused. "You can be glad fast-penta has replaced torture, eh?"

Kly's nephew-in-law helped him saddle up the sorrel, and buckle on the mailbags. The mailman adjusted his hat, and climbed up.

"If I don't keep my schedule, it will be near-impossible for the Gen'ral to contact me," he explained. "Got to go, I'm late already. I'll be back. You and the boy stay inside, out of sight, as much as you can, m'lady." He turned his horse toward the bare-branched woods. The animal blended quickly into the red-brown native scrub.

Cordelia found Kly's last advice all too easy to follow. She spent most of the next four days in her cot-bed. The dull silence of hours went by in a fog, a relapse into the frightening fatigue she'd experienced after the placental transfer operation and its near-lethal complications. Conversation provided no diversion. The hill-folk were as laconic as Bothari. It was the threat of fast-penta, Cordelia thought. The less you knew, the less you could tell. The old woman Sonia's eyes probed Cordelia curiously, but she never asked anything beyond, "You hungry?" Cordelia didn't even know her last name.

Baths. After the first one, Cordelia did not ask again. The old couple worked all afternoon to haul and heat enough water for herself and Gregor. Their simple meals were nearly as much labor. No *Pull Tab To Heat Contents* up here. Technology, a woman's best friend. Unless the technology appeared in the form of a nerve disruptor in the hand of some dead-eyed soldier hunting you down carelessly as an animal.

Cordelia counted over the days since the coup, since all hell had broken loose. What was happening in the larger world? What response from the space forces, from planetary embassies, from conquered Komarr? Would Komarr seize the chaos to revolt, or had Vordarian taken them by surprise too? *Aral, what are you doing out there?*

Sonia, though she asked no questions, would now and then return from outings and drop bits of local news. Vordarian's troops, headquartered in Piotr's residence, were close to abandoning the search of the lake bottom. Hassadar was sealed, but refugees escaped in a trickle; someone's children, smuggled out, had arrived to stay with relatives nearby. At Vorkosigan Surleau most of Piotr's armsmen's families had escaped except Armsman Vogti's wife and very aged mother, who had been taken away in a groundcar, no one knew where.

"And, oh yes, very strange," Sonia added. "They took Karla Hysopi. That hardly makes sense. She was only the widow of a retired regular Service sergeant, what use do they expect to make of her?"

Cordelia froze. "Did they take the baby, too?"

"Baby? Donnia didn't say about a baby. Grandchild, was it?"

Bothari was sitting by the window sharpening his knife on Sonia's kitchen whetstone. His hand paused in mid-stroke. He looked up to meet Cordelia's alarmed eyes. Beyond a tightening of his jaw his face did not change expression, yet the sudden increase of tension in his body made Cordelia's stomach knot. He looked back down at what he was doing, and took a longer, firmer stroke that hissed along the whetstone like water on coals.

"Maybe . . . Kly will know something more, when he comes back," Cordelia quavered.

"Belike," said Sonia doubtfully.

At last, on schedule, on the evening of the seventh day, Kly rode into the clearing on his sorrel horse. A few minutes later Armsman Esterhazy rode in behind him. He was dressed in hillman's togs, and his mount was a lean and spindle-shanked hill horse, not one of Piotr's big glossy beasts. They put their horses away and came in to a dinner Sonia had apparently fixed this night of Kly's rounds for eighteen years.

After dinner they pulled up chairs to the stone fireplace, and Kly and Esterhazy briefed Cordelia and Bothari in low tones. Gregor sat by Cordelia's feet.

"Since Vordarian has greatly widened his search area," Esterhazy began, "Count and Lord Vorkosigan have decided that the mountains are still the best place to hide Gregor. As the search radius grows enemy forces will be spread thinner and thinner."

"Locally, Vordarian's forces are still hunting up and down the caves," Kly put in. "There's about two hundred men still up there. But as soon as they finish finding each other, I expect they'll pull out. I hear they've given up on finding you in there, Milady. Tomorrow, Sire," Kly glanced down and addressed Gregor directly, "Armsman Esterhazy will take you to a new place, a lot like this one. You'll have a new name for a while, for pretend. And Armsman Esterhazy will pretend he's your da. Think you can do that?"

Gregor's hand tightened on Cordelia's skirt. "Will Lady Vorkosigan pretend she's my ma?"

"We're going to take Lady Vorkosigan back to Lord Vorkosigan, at Tanery Base Shuttleport." At Gregor's alarmed look Kly added, "There's a pony, where you're going. And goats. The lady there might teach you how to milk the goats."

Gregor looked doubtful, but did not fuss further, though the next morning as he was put up behind Esterhazy on the shaggy horse he looked near to tears.

Cordelia said anxiously, "Take care of him, Armsman."

Esterhazy gave her a driven look. "He's my Emperor, Milady. He holds my oath."

"He's also a little boy, Armsman. Emperor is . . . a delusion you all have in your heads. Take care of the Emperor for Piotr, yes, but you take care of Gregor for me, eh?"

Esterhazy met her eyes. His voice softened. "My little boy is four, Milady."

He did understand, then. Cordelia swallowed relief and grief. "Have you . . . heard anything from the capital? About your family?"

"Not yet," said Esterhazy bleakly.

"I'll keep my ears open. Do what I can."

"Thank you." He gave her a nod, not as retainer to his lady, but as one parent to another. No other word seemed necessary.

Bothari was out of earshot, having returned to the cabin to pack up their few supplies. Cordelia went to Kly's stirrup, as he prepared to swing his black and white horse about and lead Esterhazy and Gregor on their way. "Major. Sonia passed on a rumor that Vordarian's troops took Mistress Hysopi. Bothari had hired her to foster his baby girl. Do you know if they took Elena—the baby—too?"

Kly lowered his voice. "'Twas the other way around, as I have it. They went for the baby, Karla Hysopi raised hell, so they took her too even though she wasn't on the list."

"Do you know where?"

He shook his head. "Somewhere in Vorbarr Sultana. Belike your husband's Intelligence will know exactly, by now."

"Have you told the Sergeant yet?"

"His brother armsman told him, last night."

"Ah."

Gregor looked back over his shoulder at her as they rode away, until they were obscured from sight by the tree-boles.

For three days Kly's nephew guided them through the mountains, Bothari on foot leading Cordelia on a bony-hipped little hill horse with a sheepskin pad cinched to its back. On the third afternoon, they came to a cabin which sheltered a skinny youth who led them to a shed that held, wonder of wonders, a rickety lightflyer. He loaded up the backseat with Cordelia and six jugs of maple syrup. Bothari shook hands silently with Kly's nephew, who mounted the little horse and vanished into the woods.

Under Bothari's narrow eye, the skinny youth coaxed his vehicle into the air. Brushing treetops, they followed ravines and ridges up over the snow-frosted spine of the mountains and down the other side, out of Vorkosigan's District. They came at dusk to a little market town. The youth brought his flyer down in a side street. Cordelia and Bothari helped him carry his gurgling produce to a small grocer's shop, where he bartered the syrup for coffee, flour, soap, and power cells.

Upon returning to his lightflyer, they found that a battered groundtruck had pulled up and parked behind it. The youth exchanged no more than a nod with its driver, who hopped out and slid the door to the cargo bay aside for Bothari and Cordelia. The bay was a quarter full of fiber sacks of cabbages. They did not make very good pillows, though Bothari did his best to arrange Cordelia a nest of them as the truck rocked along above the dismally uneven roads. Bothari then sat wedged against the side of the cargo bay and compulsively polished the edge of his knife to molecular sharpness with a makeshift strop, a bit of leather he'd begged from Sonia. Four hours of this and Cordelia was ready to start talking to the cabbages.

The truck thumped to a halt at last. The door slid aside, and first Bothari then Cordelia emerged to find themselves in the middle of nowhere: a gravel-surfaced road over a culvert, in the dark, in the country, in an unfamiliar district of unknown loyalties.

"They'll pick you up at Kilometer Marker Ninety-six," the truck driver said, pointing to a white smudge in the dimness that appeared to be merely a painted rock.

"When?" asked Cordelia desperately. For that matter, who were *they*?

"Don't know." The man returned to his truck and drove off in a spray of gravel from the hoverfan, as if he were already pursued.

Cordelia perched on the painted boulder and wondered morbidly which side was going to leap out of the night first, and by what test she might tell them apart. Time

passed, and she entertained an even more depressed vision
of no one picking them up at all.

But at last a darkened lightflyer floated down out of the
night sky, its engines pitched to eerie near-silence. Its
landing feet crunched in the gravel. Bothari crouched
beside her, his useless knife gripped in his hand. But the
man awkwardly levering himself up out of the passenger
seat was Lieutenant Koudelka. "Milady?" he called uncertainly to the two human scarecrows. "Sergeant?" A breath
of pure delight puffed from Cordelia as she recognized the
pilot's blonde head as Droushnakovi. *My home is not a
place, it is people, sir. . . .*

With Bothari's hand on her elbow, at Koudelka's anxious gesture Cordelia fell gratefully into the padded
backseat of the flyer. Droushnakovi cast a dark look over
her shoulder at Bothari, wrinkled her nose, and asked,
"Are you all right, Milady?"

"Better than I expected, really. Go, go."

The canopy sealed, and they rose into the air. Vent fans
powered up, cycling filtered air. Colored lights from the
control interface highlighted Kou's and Drou's faces. A
technological cocoon. Cordelia glanced at systems readouts over Droushnakovi's shoulder, and then up through
the canopy; yes, dark shapes paced them, guardian military
flyers. Bothari saw them, too, his eyes narrowing in approval. Some fraction of tension eased from his body.

"Good to see you two—" some subtle cue of their body
language, some hidden reserve, kept Cordelia from adding
together again. "I gather you got that accusation about
the comconsole sabotage straightened out in good order?"

"As soon as we got the chance to stop and fast-penta
that guard corporal, Milady," Droushnakovi answered. "He
didn't have the nerve to suicide before questioning."

"He was the saboteur?"

"Yes," answered Koudelka. "He'd intended to escape
to Vordarian's troops when they arrived to capture us.
Vordarian apparently suborned him months ago."

"That accounts for our security problems. Or does it?"

"He passed information about our route, the day of

the sonic grenade attempt." Koudelka rubbed at his sinuses in memory.

"So it was Vordarian behind that!"

"Confirmed. But the guard doesn't seem to have known anything about the soltoxin. We turned him inside out. He wasn't a high-level conspirator, just a tool."

Nasty flow of thought, but, "Has Illyan reported in yet?"

"Not yet. Admiral Vorkosigan hopes he may be hiding in the capital, if he wasn't killed in the first fighting."

"Hm. Well, you'll be glad to know Gregor's all right—"

Koudelka held up an interrupting hand. "Excuse me, Milady. The Admiral ordered—you and the Sergeant are not to debrief anything about Gregor to anyone except Count Piotr or himself."

"All right. Damn fast-penta. How is Aral?"

"He's well, Milady. He ordered me to bring you up to date on the strategic situation—"

Screw the strategic situation, what about my baby? Alas, the two seemed inextricably intertwined.

"—and answer any questions you had."

Very well. "What about our baby? Pi—Miles?"

"We've heard nothing bad, Milady."

"What does that mean?"

"It means we've heard nothing," Droushnakovi put in glumly.

Koudelka shot her an irate look, which she shrugged off with a twitch of one shoulder.

"No news may be good news," Koudelka went on. "While it's true Vordarian holds the capital—"

"And therefore ImpMil, yes," said Cordelia.

"And he's publicizing names of hostages related to anyone in our command structure, there's been no mention of, of your child, in the lists. The Admiral thinks Vordarian simply doesn't realize that what went into the replicator was viable. Doesn't know what he's got."

"Yet," bit off Cordelia.

"Yet," Koudelka conceded reluctantly.

"All right. Go on."

"The overall situation isn't as bad as we feared at first.

Vordarian holds Vorbarr Sultana, his own District and its military bases, and he's put troops in Vorkosigan's District, but he only has about five district counts who are his committed allies. About thirty of the other counts were caught in the capital, and we can't tell their real allegiance while Vordarian holds guns to their heads. Most of the twenty-three remaining Districts have reiterated their oaths to my Lord Regent. Though a couple are waffling, who have relatives in the capital or who are in dicey strategic positions as potential battlefields."

"And the space forces?"

"I was just coming to them, yes, Milady. Over half of their supplies come up from the shuttleports in Vordarian's District. For the moment, they're still holding out for a clear result rather than moving in to create one. But they've refused to openly endorse Vordarian. It's a balance, and whoever can tip it their way first will start a landslide. Admiral Vorkosigan seems awfully confident." Cordelia was not sure from the lieutenant's tone if he altogether shared that confidence. "But then, he has to. For morale. He says Vordarian lost the war the hour Negri got away with Gregor, and the rest is just maneuvering to limit the losses. But Vordarian holds Princess Kareen."

"Doubtless one of the losses Aral is anxious to limit. Is she all right? Vordarian's goons haven't abused her?"

"Not as far as we know. She seems to be under house arrest in her own rooms in the Imperial Residence. Several of the more important hostages have been secluded there."

"I see." She glanced sideways in the dim cabin at Bothari, who did not change expression. She waited for him to ask after Elena, but he said nothing. Droushnakovi stared bleakly into the night, at the mention of Kareen.

Had Kou and Drou made up? They seemed cool, civil, all duty and on duty. But whatever surface apologies had passed, Cordelia sensed no healing in them. The secret adoration and will-to-trust was all gone from the blue eyes that now and then flicked from the control interface to the man in the passenger seat. Drou's glances were merely wary.

Lights glowed ahead on the ground, the spatter of a middle-sized city, and beyond it, the jumbled geometrics of a sprawling military shuttleport. Drou went through code-check after code-check, as they approached. They spiraled down to a pad that lit for them, peopled with armed guards. Their guard-flyers passed on overhead to their own landing zones.

The guards surrounded them as they exited the flyer, and escorted them as fast as Koudelka's pace would permit to a lift tube. They went down, took a slide-walk, and went down again through blast doors. Tanery Base clearly featured a hardened underground command post. Welcome to the bunker. And yet a throat-catching whiff of familiarity shook Cordelia for a terrifying moment of confusion and loss. Beta Colony did a lot better on the interior decorating than these barren corridors, but she might have descended to the utility level of some buried Betan city, safe and cool. . . . *I want to go home.*

There were three green-uniformed officers, talking in a corridor. One was Aral. He saw her. "Thank you, dismissed, gentlemen," he said in the middle of someone's sentence, then more consciously, "We'll continue this shortly." But they lingered to goggle.

He looked no worse than tired. Her heart ached to look at him, and yet . . . *Following you has brought me here. Not to the Barrayar of my hopes, but to the Barrayar of my fears.*

With a voiceless "Ha!" he embraced her, hard to him. She hugged him back. *This is a good thing. Go away, World.* But when she looked up the World was still waiting, in the form of seven watchers all with agendas.

He held her away, and scanned her anxiously up and down. "You look terrible, dear Captain."

At least he was polite enough not to say, You *smell* terrible. "Nothing a bath won't cure."

"That is not what I meant. Sickbay for you, before anything." He turned to find Sergeant Bothari first in line.

"Sir, I must report in to my lord Count," Bothari said.

"Father's not here. He's on a diplomatic mission from

me to some of his old cronies. Here, you, Kou—take Bothari and set him up with quarters, food chits, passes, and clothes. I'll want your personal report immediately I've seen to Cordelia, Sergeant."

"Yes, sir." Koudelka led Bothari away.

"Bothari was amazing," Cordelia confided to Aral. "No—that's unjust. Bothari was Bothari, and I shouldn't have been amazed at all. We wouldn't have made it without him."

Aral nodded, smiling a little. "I thought he would do for you."

"He did indeed."

Droushnakovi, taking up her old position at Cordelia's elbow the moment Bothari vacated it, shook her head in doubt, and followed along as Aral steered Cordelia down the corridor. The rest of the parade followed less certainly.

"Hear any more about Illyan?" Cordelia asked.

"Not yet. Did Kou brief you?"

"A sketch, enough for now. I don't suppose any more word's come in on Padma and Alys Vorpatril, then, either?"

He shook his head regretfully. "But neither are they on the list of Vordarian's confirmed captures. I think they're hiding in the city. Vordarian's side is leaking information like a sieve, we'd know if any arrest that important had happened. I can only wonder if our own arrangements are so porous. That's the trouble with these damned civil affrays, everybody has a brother—"

A voice from down the corridor hailed loudly, "Sir! Oh, sir!" Only Cordelia felt Aral flinch, his arm jerking under her hand.

An HQ staffer led a tall man in black fatigues with colonel's tabs on the collar toward them. "There you are, sir. Colonel Gerould is here from Marigrad."

"Oh. Good. I have to see this man now. . . ." Aral looked around hurriedly, and his eye fell on Droushnakovi. "Drou, please escort Cordelia to the infirmary for me. Get her checked, get her—get her everything."

The colonel was no HQ desk pilot. He looked, in fact, as if he'd just flown in from some front line, wherever the "front" was in this war for loyalties. His fatigues were dirty and wrinkled and looked slept-in, their smoke-stink eclipsing Cordelia's mountain-reek. His face was lined with fatigue. But he looked only grim, not beaten. "The fighting in Marigrad has gone house-to-house, Admiral," he reported without preamble.

Vorkosigan grimaced. "Then I want to hopscotch it. Come with me to the tactics room—*what* is that on your arm, Colonel?"

A wide piece of white cloth and a narrower strip of brown circled the officer's black upper left sleeve. "ID, sir. We couldn't tell who we were shooting at, up close. Vordarian's people are wearing red and yellow, 's as close as they could come to maroon and gold, I guess. That's supposed to be brown and silver for Vorkosigan, of course."

"That's what I was afraid of." Vorkosigan looked extremely stern. "Take it off. Burn it. And pass the word down the line. You already have a uniform, Colonel, issued to you by the Emperor. That's who you're fighting for. Let the traitors alter their uniforms."

The colonel looked shocked at Vorkosigan's vehemence, but, after a beat, enlightened; he stripped the cloth hastily from his arm and stuffed it in his pocket. "Right, sir."

Aral let go of Cordelia's hand with a palpable effort. "I'll meet you in our quarters, love. Later."

Later in the week, at this rate. Cordelia shook her head helplessly, took in one last view of his stocky form as if her intensity could somehow digitize and store him for retrieval, and followed Droushnakovi into Tanery Base's underground warren. At least with Drou, Cordelia was able to overrule Vorkosigan's itinerary and insist on a bath first. Almost as good, she found half a dozen new outfits in her correct size, betraying Drou's palace-trained good taste, waiting for her in a closet in Aral's quarters.

The base doctor had no charts; Cordelia's medical records were of course all behind enemy lines in Vorbarr Sultana at present. He shook his head and keyed up a new form on his report panel. "I'm sorry, Lady Vorkosigan. We'll simply have to begin at the beginning. Please bear with me. Do I understand correctly you've had some sort of female trouble?"

No, most of my troubles have been with males. Cordelia bit her tongue. "I had a placental transfer, let me see, three plus," she had to count it up on her fingers, "about five weeks ago."

"Excuse me, a what?"

"I gave birth by surgical section. It did not go well."

"I see. Five weeks post-partum." He made a note. "And what is your present complaint?"

I don't like Barrayar, I want to go home, my father-in-law wants to murder my baby, half my friends are running for their lives, and I can't get ten minutes alone with my husband, whom you people are consuming before my eyes, my feet hurt, my head hurts, my soul hurts . . . it was all too complicated. The poor man just wanted something to put in his blank, not an essay. "Fatigue," Cordelia managed at last.

"Ah." He brightened, and entered this factoid on his report panel. "Post-partum fatigue. This is normal." He looked up and regarded her earnestly. "Have you considered starting an exercise program, Lady Vorkosigan?"

CHAPTER FOURTEEN

"Who are Vordarian's men?" Cordelia asked Aral in frustration. "I've been running from them for weeks, but it's like I've only glimpsed them in a rearview mirror. Know your enemy and all that. Where does he get this endless supply of goons?"

"Oh, not endless." Aral smiled slightly, and took another bite of stew. They were—miracle!—alone at last, in his simple underground senior officer's apartment. Their supper had been brought in on a tray by a batman, and spread on a low table between them. Aral had then, to Cordelia's relief, ejected this hovering minion with a "Thank you, Corporal, that will be all."

Aral swallowed his bite and continued, "Who are they? For the most part, anyone who was caught with an officer up along his chain of command who elected Vordarian's side, and who hasn't worked up the nerve, or in some cases the wit, to either frag the officer or desert his unit and report in elsewhere. And obedience and unit cohesion is deeply inculcated in these men. 'When the going gets rough, stick to your unit' is literally drilled into them. So the unfortunate fact that their officer is leading them into treason makes clinging to their squad-brothers even more natural. Besides," he grinned bleakly, "it's only treason if Vordarian loses."

"And is Vordarian losing?"

"As long as I live, and keep Gregor alive, Vordarian cannot win." He nodded in conviction. "Vordarian is imputing crimes to me as fast as he can invent them. Most serious is the rumor he's floating that I've made away with Gregor and seek the Imperium for myself. I judge this a ploy to smoke out Gregor's hiding place. He knows that Gregor's not with me. Or he'd be tempted to lob a nuclear in here."

Cordelia's lips curled in aversion. "So does he want to capture Gregor, or kill him?"

"Kill only if he can't capture. I will, when the time is right, produce Gregor."

"Why not right now?"

He sat back with a tired sigh, and pushed away his tray with a few bites of stew and a ragged bread shred still left in his bowl. "Because I wish to see how many of Vordarian's forces I can woo back to my side before the denouement. Desert to me is not quite the right term . . . come over, maybe. I don't wish to inaugurate my second year of office with four thousand military executions. All below a certain rank can be given a blanket pardon on the grounds that they were oath-bound to follow their officers, but I want to save as many of the senior men as I can. Five district counts and Vordarian are doomed now, no hope for them. *Damn* him for starting this."

"What are Vordarian's troops doing? Is this a sitzkrieg?"

"Not quite. He's wasting a lot of his time and mine, trying to gain a couple of useless strong points, like the supply depot at Marigrad. We oblige and draw him in, or out. It keeps Vordarian's commanders occupied, and their minds off the real high ground, which are the space-based forces. If only I had Kanzian!"

"Have your intelligence people located him yet?" The admired Admiral Kanzian was one of the two men in the Barrayaran High Command whom Vorkosigan regarded as his superiors in strategy. Kanzian was an advanced space operations specialist; the space-based forces had great faith in him. "No horse manure stuck on *his* boots," was the way Kou had once expressed it, to Cordelia's amusement.

"No, but Vordarian doesn't have him either. He's vanished. Hope to God he wasn't caught in some stupid street cross-fire and is lying unidentified on a slab somewhere. What a waste that would be."

"Would going up help? To sway the space forces?"

"Why d'you think I'm troubling to hold Tanery Base? I've considered the pros and cons of moving my field HQ aboard ship. I think not yet; it could be misinterpreted as the first step in running away."

Running away. What a seductive thought. Far, far away from all this lunacy, till it was all reduced to the single dimension of a minor filler in some galactic news vid. But . . . run away from Aral? She studied him, as he sat back on the padded sofa, staring at but not seeing the remains of his supper. A weary middle-aged man in a green uniform, of no particular handsomeness (except perhaps for the sharp grey eyes); a hungry intellect at constant internal war with fear-driven aggression, each fueled by a lifetime crowded with bizarre experience, Barrayaran experience. *You should have fallen in love with a happy man, if you wanted happiness. But no, you had to fall for the breathtaking beauty of pain. . . .*

The two shall be made one flesh. How literal that ancient pious mouthing had turned out to be. One little scrap of flesh, prisoned in a uterine replicator behind enemy lines, bound them now like siamese twins. And if little Miles died, would that bond be slashed?

"What . . . what are we doing about Vordarian's hostages?"

He sighed. "That is the hard nut in the center. Stripped of everything else, as we are gradually doing, Vordarian still holds over twenty district counts and Kareen. And several hundred lesser folk."

"Such as Elena?"

"Yes. And the city of Vorbarr Sultana itself, for that matter. He could threaten to atomize the city, at the end, to get passage off-planet. I've toyed with the idea of dealing. Have him assassinated later. Can't just let him go free, it would be unjust to all those who've died already in loyalty to me. What burning could satisfy those betrayed souls? No.

"So we're planning various rescue-raid options, for the end. The moment when the shift in men and loyalties reaches critical mass, and Vordarian really starts to panic. Meanwhile we wait. In the end . . . I'll sacrifice hostages before I'll let Vordarian win." His unseeing stare was black, now.

"Even Kareen?" *All the hostages? Even the tiniest?*

"Even Kareen. She is Vor. She understands."

"The surest proof I am not Vor," said Cordelia glumly. "I don't understand any of this . . . stylized madness. I think you should all be in therapy, every last one of you."

He smiled slightly. "Do you think Beta Colony could be persuaded to send us a battalion of psychiatrists as humanitarian aid? The one you had that last argument with, perhaps?"

Cordelia snorted. Well, Barrayaran history did have a sort of weird dramatic beauty, in the abstract, at a distance. A passion play. It was close-up that the stupidity of it all became more palpable, dissolving like a mosaic into meaningless squares.

Cordelia hesitated, then asked, "Are we playing the hostage game?" She was not sure she wanted to hear the answer.

Vorkosigan shook his head. "No. That's been my toughest argument, all week, to look men in the eye who have wives and children up in the capital, and say No." He arranged his cutlery neatly on his tray, in its original pattern, and added in a meditative tone, "But they aren't looking widely enough. This is not, so far, a revolution, merely a palace coup. The population is inert, or rather, lying low, except for some informers. Vordarian is making his appeals to the elite conservatives, old Vor, and the military. The Count can't count. The new technoculture is producing plebe progressives as fast as our schools can crank them out. They are the majority of the future. I wish to give them some method besides colored armbands to distinguish the good guys from the bad guys. Moral suasion is a more powerful force than Vordarian suspects. What old Earth general said that the moral is to the physical as three to one? Oh, Napoleon, that was it. Too bad he didn't follow his own advice. I'd put it as five to one, for this particular war."

"But do your powers balance? What about the physical?"

Vorkosigan shrugged. "We each have access to enough weapons to lay Barrayar waste. Raw power is not really the issue. But my legitimacy is an enormous advantage, as long as weapons must be manned. Hence Vordarian's attempts to undercut that legitimacy with his accusations about my doing away with Gregor. I propose to catch him in his lie."

Cordelia shivered. "You know, I don't think I would care to be on Vordarian's side."

"Oh, there are still a few ways he could win. My death is entailed in all of them. Without me as a focus, the only Regent anointed by the late Ezar, what's to choose? Vordarian's claim is then as good as anyone's. If he killed me, and got possession of Gregor, or vice versa, he could conceivably consolidate from there. Till the next coup, and train of revolts and vengeance-killings rebounding into the indefinite future . . ." His eyes narrowed, as he contemplated this dark vision. "That's my worst nightmare. That this war won't stop if we lose, till another Dorca Vorbarra the Just arises to put an end to another Bloody Century. God knows when. Frankly, I don't see a man of that calibre among my generation."

Check your mirror, thought Cordelia somberly.

"Ah, so *that's* why you wanted me to see the doctor first," Cordelia teased Aral that night. The doctor, once Cordelia had adjusted a few of his confused assumptions, had examined her meticulously, changed his prescription from exercise to rest, and cleared her to resume marital relations, with caution. Aral merely grinned, and made love to her as if she were spun glass. His own recovery from the soltoxin was nearly complete, she judged from this. He slept like a rock, only warmer, till the comconsole woke them at dawn. There must have been some military conspiracy at work, for it not to have lit up before then. Cordelia pictured some understaffer confiding to Kou, "Yeah, let's let the Old Man get laid, maybe he'll mellow out. . . ."

Still, the miserable fatigue-fog lifted faster this time. Within a day, with Droushnakovi for escort, Cordelia was up and exploring her new surroundings.

She ran across Bothari in the base gymnasium. Count Piotr had not yet returned, so once he'd debriefed to Aral Bothari had no duties either. "Got to keep in training," he told her shortly.

"You been sleeping?"

"Not much," he said, and resumed his running. Compulsively, too long, far past the optimum effect-for-time-spent trade-off. He sweated to fill time and kill thought, and Cordelia silently wished him luck.

She caught up on the details of the war from Aral and Kou and the controlled newsvids. What counts were allied, who was known hostage and where, what units were deployed on each side and which were ripped apart and scattered to both; where fighting had taken place, what damages, which commanders had renewed oath . . . knowledge without power. No more, she judged, than her intellectualized version of Bothari's endless running; and even less useful for distracting her mind from unbroken concentration on all the horrors and disasters, past or impending, that she could presently do nothing about.

She preferred her military history with more temporal displacement. A century or two in the past, say. She imagined some cool future scholar looking through a time-telescope at her, and gave him a mental rude gesture. Anyway, she now realized, the military histories she'd read had left out the most important part; they never told what happened to people's babies.

No—they were all babies, out there. Every mother's son in a black uniform. One of Aral's reminiscences floated up in her memory, velvet voice rumbling, "It was about that time that soldiers started looking like children to me. . . ."

She pushed away from the vidconsole, and went to search the bathroom for medication for pain.

On the third day she passed Lieutenant Koudelka in a corridor, stumping along at a near run, his face flushed with excitement.

"What's up, Kou?"

"Illyan's here. And he's brought Kanzian with him!"

Cordelia followed him to a briefing room. Droushnakovi had to lengthen even her long stride to keep up. Aral, flanked by two staffers, sat with his hands clasped on the table before him, listening with utmost attention. Commander Illyan sat on the edge of the table, swinging one leg in rhythm to his voice. A bandage on his left arm was stained with yellow seepage. He was pale and dirty, but his eyes shone in triumph, gilded with a touch of fever. He wore civilian gear that looked as if it had been stolen out of someone's laundry, and then rolled downhill in.

An older man was sitting beside Illyan—a staffer handed the man a drink, which Cordelia recognized as a potassium-salts-laced fruit-flavored pick-me-up for the metabolically depleted. He tasted it dutifully, and made a face, looking as if he would have preferred some more old-fashioned revivifier such as brandy. Overweight and undertall, greying where he was not balding, Admiral Kanzian was not a very martial-looking man. He looked grandfatherly—though only if one's grandfather was a research professor. His face was held together with an intensity of intellect that seemed to give the term "military science" real clout. Cordelia had met him in uniform; his air of quiet authority seemed unaffected by civilian shirt and slacks that might have come from the same laundry basket as Illyan's.

Illyan was saying, "—and then we spent the next night in the cellar. Vordarian's squad came back the next morning, but—Milady!"

His grin of greeting was blunted by a flash of guilt, as he glanced to and away from her waist. She'd rather he kept piffling on, excited, about his adventures, but her arrival seemed to deflate him, ghost of his most notable failure at his banquet of victory.

"Wonderful to see you both, Simon, Admiral." They exchanged nods; Kanzian made to rise, but was unanimously waved back to his seat, which made his lip twist in bemusement. Aral signed her to sit next to him.

Illyan continued in a more clipped fashion. His past two weeks of hide-and-seek with Vordarian's forces seemed to parallel Cordelia's, though in the far more complex setting of the seized capital. But Cordelia recognized the familiar terrors under his plain words. He brought his tale swiftly up to the present moment. Kanzian nodded an occasional confirmation.

"Well done, Simon," said Vorkosigan when Illyan concluded. He nodded toward Kanzian. "Extremely well done."

Illyan smiled. "Thought you'd like it, sir."

Vorkosigan turned to Kanzian. "As soon as you feel able, I would like to brief you in the tac room, sir."

"Thank you, my lord. I've been out of communications—except for Vordarian's newscasts—since I escaped Headquarters. Though there was much to be deduced from what we did see. By the way, I commend your strategy of restraint. Good so far. But you're close to its limits."

"So I've sensed, sir."

"What's Jolly Nolly doing at Jumppoint Station One?"

"Not answering his tightbeam. Last week his understaffers were offering an amazing array of excuses, but their ingenuity finally dried up."

"Ha. I can just picture it. His colitis must be in wonderful form. I'll bet not all of those 'indisposeds' were lies. I think I should begin with a private chat with Admiral Knollys, just the two of us."

"I would appreciate that, sir."

"We will discuss the inevitabilities of time. And the defects of a potential commander who bases an entire strategy on an assassination he then does not succeed in carrying out." Kanzian frowned judgmentally. "Not well constructed, to let your whole war turn on one event. Vordarian always did have a tendency to pop off."

Cordelia, aside, caught Illyan's eye. "Simon. Did you pick up any information at all, while you were trapped in Vorbarr Sultana, about the Imperial Military Hospital? Vaagen and Henri's lab?" *My baby?*

Regretfully, he shook his head. "No, Milady." Illyan glanced in turn at Vorkosigan. "My lord, is it true about Captain Negri's death? We'd only had it from rumor, and Vordarian's propaganda broadcasts. Thought it might have been a lie."

"Negri is dead. Unfortunately." Vorkosigan grimaced.

Illyan sat upright in alarm. "And the Emperor, too?"

"Gregor is safe and well."

Illyan slumped again. "Thank God. Where?"

"Elsewhere," said Vorkosigan dryly.

"Oh. Quite, sir. Beg pardon."

"As soon as you've hit sickbay and the showers, Simon, I have some housecleaning chores for you," Vorkosigan continued. "I want to know just exactly how ImpSec was blindsided by Vordarian's coup. I have no wish to malign the dead—and God knows the man paid for his mistakes—but Negri's old personal system for running ImpSec, with all his little secret compartments shared only with Ezar, has to be taken completely apart. Every component, every man re-examined, before it's all put back together. That will be your first job as the new Chief of Imperial Security. Captain Illyan."

Illyan's face went from pale-tired to green-white. "Sir— you want me to step into *Negri's* shoes?"

"Shake them out, first," Vorkosigan advised dryly. "And with dispatch, if you please. I cannot produce the Emperor until ImpSec is again fit to guard him."

"Yes, sir." Illyan's voice was thin with his staggerment.

Kanzian levered out of his seat, shrugging off the help of an anxious staff officer. Aral squeezed Cordelia's hand under the table, and rose to accompany the nucleus of his new General Staff. As they all exited, Kou grinned over his shoulder at Cordelia and whispered, "Things are looking up, eh?"

She smiled bleakly back at him. Vorkosigan's words echoed in her head. *When the shift in men and loyalties reaches the critical point, and Vordarian starts to panic* . . .

The trickle of refugees appearing at Tanery Base became a steady stream, as the week wore on. The most spectacular after Kanzian was the breakout of Prime Minister Vortala from Vordarian's house arrest. He arrived with several wounded liveried men and a hair-raising tale of bribery, trickery, chase, and exchange-of-fire. Two lesser Imperial Ministers also turned up, one on foot. Morale rose with each notable addition; the base's atmosphere grew electric with anticipation of action. The question exchanged by staffers in corridors became not, "Who's come in?" but "Who's come in this morning?" Cordelia tried to appear cheered by it all, hugging her dread to her private mind. Vorkosigan grew both pleased and tenser.

As instructed, Cordelia rested a lot in Vorkosigan's quarters. All too soon she felt re-energized enough to start beating on the walls. She then tried varying the prescription with a few experimental push-ups and knee-bends (but not sit-ups). She was just contemplating the merits and drawbacks of going to join Bothari in the gym, when the comconsole chimed.

Koudelka's apprehensive face appeared over the vid plate. "Milady, m'lord requests you join him now in Briefing Room Seven. Something's come in he wants you to see."

Cordelia's stomach twisted. "All right. On my way."

An array of men were waiting in Briefing Room Seven, clustered around a vidconsole in low-voiced debate. Staffers, Kanzian, Minister Vortala himself. Vorkosigan looked up and gave her a brief, unfelt smile.

"Cordelia. I'd like your opinion on something that's come in."

Flattering, but, "What sort of something?"

"Vordarian's latest special report has a new twist. Kou, replay the vid, please."

Vordarian's propaganda broadcasts from the capital were mostly subjects for derision, among Vorkosigan's men. Their faces looked rather more serious, this time.

Vordarian appeared in what was recognizably one of the state rooms of the Imperial Residence, the formal and serene Blue Room. Ezar Vorbarra used to make his rare public pronouncements from that background. Vorkosigan frowned.

Vordarian, in full dress greens, was seated on an ivory silk sofa, Princess Kareen at his side. Her dark hair was pulled back severely from her oval face with jeweled combs. She wore a striking black gown, somber and formal.

Vordarian spoke only a few earnest words, invoking the viewers' attention. Then the vid cut away to the great chamber of the Council of Counts at Vorhartung Castle. The vid zoomed in on the Lord Guardian of the Speaker's circle, dressed in his full regalia. The vid did not show what, besides its own pickup, was aimed at the Lord Guardian's head, but something in his repeated looks, just to one side instead of directly at the focus, made Cordelia place a lethally armed man, or maybe a squad, in that unseen position.

The Lord Guardian raised a plastic flimsy, and began, "I quote—due to the—"

"Ah, slick!" murmured Vortala, and Koudelka paused the vid to say, "I beg your pardon, Minister?"

"The I-quote—he's just legally distanced himself from the words about to come off that flimsy and out his mouth. Didn't catch that, the first time. Good, Georgos, good," Vortala addressed the paralyzed figure. "Go on, Lieutenant, I didn't mean to interrupt."

The holovid image continued, "—vile murder of the child-Emperor Gregor Vorbarra, and betrayal of his sacred oaths by the would-be usurper Vorkosigan, the Council of Counts declares the false Regent faithless, outcast, stripped of powers and outlawed. This day the Council of Counts confirms Commodore Count Vidal Vordarian

as Prime Minister and acting Regent for Dowager-Princess
Kareen Vorbarra, forming an emergency caretaker government until such time as a new heir may be found and
confirmed by the Council of Counts and Council of
Ministers in full council assembled."

He continued with further legalities, as the vid panned
the chamber. "Freeze it, Koudelka," Vortala demanded.
His lips moved as he counted. "Ha! Not even one-third
present. He doesn't have near a quorum. Who does he
think he's fooling?"

"Desperate man, desperate measures," Kanzian murmured as the holo continued at Koudelka's touch.

"Watch Kareen," Vorkosigan said to Cordelia.

The holo cut back to Vordarian and the Princess.
Vordarian went on in such mealy terms, it took Cordelia
a moment to unravel the fact that in the phrase "personal
protector," Vordarian was announcing an engagement of
marriage. His hand closed earnestly over Kareen's, though
his eye contact was reserved for the holovid. Kareen lifted
her hand to receive a ring without changing her calm
expression in the slightest. The vid closed with solemn
music. The End. They were thankfully spared Betan-style
post-mortem commentary; apparently, nobody ever asked
the Barrayaran-in-the-street much of anything, at least
until major rioting raised the volume to a level no one
dared ignore.

"How would you analyze Kareen's reaction?" Aral asked
Cordelia.

Cordelia's brows rose. "What reaction? How, analyze?
She never said a word!"

"Just so. Does she looked drugged to you? Or under
compulsion? Or was that real assent? Is she duped by
Vordarian's propaganda, or what?" Frustrated, Vorkosigan
eyed the space where the woman's image had lately been.
"She's always been reserved, but that was the most
unreadable performance I've ever seen."

"Run it again, Kou," said Cordelia. She had him stop
at the best views of Kareen. She studied the frozen face,
scarcely less animate than when the holo was running.

"She doesn't look woozy or sedated. And her eyes don't look aside the way the Speaker's did."

"Nobody threatening her with a weapon?" Vortala guessed.

"Or perhaps she simply doesn't care," Cordelia suggested grimly.

"Assent, or compulsion?" Vorkosigan repeated.

"Maybe neither. She's been dealing with this sort of nonsense all her adult life . . . what do you expect of her? She survived three years of marriage with Serg, before Ezar sheltered her. She must be a bona fide expert in guessing what not to say and when not to say it."

"But to publicly submit to Vordarian—if she thinks he's responsible for Gregor's death . . ."

"Yes, what does she believe? If she truly thinks her son is dead—even if she doesn't believe you killed him— then all she has left to look out for is her own survival. Why risk that survival for some dramatic futility, if it won't help Gregor? What does she owe you, owe us, after all? We've all failed her, as far as she knows."

Vorkosigan winced.

Cordelia went on, "Vordarian's been controlling her access to information, surely. She may even be convinced he's winning. She's a survivor; she's survived Serg and Ezar, so far. Maybe she means to survive you and Vordarian both. Maybe the only revenge she thinks she'll ever get is to live long enough to spit on all your graves."

One of the staff officers muttered, "But she's Vor. She should have defied him."

Cordelia favored him with a glittery grin. "Oh, but you never know what any Barrayaran woman thinks by what she says in front of Barrayaran men. Honesty is not exactly rewarded, you know."

The staffer gave her an unsettled look. Drou smiled sourly. Vorkosigan blew out his breath. Koudelka blinked.

"So, Vordarian gets tired of waiting and appoints himself Regent," Vortala murmured.

"And Prime Minister," Vorkosigan pointed out in return. "Indeed, he swells."

"Why not go straight for the Imperium?" asked the staff officer.

"Testing the waters," said Kanzian.

"It's coming, later in the script," opined Vortala.

"Or maybe sooner, if we force his hand a bit," suggested Kanzian. "The last and fatal step. We must consider how to rattle him just a little more."

"Not much longer," Vorkosigan said firmly.

The ghostly mask of Kareen's face hung before Cordelia's mind's eye all that day, and returned at her waking the next morning. What did Kareen think? What did Kareen feel, for that matter? Perhaps she was as numb as the evidence suggested. Perhaps she was biding her time. Perhaps she was all for Vordarian. *If I knew what she believed, I'd know what she was doing. If I knew what she was doing, I'd know what she believed.*

Too many unknowns in this equation. *If I were Kareen* . . . Was this a valid analogy? Could Cordelia reason from herself to another? Could anyone? They had likenesses, Kareen and herself, both women, near in age, mothers of endangered sons. . . . Cordelia took Gregor's shoe from her meager pile of mountain souvenirs, and turned it in her hand. *Mama grabbed me back, but my shoe came off in her hand. I should have fastened it tighter.* . . . Maybe she should trust her own judgment. Maybe she knew exactly what Kareen was thinking.

When the comconsole chimed, close to the time of yesterday's call, Cordelia shot to answer it. A new broadcast from the capital, new evidence, something to break that circle of unreason? But the face that materialized over the vidplate was not Koudelka, but a stranger with Intelligence insignia on his collar.

"Lady Vorkosigan?" he began deferentially.

"Yes?"

"I'm Major Sircoj, duty-officer at the main portal. It's my job to screen everyone new reporting in, men who've left traitor-units and so on, and to collect any new intelligence they've brought with them. We had a man turn up half an hour ago who says he escaped the capital, who refuses to voluntarily debrief. We've confirmed his claim that he's had anti-interrogation conditioning—if we try to fast-penta him, it'll kill him. He keeps asking—actually, insisting—to speak with you. He could be an assassin."

Cordelia's heart pounded. She leaned into the holovid as if she might climb through it. "Did he bring anything with him?" she demanded breathlessly. "Like a canister, about half a meter high—lots of blinking lights, and big red letters on top that say This End Up? Looks mysterious as hell, guaranteed to send any security guard into fits—his name, Major!"

"He brought nothing but the clothes he's standing in. He's not in good shape. His name is Vaagen, Captain Vaagen."

"I'll be right there."

"No, Milady! The man is practically raving. Could be dangerous, I can't let you—"

She left him talking to an empty room. Droushnakovi had to break into a run to catch up with her. Cordelia made it to the main portal Security offices in less than seven minutes, and paused in the corridor to catch her breath. To catch her soul, that wanted to fly out her mouth. Calm. Calm. Raving apparently cut no ice with Sircoj.

She lifted her chin and entered the office. "Tell Major Sircoj that Lady Vorkosigan is here to see him," she told the clerk, who raised impressed brows and obediently bent to his comconsole.

Sircoj appeared in a few endless minutes—through *that* door, Cordelia mentally marked his route. "I must see Captain Vaagen."

"Milady, he could be dangerous," Sircoj began exactly where she'd cut him off before. "He could be programmed in some unexpected way."

Cordelia considered unexpectedly grabbing Sircoj by the throat and attempting to squeeze reason into him. Impractical. She took a deep breath. "What will you let me do? Can I at least see him on vid?"

Sircoj looked thoughtful. "That might be all right. A cross-check on our identification, and we can record. Very well."

He took her into another room, and keyed up a monitor viewer. Her breath blew out with a small moan.

Vaagen was alone in a holding room, pacing from wall to wall. He wore green uniform trousers and a brown-stained white shirt. He was terribly changed from the trim and energetic scientist she'd last seen in his lab at ImpMil. Both his eyes were ringed with red-purple blotches, one lid swollen nearly shut; the slit glowed a frightening blood-scarlet. He moved bent-over. Bathless, sleepless, swollen lips . . .

"You get a medtech for that man!" Cordelia realized she'd yelled when Sircoj jumped.

"He's been triaged. His condition is not life-threatening. We can start treating him just as soon as he's security-cleared," said Sircoj doggedly.

"Then you put him on-line with me," Cordelia said through set teeth. "Drou, go back to the office, call Aral. Tell him what's going on."

Sircoj looked worried at this, but stuck valiantly to his procedures. More endless seconds, while someone went back to the prison-area and took Vaagen to a comconsole.

His face came up over the plate at last; Cordelia could see her own face reflected in the passionate intensity in his. Connected at last.

"Vaagen! What happened?"

"Milady!" His hands clenched, trembling, as he leaned on them toward the vid pickup. "The idiots, the morons, the ignorant, stupid—" he sputtered into helpless obscenities, then caught his breath and began again, quickly, concisely, as if her image might be snatched away again at any moment.

"We thought we might be all right at first, after the first two days' fighting trailed off. We hid the replicator at ImpMil, but nobody came. We lay low, and took turns sleeping in the lab. Then Henri managed to smuggle his wife out of town, and we both stayed. We tried to continue the treatments in secret. Thought we might wait it out, wait till rescue. Things had to break, one way or another. . . .

"We'd almost stopped expecting them, but they came. Last—yesterday." He rubbed a hand through his hair as if seeking some connection between real-time and nightmare-time, where clocks ran crazy. "Vordarian's squad. Came looking for the replicator. We locked the lab, they broke in. Demanded it. We refused, refused to talk, they couldn't fast-penta either of us. So they beat us up. Beat him to *death*, like street scum, like he was nobody, all that intelligence, all that education, all that promise *wasted*, dropped by some mumbling moron swinging a gun butt. . . ." Tears were running down his face.

Cordelia stood white and stricken; bad, bad attack of defective deja vu. She'd played the lab scene in her head already a thousand times, but she'd never seen Dr. Henri dead on the floor, nor Vaagen beaten senseless.

"Then they ripped into the lab. Everything, all the treatment records. All Henri's work on burns, gone. They didn't have to do that. All gone for nothing!" His voice cracked, hoarse with fury.

"Did they . . . find the replicator? Dump it out?" She could see it; she had seen it over and over, spilling. . . .

"They found it, finally. But then they took it. And then let *me* go." He shook his head from side to side.

"Took it," she repeated stupidly. Why? What sense, to take the technology and not the techs? "And let you go. To run to us, I suppose. To give us the word."

"You have it, Milady."

"Where, do you suppose? Where did they take it?"

Vorkosigan's voice spoke beside her. "The Imperial Residence, most likely. All the best hostages are being kept there. I'll put Intelligence right on it." He stood, feet planted, grey-faced. "It seems we're not the only side turning up the pressure."

CHAPTER FIFTEEN

Within two minutes of Vorkosigan's arrival at main portal Security, Captain Vaagen was flat on a float pallet and on his way to the infirmary, with the top trauma doctor on the base being paged for rendezvous. Cordelia reflected bitterly on the nature of chain of command; all truth and reason and urgent need were not enough, apparently, to lend causal power to one outside that chain.

Further interrogation of the scientist had to wait on his medical treatment. Vorkosigan used the time to put Illyan and his department on the new problem. Cordelia used the time to pace in circles in the infirmary's waiting area. Droushnakovi watched her in silent worry, not so foolish as to offer up reassurances they both knew to be empty.

At last the trauma man emerged from surgery to announce Vaagen conscious and oriented enough for a brief—he emphasized the brief—questioning. Aral came, trailing Koudelka and Illyan, and they all trooped in to find Vaagen in an infirmary bed, with his eye patched and an IV running fluids and meds.

Vaagen's hoarse and weary voice added a few horrific

details, but nothing to change the word-picture he'd first given Cordelia.

Illyan listened with steady attention. "Our people at the Residence confirm," he reported when Vaagen ran down, depressed whisper trailing to silence. "The replicator was apparently brought in yesterday, and has been placed in the most heavily guarded wing, near Princess Kareen's quarters. Our loyalists don't know what it is, they think it's some kind of a device, maybe a bomb to take out the Residence and everyone in it in the final battle."

Vaagen snorted, coughed, and winced.

"Do they have anyone tending it?" Cordelia asked the question no one else had, so far. "A doctor, a medtech, anyone?"

Illyan frowned. "I don't know, Milady. I can try to find out, but every extra communication endangers our people up there."

"Mm."

"The treatment's interrupted anyway," Vaagen muttered. His hand fiddled with the edge of his sheet. "Bitched to hell."

"I realize you've lost your notes, but could you . . . reconstruct your work?" Cordelia asked diffidently. "If you got the replicator back, that is. Take up where you left off."

"It wouldn't be where we left off, by the time we got it back. And it wasn't all in my head. Some of it was in Henri's."

Cordelia took a deep breath. "As I recall, these Escobaran portable replicators run on a two-week service cycle. When did you last recharge the power, and change the filters and add nutrients?"

"Power cell's good for months," Vaagen corrected. "Filters are more of a problem. But the nutrient solution will be the first limiting factor it'll hit. At its hyped-up metabolic rate, the fetus would starve a couple of days before the system choked on its waste. Breakdown products might overload the filters pretty soon after lean-tissue metabolism began, though."

She avoided Aral's gaze and looked straight at Vaagen, who looked straight back with his one good eye, more than physical pain in his face. "And when did you and Henri last service the replicator?"

"The fourteenth."

"Less than six days left," Cordelia whispered, appalled.

"About . . . about that. What day is this?" Vaagen looked around in an uncharacteristic uncertainty that hurt Cordelia's heart to watch.

"The time limit applies only if it's not being properly taken care of," Aral put in. "The Residence physician, Kareen and Gregor's man—wouldn't he realize something was needed?"

"Sir," Illyan said, "the Princess's physician was reported killed in the first day's fighting at the Residence. Two cross-confirmations—I have to consider it certain."

"They could let Miles die out of sheer ignorance up there," Cordelia realized in dismay. "As well as on purpose." Even one of their own secret loyalists, under the heroic impression he was defusing a bomb, could be a menace to her child.

Vaagen twisted in his sheets. Aral caught Cordelia's eye, and jerked his head toward the door. "Thank you, Captain Vaagen. You have done us extraordinary service. Beyond duty."

"Screw duty," Vaagen muttered. "Bitched to hell . . . damned ignorant goons . . ."

They withdrew, to leave Vaagen to his unrestful recovery. Vorkosigan dispatched Illyan to his multiplied duties.

Cordelia faced Aral. "Now what?"

His lips were a flat, hard line, his eyes half-absent with calculation, the same calculations she was running, Cordelia guessed, complicated by a thousand added factors she could only imagine. He said slowly, "Nothing's changed, really. From before."

"It is changed. Whatever the difference there is between being in hiding, and being a prisoner. But why did Vordarian wait till now for this capture? If he was ignorant of Miles's existence before this, who told him of it? Kareen, maybe, when she decided to cooperate?"

Droushnakovi looked sick at this suggestion.

Aral said, "Maybe Vordarian's playing with us. Maybe he was always keeping the replicator in reserve, till he most needed a new lever."

"Our son. In reserve," Cordelia corrected. She stared into those half-there grey eyes, willing *See me, Aral!* "We have to talk about this." She towed him down the corridor to the nearest private room, a doctors' conference chamber, and turned up the lights. Obediently, he seated himself at the table, Kou at his elbow, and waited for her. She sat down opposite him. *We've always sat on the same side, before. . . .* Drou stood behind her.

Aral watched her warily. "Yes, Cordelia?"

"What's going on in your head?" she demanded. "Where are we, in this?"

"I . . . regret. In hindsight. Regret not sending a raid earlier. The Residence is a far more difficult fortress to penetrate right now than the military hospital, dangerous as a raid on ImpMil would have been. And yet . . . I could not change that choice. When men on my own staff were asked to wait and sweat, I could not risk men and expend resources for my private benefit. Miles's . . . position, gave me the power to demand their loyalty in the face of Vordarian's pressure. They knew I asked no risk of them and theirs I was unwilling to share myself."

"But now the situation's changed," Cordelia pointed out. "Now you aren't sharing the same risks. Their relatives have all the time there is. Miles has only six days, minus the time we spend arguing." She could feel that clock ticking, in her head.

He said nothing.

"Aral . . . in all our time here, what favor have I ever asked of you, of your official powers?"

A sad half-smile quirked across his lips, and vanished. His eyes were wholly on her, now. "Nothing," he whispered. They both sat tensely, leaning toward the other, his elbows planted and hands clasped near his chin, her hands out flat before her, controlled.

"I'm asking now."

"Now," he said after a long hesitation, "is an extremely delicate time, in the overall strategic situation. We are right now engaged in secret negotiations with two of Vordarian's top commanders to sell him out. The space forces are about to commit. We are on the verge of being able to shut Vordarian down without a major set-battle."

Cordelia's thought was diverted just long enough to wonder how many of Vorkosigan's commanders were secretly negotiating right now to sell *them* out. Time would tell. Time.

Vorkosigan continued, "If—*if* we bring this negotiation off as I wish, we will be in a position to rescue most of the hostages in one major surprise raid, from a direction Vordarian does not expect."

"I'm not asking for a big raid."

"No. But I'm telling you that a small raid, particularly if things went wrong, might seriously interfere with the success of the larger, later one."

"Might."

"Might." He tilted his head in concession to the uncertainty.

"Time?"

"About ten days."

"Not good enough."

"No. I will try to speed things up. But you understand—if I botch this chance, this timing, several thousand men could pay for my mistakes with their lives."

She understood clearly. "All right. Suppose we leave the armies of Barrayar out of this for the moment. Let me go. With maybe a liveried man or two, and pinpoint—downright hypodermic—secrecy. A totally private effort."

His hands slapped to the table, and he sputtered, "No! God, Cordelia!"

"Do you doubt my competence?" she asked dangerously. *I sure do.* Now was not the moment to admit this, however. "Is that 'Dear Captain' just a pet name for a pet, or did you mean it?"

"I have seen you do extraordinary things—"

You've also seen me fall flat on my face, so?

"—but you are not expendable. God. That really would make me terminally crazy. To wait, not knowing . . ."

"You ask that of me. To wait, unknowing. You ask it every day."

"You are stronger than I. You are strong beyond reason."

"Flattering. Not convincing."

His thought circled hers; she could see it in his knife-keen eyes. "No. No haring off on your own. I forbid it, Cordelia. Flat, absolutely. Put it right out of your mind. I cannot risk you both."

"You do. In this."

His jaw clamped; his head lowered. Message received and understood. Koudelka, sitting worriedly beside him, glanced back and forth between the two of them in consternation. Cordelia could sense the pressure of Drou's hand, white-tight on the back of her chair.

Vorkosigan looked like something being ground between two great stones; she had no desire to see him smeared to powder. In a moment, he would demand her word to confine herself to Base, to dare no risk.

She opened her hand, curving up on the tabletop. "I would choose differently. But no one appointed me Regent of Barrayar."

The tension ran out of him with a sigh. "Insufficient imagination." *A common failing, among Barrayarans, my love.*

Returning to Aral's quarters, Cordelia found Count Piotr in the corridor, just turning away from their door. He was quite changed from the exhausted wild man who'd left her on a mountain trail. Now he was dressed in the sort of quietly upper-class clothes favored by retired Vor lords and senior Imperial ministers; neat trousers, polished half-boots, an elaborate tunic. Bothari loomed at his shoulder, once again costumed in his formal brown-and-silver livery. Bothari carried a thick coat folded over his arm, by which Cordelia deduced Piotr had just blown in from his diplomatic mission to some fellow District count to the wintery north of Vordarian's holdings. Vorkosigan's people certainly seemed to be able to move at will now, outside the heartlands held by Vordarian.

"Ah. Cordelia." Piotr gave her a formal, cautious nod; not reopening hostilities here. That was fine with Cordelia. She was not sure she had any will to fight left in her gnawed-out heart.

"Good day, sir. Was your trip a success?"

"Indeed it was. Where is Aral?"

"Gone to Sector Intelligence, I believe, to consult with Illyan about the most recent reports from Vorbarr Sultana."

"Ah? What's happening?"

"Captain Vaagen turned up at our door. He'd been beaten half-senseless, but he still somehow made it from the capital—it seems Vordarian finally woke up to the fact that he had another hostage. His squad looted Miles's replicator from ImpMil, and took it back to the Imperial Residence. I expect we'll hear more from him soon about it, but he's doubtless waited to give us the full pleasure of Captain Vaagen's tale, first."

Piotr threw back his head in a sharp, bitter laugh. "Now *there's* an empty threat."

Cordelia unclenched her jaw long enough to say, "What do you mean, sir?" She knew perfectly well what he meant, but she wanted to see him run to his limit. *All the way, damn you; spit it all out.*

His lips twitched, half frown, half smile. "I mean Vordarian inadvertently offers House Vorkosigan a service. I'm sure he doesn't realize it."

You wouldn't say that if Aral were standing here, old man. Did you set this up? God, she couldn't say that to him—"Did you set this up?" Cordelia demanded tightly.

Piotr's head jerked back. "I don't deal with traitors!"

"He's of your Old Vor party. Your true allegiance. You always said Aral was too damned progressive."

"You dare accuse me—!" His outrage edged into plain rage.

Her rage was shadowing her vision with red. "I know you are an attempted murderer, why not an attempted traitor, too? I can only hope your incompetence holds good."

His voice was breathy with fury. "Too far!"

"No, old man. Not nearly far enough."

Drou looked absolutely terrorized. Bothari's face was a stony blank. Piotr's hand twitched, as if he wanted to strike her. Bothari watched that hand, his eyes glittering oddly, shifting.

"While dumping that mutant out of its can is the best favor Vidal Vordarian could do me, I am hardly likely to let him know it," Piotr bit out. "It will be far more amusing to watch him try to play a joker as if it were an ace, and then wonder what went wrong. Aral knows—I imagine he's relieved as hell, to have Vordarian do his job for him. Or have you bewitched him into planning something spectacularly stupid?"

"Aral's doing nothing."

"Oh, good boy. I was wondering if you'd stolen his spine permanently. He is Barrayaran after all."

"So it seems," she said woodenly. She was shaking. Piotr was not in much better case.

"This is a side-issue," he said, as much to himself as her, trying to regain his self-control. "I have major issues to pursue with the Lord Regent. Farewell, Milady." He tilted his head in ironic effort, and turned away.

"Have a nice day," she snarled to his back, and flung herself through the door into Aral's quarters.

She paced for twenty minutes, back and forth, before she trusted herself enough to speak even to Drou, who had squeezed into a corner seat as if trying to make herself small.

"You don't really think Count Piotr is a traitor, do you, Milady?" Droushnakovi asked, when Cordelia's steps finally slowed.

Cordelia shook her head. "No . . . no. I just wanted

to hurt him back. This place is getting to me. Has gotten to me." Wearily, she sank into a seat and leaned her head back against the padding. After a silence she added, "Aral's right. I have no right to risk. No, that's not quite correct. I have no right to *failure*. And I don't trust myself anymore. I don't know what's happened to my edge. Lost it in a strange land." *I can't remember. Can't remember how I did it.* She and Bothari were twins, right enough, two personalities separately but equally crippled by an overdose of Barrayar.

"Milady . . ." Droushnakovi plucked at her skirts, looking down into her lap. "I was in Imperial Residence Security for three years."

"Yes . . ." Her heart lurched, gulped. As an exercise in self-discipline, Cordelia closed her eyes and did not open them again. "Tell me about that, Drou."

"Negri trained me himself. Because I was Kareen's body servant, he always said I would be the last barrier between Kareen and Gregor and—and anything that was bad enough to get that far. He showed me everything about the Residence. He used to drill me about it. He showed me things I don't think he showed anybody else. We had five emergency escape routes worked out, in our disaster drills. Two of them were common Security procedure. One of them he showed only to a few top staffers like Illyan. The other two—I don't know that anybody knew about them but Negri and Emperor Ezar. And I'm thinking . . ." she moistened her lips, "a secret route out of something ought to be an equally secret route in. Don't you think?"

"Your reasoning interests me extremely, Drou. As Aral might say. Go on." Cordelia still did not open her eyes.

"That's about it. If I could somehow get to the Residence, I bet I could get in. If Vordarian's just taken over all the standard Security arrangements and beefed them up."

"And get back out?"

"Why not?"

Cordelia found she had to remember to breathe. "Who do you work for, Drou?"

"Captain—" she started to answer, but slowed self-consciously. "Negri. But he's dead. Commander—Captain Illyan, now, I suppose."

"Let me rephrase that." Cordelia opened her eyes at last. "Who did you put your life on the line for?"

"Kareen. And Gregor, of course. They were kind of the same thing."

"Still are. This mother bets." She caught Drou's blue gaze. "And Kareen gave you to me."

"To be my mentor. We thought you were a soldier."

"Never. But that doesn't mean I never fought." Cordelia paused. "What do you want to trade for, Drou? Your life in my hand—I shall not say oath-sworn, that's for those other idiots—for what?"

"Kareen," Droushnakovi answered steadily. "I've watched them, here, gradually reclassifying her as expendable. Every day for three years, I put my life on the line because I believed that her life was important. You watch someone that closely for that long, you don't have too many illusions about her. Now they seem to think I should just switch off my loyalty, like some guard-machine. There's something wrong with that. I want to—to at least try for Kareen. In exchange for that—whatever you will, Milady."

"Ah." Cordelia rubbed her lips. "That seems . . . equitable. One expendable life for another. Kareen for Miles." She sank down in the chair in deep meditation.

First you see it. Then you do it. "It's not enough." Cordelia shook her head at last. "We need . . . someone who knows the city. Someone with muscle, for backup. A weapons-man, a sleepless eye. I need a friend." The corners of her lips turned up in a very small smile. "Closer than a brother." She rose and walked to the comconsole.

"You asked to see me, Milady?" said Sergeant Bothari. "Yes. Please come in."

Senior officers' quarters did not intimidate Bothari, but his brow furrowed nonetheless as Cordelia gestured him to a seat. She took Aral's usual spot across the low table from him. Drou sat again in the corner, watching in reserved silence.

Cordelia regarded Bothari, who regarded her in return. He looked all right physically, though his face was grooved with tension. She sensed, as with a third eye, frustrated energies coursing through his body; arcs of rage, nets of control, a tangled electric knot of dangerous sexuality under it all. Reverberating energies, building up and up without release, in desperate need of ordered action lest they break out wildly on their own. She blinked, and refocused on his less terrifying surface; a tired-looking ugly man in an elegant brown uniform.

To her surprise, Bothari began. "Milady. Have you heard anything new about Elena?"

Wondering why I called you here? To her shame, she had almost forgotten Elena. "Nothing new, I'm afraid. She is reported being kept along with Mistress Hysopi in that downtown hotel that Vordarian's Security commandeered when they ran out of cells, with a lot of other second- and third-tier hostages. She hasn't been moved to the Residence or anything." Elena was not, unlike Kareen, in the direct line of Cordelia's secret mission. If he asked, how much dare she promise?

"I was sorry to hear about your son, Milady."

"My mutant, as Piotr would say." She watched him; she could read his shoulders and spine and gut better than that blank beaky face.

"About Count Piotr," he said, and stopped. His hands hooked each other, between his knees, and flexed. "I had thought to speak to the admiral. I hadn't thought to speak to you. I should have thought of you."

"Always." Now what?

"Man came up to me yesterday. In the gym. Not in uniform, no rank or nametag. He offered me Elena. Elena's life, if I would assassinate Count Piotr."

"How tempting," Cordelia choked, before she could stop herself. "What, uh, guarantees did he offer?"

"That question came to me, pretty shortly. There I would be, in deep shit, maybe executed, and who would care for a, a dead man's bastard then? I figured it for a cheat, just another cheat. I went back to look for him, been on the lookout, but I never spotted him since." He sighed. "It almost seems like a hallucination, now."

The expression on Drou's face was a study in the deepest unreassurance, but fortunately Bothari was turned away from her and did not notice. Cordelia shot her a small quelling frown.

"Have you been having hallucinations?" Cordelia asked.

"I don't think so. Just bad dreams. I try not to sleep."

"I . . . have a dilemma of my own," Cordelia said. "As you heard me tell Piotr."

"Yes, Milady."

"Had you heard about the time limit?"

"Time limit?"

"If it's not serviced, the replicator will start to fail to support Miles in less than six days. Aral argues that Miles is in no more danger than any of his staffers' families. I disagree."

"Behind his back, I've heard some say otherwise."

"Ah?"

"They say it's a cheat. The admiral's son is some sort of mutant, non-viable, while they risk whole children."

"I don't think he realizes . . . anyone says that."

"Who would repeat it to his face?"

"Very few. Maybe not even Illyan." Though Piotr probably wouldn't fail to pass it on, if he picked it up. "Dammit! No one, on either side, would hesitate to dump that replicator." She brooded, and began again. "Sergeant. Who do you work for?"

"I am oath-sworn Armsman to Count Piotr," Bothari recited the obvious. He was watching her closely now, a weird smile tugging at one corner of his mouth.

"Let me rephrase that. I know the official penalties for an armsman going AWOL are fearsome. But suppose—"

"Milady." He held up a hand; she paused in mid-breath. "Do you remember, back on the front lawn at Vorkosigan Surleau when we were loading Negri's body into the

lightflyer, when my Lord Regent told me to obey your
voice as his own?"

Cordelia's brows went up. "Yes . . . ?"

"He never countermanded that order."

"Sergeant," she breathed at last, "I'd never have
guessed you for a barracks-lawyer."

His smile grew a millimeter tighter. "Your voice is as
the voice of the Emperor himself. Technically."

"Is it, now," she whispered in delight. Her nails dug
into her palms.

He leaned forward, his hands now held rock-still
between his knees. "So, Milady. What were you saying?"

The motor pool staging bay was an echoing low vault,
its shadows slashed by the lights from a glass-walled office.
Cordelia stood waiting in the darkened lift tube portal,
Drou at her shoulder, and watched through the distant
rectangle of glass as Bothari negotiated with the transport officer. General Vorkosigan's Armsman was signing
out a vehicle for his oath-lord. The passes and IDs Bothari
had been issued apparently worked just fine. The motor
pool man fed Bothari's cards to his computer, took
Bothari's palm print on his sensor-pad, and dispatched
orders with snap and hustle.

Would this simple plan work? Cordelia wondered desperately. And if it didn't, what alternative had they? Their
planned route sketched itself in her mind, red light-lines
snaking over a map. Not north toward their goal, but due
south first, by groundcar into the next loyal District. Ditch
the distinctive government vehicle, take the monorail west
to yet another District, then northwest to another; then
due east into Count Vorinnis's neutral zone, focus of so
much diplomatic attention from both sides. Piotr's comment echoed in her memory, "I swear, Aral, if Vorinnis
doesn't quit trying to play both ends against the middle,
you ought to hang him higher than Vordarian when this
is over." Then into the capital District itself, then, somehow, into the sealed city. A daunting number of kilometers to cover. Three times the distance of the direct route.

So much time. Her heart swung north like a compass needle.

The first and last Districts would be the worst. Aral's forces could be almost more inimical to this excursion than Vordarian's. Her head spun with the cumulative impossibility of it all.

Step by step, she told herself firmly. One step at a time. Just get off Tanery Base; that, they could do. Divide the infinite future into five-minute blocks, and take them one by one.

There, the first five minutes down already, and a swift and shining general staff car appeared from underground storage. A small victory, in reward for a little patience and daring. What might great patience and daring yet bring?

Judiciously, Bothari inspected the vehicle, as if in doubt that it was quite fit for his master. The transport officer waited anxiously, and seemed to deflate with relief when the great general's Armsman, after running his hand over the canopy and frowning at some minute speck of dust, gave it a grudging acceptance. Bothari brought the vehicle around to the lift tube portal and parked it, neatly blocking the office's view of the entering passengers.

Drou bent to pick up their satchel, packed with a very odd variety of clothing including Bothari's and Cordelia's mountain souvenirs, and their thin assortment of weapons. Bothari set the polarization on the rear canopy to mirror-reflection, and raised it.

"Milady!" Lieutenant Koudelka's anxious voice called from the lift tube entry behind them. "What are you doing?"

Cordelia's teeth closed on vile words. She converted her savage expression to a light, surprised smile, and turned. "Hello, Kou. What's up?"

He frowned, looking at her, at Droushnakovi, at the satchel. "I asked first." He was out of breath; he must have been chasing them down for some minutes, after not finding her in Aral's quarters. An ill-timed errand.

Cordelia kept her smile fixed, as her mind blinked on a vision of a Security team piling out of the lift tube to arrest her, or at least her plans. "We're . . . going into town."

His lips thinned in skepticism. "Oh? Does the Admiral know? Where's Illyan's outer-perimeter team, then?"

"Gone on ahead," said Cordelia blandly.

The vague plausibility actually raised a flicker of doubt in his eyes. Alas, only for a moment. "Now, wait just a bloody minute—"

"Lieutenant," Sergeant Bothari interrupted. "Take a look at this." He gestured toward the rear passenger compartment of the staff car.

Koudelka leaned to look. "What?" he said impatiently.

Cordelia winced as Bothari's open hand chopped down across the back of Koudelka's neck, and winced again at the heavy *thud* of Koudelka's head hitting the far side of the compartment's interior after a powerful boost-assist to neck and belt by Bothari. His swordstick clattered to the pavement.

"In." Bothari's voice was a strained low growl, accompanied by a quick glance across the bay toward the glass-walled transport office.

Droushnakovi flung the satchel into the compartment and dove in after Koudelka, shoving his long loose limbs out of the way. Cordelia grabbed up the stick and piled in after. Bothari stood back, saluted, closed the mirrored canopy, and entered the driver's compartment.

They started smoothly. Cordelia had to control irrational panic as Bothari stopped at the first checkpoint. She could see and hear the guards so clearly, it was difficult to remember they saw only the reflections of their own hard eyes. But apparently General Piotr could indeed pass anywhere at will. How pleasant, to be General Piotr. Though in these trying times, probably not even Piotr could have entered Tanery Base without that rear canopy being opened and scanned. The final gate crew that waved them out was busily engaged in just such an inspection of a large incoming convoy of freight haulers. Their timing was just as Cordelia had planned and prayed.

Cordelia and Droushnakovi finally got the sprawling

Koudelka straightened up between them. His first alarming flaccidity was passing off. He blinked and moaned. Koudelka's head, neck, and upper torso were of the few areas of his body not rewired; Cordelia trusted nothing inorganic was broken.

Droushnakovi's voice was taut with worry. "What'll we do with him?"

"We can't dump him out on the road, he'd run back and give the word," said Cordelia. "Yet if we cinched him to a tree out of sight somewhere, there's a chance he might not be found . . . we'd better tie him up, he's coming around."

"I can handle him."

"He's had enough handling, I'm afraid."

Droushnakovi managed to immobilize Koudelka's hands with a twisted scarf from the satchel; she was quite good at clever knots.

"He might prove useful," mused Cordelia.

"He'll betray us," frowned Droushnakovi.

"Maybe not. Not once we're in enemy territory. Once the only way out is forward."

Koudelka's eyes stopped jerking, following some invisible starry blur, and came at last into focus. Both his pupils were still the same size, Cordelia was relieved to note.

"Milady—Cordelia," he croaked. His hands yanked futilely at the silky bonds. "This is crazy. You'll run right into Vordarian's forces. And then Vordarian will have two handles on the Admiral, instead of just one. And you and Bothari know where the Emperor is!"

"Was," corrected Cordelia. "A week ago. He's been moved since then, I'm sure. And Aral has demonstrated his capacity to resist Vordarian's leverage, I think. Don't underestimate him."

"Sergeant Bothari!" Koudelka leaned forward, appealing into the intercom. The front canopy was also silvered, now.

"Yes, Lieutenant?" Bothari's bass monotone returned.

"I order you to turn this vehicle around."

A slight pause. "I'm not in the Imperial Service any-more, sir. Retired."

"Piotr didn't order this! You're Count Piotr's man."

A longer pause; a lower tone. "No. I am Lady Vorkosigan's dog."

"You're off your meds!"

How such could travel over a purely audio link Cordelia was not sure, but a canine grin hung in the air before them.

"Come on, Kou," Cordelia coaxed. "Back me. Come for luck. Come for life. Come for the adrenaline rush."

Droushnakovi leaned over, a sharp smile on her lips, to breathe in Koudelka's other ear, "Look at it this way, Kou. Who else is ever going to give you a chance at field combat?"

His eyes shifted, right and left, between his two cap-tors. The pitch of the groundcar's power-whine rose, as they arrowed into the growing twilight.

CHAPTER SIXTEEN

Illegal vegetables. Cordelia sat in bemused contemplation between sacks of cauliflower and boxes of cultivated
brillberries as the creaking hovertruck coughed along.
Southern vegetables, that flowed toward Vorbarr Sultana
on a covert route just like hers. She was half-certain that
under that pile were a few sacks of the same green cabbages she'd traveled with two or three weeks ago, migrat-
ing according to the strange economic pressures of the
war.

The Districts controlled by Vordarian were now under
strict interdiction by the Districts loyal to Vorkosigan.
Though starvation was still a long way off, food prices in
the capital of Vorbarr Sultana had skyrocketed, in the face
of hoarding and the coming winter. So poor men were
inspired to take chances. And a poor man already taking
a chance was not averse to adding a few unlisted passengers to his load, for a bribe.

It was Koudelka who'd generated the scheme, abandoning his urgent disapproval, drawn in to their
strategizing almost despite himself. It was Koudelka who'd
found the produce wholesale warehouses in the town in
Vorinnis's District, and cruised the loading docks for

independents striking out with their loads. Though it was
Bothari who'd ruled the size of the bribe, pitifully small
to Cordelia's mind, but just right for the parts they now
played of desperate countryfolk.

"My father was a grocer," Koudelka had explained
stiffly, when selling his scheme to them. "I know what
I'm doing."

Cordelia had puzzled for a moment what his wary
glance at Droushnakovi meant, till she recalled Drou's
father was a soldier. Kou had talked of his sister and
widowed mother, but it was not till that moment that
Cordelia realized Kou had edited his father from his
reminiscences out of social embarrassment, not any lack
of love between them. Koudelka had vetoed the choice
of a meat truck for transport: "It's more likely to be
stopped by Vordarian's guards," he'd explained, "so they
can shake down the driver for steaks." Cordelia wasn't sure
if he was speaking from military or food service experience, or both. In any case, she was grateful not to ride
with grisly refrigerated carcasses.

They dressed for their parts as best they could, pool-
ing the satchel and the clothes they stood in. Bothari and
Koudelka played two recently discharged vets, looking to
better their sorry lot, and Cordelia and Drou two
countrywomen co-scheming with them. The women were
decked in a realistically odd combination of worn mountain dress and upper-class castoffs apparently acquired
from some secondhand shop. They managed the right
touch of mis-fittedness, of women not wearing originals,
by trading garments.

Cordelia's eyes closed in exhaustion, though sleep was
far from her. Time ticked in her brain. It had taken them
two days to get this far. So close to their goal, so far from
success . . . Her eyes snapped open again when the truck
halted and thumped to the ground.

Bothari eased through the opening to the driver's
compartment. "We get out here," he called lowly. They
all filed through, dropping to the city curb. Their breath
smoked in the chill. It was pre-dawn dark, with fewer

lights about than Cordelia thought there ought to be. Bothari waved the transport on.

"Didn't think we should ride all the way in to the Central Market," Bothari grunted. "Driver says Vorbohn's municipal guards are thick there this time of day, when the new stocks come in."

"Are they anticipating food riots?" Cordelia asked.

"No doubt, plus they like to get theirs first," said Koudelka. "Vordarian's going to have to put the army in soon, before the black market sucks all the food out of the rationing system." Kou, in the moments he forgot to pretend himself an artificial Vor, displayed an amazing and detailed grasp of black-market economics. Or, how *had* a grocer bought his son the education to gain entry to the fiercely competitive Imperial Military Academy? Cordelia grinned under her breath, and looked up and down the street. It was an old section of town, pre-dating lift tubes, no buildings more than six flights high. Shabby, with plumbing and electricity and light-pipes cut into the architecture, added as afterthoughts.

Bothari led off, seeming to know where he was going. The maintenance did not improve, in their direction of transit. Streets and alleys narrowed, channeling a moist aroma of decay, with an occasional whiff of urine. Lights grew fewer. Drou's shoulders hunched. Koudelka gripped his stick.

Bothari paused before a narrow, ill-lit doorway bearing a hand-lettered sign, *Rooms*. "This'll do." The door, an ancient non-automatic that swung on hinges, was locked. He rattled it, then knocked. After a long time, a little door within the door opened, and suspicious eyes stared out.

"Whatcha want?"

"Room."

"At this hour? Not damned likely."

Bothari pulled Drou forward. The stripe of light from the opening played over her face.

"Huh," grunted the door-muffled voice. "Well . . ." Some clinking of chains, the grind of metal, and the door swung open.

They all huddled in to a narrow hallway featuring stairs, a desk, and an archway leading back to a darkened chamber. Their host grew even grumpier when he learned they desired only one room among the four of them. Yet he did not question it; apparently their real desperation lent their pose of poverty a genuine edge. With the two women and especially Koudelka in the party, no one seemed to leap to identify them as secret agents.

They settled into a cramped, cheap upstairs room, giving Kou and Drou first shot at the beds. As dawn seeped through the window, Cordelia followed Bothari back downstairs to forage.

"I should have realized we'd need to bring rations, to a city under siege," Cordelia muttered.

"It's not that bad yet," said Bothari. "Ah—best you don't talk, Milady. Your accent."

"Right. In that case, strike up a conversation with this fellow, if you can. I want to hear the local view of things."

They found the innkeeper, or whatever he was, in the little room beyond the archway, which, judging from a counter and a couple of battered tables with chairs, doubled as a bar and a dining room. The man reluctantly sold them some seal-packed food and bottled drinks at inflated prices, while complaining about the rationing and angling for information about them.

"I been planning this trip for months," said Bothari, leaning on the bar, "and the damned war's bitched it."

The innkeep made an encouraging noise, one entrepreneur to another. "Oh? What's your strat?"

Bothari licked his lips, eyes narrowing in thought. "You saw that blonde?"

"Yo?"

"Virgin."

"No way. Too old."

"Oh, yeah. She can pass for class, that one. We were gonna sell it to some Vor lord at Winterfair. Get us a grubstake. But they've all skipped town. Could try for a rich merchant, I guess. But she won't like it. I promised her a real lord."

Cordelia hid her mouth behind her hand, and tried not to emit any attention-drawing noises. It was an excellent thing Drou was not there to learn Bothari's idea of a cover story. Good God. Did Barrayaran men actually pay for the privilege of committing that bit of sexual torture upon uninitiated women?

The 'keep glanced at Cordelia. "You leave her alone with your partner without her duenna, you could lose what you came to sell."

"Naw," said Bothari. "He would if he could, but he took a nerve-disruptor bolt, once. Below the belt, like. He's out on medical discharge."

"What're you out on?"

"Discharged without prejudice."

This was a code-phrase for, Quit or be housed in the stockade, as Cordelia understood it, the ultimate fate of chronic troublemakers who fell just, but only just, short of felony.

"You put up with a spastic?" The 'keep jerked his head, indicating their upstairs room and its inhabitants.

"He's the brains of the outfit."

"Not too many brains, to come up here and try to do that bit of business now."

"Yeah. I think I could've had a better price for that same piece of meat here if I'd had her butchered and dressed."

"You got that right," snorted the 'keep glumly, eyeing the food piled on the counter before Cordelia.

"She's too good to waste, though. Guess I'll have to find something else, till this mess blows over. Kill some time. Somebody may be hiring muscle. . . ." Bothari let this trail off. Was he running out of inspiration?

The 'keep studied him with interest. "Yo? I've had something in my eye I could use a, like, agent for. Been afraid for a week somebody else'd go after it first. You could be just what I need."

"Yo?"

The 'keep leaned forward across the bar, confidentially. "Count Vordarian's boys are giving out some fat rewards, down at ImpSec, for information-leading-to. Now, I wouldn't normally mess with ImpSec whoever was running it this week, but there's a strange fellow down the street who's taken a room. And he keeps to it, 'cept when he goes out for food, more food than one man might eat . . . he's got someone in there with him no one ever sees. And he sure isn't one of us. I can't help thinking he might be . . . worth something to somebody, eh?"

Bothari frowned judiciously. "Could be dangerous. Admiral Vorkosigan blows back into town, they'll be looking real hard for that little list of informers. And you have an address."

"But you don't, seems. If you'd front it, I could give you a ten percent split. I think he's big, that fellow. He's sure scared."

Bothari shook his head. "I been out-country, and I came up here—can't you smell it, here in the city? Defeat, man. Vordarian's people look downright morbid to me. I'd think real carefully 'bout that list, if I was you."

The 'keep's lips tightened in frustration. "One way or another, opportunity's not going to last."

Cordelia grabbed for Bothari's ear to whisper, "Play along. Find out who it is. Could be an ally." After a moment's thought she added, "Ask for fifty percent."

Bothari straightened, nodded. "Fifty-fifty," he said to the 'keep. "For the risk."

The 'keep frowned at Cordelia, but respectfully. He said reluctantly, "Fifty percent of something's better than a hundred percent of nothing, I suppose."

"Can you get me a look at this fellow?" asked Bothari. "Maybe."

"Here, woman." Bothari piled the packages in Cordelia's arms. "Take these back to the room."

Cordelia cleared her throat, and tried for an imitation mountain accent. "You be careful belike. City man'll take you."

Bothari favored the 'keep with an alarming grin. "Ah, he wouldn't try and cheat an old vet. More than once."

The 'keep smiled back nervously.

❖   ❖   ❖

Cordelia dozed uneasily, and jerked awake as Bothari returned to their little room. He checked the hallway carefully before closing the door behind him. He looked grim.

"Well, Sergeant? What did you find out?" What if their fellow-hider turned out to be someone as strategically important as, say, Admiral Kanzian? The thought frightened her. How could she resist being turned aside from her personal mission if some greater good were too crystal-clear. . . . Kou on a pallet on the floor, and Drou on the other cot, both blinking sleep, sat up on their elbows to listen.

"It's Lord Vorpatril. Lady Vorpatril, too."

"Oh, no." She sat upright. "Are you certain?"

"Oh, yes."

Kou scrubbed at his scalp, hair bent with sleep. "Did you make contact with them?"

"Not yet."

"Why not?"

"It's Lady Vorkosigan's call. Whether to divert from our primary mission."

And to think she'd wished for command. "Do they seem all right?"

"Alive, lying low. But—that git downstairs can't have been the only one to spot them. I've spiked him for now, but somebody else could get greedy any time."

"Any sign of the baby?"

He shook his head. "She hasn't had it yet."

"It's late! She was due over two weeks ago. How hellish." She paused. "Do you think we could escape the city together?"

"The more people in a party, the more conspicuous," Bothari said slowly. "And I caught a glimpse of Lady Vorpatril. She's real conspicuous. People'd notice her."

"I don't see how joining us now would improve their position. Their cover's worked for several weeks. If we succeed at the Residence, maybe we can try for them on the way back. Certainly have Illyan send loyalist agents to help them, if we get back . . ." Damn. If she were an official raid, she'd have just the contacts the Vorpatrils needed. But then, if she were an offical raid, she doubtless would not have come this way. She sat thinking. "No. No contact yet. But we'd better do something to discourage your friend downstairs."

"I have," said Bothari. "Told him I knew where I could get a better price, and not risk my head later. We may be able to bribe him to help us."

"You'd trust him?" said Droushnakovi doubtfully.

Bothari grimaced. "As far as I can see him. I'll try to keep an eye on him, while we're here. 'Nother thing. I caught a broadcast on his vid in the back room. Vordarian had himself declared Emperor last night."

Kou swore. "So he's finally gone and done it."

"But what does it mean?" asked Cordelia. "Does he feel himself strong, or is it a move of desperation?"

"Last-ditch ploy to try to sway the space forces, I'd guess," said Kou.

"Will it really attract more men than it offends?"

Kou shook his head. "We have a real fear of chaos, on Barrayar. We've tried it. It's nasty. The Imperium has been identified as a source of order ever since Dorca Vorbarra broke the power of the warring counts and unified the planet. Emperor is a real power-word, here."

"Not to me," Cordelia sighed. "Let's get some rest. Maybe by this time tomorrow it'll all be over." Hopeful/gruesome thought, depending on how it was construed. She counted the hours over for the thousandth time, one day left to penetrate the Residence, two to get back to Vorkosigan's territories . . . not much to spare. She felt as if she was flying, faster and faster. And running out of turning room.

Last chance to call the whole thing off. A fine misting rain had brought early dusk to the city. Cordelia stared out the dirty window into the slick street, striped with the reflections of a few sickly amber-haloed streetlights. Only a few bundled shapes hurried along, heads down.

It was as if war and the winter had inhaled autumn's last breath, and blew back out a deathly silence. *Nerves,* Cordelia told herself, straightened her back, and led her little party downstairs.

The desk was deserted. Cordelia was just deciding to skip such formalities as checking out—they had, after all, paid in advance—when the 'keep came stomping in through the front door, shaking cold drops from his jacket and swearing. He spotted Bothari.

"You! It's all your fault, you gutless git. We missed it, we bloody missed it, and now someone else will collect. That reward could've been mine, should've been mine—"

The 'keep's invective was cut off with a thump as Bothari pinned him to the wall. The man's toes stretched for the floor as Bothari's suddenly feral face leaned into his. *"What happened?"*

"One of Vordarian's squads picked up that fellow. Looks like he led them back to his partner, too." The 'keep's voice wavered between anger and fear. "They've got them both, and I've got nothing!"

"Got them?" Cordelia repeated sickly.

"Picking 'em off right now, damn it."

There might still be a chance, Cordelia realized. Command decision or tactical compulsion, it hardly mattered now. She grabbed a stunner out of the satchel; Bothari stepped back and she buzzed the 'keep where he stood openmouthed. Bothari shoved his inert form behind the desk. "We have to try for them. Drou, break out the rest of the weapons. Sergeant, lead us there. Go!"

And so she found herself running down the street toward a scene any right-minded Barrayaran would run the other way to avoid, a night-arrest by security forces. Drou kept up with Bothari; Koudelka, burdened with the satchel, lagged behind. Cordelia wished the mist were thicker.

The Vorpatrils' bolt-hole turned out to be two blocks down and one over, in a shabby narrow building much like the one they'd spent the day in. Bothari held up a hand, and they peered cautiously around the corner, then drew back. Two Security groundcars were parked out front of the little hostel, covering the entrance. But for themselves, the area was strangely deserted. Koudelka came panting up behind.

"Droushnakovi," said Bothari, "circle around. Get a cross-fire position covering the other side of those groundcars. Watch out, they're sure to have men at the back door."

Yes, street tactics were clearly Bothari's call. Drou nodded, checked her weapons' charges, and walked as if casually across the corner, not even turning her head. Once out of the enemy's line of sight, she flowed into a silent run.

"We got to get a better position," Bothari muttered, risking his head once more around the corner. "Can't bloody see."

"A man and a woman walk down the street," Cordelia visualized desperately. "They stop to talk in a doorway. They goggle curiously at the security men, who are engrossed in their arrest—would we pass?"

"Not for long," said Bothari, "once they spot our energy weapons on their area scanners. But we'd last longer than two men. It's going to move fast, when it moves. Might pass just long enough. Lieutenant, cover us from here. Have the plasma arc ready, it's all we've got to stop a vehicle."

Bothari shoved his nerve disruptor out of sight under his jacket. Cordelia tucked her stunner in the waistband of her skirt, and lightly took Bothari's arm. They strolled around the corner.

This was a really stupid idea, Cordelia decided, matching steps to Bothari's booted stride. They should have set up hours ago, if they'd been going to try an ambush like this. Or they should have hooked Padma and Alys out hours ago. And yet—how long ago had Padma been spotted? Might they have fallen into some long-laid trap, and gone down together? *No might-have-beens. Pay attention to the now.*

Bothari's steps slowed, as they approached a deep shadowed doorway. He swung her in, and leaned with his arm on the wall, close to her. They were near enough now to the arrest scene to catch voices. Snatches of crackle from the comm links carried clearly in the damp air.

Just in time. Despite the shabby shirt and trousers, Cordelia readily recognized the dark-haired man pinned against the groundcar by one guard as Captain Vorpatril. His face was marred with a grated, bleeding contusion and swollen lips, pulled back in a stereotypical fast-penta-induced smile. The smile slipped to anguish, and back again, and his giggles choked on moans.

Black-clad security men were bundling a woman out the hostel door and into the street. The security team's attention was drawn to her; Cordelia's and Bothari's, too.

Alys Vorpatril wore only a nightgown and robe, with her feet jammed bare into flat shoes. Her dark hair was loose, flowing down wildly around her white face; she looked a fair madwoman. She was indeed conspicuously pregnant, black robe falling open around her white-gowned belly. The guard manhandling her had her arms locked behind her; her legs splayed for balance against his backward pull.

The guard commander, a full colonel, checked a report panel. "That's it, then. The lord and the heir." His eye locked to Alys Vorpatril's abdomen; he shook his head as if to clear it, and spoke into his comm link. "Pull back, boys, we're done here."

"What the hell are we supposed to do about this, Colonel?" asked his lieutenant uneasily. His voice blended fascination with dismay as he walked over to Lady Vorpatril and lifted her gown high. She had gained weight, these last two months; her chin and breasts were rounded, thighs thickened, belly padded out. He poked a curious finger deep into that soft white flesh. She stood silent, trembling, face on fire with rage at his liberty and eyes glistening dark with tears of fear. "Our orders are to kill the lord and the heir. It doesn't say her. Are we supposed to sit around and wait? Squeeze? Cut her open? Or," his voice went persuasive, "maybe just take her back to HQ?"

The guard holding her from behind grinned and ground his hips into her buttocks, mock-thrusts of unmistakable meaning. "We don't have to take her straight back, do we? I mean, this is Vor meat. What a chance."

The colonel stared at him, and spat disgust. "Corporal, you're perverted."

Cordelia realized with a shock that Bothari's riveted attention to the scene before them was no longer tactical. He was deeply aroused. His eyes seemed to glaze as she watched; his lips parted.

The guard colonel pocketed his comm link, and drew his nerve disruptor. "No." He shook his head. "We make this quick and clean. Step aside, Corporal."

Strange mercies . . .

The guard expertly popped Alys's knees and shoved her down, stepping back. Her hands flung out to the pavement, too late to save her swollen belly from a hard smack. Padma Vorpatril moaned through his fast-penta haze. The guard colonel raised his nerve disruptor and hesitated, as if uncertain whether to aim it at her head or torso.

"*Kill them,*" Cordelia hissed in Bothari's ear, jerked out her stunner, and fired.

Bothari snapped not only awake, but over into some berserker mode; his nerve disruptor bolt hit the guard colonel at the same moment as Cordelia's stunner beam did, though she had drawn first. Then he was moving, a dark blur leaping behind a parked vehicle. He snapped off shots, blue crackles that electrified the air; two more guards fell as the rest took cover behind their groundcars.

Alys Vorpatril, still on the pavement, curled up in a tight ball, trying to cover her abdomen with her arms and legs. Padma Vorpatril, penta-drunk, staggered bewilderedly toward her, arms out, apparently with some similar idea in mind. The guard lieutenant, rolling on the pavement toward cover, aimed his nerve disruptor at the distraught man.

The guard lieutenant's pause for accuracy was fatal; Droushnakovi's nerve disruptor cross-fire and Cordelia's stunner beam intersected upon his body—a millisecond too late. His nerve disruptor bolt took Padma Vorpatril squarely in the back of his head. Blue sparks danced, dark hair sparked orange, and Padma's body arced in a violent convulsion and fell twitching. Alys Vorpatril wailed, a short sharp cry cut off by a gasp. On her hands and knees, she seemed momentarily frozen between trying to crawl toward him, or away.

Droushnakovi's cross-fire vantage was perfect. The last guard was killed while still trying to raise the canopy of the armored groundcar. A driver, shielded inside the second vehicle, prudently chose to try and speed away. Koudelka's plasma arc bolt, set on high power, blasted into the groundcar as it accelerated past the corner. It skidded wildly, dragging an edge and trailing sparks, and crashed into the side of a brick building.

Yes, and didn't my whole strategy for this mission turn on our staying invisible? Cordelia thought dizzily, and ran forward. She and Droushnakovi reached Alys Vorpatril at the same moment; together they hoisted the shuddering woman to her feet.

"We have to get out of here," said Bothari, rising from his firing-crouch and coming toward them.

"No shit," agreed Koudelka, limping up and staring around at the sudden and spectacular carnage. The street was amazingly quiet. Not for long, Cordelia suspected.

"This way." Bothari pointed up an alley, narrow and dark. "Run."

"Shouldn't we try to take that car?" Cordelia gestured to the body-draped vehicle.

"No. Traceable. And it can't fit where we're going."

Cordelia was not sure if the wild-faced, weeping Alys was able to run anywhere, but she stuck her stunner back in her waistband and took one of the pregnant woman's arms. Drou took the other, and together they guided her in the sergeant's wake. At least Koudelka was no longer the slowest of the party.

Alys was crying, yet not hysterical; she glanced only once over her shoulder at her husband's body, then concentrated grimly on trying to run. She did not run well. She was hopelessly unbalanced, her arms wrapping her belly in an attempt to take up the shocks of her heavy footsteps. "Cordelia," she gasped. An acknowledgment of recognition; there was no time or breath for demands of explanation.

They had not lurched more than three blocks when Cordelia began to hear sirens from the area they were fleeing. But Bothari seemed controlled again, unpanicked. They traversed another narrow alley, and Cordelia realized they had crossed into a region of the city with no streetlights, or indeed any lights at all. Her eyes strained in the misty shadows.

Alys stopped suddenly, and Cordelia skidded to a halt, almost jerking the woman off her feet. Alys stood for half a minute, bent over, gasping.

Cordelia realized that beneath its deceptive padding of fat, Alys's abdomen was hard as a rock; the back of her robe was soaking wet. "Are you going into labor?" she asked. She didn't know why she made that a question, the answer was obvious.

"This has been going on—for a day and a half," Alys blurted. She seemed unable to straighten. "I think my water broke back there, when that bastard knocked me down. Unless it's blood—should have passed out by now, if all that was blood—it hurts so much worse, now. . . ." Her breath slowed; she pulled her shoulders back with effort.

"How much longer?" asked Kou in alarm.

"How should I know? I've never done this before. Your guess is as good as mine," Lady Vorpatril snapped. Hot anger to warm cold fear. It wasn't enough warmth, a candle against a blizzard.

"Not much longer, I'd say," came Bothari's voice out of the dark. "We'd better go to ground. Come on."

Lady Vorpatril could no longer run, but managed a rapid waddle, stopping helplessly every two minutes. Then every one minute.

"Not going to make it all the way," muttered Bothari. "Wait here." He disappeared up a side—alley? The passages all seemed alleys here, cold and stinking, much too narrow for groundcars. They had passed exactly two people in the maze, huddled to one side of a passage in a heap, and stepped carefully around them.

"Can you do anything to, like, hold back?" asked Kou, watching Lady Vorpatril double over again. "We ought to . . . try and get a doctor or something."

"That's what that idiot Padma went out for," Alys ground out. "I begged him not to go . . . oh, God!" After another moment she added, in a surprisingly conversational tone, "The next time you're vomiting your guts out, Kou, let me suggest you just close your mouth and swallow hard . . . it's not exactly a voluntary reflex!" She straightened again, shivering violently.

"She doesn't need a doctor, she needs a flat spot," Bothari spoke from the shadows. "This way."

He led them a short distance to a wooden door, formerly nailed shut in an ancient solid stuccoed wall. Judging from the fresh splinters, he'd just kicked it open. Once inside, with the door pulled tight-shut again, Droushnakovi at last dared pull a hand-light from the satchel. It illuminated a small, empty, dirty room. Bothari swiftly prowled its perimeters. Two inner doors had been broken open long ago, but beyond them all was soundless and lightless and apparently deserted. "It'll have to do," said Bothari.

Cordelia wondered what the hell to do next. She knew all about placental transfers and surgical sections now, but for so-called normal births she had only theory to go on. Alys Vorpatril probably had even less grasp of the biology, Drou less still, and Kou was downright useless. "Has anyone here ever actually been in on one of these, before?"

"Not I," muttered Alys. Their looks met in rather too clear an understanding.

"You're not alone," said Cordelia stoutly. Confidence should lead to relaxation, should lead to something. "We'll all help."

Bothari said—oddly reluctantly—"My mother used to do a spot of midwifery. Sometimes she'd drag me along to help. There's not that much to it."

Cordelia controlled her brows. That was the first time she'd heard the sergeant say word one about either of his parents.

The sergeant sighed, clearly realizing from their array of looks that he'd just put himself in charge. "Lend me your jacket, Kou."

Koudelka divested the garment gallantly, and made to wrap it around the shaking Lady Vorpatril. He looked a little more dismayed when the sergeant put his own jacket around Lady Vorpatril's shoulders, then made her lie down on the floor and spread Koudelka's jacket under her hips. She looked less pale, lying down, less like she was about to pass out. But her breath stopped, then she cried out, as her abdominal muscles locked again.

"Stay with me, Lady Vorkosigan," Bothari murmured to Cordelia. For what? Cordelia wondered, then realized why as he knelt and gently pushed up Alys Vorpatril's nightgown. *He wants me for a control mechanism.* But the killing seemed to have bled off that horrifying wave of lust that had so distorted his face, back in the street. His gaze now was only normally interested. Fortunately, Alys Vorpatril was too self-absorbed to notice that Bothari's attempt at an expression of medical coolness was not wholly successful.

"Baby's head's not showing yet," he reported. "But soon."

Another spasm, and he looked around vaguely and added, "I don't think you'd better scream, Lady Vorpatril. They'll be looking by now."

She nodded understanding, and waved a desperate hand; Drou, catching on, rolled up a bit of cloth into a rag rope, and gave it to her to bite.

And so the tableau hung, for spasm after uterine spasm. Alys looked utterly wrung, crying very quietly, unable to stop her body's repeated attempts to turn itself inside out long enough to catch either breath or balance. The baby's head crowned, dark haired, but seemed unable to go further.

"How long is this supposed to take?" asked Kou, in a

voice that tried to sound measured, but came out very worried.

"I think he likes it where he is," said Bothari. "Doesn't want to come out in the cold." This joke actually got through to Alys; her sobbing breath didn't change, but her eyes flashed in a moment of gratitude. Bothari crouched, frowned judiciously, hunkered around to her side, placed a big hand on her belly, and waited for the next spasm. Then he leaned.

The infant's head popped out, between Lady Vorpatril's bloody thighs, quick as that.

"There," said the sergeant, sounding rather satisfied. Koudelka looked thoroughly impressed.

Cordelia caught the head between her hands, and eased the body out with the next contraction. The baby boy coughed twice, sneezed like a kitten in the awed silence, inhaled, grew pinker, and emitted a nerve-shattering wail. Cordelia nearly dropped him.

Bothari swore at the noise. "Give me your swordstick, Kou."

Lady Vorpatril looked up wildly. "No! Give him back to me, I'll make him be quiet!"

"Wasn't what I had in mind," said Bothari with some dignity. "Though it's an idea," he added as the wails went on. He pulled out the plasma arc and heated the sword briefly, on low power. Sterilizing it, Cordelia realized.

Placenta followed cord on the next contraction, a messy heap on Kou's jacket. She stared with covert fascination at the spent version of the supportive organ that had been of so much concern in her own case. *Time. This rescue's taken so much time. What are Miles's chances down to now?* Had she just traded her son's life for little Ivan's? Not-so-little Ivan, actually, no wonder he'd given his mother so much trouble. Alys must be blessed with an unusually wide pelvic arch, or she'd never have made it though this nightmare night alive.

After the cord drained white, Bothari cut it with the sterilized blade, and Cordelia self-knotted the rubbery thing as best she could. She mopped off the baby and wrapped him in their spare clean shirt, and handed him at last into Alys's outstretched arms.

Alys looked at the baby and began crying again, muffled sobs. "Padma said . . . I'd have the best doctors. Padma said . . . there'd be no pain. Padma said he'd stay with me . . . damn you, Padma!" She clutched Padma's son to her. In an altered tone of mild surprise, she added, "Ow!" Infant mouth had found her breast, and apparently had a grip like a barracuda.

"Good reflexes," observed Bothari.

CHAPTER SEVENTEEN

"For God's sake, Bothari, we can't take her in *there*," hissed Koudelka.

They stood in an alley deep in the maze of the caravanserai. A thick-walled building bulked an unusual three stories high in the cold, wet darkness. High on its stuccoed face, scabrous with peeling paint, yellow light glinted through carved shutters. An oil lamp burned dimly above a wooden door, the only entrance Cordelia could see.

"Can't leave her out here. She needs heat," replied the sergeant. He carried Lady Vorpatril in his arms; she clung to him, wan and shivering. "It's a slow night anyway. Late. They're closing down."

"What is this place?" asked Droushnakovi.

Koudelka cleared his throat. "Back in the Time of Isolation, when this was the center of Vorbarr Sultana, it was a lord's Residence. One of the minor Vorbarra princes, I think. That's why it's built like a fortress. Now it's a . . . sort of inn."

Oh, so this is your whorehouse, Kou, Cordelia managed not to blurt out. Instead she addressed Bothari, "Is it safe? Or is it likely to be stocked with informers like that last place?"

524

"Safe for a few hours," Bothari judged. "A few hours is all we have anyway." He set Lady Vorpatril down, handing her off to Droushnakovi, and slipped inside after a muffled conversation through the door with some guardian. Cordelia tucked little Ivan more firmly to her, tugging her jacket over him for all the warmth she could share. Fortunately, he had slept quietly through their several-minutes hike from the abandoned building to this place. In a few moments Bothari returned, and motioned them to follow.

They passed through an entryway, almost like a stone tunnel, with narrow slits in the walls and holes every half-meter above. "For defense, in the old days," whispered Koudelka, and Droushnakovi nodded understanding. No arrows or boiling oil awaited them tonight, though. A man as tall as Bothari, but wider, locked the door again behind them.

They came out in a large, dim room that had been converted into some sort of bar/dining room. It was occupied only by two dispirited-looking women in robes and a man snoring with his head on the table. As usual, an extravagant fireplace glowed with coals of wood.

They had a guide, or hostess. A rangy woman beckoned them silently toward the stairs. Fifteen years ago, or even ten years ago, she might have achieved a leggy aquiline look; now she was bony and faded, mis-clad in a gaudy magenta robe with drooping ruffles that seemed to echo her inherent sadness. Bothari swept up Lady Vorpatril and carried her up the steep stairs. Koudelka stared around uneasily, and seemed to brighten slightly upon not finding someone.

The woman led them to a room off an upstairs hallway. "Change the sheets," muttered Bothari, and the woman nodded and vanished. Bothari did not set the exhausted Lady Vorpatril down. The woman returned in a few minutes, and whisked off the bed's rumpled coverings and replaced them with fresh linens. Bothari laid Lady Vorpatril in the bed and backed up. Cordelia tucked the sleeping infant in her arm, and Lady Vorpatril managed a grateful nod.

The—housewoman, Cordelia decided she would think of her—stared with a spark of interest at the baby. "That's a new one. Big boy, eh?" her voice swung to a tentative coo.

"Two weeks old," stated Bothari in a repelling tone.

The woman snorted, hands on hips. "I do my bit of midwifery, Bothari. Two hours, more like."

Bothari shot Cordelia an odd look, almost a flash of fear. The housewoman held up a hand to ward off his frown. "Whatever you say."

"We should let her sleep," said Bothari, "till we're sure she isn't going to bleed."

"Yes, but not alone," said Cordelia. "In case she wakes up disoriented in a strange place." In the range of strange, Cordelia suspected, this place qualified as downright alien for the Vor woman.

"I'll sit with her a while," volunteered Droushnakovi. She glowered suspiciously at the housewoman, who was apparently leaning too near the baby for her taste. Cordelia didn't think Drou was at all fooled by Koudelka's pretense that they had stumbled into some sort of museum. Nor would Lady Vorpatril be, once she'd rested enough to regain her wits.

Droushnakovi plunked down in a shabby padded armchair, wrinkling her nose at its musty smell. The others withdrew from the room. Koudelka went off to find whatever this old building used for a lavatory, and to try and buy them some food. An underlying tang to the air suggested to Cordelia that nothing in the caravanserai was hooked up to the municipal sewerage. No central heating, either. At Bothari's frown, the housewoman made herself scarce.

A sofa, a couple of chairs, and a low table occupied a space at the end of the hall, lit by a red-shaded battery-driven lamp. Wearily, Bothari and Cordelia sat there. With the pressure off for a moment, not fighting the strain, Bothari looked ragged. Cordelia had no idea what she looked like, but she was certain it wasn't her best.

"Do they have whores on Beta Colony?" Bothari asked suddenly.

Cordelia fought mental whiplash. His voice was so tired the question sounded almost casual, except that Bothari never made casual conversation. How much had tonight's violent events disturbed his precarious balance, stressed his peculiar fault lines? "Well . . . we have the L.P.S.T.s," she answered cautiously. "I guess they fill some of the same social functions."

"Ellpee Estees?"

"Licensed Practical Sexuality Therapists. You have to pass the government boards, and get a license. You're required to have at least an associate degree in psychotherapy. Except that all three sexes take up the profession. The hermaphrodites make the most money, they're very popular with the tourists. It's not . . . not a high social status job, but neither are they dregs. I don't think we have dregs on Beta Colony, we sort of stop at the lower middle class. It's like . . ." she paused, struggling for a cultural translation, "sort of like being a hairdresser, on Barrayar. Delivering a personal service to professional standards, with a bit of art and craft."

She'd actually managed to boggle Bothari, surely a first. His brow wrinkled. "Only Betans would think you needed a bleeding university degree. . . . Do *women* hire them?"

"Sure. Couples, too. The . . . the teaching element is rather more emphasized, there."

He shook his head, and hesitated. He shot her a sidelong look. "My mother was a whore." His tone was curiously distant. He waited.

"I'd . . . about figured that out."

"Don't know why she didn't abort me. She could have, she did those as well as midwifery. Maybe she was looking to her old age. She used to sell me to her customers."

Cordelia choked. "Now . . . now *that* would not have been allowed, on Beta Colony."

"I can't remember much about that time. I ran away when I was twelve, when I got big enough to beat up her damned customers. Ran with the gangs, till I was sixteen, passed for eighteen, and lied my way into the

Service. Then I was out of here." His palms slid across each other, indicating how slick and fast his escape.

"The Service must have seemed like heaven, in comparison."

"Till I met Vorrutyer." He stared around vaguely. "There were more people around here, back then. It's almost dead here now." His voice went meditative. "There's a great deal of my life I can't remember very well. It's like I'm all . . . patchy. Yet there are some things I want to forget and can't."

She wasn't about to ask, What? But she made an I-am-listening noise, down in her throat.

"Don't know who my father was. Being a bastard here is damn near as bad as being a mutant."

" 'Bastard' is used as a negative description of a personality, but it doesn't really have an objective meaning, in the Betan context. Unlicensed children aren't the same thing, and they're so rare, they're dealt with on a case-by-case basis." *Why is he telling me all this? What does he want of me? When he started, he seemed almost fearful; now he looks almost contented. What did I say right?* She sighed.

To her secret relief, Koudelka returned about then, bearing actual fresh sandwiches of bread and cheese, and bottled beer. Cordelia was glad for the beer; she'd have been dubious of the water in this place. She chased her first bite with a grateful swallow, and said, "Kou, we have to re-arrange our strategy."

He settled awkwardly beside her, listening seriously. "Yes?"

"We obviously can't take Lady Vorpatril and the baby with us. And we can't leave her here. We left five corpses and a burning groundcar for Vordarian's security. They're going to be searching this area in earnest. But for just a little while longer, they will still be hunting for a very pregnant woman. It gives us a time window. We have to split up."

He filled a hesitant moment with a bite of sandwich. "Will you go with her, then, Milady?"

She shook her head. "I must go with the Residence team. If only because I'm the only one who can say, This is impossible now, it's time to quit. Drou is absolutely required, and I need Bothari." *And, in some strange way, Bothari needs me.* "That leaves you."

His lips compressed bitterly. "At least I won't slow you down."

"You're not a default choice," she said sharply. "Your ingenuity got us in to Vorbarr Sultana. I think it can get Lady Vorpatril out. You're her best shot."

"But it feels like you're running into danger, and I'm running away."

"A dangerous illusion. Kou, think. If Vordarian's goons catch her again, they'll show her no mercy. Nor you, nor especially the baby. There is no 'safer.' Only mortal necessity, and logic, and the absolute need to keep your head."

He sighed. "I'll try, Milady."

" 'Try' is not good enough. Padma Vorpatril 'tried.' You bloody *succeed,* Kou."

He nodded slowly. "Yes, Milady."

Bothari left to scrounge clothing for Kou's new persona of poor-young-husband-and-father. "Customers are always leaving things," he remarked. Cordelia wondered what he could collect here in the way of street clothes for Lady Vorpatril. Kou took food in to Lady Vorpatril and Drou. He returned with a very bleak expression on his face, and settled again beside Cordelia.

After a time he said, "I guess I understand now why Drou was so worried about being pregnant."

"Do you?" said Cordelia.

"Lady Vorpatril's troubles make mine look . . . pretty small. God, that looked painful."

"Mm. But the pain only lasts a day." She rubbed her scar. "Or a few weeks. I don't think that's it."

"What is, then?"

"It's . . . a transcendental act. Making life. I thought about that, when I was carrying Miles. 'By this act, I bring one death into the world.' One birth, one death, and all the pain and acts of will between. I didn't understand certain Oriental mystic symbols like the Death-mother, Kali, till I realized it wasn't mystic at all, just plain fact. A Barrayaran-style sexual 'accident' can start a chain of causality that doesn't stop till the end of time. Our children change us . . . whether they live or not. Even though your child turned out to be chimerical this time, Drou was touched by that change. Weren't you?"

He shook his head in bafflement. "I wasn't thinking about all that. I just wanted to be normal. Like other men."

"I think your instincts are all right. They're just not enough. I don't suppose you could get your instincts and your intellect working together for once, instead of at cross-purposes?"

He snorted. "I don't know. I don't know . . . how to get through to her now. I said I was sorry."

"It's not all right between you two, is it?"

"No."

"You know what's bothered me most, on the journey up here?" said Cordelia.

"No . . ."

"I couldn't say goodbye to Aral. If . . . anything happens to me—or to him, for that matter—it will leave something hanging, unraveled, between us. And no way to ever make it right."

"Mm." He folded a little more into himself, slumped in the chair.

She meditated a bit. "What have you tried besides 'I'm sorry'? How about, 'How do you feel? Are you all right? Can I help? I love you,' there's a classic. Words of one syllable. Mostly questions, now I think on it. Shows an interest in starting a conversation, y'know?"

He smiled sadly. "I don't think she wants to talk to me anymore."

"Suppose," she leaned her head back, and stared unseeing down the hallway. "Suppose things hadn't taken such a wrong turn, that night. Suppose you hadn't panicked. Suppose that idiot Evon Vorhalas hadn't interrupted with his little horror show." There was a thought. Too

painful, that might-not-have-been. "Drop back to square
one. There you were, cuddling happily." Aral had used
that word, cuddling. It hurt too much to think of Aral
just now, too. "You part friends, you wake up the next
morning, er, aching with unrequited love . . . what happens next, on Barrayar?"

"A go-between."

"Ah?"

"Her parents, or mine, would hire a go-between. And
then they'd, well, arrange things."

"And you do what?"

He shrugged. "Show up on time for the wedding and
pay the bill, I guess. Actually, the parents pay the bill."

No wonder the man was at a loss. "Did you want a
wedding? Not just to get laid?"

"Yes! But . . . Milady, I'm just about half a man, on
a good day. Her family'd take one look at me and laugh."

"Have you ever met her family? Have they met you?"

"No . . ."

"Kou, are you listening to yourself?"

He looked rather shamefaced. "Well . . ."

"A go-between. Huh." She stood up.

"Where are you going?" he asked nervously.

"Between," she said firmly. She marched down the hall
to Lady Vorpatril's door, and stuck her head in.
Droushnakovi was sitting watching the sleeping woman.
Two beers and the sandwiches sat untouched on a bedside table.

Cordelia slipped within, and closed the door gently.
"You know," she murmured, "good soldiers never pass up
a chance to eat or sleep. They never know how much
they'll be called on to do, before the next chance."

"I'm not hungry." Drou too had a folded-in look, as
if caught in some trap within herself.

"Want to talk about it?"

She grimaced uncertainly, and moved away from the
bed to a settee in the far corner of the room. Cordelia
sat beside her. "Tonight," she said lowly, "was the first
time I was ever in a real fight."

"You did well. You found your position, you reacted—"

"No." Droushnakovi made a bitter hand-chopping gesture. "I didn't."

"Oh? It looked good to me."

"I ran around behind the building—stunned the two security men waiting at the back door. They never saw me. I got to my position, at the building's corner. I watched those men, tormenting Lady Vorpatril in the street. Insulting and staring and pushing and poking at her . . . it made me so angry, I switched to my nerve disruptor. I wanted to kill them. Then the firing started. And . . . and I hesitated. And Lord Vorpatril died because of it. My fault—"

"Whoa, girl! That goon who shot Padma Vorpatril wasn't the only one taking aim at him. Padma was so penta-soaked and confused, he wasn't even trying to take cover. They must have double-dosed him, to force him to lead them back to Alys. He might as easily have died from another shot, or blundered into our own cross-fire."

"Sergeant Bothari didn't hesitate," Droushnakovi said flatly.

"No," agreed Cordelia.

"Sergeant Bothari doesn't waste energy feeling . . . sorry, for the enemy, either."

"No. Do you?"

"I feel sick."

"You kill two total strangers, and expect to feel jolly?"

"Bothari does."

"Yes. Bothari enjoyed it. But Bothari is not, even by Barrayaran standards, a sane man. Do you aspire to be a monster?"

"You call him that!"

"Oh, but he's *my* monster. My good dog." She always had trouble explaining Bothari, sometimes even to herself. Cordelia wondered if Droushnakovi knew the Earth-historical origin of the term, scapegoat. The sacrificial animal that was released yearly into the wilderness, to carry the sins of its community away . . . Bothari was surely her beast of burden; she saw clearly what he did for her. She was less certain what she did for him, except that he seemed to find it desperately important. "I, for one, am glad you are heartsick. Two pathological killers in my service would be an excess. Treasure that nausea, Drou."

She shook her head. "I think maybe I'm in the wrong trade."

"Maybe. Maybe not. Think what a monstrous thing an army of Botharis would be. Any community's arm of force—military, police, security—needs people in it who can do the necessary evil, and yet not be made evil by it. To do only the necessary, and no more. To constantly question the assumptions, to stop the slide into atrocity."

"The way that security colonel quashed that obscene corporal."

"Yes. Or the way that lieutenant questioned the colonel . . . I wish we might have saved him," Cordelia sighed.

Drou frowned deeply, into her lap.

"Kou thought you were angry with him," said Cordelia.

"Kou?" Droushnakovi looked up dimly. "Oh, yes, he was just in here. Did he want something?"

Cordelia smiled. "Just like Kou, to imagine all your unhappiness must center on him." Her smile faded. "I'm going to send him with Lady Vorpatril, to try and smuggle her and the baby out. We'll go our separate ways as soon as she's able to walk."

Drou's face grew worried. "He'll be in terrible danger. Vordarian's people will be rabid over losing her and the young lord tonight."

Yes, there was still a Lord Vorpatril to disturb Vordarian's genealogical calculations, wasn't there? Insane system, that made an infant seem a mortal danger to a grown man. "There's no safety for anybody, till this vile war is ended. Tell me. Do you still love Kou? I know you're over your initial starry-eyed infatuation. You see his faults. Egocentric, and with a bug in his brain about his injuries, and terribly worried about his masculinity. But he's not stupid. There's hope for him. He has an interesting life ahead of him, in the Regent's service." Assuming they all lived through the next forty-eight hours. A passionate desire to live was a good thing to instill in her agents, Cordelia thought. "Do you want him?"

"I'm . . . bound to him, now. I don't know how to explain . . . I gave him my virginity. Who else would have me? I'd be ashamed—"

"Forget that! After we bring off this raid, you're going to be covered in so much glory, men will be lining up for the status of courting you. You'll have your pick. In Aral's household, you'll have a chance to meet the best. What do you want? A general? An Imperial minister? A Vor lordling? An off-world ambassador? Your only problem will be choosing, since Barrayaran custom stingily only allows you one husband at a time. A clumsy young lieutenant hasn't got a prayer of competing with all those polished seniors."

Droushnakovi smiled, a bit skeptically, at Cordelia's painted vision. "Who says Kou won't be a general himself someday?" she said softly. She sighed, her brow creasing. "Yes. I still want him. But . . . I guess I'm afraid he'll hurt me again."

Cordelia thought that one over. "Probably. Aral and I hurt each other all the time."

"Oh, not you two, Milady! You seem so, so perfect."

"Think, Drou. Can you imagine what mental state Aral is in right this minute, because of my actions? I can. I do."

"Oh."

"But pain . . . seems to me an insufficient reason not to embrace life. Being dead is quite painless. Pain, like time, is going to come on regardless. Question is, what glorious moments can you win from life in addition to the pain?"

"I'm not sure I follow that, Milady. But . . . I have a picture, in my head. Of me and Kou, on a beach, all alone. It's so warm. And when he looks at me, he sees me, really sees me, and loves me. . . ."

Cordelia pursed her lips. "Yeah . . . that'll do. Come with me."

The girl rose obediently. Cordelia led her back in to

the hall, forcefully arranged Kou at one end of the sofa, sat Drou down on the other, and plopped down between them. "Drou, Kou has a few things to say to you. Since you apparently speak different languages, he's asked me to be his interpreter."

Kou made an embarrassed negative motion over Cordelia's head.

"That hand signal means, I'd rather blow up the rest of my life than look like a fool for five minutes. Ignore it," Cordelia said. "Now, let me see. Who begins?"

There was a short silence. "Did I mention I'm also playing the parts of both your parents? I think I shall begin by being Kou's Ma. Well, son, and have you met any nice girls yet? You're almost twenty-six, you know. I saw that vid," she added in her own voice as Kou choked. "I have her style, eh? And her content. And Kou says, Yes, Ma, there's this gorgeous girl. Young, tall, smart— and Kou's Ma says, Tee hee! And hires me, your friendly neighborhood go-between. And I go to your father, Drou, and say, there's this young man. Imperial lieutenant, personal secretary to the Lord Regent, war hero, slated for the inside track at Imperial HQ—and he says, Say no more! We'll take him. Tee-hee. And—"

"I think he'll have more to say than that!" interrupted Kou.

Cordelia turned to Droushnakovi. "What Kou just said was, he thinks your family won't like him 'cause he's a crip."

"No!" said Drou indignantly. "That's not so—"

Cordelia held up a restraining hand. "As your go-between, Kou, let me tell you. When one's only lovely daughter points and says firmly, Da, I want *that* one, a prudent Da responds only, Yes, dear. I admit, the three large brothers may be harder to convince. Make her cry, and you could have a serious problem in the back alley. By which I presume you haven't complained to them yet, Drou?"

She stifled an involuntary giggle. "No!"

Kou looked as if this was a new and daunting thought.

"See," said Cordelia, "you can still evade fraternal retribution, Kou, if you scramble." She turned to Drou. "I
know he's been a lout, but I promise you, he's a train-
able lout."

"I *said* I was sorry," said Kou, sounding stung.

Drou stiffened. "Yes. Repeatedly," she said coldly.

"And *there* we come to the heart of the matter,"
Cordelia said slowly, seriously. "What Kou actually means,
Drou, is that he isn't a bit sorry. The moment was won-
derful, you were wonderful, and he wants to do it again.
And again and again, with nobody but you, forever, socially
approved and uninterrupted. Is that right, Kou?"

Kou looked stunned. "Well—yes!"

Drou blinked. "But . . . that's what I wanted you to say!"

"It was?" He peered over Cordelia's head.

This go-between system may have some real merits. But
also its limits. Cordelia rose from between them, and
glanced at her chrono. The humor drained from her spirit.
"You have a little time yet. You can say a lot in a little
time, if you stick to words of one syllable."

CHAPTER EIGHTEEN

Pre-dawn in the alleys of the caravanserai was not so pitchy-black as night in the mountains. The foggy night sky reflected back a faint amber glow from the surrounding city. The faces of her friends were grey blurs, like the very earliest of ancient photographs; Cordelia tried not to think, *Like the faces of the dead.*

Lady Vorpatril, cleaned and fed and rested a few hours, was still none too steady, but she could walk on her own. The housewoman had contributed some surprisingly sober clothes for her, a calf-length grey skirt and sweaters against the cold. Koudelka had exchanged all his military gear for loose trousers, old shoes, and a jacket to replace the one that had suffered from its emergency obstetrical use. He carried baby Lord Ivan, now makeshift-diapered and warmly wrapped, completing the picture of a timid little family trying to make it out of town to the wife's parents in the country before the fighting started. Cordelia had seen hundreds of refugees just like them, in passing, on her way into Vorbarr Sultana.

Koudelka inspected his little group, ending with a frowning look at the swordstick in his hand. Even when seen as a mere cane, the satin wood, polished steel ferrule,

and inlaid grip did not look very middle-class. Koudelka
sighed. "Drou, can you hide this somehow? It's conspicuous as hell with this outfit, and more of a hindrance than
a help when I'm trying to carry this baby."

Droushnakovi nodded, and knelt and wrapped the stick
in a shirt, and stuffed it into the satchel. Cordelia remembered what had happened the last time Kou had carried
that stick down to the caravanserai, and stared nervously
into the shadows. "How likely are we to be jumped by
someone, at this hour? We don't look rich, certainly."

"Some would kill you for your clothes," said Bothari
glumly, "with winter coming on. But it's safer than usual.
Vordarian's troops have been sweeping the quarter for
'volunteers,' to help dig those bomb shelters in the city
parks."

"I never thought I'd approve of slave labor," Cordelia
groaned.

"It's nonsense anyway," Koudelka said. "Tearing up the
parks. Even if completed they wouldn't shelter enough
people. But it looks impressive, and it sets up Lord
Vorkosigan as a threat, in people's minds."

"Besides," Bothari lifted his jacket to reveal the silvered
gleam of his nerve disruptor, "this time I've got the right
weapon."

This was it, then. Cordelia embraced Alys Vorpatril,
who hugged her back, murmuring, "God help you,
Cordelia. And God rot Vidal Vordarian in hell."

"Go safely. See you back at Tanery Base, eh?" Cordelia
glanced at Koudelka. "Live, and so confound our
enemies."

"We'll tr—we will, Milady," said Koudelka. Gravely, he
saluted Droushnakovi. There was no irony in the military
courtesy, though perhaps a last tinge of envy. She returned
him a slow nod of understanding. Neither chose to con-
fuse the moment with further words. The two groups
parted in the clammy darkness. Drou watched over her
shoulder till Koudelka and Lady Vorpatril turned out of
sight, then picked up the pace.

They passed from black alleys to lit streets, from

deserted darkness to occasional other human forms,
hurrying about early winter morning business. Everybody
seemed to cross streets to avoid everybody else, and
Cordelia felt a little less noticeable. She stiffened inwardly
when a municipal guard groundcar drove slowly past them,
but it did not stop.

They paused, across the street, to be certain their target
building had been unlocked for the morning. The structure was multi-storied, in the utilitarian style of the building boom that had come on the heels of Ezar Vorbarra's
ascent to power and stability thirty-plus years ago. It was
commercial, not governmental; they crossed the lobby,
entered the lift tubes, and descended unimpeded.

Drou began seriously looking over her shoulder when
they reached the sub-basement. "*Now* we look out of
place." Bothari kept watch as she bent and forced a lock
to a utility tunnel. She led them down it, taking two cross-
turns. The passage was clearly used frequently, as the
lights remained on. Cordelia's ears strained for footsteps
not their own.

An access cover was bolted to the floor. Droushnakovi
loosened it quickly. "Hang and drop. It's not much more
than two meters. It'll likely be wet."

Cordelia slid into the dark circle, landing with a splash.
She lit her hand-light. The water, slick and black and
shimmering, came to her booted ankles in the synthacrete
tube. It was icy cold. Bothari followed. Drou knelt on his
shoulders, to coax the cover back into place, then splashed
down beside her. "There's about half a kilometer of this
storm sewer. Come on," she whispered. This close to their
goal, Cordelia needed no urging to hurry.

At the half-kilometer, they climbed into a darkened
orifice high on the curving wall that led to a much older
and smaller tunnel, made of time-blackened brick. Knees
and backs bent, they shuffled along. It must be particularly painful for Bothari, Cordelia reflected. Drou slowed,
and began tapping on the tunnel's roof with the steel ferrule of Koudelka's stick. When the ticks became hollow
tocks, she stopped. "Here. It's meant to swing downward.

Watch it." She released the sheath, and slid the blade carefully between a line of slimy bricks. A click, and the false-brick-lined panel flopped down, nearly cracking her head. She returned the sword to its casing. "Up." She pulled herself through.

They followed to find themselves in another ancient drain, even narrower. It sloped more steeply upward. They crouched along, their clothes brushing the sides and picking up damp stains. Drou rose suddenly, and clambered out over a pile of broken bricks into a dark, pillared chamber.

"What is this place?" whispered Cordelia. "Too big for a tunnel . . ."

"The old stables," Drou whispered back. "We're under the Residence grounds, now."

"It doesn't sound so secret to me. Surely they must appear in old drawings and elevations. People—Security— must know this is here." Cordelia stared into the dim, musty recesses, past pale arches picked out by their wavering hand-lights.

"Yes, but this is the cellar of the *old* old stables. Not Dorca's, but Dorca's great-uncle's. He kept over three hundred horses. They burned down in a spectacular fire about two hundred years ago, and instead of rebuilding on the site, they knocked them flat and put up the *new* old stables on the east side, downwind. Those got converted to staff apartments in Dorca's day. Most of the hostages are being kept over there now." Drou marched firmly forward, as if sure of her ground. "We're to the north of the main Residence now, under the gardens Ezar designed. Ezar apparently found this old cellar and arranged this passage with Negri, thirty years ago. A bolt-hole that even their own Security didn't know about. Trusting, eh?"

"Thank you, Ezar," Cordelia murmured wryly.

"Once we're out of Ezar's passage, the real risk starts," the girl commented.

Yes, they could still pull out now, retrace their steps and no one the wiser. *Why have these people so blithely handed me the right to risk their lives? God, I hate command.* Something skittered in the shadows, and somewhere, water dripped.

"Here," said Droushnakovi, shining her light on a pile of boxes. "Ezar's cache. Clothes, weapons, money—Captain Negri had me add some women's and boy's clothes to it just last year, at the time of the Escobar invasion. He was keyed up for trouble about it, but the riots never reached here. My clothes should only be a little big for you."

They discarded their beslimed street clothes. Droushnakovi shook out clean dresses, suitable for senior Residence womenservants too superior for menial's uniforms; the girl had worn them for just such service. Bothari unbundled his black fatigue uniform again from the satchel, and donned it, adding correct Imperial Security insignia. From a distance he made a proper guard, though he was perhaps a little too rumpled to pass inspection up close. As Drou had promised, a complete array of weapons lay fully charged in sealed cases. Cordelia chose a fresh stunner, as did Drou; their eyes met. "No hesitation this time, eh?" Cordelia murmured. Drou nodded grimly. Bothari took one of each, stunner, nerve disruptor, and plasma arc. Cordelia trusted he wouldn't clank when he walked.

"You can't fire that thing indoors," Droushnakovi objected to the plasma arc.

"You never know," shrugged Bothari.

After a moment's thought, Cordelia added the swordstick, tightening a loop of her belt around its grip. A serious weapon it wasn't, but it had proved an unexpectedly useful tool on this trip. *For luck.* Then from the last depths of the satchel, Cordelia pulled what she privately considered to be the most potent weapon of all.

"A shoe?" said Droushnakovi blankly.

"Gregor's shoe. For when we make contact with Kareen. I rather fancy she still has the other." Cordelia nested it deeply in the inner pocket of one of Drou's Vorbarra-crested boleros, worn over Cordelia's dress to complete the picture of an inner Residence worker.

When their preparations were as complete as possible,

Drou led them again into narrowing darkness. "Now we're under the Residence itself," she whispered, turning sideways. "We go up this ladder, between the walls. It was added after, there's not much space."

This proved an understatement. Cordelia sucked in her breath and climbed after her, sandwiched flat between two walls, trying not to accidently touch or thump. The ladder was made, naturally, of wood. Her head throbbed with exhaustion and adrenaline. She mentally measured the width. Getting the uterine replicator back down this ladder was going to be a bitch. She told herself sternly to think positively, then decided that was positive. *Why am I doing this? I could be back at Tanery Base with Aral right now, letting these Barrayarans kill each other all day long, if it is their pleasure. . . .*

Above her, Drou stepped aside onto some sort of tiny ledge, a mere board. When Cordelia came up beside her, she gestured "stop" and extinguished her hand-light. Drou touched some silent latch mechanism, and a wall panel swung outward before them. Clearly, everything had been kept well oiled right up to Ezar's death.

They looked out into the old Emperor's bedchamber. They had expected it to be empty. Drou's mouth opened in a voiceless O of dismay and horror.

Ezar's huge old carved wooden bed, the one he'd for-God's-sake *died* in, was occupied. A shaded light, dimmed to an orange glow, cast highlight and shadow across two bare-torsoed, sleeping forms. Even in this foreshortened view, Cordelia instantly recognized the dish-face and moustache of Vidal Vordarian. He sprawled across four-fifths of the bed, his heavy arm flung possessively across Princess Kareen. Her dark hair was tumbled on the pillow. She slept in a tight, tiny ball in the upper corner of the bed, facing outward, white arms clutched to her chest, nearly in danger of falling out.

Well, we're reached Kareen. But there's a hitch. Cordelia shivered with the impulse to shoot Vordarian in his sleep. But the energy discharge must set off alarms. Until she had Miles's replicator in her hand, she was not ready to run for it. She motioned Drou to close the panel again, and breathed "Down," to Bothari, waiting beneath her. They reversed their painstaking four-flight climb. Back in the tunnel, Cordelia turned to face the girl, who was crying quite silently.

"She's sold out to him," Droushnakovi whispered, her voice shaking with grief and revulsion.

"If you'll explain to me what power-base you imagine she has to resist the man right now, I'd be interested to hear it," said Cordelia tartly. "What do you expect her to do, fling herself out a window to avoid a fate worse than death? She did fates worse than death with Serg, I don't think they hold any more emotion for her."

"But if only we'd got here sooner, I might—we might have saved her."

"We still might."

"But she's really sold out!"

"Do people lie in their sleep?" asked Cordelia. At Drou's confused look, she explained. "She didn't look like a lover to me. She lay like a prisoner. I promised we'd try for her, and we will." *Time.* "But we'll go for Miles first. Let's try the second exit."

"We'll have to pass through more monitored corridors," Droushnakovi warned.

"Can't be helped. If we wait, this place will start waking up, and we'll hit more people."

"They're coming on duty in the kitchens right now," sighed Drou. "I used to stop in for coffee and hot pastries, some days."

Alas, a commando raid could not knock off for breakfast. This was it. Go or no-go? Was it bravery, or stupidity, that drove her on? It couldn't be bravery, she was sick with fear, the same hot acid nausea she'd felt just before combat during the Escobar war. Familiarity with the sensation didn't help. *If I do not act, my child will die.* She would simply have to do without courage. "Now," Cordelia decided. "There will be no better chance."

Up the narrow ladder again. The second panel opened in the old Emperor's private office. To Cordelia's relief it still remained dark and unused, untouched since it had been cleaned out and locked after Ezar's death last spring. His comconsole desk, with all its Security overrides, was disconnected, wiped of secrets, dead as its owner. The windows were still dark, with the tardy winter morning.

Kou's stick banged against Cordelia's calf as she strode across the room. It did look odd, hitched to her waist too obviously like a sword. On a bureau in the office was a wide antique tray holding a flat ceramic bowl, typical of the knickknacks that cluttered the Residence. Cordelia laid the stick across the tray and lifted it solemnly, servant-fashion.

Droushnakovi nodded approval. "Carry it halfway between your waist and your chest," she whispered. "And keep your spine straight, they always told me."

Cordelia nodded. They closed the panel behind them, straightened themselves, and entered the lower corridor of the north wing.

Two Residence serving women and a security guard. At first glance, they looked perfectly natural in this setting, even in these troubled times. A guard corporal standing duty at the foot of the Petite Stairway at the corridor's west end came to attention at the sight of Bothari's ImpSec and rank tabs; they exchanged salutes. They were passing out of sight up around the stairs' curve before he looked again, harder. Cordelia steeled herself not to break into a panicked run. A subtle piece of misdirection; the two women couldn't be a threat, they were already guarded. That their guard could be the threat, might escape the corporal for minutes yet.

They turned into the upper corridor. There. Behind *that* door, according to the loyalists' reports, Vordarian kept the captured replicator. Right under his eye. Perhaps as a human shield; any explosive dropped on Vordarian's quarters must kill tiny Miles as well. Or did the Barrayaran think of her damaged child as human?

Another guard stood outside that door. He stared at them suspiciously, his hand touching his sidearm. Cordelia and Droushnakovi walked on by without turning their heads. Bothari's exchanged salute flowed smoothly into a clip to the man's jaw that snapped his head back into the wall. Bothari caught him before he dropped. They swung the door open and dragged the guard inside; Bothari took his place in the corridor. Silently, Drou closed the door.

Cordelia stared wildly around the little chamber, looking for automatic monitors. The room might formerly have been a bedroom of the sort once slept in by bodyservants to be near their Vorish masters, or perhaps an unusually large wardrobe; it didn't even have a window overlooking some dull inner court. The portable uterine replicator sat on a cloth-covered table in the exact center of the room. Its lights still glowed their reassuring greens and ambers. No feral red eyes warned of malfunction yet. A breath half-agony, half-relief, tore from Cordelia's lips at the sight of it.

Droushnakovi gazed around the room unhappily.

"What's wrong, Drou?" whispered Cordelia.

"Too easy," the girl muttered.

"We're not done yet. Say 'easy' an hour from now." She licked her lips, shaken by secret subliminal agreement with Droushnakovi's evaluation. No help for it. Grab and go. Speed, not secrecy, was their hope now.

She set the tray down on the table, reached for the replicator's carrying handle, and stopped. Something, something wrong . . . she stared more closely at the readouts. The oxygenation monitor wasn't even functioning. Though its indicator light glowed green, the nutrient fluid level read 00.00. *Empty.*

Cordelia's mouth opened in a silent wail. Her stomach churned. She leaned closer, eyes devouring all the illogical hash of false readouts. Her hagridden nightmare, made suddenly and horribly real—had they dumped it on the floor, into a drain, down a toilet? Had Miles died quickly, mercifully smashed, or had they let the tiny infant, bereft of life-support, twitch to death in agony while they watched? Perhaps they hadn't even bothered to watch. . . .

The serial number. Look at the serial number. A hopeless hope, but . . . she forced her blurring eyes to focus, her racing mind to try and remember. She had fingered that number, pensively, back in Vaagen and Henri's lab, meditating upon this piece of technology and the distant world that had created it—and this number didn't match. Not the same replicator, not Miles's! One of the sixteen others, used to bait this trap.

Her heart sank. How many other traps were laid? She pictured herself running frantically from replicator to replicator, like a distraught child in some cruel game of keep-away, searching. . . . *I shall go mad.*

No. Wherever the real replicator was, it was near to Vordarian's person. Of that, she was sure. She knelt beside the table, putting her head down a moment to fight the blood-drained black balloons that clouded her vision and threatened to empty her mind of consciousness. She lifted the cloth. *There.* A pressure-sensor. Was this Vordarian's own clever idea? Slick and vicious. Drou bent to follow her gesture.

"A trap," whispered Cordelia. "Lift the replicator, and the alarms go off."

"If we disarm it—"

"No. Don't bother. It's false bait. Not the right replicator. It's an empty, with the controls buggered to make it look like it's running." Cordelia tried to think clearly through the pounding in her skull. "We'll have to retrace our steps. Back down, and up. I hadn't expected to encounter Vordarian here. But I guarantee he'll know where Miles is. A little old-fashioned interrogation. We'll be working against time. When the alarm goes up—"

Footsteps thudded in the corridor, and shouts. The chirping buzz of stunner fire. Swearing, Bothari flung himself backward through the door. "That's done it. They've spotted us."

When the alarm goes up, it's all over, Cordelia's thought completed itself, in a vertigo of loss. No window, one door, and they'd just lost control of their only exit. Vordarian's trap had worked after all. *May Vidal Vordarian rot in hell. . . .*

Droushnakovi clutched her stunner. "We won't surrender you, Milady. We'll fight to the end."

"Rubbish," snapped Cordelia. "There's nothing our deaths would buy here but the deaths of a few more of Vordarian's goons. Meaningless."

"You mean we should just quit?"

"Suicidal glory is the luxury of the irresponsible. We're not giving up. We're waiting for a better opportunity to win. Which we can't take if we're stunned or nerve-fried." Of course, if that had been the real replicator on the table . . . she was insane enough by now to sacrifice these people's lives for her son's, Cordelia reflected ruefully, but not yet mad enough to trade them for nothing. She hadn't grown that Barrayaran yet.

"You give yourself to Vordarian as a hostage," Bothari warned.

"Vordarian has held me hostage since the day he took Miles," Cordelia said sadly. "This changes nothing."

A few minutes of shouted negotiations through the door accomplished their surrender, despite the hair-trigger nerves of the security guards. They tossed out their weapons. The guards ran a scan for power packs to be sure, then four of them piled into the little room to frisk their new prisoners. Two more waited outside as backup. Cordelia made no sudden moves to startle them. A guard frowned puzzlement when the interesting lump in Cordelia's vest turned out to be only a child's shoe. He laid it on the table next to the tray.

The commander, a man in the maroon and gold Vordarian livery, spoke into his wrist comm. "Yes. We're secured here. Tell m'lord. No, he said to wake him. You want to explain why you didn't? Thank you."

The guards did not prod them into the corridor, but waited. The still-unconscious man Bothari had clipped was dragged out. The guards placed Cordelia, arms outstretched to the wall and legs straddled, in a row with Bothari and Droushnakovi. She was dizzy with despair. But Kareen would come to her sometime, even as a prisoner. Must come to her. All she needed was thirty

seconds with Kareen, maybe less. *When I see Kareen, you
are a dead man, Vordarian. You may walk and talk and
give orders, unconscious of your demise for weeks, but
I'll seal your fate as surely as you've sealed my son's.*

The reason for the wait materialized at last; Vordarian
himself, in green uniform trousers and slippers, bare-
chested, shouldered his way through the doorway. He was
followed by Princess Kareen, clutching a dark red velvet robe around her. Cordelia's heart hammered at a
doubled rate. *Now?*

"So. The trap worked," Vordarian began complacently,
but added a genuinely shocked "Huh!" as Cordelia pushed
away from the wall and turned to face him. A hand signal stopped a guard from shoving her back into position.
The shock on Vordarian's face gave way to a wolfish grin.
"My God, did it work! Excellent!" Kareen, hovering
behind him, stared at Cordelia in bewildered
astonishment.

MY trap worked, Cordelia thought, stunned with her
opportunity. *Watch me. . . .*

"That's the thing, my lord," said the liveried man, not
at all happily. "It didn't work. We didn't pick this party
up at the outer perimeter of the Residence and clear their
way, they just bloody turned up—without triggering anything. That shouldn't have happened. If I hadn't come
along looking for Roget, we might not have spotted 'em."

Vordarian shrugged, too delighted by the magnitude
of his prey to issue some trifling censure. "Fast-penta
that frill," he pointed at Droushnakovi, "and I imagine
you'll find out how. She used to work in Residence
Security."

Droushnakovi glowered over her shoulder at Princess
Kareen in hurt accusation; Kareen unconsciously pulled
her robe up more closely about her neck, her dark eyes
full of equally hurt question.

"Well," said Vordarian, still smiling at Cordelia, "is my
Lord Vorkosigan so thin of troops he sends his wife to
do their work? We cannot lose." He smiled at his guards,
who smiled back.

Damn, I wish I'd shot this lout in his sleep. "What have you done with my son, Vordarian?"

Vordarian said through his teeth, "An outworlder frill will never gain power on Barrayar by scheming to give a mutant the Imperium. That, I guarantee."

"Is that the official line, now? I don't want power. I just object to idiots having power over me."

Behind Vordarian, Kareen's lips quirked sadly. *Yes, listen to me, Kareen!*

"Where's my son, Vordarian?" Cordelia repeated doggedly.

"He's Emperor Vidal now," Kareen remarked, her glance going back and forth between them, "if he can keep it."

"I will," Vordarian promised. "Aral Vorkosigan has no better a blood-claim than my own. And I will protect where Vorkosigan's party has failed. Protect and preserve the real Barrayar." His head shifted; apparently this assertion was directed over his shoulder to Kareen.

"We have not failed," Cordelia whispered, meeting Kareen's eyes. *Now.* She lifted the shoe from the table, and stretched out her arm with it; Kareen's eyes widened. She darted forward and grabbed it. Cordelia's hand spasmed like a dying runner's giving up the baton in some mortal relay race. Fierce certainty bloomed like fire in her soul. *I have you now, Vordarian.* The sudden movement sent a ripple through the armed guards. Kareen examined the shoe with passionate intensity, turning it in her hands. Vordarian's brows rose in bafflement, then he dismissed Kareen from his attention and turned to his liveried guard commander.

"We'll keep all three of these prisoners here in the Residence. I'll personally attend the fast-penta interrogations. This is a spectacular opportunity—"

Kareen's face, when she lifted it again to Cordelia, was terrible with hope.

Yes, thought Cordelia. *You were betrayed. Lied to. Your son lives; you must move and think and feel again, no more the walking numbness of a dead spirit* beyond pain. This is no gift I've brought you. It is a curse.

"Kareen," said Cordelia softly, "where is my son?"

"The replicator is on a shelf in the oak wardrobe, in the old Emperor's bedchamber," Kareen replied steadily, locking her eyes to Cordelia's. "Where is mine?"

Cordelia's heart melted in gratitude for her curse, live pain. "Safe and well, when I last saw him, as long as this pretender," she jerked her head at Vordarian, "doesn't find out where. Gregor misses you. He sends his love." Her words might have been spikes, pounded into Kareen's body.

That got Vordarian's attention. "Gregor is at the bottom of a lake, killed in the flyer crash with that traitor Negri," he said roughly. "The most insidious lie is the one you want to hear. Guard yourself, my lady Kareen. I could not save him, but I will avenge him. I promise you that."

Uh-oh. Wait, Kareen. Cordelia bit her lip. *Not here. Too dangerous. Wait your best opportunity. Wait till the bastard's asleep, at least*—but if even a Betan hesitated to shoot her enemy sleeping, how much less a Vor? *She is true Vor. . . .*

An unfriendly smile crinkled Kareen's lips. Her eyes were alight. "This has never been immersed," she said softly.

Cordelia heard the murderous undertones ringing like a bell; Vordarian, apparently, only heard the breathiness of some girlish grief. He glanced at the shoe, not grasping its message, and shook his head as if to clear it of static. "You'll bear another son someday," he promised her kindly. "Our son."

Wait, wait, wait, Cordelia screamed inside.

"Never," whispered Kareen. She stepped back beside the guard in the doorway, snatched his nerve disruptor from his open holster, aimed it point-blank at Vordarian, and fired.

The startled guard knocked her hand up; the shot went wide, crackling into the ceiling. Vordarian dove behind the table, the only furniture in the room, rolling. His liveried man, in pure spinal reflex, snapped up his nerve disruptor and fired. Kareen's face muscles locked in death-agony as the blue fire washed around her head; her mouth pulled open in a last soundless cry. *Wait,* Cordelia's thought wailed.

Vordarian, utterly horrified, bellowed "No!", scrambled to his feet, and tore a nerve disruptor from the hand of another guard. The liveried man, realizing the enormity of his error, tossed his weapon away as if to divorce himself from his action. Vordarian shot him.

The room tilted around her. Cordelia's hand locked around the hilt of the swordstick and triggered its sheath flying into the head of one guard, then brought the blade smartly down across Vordarian's weapon-wrist. He screamed, and blood and the nerve disruptor flew wide. Droushnakovi was already diving for the first discarded nerve disruptor. Bothari just took his target out with one lethal hand-blow to the neck. Cordelia slammed the door shut against the guards in the corridor, surging forward. A stunner charge buzzed into the walls, then three blue bolts in rapid succession from Droushnakovi took out the last of Vordarian's men.

"*Grab* him," Cordelia yelled to Bothari. Vordarian, shaking, his left hand clamped around his half-severed right wrist, was in poor condition to resist, though he kicked and shouted. His blood ran the color of Kareen's robe. Bothari locked Vordarian's head in a firm grip, nerve disruptor pressed to his skull.

"Out of here," snarled Cordelia, and kicked the door back open. "To the Emperor's chamber." *To Miles.* Vordarian's other guards, preparing to fire, held back at the sight of their master.

"Back off!" Bothari roared, and they fell away from the door. Cordelia grabbed Droushnakovi by the arm, and they stepped over Kareen's body. Her ivory limbs lay muddled in the red fabric, abstractly beautiful forms even in death. The women kept Bothari and Vordarian between themselves and Vordarian's troops, and retreated down the corridor.

"Pull that plasma arc out of my holster and start firing,"

Bothari savagely directed Cordelia. Yes; Bothari had managed to retrieve it in the melee, probably why his body count hadn't been higher.

"You can't set fire to the *Residence*," Drou gasped in horror.

A fortune in antiquities and Barrayaran historical artifacts were housed in this wing alone, no doubt. Cordelia grinned wildly, grabbed the weapon, and fired back down the corridor. Wooden furniture, wooden parquetry, and age-dry tapestries roared into flame as the beam's searing fingers touched them.

Burn, you. Burn for Kareen. Pile a death-offering to match her courage and agony, blazing higher and higher— As they reached the door of the old Emperor's bedchamber, she fired the hallway in the opposite direction for good measure. *THAT for what you've done to•me, and to my boy—*the flames should hold back pursuit for a few minutes. She felt as though her body were floating, light as air. *Is this how Bothari feels, when he kills?*

Droushnakovi went for the wall panel to the secret ladder. She was functioning steadily now, as if her hands belonged to a different body than her tear-ravaged face. Cordelia dropped the sword on the bed and raced straight for the huge old carved oak wardrobe that stood against the near wall, and flung its doors wide. Green and amber lights glowed in the dim recesses of the center shelf. *God, don't let it be another decoy.* . . . Cordelia wrapped her arms around the canister and lifted it out into the light. The right weight, this time, heavy with fluids; the right readouts, the right numbers. The right one.

Thank you, Kareen. I didn't mean to kill you. Surely she was mad. She didn't feel anything, no grief or remorse, though her heart was racing and her breath came in gasps. A shocky combat-high, that immortal rush that made men charge machine guns. So this was what the war-addicts came for.

Vordarian was still struggling against Bothari's grip, swearing horribly. "You won't escape!" He stopped bucking, and tried to catch Cordelia's eyes. He took a deep breath. "Think, Lady Vorkosigan. You'll never make it. You must have me for a shield, but you can't carry me stunned. Conscious, I'll fight you every meter of the way. My men will be all over you, out there." His head jerked toward the window. "Stun us all and take you prisoner." His voice went persuasive. "Surrender now, and you'll save your lives. That one's life, too, if it means so much to you." He nodded to the replicator Cordelia held in her arms. Her steps were heavier than Alys Vorpatril's, now.

"I never gave orders for that fool Vorhalas to kill Vorkosigan's heir," Vordarian continued desperately into her silence. Blood leaked rapidly between his fingers. "It was only his father, with his fatal progressive policies, who threatened Barrayar. Your son might have inherited the Countship from Piotr with my goodwill. Piotr should never have been divided from his party of true allegiance. It's a crime, what Lord Aral has put Piotr through—"

So. It was you. Even at the very beginning. Blood loss and shock were making a jerky parody of Vordarian's usual smooth delivery of political argument. It was as if he sensed he could talk his way out of retribution, if only he hit on the right key words. Somehow, Cordelia doubted he would. Vordarian was not gaudily evil like Vorrutyer had been, not personally degraded like Serg; yet evil had flowed from him nonetheless, not from his vices, but from his virtues: the courage of his conservative convictions, his passion for Kareen. Cordelia's head ached, vilely.

"We'd never proved you were behind Evon Vorhalas," Cordelia said quietly. "Thank you for the information."

That shut him up, for a moment. His eyes shifted uneasily to the door, soon to burst inward, ignited by the inferno behind it.

"Dead, I'm no use to you as a hostage," he said, drawing himself up in dignity.

"'You're no use to me at all, Emperor Vidal," said Cordelia frankly. "There are at least five thousand casualties in this war so far. Now that Kareen is dead, how long will you keep fighting?"

"Forever," he snarled whitely. "I will avenge her—avenge them all—"

Wrong answer, Cordelia thought, with a curious light-headed sadness. "Bothari." He was at her side instantly. "Pick up that sword." He did so. She set the replicator on the floor and laid her hand briefly atop his, wrapped around the hilt. "Bothari, execute this man for me, please." Her tone sounded weirdly serene in her own ears, as if she'd just asked Bothari to pass the butter. Murder didn't really require hysterics.

"Yes, Milady," Bothari intoned, and lifted the blade. His eyes gleamed with joy.

"What?" yelped Vordarian in astonishment. "You're a Betan! You can't do—"

The flashing stroke cut off his words, his head, and his life. It was really extremely neat, despite the last spurts of blood from the stump of his neck. Vorkosigan should have loaned Bothari's services the day they'd executed Carl Vorhalas. All that upper body strength, combined with that extraordinary steel . . . the bemused gyration of her thought snapped back to near-reality as Bothari fell to his knees with the body, dropping the swordstick and clutching his head. He screamed. It was as if Vordarian's death cry had been forced out of Bothari's throat.

She dropped beside him, suddenly afraid again, though she'd been numb to fear, white-out overloaded, ever since Kareen had grabbed for the nerve disruptor and triggered all this chaos. Keyed by similar stimuli, Bothari was having the forbidden flashback, Cordelia guessed, to the mutinous throat-cutting that the Barrayaran high command had decreed he must forget. She cursed herself for not forseeing this possibility. Would it kill him?

"This door is hot as hell," Droushnakovi, white and shaken, reported from beside it. "Milady, we have to get out of here *now.*"

Bothari was gasping raggedly, hands still pressed to his head, yet even as she watched his breathing grew marginally less disrupted. She left him, to crawl blindly over the floor. She needed something, something moisture-proof. . . .

There, at the bottom of the wardrobe, was a sturdy plastic bag containing several pairs of Kareen's shoes, no doubt hastily transported by some maidservant when Vordarian had Imperially decreed Kareen move in with him. Cordelia emptied out the shoes, stumbled back around the bed, and collected Vordarian's head from the place where it had rolled to a stop. It was heavy, but not so heavy as the uterine replicator. She pulled the drawstrings tight.

"Drou. You're in the best shape. Carry the replicator. Start down. Don't drop it." If she dropped Vordarian, Cordelia decided, it would scarcely do him further harm.

Droushnakovi nodded and grabbed up both the replicator and the abandoned swordstick. Cordelia wasn't sure if she retrieved the latter for its newly acquired historical value, or from some fractured sense of obligation for one of Kou's possessions. Cordelia coaxed Bothari to his feet. Cool air was rushing up out of the panel opening, drawn by the fire beyond the door. It would make a neat flue, till the burning wall crashed in and blocked the entry. Vordarian's people were going to have a very puzzling time, poking through the embers and wondering where they'd gone.

The descent was nightmarish, in the compressed space, with Bothari whimpering below her feet. She could carry the bag neither beside nor in front of her, so had to balance it on one shoulder and go one-handed, palm slapping down the rungs and her wrist aching.

Once on the level, she prodded the weeping Bothari ruthlessly forward, and wouldn't let him stop till they came again to Ezar's cache in the ancient stable cellar.

"Is he all right?" Droushnakovi asked nervously, as Bothari sat down with his head between his knees.

"He has a headache," said Cordelia. "It may take a while to pass off."

Droushnakovi asked even more diffidently, "Are *you* all right, Milady?"

Cordelia couldn't help it; she laughed. She choked down the hysteria as Drou began to look really scared. "No."

CHAPTER NINETEEN

Ezar's cache included a crate of currency, Barrayaran marks of various denominations. It also included a choice of IDs tailored to Drou, not all of which were obsolete. Cordelia put the two together, and sent Drou out to purchase a used groundcar. Cordelia waited by the cache while Bothari slowly uncurled from his tight fetal ball of pain, recovering enough to walk.

Getting back out of Vorbarr Sultana had always been the weak part of her plan, Cordelia felt, perhaps because she'd never really believed they'd get this far. Travel was tightly restricted, as Vordarian sought to keep the city from collapsing under him should its frightened populace attempt to stream away. The monorail required passes and cross-checks. Lightflyers were absolutely forbidden, targets of opportunity for trigger-happy guards. Groundcars had to cross multiple roadblocks. Foot travel was too slow for her burdened and exhausted party. There were no good choices.

After an eternity, pale Drou returned, to lead them back through the tunnels and out to an obscure side street. The city was dusted with sooty snow. From the direction of the Residence, a kilometer off, a darker cloud boiled up to mix with the winter-grey sky; the fierce fire was still not under control, apparently. How long would Vordarian's decapitated command structure keep functioning? Had word of his death leaked out yet?

As instructed, Drou had found a very plain and unobtrusive old groundcar, though there had been enough funds to buy the most luxurious new vehicle the city still held. Cordelia wanted to save that reserve for the checkpoints.

But the checkpoints were not as bad as Cordelia had feared. Indeed, the first was empty, its guards pulled back, perhaps, to fight the fire or seal the perimeter of the Residence. The second was crowded with vehicles and impatient drivers. The inspectors were perfunctory and nervous, distracted and half-paralyzed by who-knew-what rumors coming from downtown. A fat wad of currency, handed out under Drou's perfect false ID, disappeared into a guard's pocket. He waved Drou through, driving her "sick uncle" home. Bothari looked sick enough, for sure, huddled under a blanket that also hid the replicator. At the last checkpoint Drou "repeated" a likely version of a rumor of Vordarian's death, and the worried guard deserted on the spot, shedding his uniform in favor of a civilian overcoat and vanishing down a side street.

They zigzagged over bad side roads all afternoon to reach Vorinnis's neutral District, where the aged groundcar died of a fractured power-train. They abandoned it and took to the monorail system then, Cordelia driving her exhausted little party on, racing the clock in her head. At midnight, they reported in at the first military installation over the next loyalist border, a supply depot. It took Drou several minutes of argument with the night duty officer to persuade him to 1) identify them, 2) let them in, and 3) let them use the military comm net to call Tanery Base to demand transport. At that point the D.O. abruptly became a lot more efficient. A high-speed air shuttle with a hot pilot was scrambled to pick them up.

Approaching Tanery Base at dawn from the air, Cordelia felt the most unpleasant flash of deja vu. It was so like her first arrival from the mountains, she had the sense of being caught in a time loop. Perhaps she'd died and gone to hell, and her eternal torment would be to repeat the last three weeks' events over and over, endlessly. She shivered.

Droushnakovi watched her with concern. The exhausted Bothari dozed, in the air shuttle's passenger cabin. Illyan's two ImpSec men, identical twins for all Cordelia could tell to Vordarian's ones they'd murdered back at the Residence, maintained a nervous silence. Cordelia held the uterine replicator possessively on her lap. The plastic bag sat between her feet. She was irrationally unable to let either item out of her sight, though it was clear Drou would much rather the bag had ridden in the luggage compartment.

The air shuttle touched neatly down on its landing pad, and its engines whined to silence.

"I want Captain Vaagen, and I want him *now*," Cordelia repeated for the fifth time as Illyan's men led them underground into the Security debriefing area.

"Yes, Milady. He's on his way," the ImpSec man assured her again. She glowered suspiciously at him.

Cautiously, the ImpSec men relieved them of their personal arsenal. Cordelia didn't blame them; she wouldn't have trusted her wild-looking crew with charged weapons either. Thanks to Ezar's cache the women were not ill dressed, though there had been nothing in Bothari's size, so he'd retained his smoked and stinking black fatigues. Fortunately the dried blood spatters didn't show much. But all their faces were hollow-eyed, grooved and shadowed. Cordelia shivered, and Bothari's hands and eyelids twitched, and Droushnakovi had a distressing tendency to start crying, silently, at random moments, stopping as suddenly as she started.

At long last—only minutes, Cordelia told herself firmly—Captain Vaagen appeared, a tech at his side. He wore undress greens, and his steps were quick, up to Vaagen-speed again. The only residue of his injuries seemed to be a black patch over his eye; on him, it looked good, giving him a fine piratical air. Cordelia trusted the patch was only a temporary part of ongoing treatment.

"Milady!" He managed a smile, the first to shift those facial muscles in a while, Cordelia sensed. His one eye gleamed triumph. "You got it!"

"I hope so, Captain." She held up the replicator, which she had refused to let the ImpSec men touch. "I hope we're in time. There aren't any red lights yet, but there was a warning beeper. I shut it off, it was driving me crazy."

He looked the device over, checking key readouts. "Good. Good. Nutrient reservoir is very low, but not quite depleted yet. Filters still functioning, uric acid level high but not over tolerance—I think it's all right, Milady. Alive, that is. What this interruption has done to my calcification treatments will take more time to determine. We'll be in the infirmary. I should be able to begin servicing it within the hour."

"Do you have everything you need there? Supplies?"

His white teeth flashed. "Lord Vorkosigan had me begin setting up a lab the day after you left. Just in case, he said."

Aral, I love you. "Thank you. Go, go." She surrendered the replicator into Vaagen's hands, and he hurried out with it.

She sat back down like a marionette with the strings cut. Now she could allow herself to feel the full weight of her exhaustion. But she could not stop quite yet. She had one very important debriefing yet to accomplish. And not to these hovering ImpSec twits, who pestered her—she closed her eyes and pointedly ignored them, letting Drou stammer out answers to their foolish questions.

Desire warred with dread. She wanted Aral. She had defied Aral, most openly. Had it touched his honor, scorched his—admittedly, unusually flexible—Barrayaran male ego beyond tolerance? Would she be frozen out of his trust forever? No, that suspicion was surely unjust. But his public credibility among his peers, part of the delicate psychology of power—had she damaged it? Would some damnable unforseen political consequence rebound out of all this, back on their heads? Did she care? Yes, she decided sadly. It was hell to be so tired, and still care.

"Kou!"

Drou's cry snapped Cordelia's eyes open. Koudelka was limping into the main portal Security debriefing office. Good Lord, the man was back in uniform, shaved and sharp. Only the grey rings under his eyes were non-regulation.

Kou and Drou's reunion, Cordelia was delighted to note, was not in the least military. The staff soldier was instantly plastered all over with tall and grubby blonde, exchanging muffled un-regulation greetings like *darling, love, thank God, safe, sweet*. . . . The ImpSec men turned away uncomfortably from the blast of naked emotion radiating from their faces. Cordelia basked in it. A far more sensible way to greet a friend than all that moronic saluting.

They parted only to see each other better, still holding hands. "You made it," chortled Droushnakovi. "How long have you—is Lady Vorpatril—?"

"We only made it in about two hours ahead of you," Kou said breathlessly, reoxygenating after a heroic kiss. "Lady Vorpatril and the young lord are bedded down in the infirmary. The doctor says she's suffering mainly from stress and exhaustion. She was incredible. We had a couple of bad moments, getting past Vordarian's Security, but she never cracked. And you—you did it! I passed Vaagen in the corridor, with the replicator—you rescued m'lord's son!"

Droushnakovi's shoulders sagged. "But we lost Princess Kareen."

"Oh." He touched her lips. "Don't tell me—Lord Vorkosigan instructed me to bring you all to him the instant you arrived. Debrief to him before anyone. I'll take you to him now." He waved away the ImpSec men like flies, something Cordelia had been longing to do.

Bothari had to help her rise. She gathered up the yellow plastic bag. She noted ironically that it bore the name and logo of one of the capital's most exclusive women's clothiers. *Kareen encompasses you at last, you bastard.*

"What's that?" asked Kou.

"Yes, Lieutenant," the urgent ImpSec man put in, "please—she's refused to let us examine it in any way. By regulations, we shouldn't let her carry it into the base."

Cordelia pulled open the top of the bag and held it out for Kou's inspection. He peered within.

"*Shit.*" The ImpSec men surged forward as Koudelka jumped back. He waved them down. "I . . . I see," he swallowed. "Yes, Admiral Vorkosigan will certainly want to see *that.*"

"Lieutenant, what should I put on my inventory?" the ImpSec man—whined, Cordelia decided, was what he was doing. "I have to register it, if it's going in."

"Let him cover his ass, Kou," Cordelia sighed.

Kou peeked again, his lips twisting into a very crooked grin. "It's all right. Put it down as a Winterfair gift for Admiral Vorkosigan. From his wife."

"Oh, Kou," Drou held out his sword. "I saved this. But we lost the casing, I'm sorry."

Kou took it, looked at the bag, made the connection, and carried it more carefully. "That's . . . that's all right. Thank you."

"I'll take it back to Siegling's and get a duplicate casing made," Cordelia promised.

The ImpSec men gave way before Admiral Vorkosigan's top aide. Kou led Cordelia, Bothari, and Drou into the base. Cordelia pulled the drawstring tight, and let the bag swing from her hand.

"We're going down to the Staff level. The admiral's been in a sealed meeting for the last hour. Two of Vordarian's top officers came in secretly last night. Negotiating to sell him out. The best hostage-rescue plan hinges on their cooperation."

"Did they know about this yet?" Cordelia held up the bag.

"I don't think so, Milady. You've just changed everything." His grin grew feral, and his uneven stride lengthened.

"I expect that raid is still going to be required,"

Cordelia sighed. "Even in collapse, Vordarian's side is still dangerous. Maybe more dangerous, in their desperation." She thought of that downtown Vorbarr Sultana hotel, where Bothari's baby girl Elena was, as far as she knew, still housed. Lesser hostages. Could she persuade Aral to apportion a few more resources for lesser hostages? Alas, she had probably not put all the soldiers out of work even yet. *I tried. God, I tried.*

They went down, and down, to the nerve center of Tanery Base. They came to a highly secured conference chamber; a lethally armed squad stood ramrod-guard outside it. Koudelka wafted them past. The doors slid aside, and closed again behind them.

Cordelia took in the tableau, that paused to look back up at her from around the polished table. Aral was in the center, of course. Illyan and Count Piotr flanked him on either side. Prime Minister Vortala was there, and Kanzian, and some other senior staffers all in formal dress greens. The two double-traitors sat across, with their aides. Clouds of witnesses. She wanted to be alone with Aral, be rid of the whole bloody mob of them. *Soon.*

Aral's eyes locked to hers in silent agony. His lips curled in an utterly ironic smile. That was all; and yet her stomach warmed with confidence again, sure of him. No frost. It was going to be all right. They were in step again, and a torrent of words and hard embraces could not have communicated it any better. Embraces would come, though, the grey eyes promised. Her own lips curved up for the first time since—when?

Count Piotr's hand slapped down hard upon the table. "Good God, woman, where have you *been*?" he cried furiously.

A morbid lunacy overtook her. She smiled fiercely at him, and held up the bag. "Shopping."

For a second, the old man nearly believed her; conflicting expressions whiplashed over his face, astonishment, disbelief, then anger as it penetrated he was being mocked.

"Want to see what I bought?" Cordelia continued, still

floating. She yanked the bag's top open, and rolled
Vordarian's head out across the table. Fortunately, it had
ceased leaking some hours back. It stopped faceup before
him, lips grinning, drying eyes staring.

Piotr's mouth fell open. Kanzian jumped, the staffers swore, and one of Vordarian's traitors actually fell
out of his chair, recoiling. Vortala pursed his lips and
raised his brows. Koudelka, grimly proud of his key role
in stage-managing this historic moment in one-
upsmanship, laid the swordstick on the table as further
evidence. Illyan puffed, and grinned triumphantly through
his shock.

Aral was perfect. His eyes widened only briefly, then
he rested his chin on his hands and gazed over his father's
shoulder with an expression of cool interest. "But of
course," he breathed. "Every Vor lady goes to the capital to shop."

"I paid too much for it," Cordelia confessed.

"That, too, is traditional." A sardonic smile quirked his
lips.

"Kareen is dead. Shot in the melee. I couldn't save her."

He opened his hand, as if to let the nascent black
humor fall through his fingers. "I see." He raised his eyes
again to hers, as if asking *Are you all right?*, and apparently finding the answer, *No.*

"Gentlemen. If you will be pleased to excuse yourselves for a few minutes. I wish to be alone with my
wife."

In the shuffle of the men rising to their feet, Cordelia
caught a mutter, "Brave man . . ."

She nailed Vordarian's men by eye, as they backed from
the table. "Officers. I recommend that when this conference resumes, you surrender unconditionally upon Lord
Vorkosigan's mercy. He may still have some." *I certainly
don't*, was the unspoken cap to that. "I'm tired of your
stupid war. End it."

Piotr edged past her. She smiled bitterly at him. He
grimaced uneasily back. "It appears I underestimated you,"
he murmured.

"Don't you ever . . . cross me again. And stay away from my son."

A look from Vorkosigan held back her outpouring of rage, quivering on the lip of her cup. She and Piotr exchanged wary nods, like the vestigial bows of two duelists.

"Kou," said Vorkosigan, staring bemusedly at the grisly object lying by his elbow. "Will you please arrange for this thing to be removed to the base morgue. I don't fancy it as a table decoration. It will have to be stored till it can be buried with the rest of him. Wherever that may be."

"Sure you don't want to leave it there to inspire Vordarian's staffers to come to terms?" said Kou.

"No," said Vorkosigan firmly. "It's had a sufficiently salutary effect already."

Gingerly, Kou took the bag from Cordelia, opened it, and used it to capture Vordarian's head without actually touching it.

Aral's eye took in her weary team, Droushnakovi's grief, Bothari's compulsive twitching. "Drou. Sergeant. You are dismissed to wash and eat. Report back to me in my quarters after we finish here."

Droushnakovi nodded, and the sergeant saluted, and they followed Koudelka out.

Cordelia fell into Aral's arms as the door sighed shut, into his lap, catching him as he rose for her. They both landed with enough force to threaten the balance of the chair. They embraced each other so tightly, they had to back off to manage a kiss.

"Don't you ever," he husked, "pull a stunt like that again."

"Don't you ever let it become necessary, again."

"Deal."

He held her face away from his, between his hands, his eyes devouring her. "I was so afraid for you, I forgot to be afraid for your enemies. I should have remembered. Dear Captain."

"I couldn't have done a thing, alone. Drou was my eyes, Bothari my right arm, Koudelka our feet. You must forgive Kou for going AWOL. We sort of kidnapped him."

"So I heard."

"Did he tell you about your cousin Padma?"

"Yes," a grieved sigh. He stared back through time. "Padma and I were the only survivors of Mad Yuri's massacre of Prince Xav's descendants, that day. I was eleven. Padma was one, a baby . . . I always thought of him as the baby, ever after. Tried to watch out for him . . . Now I'm the only one left. Yuri's work is almost done."

"Bothari's Elena. She must be rescued. She's a lot more important than that barn full of counts at the Residence."

"We're working on that right now," he promised. "Top priority, now that you've removed Emperor Vidal from consideration." He paused, smiling slowly. "I fear you've shocked my Barrayarans, love."

"Why? Did they think they had a monopoly on savagery? Those were Vordarian's last words. 'You're a Betan. You can't do.' "

"Do what?"

"*This*, I suppose he would have said. If he'd had the chance."

"A lurid trophy, to carry on the monorail. Suppose someone had asked you to open your bag?"

"I would have."

"Are you . . . quite all right, love?" His mouth was serious, under his smile.

"Meaning, have I lost my grip? Yes, a little. More than a little." Her hands still shook, as they had for a day, a continuing tremula that did not pass off. "It seemed . . . necessary, to bring Vordarian's head along. I hadn't actually thought about mounting it on the wall of Vorkosigan House along with your father's hunting trophies, though it's an idea. I don't think I consciously realized why I was hanging on to it till I walked into this room. If I'd staggered in here empty-handed and told all those men I'd killed Vordarian, and undeclared their little war, who'd have believed me? Besides you."

"Illyan, perhaps. He's seen you in action before. The others . . . you're quite right."

"I think I also had some idea stuck in my mind from ancient history. Didn't they used to publicly display the bodies of slain rulers, to scotch pretenders? It seemed appropriate. Though Vordarian was almost a side-issue, from my point of view."

"Your ImpSec escort reported to me you'd recovered the replicator. Was it still working?"

"Vaagen has it now, checking it. Miles is alive. Damage unknown. Oh. It seems Vordarian had some hand in setting up Evon Vorhalas. Not directly, through some agent."

"Illyan suspected it." His arms tightened around her.

"About Bothari," she said. "He's not in good shape. Way overstressed. He needs real treatment, medical, not political. That memory wipe was a horror show."

"At the time, it saved his life. My compromise with Ezar. I had no power then. I can do better now."

"You'd better. He's fixated on me like a dog. His words. And I've used him like one. I owe him . . . everything. But he scares me. Why *me*?"

Vorkosigan looked very thoughtful. "Bothari . . . does not have a good sense of self. No strong center. When I first met him, at his most ill, his personality was close to separating into multiples. If he were better educated, not so damaged, he would have made an ideal spy, a deep-penetration mole. He's a chameleon. A mirror. He becomes whatever is required of him. Not a conscious process, I don't think. Piotr expects a loyal retainer, and Bothari plays the part, deadpan as you please. Vorrutyer wanted a monster, and Bothari became his torturer. And victim. I demanded a good soldier, and he became one for me. You . . ." his voice softened, "you are the only person I know who looks at Bothari and sees a hero. So he becomes one for you. He clings to you because you create him a greater man than he ever dreamed of being."

"Aral, that's crazed."

"Ah?" He nuzzled her hair. "But he's not the only man you have that peculiar effect upon. Dear Captain."

"I'm afraid I'm not in much better shape than Bothari. I botched it, and Kareen died. Who will tell Gregor? If it weren't for Miles, I'd quit. You keep Piotr off me, or I swear, next time I'll try and take him apart." She was shaking again.

"Sh." He rocked her, a little. "I think you can at least leave the mopping up to me, eh? Will you trust me again? We'll make something of these sacrifices. Not vain."

"I feel dirty. I feel sick."

"Yes. Most sane people do, coming in off a combat mission. It's a very familiar state of mind." He paused. "But if a Betan can become so Barrayaran, maybe it's not so impossible for Barrayarans to become a little more Betan. Change *is* possible."

"Change is inevitable," she asserted. "But you can't manage it Ezar's way. This isn't Ezar's era anymore. You have to find your own way. Remake this world into one Miles can survive in. And Elena. And Ivan. And Gregor."

"As you will, Milady."

On the third day after Vordarian's death, the capital fell to loyal Imperial troops; if not without a shot being fired, at least not nearly so bloodily as Cordelia had feared. Only two pockets of resistance, at ImpSec and at the Residence itself, had to be cleared out by ground troops. The downtown hotel with its hostages was surrendered intact by its garrison, after hours of intense covert negotiations. Piotr gave Bothari a one-day leave to personally retrieve his child and her fosterer and escort them home. Cordelia slept through the night for the first time since her return.

Evon Vorhalas had been commanding ground troops for Vordarian in the capital, in charge of the last defense of the space communications center in the military headquarters complex. He died in the final flurry of fighting, shot by his own men when he spurned an offer of amnesty in return for their surrender. In a way, Cordelia was relieved. The traditional punishment for treason upon the part of a Vor lord was public exposure and death by starvation. The late Emperor Ezar had not hesitated to maintain the gruesome tradition. Cordelia could only pray that Gregor's reign would see the custom end.

Without Vordarian to hold it together, his rebel coalition shattered rapidly into disparate factions. An extreme conservative Vor lord in the city of Federstok raised his standard and declared himself Emperor, succeeding Vordarian; his pretendership lasted somewhat less than thirty hours. In an eastern coastal District belonging to one of Vordarian's allies, the Count suicided upon capture. An anti-Vor group declared an independent republic in the chaos. The new Count, an infantry colonel from a collateral family line who had never anticipated such honors falling upon him, took instant and effective exception to this violent swing to the over-progressive. Vorkosigan left it to him and his District militia, reserving Imperial troops for "non-District-internal matters."

"You can't go halfway and stop," Piotr muttered forebodingly, at this delicacy.

"One step at a time," Vorkosigan returned grimly, "I can walk around the world. Watch me."

On the fifth day, Gregor was returned to the capital. Vorkosigan and Cordelia together undertook to tell him of the death of Kareen. He cried in bewilderment. When he quieted, he was taken for a ride in a groundcar with a transparent force-screen, reviewing some troops; in fact, the troops were reviewing him, that he might be seen to be alive, finally dispelling Vordarian's rumors of his death. Cordelia rode with him. His silent shockiness hurt her to the heart, but it was better from her point of view than parading him first and then telling him. If she'd had to endure his repeated queries of when he would see his mother again, all during the ride, she would have broken down herself.

The funeral for Kareen was public, though much less elaborate than it would have been in less chaotic circumstances. Gregor was required to light an offering pyre for the second time in a year. Vorkosigan asked

Cordelia to guide Gregor's hand with the torch. This part
of the funeral ceremony seemed almost redundant, after
what she'd done to the Residence. Cordelia added a
thick lock of her own hair to the pile. Gregor clung close
to her.

"Are they going to kill me, too?" he whispered to her.
He didn't sound frightened, just morbidly curious. Father,
grandfather, mother, all gone in a year; no wonder he felt
targeted, confused though his understanding of death was
at his age.

"No," she said firmly. Her arm tightened around his
shoulders. "I won't let them." God help her, this base-
less assurance actually seemed to console him.

I'll look after your boy, Kareen, Cordelia thought as
the flames rose up. The oath was more costly than any
gift being burned, for it bound her life unbreakably to
Barrayar. But the heat on her face eased the pain in her
head, a little.

Cordelia's own soul felt like an exhausted snail, shelled
in a glassy numbness. She crept like an automaton through
the rest of the ceremony, though there were flashes when
her surroundings made no sense at all. The assorted
Barrayaran Vor reacted to her with a frozen, deep formality. *They doubtless figure me for crazy-dangerous, a
madwoman let out of the attic by overindulgent relations.*
It finally dawned on her that their exaggerated courtesies signified *respect.*

It made her furious. All Kareen's courage of endurance
had bought her nothing, Lady Vorpatril's brave and bloody
birth-giving was taken for granted, but whack off some
idiot's head and you were really somebody, by God—!

It took Aral an hour, when they returned to his quarters, to calm her down, and then she had a crying jag.
He stuck it out.

"Are you going to use this?" she asked him, when sheer
weariness returned her to a semblance of coherence.
"This, this . . . amazing new *status* of mine?" How she
loathed the word, acid in her mouth.

"I'll use anything," he vowed quietly, "if it will help

me put Gregor on the throne in fifteen years a sane and competent man, heading a stable government. Use you, me, whatever it takes. To pay this much, then fail, would not be tolerable."

She sighed, and put her hand in his. "In case of accident, donate my remaining body parts, too. It's the Betan way. Waste not."

His lip curled up helplessly. Face-to-face, they rested their foreheads together for a moment, bracing each other. "Want not."

Her silent promise to Kareen was made policy when she and Aral, as a couple, were officially appointed Gregor's guardians by the Council of Counts. This was legally distinct somehow from Aral's guardianship of the Imperium as Regent. Prime Minister Vortala took time to lecture her and make it clear her new duties involved no political powers. She did have economic functions, including trusteeship of certain Vorbarra holdings that were separate from Imperial properties, appending strictly to Gregor's title as Count Vorbarra. And by Aral's delegation, she was given oversight of the Emperor's household. And education.

"But, Aral," said Cordelia, stunned. "Vortala emphasized I was to have no power."

"Vortala . . . is not all-wise. Let's just say, he has a little trouble recognizing as such some forms of power which are not synonymous with force. Your window of opportunity is narrow, though; at age twelve Gregor will enter a pre-Academy preparatory school."

"But do they realize . . . ?"

"I do. And you do. It's enough."

CHAPTER TWENTY

One of Cordelia's first orders was to assign Droushnakovi back to Gregor's person, for his emotional continuity. This did not mean giving up the girl's company, a comfort to which Cordelia had grown deeply accustomed, because upon Illyan's renewed insistence Aral finally took up living quarters in the Imperial Residence. It eased Cordelia's heart, when Drou and Kou were wed a month after Winterfair.

Cordelia offered herself as a go-between for the two families. For some reason, Kou and Drou both turned the offer down, hastily, though with profuse thanks. Given the bewildering pitfalls of Barrayaran social custom, Cordelia was just as happy to leave it to the experienced elderly lady the couple did contract.

Cordelia saw Alys Vorpatril often, exchanging domestic visits. Baby Lord Ivan was, if not exactly a comfort to Alys, certainly a distraction in her slow recovery from her physical ordeal. He grew rapidly despite a tendency to fussiness, an iatrogenic trait, Cordelia realized after a while, triggered by Alys's fussing over him. Ivan should have three or four sibs to divide her attention among, Cordelia decided, watching Alys burp him on her shoulder while planning aloud his educational attack, come age eighteen, upon the formidable Imperial Military Academy entrance examinations.

Alys Vorpatril was drawn off her embittered mourning for Padma and her planning of Ivan's life down to the last detail, when she was given a look at a picture of the wedding dress Drou was drooling over.

"No, no, no!" she cried, recoiling. "All that lace—you would look as furry as a big white bear. Silk, dear, long falls of silk is what you need—" and she was off. Motherless, sisterless Drou could scarcely have found a more knowledgeable bridal consultant. Lady Vorpatril ended by making the dress one of her several presents, to be sure of its aesthetic perfection, along with a "little holiday cottage" which turned out to be a substantial house on the eastern seashore. Come summer, Drou's beach dream would come true. Cordelia grinned, and purchased the girl a nightgown and robe with enough tiers of lace layered on them to satiate the most frill-starved soul.

Aral lent the hall: the Imperial Residence's Red Room and adjacent ballroom, the one with the beautiful marquetry floor, which to Cordelia's immense relief had escaped the fire. In theory, this magnificent gesture was required to ease Illyan's Security headaches, as Cordelia and Aral were to stand among the principal witnesses. Personally, Cordelia thought converting ImpSec into wedding caterers a promising turn of events.

Aral looked over the guest list and smiled. "Do you realize," he said to Cordelia, "every class is represented? A year ago this event, here, would not have been possible. The grocer's son and the non-com's daughter. They bought it with blood, but maybe next year it can be bought with peaceful achievement. Medicine, education, engineering, entrepreneurship—shall we have a party for librarians?"

"Won't those terrible Vorish crones all Piotr's friends are married to complain about social over-progressiveness?"

"With Alys Vorpatril behind this? They wouldn't dare."

The affair grew from there. By a week in advance Kou

and Drou were considering eloping out of sheer panic, having lost all control of everything whatsoever to their eager helpers. But the Imperial Residence's staff brought it all together with practiced ease. The senior housewoman flew about, chortling, "And here I was afraid we weren't going to have anything to do, once the admiral moved in, but those dreadful boring General Staff dinners."

The day and hour came at last. A large circle made of colored groats was laid out on the floor of the Red Room, encompassed by a star with a variable number of points, one for each parent or principal witness to stand at: in this case, four. In Barrayaran custom a couple married themselves, speaking their vows within the circle, requiring neither priest nor magistrate. Practically, a coach, called appropriately enough the Coach, stood outside the circle and read the script for the fainthearted or faint-headed to repeat. This dispensed with the need for higher neural functions such as learning and memory on the part of the stressed couple. Lost motor coordination was supplied by a friend each, who steered them to the circle. It was all very practical, Cordelia decided, as well as splendid.

With a grin and a flourish Aral placed her at her assigned star point, as if setting out a bouquet, and took his own place. Lady Vorpatril had insisted on a new gown for Cordelia, a sweeping length of blue and white with red floral accents, color-coordinated with Aral's ultra-formal parade red-and-blues. Drou's proud and nervous father also wore his red-and-blues and held down his point. Strange to think of the military, which Cordelia normally associated with totalitarian impulses, as the spearhead of egalitarianism on Barrayar. The Cetagandans' gift, Aral called it; their invasion had first forced the promotion of talent regardless of origin, and the waves of that change were still traveling through Barrayaran society.

Sergeant Droushnakovi was a shorter, slighter man than Cordelia had expected. Either Drou's mother's genes, better nutrition, or both had boosted all his children up taller than himself. All three brothers, from the captain to the corporal, had been broken loose from their military assignments to attend, and stood now in the big outer circle of other witnesses along with Kou's excited younger sister. Kou's mother stood on the star's last point, crying and smiling, in a blue dress so color-perfect Cordelia decided Alys Vorpatril must have somehow gotten to her, too.

Koudelka marched in first, propped by his stick with its new cover and Sergeant Bothari. Sergeant Bothari wore the most glittery version of Piotr's brown and silver livery, and whispered helpful, horribly suggestive advice like "If you feel really nauseous, Lieutenant, put your head down." The very thought turned Kou's face greener, an extraordinary color-contrast with his red-and-blues that Lady Vorpatril would no doubt have disapproved.

Heads turned. *Oh, my.* Alys Vorpatril had been absolutely right about Drou's gown. She swept in, as stunningly graceful as a sailing ship, a tall clean perfection of form and function, ivory silk, gold hair, blue eyes, white, blue, and red flowers, so that when she stepped up beside Kou one suddenly realized how tall he must be. Alys Vorpatril, in silver-grey, released Drou at the circle's edge with a gesture like some hunting goddess releasing a white falcon, to soar and settle on Kou's outstretched arm.

Kou and Drou made it through their oaths without stammering or passing out, and managed to conceal their mutual embarrassment at the public declaration of their despised first names, Clement and Ludmilla.

("My brothers used to call me Lud," Drou had confided to Cordelia during the practice yesterday. "Rhymes with mud. Also thud, blood, crud, dud, and cud."

"You'll always be Drou to me," Kou had promised.)

As senior witness Aral then broke the circle of groats with a sweep of one booted foot and let them out, and the music, dancing, eating and drinking began.

The buffet was incredible, the music live, and the drinking . . . traditional. After the first formal glass of the good wine Piotr'd sent on, Cordelia drifted up to Kou and murmured a few words about Betan research on the detrimental effects of ethanol on sexual function, after which he switched to water.

"Cruel woman," Aral whispered in her ear, laughing.

"Not to Drou, I'm not," she murmured back.

She was formally introduced to the brothers, now brothers-in-law, who regarded her with that awed respect that made her teeth grind. Though her jaw eased a bit when a rhyming brother was waved to silence by Dad to make room for some comment by the bride on the topic of hand-weapons. "Quiet, Jos," Sergeant Droushnakovi told his son. "You've never handled a nerve disruptor in combat." Drou blinked, then smiled, a gleam in her eye.

Cordelia seized a moment with Bothari, whom she saw all too seldom now that Aral had split his household from Piotr's.

"How is Elena doing, now she's back home? Has Mistress Hysopi recovered from it all yet?"

"They're well, Milady," Bothari ducked his head, and almost-smiled. "I visited about five days ago, when Count Piotr went down to check on his horses. Elena, um, creeps. Put her down and look away a minute, you look back and she's moved. . . ." He frowned. "I hope Carla Hysopi stays alert."

"She saw Elena safely through Vordarian's war, I suspect she'll handle crawling with equal ease. Courageous woman. She should be in line for some of those medals they're handing out."

Bothari's brow wrinkled. "Don't know they'd mean much to her."

"Mm. She does understand she can call on me for anything she needs, I trust. Any time."

"Yes, Milady. But we're doing all right for the moment." A flash of pride, there, in that statement of sufficiency. "It's very quiet down at Vorkosigan Surleau, in the winter. Clean. A right and proper place for a baby." *Not like the place I grew up in,* Cordelia could almost hear him add. "I mean her to have everything right and proper. Even her da."

"How are you doing, yourself?"

"The new med is better. Anyway, my head doesn't feel

like it's stuffed with fog anymore. And I sleep at night. Besides that I can't tell what it's doing."

Its job, apparently; he seemed relaxed and calm, almost free of that sinister edginess. Though he was still the first person in the room to look over to the buffet and ask, "Is *he* supposed to be up?"

Gregor, in pajamas, was creeping along the edge of the culinary array, trying to look invisible and nail down a few goodies before he was spotted and taken away again. Cordelia got to him first, before he was either stepped on by an unwary guest, or recaptured by Security forces in the persons of the breathless maidservant and terrified bodyguard who were supposed to be filling in for Drou. They were followed up by a paper-white Simon Illyan. Fortunately for Illyan's heart, Gregor had apparently only been formally missing for about sixty seconds. Gregor shrank into her skirts as the hyperventilating adults loomed over him.

Drou, who had noticed Illyan touch his comm, turn pale, and start to move, checked in by sheer force of habit. "What's the matter?"

"How'd he get away?" snarled Illyan to Gregor's keepers, who stammered out something inaudible about *thought he was asleep* and *never took my eyes off*.

"He's not away," Cordelia put in tartly. "This is his home. He ought to be at least able to walk about inside, or why do you keep all those bloody useless guards on the walls out there?"

"Droushie, can't I come to your party?" Gregor asked plaintively, casting around desperately for an authority to outrank Illyan.

Drou looked at Illyan, who looked disapproving. Cordelia broke the deadlock without hesitation. "Yes, you can."

So, under Cordelia's supervision, the Emperor danced with the bride, ate three cream cakes, and was carried away to bed satisfied. Fifteen minutes was all he'd wanted, poor kid.

The party rolled on, elated. "Dance, Milady?" Aral inquired hopefully at her elbow.

Dare she try it? They were playing the restrained rhythms of the mirror-dance—surely she couldn't go too wrong. She nodded, and Aral drained his glass and led her onto the polished marquetry. Step, slide, gesture: concentrating, she made an interesting and unexpected discovery. Either partner could lead, and if the dancers were alert and sharp, the watchers couldn't tell the difference. She tried some dips and slides of her own, and Aral followed smoothly. Back and forth the lead passed like a ball between them, the game growing ever more absorbing, until they ran out of music and breath.

The last snows of winter were melting from the streets of Vorbarr Sultana when Captain Vaagen called from ImpMil for Cordelia.

"It's time, Milady. I've done all I can do in vitro. The placenta is ten months old and clearly senescing. The machine can't be boosted any more to compensate."

"When, then?"

"Tomorrow would be good."

She barely slept that night. They all trooped down to the Imperial Military Hospital the next morning, Aral, Cordelia, Count Piotr flanked by Bothari. Cordelia was not at all sure she wanted Piotr present, but until the old man did them all the convenience of dropping dead, she was stuck with him. Maybe one more appeal to reason, one more presentation of the facts, one more try, would do the trick. Their unresolved antagonism grieved Aral; at least let the onus for fueling it fall on Piotr, not herself. *Do your worst, old man. You have no future except through me. My son will light your offering pyre.* She was glad to see Bothari again, though.

Vaagen's new laboratory was an entire floor in the most up-to-date building in the complex. Cordelia'd had him moved from his old lab on account of ghosts, having come in for one of her frequent visits soon after their return to Vorbarr Sultana to find him in a state of near-paralysis, unable to work. Every time he entered the room, he'd said, Dr. Henri's violent and senseless death replayed in his memory. He could not step on the floor near the place where Henri's body had fallen, but had to walk wide around; little noises made him jump and twitch. "I am a man of reason," he'd said hoarsely. "This superstitious nonsense means nothing to me." So Cordelia had helped him burn a private offering to Henri in a brazier on the lab floor, and disguised the move as a promotion.

The new lab was bright and spacious and free of revenant spirits. Cordelia found a mob of men waiting when Vaagen ushered her in: researchers assigned to Vaagen to explore replicator technology, interested civilian obstetricians including Dr. Ritter, Miles's own pediatrician-to-be, and his consulting surgeon. The changing of the guard. Mere parents needed determination to elbow their way in.

Vaagen bustled about, happily important. He still wore his eyepatch, but promised Cordelia he would take the time for the last round of surgery to restore his vision very soon now. A tech trundled out the uterine replicator and Vaagen paused, as if trying to figure out how to put the proper drama and ceremony into what Cordelia knew for a very simple event. He settled on turning it into a technical lecture for his colleagues, detailing the composition of the hormone solutions as he injected them into the appropriate feed-lines, interpreting readouts, describing the placental separation going on within the replicator, the similarities and differences between replicator and body births. There were several differences Vaagen didn't mention. *Alys Vorpatril should see this,* Cordelia thought.

Vaagen looked up to see her watching him, paused self-consciously, and smiled. "Lady Vorkosigan." He gestured to the replicator's latch-seals. "Would you care to do the honors?"

She reached, hesitated, and looked around for Aral. There he was, solemn and attentive at the edge of the crowd. "Aral?"

He strode forward. "Are you sure?"

"If you can open a picnic cooler, you can do this." They each took a latch and raised them in unison, breaking the sterile seal, and lifted the top off. Dr. Ritter moved in with a vibra-scalpel, cutting through the thick felt mat of nutrient tubing with a touch so delicate the silvery amniotic sac beneath was unscored, then cut Miles free of his last bit of biological packaging, clearing his mouth and nose of fluids before his first surprised inhalation. Aral's arm, around her, tightened so hard it hurt. A muffled laugh, no more than a breath, broke from his lips; he swallowed and blinked to bring his features, suffused with elation and pain, back under strict control.

Happy birthday, thought Cordelia. *Good color . . .*

Unfortunately, that was about all that was really good. The contrast with baby Ivan was overwhelming. Despite the extra weeks of gestation, ten months to Ivan's nine-and-a-half, Miles was barely half Ivan's size at birth, and far more wizened and wrinkled. His spine was noticeably deformed, and his legs were drawn up and locked in a tight bend. He was definitely a male heir, though, no question about that. His first cry was thin, weak, nothing at all like Ivan's angry, hungry bellow. Behind her, she heard Piotr hiss with disappointment.

"Has he been getting enough nutrition?" she asked Vaagen. It was hard to keep the accusation out of her tone.

Vaagen shrugged helplessly. "All he would absorb."

The pediatrician and his colleague laid Miles out under a warming light, and began their examination, Cordelia and Aral on either side.

"This bend will straighten out on its own, Milady," the pediatrician pointed. "But the lower spine should have surgical correction as early as possible. You were right, Vaagen, the treatment to optimize skull development also fused the hip sockets. That's why the legs are locked in that strange position, m'lord. He'll require surgery to crack those bones loose and turn them around before he can start to crawl or walk. I don't recommend that in the first year, on top of the spinal work, let him gain strength and weight first—"

The surgeon, testing the infant's arms, swore suddenly

and snatched up his diagnostic viewer. Miles mewed. Aral's hand clenched, by his trouser seam. Cordelia's stomach sank. "Hell!" said the surgeon. "His humerus just snapped. You're right, Vaagen, the bones are abnormally brittle."

"At least he has bones," sighed Vaagen. "He almost didn't, at one point."

"Be careful," said the surgeon, "especially of the head and spine. If the rest are as bad as the long bones, we're going to have to come up with some kind of reinforcement. . . ."

Piotr stamped toward the door. Aral glanced up, his lips thinning to a frown, and excused himself to follow. Cordelia was torn, but once observation assured her that the bone-setting was under way and the doctors' new caution would protect Miles from further damage today, she left their ingenious heads bent over him and followed Aral.

In the corridor, Piotr was stalking up and down. Aral stood at parade rest, unmoved and unmoving. Bothari was a silent witness in the background.

Piotr turned and saw her. "You! You've strung me along. This is what you call 'great repairs'? Gah!"

"They are great repairs. Miles is unquestionably much better than he was. Nobody promised perfection."

"You lied. Vaagen lied."

"We did not," denied Cordelia. "I tried to give you accurate summaries of Vaagen's experiments all the way along. What he's delivered is about what his reports led us to expect. Check your ears."

"I see what you're trying, and it won't work. I've just told him," he pointed at Aral, "this is where I stop. I don't want to see that mutant again. Ever. While it lives, if it lives, and it looks pretty damned sickly to me, don't bring it around my door. As God is my judge, woman, you won't make a fool of me."

"That would be redundant," snapped Cordelia.

Piotr's lips curled in a silent snarl. Cheated of a cooperative target, he turned on Aral. "And you, you spineless, skirt-smothered—if your elder brother had lived—" Piotr's mouth clamped shut abruptly, too late.

Aral's face drained to a grey hue Cordelia had seen but twice before; both times he'd been a breath and a chance away from committing murder. Piotr had joked about Aral's famous rages. Only now did Cordelia realize Piotr, though he may have witnessed his son in irritation, had never seen the real thing. Piotr seemed to realize it, too, dimly. His brows lowered; he stared, off-balanced.

Aral's hands locked to each other, behind his back. Cordelia could see them shake, white-knuckled. His chin lifted, and he spoke in a whisper.

"If my brother had lived, he would have been perfect. You thought so; I thought so; Emperor Yuri thought so, too. So ever after you've had to make do with the left-overs from that bloody banquet, the son Mad Yuri's death squad overlooked. We Vorkosigans, we can make do." His voice fell still further. "But *my* firstborn will live. I will not fail him."

The icy statement was a near-lethal cut across the belly, as fine a slash as Bothari could have delivered with Koudelka's swordstick, and very accurately placed. Truly, Piotr should not have lowered the tone of this discussion. The breath huffed from him in disbelief and pain.

Aral's expression grew inward. "I will not fail him *again*," he corrected himself lowly. "A second chance you were never given, sir." Behind his back his hands unclenched. A small jerk of his head dismissed Piotr and all Piotr might say.

Blocked twice, visibly suffering from his profound misstep, Piotr looked around for a target of opportunity upon which to vent his frustration. His eye fell on Bothari, watching blank-faced.

"And you. Your hand was in this from beginning to end. Did my son place you as a spy in my household? Where do your loyalties lie? Do you obey me, or him?"

An odd gleam flared in Bothari's eye. He tilted his head toward Cordelia. "Her."

Piotr was so taken aback, it took him several seconds to regain his speech. "Fine," he sputtered at last. "She can have you. I don't want to see your ugly face again.

Don't come back to Vorkosigan House. Esterhazy will deliver your things before nightfall."

He wheeled and marched away. His grand exit, already weak, was spoiled when he looked back over his shoulder before he rounded the corner.

Aral vented a very weary sigh.

"Do you think he means it this time?" Cordelia asked. "All that never-ever stuff?"

"Government concerns will require us to communicate. He knows that. Let him go home and listen to the silence for a bit. Then we'll see." He smiled bleakly. "While we live, we cannot disengage."

She thought of the child whose blood now bound them, her to Aral, Aral to Piotr, and Piotr to herself. "So it seems." She looked an apology to Bothari. "I'm sorry, Sergeant. I didn't know Piotr could fire an oath-armsman."

"Well, technically, he can't," Aral explained. "Bothari was just reassigned to another branch of the household. You."

"Oh." *Just what I always wanted, my very own monster. What am I supposed to do, keep him in my closet?* She rubbed the bridge of her nose, then regarded her hand. The hand that had encompassed Bothari's on the swordstick. So. And so. "Lord Miles will need a bodyguard, won't he?"

Aral tilted his head in interest. "Indeed."

Bothari looked suddenly so intently hopeful, it made Cordelia catch her breath. "A bodyguard," he said, "and backup. No raff could give him a hard time if . . . let me help, Milady."

Let me help. Rhymes with *I love you,* right? "It would be . . ." *impossible, crazy, dangerous, irresponsible,* "my pleasure, Sergeant."

His face lit like a torch. "Can I start now?"

"Why not?"

"I'll wait for you in there, then." He nodded toward Vaagen's lab. He slipped back through the door. Cordelia could just picture him, leaning watchfully against the wall—she trusted that malevolent presence wouldn't make the doctors so nervous they would drop their fragile charge.

Aral blew out his breath, and took her in his arms. "Do you Betans have any nursery tales about the witch's name-day gifts?"

"The good and bad fairies seem to all be out in force for this one, don't they?" She leaned against the scratchy fabric of his uniformed shoulder. "I don't know if Piotr meant Bothari for a blessing or a curse. But I bet he really will keep the raff off. Whatever the raff turns out to be. It's a strange list of birthday presents we've given our boychick."

They returned to the lab, to listen attentively to the rest of the doctors' lecture on Miles's special needs and vulnerabilities, arrange the first round of treatment schedules, and wrap him warmly for the trip home. He was so small, a scrap of flesh, lighter than a cat, Cordelia found when she at last took him up in her arms, skin to skin for the first time since he'd been cut from her body. She had a moment's panic. *Put him back in the vat for about eighteen years, I can't handle this. . . .* Children might or might not be a blessing, but to create them and then fail them was surely damnation. Even Piotr knew that. Aral held the door open for them.

Welcome to Barrayar, son. Here you go: have a world of wealth and poverty, wrenching change and rooted history. Have a birth; have two. Have a name. Miles means "soldier," but don't let the power of suggestion overwhelm you. Have a twisted form in a society that loathes and fears the mutations that have been its deepest agony. Have a title, wealth, power, and all the hatred and envy they will draw. Have your body ripped apart and re-arranged. Inherit an array of friends and enemies you never made. Have a grandfather from hell. Endure pain, find joy, and make your own meaning, because the universe certainly isn't going to supply it. Always be a moving target. Live. Live. Live.

EPILOGUE

"Dammit, Vaagen," Cordelia panted under her breath. "You never told me the little bugger was going to be *hyperactive*."

She galloped down the end stairs, through the kitchen, and out onto the terrace at the end of the rambling stone residence. Her gaze swept the lawn, probed the trees, and scanned the long lake sparkling in the summer sun. No movement.

Aral, dressed in old uniform trousers and a faded print shirt, came around the house, saw her, and opened his hands in a no-luck gesture. "He's not out here."

"He's not inside. Down, or up, d'you think? Where's little Elena? I bet they're together. I forbade him to go down to the lake without an adult, but I don't know. . . ."

"Surely not the lake," said Aral. "They swam all morning. I was exhausted just watching them. In the fifteen minutes I timed it, he climbed the dock and jumped back in nineteen times. Multiply that by three hours."

"Up, then," decided Cordelia. They turned and trudged together up the hill on the gravel path lined with native,

584

Earth-import, and exotic shrubbery and flowers. "And to think," Cordelia wheezed, "I prayed for the day he would walk."

"It's five years pent-up motion all let loose at once," Aral analyzed. "In a way, it's reassuring that all that frustration didn't turn in on itself and become despair. For a time, I was afraid it might."

"Yes. Have you noticed, since the last operation, that the endless chatter's dried up? At first I was glad, but do you suppose he's going to go mute? I didn't even know that refrigeration unit was supposed to come apart. A mute engineer."

"I think the, er, verbal and mechanical aptitudes will come into balance eventually. If he survives."

"There's all of us adults, and one of him. We ought to be able to keep up. Why do I feel like he has us outnumbered and surrounded?" She crested the hill. Piotr's stable complex lay in the shallow valley below, half a dozen red-painted wood and stone buildings, fenced paddocks, pastures planted to bright green Earth grasses. She saw horses, but no children. Bothari was ahead of them, though, just exiting one building and entering another. His bellow carried up to them, thinned by distance. "Lord Miles?"

"Oh, dear, I hope he's not bothering Piotr's horses," said Cordelia. "Do you really think this reconciliation attempt will work, this time? Just because Miles is finally walking?"

"He was civil, last night at dinner," said Aral, judiciously hopeful.

"*I* was civil, last night at dinner," Cordelia shrugged. "*He* as much as accused me of starving your son into dwarfism. Can I help it if the kid would rather play with his food than eat it? I just don't know about stepping up the growth hormone, Vaagen's so uncertain about its effect on bone friability."

A crooked smile stole over Aral's face. "I did think the dialogue with the peas marching to surround the bread-roll and demand surrender was rather ingenious. You could almost picture them as little soldiers in Imperial greens."

"Yes, and you were no help, laughing instead of terrorizing him into eating like a proper Da."

"I did not laugh."

"Your eyes were laughing. He knew it, too. Twisting you round his thumb."

The warm organic scent of horses and their inevitable by-products permeated the air as they approached the buildings. Bothari re-appeared, saw them, and waved an apologetic hand. "I just saw Elena. I told her to get down out of that loft. She said Lord Miles wasn't up there, but he's around here somewhere. Sorry, Milady, when he talked about looking at the animals, I didn't realize he meant immediately. I'm sure I'll find him in just a moment."

"I was hoping Piotr would offer a tour," Cordelia sighed.

"I thought you didn't like horses," said Aral.

"I loathe them. But I thought it might get the old man talking to him, like a human being, instead of over him like a potted plant. And Miles was so excited about the stupid beasts. I don't like to linger here, though. This place is so . . . Piotr." *Archaic, dangerous, and you have to watch your step.*

Speak of the devil. Piotr himself emerged from the old stone tack storage shed, coiling a web rope. "Hah. There you are," he said neutrally. He joined them sociably enough, though. "I don't suppose you would like to see the new filly."

His tone was so flat, she couldn't tell if he wanted her to say yes, or no. But she seized the opportunity. "I'm sure Miles would."

"Mm."

She turned to Bothari. "Why don't you go get—" But Bothari was staring past her, his lips rippling in dismay. She wheeled.

One of Piotr's most enormous horses, quite naked of bridle, saddle, halter, or any other handle to grab, was trotting out of the barn. Clinging to its mane like a burr was a dark-haired, dwarfish little boy. Miles's sharp features shone with a mixture of exaltation and terror. Cordelia nearly fainted.

"My imported stallion!" yelped Piotr in horror.

In pure reflex, Bothari snatched his stunner from its holster. He then stood paralyzed with the uncertainty of what to shoot and where. If the horse went down and rolled on its little rider—

"Look, Sergeant!" Miles's thin voice called eagerly. "I'm taller than you!"

Bothari started to run toward him. The horse, spooked, wheeled away and broke into a canter.

"—and I can run faster, too!" The words were whipped away in the bounding motion of the gait. The horse shied out of sight around the stable.

The four adults pelted after. Cordelia heard no other cry, but when they turned the corner Miles was lying on the ground, and the horse had stopped further on and lowered its head to nibble at the grass. It snorted in hostility when it saw them, raised its head, danced from foot to foot, then snatched a few more bites.

Cordelia fell to her knees beside Miles, who was already sitting up and waving her away. He was pale, and his right hand clutched his left arm in an all-too-familiar signal of pain.

"You see, Sergeant?" Miles panted. "I can ride, I *can*."

Piotr, on his way toward his horse, paused and looked down.

"I didn't mean to say you weren't *able*," said the sergeant in a driven tone. "I meant you didn't have *permission*."

"Oh."

"Did you break it?" Bothari nodded to the arm.

"Yeah," the boy sighed. There were tears of pain in his eyes, but his teeth set against any quaver entering his voice.

The sergeant grumbled, and rolled up Miles's sleeve, and palpated the forearm. Miles hissed. "Yep." Bothari pulled, twisted, adjusted, took a plastic sleeve from his pocket, slipped it over the arm and wrist, and blew it up. "That'll keep it till the doctor sees it."

"Hadn't you better . . . containerize that horrendous horse?" Cordelia said to Piotr.

" 'S not h'rrendous," Miles insisted, scrambling to his feet. "It's the prettiest."

"You think so, eh?" said Piotr roughly. "How do you figure that? You like brown?"

"It moves the springiest," Miles explained earnestly, bouncing in imitation.

Piotr's attention was arrested. "And so it does," he said, sounding bemused. "It's my hottest dressage prospect. . . . You like horses?"

"They're great. They're wonderful." Miles pirouetted.

"I could never much interest your father in them." Piotr gave Aral a dirty look.

Thank God, thought Cordelia.

"On a horse, I could go as fast as anybody, I bet," said Miles.

"I doubt it," said Piotr coldly, "if that was a sample. If you're going to do it, you have to do it right."

"Teach me," said Miles instantly.

Piotr's brows shot up. He glanced at Cordelia, and smiled sourly. "If your mother gives permission." He rocked on his heels, in certain smug safety, knowing Cordelia's rooted antipathy to the beasts.

Cordelia bit her tongue on *Over my dead body,* and thought fast. Aral's intent eyes were signaling something, but she couldn't read it. Was this a new way for Piotr to try and kill Miles? Take him out and get him smashed, trampled, broken . . . tired out? Now there was a thought. . . .

Risk, or security? In the few months since Miles had at last acquired a full range of motion, she'd run on panicked overdrive, trying to save him from physical harm; he'd spent the same time near-frantically trying to escape her supervision. Much more of this struggle, and either she'd be insane, or he would.

If she could not keep him safe, perhaps the next best

thing was to teach him competence at living dangerously. He was almost undrownable already. His big grey eyes were radiating a desperate, silent plea at her, *Let me, let me, let me . . .* with enough transmission energy to burn through steel. *I would fight the world for you, but I'm damned if I can figure out how to save you from yourself. Go for it, kid.*

"Yes," she said. "If the sergeant accompanies you."

Bothari shot her a look of horrified reproach. Aral rubbed his chin, his eyes alight. Piotr looked utterly taken aback to have his bluff called.

"Good," said Miles. "Can I have my own horse? Can I have *that* one?"

"*No,* not that one," said Piotr indignantly. Then drawn in, added, "Perhaps a pony."

"Horse," said Miles, watching his face.

Cordelia recognized the Instant Re-Negotiation Mode, a spinal reflex, as far as she could tell, triggered by the faintest concession. The kid should be put to work beating out treaties with the Cetagandans. She wondered how many horses he'd finally end up with. "A pony," she put in, giving Piotr the support that he did not yet recognize how badly he was going to need. "A gentle pony. A gentle *short* pony."

Piotr pursed his lips, and gave her a challenging look. "Perhaps you can work up to a horse," he said to Miles. "Earn it, by learning well."

"Can I start now?"

"You have to get your arm set first," said Cordelia firmly.

"I don't have to wait till it *heals,* do I?"

"It will teach you not to run around breaking things!"

Piotr regarded Cordelia through half-lidded eyes. "Actually, proper dressage training starts on a lunge line. You aren't permitted to use your arms till you've developed your seat."

"Yeah?" said Miles, hanging worshipfully on his words. "What else—?"

By the time Cordelia withdrew to hunt up the personal

physician who accompanied the Lord Regent's traveling circus, ah, entourage, Piotr had recaptured his horse—rather efficiently, though Cordelia wondered if the sugar in his pockets was cheating—and was already explaining to Miles how to make a simple line into an effective halter, which side of the beast to stand on, and what direction to face while leading. The boy, barely waist-high to the old man, was taking it in like a sponge, upturned face passionately intent.

"Want to lay a side-bet, who's leading who on that lunge line by the end of the week?" Aral murmured in her ear.

"No contest. I must say, the months Miles spent immobilized in that dreadful spinal brace did teach him how to do charm. The most efficient long-term way to control those about you, and thus exert your will. I'm glad he didn't decide to perfect whining as a strategy. He's the most willful little monster I've ever encountered, but he makes you not notice."

"I don't think the Count has a chance," Aral agreed.

She smiled at the vision, then glanced at him more seriously. "When my father was home on leave one time from the Betan Astronomical Survey, we made model gliders together. Two things were required to get them to fly. First we had to give them a running start. Then we had to let them go." She sighed. "Learning just when to let go was the hardest part."

Piotr, his horse, Bothari, and Miles turned out of sight into the barn. By his gestures, Miles was asking questions at a rapid-fire rate.

Aral gripped her hand as they turned to go up the hill. "I believe he'll soar high, dear Captain."

AUTHOR'S AFTERWORD

I was asked by my publisher if I would like to contribute a preface to *Cordelia's Honor*. Upon reflection, I decided I'd rather write an afterword. For one thing, it was a horrifying thought that anything at all should further delay new readers from meeting my characters; secondly, discursive comments about a book make ever so much more sense *after* people have read it.

I'd like to thank Baen Books for this combined edition of *Shards of Honor* and *Barrayar*. Here at last in one set of covers is the whole story arc, very much as I originally conceived its shape, if not its details. As a longtime series reader, and now writer, I'm very aware of the pitfalls of what I've come to believe is another story form, as distinct from the novel as the novel is from the short story. A proper series in this sense is neither an extension of the novel (as in the multi-volume single story) nor a replication (as when essentially the same story is told over and over, cookie-cutter fashion), but another animal altogether, with its own internal demands. In addition, one must assume that readers, as I did when reading my own favorite series, will encounter the books in utterly random order. Therefore each series novel must

simultaneously be a complete tale in itself, and uphold
its unique place in the growing structure; it must be two
books at once. The understructure must be global and
timeless as well as linear and sequential. The series landscape must satisfy its readers regardless of what direction they chance to travel through it, or how often.

I had no more idea of all this when I started writing
the Vorkosigan series than I had of what my own life
would be like when I started living it. A brief history of
how I came to write these two books may illustrate both.

I began what was to become *Shards of Honor* in
December of 1982. Inspired by the example of a new-
writer friend, and by the economic pressures of the rust-
belt Midwest town in which I was living, I set out to Write
A Novel. My writing career has been on-the-job training
throughout, and this was no exception; my only plan of
how to structure my material was to plant an eavesdropping device in my main character's brain and follow her
through her first weeks of action. This brought Cordelia
and me to the end of what later became the first section of *Shards*. (It then had the working title of *Mirrors*.)
I now had in hand a messy first draft of about a hundred pages of narrative, with no chapter breaks, that
clearly wasn't long enough to be a novel. I paused briefly,
flirted with a really bad scenario about a convenient alien
invasion that would force Barrayar and Beta to ally, decided "Why should I make things easy on my characters?",
and plunged on to the much better and more inherent
idea of the Escobar invasion, thus accidentally discover-
ing my first application of the rule for finding plots for
character-centered novels, which is to ask "So what's the
worst possible thing I can do to *this* guy?" And then do
it.

Thus I already knew, at this early date, that Aral and
Cordelia would have a physically handicapped son in
Barrayar's intensely militaristic culture, though I did not
yet know how it would come about. Though I was not really
aware of it when I was writing Chapter One, Ensign
Dubauer is clearly the first statement of this theme. I had

a toddler myself at that time, and I thought of the injured ensign as a 180-pound one-year-old, and amused myself putting Aral and Cordelia through reflections of my own harried parental tribulations—which incidentally allowed them to unconsciously scope each other out as potential parents. The birth of a child is the proper climax, after all, of any romance that starts out "boy meets girl," if the romance is not falsely truncated. So I knew even then that the *end* of the story should be Miles's birth.

I wrote industriously through the spring and early summer of 1983. The book had now acquired the opposite problem from that of mid-winter, of being too short; it was now getting *longer*, but not getting any closer to the end. (I've experienced that phenomenon subsequently on other books, one of which managed to stay three chapters from the end for at least five chapters straight, so now it doesn't daunt me so much.) Since it was apparent that this really was going to be a book, and not just another false start in life, marketing considerations began to come into play. Editors' slush piles of unsolicited manuscripts from unknowns were enormous, I was told; a thinner book had a better chance of being read first than a fat one. Besides, new characters with entire attached subplots were arriving on page 378, all demanding development at length, my internal clue that I had overshot the end and was already into the sequel, unless this was going to be a multi-volume novel as fat as a major fantasy trilogy.

The last scene I wrote back in '83 before making the decision to go back and cut it short was Cordelia's conversation with Dr. Vaagen; the introduction of Droushnakovi, Koudelka's swordstick and depression, Cordelia's first encounters with Barrayaran culture, with Padma and Alys, with the Vorhalas clan, and the soltoxin attack were already written then. I did not yet have the ideas for the war of Vordarian's Pretendership; the action-plot upon which all this good stuff then hung was much weaker, making the decision to stop easier, if still a little heartbreaking.

With much labor, and a lot of help from writer-friends,

I revised and put *Mirrors* into proper submission format. I then went on to write the book which became *The Warrior's Apprentice* (which, for you fellow Dumas fans out there, I thought of for a while as *Twenty Years After*, though it opens seventeen years after the events of *Shards*). Though I hoped to develop a series, I didn't dare count on it; series books might float together, but they also can sink together, and I wanted to make sure each novel had its own lifeboat. So the each-book-independent format, which I later came to regard as a Really Good Artistic Idea, began as a mere survival plan. *Mirrors* came back rejected from its first submission when I was about halfway through *Warrior's*, with an editorial suggestion that I tighten it; I set it aside till the second book was finished, then turned my attention to one last edit, cutting altogether about 80 pages, mostly in sentence or paragraph lengths. It was a good learning experience; I've written more tightly ever since, and no, there isn't much of it I'd put back now if I could. Trust me on this one. In the late summer of '85, about the time I was finishing *Ethan of Athos*, *Warrior's* made it in over the transom at Baen Books, and I was abruptly elevated from slush-pile wannabe to real author with three completed books *sold*. The re-titled *Shards of Honor* was published in June of 1986, allowing my father to see the finished book just six weeks before he died.

Having captured a publisher at last, I went on to write *Falling Free*, which was serialized in *Analog* magazine, and won me my first Nebula Award, for best SF novel of 1988. *Brothers in Arms*, *Borders of Infinity*, and *The Vor Game* followed, as the ever-lively Miles proceeded to take over his surroundings as usual. About this time—summer of 1989—Philcon, a long-established science fiction convention in Philadelphia, invited me to be a writer guest. Their program-book editor asked me for a short story or outtake to donate for their program book. I hadn't written a short story since 1986, but I thought of the soltoxin scene, reasoned that enough readers were familiar with Miles by this time to make it interesting in its own right, and took myself to my overheated attic to find the box with the old drafts. Leafing through the carbons (*Shards/Mirrors* was written in my old typewriter days, pre-word-processor), I was caught again by my own story, and the desire to finish it grew. It ought to be easy and quick, I reasoned; it was already a third written, after all.

Jim Baen was at first a little nonplussed to be offered a sequel to my then-least-selling novel, but we struck deals that fall for *Barrayar*, for a fantasy novel I'd long wanted to write, and also for a blank Miles book, contents to be announced by me later. (That one turned out to be *Mirror Dance*, which won my third best-novel Hugo.)

Still under the happy illusion about the "easy and quick" part (Hah. Novels never are. *Never*.), I started *Barrayar*, with the unenticing working title of *Shardssequel*. I wrote a new opening chapter, to reintroduce the characters and situation for new readers, cut and fit most of the old material into its new frame, and began the story again as Count Piotr argued with Cordelia and Captain Negri expired on the lawn at Vorkosigan Surleau. From that point on, the tale ran on its own legs, and turned into something I didn't expect. It turned into the book it always should have been, a *real* book, where plot, character, and theme all worked together to make a whole greater than the sum of the parts. It turned out to be *about* something, beyond itself. It's a bizarre but wonderful feeling, to arrive dead center of a target you didn't even know you were aiming for.

Shards/Barrayar, as it finally evolved, became a book about the price of becoming a parent, particularly but not exclusively a mother. Not just Aral and Cordelia, but all the other supporting couples took up and played their symphonic variations on the theme, exploring its complexities: Kou and Drou, Padma and Alys, Piotr and his dead wife, Vordarian and Serg and Kareen, and most strangely and SFnally, Bothari and the uterine replicator.

All great human deeds both consume and transform their doers. Consider an athlete, or a scientist, or an artist, or an independent business creator. In service of their goals they lay down time and energy and many other choices and pleasures; in return, they become most truly themselves. A false destiny may be spotted by the fact that it consumes without transforming, without giving back the enlarged self. Becoming a parent is one of these basic human transformational deeds. By this act, we change our fundamental relationship with the universe—if nothing else, we lose our place as the pinnacle and end-point of evolution, and become a mere link. The demands of motherhood especially consume the old self, and replace it with something new, often better and wiser, sometimes wearier or disillusioned, or tense and terrified, certainly more self-knowing, but never the same again. Cordelia undergoes such a fearsome transformation, at the climax of *Barrayar* laying down everything about her old persona, even her cherished Betan principles, to bring her child to life.

Shards and *Barrayar* between them contain most of what I presently have to say about being a mother; it's not by chance that *Barrayar* was dedicated to my children, who were my teachers in learning about this part of becoming human. Further explorations on this theme will almost certainly not return to Cordelia, but take a new start-point, though Cordelia may yet have a word to say on other topics. Growing up, I have discovered over time, is rather like housework: never finished. It's not something you do once for all. Miles and his family and friends have become my vehicle for exploring identity, in what promises to be a continuing fascination. I have not come to the end of that story yet, nor will I, till I stop learning new things about what it takes to be human.

Miles Vorkosigan/Naismith:
His Universe and Times

Chronology	Events	Chronicle
Approx. 200 years before Miles's birth	Quaddies are created by genetic engineering.	*Falling Free*
During Beta-Barrayaran War	Cordelia Naismith meets Lord Aral Vorkosigan while on opposite sides of a war. Despite difficulties, they fall in love and are married.	*Shards of Honor*
The Vordarian Pretendership	While Cordelia is pregnant, an attempt to assassinate Aral by poison gas fails, but Cordelia is affected; Miles Vorkosigan is born with bones that will always be brittle and other medical problems. His growth will be stunted.	*Barrayar*
Miles is 17	Miles fails to pass physical test to get into the Service Academy. On a trip, necessities force him to improvise the Free Dendarii Mercenaries into existence; he has	*The Warrior's Apprentice*

Chronology	Events	Chronicle
	unintended but unavoidable adventures for four months. Leaves the Dendarii in Ky Tung's competent hands and takes Elli Quinn to Beta for rebuilding of her damaged face; returns to Barrayar to thwart plot against his father. Emperor pulls strings to get Miles into the Academy.	
Miles is 20	Ensign Miles graduates and immediately has to take on one of the duties of the Barrayaran nobility and act as detective and judge in a murder case. Shortly after-wards, his first military assignment ends with his arrest. Miles has to rejoin the Dendarii to rescue the young Barrayaran emperor. Emperor accepts Dendarii as his personal secret service force.	"The Mountains of Mourning" in *Borders of Infinity* *The Vor Game*
Miles is 22	Miles and his cousin Ivan attend a Cetagandan state funeral and are caught up in Cetagandan internal politics.	*Cetaganda*

Chronology	Events	Chronicle
	Miles sends Commander Elli Quinn, who's been given a new face on Beta, on a solo mission to Kline Station.	*Ethan of Athos*
Miles is 23	Now a Barrayaran Lieutenant, Miles goes with the Dendarii to smuggle a scientist out of Jackson's Whole. Miles's fragile leg bones have been replaced by synthetics.	"Labyrinth" in *Borders of Infinity*
Miles is 24	Miles plots from within a Cetagandan prison camp on Dagoola IV to free the prisoners. The Dendarii fleet is pursued by the Cetagandans and finally reaches Earth for repairs. Miles has to juggle both his identities at once, raise money for repairs, and defeat a plot to replace him with a double. Ky Tung stays on Earth. Commander Elli Quinn is now Miles's right-hand officer. Miles and the Dendarii depart for Sector IV on a rescue mission.	"The Borders of Infinity" in *Borders of Infinity* *Brothers in Arms*

Chronology	Events	Chronicle
Miles is 25	Hospitalized after previous mission, Miles's broken arms are replaced by synthetic bones. With Simon Illyan, Miles undoes yet another plot against his father while flat on his back.	*Borders of Infinity*
Miles is 28	Miles meets his clone brother Mark again, this time on Jackson's Whole.	*Mirror Dance*
Miles is 29	Miles hits thirty; thirty hits back.	*Memory*
Miles is 30	Emperor Gregor dispatches Miles to Komarr to investigate a space accident, where he finds old politics and new technology make a deadly mix.	*Komarr*
Miles is 31	The Emperor's wedding sparks romance and intrigue on Barrayar, and Miles plunges up to his neck in both.	*A Civil Campaign*

PRAISE FOR
LOIS MCMASTER BUJOLD

What the critics say:

The Warrior's Apprentice: "Now here's a fun romp through the spaceways—not so much a space opera as space ballet.... it has all the 'right stuff.' A lot of thought and thoughtfulness stand behind the all-too-human characters. Enjoy this one, and look forward to the next."   —Dean Lambe, *SF Reviews*

"The pace is breathless, the characterization thoughtful and emotionally powerful, and the author's narrative technique and command of language compelling. Highly recommended."
—*Booklist*

Brothers in Arms: "...she gives it a genuine depth of character, while reveling in the wild turnings of her tale.... Bujold is as audacious as her favorite hero, and as brilliantly (if sneakily) successful."   —*Locus*

"Miles Vorkosigan is such a great character that I'll read anything Lois wants to write about him.... a book to re-read on cold rainy days." —Robert Coulson, *Comic Buyer's Guide*

Borders of Infinity: "Bujold's series hero Miles Vorkosigan may be a lord by birth and an admiral by rank, but a bone disease that has left him hobbled and in frequent pain has sensitized him to the suffering of outcasts in his very hierarchical era.... Playing off Miles's reserve and cleverness, Bujold draws outrageous and outlandish foils to color her high-minded adventures."   —*Publishers Weekly*

Falling Free: "In *Falling Free* Lois McMaster Bujold has written her fourth straight superb novel.... How to break down a talent like Bujold's into analyzable components? Best not to try. Best to say: 'Read, or you will be missing something extraordinary.' "   —Roland Green, *Chicago Sun-Times*

The Vor Game: "The chronicles of Miles Vorkosigan are far too witty to be literary junk food, but they rouse the kind of craving that makes popcorn magically vanish during a double feature."   —Faren Miller, *Locus*